MW00716199

William Forsyth

Cases and Opinions on Constitutional Law

SALZWASSER
VERLAG

William Forsyth

Cases and Opinions on Constitutional Law

Reprint of the original, first published in 1869.

1st Edition 2022 | ISBN: 978-3-37504-537-1

Verlag (Publisher): Salzwasser Verlag GmbH, Zeilweg 44, 60439 Frankfurt, Deutschland
Vertretungsberechtigt (Authorized to represent): E. Roepke, Zeilweg 44, 60439 Frankfurt, Deutschland
Druck (Print): Books on Demand GmbH, In de Tarpen 42, 22848 Norderstedt, Deutschland

CASES AND OPINIONS

ON

CONSTITUTIONAL LAW.

CASES AND OPINIONS

ON

CONSTITUTIONAL LAW,

AND VARIOUS POINTS OF

ENGLISH JURISPRUDENCE,

Collected and Digested from Official Documents and other Sources;

WITH NOTES.

BY

WILLIAM FORSYTH, M.A., Q.C.,

STANDING COUNSEL TO THE SECRETARY OF STATE IN COUNCIL OF INDIA,
AUTHOR OF "THE LAW RELATING TO COMPOSITION WITH CREDITORS," "HORTENSIUS,"
"HISTORY OF TRIAL BY JURY," "LIFE OF CICERO," ETC.
LATE FELLOW OF TRINITY COLLEGE, CAMBRIDGE.

"Hominum peritorum responsa sunt nobis cognoscenda."
Cic. Epist. Fragm. apud Nizolium.

LONDON:

S T E V E N S & H A Y N E S,

Law Publishers,

11, BELL YARD, TEMPLE BAR.

1869.

PREFACE.

In 1814 a book was published called "Chalmers's Opinions of Eminent Lawyers;" and, notwithstanding its faulty and inconvenient arrangement, and the quantity of useless matter with which it is encumbered, the work has always enjoyed a high reputation, and is still frequently consulted when cases occur involving questions of Constitutional Law. Lately an edition has been published in America. This is only what might have been expected with regard to a book which has made known to the world the legal Opinions, on many points of interest and importance, of such men as Lord Somers, Chief Justice Holt, Lord Hardwicke, Lord Talbot, Lord Mansfield, and others, given when they were the Law Officers of the Crown. Since then, however, there has been a complete silence and blank; and the Opinions of the Law Officers, given from time to time to the different Departments of the State during the last sixty or seventy years, have been consigned to oblivion, and buried in the dusty archives which have been practically inaccessible—

> "—— omnes illacrymabiles
> Urgentur, ignotique longá
> Nocte ——"

The idea occurred to me that I should be doing good service, not only to the Profession to which I belong, but also to the Public, if I were to rescue some of the most valuable of these Opinions from their obscurity, and publish them with explanatory Notes. Slightly varying a line of Horace, we may surely say, "Vixere fortes *post* Agamemnona multi;" and, great as were the lawyers whose Opinions have been preserved by Chalmers, there has been a succession of lawyers since equally great, who may worthily compete with them in acuteness of intellect and depth of legal knowledge. In the present Volume will be found, for the first time, the official Opinions of Lord Lyndhurst, Lord Abinger, Lord Truro, Lord Denman, Lord Cranworth, Lord Campbell, Lord St. Leonards, Lord Romilly, Lord Westbury, Lord Cairns, Lord Chelmsford, the present Lord Chancellor (Lord Hatherley), Sir William Garrow, Sir Samuel Shepherd, Sir James Marriott, Sir Christopher Robinson, Chief Justice Tindal, Chief Justice Jervis, Mr. Justice Keating, Sir William Follett, Lord Chief Justice Cockburn, Lord Chief Baron Kelly, Sir Frederick Pollock, and others.

The labour and difficulty of collecting and arranging these have been greater than I am likely to get credit for. The Opinions of the Law Officers given to the Colonial Office down to a recent period are scattered over two or three thousand manuscript volumes which are kept in the Record Office; and there is no general index to assist the search. It would, in fact, have been impossible for me to bestow the time and endure the fatigue necessary to find them, if I had not had a clue to the labyrinth supplied to me by M. Halksworth, the Librarian of the Colonial Office. But this did not extend back earlier than 1813, and I was obliged, therefore, to limit my search to the period subsequent to that date. I regret this, as no doubt much valuable matter is to be found in the manuscript volumes of an earlier date; and I hope that the same arrangement for facility of reference which has been adopted in the later volumes will be applied to the older ones, although it will be too late for my own Work, unless it should have the good fortune to reach another edition.

I have now the pleasing duty to perform of acknowledg ing the great kindness and assistance I have received in the course of my Work. To Earl Granville, the Secretary of State for the Colonies, I especially desire to tender my thanks, for the liberality and courtesy with which he assented to my application to be allowed to examine the archives, and publish the Opinions of the Law Officers in that Department. It was a thing for which there was no precedent; and if there had been a stiff adherence to official routine, I should have met with a refusal which, I venture to say, considering the value of the Opinions here for the first time made known to the world, would have been a public loss. I must express also my thanks to the Lords of the Treasury, for allowing me to select and publish some Opinions of the Law Officers; and to my friend, Mr. Greenwood, Q.C., Solicitor to the Treasury, for the kind assistance he rendered to me.

I regret that I cannot make a similar acknowledgment in the case of the Foreign Office. At the suggestion of high authority I wrote to the Earl of Clarendon a letter, which I am sure was unexceptionable in its tone, asking for permission—not to examine the archives of the Foreign Office, to which I felt there might very reasonably be an objection—but to be supplied with a few legal Opinions of old date, which could have no bearing upon any question in controversy at the present day. To my letter, however, I received no answer.

I must express my thanks to Sir Frederic Rogers, the Under-Secretary of State for the Colonies, and to Mr. Henry Holland, the Standing Counsel to that Department, for their obliging and ready assistance; also to Mr. Kingston, of the Record Office, for the very efficient aid he gave me in searching the manuscripts there; to my friend, Sir Travers Twiss, the Queen's Advocate, for the loan of two curious manuscript volumes which formerly belonged to Sir James Marriott, and of which I have made considerable use; and to my friend, Mr. Rothery, Chief Registrar of the Court of Admiralty, for two valuable manuscript Opinions.

I thought it right to obtain the consent of such *Ex* Law Officers as are still living before I made use of their Opinions; and I am happy to say that, except in two cases where I had no answer, I received the fullest and most unreserved permission to do so. And why should such Opinions not be published, provided they are of sufficiently late date to avoid questions at issue or in controversy now?

In the United States the Opinions of the Attorney Generals are published in eleven volumes, down even to the last two or three years; and surely no possible harm can ensue, but on the contrary much good may result, from knowing what the opinions have been, upon questions of Constitutional Law and public interest, of some of the greatest lawyers who have ever lived.

For reasons which will be easily understood, it was not thought expedient to publish Opinions of the Law Officers of a later date than 1856, or thereabouts; and my chief regret for this is, that I have thus been obliged to exclude the official Opinions of that distinguished lawyer and jurist, Sir Roundell Palmer. I hope that the Notes will be found useful, as I have endeavoured to bring down the law on each subject to the latest possible date.

W. F.

CONTENTS.

—◦◦—

CHAPTER I.

ON THE COMMON LAW AND STATUTE LAW APPLICABLE TO THE COLONIES.

OPINIONS.

CHAPTER II.

On the Ecclesiastical Law applicable to the Colonies.

OPINIONS.

CHAPTER III.

ON THE POWERS AND DUTIES AND CIVIL AND CRIMINAL LIABILITIES OF
GOVERNORS OF COLONIES.

OPINIONS.

CHAPTER IV.

ON VICE-ADMIRALTY JURISDICTION AND PIRACY.

OPINIONS.

CHAPTER V.

ON CERTAIN PREROGATIVES OF THE CROWN.

(1) Lands in the Colonies; (2) Grants; (3) Escheats; (4) Mines; (5) Treasure
Trove; (6) Royal Fish; (7) Felons' Goods; (8) Writ Ne exeat Regno;
(9) Proclamations (in note); (10) Cession of Territory; (11) Erection of
Courts of Justice.

OPINIONS.

CHAPTER VIII.

ON THE LEX LOCI AND LEX FORI. Pp. 239-251.

CHAPTER IX.

ON ALLEGIANCE AND ALIENS.

OPINIONS.

CHAPTER X.

ON EXTRADITION.

OPINIONS.

CONTENTS. xvii

CHAPTER XII.

ON THE REVOCATION OF CHARTERS.

OPINIONS.

CHAPTER XIII.

THE CHANNEL ISLANDS.

OPINION

CHAPTER XIV.

ON THE NATIONALITY OF A SHIP, AND OTHER MATTERS RELATING TO SHIPS.

OPINIONS.

CHAPTER XV.

On the Power of the Crown to grant Exclusive Rights of Trade.

OPINIONS.

CHAPTER XVIII.

ON MISCELLANEOUS SUBJECTS.

OPINIONS.

APPENDIX.

TABLE OF CASES.

TABLE OF STATUTES REFERRED TO.

INDEX

NAMES OF LAWYERS WHOSE OPINIONS ARE GIVEN IN THIS WORK.

Abinger, Lord (Sir James Scarlett) 6, 69, 172
Arnold, J. H. 108, 110
Atherton, Sir William 373
Beckett, Sir John 196
Cairns, Lord 79, 238, 368
Camden, Earl (Sir Charles Pratt) 1, 479
Campbell, Lord . 7, 8, 9, 10, 50, 51, 70, 72, 73, 156, 198, 199,
204, 224, 326, 341, 399, 436, 459, 464, 465
Chalmers, George 257
Chelmsford, Lord (Sir F. Thesiger) . 52, 54, 229, 328, 329, 366,
385, 402
Cockburn, Lord Chief Justice . 11, 25, 76, 77, 97, 227, 228,
332, 343, 367, 386, 404, 406, 462, 463, 468, 472, 477
Cooke, Sir John 91, 93
Cranworth, Lord (Sir R. M. Rolfe) . 7, 8, 9, 50, 51, 70, 72, 156,
198, 199, 204, 224, 326, 341, 436, 464, 465
Cushing, C. 344–366, 407
Denman, Lord 457
Dodson, Sir John . 50, 52, 73, 96, 97, 199, 227, 228, 329, 330,
332, 399
Fane, Francis 94, 152, 161, 430
Follett, Sir William Webb . 51, 73, 74, 96, 329, 383, 461
Foster, J. Leslie 99
Garrow, Sir William 4, 68, 153
Gifford, Lord 70, 95, 220, 453

SHORT BIOGRAPHICAL NOTICES

OF

DECEASED LAWYERS WHOSE OPINIONS ARE GIVEN IN THIS WORK.

Sir John King, Treasurer of the Inner Temple, 1675.

Sir William Jones, Solicitor General, 1673 ; Attorney General, 1675.

Sir Robert Sawyer, Attorney General, 1681, and again 1685 ; died, 1692.

Sir John Holt, born, 1642 ; Recorder of London, 1686 ; King's Serjeant, 1686 ; Lord Chief Justice, 1689 ; died, 1710.

Lord Somers, born, 1652 ; Solicitor General, 1689 ; Attorney General, 1692 ; Lord Keeper of the Great Seal, 1693 ; Lord Chancellor, 1697, with the title of Lord Somers ; Lord President of the Council, 1708, which office he resigned in 1710. He died in 1716.

Lord Trevor, born, 1659 ; Solicitor General, 1692 ; Attorney General, 1695 ; Chief Justice of the Common Pleas, 1701 ; Lord Privy Seal, 1726 ; President of the Council, 1730 ; died, 1730.

Sir John Hawles, Solicitor General, 1635 ; died, 1702. In 1680, Sir John Hawles published his tracts on Englishmen's Rights.

Sir John Cooke, King's Advocate, 1702.

Sir Edward Northey, Attorney General, 1701 ; reappointed, 1710 ; died, 1723.

Lord Harcourt, born, 1660 ; Solicitor General, 1702 ; Attorney General, 1707 ; reappointed, 1710 ; Keeper of the Great Seal, 1710 ; Lord Chancellor, 1712 ; died, 1727.

Sir James Montagu, Solicitor General, 1707 ; Attorney General, 1708 ; Baron of the Exchequer, 1714 ; one of the Commissioners of the Great Seal, 1718 ; Lord Chief Baron, 1722 ; died, 1723.

Lord Raymond, son of Sir Thomas Raymond, one of the Justices of the King's Bench, born, 1673 ; Solicitor General, 1710 ; Attorney General, 1720 ; one of the Justices of the King's Bench, 1724 ; Lord Chief Justice, 1725 ; a Commissioner of the Great Seal, 1725 ; died, 1733.

d

Sir William Thomson, Recorder of London, 1714; Solicitor
General, 1717; Cursitor Baron, 1726; a Baron of the Exchequer,
1729; died, 1739.

Richard West, Counsel to the Board of Trade; in 1718, Chancellor of Ireland; died, 1726.

Francis Fane succeeded Mr. West as Counsel to the Board of
Trade in 1725, and resigned that office in 1746.

Sir Clement Wearg, Solicitor General, 1723; died, 1726.

Earl Hardwicke (Philip Yorke), born, 1690; Solicitor General,
1720; Attorney General, 1724; Lord Chief Justice, 1733; Lord
Chancellor, 1737; died, 1764.

Sir Charles Talbot, Solicitor General, 1726; Lord Chancellor,
and created Lord Talbot, 1733; died, 1737.

Sir Thomas Reeve, Justice of the Pleas, 1733; Chief Justice
of the same Court, 1736; died, 1737.

Thomas Lutwyche, King's Counsel, died, 1734. He entered
the House of Commons in 1710, and sat in it till his decease.

Sir Dudley Ryder, Solicitor General, 1733; Attorney General,
1737; Lord Chief Justice, 1754; died, 1756.

Sir John Strange, Solicitor General, 1737; Recorder of London,
1739; Master of the Rolls, 1750; died, 1754.

Earl Mansfield (William Murray), born, 1705; Solicitor General,
1742; Attorney General, 1754; Lord Chief Justice, 1756; died,
1793.

Earl of Northington (Robert Henley), Attorney General, 1756;
Keeper of the Great Seal, 1757; Lord Chancellor, 1761; created
Baron Henley, 1760; Earl of Northington, 1764; Lord President
of the Council, 1766; died, 1774.

The *Hon. Charles Yorke,* born, 1722; Solicitor General, 1756;
Attorney General, 1761; again, 1765; Lord Chancellor, 1770;
died, 1770.

Sir Richard Lloyd, Solicitor General, 1754; a Baron of the
Exchequer, 1759; died, 1761.

Lord Grantley (Fletcher Norton), born, 1716; Solicitor General,
1761; Attorney General, 1763; Chief Justice in Eyre, 1769;
Speaker of the House of Commons in 1770, until 1780; created
Lord Grantley, 1782; died, 1789.

Lord Walsingham (William De Grey), Solicitor General, 1763;

Attorney General, 1766; Chief Justice of the Common Pleas, 1771; created Lord Walsingham in 1780; and died, 1781.

Sir Edward Willes, Solicitor General, 1766; one of the Justices of the King's Bench, 1768.

Sir Archibald Macdonald, born, 1746; one of the Judges for Wales in 1780; Solicitor General, 1784; Attorney General, 1788; Chief Baron of the Exchequer, 1793; created a Baronet, 1813; died, 1826.

Sir James Marriott, civilian, born, 1731; Master of Trinity Hall, Cambridge. In 1764, he was appointed the King's Advocate. He was appointed Judge of the High Court of Admiralty in the room of Sir George Hay: resigned in 1798, and died in 1803.

Sir John Willes, born, 1685; Attorney General, 1734; Chief Justice of the Common Pleas, 1737; died, 1761.

Earl Camden (Charles Pratt), born, 1713; Attorney General, 1757; Chief Justice of the Common Pleas, 1762; Lord Chancellor, 1766; died, 1794.

Lord Thurlow (Edward), born, 1732; Solicitor General, 1707; Attorney General, 1771; Lord Chancellor, 1778; died, 1806.

Chalmers, George, born, 1742; clerk to the Privy Council, 1786; died, 1825.

Sir Christopher Robinson, born, 1767; King's Advocate, 1805; Judge of the High Court of Admiralty, 1828; died, 1833.

Sir Nicolas Conyngham Tindal, born, 1776; Solicitor General, 1826; Chief Justice of the Common Pleas, 1829; died, 1846.

Lord Abinger (James Scarlett), born, 1769; Attorney General, 1827; Lord Chief Baron, 1834; died, 1844.

Lord Lyndhurst (John Singleton Copley), born at Boston, U.S., 1772; Chief Justice of Chester, 1818; Solicitor General, 1819; Attorney General, 1824; Master of the Rolls, 1826; Lord Chancellor, 1827; Lord Chief Baron, 1830; Lord Chancellor the second time, 1834; the third time, 1841; died, 1863.

Lord Gifford (Robert), born, 1779; Solicitor General, 1817; Attorney General, 1819; Chief Justice of the Common Pleas, 1824; Master of the Rolls, 1824; died, 1826.

Lord Denman (Thomas), born, 1779; Common Serjeant, 1822; Attorney General, 1830; Lord Chief Justice, 1832; died, 1854.

Lord Campbell (John), born, 1781; Solicitor General, 1832;

Attorney General, 1834; Lord Chancellor of Ireland, 1841; Chancellor of the Duchy of Lancaster, 1846; Lord Chief Justice of England, 1850; Lord Chancellor, 1859; died, 1861.

Lord Truro (*Thomas Wilde*), born, 1782; Solicitor General, 1840; Attorney General, 1841, and again, 1846; Chief Justice of the Common Pleas, 1846; Lord Chancellor, 1850; died, 1855.

Lord Cranworth (*Robert Monsey Rolfe*), born, 1790; Solicitor General, 1834; again, 1835; Baron of the Exchequer, 1839; one of the Commissioners of the Great Seal, 1850; Vice-Chancellor, 1850; Lord Justice, 1851; Lord Chancellor, 1852; a second time, 1865; died, 1868.

Sir William Horne, born, 1774; Solicitor General, 1832; Attorney General, 1832; died, 1860.

Sir Charles Wetherell, born, 1770; Solicitor General, 1824; Attorney General, 1826; died, 1846.

Sir Samuel Shepherd, born, 1761; Solicitor General, 1814; Attorney General, 1817; Chief Baron of Court of Exchequer in Scotland, 1819; died, 1841.

Sir Herbert Jenner, Queen's Advocate; Judge of Prerogative Court, and Dean of Arches Court; died, 1852.

Sir John Dodson, born, 1780; Queen's Advocate, 1834; Judge of Prerogative Court and Dean of Arches Court, 1852; died, 1858.

Sir William Webb Follett, born, 1798; Solicitor General, 1834, and again, 1841; Attorney General, 1844; died, 1845.

Sir John Jervis, born, 1802; Solicitor General, 1846; Attorney General, 1846; Chief Justice of the Common Pleas, 1850; died, 1856.

Sir William Atherton, born, 1806; Solicitor General, 1859; Attorney General, 1861; died, 1864.

Sir John Dorney Harding, born, 1809; Queen's Advocate, 1852; died, 1868.

CASES AND OPINIONS

ON

CONSTITUTIONAL LAW.

CHAPTER I.

ON THE COMMON LAW AND STATUTE LAW APPLICABLE TO THE COLONIES.

(1.) OPINION *of* MR. WEST, *Counsel to the Board of Trade* (*afterwards Lord Chancellor of Ireland*), *that the Common Law of England is the Common Law of the Colonies.* 1720.

The common law of England is the common law of the plantations, and all statutes in affirmance of the common law passed in England, antecedent to the settlement of a colony, are in force in that colony, unless there is some private Act to the contrary ; though no statutes made since those settlements, are there in force, unless the colonies are particularly mentioned. Let an Englishman go where he will, he carries as much of law and liberty with him as the nature of things will bear.

(2.) JOINT OPINION *of the Attorney and Solicitor General,* SIR CHARLES PRATT *and* HON. CHARLES YORKE, *that English subjects carry with them English laws.*

In respect to such places as have been or shall be acquired, by treaty or grant, from any of the Indian Princes or Governments, your Majesty's letters patent are not necessary ; the property of the soil vesting in the grantees by the Indian grants, subject only to your Majesty's right of sovereignty over the settlements, as English

B

settlements, and over the inhabitants, as English subjects, who carry with them your Majesty's laws wherever they form colonies, and receive your Majesty's protection, by. virtue of your royal charters.

C. PRATT.
C. YORKE.

(3.) OPINION *of the Attorney General,* SIR PHILIP YORKE, *as to the extension of the Statute Law to a Colony.* 1729.

Quære.—Whether such general statutes of England as have been made since the date of the Charter of Maryland, and wherein no mention is made of the plantations, and not restrained by words of local limitation, are, or are not, in force, without being introduced there by a particular Act of their own?

Opinion.—I am of opinion that such general statutes as have been made since the settlement of Maryland, and are not, by express words, located either to the plantations in general, or to the province in particular, are not in force there, unless they have been introduced and declared to be laws, by some Acts of Assembly of the province, or have been received there by long uninterrupted usage or practice, which may import a tacit consent of the lord proprietor and the people of the colony, that they should have the force of a law there.   P. YORKE.

By stat. 25 Geo. 2, c. 6, s. 10, it appears that the Legislature considered *usage* as sufficient to have extended an Act of Parliament to the colonies.

(4.) JOINT OPINION *of the Attorney and Solicitor General,* SIR ROBERT HENLEY, *and* HON. CHARLES YORKE, *as to how far subjects emigrating carry with them the Statute Law.* 1757.

MY LORDS,—In obedience to your Lordships' commands, signified to us by Mr. Pownall, by letter dated April 1st, 1757, accompanied with an enclosed letter and papers, which he had received from Jonathan Belcher, Esq., Chief Justice of his Majesty's colony of Nova Scotia, relating to the case of two persons convicted in the courts there, of counterfeiting and uttering Spanish dollars and pistareens, and requiring our opinion, in point of law, thereon ; we have taken the said letters and papers into our consideration, and find that the question upon which the case of those two per-

sons convicted of high treason depends, is this: Whether the Act
of Parliament, 1 Mar. c. 6, entitled " An Act that the counterfeiting of strange coins (being current within this realm), the
Queen's sign-manual or privy seal, to be adjudged treason," extends
to Nova Scotia, and is in force there, with respect to the counterfeiting Spanish dollars and pistareens in the said province?

And we are of opinion, first, that it doth not; for that the Act
is expressly restrained to the counterfeiting of foreign coin current
within this realm, of which Nova Scotia is no part.

Secondly, we are of opinion that the proposition adopted by the
Judges there, that the inhabitants of the colonies carry with them
the statute laws of this realm, is not true, as a general proposition, but depends upon circumstances: the effect of their Charter—
usage—and Acts of their Legislature; and it would be both inconvenient and dangerous to take it in so large an extent.

And thirdly, we are of opinion that the offence can only be considered as a high misdemeanor, unless there are any provisions in
any charter granted to that province, which make it a greater
offence, to which we are entirely strangers.

R. HENLEY.

May 18, 1757.   C. YORKE.

(5.) JOINT OPINION *of the Attorney and Solicitor General,*
SIR WILLIAM DE GREY *and* SIR EDWARD WILLES, *on the*
extension of Acts of Parliament to the Colonies, when they are
mentioned generally, as dominions of the Crown. 1767.

MAY IT PLEASE YOUR LORDSHIPS,—In obedience to your Lordships' commands, signified to us by Mr. Pownall's letter of the
12th of June, that we would take into our consideration an Act of
Parliament, passed in the 12th of Queen Ann., stat. 2, c. 18, entitled, " An Act for the preserving of all such ships and goods thereof
which shall happen to be forced on shore upon the coasts of this
kingdom or any other of Her Majesty's dominions;" also, one
other Act of Parliament passed the 4th of Geo. 1, c. 12, entitled
" An Act for enforcing and making perpetual an Act of the 12th
year of her late Majesty, entitled ' An Act for preserving all such
ships and goods thereof as shall happen to be forced on shore or
stranded upon the coasts of this kingdom or any other of His

B 2

Majesty's dominions,' and for inflicting the punishment of death on such as shall wilfully burn and destroy ships;" and that we would give our opinion whether the said Acts do extend to, and are in force in, his Majesty's colonies and plantations in America; we have taken the same into our consideration, and are of opinion that as the title of the Act of the 12th of Ann. stat. 2, c. 18, expressly imports to be "An Act for preserving ships and goods thereof forced on shore, or stranded upon the coasts of this kingdom or any other of Her Majesty's dominions," and the enacting part has words extending to her Majesty's dominions in general, the said Act of the 12th of Ann. extends to and is in force in his Majesty's colonies and plantations in America, notwithstanding the special promulgation of the law; and some other provisions in it are applicable only to this kingdom.

We are likewise of opinion that so much of the Act of 4th Geo. 1, c. 12, as declares the 12th of Ann. to be perpetual, extends to America. But the third clause of that Act, which introduces a new crime, by a provision altogether independent of the former part of the Act, and made to render an Act of the 1st of Ann. more effectual, we are inclined to think, does not extend to his Majesty's colonies and plantations in America, that clause being expressed in general terms, without any reference to the colonies; and the 11th of Geo. 1, c. 29, s. 7, which directs the mode of prosecution of those offences, when committed within the body of any county of this realm, or upon the high seas, making no mention of the manner of trial, if such offences should be committed in any of his Majesty's plantations or colonies in America.

W. DE GREY.

June 25, 1767. E. WILLES.

(6.) JOINT OPINION *of the King's Advocate,* SIR CHRIS-
TOPHER ROBINSON, *and the Attorney and Solicitor General,*
SIR WILLIAM GARROW *and* SIR SAMUEL SHEPHERD, *as to
the powers of Government vested in the Crown with respect to
the Colony of Berbice.* 1817.

MY LORD,—We are honoured with your Lordship's commands of the 27th ultimo, transmitting the charter of the colony of Berbice, being the conditions on which their High Mightinesses the

States-General have granted permission to the Directors of the colony of Berbice to open a free trade and navigation to the said colony for all the inhabitants of the United Netherlands; as also to deliver lands already cultivated or not on equitable terms.

And your Lordship is pleased to request that we would take the same into consideration, and report to your Lordship our opinion, whether his Royal Highness having found it necessary to dismiss the members of the present Council of Government, it is competent to his Royal Highness to direct, by an Order in Council, the manner in which another Council of Government should be formed, or whether his Royal Highness is still bound to require the late members to furnish names of other persons from which to make an election of their successors; calling our attention to the circumstance that the Berbice Association (the former directors of the colony) having been abolished previous to the surrender of the colony to his Majesty's arms, and the whole power of the directors having been at that time vested in the Government of Holland, his Royal Highness has since exercised in the colony authority both of the States-General and of the directors of the colony; and further calling our attention to the additional regulations laid down by the States-General in their resolve of the year 1780, altering in certain particulars the original charter under which the colony was established.

In obedience to your Lordship's directions, we have considered the same, and, adverting to the charter and the capitulation, we are of opinion that the full powers of Government are vested in the Crown by the conquest, and that his Royal Highness the Prince Regent having found it necessary to dismiss the present Council, the members so discharged would not be entitled to nominate their successors, as the 21st Article of the Charter, if it is adopted as the rule of Government, would not be applicable to such a case.

The original mode of nomination might be used if it was deemed expedient, but we are of opinion that it would not be obligatory, and that his Royal Highness the Prince Regent might direct by Order in Council the manner in which another Council of Government should be formed.

C. ROBINSON.

Doctors' Commons, April 22, 1817.   W. GARROW.

S. SHEPHERD.

(7.) JOINT OPINION *of the Attorney and Solicitor General,* SIR JAMES SCARLETT *and* SIR N. C. TINDAL, *on certain inquisitorial powers claimed by the House of Assembly in Antigua.* 1828.

We presume we are not called upon to consider the abstract question how far a Legislative Assembly in the colonies, without any original power given to them by their charter, or any course of usage and practice to support it, can exercise such inquisitorial powers, and enforce them by such means as are within the undisputed privilege of the English House of Commons. But conceiving the fact to be, that some analogous powers have been recognised in practice in the island of Antigua, and may be in certain cases essential for the purposes of legislation, we think it would not be expedient, on an occasion like the present, to call them in question. And we see no reason why the Attorney General of the island should refuse his attendance at the bar of the House of Assembly, or should decline answering any questions put to him, excepting such as may occasion disclosures which it would be inconsistent with the duty of his office to make, or which may have a tendency to criminate himself. It appears, however, to be unnecessary to dwell more largely on these grounds of exception, as the House of Assembly have by their 5th and 6th Resolutions expressly disclaimed their intention of breaking in upon either.

In case it should be thought necessary, upon grounds which may have occurred in the island, but which we do not comprehend, to bring the question to a judicial determination, the proper course will be by an action of trespass against the party who makes the arrest under the Speaker's warrant; in which case the powers of the House, both in general and as applied to the particular instance, may be discussed and determined on an appeal to the King in Council, the facts of the case being set out either upon a special verdict or a Bill of Exceptions.

J. SCARLETT.

Temple, January 21, 1828.   N. C. TINDAL.

(8.) JOINT OPINION *of the Attorney and Solicitor General,*
SIR WILLIAM HORNE *and* SIR JOHN CAMPBELL, *as to provisions of Charter of Justice not being at variance with Terms of Capitulation in the Mauritius.* 1833.

MY LORD,—We beg to acknowledge the receipt from your Lordship of the draft of an intended charter for the better administration of justice in the Mauritius, which you have been pleased to transmit to us for our revision, together with a letter stating the circumstances which have determined his Majesty's Government to the adoption of such a measure. In answer thereto, we have the honour to state that we have revised the draft according to your Lordship's desire, and that we do not see any reason for altering its form or the terms of its several provisions, which we presume to be in their scope and object conformable to the intention of Government, and not to be at variance with the capitulation or treaty by which his Majesty acquired tne sovereignty of that island with reference to the power of altering its laws.

W. HORNE.

Lincoln's Iun, March 26, 1833.   J. CAMPBELL.

(9.) JOINT OPINION *of the Attorney and Solicitor General,*
SIR JOHN CAMPBELL *and* SIR R. M. ROLFE, *as to sealing of writs issued for election of House of Assembly in Newfoundland.* 1837.

MY LORD,—We have to acknowledge the receipt of your Lordship's letter of the 14th instant, together with a case prepared by the Attorney General of the island of Newfoundland for the purpose of obtaining our opinion on the following points:—

1st. In case it shall be found that all the writs issued in 1832, under which the members of the House of Assembly in the island were elected and sate during all the sessions of the first General Assembly, were issued without seals, whether the Acts of the Legislature are to be deemed consequently void?

2nd. In case it should be found that two only of the fifteen members of Assembly were elected under writs issued without seals, whether such defect renders the legislative Acts of the Governor and Assembly invalid?

We beg leave to state to your Lordship that we have fully considered the case submitted to us, together with the accompanying papers, and we are clearly of opinion that no informality in the issuing of the writs can affect the validity of the acts done by the legislative body.

The absence of the seal might perhaps have justified the Sheriff or other officers to whom it was directed in treating the instrument as a nullity, and consequently refusing to proceed to an election. But the elections were, in fact, made, and we are of opinion that no objection could afterwards be raised to the form of the instruments under which the returning officers acted so as to affect the legislative power of the persons returned. Being of opinion that the legislative competency of the Assembly would not be affected by the circumstance of *all* the writs having been unsealed, we feel it hardly necessary to add, that it could not be affected by the fact that *two* of the writs issued without a seal supposing the rest to have been duly sealed.

We beg leave to add that it will be expedient for the future that all writs for the election of members of Assembly should issue under the seal of the colony, all writs being in strictness instruments under seal.

J. CAMPBELL.

Temple, October 17, 1837.   R. M. ROLFE.

(10.) JOINT OPINION *of the Attorney and Solicitor General,* SIR JOHN CAMPBELL *and* SIR R. M. ROLFE, *as to power of the Queen in Council to make laws for South Australia.* 1838.

MY LORD,—We have to acknowledge the receipt of a letter from your Lordship, of yesterday's date, transmitting to us the copy of a letter received at the Colonial Office, from the Chairman of the Colonization Commissioners for South Australia, calling your Lordship's attention to the effect which the statute of the late Session, cap. 60, may be supposed to have on the laws previously enacted in that province, and requesting us to report our opinion on the following questions :—First, whether under the statute 1 & 2 Vict. c. 60, s. 1, Her Majesty in Council has the power both to make laws and to delegate a concurrent] power of legislature to persons resident and being within the province? Secondly, whether the laws made by the local legislature, appointed under 4 Will. 4, c. 95 (1), are repealed or have lost their authority by virtue of the 1 & 2 Vict. c. 60 (2)? And if so, then, Thirdly, whether it is competent to the Queen in Council to revive the authority of such repealed or abrogated laws?

We have now the honour to report to your Lordship, in answer to the first question, that, in our opinion, the Queen has the power, by Order in Council, to make laws for the Government of the province; and that she has, concurrently with that power, the power of appointing, by warrant under the sign-manual, any three or more persons resident and being in the province, who will have the power of making laws for the colony, subject to any restrictions which Her Majesty may think fit to impose.

In answer to the second and third questions, we are clearly of opinion that all laws made under the authority of the Act 4 Will. 4, c. 95, will remain in force notwithstanding the Act of 1 Vict. c. 60.

J. CAMPBELL.
Temple, August 22, 1838. R. M. ROLFE.

(11.) JOINT OPINION *of the Attorney and Solicitor General,* SIR JOHN CAMPBELL *and* SIR R. M. ROLFE, *as to question of disqualification to sit in the House of Assembly in Newfoundland.* 1837. *

MY LORD,—We have had the honour to receive your Lordship's letter of the 16th inst., transmitting to us certain papers respecting the ejectment from the House of Assembly of Newfoundland of Mr. Power, one of the members for Conception Bay, and requesting our opinion whether the proceedings of the Assembly in this matter were according to law, and whether the seat of Mr. Power was legally vacated by his acceptance of the office of stipendiary magistrate?

(1) & (2) Both these Acts are repealed by 5 & 6 Vict. c. 61.

Having taken these papers into consideration, we have to report to your Lordship, that, in our opinion, the seat of Mr. Power was not legally vacated by his acceptance of the office in question, and that the proceedings of the Assembly of Newfoundland in this matter were contrary to law.

We think it is impossible to contend that the statutable disqualifications as to sitting in the House of Commons of the United Kingdom apply to the Assembly of Newfoundland. These disqualifications are different as to members for different parts of the United Kingdom, and cannot be applied to the members of a colonial Assembly established like that of Newfoundland.

The British House of Commons has never claimed the right by its own authority of disqualifying any persons elected by the people and not disqualified by the common law.

J. CAMPBELL.

Temple, July 20, 1837.   R. M. ROLFE.

(12.) JOINT OPINION *of the Attorney and Solicitor General,* SIR JOHN CAMPBELL *and* SIR THOMAS WILDE, *on the appointment of Magistrates in the Mauritius.* 1841.

MY LORD,—We have the honour to acknowledge the receipt of Mr. Vernon Smith's letter of the 14th inst., transmitting to us, by your Lordship's directions, copies of a correspondence between the Secretary of State and the Governor of Mauritius, together with an ordinance passed by the Governor in Council, providing for the appointment of Justices of the Peace to take cognizance of certain matters relative to merchant seamen, and requesting our opinion whether there is any objection to the confirmation by Her Majesty of the ordinance transmitted by the Governor?

Having considered this ordinance, with the accompanying documents, we have to report to your Lordship that, in our humble opinion, there is no objection to its being confirmed by Her Majesty. Although Her Majesty in Council has legislative authority in this colony, a subordinate legislative authority is deputed to the Governor with the advice and consent of the Council of Government, whereby such an ordinance as the present may be passed subject to be confirmed or disallowed by Her Majesty.

Generally speaking, it belongs to the prerogative of the Crown to appoint magistrates, but there are many precedents for this power being modified and regulated by legislative enactment.

Temple, January 22, 1841.

J. CAMPBELL.
THOS. WILDE.

(13.) JOINT OPINION *of the Attorney and Solicitor General,* SIR A. E. COCKBURN *and* SIR RICHARD BETHELL, *on the power of the Legislature of St. Helena to pass an Ordinance conferring on a foreigner power to hold land in St. Helena.* 1854.

We have had the honour of receiving Mr. Merivale's letter dated the 4th instant, stating that he was directed to ask whether, having regard to the constitution of the Island of St. Helena as described in the said letter, we were of opinion,—

1. That it would be lawful for the Legislature of St. Helena (under the direction of Her Majesty's Government) to pass an ordinance conferring on a foreigner power to hold and transfer land within the colony of St. Helena?

2. That (in the event of such a course being deemed more advisable) land might be purchased by a British subject or subjects in St. Helena, to hold it as a trustee or trustees for the French Government, or for any person or body authorized by the French Government, to do the necessary acts for keeping the land in a proper state for the purpose required; that purpose being, the fencing, watching, and protecting from injury, the spot occupied until recently by the remains of the Emperor Napoleon I. ?

We have taken the subject into our consideration, and beg to state that the difference between the island of St. Helena and the settlement of Hong Kong (to our opinion with respect to which latter place we are referred) lies in this: that Hong Kong is territory ceded by a foreign State, and therefore retaining its own laws, and not subject to English law, save so far as English law may be introduced and established by the authority of the Crown ; whereas, according to the information given us by Mr. Merivale's letter, the island of St. Helena was "occupied" by British subjects in the year 1650, who therefore carried with them such of the then existing laws of England as were applicable to the condition of a new settlement, and in which the law prohibiting aliens to hold land may probably be deemed to be included. But whether this be so or not is, we think, immaterial, because we are clearly of opinion that, even if the law against aliens being owners of land, and also the law of mortmain, be considered as having been introduced into St. Helena, it is competent to the Legislature of St. Helena, under the authority of the Act 3 & 4 Will. 4, c. 85, s. 112, and the Order in Council of 1835, to alter those laws; and we therefore think that it would be lawful for the Legislature of St. Helena (under the direction of Her Majesty's Government) to pass an ordinance conferring on a foreigner power to hold and transfer land within the colony of St. Helena.

2. We are also of opinion that the course pointed out in the second question might be adopted, but that in such a case, also, an ordinance of the legislature would be requisite, and we think the first course is to be preferred.

                                            A. E. COCKBURN.
July, 1854.   RICHARD BETHELL.

NOTES TO CHAPTER I.

Colonies acquired by Conquest.

In *Blankard* v. *Galdy*, 2 Salk. 411, it was held that in the case of an infidel country obtained by conquest, the laws do not entirely cease, but only such as are against the law of God; and that in such cases where the laws are rejected or silent, the conquered country shall be governed according to the rule of natural equity. In *Calvin's Case*, 7 Rep. 17, the rule is stated much to the same effect—namely, that " if a Christian King should conquer the kingdom of an infidel, and bring them under his subjection, then, *ipso facto*, the laws of the infidel are abrogated, for that they are not only against Christianity, but against the laws of God and of nature contained in the Decalogue; and in that case, until certain laws be established amongst them, the King by himself, and such judges as he shall appoint, shall judge them and their cases according to natural equity. But if a king conquers a Christian kingdom, he may at his pleasure alter the laws of the kingdom, but until he does so, the ancient laws remain." And see 2 P. Will. 75, Com. Dig. *Ley* (C). In *Blankard* v. *Galdy*, as reported in Comberbach, 228, the Court observed, " where it is said in Calvin's case that the laws of a conquered country do immediately cease, that may be true of laws for religion, but it seems otherwise of laws touching the government." In *Campbell* v. *Hall*,

Cowp. 209, 20 State Tr. 239, Lord Mansfield said that the laws of a conquered country continue in force until they are altered by the conqueror, and he added, that the "absurd exceptions as to pagans mentioned in Calvin's case," in all probability arose "from the mad enthusiasm of the crusaders." And he said also, addressing counsel, as reported in 20 State Tr. 294, "Don't quote the distinction for the honour of Lord Coke." But a distinction between Christian and non-Christian countries seems to be countenanced by a decision of the Judicial Committee in *Papayanni* v. *Russian Steam Company*, 2 Moore, P. C. (N. S.) 181, where it is said, that although between two Christian States all claims for jurisdiction must be founded upon treaty engagements of similar validity, the same strict rule as to precision of treaty obligations would not be required between a Christian and a non-Christian State ; and they added, "Consent may be expressed in various ways—by constant usage permitted and acquiesced in by the authorities of the State, active assent, or silent acquiescence where there must be full knowledge." Laws contrary to the fundamental principles of the British Constitution cease at the moment of conquest. Thus torture as a punishment would no longer exist : " The constitution of this country put an end to that idea :" *per* De Grey, C.J., *Fabrigas* v. *Mostyn*, 20 State Tr. 181. In *Picton's Case*, 30 State Tr. 742, Lord Ellenborough, C.J., said, " The laws that are repugnant to the rights of the conquering State cease, of course ;" upon which Mr. Nolan, one of the counsel for the prosecution, observed: " That position carried to its proper extent is all for which it is necessary that I should contend. By the laws respecting religion in the very country (Spain) from which this island ('Trinidad) has been conquered, a heretic may be burned ; and by the laws of the same country, any person converting a Roman Catholic to the Protestant religion might be burned likewise. If, therefore, the chaplain of any one of his Majesty's regiments had converted this poor girl to the Protestant faith, General Picton would have had a right, nay, it would have been his duty, to have burned this reverend person upon the principle for which his counsel must contend to-day." In *Ruding* v. *Smith*, 2 Hagg. Cons. R. 380, Lord Stowell said : " It sometimes happens that the conquered are left in possession of their own laws—more frequently the laws of the conquerors are imposed upon them ; and sometimes the conquerors, if they settle in the country, are content to adopt for their own use such part of the laws prevailing before the conquest as they may find convenient under the change of authority to retain. I presume that there is no legal difference between a conquered country and a conquered colony in this respect as far as general law is concerned ; and I am yet to seek for any principle derivable from that law which bows the conquerors of a country to the legal institutions of the conquered. Such a principle may be attended with most severe inconvenience in its operation . . . . I am perfectly aware that it is laid down generally, in the authorities referred to, 'that the laws of a conquered country *remain* till altered by the new authority.' I have to observe, first, that the word *remain* has *ex vi termini* a reference to its obligation upon those in whose usage it already existed, and not to those who are entire strangers to it, in the whole of their preceding intercourse with each other. Even with respect to the ancient inhabitants, no small portion of the ancient law is unavoidably superseded by the revolution of government that has taken place :" see *The Fama*, 5 Rob. Adm. 106.

The old Hindoo law is thus stated in the Institutes of Menu, Art. 203 : " Let him (the King) establish the laws of the conquered nations as declared in their books." It is little to the credit of our legislature that the practice of *suttee* in the East Indies was sanctioned by Act of Parliament. The stat. 37 Geo. 3, c. 142, s. 12, provided that no act done in India in consequence of the rule or law of caste, so far as respected the members of the same family only, should be deemed a crime, although the same might not be justifiable by the laws of England. But by Regulation XVII. of 1829, passed by the Governor-General in Council, the practice of *suttee* was declared illegal, and punishable by the criminal courts. All persons convicted of aiding and abetting in the sacrifice of a Hindoo widow were to be deemed guilty of culpable homicide. The preamble of this Regulation states that the practice of suttee was " revolting to the feelings of human nature," and that in abrogating it the Governor-General in Council did not intend to depart "from one of the first and most important principles of the system of British Government in India, that all classes of the people be secure in the observance of their religious usages, so long as that system can be adhered to without violation of the paramount dictates of justice and humanity " (1).

Subject to the exceptions stated by Lord Mansfield in *Campbell* v. *Hall*, Cowp. 209, 20 State Tr. 323, that the Crown cannot make any change contrary to fundamental principles, such as exempting an inhabitant from the laws of trade or from the power of Parliament, or giving him privileges exclusive of other subjects, " and so on in many other instances which might be put," the Queen in Council may impose upon a conquered country whatever laws she may think fit. " If the King refuses to grant a capitulation, and puts the inhabitants to the sword or exterminates them, all the lands belong to him. If he receives the inhabitants under his protection, and grants them their property, he has a power to fix such terms and conditions as he thinks proper." —*Campbell* v. *Hall, ubi sup.;* and see *Smith* v. *Brown*, 2 Salk. 666.

In *Jephson* v. *Riera*, 3 Knapp, 130, it was contended that Acts of Parliament or Orders in Council were the only constitutional modes by which the laws of a conquered country could be changed. But the Court held that, " as the charters of justice appeared to have been issued under the great seal, and therefore under the advice of a known responsible minister of the Crown, and as the language plainly and

(1) It is a remarkable fact that *suttee* is nowhere mentioned in the Vedas or in the Institutes of Menu, but by inveterate custom it had acquired the force of law.

explicitly declared the will of the King that the English law shall be the measure of justice in Gibraltar, the law of England has been lawfully substituted for the law of Spain." And in *Cameron* v. *Kyte* (*ibid.* 346), which was the case of a colony (Berbice) ceded by capitulation from the Dutch, and the question was as to the power of the Governor to alter the existing law, there being no such power contained in his commission, the Court said: "We do not mean to say that this portion of the King's sovereign authority may not be exercised by other means than by the Order of his Majesty in Council; that it may not be given by a commission or instruction under the King's sign-manual and signet . . . . We do not say that the King's will, intimated by the Secretary of State for the Colonies, might not be operative." Also, "the King has the whole legislative authority in a conquered colony, in so far as he may not have parted with it by capitulation or by his own voluntary grant." And in *Beaumont* v. *Barrett*, 1 Moore, P. C. 75, with reference to Jamaica : "It appears that it was a conquered island ; and, as in other territories obtained by conquest, such laws are in force there as the King, by his supreme authority, may choose to direct." But we must always understand that this power of the Crown is subject to the exceptions already stated as laid down by Lord Mansfield. The King cannot change the laws of the land : Bro. Abr. *Prerog.* The King cannot by his grant alter the law in any respect : Com. Dig. *Prerog.* (D) (1). And whatever may be the theoretical power of the Crown over a conquered territory, it is not likely that public opinion would tolerate any harsh or exceptional exercise of the prerogative ; so that, in point of fact, its situation under the Crown of England will be very much the same as that of a country acquired by settlement and occupancy. Lord Chief Justice Cockburn says, in a note to his published Charge to the Grand Jury in *R.* v. *Eyre*, in 1867, p. 19, that the question of the power to put martial law in force in Jamaica (as to which he had no doubt that it was entitled to the character of a settled colony—"the land was conquered, but the inhabitants by whom it was settled were not")—is not affected by the precedents of Demerara, Ceylon, or any other Crown colony, as in those the power of the Crown is absolute. In his Charge to the Grand Jury in another case of *R.* v. *Eyre*, in 1868, Blackburn, J., said : "When a colony is acquired by conquest, and when it had a foreign law in force . . . . I believe there is no doubt that the Crown has an option ; and one of its powers in such a case is either to leave the law which was in force in the country at that time still in force . . . or to change that law, to abolish it, and

(1) In old times the King claimed the right by his prerogative to disgavel lands, and change customary lands into military tenures. For instances see Elton's "Tenures of Kent :" London, 1867, pp. 368, 370. But it afterwards became settled law that nothing but an Act of Parliament could change a tenure inherent in the land itself. "If gavelkind lands escheat and come to the Crown by attainder, and be granted to be held by knight-service, or *per baronium*, the customary descent is not changed ; neither can it be, but by Act of Parliament, for it is a custom fixed in the land."—Hale's Hist. Com. Law, p. 312.

to substitute the English law. Whether it could go further, and substitute the English law or not, is immaterial for us to consider at present, and I express no opinion upon it."

A country reconquered from an enemy reverts to the same state that it was in before its conquest. The second acquisition is, in fact, considered rather as a resumption than a conquest : *Gumbes's Case*, 2 Knapp, 369. In such a case the doctrine of *Jus postliminii* seems to apply.

The same rule of English law as to the power of the Crown to impose law applies equally to a country obtained by cession, except that, of course, the right of legislation may be regulated by the terms of the treaty with the ceding power; and those terms ought to be inviolably observed. Thus, in *Re Adam*, 1 Moore, P. C. 470, the Court said : " The Mauritius, before its surrender to Great Britain in 1810, was a French colony, and having been surrendered on the condition that the inhabitants should preserve their religious laws and customs, we must look to the law of France as established in the colony before that event."

The following Case and Opinion are taken from Chalmers's Opinions :—

Case.—" By the Treaty of Utrecht, the King of France gave up the French part of Newfoundland to Great Britain, but the French inhabitants were allowed to remain there and enjoy their estates and settlements, provided they qualified themselves to be subjects of Great Britain, and those who would not do it had leave to go elsewhere, and take with them their moveable effects. But by her late Majesty's letter, in consideration of the King of France releasing a number of Protestant slaves out of his galleys, she did permit the French inhabitants at Placentia in Newfoundland, who were not willing to become her subjects, to sell and dispose of their leases and lands there."

Quære.—" Whether the Queen by the said letter could dispose of lands granted to the Crown by treaty ?"

Opinion.—" I am of opinion that the Queen could not by her letter dispose of lands granted to the Crown by treaty ; but if she entered into any regular agreement with the Crown of France for that purpose, she was by the law of nations engaged to do everything in her power to enable the French to have the benefit of it; which might be done by her confirming the title to such of her subjects as should pay the French a consideration in money, or otherwise, for their lands or houses.

" March 10, 1719-20.   " RICHD. WEST."

When the Crown has once granted a legislature to a conquered or ceded colony, it cannot afterwards exercise with respect to such colony its former power of legislation : *Campbell* v. *Hall*, Cowp. 204, 20 State Tr. 329, where Lord Mansfield said : " We therefore think by the two proclamations, and the commission to Governor Melville, the King had immediately and irrevocably granted to all who did or should inhabit, or who had or should have property in, the island of Grenada—

in general to all whom it should concern—that the subordinate legislation over the island should be exercised by the Assembly, with the Governor and Council, in like manner as in the other provinces under the King" (1). "After a colony or settlement has received legislative institutions, the Crown (subject to the special provisions of any Act of Parliament) stands in the same relation to that colony or settlement as it does to the United Kingdom:" *Re Lord Bishop of Natal*, 3 Moore, P. C. (N.S.) 148. And even if a constitution has not been given, but the laws of England have been granted by the Crown, it seems that its power to change them in the colony is gone. In *Calvin's Case*, 7 Rep. 14, the Court said: "And if a king took a Christian kingdom by conquest, as King Henry II. had Ireland, after King John had given unto them, being under his obedience and subjection, the laws of England for the government of that country, no succeeding King could alter the same without Parliament:" see *Re The Island of Cape Breton*, 5 Moore, P. C. 259. A question came before the Law Officers of the Crown and myself in 1867, as to whether the Indian Legislature, by virtue of the power inherent in sovereignty, irrespective of Acts of Parliament, could pass laws binding on native subjects out of British India; and we were of opinion that, having regard to the manner in which imperial legislation had been from time to time applied to the government of India, the extent of the powers of the Legislature of India depended upon the authority conferred upon it by Acts of Parliament, and we thought it unsafe to hold that the Indian Legislature had an inherent power to pass such laws. It is, however, right to mention that the then Queen's Advocate (Sir R. Phillimore) was of a different opinion.

With respect to colonies acquired by occupancy and settlement, which are in fact *plantations* in the original meaning of the word, the opinions given in the text accurately express the law: see 2 P. Will. 75; *Forbes* v. *Cochrane*, 2 B. & C. 463. "The common law is the inheritance of all the subjects of the realm; and therefore in the plantations or elsewhere, where colonies of English are settled, they are to be governed by the laws of England. So if a foreign territory, not inhabited, be obtained by the Crown of England, all laws of England bind there:" Com. Dig. *Ley* (C). "The term 'plantations,' in its common known signification, is applicable only to colonies abroad, where things are grown, or which were settled principally for the purpose of raising produce; and have never, in fact, been applied to a place like Gibraltar, which is a mere fortress and garrison, incapable of raising produce, but

Colonies acquired by Occupancy.

(1) The island of Grenada had been taken by Great Britain in the Seven Years' War, and ceded to us at the Peace of 1762. The King, by a proclamation issued in 1763, of his own authority imposed a tax of 4 per cent. on all exports; and the action was brought in the Court of King's Bench in England by the plaintiff, a British subject, who had subsequently purchased an estate and settled in the island, to recover back the sum he had been compelled to pay under this tax, in order that he might have liberty to ship his sugars to London. He maintained that such a tax could only be imposed by the authority of Parliament.

C

supplied with it from other places.   In truth, the term *plantation* in the
sense used by the Navigation Laws has never been applied either in
common understanding or in any Acts of Parliament (at least none such
could be pointed out when demanded in the course of the argument)
to any of the British dominions in Europe; not to Dunkirk, while that
was in our possession, nor at the present day to Jersey, Guernsey, or
any of the islands in the Channel :" *per* Lord Ellenborough, C.J.,
Lubbock v. *Potts,* 7 East, 455: see *Rubichon* v. *Humble,* 1 Dow. 191;
Roberdean v. *Rous,* 1 Atk. 543.   " Newfoundland is a settled, not a conquered colony, and to such colony there is no doubt that the settlers
from the mother-country carried with them such portions of its common
and statute law as was applicable to their new situation, and also the
rights and immunities of British subjects.   Their descendants have, on
the other hand, the same laws and the same rights, unless they have
been altered by Parliament.   And, upon the other hand, the Crown
possesses the same prerogatives and the same powers of government
that it does over its other subjects.   Nor has it been disputed that the
Sovereign had the right of creating a local legislative assembly, with
authority subordinate indeed to Parliament, but supreme within the
limits of the colony, for the government of its inhabitants :" *Kielley* v.
Carson, 4 Moore, P. C. 84.   " It is not disputed that the law prevailing
in the Falkland Islands must be considered to be the common law of
England, modified only by such statutes as apply to these islands :"
The Falkland Islands Company v. *The Queen,* 2 Moore, P. C. (N.S.) 273.
In *R.* v. *Brampton,* 10 East, 288, Lord Ellenborough, C.J., said : " In
the absence of any evidence to the contrary, I may suppose that the
law of England, ecclesiastical and civil, was recognised by subjects of
England in a place occupied by the King's troops, who would impliedly
carry that law with them."   But this is too broadly stated, and is certainly not true as regards ecclesiastical law.   See, as to the validity of
a marriage celebrated at the Cape of Good Hope between British subjects by the chaplain of the British forces occupying that settlement
under capitulation, the judgment of Lord Stowell in *Ruding* v. *Smith,*
2 Hagg. Cons. R. 371 ; and see *Burn* v. *Farrar,* 2 Hagg. Cons. R. 369.

Statutes
applicable to
the Colonies.
    The common law of England is the common law of the colonies,
and such statutes as have been passed in affirmance of the common
law previous to their acquisition, are in force there; but no statutes
afterwards passed are binding on their rulers, unless they are particularly mentioned: 2 P. Will. 75; *R.* v. *Vaughan,* 4 Burr. 2500.   The
question of whether a particular statute has been introduced into a
colony seems to be one of fact, and may be proved by evidence.   It
was so treated in *Gardener* v. *Fell,* 1 Jac. & Walk. 22 ; and *Freeman* v.
Fairlie, 1 Moore, Ind. App. 305.   Amongst the statutes which have been
held not to apply to the colonies are the Mortmain Acts : *Attorney
General* v. *Stewart,* 2 Mer. 143—positive regulations of Police : *R.* v.
Vaughan, 4 Burr. 2500—Statute of Frauds as to devise of lands : 2 P.

Will. 75—Penal statutes: *Blankard* v. *Galdy*, 2 Salk. 402; *Dawes* v. *Painter*, Freeman, 175—the Alien Acts: *Mayor of Lyons* v. *East India Company*, 1 Moore, P. C. 175—the Marriage Acts: *Lautour* v. *Teesdale*, 8 Taunt. 836—the Bankrupt Acts: *Clark* v. *Mullick*, 3 Moore, P. C. 252. As to Statutes of Limitation, it has been held that 21 Jac. 1, c. 16, extends to the East Indies: *East India Company* v. *Oditchurn Paul*, 7 Moore, P. C. 85. In an opinion given by Sir. A. Cockburn, A.G., and Sir R. Bethell, S.G., August, 1854, they said that neither the 21st Jac. 1, c. 2, an Act to quiet title against the Crown, nor the 9th Geo. 3, c. 16, extending and amending that Act, applies to Prince Edward's Island ; not the first of these statutes, because it only applies to lands which had been enjoyed for sixty years at the passing of the Act; nor the second, because at the time it passed Prince Edward's Island was part of the province of Nova Scotia, which had a legislative constitution of its own; and the Act not being extended to the colonies, it would not apply to Nova Scotia or Prince Edward's Island. The statute 9 Geo. 4, c: 83, s. 24, enacts that all laws and statutes within the realm of England at the time of the passing of that Act (not being inconsistent with any charter, or letters patent, or Order in Council, which might be issued in pursuance thereof), should be applied in the Courts of New South Wales and Van Diemen's Land, so far as the same could be applied within the said colonies. And it provided that the governors of those colonies, with the advice of the Legislative Councils, might, by ordinances, declare whether any particular laws or statutes extended to such colonies; but before such ordinances were made, the Supreme Courts were to adjudge and decide as to their application. And it was held in *Astley* v. *Fisher*, 6 C. B. 572, that a plea of an attorney's lien on a deed for work done in the Supreme Court of New South Wales was bad, as it did not show that the law of New South Wales was not inconsistent with the lien claimed. There Maule, J., said, " The 9 Geo. 4, c. 83, does not import into the colony *all* the English law." It has been held that the rule of the English common law, that rent due is a debt which ranks in the administration of assets as a specialty debt, does not apply to Jamaica, nor to any lands out of the jurisdiction of the English courts: *Vincent* v. *Godson*, 24 L. J. (N.S.), (Ch.) 121. See as to land in India, *Freeman* v. *Fairlie*, 1 Moore, Ind. App. 305; and as to a rule of the English bankrupt law prevailing in a colony, *Rolfe* v. *Flower*, 3 Moore, P. C. (N.S.) 365. In *Colonial Bank* v. *Warden*, 5 Moore, P. C. 354, Parke, B., said : " The 78th section of 2 & 3 Vict. c. 41, says, ' all moveable estate and effects of the bankrupt, wherever situate;' that would include the colonies." The English law of *felo de se*, with consequent forfeiture, does not apply to the suicide of a Hindoo in India: *Attorney General of Bengal* v. *Ranee Surnomoye Dossee*, 9 Moore, Ind. App. 387; see *Bentinck* v. *Willink*, 2 Hare (Ch.) 1.

Whether any particular statute has or has not force in a colony must therefore be determined by the proper tribunals—first, in the colony itself, and afterwards on appeal to the Queen in Council. All Acts which by reasonable construction must be supposed to apply to the colonies, whether passed before or after the acquisition, will be considered obligatory upon them. "The commercial intercourse of the colonies was regulated by the general laws of the British Empire, and could not be restrained or obstructed by colonial legislation :" Story, Comm. s. 178.

Power of Crown in case of Settlements.

In the case of colonies by occupancy and settlement, the Crown alone cannot legislate, but it may by virtue of its prerogative appoint governors, and erect courts of justice, and give the power of summoning representative assemblies; in other words, may grant a constitution : *Kielley* v. *Carson*, 4 Moore, P. C. 85. An exception, however, in favour of the legislative power of the Crown has been made in the case of settlements on the coast of Africa and the Falkland Islands, where by statute 6 & 7 Vict. c. 13 the Queen in Council is empowered to establish laws, institutions, and ordinances; but all such Orders in Council are to be laid before Parliament.

Barbarous or infidel countries.

When Englishmen establish themselves in an uninhabited or barbarous country, they carry with them not only the laws but the sovereignty of their own State, and those who live amongst them, and become members of their community, become also partakers of, and subject to, the same laws : *Advocate General of Bengal* v. *Ranee Surnomoye Dossee*, 2 Moore, P C. (N.S.) 59. As to the nature of the settlement made in the East Indies, see the same case, where the Court said : " If the settlement had been made in a Christian country of Europe, the settlers would have become subject to the laws of the country in which they settled. It is true that in India they retained their own laws for their own government within the factories which they were permitted by the ruling powers of India to establish ; but this was not on the ground of general international law, or because the power of England or the laws of England had any proper authority in India, but upon the principles explained by Lord Stowell in a very celebrated and beautiful passage of his judgment in the case of *The Indian Chief*, 3 Rob. Adm. 29." The passage here referred to is the following: " In the East from the oldest times an immiscible character has been kept up ; foreigners are not admitted into the general body and among the society of the nation; they continue strangers and sojourners as all their fathers were—*Doris amara suam non intermiscuit undam :* not acquiring any national character under the general sovereignty of the country, and not trading under any recognized authority of their own original country, they have been held to derive their present character from that of the association or factory under whose protection they live and carry on their trade."

Foreign acquisition vested in the Crown.

British subjects cannot take possession in their own right of a foreign country, which, if acquired, becomes vested in the Crown. The statute 53 Geo. 3, c. 155, s. 95, declared the undoubted sovereignty of the

Crown over the territorial acquisitions of the East India Company. " No point is more clearly settled in the courts of common law, than that a conquered country forms immediately part of the King's dominions :" *per* Sir W. Scott, *The Foltina,* 1 Dods, 451 ; and see, *per* Lord Mansfield, *Campbell* v. *Hall,* 20 State Tr. 323. The mere possession of a territory by an enemy's force does not of itself necessarily convert the territory so occupied into hostile territory, or its inhabitants into enemies : *per cur. Cremidi* v. *Powell,* 11 Moore, P. C. 101 ; and see *The Manilla,* 1 Edw. 3 ; *Donaldson* v. *Thompson,* 1 Camp. 429 ; *Hagedorn* v. *Bell,* 1 M. & S. 450.

Of course, all British colonies whatever are subject to the paramount authority of Parliament : see statute 7 & 8 Will. 3, c. 22, s. 9. In *Campbell* v. *Hall,* Cowp. 204, 20 State Tr. 304, Lord Mansfield said that the power of giving a constitution by the Crown to a conquered country is not exclusive of Parliament ; "there cannot exist any power in the King exclusive of Parliament," and " a country conquered by the British arms becomes a dominion of the King in right of his crown, and therefore necessarily subject to the legislative power of the Parliament of Great Britain."—*Ibid.* 324. This right of Parliament was expressly affirmed as to the American colonies by the statute 6 Geo. 3, c. 12, but afterwards as regards taxation renounced by statute 18 Geo. 3, c. 12. In his Charge to the Grand Jury in *R.* v. *Eyre,* in 1868, it was said by Blackburn, J. : " Although the general rule is that the legislative assembly has the sole right of imposing taxes on the colony, when the imperial legislature chooses to impose taxes, according to the rule of English law they have a right to do it." And again, " In the Navigation Laws there are express enactments that the colonists should not make laws to allow foreigners to trade with the colonies, and then they exercise the control which they had a right to exercise ; and when that is done, no doubt the colonial legislature cannot make a law which would be binding in contradiction to the imperial legislature."—*Ibid.* See as to Canada, 14 Geo. 3, c. 83 ; 31 Geo. 3, c. 31 ; 3 & 4 Vict. c. 35. The statute 3 & 4 Will. 4, c. 59, s. 56, enacts that all laws in any of the British possessions in America repugnant to any Act of Parliament made or thereafter to be made, " so far as such Act shall relate and mention the said possessions," are, and shall be, null and void. The next section provides that no exemption from duty in any of the British possessions abroad contained in any Act of Parliament shall extend to any duty not imposed by Act of Parliament, unless and so far only as any duty not so imposed is expressly mentioned in such exemption. Statute 22 & 23 Vict. c. 12, enacts that it shall be lawful for the legislature or other legislative authority of any of Her Majesty's possessions abroad, to which any of the provisions of the statute 54 Geo. 3, c. 15 (" An Act for the more easy Recovery of Debts in Her Majesty's Colonies of New South Wales "), or certain sections of the statute 5 & 6 Will. 4, c. 62 (as to proof by declaration instead of oath), apply, to repeal, alter,

[margin note: Colonies subject to paramount authority of Parliament.]

or amend all or any of such provisions, in like manner as if they had been originally enacted by such legislature or legislative authority. The Copyright Act (5 & 6 Vict. c. 45) says that the words " British dominions " in the Act shall include " all the colonies, settlements, and possessions of the Crown," and enacts that the Act shall extend to every part of the British dominions; and it was held in *Low* v. *Routledge*, L. R. 1 Ch. App. 42, that an alien *ami* resident in Canada who had not complied with the provisions of the Canadian Copyright Act (4 & 5 Vict. c. 6), was entitled to copyright under the Imperial Act. It was there contended that the general words " all colonies " did not include such colonies as have an independent legislature, and that the Imperial Act could not by a side-wind repeal the Canadian Act. But the Court said that the word " colonies " in the statute must extend to all colonies in the absence of a context to control it, and they could find no such context. The statute 26 & 27 Vict. c. 6, after reciting that Her Majesty has from time to time caused letters patent to be made under the great seal, intended to take effect within Her Majesty's colonies and possessions beyond the seas, enacts that no such letters patent shall (unless otherwise provided therein or by other lawful authority) take effect until the making of them has been signified therein by proclamation or other public notice.

The Documentary Evidence Act, 1868 (31 & 32 Vict. c. 37), provides that, subject to any law that may be from time to time made by the legislature of any British colony or possessions, the Act shall be in force in every such colony and possession, and it is made to extend to the Channel Islands and the Indian territories of Her Majesty. And by statute 30 & 31 Vict. c. 45, s. 16, it is made lawful for Her Majesty to empower the Admiralty by commission under the great seal to establish Vice-Admiralty Courts in any British possession, notwithstanding that such possession may have previously acquired independent legislative powers. By statute 29 & 30 Vict. c. 65, Her Majesty may, by proclamation issued with the advice of the Privy Council, declare gold coins made at any colonial branch of the Royal Mint duly established by proclamation a legal tender within any part of the British dominions.

In *Low* v. *Routledge, ubi sup.*, it was insisted in argument that an alien coming into Canada could only acquire such rights as are given by the law of Canada, and could not therefore be entitled to copyright; in support of which proposition the cases of *Donegani* v. *Donegani*, 3 Knapp. 63; *Re Adam*, 1 Moore, P. C. 460; *Brook* v. *Brook*, 3 Sm. & Giff. 481; 9 H. L. Ca. 193, S.C.; and *Hope* v. *Hope*, 8 D. M. & G. 731, were cited. But Turner, L.J., said: " On examining these cases they will be found to decide no more than this—that as to aliens coming within the British colonies, their civil rights within the colonies depend upon the colonial laws; they decide nothing as to the civil rights of aliens beyond the limits of the colonies. This argument on the part of the defendants is in truth founded on a confusion between the rights of an alien as a subject of a colony and his rights as a subject of the Crown. Every alien coming into a British colony becomes temporarily a subject of the Crown—bound by, subject to, and entitled to the benefit of the laws which affect all British subjects. He has obligations and rights both within and beyond the colony into which he comes. As to his rights within the colony, he may well be bound by its laws; but as to his rights beyond the colony, he cannot be affected by those laws, for the laws of a colony cannot extend beyond its territorial limits."—See *Craw* v. *Ramsay*, Vaugh. 274.

The *status* of a person domiciled in a colony must be determined by the law of England, but the rights and liabilities incident to such *status*, by the law of the colony : *In re Adam*, 1 Moore, P. C. 460.

When an Act of Parliament declared that all laws passed by the Validity of legislature of a colony should be valid and binding within the colony, Colonial and that the colonial Court of Appeal should be subject to such pro- Laws. visions as might be made by any Act of the colonial legislature, it was held that an Act having been passed by the colonial legislature limiting the right of appeal to causes where the sum in dispute was not less than a certain amount, a petition for leave to appeal in a case where the sum was of less amount could not be received by the King in Council, although there was a saving in the Colonial Act of the rights and prerogatives of the Crown: *Cuvillier* v. *Aylwin*, 2 Knapp, 72. The statute 6 Vict. c. 22, enacts that no law or ordinance made by the legislature of any British colony for the admission of the evidence of persons " who, being destitute of the knowledge of God and of any religious belief, are incapable of giving evidence upon oath in any court of justice," shall be null and void or invalid by reason of any repugnancy to the law of England, but such law or ordinance shall be subject to the confirmation or disallowance of Her Majesty as any other law or ordinance of the colonial legislature. A question came before the Law Officers of the Crown, Sir R. Bethell, A. G., and Hon. J. S. Wortley, S. G., in 1857, as to the confirmation by Her Majesty of an ordinance passed by the Legislature of Hong Kong "for Amending the Law of Evidence in Trial by Jury ;" and they said, in their Opinion : " The 6th Vict. c. 22 gives a power to the legislature of any British colony to make ordinances touching the admission of evidence in any judicial proceeding in such colony, although such ordinance may be repugnant to the law of England. This enactment is limited to the admission of evidence only, and the Act recognizes the obligation of Colonial Acts being in accordance with the law of England. But the 5th, 6th, 7th, and 8th enactments of the Hong Kong ordinance propose to alter most materially the established law of England in respect of the crime of perjury, and to make that punishable as perjury which by the laws of England does not amount to that offence. This is in our opinion illegal."

Recently, the powers of colonial legislatures have been enlarged
and regulated by Acts of Parliament: see statute 26 & 27 Vict. c. 84.
And by statute 28 & 29 Vict. c. 63, intituled " An Act to remove doubts
as to the validity of Colonial Laws," it is enacted that any colonial
law repugnant to the provisions of any Act of Parliament extending to
the colony to which such law may relate, or repugnant to any order or
regulation made under the authority of such Act of Parliament, or
having in the colony the force and effect of such Act, shall be read
subject to such Act, order, or regulation, and shall to the extent of such
repugnancy be void.   But no colonial law shall be void or inopera-
tive on the ground of repugnancy to the law of England, unless the
same shall be repugnant to the provisions of such Act, order, or regulation ; and no colonial law shall be void by reason only of any
instructions with reference to such law, or the subject thereof, which
may have been given to the Governor by Her Majesty, by an instrument other than the letters patent or instrument authorizing him to
assent to laws for the government of the colony.   The colonial legislatures are also empowered to establish courts of judicature, and the
representative legislatures (which are defined to be legislative bodies
of which one half are elected by inhabitants of the colony) are empowered to make laws respecting their own constitution, powers, and
procedure, provided that such laws shall have been passed in conformity with any Act of Parliament, letters patent, Order in Council,
or colonial law, for the time being in force in the colony.   The term
" colony " in this Act includes all Her Majesty's possessions abroad in
which there exists a legislature, except the Channel Islands, the Isle
of Man, and British India.   By stat. 28 & 29 Vict. c. 64, laws made by
colonial legislatures for establishing the validity of marriages contracted in their respective colonies are to have the same force and
effect within all parts of Her Majesty's dominions as they have within
the colony for which such laws were made ; but no effect or validity
is given to any marriage unless both the parties were at the time of
the marriage, according to the law of England, competent to contract
the same.   See as to the power of the Legislature of New South Wales
to pass a particular Act, *Bank of Australia* v. *Nias*, 16 Q. B. 733 ; and
see the powers of the old Irish Parliaments discussed in *Craw* v.
Ramsay, Vaugh. 292.

ent of
diction of   The jurisdiction of colonial legislatures extends to three miles from
nial   the shore.   In an opinion given by the Law Officers of the Crown—Sir
islatures.   J. Harding, Queen's Advocate ; Sir A. E. Cockburn, Attorney General ;
and Sir R. Bethell, Solicitor General—with reference to British Guiana,
Feb. 1855, they said : " We conceive that the colonial legislature cannot
legally exercise its jurisdiction beyond its territorial limits—three miles
from the shore—or, at the utmost, can only do this over persons domiciled in the colony who may offend against its ordinances even beyond
those limits, but not over other persons."   In an opinion given by Sir

J. Harding, Queen's Advocate, in Aug. 1854, on the question within what distance of the coasts of the Falkland Islands foreigners might be legally prevented from whale and seal fishing, he said : "Her Majesty's Government will be legally justified in preventing foreigners from whale and seal fishing within three marine miles (or a marine league) from the coasts, such being the distances to which, according to the modern interpretation and usage of nations, a cannon-shot is supposed to reach."

The statute 23 & 24 Vict. c. 121, after reciting that divers of Her Power of Majesty's subjects have occupied, or may hereafter occupy, places being Crown where possessions of Her Majesty, but in which no Government has been no Legisla- established by authority of Her Majesty, enacts that the provisions of tures esta-
blished. statute 6 & 7 Vict. c. 13, by which the Crown is empowered to establish by Order in Council laws, institutions, and ordinances for the government of Her Majesty's settlements on the coast of Africa and the Falkland Islands, shall extend to all possessions of Her Majesty not having been acquired by cession or conquest, nor, " except in virtue of this Act," being within the jurisdiction of the legislative authority of any of Her Majesty's possessions abroad. The statute 3 & 4 Will. 4, c. 93, empowers the Crown to appoint superintendents of trade in China, and by Order in Council to give them power and authority to make regulations for the government of British subjects in China, and to impose penalties, forfeitures, or imprisonment for the breach of such regulations. See on this *Evans* v. *Hutton*, 4 M. & G. 941.

In an opinion given by Sir A. Cockburn, A.G., and Sir R. Bethell, Power of S.G., Feb. 15, 1856, they said, that " the law and practice of Parlia- Colonial ment, as established in the United Kingdom, are not applicable to Legislatures
to commit. colonial legislative assemblies, nor does the rule of the one body furnish The *lex et* any legal analogy for the conduct of the other." The correctness of *consuetudo* this opinion has been abundantly established by decided cases. It was *Parliamenti*
does not held, indeed, in *Beaumont* v. *Barrett*, 1 Moore, P. C. 59, that the Legisla- apply. (1) tive Assembly of Jamaica had the power of imprisoning for contempt by the publication of a libel. But so far as that decision was founded upon the idea that every legislative body had the power of committing for contempt, it may be considered as overruled by *Kielley* v. *Carson*, 4 Moore, P. C. 63, where the Court decided that the House of Assembly in Newfoundland had no such power, saying : "They are a local legislature with every power reasonably necessary for the proper exercise of their functions and duties; but they have not what they have erroneously supposed themselves to possess—the same exclusive privileges which the ancient law of England has annexed to the House of Parliament." But it may be inferred from what was said in that case that frequent usage of the power of committal by a colonial legislature,

(1) See an opinion by Mr. Hargrave, in 1793, on a commitment by the Irish House of Lords for contempt and breach of privilege : " Jurisconsult Exercitations," i. 197.

and long acquiescence by the public with the sanction of the local tribunals, would raise a presumption that the power had been duly communicated by law. See also *Fenton* v. *Hampton*, 11 Moore, P. C. 347;
Doyle v. *Falconer*, L. R., 1 P. C. 328. In the last case the Court
said : "The privileges of the House of Commons, that of punishing for
contempt being one, belong to it by virtue of the *lex et consuetudo Parliamenti*, which is a law peculiar to and inherent in the two Houses of
Parliament in the United Kingdom. It cannot therefore be inferred,
from the possession of certain powers by the House of Commons by
virtue of that ancient usage and prescription, that the like powers
belong to the legislative assemblies of comparatively recent creation in
the dependencies of the Crown. Again, there is no resemblance
between a colonial House of Assembly, being a body which has no
judicial functions, and a court of justice being a court of record.
There is, therefore, no ground for saying that the power of punishing
for contempt, because it is admitted to be inherent in the one, must be
taken by analogy to be inherent in the other." They added that in the
case before them—that of the Legislature of Dominica—such a privilege might possibly have been granted by the instrument creating the
Assembly, since Dominica was a conquered or ceded colony, and the
introduction of the law of England seems to have been contemporaneous
with the creation of the Assembly. It might be possible to enlarge the
existing privileges of the Assembly by an Act of the local legislature
passed with the consent of the Crown, since such an Act seems to be
within the 3rd section of the statute 28 & 29 Vict., c. 63 ("An Act to
remove doubts as to the validity of Colonial Laws"). That extraordinary
privileges of this kind when regularly acquired would be duly recognised, had been shown by the case of *Dill* v. *Murphy*, 1 Moore, P. C.
(N. S.) 487, in which it was held that the *lex et consuetudo Parliamenti*
does not apply as part of the common law to the colonies. The House of
Keys in the Isle of Man has not in its legislative capacity the power to
commit for contempt: *Re Brown*, 33 L. J. (N. S.) Q. B. 193.

s and
of ac-
tion of
ies.

The following is a list of the British Colonies, with the modes and
dates of acquisition :—

By CAPTURE : Gibraltar, 1704 ; Malta, 1800.

By CAPITULATION : Jamaica, 1655 ; Ceylon, 1796 ; Cape of Good
Hope, 1796 ; Trinidad, 1797 ; St. Lucia, 1803 ; British Guiana, 1803 ;
Mauritius, 1810.

By CESSION : Honduras, 1670 ; Canada, 1763 ; Dominica, 1763 ;
Grenada, 1763 ; St. Vincent, 1763–1783 ; Tobago, 1763 ; Bahamas,
1783. (It seems doubtful whether the Bahamas were acquired by cession or by conquest. See Clark's "Colonial Law," p. 367.) Heligoland,
1814 ; Hong Kong, 1843 ; Labuan, 1846.

By SETTLEMENT : Newfoundland, 1497 ; New Brunswick and Nova
Scotia, 1497 (now incorporated with Canada); Prince Edward's Island,
1497 ; Barbadoes, 1605 ; Bermuda, 1609 ; Nevis, 1628 ; Turk's Island,

1629; Gambia, 1631; Antigua, 1632; Montserrat, 1632; St. Christopher, 1623–1650; St. Helena, 1661; Gold Coast, 1661; Virgin Islands, 1665; Sierra Leone, 1787; Australian colonies, from 1787 to 1859; Tasmania, 1803; New Zealand, 1814; Falkland Islands, 1765 and 1833; British Columbia, 1858.

The STRAITS SETTLEMENTS, comprising Singapore, Penang, and Malacca, were transferred from the Indian Government to the Colonial Office by Order in Council under the stat. 29 & 30 Vict. c. 115.

With respect to Constitutions, our colonies may be divided into Colonial two classes: 1, those which possess representative institutions which Constitutions have been established either directly or indirectly under the authority of Acts of Parliament; and 2, those whose Constitutions have been established by local Acts, which have afterwards received the Royal assent.

In the first class are included—

CANADA: 31 Geo. 3, c. 31; 3 & 4 Vict. c. 35; 17 & 18 Vict. c. 118; 30 Vict. c. 3.

COLUMBIA: 29 & 30 Vict. c. 67 (repealing 21 & 22 Vict. c. 99).

NEWFOUNDLAND: 5 & 6 Vict. c. 120; 10 & 11 Vict. c. 44.

NEW SOUTH WALES: 5 & 6 Vict. c. 76; 7 & 8 Vict. c. 74; 13 & 14 Vict. c. 59; 18 & 19 Vict. c. 54; 25 Vict. c. 11; 29 & 30 Vict. c. 74.

SOUTH AUSTRALIA: 5 & 6 Vict. c. 61; 13 & 14 Vict. c. 59; 25 Vict. c. 11.

WESTERN AUSTRALIA: 10 Geo. 4, c. 22; 9 & 10 Vict. c. 35.

VICTORIA: 13 & 14 Vict. c. 59; 18 & 19 Vict. c. 55; 25 Vict. c. 11.

TASMANIA (Van Diemen's Land): 5 & 6 Vict. c. 76; 7 & 8 Vict. c. 74; 13 & 14 Vict. c. 59; 25 Vict. c. 11; 29 & 30 Vict. c. 74. In an Opinion given by Sir A. Cockburn, Attorney General, and Sir R. Bethell, Solicitor General, in June, 1855, they said: " We are of opinion that the legal mode of effecting the proposed alteration in the name of the colony of Van Diemen's Land into Tasmania, is by an Order in Council, followed by the Queen's proclamation."

QUEENSLAND: 24 & 25 Vict. c. 44.

NEW ZEALAND: 3 & 4 Vict. c. 62; 15 & 16 Vict. c. 72; 20 & 21 Vict. c. 53; 25 & 26 Vict. c. 48.

In the second class are included—

ANTIGUA: Colonial Act, No. 861, 1866; No. 4, 1867. Imperial Act, 22 & 23 Vict. c. 13 (authorizing the Crown to ratify a Colonial Act extending the operation of the laws of Antigua to the island of Barbadoes).

BARBADOES, 1666. See Clarke's " Colonial Law," p. 179.

CAPE OF GOOD HOPE: By letters patent, May, 1850, the Legislature of the Cape of Good Hope was empowered to pass ordinances establishing a representative government for the colony, and ordinances constituting a Council and House of Assembly were accordingly passed by the Legislature and confirmed by Her Majesty: see *In re The Lord*

Bishop of Natal, 3 Moore, P. C. (N. S.) 118. The constitution of the House of Assembly is affected by the provisions of stat. 28 Vict. c. 5, by which British Kaffraria was incorporated with the Cape of Good Hope.

DOMINICA : Royal proclamation, 1775 ; Colonial Acts, 1863, 1865.

GRENADA : Colonial Acts.

HONDURAS : Colonial Act, 16 Vict. c. 4.

MONTSERRAT : Colonial Act, No. 350, 1866.

NEVIS : Colonial Acts, Nos. 329 and 330, 1866.

PRINCE EDWARD'S ISLAND : Colonial Acts.

ST. KITTS : Colonial Act, 1866.

ST. VINCENT : Colonial Act, 1866–1868.

VIRGIN ISLANDS : Colonial Act, 1867.

TOBAGO : Colonial Act, 1855.

Colonial Legislatures by authority of the Crown.
There is a class of colonies in which the legislative authority—generally consisting of a governor and executive and legislative councils —has been constituted by charter or letters patent from the Crown, or by virtue of commissions of governors, independently of Imperial or Colonial Acts. Amongst these are included BERMUDA, BRITISH GUIANA, BAHAMAS, CEYLON, GIBRALTAR, HELIGOLAND, HONG KONG, LABUAN, MALTA, MAURITIUS, NATAL, ST. KITTS, ST. LUCIA, TRINIDAD, TURK'S ISLAND (separated from the Bahamas Government, and annexed to that of Jamaica, by Order in Council, 1848).

ST. HELENA is governed by Orders in Council, under the authority of stat. 3 & 4 Will. 4, c. 85, s. 112.

JAMAICA is in an exceptional position since the late insurrection ; for now, by 29 Vict. c. 12, the Queen is empowered to create and constitute a government in such form and with such powers as to Her Majesty may best seem fitting, and from time to time to alter or amend such government. The constitution is, in fact, abolished. And by 6 & 7 Vict. c. 13, Her Majesty is empowered to establish by Order in Council laws, institutions, and ordinances for the government of her SETTLEMENTS ON THE COAST OF AFRICA and the FALKLAND ISLANDS. (A charter was granted to the latter in June, 1843.)

Cases relating to the Colonies.
The following are some of the principal decided cases which relate to different British colonies :—

BARBADOES : *Gill* v. *Barron,* L. R. 2 P. C. 157.

BERMUDA : *Kennedy* v. *Trott,* 6 Moore, P. C. 449 ; *Ex parte Jenkins,* L. R. 2 P. C. 258.

BRITISH GUIANA : *Re M'Dermott,* L. R. 1 P. C. 260.

CANADA : *Macdonald* v. *Lambe,* L. R. 1 P. C. 539 ; *Renaud* v. *Tourangeau,* L. R. 2 P. C. 4 ; *Kierzkowski* v. *Dorion,* L. R. 2 P. C. 291 ; (Nova Scotia) *Re Island of Cape Breton,* 5 Moore, P. C. 259 ; *Wallace* v. *M'Sweeney,* L. R. 2 P. C. 180.

CAPE OF GOOD HOPE : *Ruding* v. *Smith,* 2 Hagg. 371 ; *Long* v. *Bishop of Capetown*, 1 Moore, P. C. (N. S.) 411; *Re Lord Bishop of Natal*, 3 Moore, P. C. (N. S.) 125; *Bishop of Natal* v. *Gladstone*, L. R. 3 Eq. 1; *Murray* v. *Burgess*, L. R. 1 P. C. 362.

CEYLON: *Anstruther* v. *Arabin*, 6 Moore, P. C. 286; *Lindsay* v. *Duff*, 15 Moore, P. C. 452.

DOMINICA: *Doyle* v. *Falconer*, L. R. 1 P. C. 328.

FALKLAND ISLANDS: *Falkland Islands Company* v. *The Queen*, 1 Moore, P. C. (N. S.) 299; 2 *Ib.* 266.

GIBRALTAR: *Lubbock* v. *Potts*, 7 East, 449; *Jephson* v. *Riera*, 3 Knapp, 130.

GRENADA: *Campbell* v. *Hall*, Cowp. 204; 20 State Tr. 329.

HONDURAS: *Hodge* v. *Attorney General of Honduras*, 2 Moore, P. C. (N. S.) 325. In a case in 1851, where two persons had been tried and convicted of piracy on the high seas, at a commission court held at Honduras, an objection was taken that British Honduras did not come within the meaning of the 5th clause of the statute 12 & 13 Vict. c. 96, as being either a colony, island, plantation, dominion, fort, or factory of Her Majesty, and the question was referred to the Law Officers, Sir J. Dodson, Queen's Advocate, Sir J. Romilly, A.G., and Sir Alexander Cockburn, S.G., who were of opinion that the objection was not free from doubt; "but upon the whole, notwithstanding whatever may have been the original state of things in that settlement, we are disposed to think that at present it has become a part of the dominions of Her Majesty, and that consequently the objection is invalid."

HONG KONG: *Re Pollard*, L. R. 2 P. C. 106.

JAMAICA: *Campbell* v. *Hall*, Cowp. 204; *Beaumont* v. *Barrett*, 1 Moore, P. C. 75; *Bowerbank* v. *Bishop of Jamaica*, 2 Moore, P. C. 449.

MALTA: *Rubichon* v. *Humble*, 1 Dow. 191.

MAURITIUS: *Re Adam*, 1 Moore, P. C. 670; *Bouchecouste* v. *Dupont*, 2 Moore, P. C. (N. S.) 195; *Sérandat* v. *Saisse*, L. R. 1 P. C. 152.

NATAL: *Re Lord Bishop of Natal*, 3 Moore, P. C. (N. S.) 115; *Bishop of Natal* v. *Gladstone*, L. R. 3 Eq. 1; *Natal Land Company* v. *Good*, L. R. 1 P. C. 121.

NEW SOUTH WALES: *Devine* v. *Holloway*, 14 Moore, P. C. 290; *Lang* v. *Purves*, 15 Moore, P. C. 389; *Graham* v. *Barry*, 3 Moore, P. C. (N. S.) 207; *The Queen* v. *Murphy*, L. R. 2 P. C. 35.

NEWFOUNDLAND: *Kielley* v. *Carron*, 4 Moore, P. C. 63.

NEW ZEALAND: *The Queen* v. *Clarke*, 7 Moore, P. C. 77.

ST. HELENA: *The Queen* v. *Lees*, 27 L.J. (Q. B.) 403.

SOUTH AUSTRALIA: *Reg.* v. *Hughes*, L. R. 1 P. C. 81.

VICTORIA: *Dill* v. *Murphy*, 1 Moore, P. C. (N. S.) 487; *The Queen* v. *Dallimore*, L. R. 1 P. C. 13; *Rolfe & Bank of Australia* v. *Flower*, *ib.* 27; *The Attorney General of Victoria*, *ib.* 147.

In every colony the Governor has authority either to give or to withhold his assent to laws passed by the other branches or members of the legislature, and until that assent is given no such law is binding or valid.

Confirmation and disallowance of Colonial Acts or Ordinances.

Laws are, in some cases, passed with suspending clauses ; *i.e.*, although assented to by the Governor, they do not come into operation or take effect in the colony. until they shall have been specially confirmed by Her Majesty. And in other cases (as, for example, in the British North America Act, 1867, 30 Vict. c. 3, s. 55) Parliament has for the same purpose empowered the Governor to reserve laws for the Crown's assent, instead of himself assenting or refusing his assent to them.

Every law which has received the Governor's assent (unless it contains a suspending clause) comes into operation immediately or at the time specified in the law itself. But the Crown retains power to disallow the law; and if such power be exercised at any time afterwards, the law ceases to have operation from the date at which such disallowance is published in the colony.

In colonies having representative assemblies the disallowance of any law, or the Crown's assent to a reserved bill, or the confirmation of a law passed without a suspending clause, is signified by Order in Council.

In Crown colonies the allowance or disallowance of any law is generally signified by a despatch.

In some cases a period is limited, after the expiration of which local enactments, though not actually disallowed, cease to have the authority of law in the colony, unless before that time Her Majesty's confirmation of them shall have been signified there; but the general rule is otherwise. Each Governor receives special directions not to assent to Acts except under certain conditions, which are specified in his instructions.

In an opinion given by the Attorney and Solicitor General, Sir Charles Wetherell and Sir Nicolas Tindal, in March, 1828, respecting the execution of sentences passed in Jamaica upon two convicts under a particular Colonial Act, they said : " We are of opinion that, in consequence of the disallowance of the Act in question, M'Kay cannot be lawfully executed, but ought to be discharged; and that upon the same ground Hall cannot be lawfully imprisoned for the remainder of his sentence, but ought to be discharged."

East
&c.

The first Act of Parliament which gave authority to the Governor-General and Council at Fort William, in Bengal, to make rules and regulations "for the good order and civil government" of the East India Company's settlement at Fort William, and to impose "reasonable fines and forfeitures" for the breach of such rules and regulations, was 13 Geo. 3, c. 63, s. 36 (1773), usually called "The Regulating Act." This was followed by other Acts: 21 Geo. 3, c. 70, s. 23 ; 37 Geo. 3, c. 142, s. 8 ; 39 & 40 Geo. 3, c. 79, s. 18 ; 53 Geo. 3, c. 155, s. 6. By Regulation III. of 1793, in cases coming within the jurisdiction of the zillah and city courts, for which no specific rule may exist, the judges are to act according to justice, equity, and good conscience.

The legislative authority in the East Indies was vested by statute, 3 & 4 Will. 4, c. 85, s. 43, in the Governor-General of India in Council, who had the power of making laws and regulations for all persons, whether British or native, foreigners or others, and for all places and things within the British territories in India, and " for all servants of the (East India) Company within the dominions of Princes and States in alliance with the said Company." But it was expressly enacted that the Governor-General in Council should not have the power of making any laws or regulations contrary to that Act or the Mutiny Acts, " or any provisions of any Act hereafter to be passed in anywise affecting the said Company, or the said territories, or the inhabitants thereof, or any laws or regulations which shall in any way affect any prerogative of the Crown, or the authority of Parliament, or the constitution or rights of the said Company, or any part of the unwritten laws or constitution of the United Kingdom of Great Britain and Ireland, whereon may depend in any degree the allegiance of any person to the Crown of the United Kingdom, or the sovereignty or dominion of the said Crown over any part of the said territories."

This section of the Act was repealed by " The Indian Councils Act, 1861," 24 & 25 Vict. c. 67, but was, in effect, re-enacted by sect. 22 of the last-mentioned Act. And by statute 28 Vict. c. 18, s. 1, the Governor-General of India has power, at meetings for the purpose of making laws and regulations, to make them for all British subjects of Her Majesty within the dominions of Princes and States in India in alliance with Her Majesty, whether in the service of the Government of India or otherwise. The statute 24 & 25 Vict. c. 67 provides that the Governor-General shall transmit to the Secretary of State for India an authentic copy of every law or regulation assented to by him, and Her Majesty may signify through the Secretary of State for India in Council her disallowance of such law, which shall thereby become void and be annulled. The same statute also provides, by sect. 24, that no law or regulation made by the Governor-General in Council (subject to the power of disallowance by the Crown as thereinbefore provided) shall be deemed invalid by reason only that it affects the prerogative of the Crown. It also by sect. 28 enables the Governors of Madras and Bombay to make rules and orders for the conduct of business in their Councils; and by sect. 42 the Governor of each of those presidencies in Council has power, subject to the provisions of the Act, to make laws and regulations for the peace and good government of such presidency; but by sect. 43 they are expressly prohibited from making laws or regulations on certain specified subjects.

In illustration of the difficulties that have now and then occurred with respect to the extent of legislative authority in India, I may mention the question of patents. Grave doubts were entertained whether, during the government of the East India Company, the prerogative of the Crown to grant patents in India was or was not in abeyance, and

in 1856 a patent law was passed by the Governor-General in Council :
Act VI. of 1856. But this Act had not the previous sanction of the
Crown, as required by statute 16 & 17 Vict. c. 95, s. 26 (now repealed
by 24 & 25 Vict. c. 67), and it was doubtful, therefore, whether it was
not *ultrà vires*. It was repealed by Act IX. of 1857, and a new patent
law was enacted by Act XV. of 1859 ; which recites that Her
Majesty's law officers had given it as their opinion that the Legislative
Council of India was not competent to pass Act VI. of 1856 without
previously obtaining the sanction of the Crown. This Act is now the
governing Act as to patents in India.

Another question arose with respect to the validity of Act I. of 1849,
by which jurisdiction was given over offences committed by *all* British
subjects in foreign States; and the Law Officers of the Crown and myself were of opinion, in 1866, that in the case of offences committed
in foreign states by *native* Indian subjects of the Crown, the Governor-
General in Council had not the power to make laws for their apprehension and punishment in British India, for we thought that the power
was restricted by statute 24 & 25 Vict. c. 67, s. 22, and 28 Vict. c. 17.

The government of the British territories in India was taken from
the East India Company and vested in Her Majesty by the " Act for
the better Government of India," 21 & 22 Vict. c. 106.

The following chronological statement of the principal events in
the history of the East India Company, may be found useful :—

1600. Dec. 31.—Charter granted by Elizabeth, limited to fourteen
years.

1609. May 31.—Second charter granted by James I., " for ever."

1613.—Firman from Mogul Emperor to East India Company, allowing
them to establish factories at Surat and elsewhere on Malabar
Coast. This was the beginning of their establishment in
India.

1616.—East India Company occupied Surat, Calicut (on Malabar
coast), and Masulipatam (on coast of Coromandel).

1624.—Firman from Mogul Emperor, permitting East India Company
to trade with Bengal at port of Piplee in Midnapore.

1638.—Fort St. George erected at Madras-patam.

1640.—East India Company first permitted to establish a factory at
Hooghly (Calcutta), in the beginning of Shah Shuja's
government of Bengal.

1653.—Fort St. George erected into a Presidency.

1661. April 3.—Letters patent of Charles II., ratifying charter.

1661.—Charter granted by Charles II., granting to East India Company power to make peace or war with any prince not
Christian, and to seize and send to England unlicensed
traders.

1669. March 27.—Letters patent of Charles II., granting Bombay to

East India Company, "to be held of the King in free and common soccage, as of the Manor of East Greenwich, on the payment of the annual rent of £10." Authority also granted to Company to exercise all political powers necessary for the defence and government of the place. (Bombay was ceded to British Crown by King of Portugal under treaty, June 23, 1661.)

1673.—St. Helena granted to East India Company by charter.

1683–5.—"The servants of the Company were now invested with unlimited power over the British people in India."—Mill's History of British India, i. 119. But, query, how and by what authority?

1687.—Bombay erected into a regency, with unlimited power over the rest of the Company's settlements.

„   Madras erected into a corporate town, governed by mayor and aldermen. There was a discussion in the Privy Council whether the charter should be under the King's or Company's seal.—Mill's History of British India, i. 121.

1689.—Instructions from Court of Directors, pointing to increase of territorial and political powers.

1698–9.—East India Company obtained permission from Emperor Aurungzebe to *purchase* the villages of Soota Nuttee (or Chutta Nuttee), Govindpore, and Calcutta; and began to build Fort William. The station made a Presidency.

1698. Sept. 5.—Charter by William III., incorporating a second East India Company under name of "English Company," the old Company being known as "The London Company."

1702. July 22.—Indenture tripartite between Queen Anne, the old Company, and the new Company.

1708. Sept. 29.—Earl Godolphin's award.

1709. March 22.—Surrender of rights of old Company, and all rights vested in "United Company of Merchants of England trading to the East Indies."

1753.—Letters patent creating courts of judicature at Calcutta, Madras, and Bombay.

1756.—Suraja Dowla became Subahdar of Bengal.

„   Aug. 5.—Calcutta taken, and English thrown into the "Black Hole."

1757. Jan. 2.—Calcutta retaken by Lord Clive.

„   Battle of Plassey. (June 23.) First treaty with Nabob of Bengal. Grant to East India Company of twenty-four Pergunnahs. East India Company permitted to fortify Calcutta, and erect a Mint.

1760.—Treaty with Meer Kossim Ally Khan, by which East India Company obtained possession of Burdwan, Midnapore, and Chittagong.

1765.—Grant of the Dewanny by the Emperor Shah Allum to the East India Company of Bengal, Behar, and Orissa.

D

84 CASES AND OPINIONS ON CONSTITUTIONAL LAW.

1772.—First Regulating Act, 13 Geo. 3, c. 16.
1773.—Act authorising the erection of Supreme Court of Judicature, 13 Geo. 3, c. 63.
1833.—The East India Company ceased to be a trading company, but continued to hold the government of India in trust for the Crown, by 3 & 4 Will. 4, c. 85.
1858.—The government of India taken from the East India Company, and vested in Her Majesty, by 21 & 22 Vict. c. 106.

Actions on colonial judgments.

As to actions brought in this country upon colonial judgments, see *Carpenter* v. *Thornton*, 3 B. & Al. 52 (doubtful); *Henley* v. *Soper*, 8 B. & C. 16; *Henderson* v. *Henderson*, 6 Q. B. 288; *Russell* v. *Smyth*, 9 M. & W. 810; *Sadler* v. *Robins*, 1 Camp. 253; *Obicini* v. *Bligh*, 8 Bing. 335; *Hutchinson* v. *Gillespie*, 25 L. J. (Ex.) 103; *Frith* v. *Wollaston*, 7 Ex. R. 194; *Bank of Australia* v. *Nias*, 16 Q. B. 717; *Buchanan* v. *Rucker*, 1 Camp. 63; 9 East, 192, S.C.; *Ferguson* v. *Mahon*, 11 Ad. & Ell. 179; *Cowan* v. *Braidwood*, 1 M. & G. 882; *Reynolds* v. *Fenton*, 3 C. B. 187; *Vallee* v. *Dumerque*, 4 Ex. R. 290. '

CHAPTER II.

ON THE ECCLESIASTICAL LAW APPLICABLE TO THE COLONIES.

(1.) OPINION *of the Attorney General,* SIR EDWARD NORTHEY, *as to Roman Catholic Priests in the Colonies.* 1705.

To the Right Honourable the Lords Commissioners for Trade and Plantations.

MAY IT PLEASE YOUR LORDSHIPS,—In obedience to your Lordships' commands, signified to me by Mr. Popple, Jun., your Secretary, I have considered of the annexed extract of a letter from Colonel Seymour, Governor of Maryland, relating to the Jesuits and papists there; and the extract also sent me, of the grant of the province of Maryland to Lord Baltimore, relating to the ecclesiastical power; and the questions proposed thereon, whether the laws of England against Romish priests are in force in the plantations, and whether her Majesty may not direct Jesuits, or Romish priests, to be turned out of Maryland?

And as to the said clause in the grant of the province of Maryland to Lord Baltimore, relating to the ecclesiastical power, I am of opinion the same doth not give him any power to do anything contrary to the ecclesiastical laws of England, but he hath only the advowsons of, and power to erect and consecrate churches, and such power as the Bishop of Durham had as Earl Palatine in his County Palatine, who was subject to the laws of England; and the consecrations of chapels ought to be, as in England, by orthodox ministers only.

As to the question, whether the laws of England against Romish priests are in force in the plantations, by the statute 27mo. of Elizabeth, cap. 2, every Jesuit, seminary priest, or other such priest, deacon, or religious or ecclesiastical person, born within this realm or any other her Majesty's dominions, made, ordained, or

D 2

professed, by any authority or jurisdiction, derived, challenged, or pretended, from the see of Rome, who shall come into, or be, or remain in any part of this realm or any other of her Majesty's dominions, is guilty of high treason. It is plain that law extended to all the dominions the Queen had when it was made; but some doubt hath been made, whether it extendeth to dominions acquired after, as the plantations have been.

By the statute 11mo. William, for preventing the further growth of Popery, it is provided that, if any popish bishop, priest, or Jesuit whatsoever, shall say mass, or exercise any other part of the office or function of a popish bishop or priest, within this realm, or the dominions thereunto belonging, such person, being thereof lawfully convicted, shall be adjudged to perpetual imprisonment, in such place within this kingdom as her Majesty, by the advice of her Privy Council, shall appoint. I am of opinion this law extends to the plantations, they being dominions belonging to the realm of England, and extends to all priests, foreigners as well as natives.

As to the question, whether her Majesty may not direct Jesuits or Romish priests to be turned out of Maryland, I am of opinion, if the Jesuits or priests be aliens, not made denizens or naturalized, her Majesty may by law compel them to depart Maryland; if they be her Majesty's natural-born subjects, they cannot be banished from her Majesty's dominions, but may be proceeded against on the last before-mentioned law.

October 18, 1705.   EDW. NORTHEY.

(2.) JOINT OPINION *of the Attorney and Solicitor General,* SIR PHILIP YORKE *and* SIR CLEMENT WEARG, *on Convocations or Synods of the Clergy or Dissenting Ministers in New England.* 1725.

To their Excellencies the Lords Justices.

MAY IT PLEASE YOUR EXCELLENCIES,—In humble obedience to your Excellencies' commands, signified to us by Mr. Delafaye, we have considered the several matters referred to us by letter of the 24th inst., transmitting to us the enclosed copies of some letters which his Grace the Duke of Newcastle had received from the Lord Bishop of London, concerning an address from the

General Convention of the Independent Ministers in New England, to the Lieutenant-Governor, Council, and House of Burgesses there, desiring them to call the several churches in that province, to meet, by their pastors and messengers, in a synod, to which the said Council and House of Representatives have given their consent, and directing us to inquire into this matter, and report our opinions upon several questions proposed in the said letter.

And we humbly certify your Excellencies, that, as to the several matters of fact contained in the said letters and papers therewith transmitted, we have been obliged to take the same as they are therein stated, having at present no opportunity of obtaining strict regular proof; and, therefore, such parts of this report as arise out of those facts, are grounded upon a supposition that the relations contained in those letters and papers are true.

The address of the General Convention of Ministers is mentioned to be in these words, to wit:—

"To the very Honourable William Dummer, Esq., Lieutenant-Governor and Commander-in-Chief, and to the Honourable the Councillors, to the Honourable the Representatives, in the great and General Court of his Majesty's province of the Massachusetts Bay, assembled, and now sitting, a memorial and an address humbly presented.

"At a General Convention of Ministers from several parts of the province, at Boston, 27th May, 1725:

"Considering the great and visible decay of piety in the country, and the growth of many miscarriages, which we may fear has provoked the glorious Lord, in a series of various judgments, wonderfully to distress us; considering also, the laudable example of our predecessors, to recover and establish the faith and order of the Gospel in the churches, and provide against what immoralities might threaten to impair them, in the way of general synods convened for that purpose; and considering that forty-five years have now rolled away since these churches have now seen any such convention;—it is humbly desired that the honoured General Court would express their concern for the great interests of religion in the country, by calling the several churches in the province to meet, by their pastors and messengers, in a synod, and from thence offer their advice upon that weighty case, which the circumstances of the day do loudly call to be considered: 'What are the miscarriages whereof we have reason to think the judgments of Heaven upon us call us to be more generally sensible, and what may be the most evangelical and effectual expedients to put a stop to those or the like miscarriages?' This proposal we humbly make, in hopes that if it be prosecuted, it may be followed by many desirable consequences, worthy the study of those whom God has made, and we are so happy to enjoy, as the nursing fathers of our churches."

Upon this address it is represented, that on the 3rd of June last, the Council voted, " That the synod and assembly proposed in this memorial will be agreeable to this Board, and the reverend ministers are desired to take their own time for the said assembly; and it is earnestly wished the issue thereof may be a happy reformation in all the articles of a Christian life, among his Majesty's good subjects of this province."

That this resolution was sent down to the House of Representatives for concurrence, and in that House, June 11, 1715, it was read and referred to the next session, for further consideration.

That this resolution of the House of Representatives was sent up to the Council for their concurrence, and in Council, June 19, 1725, read and concurred, and the Lieutenant-Governor subscribed his consent thereto.

It appears, that against this application of the convention of ministers, for a synod, a memorial was presented by Timothy Cutler and Samuel Myles, ministers of the Established Church of England, to the Lieutenant-Governor, Council, and House of Representatives, in General Court assembled, a copy of which is hereunto annexed, and contains several reasons against the address of the Convention of Ministers.

Upon this memorial, the Council, on the 22nd of June, 1725, resolved, that it contained an indecent reflection on the proceedings of that Board, with several groundless insinuations, and voted that it should be dismissed, to which resolution the House of Representatives agreed.

As to the questions contained in Mr. Delafaye's letter, we beg leave to submit our thoughts upon them to your Excellencies' consideration, separately and distinctly.

The first question is: whether such pastors and messengers have any power to meet in a synod without the King's license?

In order to form an opinion upon this point, we have perused the charter, which is the fundamental constitution of this province, and have looked into their printed Acts of Assembly, as far as the year 1722.

The charter bears date 7° Octobris, 3° Will. et Mariæ, A.D. 1691, and recites two former charters, one granted 3 Nov. 18 Jac. 1, and the other 4 Mar. 4 Car. 1, which was vacated, by judgment upon a *scire facias*, in Trinity term, 1684. In this charter, nothing is contained, tending to the establishment of any kind of church government or ecclesiastical authority in this colony, but there is the following clause: "For the greater ease and encouragement of our loving subjects inhabiting our said province or territory of Massachusetts Bay, and of such as shall come to inhabit there, we do, by these presents, for us, our heirs and successors, grant, establish and ordain, that for ever hereafter there shall be a liberty of conscience allowed in the worship of God to all Christians (except papists) inhabiting, or which shall inhabit or be resident within, our said province or territory."

By the power given by this charter to the General Court or Assembly to make laws and impose taxes, they are authorised to dispose of matters and things, whereby the subjects, inhabitants of the said province, may be religiously, peaceably, and civilly governed, protected and defended, so as their good life and orderly conversation may bring the Indian natives of the country to the knowledge and obedience of the only true God and Saviour of mankind, and the Christian faith, which King Charles I., in his said letters patent, declared was his royal intention, and the adventurers' free profession to be the principal end of the said plantation; and for the better maintaining liberty of conscience thereby granted to all persons, at any time being and residing within the said province or territory.

In the Acts of Assembly, we find nothing relating to ecclesiastical authority; but there are some Acts directing that every town shall be provided of one or more able, learned and orthodox minister or ministers, without defining what they intend by that description, and there are other Acts, appointing methods for maintaining them·

And in the second year of his Majesty's reign, an Act passed, whereby it is enacted, that upon representation made to the General Court or Assembly, that any town or district is destitute of a minister, qualified as by law is provided, or do neglect to make due provision for the support of their minister, the General Assembly shall provide and send an able, learned, orthodox minister, of good conversation, being first recommended by three or more of the settled ordained ministers, or may lay a tax for the maintenance of the minister.

From these letters patent and laws, we cannot collect that there is any regular establishment of a national or provincial church in this colony, so as to warrant the holding of convocations or synods of the clergy; but if such synods might be holden, yet we take it to be clear, in point of law, that his Majesty's supremacy in ecclesiastical affairs, being a branch of his prerogative, does take place in the plantations, and that synods cannot be held, nor is it lawful for the clergy to assemble as in a synod, without his royal license.

The second question is: how far his Majesty's prerogative may be concerned, in which an application, not to the Lieutenant-Governor, as representing his Majesty's person, but to him and the Council and House of Representatives?

We conceive such application to be a contempt of his Majesty's prerogative, as it is a public acknowledgment that that power resides in the legislative body of the province which by law is vested only in his Majesty; and the Governor, Council, and Assembly intermeddling therein, was an invasion of his royal authority, which it was the particular duty of the Governor to have withstood and rejected.

The next question is: whether the consent of the Council and House of Representatives be a sufficient authority for their holding a synod?

We are of opinion such consent will not be a sufficient authority; but we beg leave to observe, that it does not appear, by the papers transmitted to us, that the Council and Assembly have given their consent thereto, but that the House of Representatives, upon reading the resolution of the Council, adjourned the further consideration thereof till the next session, to which resolution of adjournment the Council concurred and the Governor subscribed his consent.

The next question is: if this pretended synod should be actually sitting when the Lords Justices' directions in this matter are received by the Lieutenant-Governor, what can be done to put an end to their meeting?

We humbly apprehend, that in case such synod should be actually sitting, yet the Lieutenant-Governor, by order from his Majesty or your Excellencies, may cause them to cease their meeting ; and that for this purpose it may be proper that he should be directed to signify to them, that their assembly is against law, and a contempt of his Majesty's prerogative, and that they do forbear to meet any more ; and if, notwithstanding that, they shall continue to hold their assembly, that the principal actors therein be prosecuted, by information, for a misdemeanor. But we apprehend no formal act should be done to dissolve them, because that may imply that they had a right to assemble.

The principal difficulty in this case will be, if there should be an Act of the General Court or Assembly to warrant their meeting. And we conceive, that if such Act should pass in the nature only of the resolution above-mentioned, it will have no effect; but if it should have the regular form of a law, it will admit of great doubts whether it will be agreeable to the powers granted by the charter, and therefore, we humbly apprehend, it will be fit for his Majesty to disallow it. But it is difficult to give an opinion upon the effect and consequence of such an Act without seeing the Act itself.

The last question is: what authority those ministers have to meet in a general convention, and being so assembled, to make and present addresses, or to do any other public act?

We apprehend that such meeting is not unlawful provided they do not take upon them to do any authoritative act, being only a voluntary society ; and they may lawfully make addresses, either to the Crown or to the General Court or Assembly, in case the subject-matter of such addresses be lawful.

It being taken notice of in the address of the General Convention of Ministers, that such a synod as is now desired was holden forty-five years ago, we cannot help observing to your Excellencies, that this computation falls in with the year 1680, and that the former charter, upon which the government of this province depended, was repealed by *scire facias* in the year 1684, and the new charter granted in the year 1691; from whence it appears, that such synod or assembly was holden a short time before the repealing of their old charter, but none since the granting of the new one.

All which is humbly submitted to your Excellencies' great wisdom.

P. YORKE.

September 29, 1725.   C. WEARG.

(3.) OPINION *of the Attorney General,* SIR EDWARD NORTHEY, *on the Right of Presentation to Benefices in Virginia.* 1703.

On consideration of the laws of Virginia, provision being made by the Act entitled, "Church to be built, or Chapel of Ease," for the building a church in each parish; and by the Act entitled "Ministers to be Inducted," that ministers of each parish shall be inducted on the presentation of the parishioners; and the church-wardens, being, by the Act entitled "Churchwardens," to keep the church in repair, and provide ornaments, to collect the minister's dues; and by the "Act for the better support and maintenance of the Clergy," provision being made for the ministers of the parishes; and by the said Act for inducting ministers, the Governor being to induct the minister to be presented, and thereby he being constituted ordinary, and as bishop of the plantation, and with a power to punish ministers preaching contrary to that law, I am of the opinion, the advowsons and the right of presentation to the churches, is subject to the laws of England, there being no express law of that plantation made further concerning the same; therefore, when the parishioners present their clerk, and he is inducted by the Governor (who is and must induct on the presentation of the parishioners), the incumbent is in for his life, and cannot be displaced by the parishioners. If the parishioners do not present a minister to the Governor within six months after any church shall become void, the Governor, as ordinary, shall and may collate a clerk to such church by lapse, and his collatee shall hold the church for his life; if the parishioners have never presented, they have a reasonable time to present a minister; but if they will not present, being required so to do, the Governor may also, in their default, collate a minister. In inducting ministers by the Governor, on the presentation of the parishes, or on his own collation, he is to see the ministers be qualified, according as that Act for inducting ministers requires. In case of the avoidance of any church, the Governor, as ordinary of the plantation, is, according to the statute of 28th Henry 8, cap. 11, s. 5, to appoint a minister to officiate till the parish shall present one, or the six months be lapsed; and such person appointed to officiate in the vacancy, is to be paid for his service out of the profits thereof, from the time the church becomes void by the law above stated. In this case no minister is to officiate as such till he hath showed to the Governor he is qualified, according as the said Act for induction directs; if the vestry do not levy the tobacco for the minister, the courts there must decree the same to be levied.

July 29, 1703. EDWARD NORTHEY.

(4.) OPINION *of the Attorney General,* SIR EDWARD NORTHEY, *on the granting of Letters of Administration on the same Estate, both in England and in the Colonies.* 1707.

To the Right Honourable the Lords Commissioners for Trade and Plantations. ♦

MAY IT PLEASE YOUR LORDSHIPS,—In obedience to your Lordships' commands, signified to me by Mr. Popple, I have considered of the enclosed extract of Lord Cornbury's instructions, and of his letter relating to the granting letters of administration; and your Lordships having required my opinion thereon, and what may be fit for her Majesty to do in all the plantations on the like occasions, I do most humbly certify to your Lordships, that by law, where a man dies intestate in the plantations, having a personal estate there, and also any personal estate, or debts owing, here in England, the right of granting administration belongs to the Archbishop of Canterbury; and if administration be granted, in the plantations, also (which may be), that administrator will be accountable to the administrator in England, but will be allowed the payment of just debts, if paid in the order the law allows of—that is to say, the whole personal estate, in England and the plantations, will be liable to all the intestate's debts

in both places, and out of the whole, first, debts owing to her
Majesty, then judgments, statutes and recognizances, then bonds,
then debts, without speciality, both there and in England, are to
be satisfied; and the administrator in the plantations will not be
allowed the payment of any debts, without speciality, if there be
debts of a superior nature unsatisfied in England; for every administrator is bound to take care to apply the intestate's assets to
discharge his debts, in the order the law directs, and it matters not
whether the debts were contracted in England or the plantations.
If there be debts of equal nature in England and the plantations,
the administrator may discharge which he pleases, before he be
sued for any other of the like nature. This, indeed, is some difficulty on administrators, but it is no more there than in England;
and attempts have been made by Acts of Assembly, in some of the
plantations—particularly, as I remember, in Pennsylvania—to appropriate the effects in the plantations, of persons dying there, to
the discharging debts contracted there; but those Acts have been
repealed here, as being prejudicial to this kingdom. I am also of
opinion, that when the letters of administration arrive at the plantations, under the seal of the Prerogative Court of Canterbury, they
are to be allowed there, and the authority of the administration
granted in the plantations from that time ceases.

March, 1707.   EDW. NORTHEY.

(5.) OBSERVATIONS by the King's Advocate, SIR JAMES
MARRIOTT, on enforcing residence at a living in Barbadoes, in
the Case of the REV. MR. BARNARD (1). 1764.

It is stated that the Governor of Barbadoes institutes to all
livings in the island of Barbadoes.

That no law of the island enforces residence.

That the Royal institutions are silent.

That there is no judicature there to inflict the penalty of the
Act of Parliament.

The question is, how residence can be enforced?

It appears that the commission granted by George I. to Bishop

(1) From a MS. in the possession of Sir Travers Twiss, Queen's Advocate,
which formerly belonged to Sir James Marriott, King's Advocate.

Gibson, then Bishop of London, empowering him to act in *all respects* by his commissaries as diocesan of the colonies, was personal, and was never obeyed nor held to be sufficient.

The jurisdiction of the Bishops of London in the colonies, on the foot of custom, is not established nor exercised effectually ; nor does anything appear further than that, upon the first setting-up a Virginia Company, they were recommended by the then Government to apply to the Bishop of London to assist them in sending some clergymen of the Church of England to reside in that infant colony.

Nothing more has passed since, than merely on a supposition that the Bishops of London had jurisdiction (of some sort or other) in the colonies; and so all the instructions to the governors have ordered them to give countenance to the Bishop of London's jurisdiction accordingly.

The jurisdiction, therefore, of the Bishops of London and all other ecclesiastical authority is out of the present question.

It seems to rest entirely on the Act of the 21st Hen. 8, called the "Act of Non-residence," to the penalty of which Mr. Barnard is liable whenever any person shall sue him for the same. He is liable to the penalty of £10 for every default.

The word "default" is defined by Bracton to be an omission of anything which ought to be done ; if so, the penalty for every month's omission will fall heavily on Mr. Barnard in the course of every year's absence, and he may be sued for the amount of all the gross sum chargeable for every month's non-residence.

But if the word "default" does not mean omission, *toties quoties*, but a defect in the course of a year taken altogether, and legal conviction thereupon, then the penalty of £10 for such annual default would certainly be insufficient to enforce residence as is necessary, and Mr. Barnard will avail himself of the advantage.

But there seems a difficulty in complying with the request of the Governor, that his Majesty should grant fresh instructions to his governors in the colonies in cases of non-residence, to declare the living vacant, and to institute other rectors.

It is apprehended that his Majesty cannot empower any governor, by their authority under his commission, to deprive clergymen of their freeholds. His Majesty's supremacy is exercised in ecclesiastical causes, as well as in civil, in the same manner and with the same limitations; and his ecclesiastical courts and temporal courts can only deprive the subject on legal conviction of offences. His Majesty's judges are the keepers of his Majesty's conscience; they are answerable for the decrees they make, and it is the happiness and prerogative of his Majesty to judge no man's life or property in person.

If his Majesty, as supreme in all causes, ecclesiastical and civil, could by his bare instructions authorize the inflicting of penalties, he might erect of his pleasure any sort of courts whatsoever, which he cannot; and, therefore, if the penalty of the 21st of Hen. 8 is insufficient in case of non-residence in the colonies, it should seem a proper object for the consideration of Parliament to find an effectual remedy; for the legality of deprivation in consequence of the royal instructions would certainly be called in question by the American clergy.

December 25, 1764.

(6.) OPINION *of the King's Advocate*, SIR CHRISTOPHER ROBINSON, *on a Marriage performed by a Methodist Minister in Newfoundland.*

Doctors' Commons, March 3, 1817.

MY LORD,—I am honoured with your Lordship's commands, signified in Mr. Goulburn's letter of the 21st ultimo, transmitting the copy of a despatch from Vice-Admiral Pickmore, Governor of Newfoundland, relative to the conduct of a Methodist minister in that colony in performing the marriage ceremony without a compliance with the formalities of the Church of England, and in opposition to the orders of the Governor, a clergyman of the Church of England being actually resident in the colony.

And your Lordship is pleased to request that I would take the same into consideration, and report to your Lordship my opinion, whether marriages so celebrated are legal and valid; and if illegal, whether the person so celebrating them is liable to any and what penalties?

In obedience to your Lordship's directions, I have considered the same, and beg leave to refer to a report of the 11th of May, 1812, which I had the honour to make, jointly with the Attorney and Solicitor General, to the Secretary of State for the Colonial

Department, on the subject of marriages in Newfoundland, in which the general principle of the law of England was stated, as requiring the celebration of marriage by religious ceremonies for the perfect regularity of the marriage contract.

In the case represented in these papers, the certificate describes the marriage to have been celebrated according to the form of the Church of England by George Cubit, Methodist minister, "set apart (as it is expressed in his pretended letters of orders) by the authority of four private ministers in connection with the conference of the people *called Methodists.*"

It is not the case, therefore, of a person assuming ostensibly the character of a person in holy orders. But the question is, whether a marriage celebrated by a minister as above described, unconnected with local customs, or with any circumstances of special exception, is a legal and valid marriage?

The mere civil contract of parties which has constituted marriage in some countries has been considered not to be sufficient alone to perfect that relation by the ecclesiastical law of England ; and I believe it may be stated, that there has not been any positive decision to the contrary in any Court.

The issue of parties cohabiting under such contract, alone, without subsequent espousals *in facie ecclesiæ,* has been held illegitimate. It has been determined, also, by high authority at common law, that the woman was not entitled to dower ; and the conclusion is drawn from that case, in the words of the learned editor, " that *neither the contract, nor the sentence of the ecclesiastical court* (decreeing the marriage to be solemnized, without the actual celebration), was a marriage."

The terms in which the several Acts of Parliament in the reigns of Henry VIII. and Edward VI., and 12 Charles 2, c. 33, speak of marriage, further support the conclusion that no other form of marriage than that by celebration *in facie ecclesiæ* has been considered to constitute a perfect and legal marriage in the contemplation of the law of this country.

The same construction has been put on marriages celebrated by ministers not ordained by episcopal ordination, even subsequent to the Toleration Act (1). The principle of that decision, also, is

(1) *Haydon* v. *Gould,* 1 Salkeld, 119.

in some degree incidentally confirmed by a form of pleading in one case (1), setting forth, as a ground of prohibition to the proceedings of the ecclesiastical courts against the parties for incontinence, that the marriage in that instance had been celebrated under special exemptions granted to the conventicles by the Toleration Act, though the clause of the Toleration Act on which the suggestion was founded does not appear to be correctly recited.

It may be observed, also, that there has been a positive exemption of the same kind by Act of Parliament in Ireland, making the marriages of Dissenters in their own congregations legal.

On these grounds I am of opinion that the marriage described is not a legal and valid marriage.

On the other point, whether the person so celebrating marriage is liable to any and what penalties? I cannot advise that there could be any proceedings founded on the ecclesiastical law that would be applicable to the circumstances of this case. But it must be an offence, I conceive, of the nature of a misdemeanor, to assume public functions of this kind without authority, to the breach of public order, and to the prejudice of individuals; and I presume it might be punished as such by proceedings at law under the direction of the law officers of the settlement.

CHRIST. ROBINSON.

(7.) JOINT OPINION *of the King's Advocate*, SIR CHRISTOPHER ROBINSON, *and the Attorney and Solicitor General*, Sir JOHN S. COPLEY *and* SIR CHARLES WETHERELL, *on the Duties of the Governor and Bishop of a Colony in collating and instituting to Benefices.* 1825.

MY LORD,—Having considered the statements contained in your Lordship's letter, transmitting the instructions of the Governor of Barbadoes, and the patent of appointment of the Bishop, and requiring that we would report thereon—

" Whether the collation to benefices, the granting marriage licenses, probate of wills, and letters of administration, continue vested in the Governor, in the same manner, and to the same extent, as before the erection of the new bishopric; or whether

(1) *Hutchinson* v. *Brooksbanke*, Levinz, part 3, 376.

that event has diminished, or altered, the power and duties of the
Governor, in any of those respects; and especially that we will
state what are the relative duties of the Governor and the Bishop,
in collating and granting institution to benefices in the island, in
the gift of the Crown."

In obedience to your Lordship's commands, we have the honour
to report that we think the appointment of the Bishop has made
no alteration in the Governor's power to grant marriage licenses,
probates, and administrations; and we think the right of the
Governor to collate to benefices in the gift of the Crown, as is done
in England, in some cases of free chapels, is not affected by the
power given to the Bishop to grant institution, which may apply to
the patronage of private individuals. If there be no such patronage
in private individuals, the inference from the terms of the Bishop's
appointment will show, we apprehend, that it was the intention
that he should collate in all cases, and if so, we think it proper to
alter the instructions to the Governor, and direct him to present to
the Bishop for institution.

CHRISTOPHER ROBINSON.

July 16, 1825.   J. S. COPLEY.

CHARLES WETHERELL.

(8.) OPINION *of the King's Advocate*, SIR CHRISTOPHER
ROBINSON, *on the appointment of a Roman Catholic Bishop
in Canada.*

Doctors' Commons, February 21, 1826.

MY LORD,—In obedience to your Lordship's commands, I have
considered the question proposed to me by your Lordship respecting the form of appointment of a Catholic Bishop in Canada, by
direct authority of his Majesty, and I think it is one of very considerable difficulty. It has hitherto been avoided by the expedient
of adopting, by Royal approbation, the coadjutor of the preceding bishop, nominated *cum futura successione*, and consecrated in
Canada under the authority of the Pope's bull. But it may be
doubted, I think, whether that mode was consistent with the Royal
prerogative before the cession of Canada, under the French law,
or more particularly with the provisions of the statute 14 Geo. 8,
c. 83, which permits in Canada the free exercise of the religion of
the Church of Rome, *subject to the King's supremacy declared and*

E

established by 1 *Eliz.* c. 1, which last statute considered the King's supremacy as essentially opposed to the exercise of any authority by the Pope in any parts of the dominions belonging to the Imperial Crown of this realm. The Governor appears to recommend that the late coadjutor, who has been already consecrated, may be appointed Bishop of Quebec by letters patent issued under the provincial seal. The appointment of a bishop is a very high act of the royal prerogative, and has never yet been exercised, so far as I know, in any other manner, in the colonies, than by letters patent under the Great Seal. Whether that form of appointment could now be used of a Catholic Bishop, is a question on which I cannot presume to advise, and it will be proper that it should be referred to the Attorney and Solicitor General. If the appointment can be made under the provincial seal, it must be, I presume, on special instructions or warrant from his Majesty. The questions to be referred should, I humbly submit, embrace all these points—whether the appointment of a Catholic Bishop in Canada can legally be made by his Majesty, by letters patent under the Great Seal, or under the provincial seal, under special instructions or warrant from his Majesty?

Earl Bathurst, &c.   CHRISTOPHER ROBINSON.

(9.) JOINT OPINION *of the King's Advocate,* SIR JOHN DODSON, *and the Attorney and Solicitor-General,* SIR JOHN CAMPBELL *and* SIR R. M. ROLFE, *on the appointment of a Suffragan Bishop of Montreal.*

Doctors' Commons, February 3, 1836.

MY LORD,—We have received your Lordship's letter of the 2nd instant, relative to the appointment of a suffragan Bishop of Montreal, and desiring us to report our opinion, whether under the statute of 26 Hen. 8, respecting Suffragan Bishops, or for any other reason, there exists any objection in point of law to the instrument of appointment, a copy of which your Lordship has sent to us? We beg leave in answer to state to your Lordship that we have taken the subject into consideration, and we do not see any objection in point of law, under the statute of Hen. 8, or otherwise, to the proposed instrument.

The Lord Glenelg,   J. DODSON.
&c. &c. &c.   J. CAMPBELL.
                                         R. M. ROLFE.

(10.) JOINT OPINION *of the Attorney and Solicitor General,*
SIR JOHN CAMPBELL *and* SIR R. M. ROLFE, *on the incorporation of a Roman Catholic College in Prince Edward's Island.*

Temple, May 31, 1838.

MY LORD,—We have to acknowledge the receipt of your Lordship's letter of the 16th ultimo, referring us to an Act passed by the Legislature of Prince Edward's Island (No. 448), entitled " An Act to incorporate the Trustees of St. Andrew's College, and to repeal a certain Act therein mentioned," and requesting that we would state our joint opinion whether there is any reason deducible from the Act of Supremacy of Queen Elizabeth, or from any other statute or law, which should prevent the confirmation of this law by Her Majesty ? We beg leave to state to your Lordship, that, in our opinion, there is nothing in the Act of Supremacy, taken in conjunction with the subsequent statutes relative to Her Majesty's Roman Catholic subjects, which should prevent the confirmation of this law by Her Majesty in Council.　　　　　J. CAMPBELL.

The Lord Glenelg,　　　　　　　　　　R. M. ROLFE.
&c. &c. &c.

(11.) JOINT OPINION *of the Attorney and Solicitor General,*
SIR FREDERICK POLLOCK *and* SIR WILLIAM WEBB FOLLETT, *on the Authority of the Crown to interfere with and make Regulations respecting the appointment of Roman Catholic Bishops in Canada.*

Temple, April 11, 1842.

SIR,—We have the honour to acknowledge the receipt of your letter dated the 16th of October last, stating that the Reverend M. Power having been deputed by the Roman Catholic Bishop of Montreal to submit for the approval of Her Majesty's Government a proposition for dividing the diocese of Kingston into two distinct sees, and for " the formation of an ecclesiastical province to be composed of all the British North American provinces under one Archbishop or one Metropolitan See ;" and further stating, that you had received Lord Stanley's directions to state that, as preliminary to advising Her Majesty as to the course which it might be expedient to take in respect to this application, his Lordship would wish us to report to him, our opinion, whether, adverting to the Act of Supremacy, and any other Acts of Parliament relating to the exercise within the Queen's dominions of the religion of the

E 2

Church of Rome, and also adverting to the terms of the capitulation of Quebec and Montreal, in 1759 and 1760, and to the statutes 14 Geo. 3, c. 83, 31 Geo. 3, c. 31, and 3 & 4 Vict. c. 35, any authority is vested in the Queen to regulate, or in any manner interfere with, the appointment of Roman Catholic bishops or archbishops in Canada, or to determine what the number or what the character of the ecclesiastical functionaries of the Roman Catholic Church in that province shall be?

In obedience to his Lordship's commands, we have considered the subject referred to us with great care, and beg leave humbly to report that we think, under the terms of the Treaty of Paris of 1793, and of the stat. 14 Geo. 3, c. 53, s. 5, and with reference to the provisions of the statute of 1 Eliz., Her Majesty has an authority vested in her to interfere with, and to make regulations respecting, the appointment of Roman Catholic bishops and archbishops in Canada ; and with respect to the particular proposal which is mentioned in the letter, we think that the consent of the Crown is properly asked for, and that it may be lawfully given to, the division of the diocese of Kingston into two sees, if Her Majesty, in her discretion, shall think fit to do so.

But, as regards that part of the proposal which relates to the formation of an ecclesiastical province to be composed of all the British provinces in North America, and which would extend therefore over provinces not conquered, and in which there are no stipulations respecting the maintenance of the Roman Catholic religion, either by treaty or Act of Parliament: we think that the Crown cannot be properly called upon to give its sanction, and that it has no legal power to do so.

G. W. Hope, Esq.

FREDERICK POLLOCK.
W. W. FOLLETT.

(12.) JOINT OPINION of the Queen's Advocate, SIR JOHN DODSON, and the Attorney and Solicitor General, SIR FREDERICK THESIGER and SIR FITZROY KELLY, on the status of Clergymen of the Church of England, and the jurisdiction of the Bishop, in Van Diemen's Land.

Doctors' Commons, December 27, 1845.

MY LORD,—In compliance with the request contained in the letter of Mr. Under-Secretary Stephen of the 18th of October last, we have referred to the letter of Mr. Under-Secretary Hope of the 28th of August last, and to the several Acts of the Legislature of Van Diemen's Land now laid before us; and with reference to the questions submitted to us touching the proceedings adopted against certain clergymen in that colony, and the status of clergymen there, we have the honour to report to your Lordship, that having also considered the points suggested by Archdeacon Marriott, we are of opinion : that upon the appointment of a chaplain to officiate in Van Diemen's Land, whether by the Government here or in the colony, he cannot lawfully act without being licensed by the Bishop of Tasmania.

That, upon refusal by the Bishop to license, an appeal lies to the Archbishop of Canterbury, and to him only: that a license may be revoked by the Bishop. That upon the revocation of a license no formal trial is necessary : that the Bishop, however, should not act but upon what he deems sufficient cause, *or* without giving the party accused an opportunity of answering the charge against him.

That there is no form of institution or induction, or analogous to either, in Van Diemen's Land; the appointment and the license are all that can take place : that the Bishop may try, convict, and punish for ecclesiastical offences, without the aid of any new Court to be created by the local legislature or otherwise; but he must proceed judicially, with the assistance of such officers as are created by the letters patent, and decide according to the best of his judgment; there must be a distinct charge, the accused must have due notice, and a fair opportunity of answering and defending himself, and of examining his witnesses, and cross-examining the witnesses against him : that the 3 & 4 Vict. c. 86 does not extend to the colonies; that, therefore, if either of the clergymen in question was unlicensed, he could not legally officiate at all, and that if any license had been granted, the revocation of it by the Bishop was valid.

J. DODSON.

The Right Hon. the Lord Stanley,   FREDERICK THESIGER.
&c. &c. &c.   FITZROY KELLY.

(13.) JOINT OPINION *of the Queen's Advocate*, SIR J. D. HARDING, *and the Attorney and Solicitor General*, SIR FREDERICK THESIGER *and* SIR FITZROY KELLY, *on the patronage of Benefices and the appointment of Missionaries in Prince Edward's Island.*

Doctors' Commons, August 24, 1852.

SIR,—We were favoured with a letter from Mr. Elliot on the 12th instant, in which he stated that he was directed by you to request that we would intimate our opinion on the following point :—

There appeared to be in Prince Edward's Island two classes of ministers of the Church of England : some commonly designated as rectors, who enjoy, as such, certain lands attached to parish churches; others who are merely stationed at places in the island, and employed as missionaries of the Society for the Propagation of the Gospel.

Mr. Elliot also stated that he was directed to request that we would take into consideration the Local Act, 43 Geo. 3, c. 6, the annexed extracts from the commission, and instructions from the Governor of Prince Edward's Island, and the inclosed correspondence, and report to you our opinion—

What are the respective rights of the Governor, the parishioners, and the Bishop, in respect to the institution, presentation, and collation or induction of rectors ?

Has the Governor any, and what, rights or duties in respect of the appointment of missionaries of the Society for the Propagation of the Gospel to minister in the island ?

In obedience to your commands, we have perused the several documents accompanying Mr. Elliot's letter, and have the honour to report that, by the Colonial Act, 43 Geo. 3, c. 6, the patronage of all benefices is vested in the parishioners, who are entitled to present to them whenever vacancies occur. The Lieutenant-Governor, upon such a presentation, is required to induct. The clerk so presented must, however, produce a license from the Bishop of London, or from the Bishop of Nova Scotia, and he must also have publicly declared his assent and consent to the Book of Common Prayer, and must have subscribed to be conformable to the Orders and Constitution of the Church of England, and the laws there established; but the Lieutenant-Governor having ascertained that these preliminaries have been complied with, his office is merely ministerial, and he has no power to refuse induction. The Bishop's functions are confined to licensing the clerk, who is presented (of course after due examination), if such clerk has not already obtained a license from the Bishop of London.

The Lieutenant-Governor has no rights or duties in respect of the appointment of missionaries of the Society for the Propagation of the Gospel, but such missionaries cannot officiate without the license of the Bishop; and if they should do so, or fail to declare their assent to the Book of Common Prayer, or to subscribe the Articles and Canons of the Church, we think that, according to the spirit of the Colonial Act, they may be suspended and silenced by the Lieutenant-Governor and the Council.

	J. D. HARDING.
The Right Hon. Sir J. Pakington, Bart.,	FRED. THESIGER.
&c. &c. &c.	FITZROY KELLY.

NOTES TO CHAPTER II.

The foregoing Opinions give the opportunity of discussing the question of the status of the Church of England in the colonies, and how far the ecclesiastical law of England is applicable to that Church there. Of late years the question has been fully considered, and the law settled by the Judicial Committee of the Privy Council. First, in the case of *Long v. Bishop of Capetown*, 1 Moore, P. C. (N.S.) 411, where Mr. Long, the appellant, claiming to be the incumbent of a parish in the colony of the Cape of Good Hope, refused to obey certain orders which the Bishop of the diocese, in the exercise of his episcopal authority, thought fit to issue, and for such disobedience the Bishop issued against Mr. Long sentences, first of suspension, and afterwards of deprivation. The validity of these sentences was disputed, first in the colonial court, and afterwards on appeal here. The first question which the Judicial Committee considered was the authority which the Bishop possessed under and by virtue of his letters patent at the time when the sentences were pronounced. And they held that the letters patent under which the Bishop acted, having been issued after a constitutional government had been established in the Cape of Good Hope, were ineffectual to create any jurisdiction, ecclesiastical or civil, within the colony. The next point was, whether the defect of coercive jurisdiction under the letters patent had been supplied by the voluntary submission of Mr. Long? The Judicial Committee held that Mr. Long, by taking the oath of canonical obedience to the Bishop, and accepting from him a license to officiate and have the care of souls within a parish in the colony, and by accepting the appointment to the living under a deed which expressly contemplates, as one means of avoidance, the removal of the incumbent for any lawful cause, did voluntarily submit himself to the authority of the Bishop to such an extent as to enable the Bishop to deprive him of his benefice for any lawful cause. But this was on the principle of contract, the Court holding that for the purpose of the contract between the plaintiff and defendant, it was to take them as having contracted that the laws of the Church of England should, though only so far as applicable in the colony, govern both. The next question was, whether Mr. Long had been guilty of any offences which, by the laws of the Church of England, warranted the sentences against him? This depended mainly on the point whether Mr. Long was justified in refusing to take the steps which the Bishop required him to take in order to procure the election of a delegate for the parish to a synod convened by the Bishop. The Judicial Committee held that the Bishop had no power of convening a synod without the consent of either the Crown or the colonial legislature, for the purpose of making laws binding upon members of the Church of England; that the acts which they assumed to pass were illegal; and that Mr. Long was justified in refusing to assist in calling into existence a body which he was not bound by any law or duty to acknowledge. The oath of canonical obedience only means that the clergyman will obey all such commands as the Bishop by law is authorized to impose. The Court, therefore, were of opinion that the order of suspension and subsequent sentence of deprivation were not justified, and were invalid. In giving judgment, the Court said: "The Church of England in places where there is no Church established by law is in the same situation with any other religious body—in no better, but in no worse position; and the members may adopt, as the members of any other communion may adopt, rules for enforcing discipline within their body, which will be binding on those who expressly, or by implication, have assented to them."

Another point considered by the Judicial Committee in this case was, whether, supposing the sentences of the Bishop to be erroneous, Mr. Long had any remedy except by appeal to the Archbishop of Canterbury under the letters patent; and they held that even if Mr. Long might have appealed to the Archbishop — a question which they thought it unnecessary and inexpedient to discuss, as the suit in respect of which the appeal was brought respected a temporal right, in which the appellant alleged that he had been injured—he was not bound to appeal to the Archbishop, but was at liberty to resort to the Supreme Court of the colony.

This case was followed by *Re The Lord Bishop of Natal*, 3 Moore,

P. C. (N.S.) 115, which was a petition presented to Her Majesty in Council by Dr. Colenso, Bishop of Natal, complaining of the illegality of certain proceedings taken against him, and alleging the nullity of a sentence of deposition for heresy pronounced against him by the Bishop of Capetown, as metropolitan of that diocese. The petition was referred to the Judicial Committee, and several of the questions which had been considered in the case of *Long* v. *The Bishop of Capetown* came again before the Court. They held that, although in a Crown colony, properly so called, or in cases where the letters patent constituting a bishopric and appointing a bishop in a colony was made in pursuance of an Act of Parliament, a bishopric may be constituted and ecclesiastical jurisdiction conferred by the sole authority of the Crown, yet that the letters patent of the Crown will not have any such effect or operation in a colony or settlement which is possessed of an independent legislature. They held, therefore, that in the case before them the Crown had no power to confer any jurisdiction, or exercise legal authority, upon the Metropolitan of Capetown over the suffragan bishops, or over any other person ; and they said that in the case of a settled colony the ecclesiastical law of England cannot be treated as part of the law which the settlers carried with them from the mother-country (1). They said: " After a colony or settlement has received legislative institutions, the Crown (subject to the special provisions of any Act of Parliament) stands in the same relation to that colony or settlement as it does to the United Kingdom. It may be true that the Crown, as legal head of the Church, has a right to command the consecration of a bishop, but it has no power to assign to him any diocese, or give him any sphere of action within the United Kingdom. The United Church of England and Ireland is not a part of the constitution in any colonial settlement, nor can its authorities, nor those who bear office in it, claim to be recognized by the law of the colony otherwise than as members of a voluntary association." As to the question whether, supposing that the Bishop of Capetown had no jurisdiction by law, he obtained it by contract or submission on the part of the Bishop of Natal by virtue of his oath of canonical obedience, they held that it was not legally competent to the Bishop of Natal to give, or to the Bishop of Capetown to accept or exercise, any such jurisdiction.

The Bishop of Natal afterwards sued the Trustees of the Colonial Bishoprics' Fund for arrears of his salary, which they, in consequence of the decision in the last case, had withheld from him. This case, *Bishop of Natal* v. *Gladstone*, L R. 3 Eq. 1, came before Lord Romilly, M.R., in 1866, and he pronounced a decree in favour of the plaintiff. His Lordship held that the law, as declared by the Judi-

(1) In *R.* v. *Brampton*, 10 East, 288, Lord Ellenborough, C.J., said: " In the absence of any evidence to the contrary, I may suppose that the law of England, ecclesiastical and civil, was recognized by subjects of England in a place occupied by the King's troops, who would impliedly carry that law with them."—See *ante*, p. 18.

cial Committee, left all the episcopal functions to the Bishop exactly as by the law of the Church of England they belonged to his office of Bishop, and that he could perform all the acts which belong to a Bishop within the diocese of Natal which he could do if he were the Bishop of an English diocese—"with this exception, that he cannot enforce the execution of these orders without having recourse to the civil tribunals for that purpose." With respect to the passage in the judgment of the Judicial Committee in *Long* v. *Bishop of Capetown*, 1 Moore, P. C. (N.S.) 461, already quoted, as to the status of the Church of England in the colonies, his Lordship said : " These expressions have created some alarm, which has, as it appears to me, arisen from an imperfect apprehension of what is meant by them. They do not mean, as some persons seem to have supposed, that because the members of such a Church constituted a voluntary association, they may adopt any doctrines and ordinances they please, and still belong to the Church of England. All that really is meant by these words is, that where there is no State religion established by the Legislature in any colony, and in such a colony is found a number of persons who are members of the Church of England, and who establish a Church there with the doctrines, rights, and ordinances of the Church of England, it is a part of the Church of England, and the members of it are, by implied agreement, bound by all its laws. In other words, the association is bound by the doctrines, rights, rules, and ordinances of the Church of England, except so far as any statutes may exist which (though relating to this subject) are confined in their operation to the limits of the United Kingdom of England and Ireland."

The Master of the Rolls added : " The members of the Church in South Africa may create an ecclesiastical tribunal to try ecclesiastical matters between themselves, and may agree that the decisions of such a tribunal shall be final whatever may be their nature or effect. Upon this being proved the civil tribunal would enforce such decisions against all the persons who had agreed to be members of such an association— that is, against all the persons who had agreed to be bound by these decisions, and it would do so without inquiring into the propriety of such decisions. But such an association would be distinct from, and form no part of, the Church of England, whether it did or did not call itself in union and full communion with the Church of England. It would strictly and properly be an Episcopal Church, not *of*, but *in* South Africa, as it is the Episcopal Church *in* Scotland, not *of* Scotland." See the observations of the Judicial Committee in *Ex parte Jenkins*, L. R. 2 P. C. 270 : " It seems to have been supposed that the cases of *Long* v. *Bishop of Capetown*, and *In re The Lord Bishop of Natal*, are authorities for the proposition that the Bishop of Newfoundland has no legal status and cannot lawfully exercise any episcopal function within the Bermudas. The first case certainly does not go the length of that proposition, for it decided only that the Crown cannot confer coercive authority on a Bishop in a colony possessing a constitutional form of government without the consent of the Legislature. The Judicial Committee, in deciding the case of *The Bishop of Natal* v. *Gladstone,* has certainly used expressions which would restrain the power of the Crown in the creation of bishops within even narrower limits. It has been argued that the Master of the Rolls, in his judgment in *The Bishop of Natal* v. *Gladstone,* has greatly qualified the effect of the former judgment of the Privy Council. Their Lordships think that in the present case they are not called upon to express an opinion whether these two decisions can be reconciled; for they are clearly of opinion that the question whether the Bishop of Newfoundland has any lawful status, or can exercise any episcopal function, and particularly that of institution, in the Bermudas, has been set at rest conclusively by the repeated recognition of his status and functions by the colonial legislature."

In *The Bishop of Natal* v. *Gladstone,* the Master of the Rolls held that Dr. Colenso was Bishop of Natal in every sense of the word, and would remain so until he died or resigned, or until the letters patent appointing him were revoked, or until he were in some manner lawfully deprived of his see. But, in order to guard against a misapprehension which might arise from these words as if it were his opinion that the plaintiff could not by any means be removed from being Bishop of Natal, his Lordship added: "Such is not my opinion. 1 wish it to be distinctly understood that I do not mean to assert that as soon as the plaintiff's nomination by the Crown, and his appointment by letters patent, had been consummated by his consecration by the Archbishop, whatever might be his conduct or opinions, he must for ever remain Bishop of Natal and enjoy the endowments attached to that office, even though the letters patent appointing him had never been revoked. On the contrary, I entertain no doubt that if he had not performed his part in the contract entered into by him, that if he had failed to comply with 'the covenants of his trust,' he could not compel payment of his stipend. The contract he has entered into is involved in the words 'Bishop of the Church of England as by law established.' The duties, the teaching, the superintendence, the pastoral care, the watching of his flock, which appertains to a Bishop, he undertook and was bound to perform; and if, by his own wilful default, this has become impossible, I do not mean to lay down that he could maintain a suit in this Court for the payment of his salary as Bishop of Natal."

The following Opinion was afterwards given by the Solicitor General (Sir John Coleridge), Sir Roundell Palmer, and Dr. Deane, in April, 1869:—

Query.—" Assuming that the present Bishop of Natal has been guilty of an ecclesiastical offence, what steps can be taken to bring him to trial, and before what tribunal?"

Opinion.—" Any tribunal competent to decide whether the doctrinal opinions advocated by Dr. Colenso, the present Bishop of Natal, are in accordance with the doctrines of the Church of England or not, must be sought for in South Africa or in England.

60 CASES AND OPINIONS ON CONSTITUTIONAL LAW.

" The decision of the Judicial Committee in *The Bishop of Natal's Case*, 3 Moore, P. C. (N.S.) 115, is an authority for saying that the Bishop of Capetown has no jurisdiction over Dr. Colenso.

" Taking the cases of *The Bishop of Natal*, and *Long* v. *The Bishop of Capetown*, 1 Moore, P. C. (N.S.) 411, together, they appear to determine that there is no jurisdiction ecclesiastical in the metropolitan diocese (so to call it) of Capetown which can reach the Bishop of Natal.

" The colonial decision in *The Bishop of Natal* v. *Green*, sent with the Case, throws some doubt upon the condition of the colony of Natal, as assumed by the Privy Council in *The Bishop of Natal's Case;* and it may be that the letters patent granted to Dr. Colenso were valid. But if that should be so we cannot see that any tribunal, civil, criminal, or ecclesiastical, exists in Natal which can determine whether the doctrinal opinions of Dr. Colenso are erroneous or not, and can enforce its decision.

" The authority of the judgment of the Master of the Rolls in *The Bishop of Natal* v. *Gladstone*, L. R. 3 Eq. p. 1, must not be carried beyond the point determined—viz., that the Bishop of Natal, retaining his status as bishop, was entitled to receive the endowment of the see.

" The Archbishop of Canterbury, whatever may be his authority over his own suffragans, has, in our opinion, no jurisdiction, inherent or conferred by the Crown or by Parliament, which can enable him to inquire, as a Court, into the doctrines advocated by the Bishop of Natal.

" It has been suggested that the Crown as visitor, or as supreme in causes ecclesiastical, or by virtue and in exercise of some other supposed power, may be able, either by Commissioners specially appointed, or by means of the Privy Council, to hear and determine the points raised against Dr. Colenso.

" We are unable to find the slightest ground on which this suggestion can be supported.

" The Crown is supreme over all causes ecclesiastical in the same, and in no other sense, and to no greater extent than the Crown is supreme over causes temporal—that is, by law, and by means of the various established courts of law.

" The Submission of the Clergy Act (25 Hen. 8, c. 19) gave no such power to the Crown. Section 4 of that Act made it lawful for the parties grieved by any decision of an ecclesiastical judge in England to appeal to the King in Chancery, for which court of appeal the Judicial Committee of the Privy Council is now substituted. This is an appellate, and not an original jurisdiction.

" The High Commission Court, established by 1 Eliz. c. 1, is abolished by 16 Ch. 1, c. 11, and the revival of the High Commission Court or any similar court is especially provided against by 13 Ch. 2, st. 1, c. 12, and 1 Will. & M. Sess. 2, c. 2.

" With reference to the authorities referred to, intermediate in date between 1 Eliz. c. 1 and 16 Ch. 1, c. 11, it is hardly necessary to observe that they state the law as it was in force under the former of these statutes, and which ceased to be in force on the passing of the latter.

" No argument in favour of the power of the Crown can be derived from 3 & 4 Will. 4, c. 41, s. 4, by which it is enacted that it shall be lawful for his Majesty ' to refer to the Judicial Committee for hearing or consideration any such other matters as his Majesty shall think fit; and such Committee shall thereupon hear or consider the same, and shall advise his Majesty thereon in manner aforesaid.'

" To make this section applicable to the judicial determination of an ecclesiastical matter would be in effect to restore the High Commission Court. The section is to be taken as referring to questions not of judicial cognizance on which the Crown may desire to be solemnly advised by persons conversant with the law.

" The only remaining consideration is whether the merits of the case can be raised on a *scire facias* to revoke the letters patent granted to the Bishop of Natal.

" This manner of raising the question between the Bishop of Natal and his opponents was suggested by the Master of the Rolls in the case of *The Bishop of Natal* v. *Gladstone.*

" The only ground on which the letters patent would be revoked by such a proceeding is, in our opinion, that the letters were *ab initio* void, as having issued improvidently. This would leave the merits untouched.

" Indeed, if the view taken in *The Bishop of Natal* v. *Green* as to the status of the colony be correct, the letters patent might possibly be held valid.

" We are therefore of opinion that no means at present exist for trying before any tribunal competent to decide the question whether or no Dr. Colenso, the present Bishop of Natal, has advocated doctrinal opinions not in accordance with the doctrines held by the Church of England; and, assuming the present Bishop of Natal to have been guilty of an ecclesiastical offence, no steps can be taken to bring him, as such Bishop, before any tribunal.

" We do not, however, think that, upon the present materials, it would be satisfactory or proper for us to enter into the question, whether, if Dr. Colenso were present within the jurisdiction of an English ecclesiastical court, and were in this country to commit any offence against the laws ecclesiastical, he could, or not, be proceeded against, under the Church Discipline Act, as a clerk in holy orders of the Church of England."

The judgment of the Master of the Rolls, however, in *The Bishop of Natal* v. *Gladstone,* shows that there is a mode by which the question of heresy might be tried—namely, by the trustees of the Colonial Bishoprics' Fund refusing to pay the Bishop his salary on the alleged ground of heretical opinions, and distinctly raising this question in a suit instituted by him to enforce payment. The case might thus be decided in the Court of Chancery and carried on appeal to the House of Lords.

In an appeal from two orders of the Court of Chancery in Bermuda
(*Ex parte Jenkins*, L. R. 2 P. C. 258), upon an application on behalf of
the appellant, a clergyman, for a writ *de vi laicâ removendâ* to remove
any opposition to his being inducted into a parish church as rector,
the Judicial Committee decided that the Court of Chancery was justified in refusing the writ on the ground that the power of issuing such
a writ had not been expressly imposed upon the Court of Chancery in
Bermuda by the Act of the colony creating that Court. They said
that it would be an inconvenient precedent to imply the existence of a
writ not known to the Court itself as necessary to the enforcement of
the legal right obstructed merely from the creation of the Court, and a
general grant in large words of general jurisdiction. As to the writ
de vi laicâ removendâ, the Court said that it might be regarded at the
present day as an obsolete proceeding : see Fitz. *Nat. Brev.* D. 54.
They held that the appellant was duly presented by the Governor to
the rectory, and was instituted by the lawful authority of the Bishop
of Newfoundland. They said that it was a fact which would not be
disputed, that for more than a century the Crown possessed the power
of collating to all the vacant benefices in the Bermudas by direct
nomination, a power which it exercised by delegation to the successive
Governors, who were usually described as Ordinaries in their patents.
But when a Bishop or ecclesiastical ordinary was duly appointed, the
Crown, as patron, thought proper to leave to the Governor power of
nominating the clerk, but recognized, by the letters patent granted to
the Bishop, the power of institution belonging to his office. As to the
ecclesiastical authority of the Governor of a colony as ordinary, see
Basham v. *Lumley*, 3 C. and P. 489. As to a sentence of suspension
passed by the Bishop of Jamaica, and reversed for irregularity, the
party not having been cited to answer any particular charge, see
Bowerbank v. *The Bishop of Jamaica*, 2 Moore, P. C. 449. As to the
authority of a synod of a Church in connection with the Church of
Scotland in Australia, see *Lang* v. *Purves*, 15 Moore, P. C. 389, and compare *Craigdallie* v. *Aikman*, 1 Dow. 1 ; and as to a synod of the Dutch
Reformed Church at the Cape of Good Hope, *Murray* v. *Burgess*, L. R.
1 P. C. 362.

In 1813, when the British territories in India were under the
government of the East India Company, the first bishopric was established there ; and although the Bishop was appointed and consecrated
under the authority of the Crown, it was thought necessary or right to
obtain the sanction of the Legislature, and that an Act of Parliament
(53 Geo. 3. c. 155, s. 49) should be passed to give the Bishop legal status
and authority. In 1833, two additional bishoprics were founded, one
at Madras and the other at Bombay, and an Act was passed (3 & 4
Will. 4, c. 85), by the 93rd section of which it was enacted that the
Crown should have power to assign limits to the dioceses of the three
bishoprics, and from time to time to alter and vary the same limits
respectively, and to grant to such Bishops, within their dioceses, eccle-

siastical jurisdiction; and by section 94, the Bishop of Calcutta was to be Metropolitan in India.

On a question which came before the Queen's Advocate (Sir Travers Twiss), Mr. Pontifex, and myself, in 1868, as to whether the Crown had the power to vary by letters patent the limits of the dioceses of Calcutta, Madras, and Bombay, we were of opinion that, having regard to the statute 3 & 4 Will. 4, c. 85, s. 93, the Crown had such power; but it was so doubtful whether there was any power in the Crown to alter and vary by letters patent the limits of the existing archdeaconries of Calcutta, Madras, and Bombay respectively, that we advised that, if the scheme were carried out, an Act of Parliament should be obtained for the purpose. We added that the Crown, in our opinion, had not the power to grant by letters patent to the bishops of the respective dioceses in India, jurisdiction over congregations of the Church of England in places not within the dominions of the Crown.

If a will be made in this country and proved in the Prerogative Court, the probate will not extend to property in the colonies. Nor will a grant of administration obtained here, although the intestate was resident and died in this country: *Burn* v. *Cole*, Amb. 416; *Atkins* v. *Smith*, 2 Atk. 63; *Thorne* v. *Watkins*, 2 Ves. Sen. 35. And if the testator was domiciled here, the Judge of Probate in the colony is bound by the probate here, and ought to grant it to the same person: *per* Lord Mansfield, in *Burn* v. *Cole*, *ubi sup.* If the testator is domiciled in a colony, the will should be proved in the Probate Court there, and a copy transmitted to, and proved in, the Ecclesiastical Court here, as an original will: Williams on Executors, 303, 308 (4th edit.). See *Hare* v. *Nasmyth*, 2 Add. 25. A probate obtained in the proper ecclesiastical court here extends to all the personal property of the deceased, wherever situate at the time of his death, including the colonies and any country abroad: *Whyte* v. *Rose*, 3 Q. B. 493 (in Error); see *Swift* v. *Nun*, 26 L. J. (Ex.)(N.S.) 365. A grant of administration obtained here will not extend to the colonies, though the intestate died and was resident here.

Effect of Letters of Administration in the Colonies.

It has been held that a foreign plantation, though an inheritance, was to be looked upon as a chattel to pay debts, and a testamentary thing: *Noell* v. *Robinson*, 2 Ventr. 358; see also *Blankard* v. *Galdy*, 4 Mod. 215. And as to property in any of the British plantations in America, see statute 5 Geo. 2, c. 7, repealed as to negroes by statute 37 Geo. 3, c. 119: see *Thomson* v. *Grant*, 1 Russ. 540; and *Manning* v. *Spooner*, 3 Ves. 118.

The compensation money for slaves in Jamaica was held to be legal assets in *Lyon* v. *Colville*, 1 Coll. 449. The term British plantations in America, in statute 5 Geo. 2, c. 7, includes the West Indies, and it has been held that although estates there were made legal assets by that statute, they might be devised so as to make them equitable assets: *Charlton* v. *Wright*, 12 Sim. 274. As to the East Indies, see statute 39 & 40 Geo. 3, c. 79, s. 21; 55 Geo. 3, c. 84; Act of the Governor-General of India in Council VII. of 1849, and Act II. of 1850.

CHAPTER III.

ON THE POWERS AND DUTIES AND THE CIVIL AND CRIMINAL LIABILITIES OF GOVERNORS OF COLONIES.

(1.) JOINT OPINION *of the Attorney and Solicitor General,* SIR THOMAS TREVOR *and* SIR JOHN HAWLES, *as to how a Lieutenant-Governor could be tried for Misdemeanor.* 1701.

To the Right Honourable the Lords Commissioners for Trade and Plantations.

In answer to your Lordships' *quæries,* signified to us by Mr. Popple the 30th of April last, relating to offences committed by Captain Norton, and against the Act for regulating abuses in the plantation trade:

First: We are of opinion that, for such offence or wilful neglect, the Lieutenant-Governor, Captain Norton, may be indicted and tried in the Court of King's Bench, by virtue of the Act for punishing governors of plantations for offences committed by them in the plantations. But we doubt whether he will incur the penalty of £1000 by the Act, made the 7th and 8th of the King, for regulating abuses in the plantation trade; for the words of the Act extend only to Governors and Commanders-in-Chief, and is given only for the offence of not taking the oaths or putting the Acts in execution; but he will be finable at the discretion of the Court.

Secondly: We think a foreigner endenized is qualified to be master of a ship trading to the plantations, unless there be a provision in the letters patent of denization, that such denization shall not enable him to be master of a ship, which is usually inserted for that purpose; but hath been omitted in some denizations of French Protestants since the reign of his present Majesty, by Order of Council.

Thirdly: We are of opinion, that a Scotchman is to be accounted as an Englishman within the Act, every Scotchman being a natural-born subject.

                                        THOS. TREVOR.
June 4, 1701.   JOHN HAWLES.

(2.) OPINIONS *of* MR. REEVE (*afterwards Chief Justice of the Common Pleas*), *and* MR. LUTWYCHE, *King's Counsel, on the effect of the Demise of the Crown on a Colonial Act granting a salary to the Governor of a Colony.* 1727.

I am of opinion that this Act is not determined by the demise of his Majesty King George, but will remain in force as long as Mr. Worsley continues Governor of Barbadoes, and shall personally reside in the island. It is observable that the tax, &c., is granted to his Majesty, his heirs and successors, during the continuance of the Act : it is limited to continue for so long time as Mr. Worsley shall continue to be his Majesty's Captain-General, &c. Yet, I conceive these words will have the same construction as if it had been limited to continue so long as Mr. Worsley should be the King's Captain-General ; and as the King, in law, never dies, I conceive the demise of King George I. will not be a determination of this Act.

January 15, 1727.   THOMAS REEVE.

I am of opinion that upon the demise of his late Majesty, the Act for granting the £6000 *per annum* did not determine ; for I think it is clear that the Governor's commission continued for the space of six months after the death of the King, by virtue of an Act of Parliament in Queen Anne's reign, unless the commission was superseded in the meantime ; and if the commission was determined by ending at the six months, I am of opinion that the Act had determined also, though the Governor had been appointed afterwards, because he once ceased to be Governor under any commission. But if the fact was, that within the six months he had a new commission, it is doubtful whether his continuing Governor without intermission will not be sufficient to entitle him to the £6000 *per annum* by the Act; and upon consideration of these

F

three clauses, I am inclinable to think that it will entitle him so
long as he remains Governor, and continues without intermission;
but perhaps it might be made plainer by seeing the whole Act.

February 1, 1728.   T. LUTWYCHE.

(3.) JOINT OPINION *of the Attorney and Solicitor General,*
SIR THOMAS TREVOR *and* SIR JOHN HAWLES, *on the determination of a Governor's Commission.* 1700.

To the Right Honourable the Lords Commissioners of Trade and
Plantations.

MAY IT PLEASE YOUR LORDSHIPS,—Upon perusal of their Excellencies the Lords Justices' letter to the President and Council
of Nevis, dated the 29th September, 1698, and of a copy of a
commission granted by his Majesty to Colonel Fox, dated the
15th November, 1699, we are humbly of opinion, that the
powers and authorities given by the Lords Justices to the President and Council of Nevis were determined by the commission to Colonel Fox, upon the arrival of Colonel Fox there
and publication of his commission, and we conceive he might upon
his coming there before Colonel Codrington, by virtue of his
commission, dispossess the President and Council, and assume to
himself that government until the arrival of Colonel Codrington
there.   ⸲
                                                   THOMAS TREVOR.
    August 9, 1700.   JOHN HAWLES.

(4.) OPINION *of* MR. WEST (*afterwards Lord Chancellor of
Ireland*), *as to whether a Governor can vote as a Councillor.*
1725.

To the Right Honourable the Lords Commissioners for Trade and
Plantations.

MY LORDS,—In obedience to your Lordships' commands, signified to me by letter from Mr. Popple, dated the 24th day of
November last, I have considered the following *quære*, whether a
Governor can vote, as a Councillor, in the passing of bills, when
the Council sit in their legislative capacity ?

Upon consideration of which, and of the Governor's commission and instructions, I am of opinion that a Governor cannot, by law, vote as a Councillor in the passing of bills, when the Council sit in their legislative capacity.

January 8, 1724-5.   RICHARD WEST.

(5.) OPINION *of the Attorney General*, SIR JOHN WILLES, *on the right of the Proprietor of Maryland to appoint to Offices under the King's Charter.* 1737.

Quære 1. Whether by the Charter of Maryland, the Lord Proprietor has not a right to the nomination of all officers in general, civil as well as military?

Answer. I am of opinion that by the Charter of Maryland, the Lord Proprietor has a right to nominate and appoint all officers in general, as well civil as military.

Quære 2. Whether there is anything particular in the nature of the office of Treasurer, of either shore, to exempt it from the said nomination?

Answer. It does not appear to me, that there is anything so particular in the nature of the office of Treasurer, of either shore, as to take the right of nomination to this office from the Lord Proprietor, and to give it to any other persons.

Quære 3. Whether a few precedents in this case, of a Treasurer being appointed by tripartite concurrence of both Houses of Assembly and the Governor, can or do overthrow his Lordship's right?

Answer. All the precedents, except one, being between 1692 and 1716, when my Lord Baltimore was out of possession, I am of opinion that they will not overthrow his Lordship's right, founded upon such plain words in the Charter.

Quære 4. Whether the precedents, hereunto annexed, do divest the Lord Proprietor of his right of nomination to the office of Treasurer or Treasurers, so nominated, they giving the security the law directs?

Answer. The Treasurer or Treasurers, when nominated by the

F 2

Proprietor, must give such security as the law directs. To the other part of this *quære* I have given an answer already.

January 22, 1736-7.   J. WILLES.

(6.) JOINT OPINION *of the Attorney and Solicitor General,* SIR WILLIAM GARROW *and* SIR SAMUEL SHEPHERD, *as to the devolution of the authority of Governor of a Colony.*

Lincoln's Inn, November 24, 1814.

MY LORD,—We have had the honour to receive your Lordship's letter of yesterday's date, stating that his Royal Highness the Prince Regent, having judged it expedient to direct Lieutenant-General Sir G. Prevost, his Majesty's Captain-General and Governor-in-Chief of the provinces of Upper and Lower Canada, to deliver over all the civil and military powers with which he may be invested, to the senior General Officer for the time being in Canada ; and doubts having been entertained whether, consistently with the terms of his Majesty's commission under the great seal, bearing date the 21st day of October, 1811, he can comply with such instruction, so long as he may remain in the province, in which the severity of the season may for a length of time detain him, your Lordship is pleased to transmit to us the extract of your despatch to Sir G. Prevost, which conveys the instruction before mentioned, together with the copy of Sir G. Prevost's commission and other papers, and to desire that we will take the same into our consideration, and report to your Lordship, for the information of his Royal Highness the Prince Regent, our opinion upon the point in question, and also whether any Act short of an absolute and entire revocation of the commission can, during the presence of Sir G. Prevost in the province, suspend the powers with which he is invested by the said commission.

    We have accordingly considered the same, and have the honour to report to your Lordship, that we observe by the commission to which your Lordship has been pleased to refer us, that his Majesty directed the Governor, in the case of his absence from either of the provinces of Upper Canada and Lower Canada, to deliver the seal of the said provinces respectively into the charge of the Lieutenant-Governor or person administering the government there, until his Majesty should think fit to authorize him, by instrument under his royal sign-manual, to commit the custody thereof to such person as might be appointed by his Majesty for that purpose. It does not appear that in any case but that of absence the authority of the Governor could be devolved on any other person; we beg therefore very humbly to submit as our opinion, that the Lieutenant-General and Governor cannot, consistently with the terms of his commission, deliver over his civil and military powers to any other person during his personal residence within the local limits of his Government; and we further beg leave to submit as our opinion, that no act short of an absolute and entire revocation of the commission can, during the presence of Sir G. Prevost in the provinces, suspend the powers with which he is invested by the said commission.

The Right Hon. Earl of Bathurst,
&c. &c. &c.

W. GARROW.
S. SHEPHERD.

(7.) CASE and JOINT OPINION *of the Attorney and Solicitor General,* SIR J. SCARLETT *and* SIR EDWARD B. SUGDEN, *as to power of Governor to revoke assignment of a Convict.*

December 24, 1829.

Case.—The Secretary of State is desirous to be advised whether, under the 9th section of 9 Geo. 4, c. 83, a Governor can revoke the assignment of a convict of whose sentence it is not intended to grant any remission, general or partial.

Opinion.—We are of opinion that under the 9th section of 9 Geo. 4, c. 83, a Governor can revoke the assignment of a convict of whose sentence it is not intended to grant any remission, and we think that there is nothing either in the context or the apparent policy of the Act which militates against this construction.

J. SCARLETT.
EDWARD B. SUGDEN.

(8.) JOINT OPINION *of the Attorney and Solicitor General,*
SIR JOHN CAMPBELL *and* SIR R. M. ROLFE, *as to power of
Governor to suspend a Colonial Officer appointed by Order in
Council.*

Temple, August 6, 1838.

MY LORD,—We have had the honour to receive your Lordship's
letter of the 4th instant, asking our opinion on the question whether,
under 4 & 5 Will. 4, c. 95, the Governor of South Australia has
the power to suspend any colonial officer appointed by an Order
in Council, and whether notwithstanding an Act of Suspension any
such officer would continue *de jure* to hold his appointment?

In answer, we beg to state that in our opinion the Governor has
the power of suspension, and that an officer so suspended would
from thenceforth cease to be entitled to exercise any of the functions
or to derive any of the emoluments of his office till her Majesty's
pleasure should be made known.

The officer must be considered holding during the pleasure of
the Crown, and we think the Governor has the power of suspension
under his commission and instructions from the Crown.

This power is not conferred upon him by 4 & 5 Will. 4, c. 95, but
there is nothing in that Act by which the prerogative of the Crown
in this respect is abridged.

The Lord Glenelg,   J. CAMPBELL.
&c. &c. &c.   R. M. ROLFE.

(9.) JOINT OPINION *of the King's Advocate,* SIR C. ROBIN-
SON, *and the Attorney and Solicitor General,* SIR R. GIFFORD
and SIR J. COPLEY, *on the notification of the Demise of the
Crown in a Colony.*

Doctors' Commons, May 21, 1821.

MY LORD,—We are honoured with your Lordship's commands of
the 14th instant, transmitting the copy of a despatch from the
officer administering the civil government of the island of Ceylon,
stating the circumstances under which the clergy and the Supreme
Court of Ceylon had acted upon the information of his late

Majesty's demise, although not conveyed to them through the channel of the Governor; and requesting instructions how far their conduct in doing so was legal.

And your Lordship is pleased to desire that we would take the same into consideration, and report to your Lordship our opinion:

1. Whether a notification from the Bishop to his clergy is not a sufficient authority to them to change the Church Service of the colony according to the form prescribed by his Majesty's Order in Council even before any proclamation has been issued by the Governor?

2. Whether the courts of justice of the colony, after such change in the Church Service, can properly retain the form of process used by them, or whether they are at liberty to change such form upon what they may consider satisfactory evidence of the demise of the Crown, even although that event may not have been officially notified in a proclamation by the Governor?

In obedience to your Lordship's commands, we have the honour to report that we are of opinion that the notification of the Governor is not absolutely necessary to establish legal evidence of the demise of the Crown.

We think the Bishop's directions to his clergy, founded on the Order in Council, might be sufficient authority to them to make the change prescribed, and that the Supreme Court of Justice might also make the necessary change in the forms of process, although no proclamation had been issued by the Governor. But we think such an act should be considered as an exception to the more regular mode of waiting for public instructions from the Governor, and to be justified only by peculiar circumstances, and on the ground of the inconvenience that might be likely to ensue from longer delay.

CHRISTOPHER ROBINSON.

The Earl Bathurst,   R. GIFFORD.
&c. &c. &c.   J. COPLEY.

(10.) JOINT OPINION *of the Attorney and Solicitor General,*
SIR JOHN CAMPBELL *and* SIR R. M. ROLFE, *as to effect of
Demise of the Crown on the Commission of the Governor of a
Colony.*

Temple, March 12, 1839.

MY LORD,—We have to acknowledge the receipt of a letter
from Lord Glenelg, dated the 18th ultimo, transmitting to us the
copy of a despatch from the Governor of the Cape of Good Hope,
with the reports therein enclosed of the proceedings which were had
in October last, before the Commissioners for the trial of offences
committed at sea, on the trial of the commander and first mate of
the barque "Blake" for murder, and of another mate for cruelly
ill-treating an apprentice. His Lordship requested us to report our
opinion, whether on the ground stated by the prisoners' counsel, or
on any other grounds, there is any sufficient reason for doubting
the validity of the commission under which the prisoners were
tried.

The doubts suggested as to the validity of the commission were
founded on the circumstance that more than six calendar months
had, at the date of the trial (October, 1838), elapsed since the
demise of his late Majesty King William IV. But we are of
opinion that these doubts are altogether unfounded. By the 1 Will.
4, c. 4, it was expressly enacted that no commission or warrant
for the exercise of any office or employment, civil or military,
within any of his Majesty's plantations or foreign possessions
should, by reason of any future demise of the Crown, become void
until the expiration of eighteen calendar months next after any
such demise; all commissions, therefore, which were in force at the
Cape of Good Hope on the day of the death of his late Majesty
(June 20, 1837), continued in force until the 20th of December,
1838, which was long after the trial. The same statute continued
in force all colonial commissions which existed at the demise of
George IV. until they should be superseded by a new commission.
And this explains the circumstance stated by the Commissioners,
that their commission bears date the 10th of March, 1832, being
nearly two years after the death of King George IV.

The Marquess of Normanby,   J. CAMPBELL.
&c. &c. &c.   R. M. ROLFE.

(11.) JOINT OPINION *of the Attorney and Solicitor General,* SIR JOHN CAMPBELL *and* SIR THOMAS WILDE, *as to appointment of Members of the Legislative Council of Canada.*

Temple, March 20, 1841.

MY LORD,—With reference to Mr. Vernon Smith's letter of this day's date, respecting the mode of appointing the members of the first Legislative Council of the United Province of Canada, under 3 & 4 Vict. c. 35, s. 4, we have the honour to report to your Lordship that we are clearly of opinion they must all be appointed by one instrument under the royal sign-manual, authorizing the Governor of Canada in Her Majesty's name, by one instrument under the great seal of the province, to summon them.

The instrument under the royal sign-manual will follow the words of the Act of Parliament, and authorize the Governor by an instrument under the great seal to summon; but we humbly conceive that instructions should be given to the Governor to execute this authority by *one* instrument under the great seal of the province, naming all the members of the Legislative Council.

The Right Hon. Lord John Russell,   J. CAMPBELL.
  &c. &c. &c.   THOS. WILDE.

(12.) JOINT OPINION *of the Queen's Advocate,* SIR J. DODSON, *and the Attorney and Solicitor General,* SIR FREDERICK POLLOCK *and* SIR WILLIAM FOLLETT, *as to Power of the Government of Canada to grant an exclusive Right of Ferry between that Province and the United States.*

Temple, March 12, 1842.

SIR,—We beg to acknowledge the receipt of your letter of the 24th ult., wherein you state you had been directed by Lord Stanley to transmit to us the enclosed copy of a despatch from the Governor-General of Canada, submitting a question which has arisen respecting the power of the Provincial Government to grant an exclusive right of ferriage over rivers dividing the British territory from the adjoining States.

And you were pleased to request we would take this subject into our consideration, and report to his Lordship our opinion whether

the Government of Canada possesses the exclusive right of regulating the ferries between that province and the United States.
In obedience to his Lordship's commands, we have taken this
matter into our consideration, and beg to report that if we are to
understand the question submitted to us to be, whether the Government of Canada has the power to grant to any individual the right
of conveying passengers to and from the American shore to the
exclusion of all other persons, English or American, we are of
opinion that the Governor of Canada has no such legal power; and
if it be desirable that any regulations should be adopted with
respect to the intercourse between the two shores, we think that it
should be made the subject of a treaty between the two governments, and be sanctioned by an Act of the Legislature.

G. W. Hope, Esq.,
&c. &c. &c.

J. DODSON.
FRED. POLLOCK.
W. W. FOLLETT.

(13.) *Extract from* JOINT OPINION *of the Attorney and Soli-
citor General,* SIR FREDERICK POLLOCK *and* SIR WILLIAM
FOLLETT, *on the necessity of the concurrence of the Council of a
Colony in granting leave of absence to Public Officers.*

Temple, December 17, 1842.

In obedience to your Lordship's commands, we have taken this
matter into our consideration, and have the honour to report, for
your Lordship's information, that we are of opinion that neither
on any of the grounds suggested, nor on any other grounds that
occur to us, can the concurrence of the Council in St. Lucia, or in
any other colony, be lawfully dispensed with in granting leave of
absence to public officers generally, or to any particular class of
public officers.

The first Act, 22 Geo. 3, c. 75, is expressly made to apply to
any colony or plantation now or at any time thereafter belonging
to the Crown of Great Britain ; there is, therefore, no foundation
for the suggestion that the statute does not apply to colonies
acquired since the passing of the statute.

The second statute, 54 Geo. 3, c. 61, extends the enactments of
the first to all officers however appointed, if appointed by any in-

strument; and it appears to us that the two statutes taken together
are of universal application to all the colonies, and to all officers
appointed by any instrument whatever. Any inconvenience arising
from this must be remedied by the Legislature.

FREDERICK POLLOCK.

W. W. FOLLETT.

(14.) JOINT OPINION *of the Attorney and Solicitor General,*
SIR J. JERVIS *and* SIR J. ROMILLY, *on the Grant of a Conditional Pardon for Murder in British Guiana.*

Temple, December 12, 1849.

MY LORD,—We are honoured with your Lordship's command,
contained in Mr. Merivale's letter of the 21st ultimo, in which he
stated that he was directed by your Lordship to transmit to us the
enclosed papers, with a request that we would favour you with our
joint opinion on the following question :—

A criminal has been convicted of murder by the Supreme Court
of Criminal Justice in Demerara and Essequibo. The Governor
wishes to extend to this offender the mercy of the Crown, subject
to the condition of imprisonment for life—a punishment which is
recognized by the law of British Guiana.

But he has been advised that his power to do so is doubtful. It
is derived from his commission, which authorizes him to grant to
any offender " a free and unconditional pardon, or a pardon subject
to such conditions as by any law in force in the said colony may
be thereunto annexed."

But it is stated that by the Dutch law, in force in British
Guiana prior to the capitulation, no pardon could be granted
by the Governor in cases of murder; and, consequently, that no
such law is in force in the colony as is contemplated by the
commission.   The questions, therefore, on which our advice was
requested, were—

1st. Whether we considered that the Governor possesses the
power which he wishes to exercise ? and,

2nd. If we should be of opinion that he does not, what is the
most advisable course, both in order to grant the pardon in the
present instance, subject to the requisite condition, and also to
obviate the occurrence of the same difficulty ?

Mr. Merivale also stated that he was directed to annex copies of the Governor's despatch on this subject, and the opinion given by the Attorney General of British Guiana, and extracts of so much of the Governor's commission and instructions as regard the question.

In obedience to your Lordship's command, we have considered the various documents submitted to us, and have the honour to report that, in our opinion, the Governor does possess the power which he wishes to exercise. The conditions referred to in the patent do not depend upon the nature of the crime pardoned, but upon the legality of the conditions themselves.

> The Right Hon. Earl Grey,   JOHN JERVIS.
> &c. &c. &c.   JOHN ROMILLY.

(15.) JOINT OPINION *of the Attorney and Solicitor General,* SIR A. E. COCKBURN *and* SIR RICHARD BETHELL, *on the Grant of a Conditional Pardon by the Governor of a Colony in virtue of the general power to pardon conveyed by his Commission.*

Temple, February 16, 1853.

MY LORD DUKE,—We were honoured with your commands, contained in Mr. Merivale's letter of the 9th instant, in which he stated that he was directed by your Grace to request that we would favour you with an answer to the following question :—

Whether the Governor of Barbadoes can, by virtue of the power entrusted to him by his commission, commute sentences of death passed by a criminal court in Barbadoes to imprisonment for a term of years ?

Mr. Merivale was also directed to annex an extract of the commission of the Governor, and also a despatch received on the subject from the Governor of Barbadoes.

In obedience to your Grace's commands, we have considered the documents transmitted to us, and have the honour to report that the power to grant conditional pardons has always been held to be incidental to the general power to pardon vested in the Crown as part of its prerogative.

By means of such conditional pardons, the Crown was enabled to commute the punishment of death for that of transportation, a

punishment unknown to the common law, independently of any
statutory enactment.

We are of opinion, that the power to pardon, conferred on the
Governor of Barbadoes by his commission, carries with it the
power to commute the sentence of death for a minor punishment,
by means of a pardon conditional upon the delinquent undergoing
the substituted punishment.

His Grace the Duke of Newcastle,   A. E. COCKBURN.
    &c.   &c.   &c.   RICHARD BETHELL.

(16.) JOINT OPINION *of the Attorney and Solicitor General,*
SIR A. E. COCKBURN *and* SIR R. BETHELL, *that the Power of
Pardon is not vested in the Superintendent of Honduras.*

Temple, July 3, 1854.

SIR,—We were honoured with his Grace the Duke of Newcastle's
commands, contained in Mr. Merivale's letter of the 13th April
last, in which he stated that he was directed by his Grace to transmit to us copy of a correspondence between the Colonial Office
and the Local Government of Honduras, on the question of the
exercise of the prerogative of mercy by the Superintendent of that
settlement.

And he further stated that he was to request that we would take
these papers into consideration, and report to his Grace whether, in
our opinion, the Superintendent of Honduras possesses, under his
commission from the Governor of Jamaica, and the Act of the
public meeting (*sic*) " to amend the system of government of British Honduras " (copies of which were annexed), or otherwise, power
to exercise her Majesty's prerogative of pardon.

Mr. Merivale concluded by stating that his Grace did not think
it necessary to do more than direct our attention to the peculiar
circumstances of the settlement of Honduras, and the Acts relating
to it (57 Geo. 3, c. 53, and 59 Geo. 3, c. 54) which had been frequently under our and our predecessors' consideration : and also to
a letter from Her Majesty's Law Officers, dated the 14th March,
1851, in which the opinion was intimated that the recitals of those
Acts are not at present fully applicable to the settlement.

In obedience to the above request, we have fully considered the
Acts of Parliament, the Superintendent's commission, and also the

Colonial Act to which the letter refers, and have the honour to report—

That we think the power to exercise Her Majesty's prerogative of pardon was not, at the time when the Act of the public meeting was passed, a power that was vested in, or could be lawfully exercised by, the Superintendent; and that section 44 of the last-mentioned Act must be construed as vesting in the officer administering the government of Honduras such powers only as theretofore had been lawfully exercised by the Superintendent; and that in our opinion the Superintendent of Honduras does not possess the power to exercise Her Majesty's prerogative of pardon.

The Right Hon. Sir G. Grey, Bart.,   A. E. COCKBURN.
&c.   &c.   &c.   RICHARD BETHELL.

(17.) JOINT OPINION *of the Attorney and Solicitor General,* SIR R. BETHELL *and* SIR H. S. KEATING, *as to the legal meaning of the phrase " Governor in Council."*

Lincoln's Inn, December 17, 1857.

SIR,—We were honoured with your commands, signified in Mr. Merivale's letter of the 11th of December instant, in which he stated that he was directed by you to send to us copy of a despatch from the Governor of the Bahamas, and to request that we would favour you with our advice as to the answer to be returned to the Governor's question : namely, whether, where any act is to be done under colonial enactment (confirmed by the Crown) by the Governor, in either of the three forms specified in the despatch, the personal presence of the Governor in the Council is necessary to the legal performance of the act?

In obedience to the request contained in Mr. Merivale's letter, we have the honour to report—

That we have considered the despatch from the Governor of the Bahamas. The royal instructions treat the presence of the Governor as necessary at every meeting of the Executive Council. They dispense with his presence in cases only of some insuperable impediment.

Whenever the Governor is physically able to attend, he is bound to be present. Of the three forms of expression cited in the despatch as contained in Colonial Acts confirmed by the Crown, we are of opinion that where a colonial enactment enjoins certain things to be done "by the Governor in Council," the Governor must be present, and the royal instructions do not control the Act so as to admit of the things being done in the absence of the Governor, even though such absence be caused by some insuperable impediment.

Secondly and Thirdly.—Where the Colonial Acts enjoin certain things to be done "by the Governor, with the advice of the Executive Council," or simply to be done "with the advice and consent of the Executive Council," the forms of expression do not require the actual presence of the Governor in Council as a necessary condition, but the enactments, of course, do not control or dispense with the necessity of obeying the instructions; and in these two latter cases, therefore, whenever the attendance of the Governor is prevented by an insuperable impediment, the Act may be done by the Council, with the subsequent concurrence of the Governor.

The Right Hon. H. Labouchere, M.P., RICHARD BETHELL.
  &c. &c. &c.   HENRY S. KEATING.

(18.) OPINION *of the Solicitor General,* SIR HUGH CAIRNS, *as to Legality of Government of a Colony administered by Officer appointed by the Governor in the absence of the Officer on whom that function devolved by Royal Charter.*

Lincoln's Inn, July, 1858.

SIR,—I am honoured with Mr. Merivale's letter of the 10th instant, stating that he was directed by you to transmit to me for my opinion thereon the following Case, with its enclosures :—

By the Royal Charter of 1850, which provides for the government of the Gold Coast, it was ordained that in case of the Governor's death or absence, the government should devolve on the Lieutenant-Governor; and if there should be no Lieutenant-Governor, on the Judicial Assessor; and if there should be no Judicial Assessor, on the Senior Puisne Justice.

That it has lately, however, been deemed expedient to issue a supplementary charter altering the preceding provision for the administration of the government, so far that in case of the Governor's death or absence, if there should be no Lieutenant-Governor, the government is appointed to devolve on the Colonial Secretary.

That the Governor having reported in a despatch that, being about to absent himself, and the Colonial Secretary being actually absent, he had appointed the Senior Justice to administer the government during his absence; and to request that I would favour you with my opinion, whether the Governor's appointment of the Senior Justice to administer the government was legally consistent with the terms of the original (as amended by the supplementary) charter, and, if not, what steps should be taken to repair the error which may have been committed?

In compliance with your request, I have taken the subject into consideration, and have the honour to report—

That I am of opinion that the Governor's appointment of the Senior Justice to administer the government was not legally consistent with or warranted by the terms of the original (as amended by the supplementary) charter. The error committed should be repaired either by the Governor or Colonial Secretary resuming the government, or by a Royal Warrant confirming the appointment of the Senior Justice *pro hac vice*; and, in either case, if any act of importance has been done in the meantime by the Senior Justice, it should be legalized by a Bill of Indemnity.

The Right Hon. Sir E. B. Lytton, Bart.,   H. McC. CAIRNS.
&c.   &c.   &c.

NOTES TO CHAPTER III.

of or of   The Governor of a colony has not a delegation of the whole royal power, as between him and a subject, which is not expressly given by his commission; nor does any commission to Colonial Governors convey such an extensive authority. They have merely a limited authority from the Crown, and their assumption of an act of sovereign power out of the limits of the authority so given to them is purely void: *Cameron* v. *Kyte*, 3 Knapp, P. C. 332. "If it be said that the Governor of a colony is *quasi* Sovereign, the answer is that he does not even represent the Sovereign generally, having only the functions delegated to him by the terms of his commission, and being only the officer to execute the specific powers with which that commission clothes him:" *per cur.* *Hill* v. *Bigge*, 3 Moore, P. C. 476. The civil superintendent of a colony who was an officer in a regiment, and who was appointed military commandant there, was held to continue in command of the troops, notwithstanding that his own regiment was disbanded, and he was put on half-pay: *Bradley* v. *Arthur*, 4 B. & C. 292.   There Bayley, J., said: "The Crown exercises its judgment, and the persons who from time to time shall have the command in particular places, and the person under the Crown entrusted with the care of a whole district, must from time to time say who shall be the person exercising the military command within particular parts of that district;" and *per* Holroyd, J.: "By looking into the Articles of War, particularly sections 18 & 22, it appears to be taken for granted that it is within the prerogative of the Crown, that not only the Crown itself, but also, under certain circumstances, a Governor, may grant commissions and make appointments."

The question of whether the Governor of a colony has, by virtue of his authority as representing the Crown, power to make grants of waste lands, was raised, but not decided, in *The Queen* v. *Clarke*, 7 Moore, P. C. 77: see *Robertson* v. *Dumaresq*, 2 Moore, P. C. (N.S.) 66.

It was held in *The Queen* v. *Hughes*, L. R. 1 P. C. 81, that leases granted by the Governor of South Australia under powers conferred upon him by a Colonial Act, and sealed with the public seal of the province, but not enrolled or recorded in any court, are not in themselves records, and cannot be annulled or quashed by a writ of *scire facias*. The case of *The Queen* v. *Clarke*, 7 Moore, P. C. 77, was there commented upon, and shown to be no authority for a contrary doctrine. The proper mode of proceeding in such a case is by writ of intrusion, which lies in every case in which a trespass is committed on the lands of the Crown, or a person enters on the same without title; or by information in Chancery, which may be used to speak the right of the Crown to property, as in *The Attorney General* v. *Chambers*, 4 D. M. & G. 206.

In a recent case, where the question was whether the Governor of a colony, who was absent at the time of the seizure of some slaves, or the acting Governor, was entitled to the bounties payable under statute 5 Geo. 4, c. 113, 11 Geo. 4, & 1 Wm. 4, c. 55, Dr. Lushington held the Governor was entitled: *Re Sierra Leone*, Br. & Lush, Adm. 148.

By several statutes it is provided that the word "Governor" in the particular statute shall mean the officer for the time being administering the government of any colony: *e.g.* see 12 & 13 Vict. c. 96, s. 5.

Under the statute 22 Geo. 3, c. 75, s. 2, the Governor and Council of a colony have the power to remove a judge from his office for misbehaviour: *Willis* v. *Gipps*, 5 Moore, P. C. 379; *Montagu* v. *Lieutenant-Governor of Van Diemen's Land*, 6 Moore, P. C. 489.

In *Ex parte Robertson, in re The Governor-General of New South Wales*, 11 Moore, P. C. 288, where the appellant, a commissioner of Crown lands "in the colony of New South Wales created under a Colonial Act, and holding the office during the pleasure of the Governor," had been dismissed by the Governor, the Court held that it was not a matter of great importance whether the office might be said to be held by patent or not. They said: "Their Lordships are all of opinion that the practice of this Court is not to enter into the consideration of such a dismissal unless by the express command of Her Majesty. They do

G

not enter into the consideration of such acts as are done by the Governor and Council of a colony in the exercise of the power and authority committed to them, whereby they dismiss persons from holding situations in that colony, they holding them not by any patent right, but simply and only during the pleasure of the Governor himself. Therefore, upon that ground we are of opinion that the original petition cannot be sustained."

Lord Stowell held that the notification of a blockade by a naval commander on a foreign station, although done without authority from the Government at home, was legal: *In re Rolla*, 6 Rob. Adm., 364. But with respect to his dictum in that case that a naval commander on a distant station may be reasonably supposed to carry with him such a portion of the sovereign authority delegated to him as may be necessary for the exigencies of the service, the Judicial Committee, in *Cameron* v. *Kyle, ubi sup.*, observed that it was clear that he was speaking of such an authority being from the very nature of the case necessarily incident to the functions of a commander carrying on war in a distant part of the globe; "but no such necessity exists in the case of a Governor of a colony for the exercise of powers of sovereignty out of the ordinary and usual course:" see *Northcote* v. *Douglas*, 10 Moore, P. C. 37.

In *Bryan* v. *Arthur*, 11 Ad. & Ell. 108, it was held that under statute 3 Geo. 4, c. 83, s. 9, the Governor of New South Wales and Van Diemen's Land had power to revoke assignments of convicts without any remission of their sentences.

In 1842 an Order in Council was made for a commission under the Great Seal, empowering the Governor of New South Wales to exercise the royal prerogative of pardon, in the case of criminals convicted of treason and murder in that colony: MS. Council Register, 1842, p. 386.

Effect of demise of the Crown on Governor's commission.   Hallam says (Const. Hist. iii. 262, 3rd edit.) that we owe the provision which makes the commissions of the judges run *quamdiu se bene gesserint*, instead of *durante bene placito*, to the Act of Settlement, " not, as ignorance and adulation have perpetually asserted, to his late Majesty George III." But this is a mistake. The statute which first altered the form of the commissions was 12 & 13 Will. 3, c. 2, s. 3; but as it was decided at the accession of Anne that the patents of the judges terminated by the demise of the Crown, this was remedied by the Act of Settlement (6 Anne, c. 7, s. 8), which enacts that all officers, including the judges, shall act upon their former patents for the space of six months after any demise of the Crown, unless sooner removed by the next succession. And by statute 1 Geo. 3, c. 23, the commissions of the judges are to remain in full force during their good behaviour, notwithstanding the demise of the Crown, without any limitation of time. It was this Act which gave rise to the mistake which Hallam ascribes to "ignorance and adulation:" see *Devine* v. *Holloway*, 14 Moore, P. C. 290.

A power of attorney is revoked by the death of the person who granted it, and a contract afterwards made under the authority given by it, though without notice of the death, is void : *Watson* v. *King*, 4 Camp. 272; and see the note to *Smart* v. *Sanders*, 5 C. B. 917. And so, although the act was appointed to be done after the death of the principal, " A letter of attorney to deliver livery of seisin after the decease of the feoffer is void :" Co. Litt. 52 b. In the note there it is said, " by devise or by special custom authority may be created executory after the party's death." By the civil law a sale by an agent after the death of the principal, but before notice, binds the property : Dig. lib. 17, tit. 1, l. 26.

In general, a ministerial officer can appoint a deputy unless the office is to be exercised by the ministerial officer in person. But where the office partakes of a judicial and ministerial character, although a deputy may be made for the performance of ministerial acts, one cannot be made for the performance of a judicial act. A sheriff, therefore, cannot make a deputy to hold an inquisition under a writ of inquiry, although he may appoint a deputy to serve a writ : Com. Dig., *Officer*, D. Appointment of deputy.

In *Lane* v. *Cotton*, 1 Salk. 18, Holt, C.J., said : " What is done by the deputy is done by the principal, and it is the act of the principal, who may displace him at pleasure, even though he were constituted for life, *vide* Hob. 13, 1 Mod. 85 ; and the act of the deputy may forfeit the office of the principal : 39 Hen. 6, c. 34."—See *Campbell* v. *Hewlitt*, 16 Q. B. 258.

It was said by Lord Abinger, C.B., in *Jewison* v. *Dyson*, 9 M. & W. 585, that many officers may be called judicial to a certain extent who are not judicial within the general meaning of the law, which says that the Crown cannot delegate to another its right to appoint judicial officers. That rule is confined to judicial officers who determine causes *inter partes*. In that case the question was, whether the Crown, in right of the Duchy of Lancaster, had the exclusive right, under a charter of Edward III., of appointing a coroner within the province of Pontefract. The Crown may, by charter in express words, grant to a commonalty or corporation the power to make another commonalty or corporation : Bro. Abr. *Prerog.* 53 ; and see *The Queen* v. *Dulwich College*, 21 L. J. (N.S.) (Q.B.) 36, where, *per* Lord Campbell, C.J., " The Crown could not delegate the appointment of magistrates." A deputy cannot make a deputy, on the principle that *delegatus non potest delegare :* Com. Dig., *Viscount* B. 7 Vin. Abr. 556.

The statute 22 Geo. 3, c. 75, enacts that no office to be exercised in any colony shall be granted by patent for any longer term than while the grantee shall discharge the duty thereof *in person* and behave well therein. This statute was passed to put an end to the practice of exercising offices in the colonies by deputy while the holders were resident in this country : see *Montagu* v. *Lieutenant-Governor of Van Diemen's*

Land, 6 Moore, P. C. 489. Where the Judge of a Vice-Admiralty Court (at Sierra Leone), who was also Chief Justice, with the concurrence of the Governor, appointed a Deputy Judge of the court, and left for England, and the Deputy Judge died soon afterwards, and then the acting Chief Justice, with the concurrence of the Governor, appointed another Deputy Judge of the Vice-Admiralty Court, it was contended that such deputy was illegally appointed, and had no jurisdiction ; but the Judicial Committee said that they had no doubt whatever that he was duly appointed, and had full jurisdiction : *Rolet* v. *The Queen*, L. R. 1 P. C. 198; see 26 Vict. c. 24, s. 4.

Civil liability of Governor.
With respect to the civil liability of the Governor of a colony to an action brought against him in this country for a wrong committed by him while holding the office of Governor, the leading cases are— *Mostyn* v. *Fabrigas*, Cowp. 161 ; *Campbell* v. *Hall*, Cowp. 204; and see also *Wall* v. *Macnamara*, 1 T. R. 536 ; *Wilkins* v. *Despard*, 5 T. R. 112 ; *Wytham* v. *Dutton*, 3 Mod. 160 ; *Way* v. *Yally*, 6 Mod. 195 ; *Rafael* v. *Verelst*, 2 W. Bl. 982, 1055 ; *Glynn* v. *Houston*, 2 M. & G. 337 ; *Basham* v. *Lumley*, 3 C. & P. 489 ; *Phillips* v. *Eyre*, L. R. 4 Q. B. 225, which clearly establish the principle that a Governor is liable to an action in this country for a wrong done by him during his government. In *Lord Bellamont's Case*, 2 Salk. 625, the Attorney General moved for a trial at bar in an action against the Governor of New York for matter done by him as governor, and it was granted " because the King defended it."

In *Phillips* v. *Eyre*, *ubi sup.*, it was decided that a Colonial Act of Indemnity, by which the right of action in respect of an act otherwise lawfully done by the Governor of the colony, is taken away before an action has been brought in this country, is a good defence to such action (1). In *Dutton* v. *Howell*, Show. Parl. Ca. 24, it was held that the Governor of a colony could not be sued in this country for imprisoning a person guilty of official delinquency under his government; but this proceeded on the ground that the Governor and his Council had acted judicially : see *Hill* v. *Bigge*, 3 Moore, P. C. 482; and as to the non-liability of a judicial officer, *Kemp* v. *Neville*, 10 C. B. (N.S.) 523. The Governor of a colony may be sued in an action of debt in one of the Courts of the colony, but it seems that he would not be liable while resident in his government to be taken in execution upon judgment recovered : *Hill* v. *Bigge*, *ubi sup.*, 465. In that case the Court commented upon the dictum of Lord Mansfield, in *Fabrigas* v. *Mostyn*, that " the Governor is in the nature of a viceroy, and that, therefore, locally during his government no civil or criminal action will lie against

(1) Two of the earliest instances of Acts of Indemnity in this country are the statutes passed 7 Edw. 2: (1) *Ne quis occasionetur pro reditu Petri de Gaveston;* (2) *Ne quis occasionetur pro captione et morte Petri de Gaveston.* But these are said to have been repealed within a year after they were passed. By statute 15 Edw. 2, an indemnity was granted to all persons for felonies and transgressions done in the case of the two Le Despencers : but this indemnity was afterwards revoked.

him"(1); and pointed out the difference between the liability to be sued and the liability to process in execution; and also upon the case of *Tandy* v. *Earl of Westmoreland*, 27 State Tr. 1264. The same distinction between liability to action and liability to process of execution was thought to apply to the case of ambassadors in *Taylor* v. *Best*, 14 C. B. 487; but the contrary was decided in *The Magdaléna Steam Navigation Company* v. *Marten*, 28 L. J. (Q.B.) 310.

As to the extent of protection from civil liability accorded to public officers on grounds of policy, see *Lane* v. *Cotton*, 1 Salk. 17; *Whitfield* v. *Lord Despencer*, Cowp. 754; *Cunningham* v. *Collier*, 4 Doug. 233; *Le Caux* v. *Eden*, 2 Doug. 594; *Allen* v. *Waldegrave*, 2 J. B. Moore, 621; *Macbeath* v. *Haldemand*, 1 T. R. 172; *Unwin* v. *Wolseley*, 1 T. R. 674; *Myrtle* v. *Beaver*, 1 East, 135; *Rice* v. *Chute*, 1 East, 579; *Nicholson* v. *Mounsey*, 15 East, 384; *Oliver* v. *Bentinck*, 3 Taunt. 456; *Gidley* v. *Lord Palmerston*, 3 Brod. & B. 275; *Hodgkinson* v. *Fernie*, 26 L. J. (C.P.) 217; *Buron* v. *Denman*, 2 Ex. R. 167; *Broughton* v. *Jackson*, 21 L. J. (Q.B.) 265; *Auty* v. *Hutchinson*, 6 C. B. 266; *Tobin* v. *The Queen*, 33 L. J. (C.P.) 199; *Priddy* v. *Rose*, 3 Mer. 102; *Dickson* v. *Viscount Combermere*, 3 Fost. & Fin. 585; *The Athol*, 1 W. Rob. Adm. 374.

In a case where several actions for false imprisonment were brought by sailors belonging to a merchant vessel which had been captured by a privateer with a *letter of marque*, but liberated by the Court of Admiralty, against the captain of the privateer, Lord Mansfield said : "This is a new attempt which, if it succeeded, would destroy the British navy. If an action at law should lie by the owners, and every man on board a ship taken as prize, against the captain and every man on board his ship, the sea would be safe for the trade of our enemies, however great our naval superiority :" *Lindo* v. *Rodney*, 2 Doug. 613.

Where some slaves escaped from a territory where slavery was lawful, and got on board a British ship of war in the high seas, it was held that the owner could not maintain an action against the commander of the ship for harbouring the slaves after notice : *Forbes* v. *Cochrane*, 2 B. & C. 448. There Bayley, J., said that if it could be made out that the defendants acted *malá fide*, they would be liable to an action, but in order to support an action against a person who fills a public office like that which the defendants filled, it is essential to shew *mala fides*. And, *per* Holroyd, J.: "I have given my opinion upon this question supposing that there would be a right of action against these defendants, if a wrong had been actually done by them; but I am by no means clear that even under such circumstances any action would have been maintainable against them by reason of their particular situation as officers acting in discharge of a public duty, in a place *flagrante bello*."

Although not liable to actions of contract at the suit of individuals for

(1) This is in accordance with the Roman law : " In jus vocari non oportet neque consulem, neque præfectum, neque prætorem, neque proconsulem, neque cæteros magistratus qui imperium habent, et qui coercere aliquem possunt, et jubere in carcerem duci."—Dig. ii. tit. 4, § 2.

86   CASES AND OPINIONS ON CONSTITUTIONAL LAW.

goods supplied for the public service, public officers may be compelled by *mandamus* to perform their duty in paying over monies in their hands: *R.* v. *Lords Commissioners of the Treasury,* 4 Ad. & Ell. 286. (In the *Banker's Case,* 14 State Tr. 1, temp. Wm. III., the proceeding was by petition to the Court of Exchequer : see 12 & 13 Wm. 3, c. 12, s. 5.) *The Queen* v. *The Lords of the Treasury,* 16 Q. B. 357; *Ex parte Sir Charles Napier,* 21 L. J. (Q.B.) 332.

Privileged communication.   As to how far orders given by the Governor of a colony, or by a public officer to a subordinate, are privileged communications, see *Anderson* v. *Hamilton,* 2 Brod. & Bing. 156 (note); *Cooke* v. *Maxwell,* 2 Stark. 183; *Wyatt* v. *Gore,* Holt, 299; *Lee* v. *Birrell,* 3 Camp. 337; *Horne* v. *Bentinck,* 2 Brod. & Bing. 130; *Fairman* v. *Ives,* 5 B. & Al. 642; *Blagg* v. *Sturt,* 10 Q. B. 899, s. c. in Error, 906.   See also the *Trial of the Seven Bishops,* 12 State Tr. 349, where the Clerk of the Privy Council gave evidence as to what passed in the council chamber.

And as to the rule of public policy in Government prosecutions which protects a witness from answering questions to discover the informer, see *Attorney General* v. *Briant,* 15 M. & W. 169; *Rex* v. *Hardy,* 24 State Tr. 753, 808, 816; *Rex* v. *Watson,* 32 State Tr. 102.

Act of State.   A Governor is not liable to a suit for an act done by him in his political capacity as an act of State : *Tandy* v. *Earl of Westmoreland,* 27 State Tr. 1264; *Nabob of Carnatic* v. *East India Company,* 1 Ves. Sr. 371; 2 Ves. Sen. 56; *Elphinstone* v. *Bedreechund,* 1 Knapp, 316; *Buron* v. *Denman,* 2 Ex. R. 167; *Secretary of State in Council* v. *Kammachee Boye Sahaba,* 13 Moore, P. C. 22; *Wadeer (ex-Rajah of Coorg)* v. *East India Company,* 29 Beav. 300.

Criminal liability of Governor.   With respect to the criminal liability of a Governor, it is enacted by statute 11 & 12 Wm. 3, c. 12, intituled " An Act to punish Governors of Plantations in this Kingdom for crimes by them committed in the Plantations," that such offences shall be tried in the Court of Queen's Bench in England, or before such Commissioners, and in such county of this realm, as shall be assigned by Her Majesty's commission.   And by statute 42 Geo. 3, c. 85, any person employed in the service of the Crown in any civil or military station, office, or capacity within Great Britain, who shall commit any crime, misdemeanor, or offence in the execution, or under colour, or in the exercise of his office, may be prosecuted in the Court of Queen's Bench.   It has been held that these statutes do not extend to felonies : *Rex* v. *Shawe,* 5 M. & S. 403.   Ex-Governor Wall was tried in 1802 for a murder committed by him by inflicting excessive corporal punishment in the island of Goree in 1782, he being at that time Governor of the island, and he was convicted and hanged (1): 28 State Tr. 51.

(1) Lord Campbell says, in his " Lives of the Chief Justices," iii. 149 : " Then a very young man, just entered at Lincoln's Inn, I was present at the trial, and carried away by the prevalent vengeful enthusiasm, I thought that all was right; but after the lapse of half a century, having dispassionately examined the whole proceeding, I came to a very different conclusion."

In 1804, General Picton was tried for a misdemeanor in causing torture to be inflicted upon a mulatto woman in the island of Trinidad, of which he had been Governor. Lord Ellenborough left to the jury the question whether the punishment of torture was allowed by the law of Trinidad at the time of the cession of the island by Spain to England. They found that there was no such law existing at the time of the cession, and a verdict of guilty was recorded. A rule for a new trial was afterwards made absolute; and on the second trial the jury found a special verdict, setting out the facts of the case, and stating that, whether the defendant were upon these facts guilty or not they were wholly ignorant. They found that by the law of Spain torture existed in the island at the time of the cession of the island, and that no malice existed in the mind of the defendant independent of the illegality of the act. The proceedings lasted from 1809 until 1812, when the Court ordered the defendant's recognizances to be respited until further orders; and no judgment was finally pronounced. The prosecution was still pending when General Picton fell at Waterloo : 30 State Tr. 225–956.

In *Wall* v. *Macnamara*, cited in *Johnstone* v. *Sutton*, 1 T. R. 536, Lord Mansfield said : " In trying the legality of acts done by military officers in the exercise of their duty, particularly beyond the seas, where cases may occur without the possibility of application for proper advice, great latitude ought to be allowed, and they ought not to suffer for a slip of form if their intention appears by the evidence to have been upright ; it is the same as when complaints are brought against inferior civil magistrates, such as justices of the peace, for acts done by them in the exercise of their civil duty. There the principal inquiry to be made by a court of justice is, how the heart stood? And if there appears to be nothing wrong, then great latitude will be allowed for misapprehension or mistake." And in *Mostyn* v. *Fabrigas*, Cowp. 161, the same great judge said : " I can conceive cases in time of war in which a Governor would be justified, though he acted very arbitrarily, in which he could not be justified in time of peace. Suppose, during a siege or invasion, the Governor . . . . . upon a general suspicion should take people up as spies ; upon proper circumstances laid before the Court, it should be very fit to see whether he had acted, as the governor of a garrison ought, according to the circumstances of the case." To this may be added what was said by Macdonald, C.B., in *Wall's Case*, 28 State Tr. 143 : " On the one hand, as the Attorney General has most liberally and most sensibly said, when a well-intentioned officer is at a great distance from his native country, having charge of a member of that country, and it shall so happen that circumstances arise which may alarm and disturb the strongest mind, it were not proper that strictness and rigour in forms and in matters of that sort should be required when you find a real, true, and genuine intention of acting for the best for the sake of the public. . . . . But, on the other hand, it is of consequence that where a commander is so circumstanced, that is,

at a distance from his native country—at a distance from inspection—
at a distance from immediate control, and not many British subjects
being there—if he shall, by reason of that distance, wanton with his
authority and his command, it will certainly be the duty of the law to
control that and to keep it within proper bounds."

It is no defence where a man is charged with a breach of public
duty, to say that the discharge of that duty belongs to a body whereof
he was only one, as in the case of a Governor and his Council, and that
the duty could only be executed by the whole body. Each individual
of the Governor and Council who does not do what in him lies to discharge his public duty, contracts by his negligence individual guilt:
Rex v. *Holland*, 5 T. R. 623.

In *Rex* v. *Bembridge*, 22 State Tr. 155, Lord Mansfield said that, "if
a man accepts an office of trust and confidence concerning the public,
especially when it is attended with profit, he is answerable to the King
for the execution of that office; and he can only answer to the King in
a criminal prosecution, for the King cannot otherwise punish his misbehaviour." And he cited 6 Mod. 96, where the Court said, "If a
man be made an officer by Act of Parliament, and misbehave himself in
his office, he is indictable for it at common law; and any public officer is
indictable for misbehaviour in his office." And where, in a criminal information against a member of the Council at Madras, the objection was
taken that it did not appear that he was legally appointed, the Court
held that it could not be sustained, saying: "In a criminal prosecution,
or in an action against a justice of the peace, or against a clergyman,
for any offences by either of them committed in their respective situations, every day's practice has settled that the exercise of their offices
is, *as against them*, proof that they are bound to discharge their respective functions:" *Rex* v. *Holland*, 5 T. R. 623; see *Rex* v. *Dobson*,
7 East, 218.

In *Reg.* v. *Eyre*, L. R. 3 Q. B. 487, it was held that under the
statute 11 & 12 Vict. c. 42, in the case of a charge of misdemeanor
alleged to have been committed by the ex-Governor of a colony, a
magistrate within whose jurisdiction the accused had come had jurisdiction to hear the case; and if he committed on the charge, it was
his duty to return the depositions into the Court of Queen's Bench,
where alone the charge could be tried.

The East
Indies.
By statute 24 Geo. 3, c. 25, s. 44, it was enacted that all British
subjects should be amenable to all courts of justice (both in India and
Great Britain) of competent jurisdiction to try offences committed in
India for all crimes and offences whatsoever by them committed in any
of the territories of any nation, prince, or state, in the same manner
as if the same had been committed within the territories directly
subject to and under the British Government in India. See also
sects. 49 and 64 as to misdemeanors committed in the East Indies by
British subjects holding offices or employments under the Crown or

under the East India Company: see also 26 Geo. 3, c. 57, s. 15.
Sections 44, 49, and 64 of the first-mentioned Act were repealed by
33 Geo. 3, c. 52, s. 146. But while they were in force, a criminal
information was filed in the Court of Queen's Bench against Holland,
who had been acting Governor of Madras, and one of the counts charged
that he " did not commence and prosecute the war against Tippoo Sultan
with all possible vigour and decision." The Court held that this was too
vague, and therefore bad. Other counts charged the defendant with
disobedience to orders, and the Court said that they were stated to have
been given by those who were empowered by the statutes to give them,
and when the orders were given they must be taken to remain in force
until they were revoked or contradicted. They held, therefore, those
counts good on demurrer. Another point taken was, that notice to the
defendant was not sufficiently averred on the record; but the Court
said that all the facts to which this objection applied arose within the
Presidency, when the defendant was one of the Council, and therefore
he was bound to take notice of them: *Rex* v. *Holland*, 5 T. R. 607.

The Governors of Jersey and Guernsey have been more than once Governors of
impeached in Parliament. This happened in the case of Otho di the Channel
Grandison, in the reign of Edward I.; William Paine, in the reign of Islands.
Edward III.; Sir Philip de Carteret, in 1642; and Colonel Russell, in
1647. But for a breach of military discipline, the Governor of either
of those islands must be tried by court-martial, as General Corbet, the
Governor of Jersey, was in 1781, for having surrendered the island to
the French without making an effective resistance. He was found
guilty, and sentenced to be superseded: see "The Constitution of
Jersey," by Le Cras (Jersey, 1857), p. 11. In the case of General
Napier, Governor of Guernsey in 1845, the Guernsey Court transmitted
a complaint against him to the Privy Council, as the Court had no
jurisdiction over him: *Ibid.*

CHAPTER IV.

ON VICE-ADMIRALTY JURISDICTION AND PIRACY.

(1.) *Letter from* J. A. STAINSBY, ESQ., *to* SIR JAMES MAR-
RIOTT, *King's Advocate* (1).

Ever since I saw you I have been very busy in ransacking
our authors who have wrote upon the origin and constitutions
of our law, to trace (if possible) those of the Admiralty, to throw a
light upon the question raised of precedence between an Attorney
General and the King's Advocate in the islands; but can meet
with nothing satisfactory, except that it is clear that though the
name of Admiral is not met with till after the Crusades commenced, yet the office was in effect among the Romans, and
voluntarily adopted by the Saxons, and that his power was upon
the *altum mare* only.   But the commissions for 150 years after the
Romans being all lost, it is no wonder we are in the dark: but it
is said in Co. Littleton, 260, that the Admiral and Court of Admiralty in Richard I.'s time was said to have been out of mind, which
must mean the office only, but not the name, as is clear from the
latter being of Saracen extraction (Enur, d, *i. e.,* great or high
lord), and brought in by Edward I. on his return from the Holy
Land; and the title of Admiral of the King's Seas occurs in 1386,
and in 4th Inst. 134, that it was generally held to have been
created by Edward III., I think probably by Edward I., as I find
by Acta Regia that the famous civilian Accursino, professor at
Bologna, was in his service and confidence, and had a pension from
him; but the constitution of it does not appear, only the title of
the index.   Perhaps the argument of Sir Leoline Jenkyns (who
was judge of that court) before the House of Lords in Charles II.'s

(1) From a M. S. in the possession of Sir Travers Twiss, Queen's Advocate,
which formerly belonged to Sir James Marriott, King's Advocate.   No date.

time, upon the statute 13 Richard 2, c. 5, made to keep it in due bounds, would throw light upon the subject. The clearest account I have met with is in Spelman's Glossary, p. 14; in Bacon on Government, part ii. p. 26; and in Mr. Solder's Notes on Fortescue de laudibus legum Angliæ, p. 69, to the above purport, and which is introduced by a modern writer (Schomberg) on the Maritime Laws of Rhodes, who informs us of the constitution of the French and Holland Courts of Admiralty, but not of ours.

As to the King's Attorney, it appears there was an officer under that name in the year 1279, 7 Edward I., and continued under that style for near 200 years, when, in 1462, in 1 Edward IV., a Solicitor General was appointed, and the Attorney had the additional term of General annexed to his office, which both continue to this day.

J. A. STAINSBY.

(2.) OPINION of the King's Advocate, SIR JOHN COOKE, on the Jurisdiction of the Court of Admiralty in the Colonies. 1702.

Ships trading contrary to the Act of Navigation (12 Car. II. c. 18) are to be prosecuted, and the penalties arising thereon to be recovered in any Court of Record : the words of the Act are general, without a particular mention of England, or of the plantations, and include the Admiralty Courts of both places, they being the King's courts, and consequently Courts of Record.

Ships trading contrary to the Act for Encouragement of Trade (15 Car. II. c. 7) are to be prosecuted, and the penalties arising thereon to be recovered in any of his Majesty's courts in the plantations, or in any Court of Record in England ; and it is certain that the Admiralty Court is the King's Court, and was so allowed to be by all the judges under their hands, anno 1632. In the eleventh paragraph of the statute, for preventing planting tobacco in England, and for regulating the plantation trade (22 & 23 Car. II. c. 26), it is said that, upon unlawful importations to, or exportations from the plantations, one moiety of the several ships, and of their ladings, shall go to the King, the other to him who shall seize and sue for the same, in any of the said plantations, in the Court of the High Admiral of England, or of any of his Vice-Admirals, or in any Court of Record in England—by which the jurisdiction of the High Court of Admiralty is plainly founded, as is likewise that of the Admiralty Courts in the plantations, which, in respect to the Admiralty of England, are Vice-Admiralty Courts; and it is observable, that both the Admiralty Courts are mentioned before the Common Law Courts, as being principally intended by the makers of that statute for such proceedings; and it is further evident by the same clause, and the two which follow in that statute, that the Admiralty jurisdiction is not so confined, but that it may hold cognizance of, and determine the offences, though the goods are valued, and seised, on land.

The three statutes above-mentioned,—viz., the 12th 15th, 22nd, & 23rd of King Charles II.—are recited in the Preamble of the last Act, relating to the plantation trade (7 & 8 Will. 3), and that last Act does sufficiently establish the Admiralty jurisdiction, in offences against the Acts of Trade, in as ample a manner, and in the same words, as it doth the jurisdiction of the courts at Westminster Hall; and if it be objected that in those two places, it is only said that the proceedings for the penalties and forfeitures arising from the offences, and not for the offences themselves, shall be had in the Courts of Admiralty, it may be answered, that the courts of Westminster have no more or other jurisdictions, for they are mentioned in the same manner as the Admiralty Courts, and not otherwise: however, the offence and the penalty is all one cause, and of the same cognizance, and are determined all at once; for to suppose otherwise, were to make one court put in execution the decree and sentence of another, which were absurd and impracticable.

Against the jurisdiction of the Admiralty Courts in the plantations, thus deduced and asserted, there is a seeming objection, from a clause of the aforesaid statute, 7th and 8th Gulielmo III., where it is declared, that upon all suits brought in the plantations, on offences against the several Acts, relating to the plantation trade, by reason of any unlawful importations, or exportations, there shall not be any jury but of natives of England, Ireland, or the plantations, from whence it may be argued, because Admiralty Courts use no juries, they are not proper courts to try such matters in.

To which objection it may, among other things, be answered, that this clause does not in the least take away the jurisdiction, which not only the same Act, but several former Acts of Trade, have given to the Admiralty Courts in the plantations, in cases of unlawful importations and exportations; for the directing the nature and manner of proceeding in one court, when two have the cognizance of the same matters, can, in no construction, take away the power of the other; but from that clause this conclusion, I conceive, may be truly and fairly drawn—viz., that none of the common law courts in the plantations should proceed in such cases but where proper jurymen may be had, so that natives of any other places but England and Ireland and the plantations, or natives even of those places who are any way interested, or who are on any other account not legally qualified, cannot serve on juries, and consequently no such trials can be had in those courts in the plantations where proper jurymen cannot be had; and in such cases the Admiralty Court, as it is always a proper court, will be then the only court to proceed in, and determine breaches of the Acts of Trade.

July 23, 1702.   J. COOKE.

(3.) OPINION *of the King's Advocate,* SIR JOHN COOKE, *on the seizure of a Spanish Brigantine, on the High Seas, by an Uncommissioned Vessel.*   1708.

MY LORDS,—In obedience to your Lordships' commands, in Mr. Popple's letter of the 25th of February, I have considered the proceedings and merits of the seizure of the Spanish brigantine therein mentioned, and am of opinion that this matter ought to be communicated to the Lord High Admiral, that directions may issue to the proper officers to proceed, in his Lordship's name, in the Court of Admiralty here, in order to have the brigantine condemned, and declared a perquisite of the Admiralty, being seized at sea by a non-commissioned ship.

Doctors' Commons, March 3, 1708.   J. COOKE.

(4.) OPINION *of* MR. FANE, *Counsel to the Board of Trade, on the Admiralty Jurisdiction in the Bahamas.* 1729.

To the Right Honourable the Lords Commissioners for Trade and Plantations.

MY LORDS,—In obedience to your Lordships' commands, signified to me by Mr. Popple's letter of the 6th of this instant (May) wherein your Lordships are pleased to desire my opinion, in point of law, whether the rights of Admiralty in the Bahama Islands are comprehended within the Lords Proprietors' surrender? I have considered of the same, and am humbly of opinion, upon perusal of the original charter of the Bahama Islands, granted by King Charles II., that there are no words in that charter which will carry a grant of Admiralty jurisdiction, and the rights and perquisites thereunto belonging, to the Lords Proprietors; and, therefore, the Lords Proprietors, or any lessee under them, could never have any legal title or pretence thereto, under the charter.

May 16, 1729.   FRAN. FANE.

(5.) OPINION *of the King's Advocate,* SIR CHRISTOPHER ROBINSON, *on the Jurisdiction of Vice-Admiralty Courts.*

Doctors' Commons, November 20, 1821.

MY LORD,—I am honoured with your Lordship's commands of the 8th instant, transmitting sundry despatches from the Governor of the Mauritius, announcing the intention of Mr. Smith, the Judge of the Vice-Admiralty Court there, to extend the jurisdiction of that court to causes over which it has hitherto assumed no control, and pointing out the inconvenience and dissatisfaction likely to result from such a proceeding.

And your Lordship is pleased to request that I would report to your Lordship my opinion how far the Court of Vice-Admiralty has properly the jurisdiction recited in the notice of the judge, and how far the colonial courts have a concurrent jurisdiction over transactions such as policies of assurance, charter-parties, &c., which, although connected with maritime affairs, have not hitherto been the subject of proceedings in any but the colonial courts?

In obedience to your Lordship's commands, I have the honour to report that the commission of the Judges of the Vice-Admiralty Courts agrees in substance with that of the High Court of Admiralty, and is an instrument of ancient date, and comprehends many subjects, which have been formerly under that jurisdiction, but have been withdrawn, or restrained, by usage or the authority of superior courts. The commission still retains its ancient form, and is acted upon under those limitations in the High Court of Admiralty, according to the principles which have been applied to it, and are as well known as any other general principles on which it proceeds; and I think the same restrictions ought to be applied to the exercise of that jurisdiction in the Vice-Admiralty Courts, except on points on which special jurisdiction may have been given by statute.

Mr. Smith appears to have interpreted the commission on these principles in the first instance. And it is scarcely consistent with the admission "*that it was not intended to interfere with the existing courts of justice*" that an EXTENDED meaning or intention should now be given to it by the notice in December, 1820, proceeding from no declaration of superior authority, but from the direction of the judge only.

Under these observations I am humbly of opinion that Mr. Smith should restrain his jurisdiction within the limits of the recognized usage and authority above referred to, and that the Court of Vice-Admiralty has not, at this time, a jurisdiction over transactions of policies of assurance, charterparties, and other civil contracts, which have been withdrawn from the general jurisdiction of the Admiralty of this kingdom.

To Earl Bathurst,　　　　　　　　　CHRIST. ROBINSON.
&c. &c. &c.

(6.) JOINT OPINION *of the King's Advocate*, SIR CHRISTOPHER ROBINSON, *and the Attorney and Solicitor General*, SIR R. GIFFORD *and* SIR J. S. COPLEY, *on a Question of Jurisdiction between the Vice-Admiralty and the Colonial Courts at the Cape of Good Hope.*

Doctors' Commons, September 8, 1821.

MY LORD,—We have had the honour to receive your Lordship's commands, transmitting several papers respecting the jurisdiction of the Vice-Admiralty Court at the Cape of Good Hope; and your

Lordship is pleased to request our opinion whether the Vice-Admiralty Court has properly cognizance of the case therein described, and similar suits, to the exclusion of the jurisdiction of the Colonial Court; or whether the Colonial Court having been continued by his Majesty in the exercise of the functions originally exercised by them under the Dutch Government, and having then had cognizance of such cases, has not now a jurisdiction over such cases to the exclusion of the Vice-Admiralty Court; and if not, whether the party seizing has an option of carrying the seizure for adjudication either into the one court or the other?

In obedience to your Lordship's commands we have taken the same into consideration, and beg leave to report to your Lordship that we think that, according to the general principle of the Navigation Laws, the Court of Vice-Admiralty would have jurisdiction over seizures for breach of those laws at the Cape of Good Hope, but concurrent with the principal Colonial Court; and we do not think that this principle is affected by the special provisions of the 49 Geo. 3, c. 17, which, though a temporary law, we presume has been continued by subsequent Acts, as it is referred to in the papers submitted to us. If, however, any serious doubts are entertained respecting the jurisdiction of the Vice-Admiralty Court, either upon the general principle or in the particular case under consideration, those doubts cannot be removed by any instructions which can be given by his Majesty's Government, or in any other manner, than by appeal from the sentence of the Vice-Admiralty Court or by legislative enactment.

CHRIST. ROBINSON.

To Earl Bathurst,
   &c. &c. &c.

R. GIFFORD.

J. S. COPLEY.

(7.) JOINT OPINION *of the Queen's Advocate*, SIR JOHN DODSON, *and the Attorney and Solicitor General*, SIR FREDERICK POLLOCK *and* SIR WILLIAM FOLLETT, *on the question whether the Supreme Court of Newfoundland could exercise Vice-Admiralty Jurisdiction out of Term.*

Temple, March 12, 1842.

SIR,—We beg to acknowledge the receipt of your letter of the 12th ult., wherein you state you had been directed by Lord Stanley to transmit to us the enclosed copy of a despatch from the Governor of Newfoundland, communicating the opinion of the Judges of the Supreme Court, that under the provisions of the imperial statute which invests them with jurisdiction in certain Admiralty cases, they can proceed in such cases in Term time only, and submitting the propriety, if that opinion be well-founded, of reviving the office of Judge of the Vice-Admiralty Court with a view to the more speedy trial of revenue suits.

And you were pleased to request that we would take the subject into our consideration, and report to his Lordship our opinion whether the Supreme Court of Newfoundland, in the exercise of the Vice-Admiralty jurisdiction conferred on it by the statute 5 Geo. 4, c. 67, is or is not at liberty to sit out of Term ; and if not, whether the existence of that Act of Parliament will not prevent the exercise by Her Majesty, in her office of Admiralty, of the power of establishing a Vice-Admiralty Court at Newfoundland ?

In obedience to his Lordship's commands, we have the honour to report that the Supreme Court of Newfoundland, in the exercise of the Vice-Admiralty jurisdiction conferred on it by the statute 5 Geo. 4, c. 67, is not at liberty to sit out of Term, and that the existence of that Act of Parliament will not prevent the exercise by Her Majesty, in her office of Admiralty, of the power of establishing a Vice-Admiralty Court at Newfoundland.

J. DODSON.

G. W. Hope, Esq.,   FREDERICK POLLOCK.
&c. &c. &c.   W. W. FOLLETT.

(8.) JOINT OPINION *of the Queen's Advocate,* SIR J. DODSON, *and the Attorney and Solicitor General,* SIR J. ROMILLY *and* SIR A. E. COCKBURN, *on the Power of the Crown to issue Commissions under* 46 Geo. 3, c. 54, *notwithstanding* 12 & 13 Vict. c. 96.

Lincoln's Inn, February 26, 1851.

MY LORD,—We were honoured with your Lordship's commands, signified in Mr. Merivale's letter of the 15th instant, in which he stated that he was directed by your Lordship to transmit to us the enclosed despatch from the Governor of Antigua. Mr. Merivale then stated that the Anegada Reef, mentioned in this despatch, is

H

off Anegada, one of the Virgin Islands, and a dependency of
Tortola ; and that he was to request that we would favour your
Lordship with our opinion on the following questions:—

Whether, since the passing of the Act " To provide for the prosecution and trial in Her Majesty's Colonies of offences committed
within the jurisdiction of the Admiralty " (12 & 13 Vict. c. 96), it
remains in Her Majesty's power to issue commissions to the colonies, as was customarily done under the 46th Geo. 3, cap. 54,
for the trial of offences specified in that Act? and whether commissions so issued before that Act are still in force?

The parties charged with the offence referred to in the Governor's
despatch were so charged within Tortola, which is a colony, having
courts of criminal justice within the meaning of the Act, but to
which no commission has ever been issued under the 46th Geo. 3,
c. 54; and our opinion was further requested whether it was
competent for the authorities of Tortola to have transferred these
parties for trial to any neighbouring colony to which such a commission has been issued by Her Majesty (if we considered such commission to be still in force).

Mr. Merivale then stated that he was directed to subjoin a paper
which was drawn up shortly before the passing of the Act 12 &
13 Vict., explanatory of the reasons for its introduction. The provision mentioned at the end of that paper, for the transmission of
persons charged with these offences from ˙one colony to another,
or to England, was withdrawn in the course of the discussions on
the Bill.

In obedience to your Lordship's command, we have perused the
several documents transmitted to us, and have the honour to report
that the 12th & 13th Vict., c. 96, appears to be an enabling
statute, not repealing any authority possessed by the Crown prior
to it; and we are therefore of opinion that, since the passing of
that Act, it remains in Her Majesty's power to issue commissions,
as was customarily done under the 46th Geo. 3, c. 54, for the
trial of offences specified in this Act, and that commissions issued
before that Act are still in force. We think that if the persons
mentioned in the despatch of the President of Tortola committed
an offence which could be tried by the maritime courts of that
island, such persons should now be tried by such court; but if the

Governor is convinced of the impossibility of obtaining an impartial trial in the colony, we think that it is competent for him to transfer such persons for trial to another colony, where there is a commission in force.

J. Dodson.

John Romilly.

A. E. Cockburn.

The Right Hon. Earl Grey,
&c. &c. &c.

(9.) Case and Joint Opinion *of the Law Officers of the Crown on the Constitution, Authority, and Powers of the Court of Admiralty in Ireland.* 1824.

Case.—The Lords Commissioners of the Admiralty are desirous of ascertaining the whole state of the law as regards the constitution, authority, and powers of the Court of Admiralty in Ireland, and the extent of the jurisdiction of the Lord High Admiral of the United Kingdom over Ireland, or the means (if any are necessary) for establishing such jurisdiction. To this end the following statement, papers, and questions are submitted for the joint opinion of his Majesty's Attorney-General of England, his Majesty's Attorney-General of Ireland, his Majesty's Solicitor-General of England, his Majesty's Advocate-General in his office of Admiralty, and the Counsel for the affairs of the Admiralty and Navy in England and Ireland respectively:—

A copy of the commission for executing the office of Lord High Admiral of the *United Kingdom.*

A copy of the letters patent to the present Judge of the High Court of Admiralty of England.

A copy of the commission by King James II., dated 8th July, 1680, being a grant of the office of Vice-Admiral in the province of Leinster. There are no patents of Vice-Admirals of provinces in Ireland recorded in the High Court of Admiralty of England between 1782 and 1801.

A copy of the latest commission granting the same office, being a grant in 1822 to the Earl of Ormond and Ossory. The appointments of Vice-Admirals of the English maritime counties are in the same form.

A copy of a commission under the seal of the High Court of

Admiralty of England, dated 18th May, 1776, appointing Warden Flood, Esq., Judge of the Court of Admiralty in Ireland by the style of his Majesty's Commissary, Deputy, and Surrogate in and throughout the kingdom of Ireland, which is the last commission of that office to be found recorded in the High Court of Admiralty of England.

There are no means of immediately obtaining a copy of any subsequent appointment of that office, which can only be procured from Dublin, but measures have been taken for obtaining it from thence forthwith.

The commissions to the Vice-Admiral of an Irish province and to Mr. Flood will show the nature of the authorities of those respective officers prior to 1782, and it will thereby be perceived that the right of appeal to the Court of Admiralty of England was saved, as well as the prerogative of that Court, " in all things concerning the premises and other affairs whatsoever." And upon this point some light may be thrown by a reference to " Sir Leoline Jenkyns's Life," vol. ii. pp. 675 and 787, where Sir Leoline, who was then Judge of the High Court of Admiralty of England, in a letter dated 23rd June, 1670, and addressed to his Royal Highness James, Duke of York, then Lord High Admiral, speaking of a Court of Appeal then in question to be erected in Dublin from the Vice-Admiralty Courts in Ireland, with resort to the Admiralty in London, says that people from the remote provinces must run through four several instances—viz., Connaught to Dublin, Dublin to London, and thence to the delegates—whereas, by the then constitution, suit could not be prolonged beyond the third instance. And he observes that it is not suggested that the Court of Appeals in Dublin is of longer standing than the time of two Judges successively, the last of whom died about 1640; and that there was not any *constat* of that among his Royal Highness' records, especially not any precedent of such a commission, nor any process from that court, as a Court of Appeal, to this Admiralty (meaning Sir Leoline's own court); and that he does not hear of any acts or records of that court, then to be seen in Dublin, whereby it might appear how far that jurisdiction had been exercised. And in a letter, dated 27th December, 1678 (page 787), he mentions an instance in which an appeal from a decision of the Court of Admiralty at Dublin was carried to the Court of Admiralty in England, and an inhibition was granted.

In the year 1782 an Act passed in the Parliament of Ireland for establishing a High Court of Admiralty in that kingdom (a copy of which Act is left herewith); and subsequently to the passing of that statute, and under its authority, a Court of Admiralty has been held at Dublin, in which suits of the following description have been entertained: viz., suits of seamen against ship master and owner for wages; by seamen against master for ill-usage; upon *respondentia* and bottomry bonds; for salvage; for collision and damage to ships; for possession of ships; to compel security to be given by one owner to the other for the safe return of the vessel when one dissents from the voyage; and suits for the condemnation of goods found derelict, &c., as *droits* to the King in his office of Admiralty.

The Court is held before Sir Henry Meredith, Bart., Doctor of the Civil Law, who acts under some species of deputation from Sir Jonah Barrington, who is the Judge of the Court, but who has been resident in France for many years. It is understood that Sir Jonah's patent recognizes the principle of his acting by deputy.

The Court is held at the Four Courts in Dublin, in an apartment provided for the purpose; and the Judge sits twice a week during term, and for some weeks after each term, and occasionally when business requires; and the Court has the following officers, viz., two surrogates, a registrar, and marshal, with advocates and proctors.

There is also, under the authority of the before-mentioned Act, a Court held as occasion requires for the trial of offences committed on sea, as described in a statute (11, 12, & 13 James 1, c. 2) passed in Ireland; and it is understood that the sitting of this court is not confined to Dublin, but when occasion calls for holding such a court, a commission under the Great Seal of Ireland issues for the purpose, in which the Judges of assize for the circuit wherein the trial is to take place are named as commissioners, and the grand and petty juries at the assizes at which the prisoner is to be tried are sworn in under that as well as the ordinary commission of the circuit.

Under the appointment of the Judge of the High Court of

102 CASES AND OPINIONS ON CONSTITUTIONAL LAW.

Admiralty of England he holds an Instance Court, in which suits, civil and maritime, of the following nature are entertained: viz., for seamen's wages against ship master or owner, or either of them; suits by seamen against masters for ill-usage; suits upon *respondentia* and bottomry bonds; suits for salvage; suits for collision and damage to ships; suits for possession of ships; suits to compel security to be given by one owner to the other for the safe return of the vessel when one dissents from the voyage; suits for the condemnation of goods found derelict, &c., as *droits* to the King in his office of Admiralty; suits for the condemnation (as *droit*) of the goods of pirates and convicts. And besides these the Court entertains suit against masters or others in the command of vessels for wearing illegal colours. The same Judge, in virtue of the King's commission and a warrant from the Lord High Admiral, holds a court for the adjudication of ships and goods taken as prize of war. The same Judge likewise presides in a court for the trial of offences committed within the jurisdiction of the Admiralty of England, which court is held under a commission issued pursuant to the statute 28 Hen. 8, c. 15, which is extended by various statutes, and *inter alia* by the statute 39 Geo. 3, c. 37, and 1 Geo. 4, c. 90. His patent as Judge of the Court of Admiralty, before referred to, purports to give him jurisdiction as follows:—

" Within the ebbing and flowing of the sea and high-water mark, or upon any of the shores or banks to them or any of them adjacent, from any of the first bridges towards the sea through England and Ireland and the dominions thereof, or elsewhere, beyond the seas." Also, " all complaints of all and singular contracts, conventions, causes, civil and maritime, contracted beyond seas and within England and Ireland, or in any part of our dominions."

" Also to arrest, and cause and command to be arrested, according to the civil laws and ancient customs of our High Court of Admiralty aforesaid, all ships, persons, things, goods, wares, and merchandizes for the premises, and every of them, and for other causes whatsoever concerning the same, wheresoever they shall be met with or found through the kingdom or dominions aforesaid."

The proceeding for wearing illegal colours seems to have been (until the passing of the Act 3 Geo. 4, c. 110) peculiar to the

Court of Admiralty of England, and founded upon the maritime
law and ancient constitutions, and was made the subject of charge
by Sir Leoline Jenkyns to the Grand Jury at a session of Oyer and
Terminer for the jurisdiction of the Admiralty of England, as
appears by Sir Christopher Robinson's Reports, vol. iii. p. 33, and
Appendix thereto.

At the Union of Great Britain and Ireland a proclamation pursuant to the Act of Union was made by his late Majesty, declaring
what ensign or colours should be borne at sea by merchant vessels
belonging to any of his Majesty's subjects, and forbidding the use
of any other ensign or colours, and expressly forbidding the use of
his Majesty's jack, or any pendant or colours usually worn by his
Majesty's ships, without particular warrant. And the Act 3 Geo. 4,
c. 110, s. 2, enacts that it should not be lawful for any subject to
wear, on board any ship, vessel, or boat whatever, the said prohibited colours under a penalty of £500, to be recovered either in
the High Court of Admiralty, or in the Court of King's Bench or
Exchequer at Westminster or Dublin, or in the Courts of Session
or Exchequer in Scotland.

Information having been transmitted to the Admiralty by the
collector of the customs at Whitehaven that Alexander Miller,
master of the British merchant ship *Jamaica*, had persisted, after
remonstrance, in wearing a pendant contrary to the proclamation
and statute before mentioned, together with an affidavit of the fact
by two witnesses, and of the seizure of the pendant by the collector, directions were given by the proctor for the Admiralty to
prosecute Miller for that offence; and thereupon, in Michaelmas
Term last, the affidavit being brought into the High Court of
Admiralty of England, and read, the Judge directed the usual warrant under seal of the Court to issue for arresting the party in
order to compel his appearance to answer for the offence.

A copy of the warrant is as follows:—

"George IV., by the grace of God, of the United Kingdom of Great Britain and Ireland, King, Defender of the Faith:
To all and singular our vice-admirals, justices of the peace, mayors,
sheriffs, bailiffs, marshals, constables, and to all other our officers,
ministers, and others, as well within liberties and franchises as
without, greeting: We do hereby empower and strictly charge and

command you, jointly and severally, that you omit not by reason of any liberty or franchise, but that you arrest, or cause to be arrested, Alexander Miller, now or late master, captain, or commander of the brigantine or vessel called the *Jamaica*, of the port of Whitehaven, in the county of Cumberland, wheresoever you shall find him, and him so arrested you keep under safe and secure arrest, so that his body may be forthcoming before us or our Judge of the High Court of our Admiralty of England, or his surrogate, in the Common Hall of Doctors' Commons, situate in the parish of Saint Benedict, near Paul's Wharf, London, on the fifteenth day after the arrest if it be a court-day, otherwise on the court-day then next following, between the usual hours for hearing of causes, to answer to such matters and articles as shall be objected against him on our behalf in our office of Admiralty for a contempt in hoisting, carrying, or wearing illegal colours, and that you duly certify us, or our said Judge or his surrogate, what you shall do in the premises, together with these presents.

"Given at London in our aforesaid Court under the great seal thereof the 18th day of November, in the year of Our Lord 1823, and of our reign the 4th.

"(Signed)   ARDEN,

"W. Townsend."   (L.S.)   "*Registrar.*"

This species of process would have been styled in the courts of common law a "*non omittas* writ of *capias ad respondendum*," and not a warrant.

By the practice of the Court this warrant is bailable. Miller having, prior to the warrant issuing, sailed on his voyage, and put into the port of Dublin in distress, where it was expected he would be detained a considerable time to repair his ship, the process was forwarded to Mr. Craig, the Admiralty agent at Dublin, and the defendant was accordingly arrested upon it, and delivered into the custody of the keeper of the gaol of Newgate in Dublin. He immediately obtained from his Majesty's Court of King's Bench there a writ of *habeas corpus*, under which he was brought before that Court, which, upon argument, decided that the warrant was not sufficient to authorize his detention, inasmuch as it did not appear on the face of it to have been *issued on oath*. But although the case took this turn, one of the grounds urged on the part of Miller was that the process of the Court of Admiralty of England could not be legally executed in Ireland; and upon a case subsequently stated to the Attorney and Solicitor General and Counsel for the Admiralty in Ireland, those officers gave an opinion that the Court of Admiralty of England had not the power of executing its warrant in Ireland, even though the objections in point of form to the warrant were removed.

The statutes which will be found to bear on the subject-matter of this case are the following, and extracts or copies of those passed in Ireland will be left herewith, viz.: 11, 12, & 13 James 1, c. 2 (Irish Act), similar in principle to the English Act 28 Hen. 8, c. 15, which requires that all treasons, felonies, robberies, murders, and confederacies committed within the jurisdiction of the Admiralty, shall be tried according to the course of the common law, and not according to that of the civil law, as had theretofore been usual. This Act of Henry VIII. not including misdemeanors, the statute 39 Geo. 3, c. 37, intituled, "An Act for remedying certain defects in the law respecting offences committed on the high seas," was passed by the British Parliament, 23 & 24 Geo. 3, c. 14 (Irish Act), intituled, " An Act for regulating the High Court of Admiralty in this kingdom." This statute, it will be seen, authorized his Majesty to appoint under the great seal of Admiralty in that kingdom, with full power to hear and determine all civil, maritime, and other causes, and gave an appeal from the sentence to the King in Chancery, directing the Lord Chancellor of Ireland, under the great seal of that kingdom, to appoint a Commission of Delegates, who, and none others, are declared to have full power finally to determine all such appeals. And the 4th section, after reciting the Act of King James abovementioned, enacts that all commissions to be issued by virtue of that statute shall be directed to the Judge of the High Court of Admiralty of Ireland, and others to be nominated by the Lord Chancellor there; which Commissioners, or any two of them, and none other, are declared to have power to hear and determine the several offences mentioned in the statute. It will be observed that in *this Act the statute of King James has been mis-recited, that part of it which requires the commission to be directed to the " Admiral or*

Admirals, or to his or their Lieutenant-General, deputy or deputies," *having been omitted.* And it may be remarked that as no Act passed in Ireland similar to the 39 Geo. 3, c. 37, there could be no jurisdiction entertained in the Irish Court of Admiralty over misdemeanors committed on the sea, the Act 23 & 24 Geo. 3, c. 14, confining the authority of the Commissioners in that court to the offences named in the Act of King James I.

In the 13th & 15th sections of the Irish Act, 23 & 24 Geo. 3, c. 4, being " An Act for regulating the Sugar Trade," &c., allusion is made to the condemnation, by an Admiralty Court in Ireland, of sugars taken as prize of war and brought into that kingdom. By the Act of Union of the two kingdoms (39 & 40 Geo. 3, c. 67, in the British Parliament, and 40 Geo. 3, c. 38, in that of Ireland), it is established in the 8th Article as follows: " That all laws in force at the time of the Union, and all the courts of civil and ecclesiastical jurisdiction within the respective kingdoms, shall remain as now by law established within the same, subject only to such alterations from time to time as circumstances may appear to the Parliament of the United Kingdom to require: provided that all writs of error and appeals depending at the time of the Union, or hereafter to be brought, and which might now be finally decided by the House of Lords of either kingdom, shall from and after the Union be finally decided by the House of Lords of the United Kingdom; and provided that from and after the Union there shall remain in Ireland an Instance Court of Admiralty for the administration of causes civil and maritime only, and that the appeal from sentences of the said Court shall be to His Majesty's delegates in his Court of Chancery in that part of the United Kingdom called Ireland, and that all laws at present in force in either kingdom which shall be contrary to any of the provisions which may be enacted for carrying these articles into effect, be from and after the Union repealed."

The questions which have been suggested as arising out of this case are as follow:

1. Whether the Court of Admiralty in Ireland is a Supreme Court or merely a Vice-Admiralty Court, and in any way dependent on the High Court of Admiralty in England?

2. What is the description of causes falling within the meaning

of the words "civil and maritime," as expressed in the 8th Article
of the Act of Union?

3. Whether the English and Irish Courts of Admiralty, respectively, have concurrent jurisdiction *in all parts of the sea?*

4. Whether *process of the High Court of Admiralty* of England
in *prize causes runs into the Irish provinces?*

5. Or process in proceedings for contempts?

6. Or process in causes civil or maritime?

7. In what manner should indictments in prosecutions instituted
in a Court of Admiralty under the Acts passed in Ireland, 11, 12,
& 13 James 1, c. 2, and 23 & 24 Geo. 3, c. 14, be entitled; whether
Admiralty of England, or Admiralty of Ireland, or Admiralty of
the United Kingdom, or the Vice-Admiralty county or province in
which the Court is held?

8. In what manner and form, and under what seal, should the
commission for holding such Court be made out?

9. Whether, if the warrant against Alexander Miller, set forth
in Case, had been executed in England, the defendant would have
been entitled to his discharge on writ of *habeas corpus?*

10. Whether any suit can be entertained in a Court of Admiralty in Ireland for wearing illegal colours?

11. And, lastly, whether there ever existed an Admiralty in Ireland?

Opinion.—1. We are of opinion that the Irish Admiralty Court
is not a Vice-Admiralty Court, nor in any way dependent on the
High Court of Admiralty in England; and that in all matters over
which it has jurisdiction there is no court superior to it, but there
is an appeal from it to the King in Chancery in Ireland.

2. We think that the words "causes civil and maritime" comprehend all matters generally cognizable by Admiralty Courts,
save only matters of prize and of criminal jurisdiction.

3. The Judge who, before the declaration of Irish independence in 1782, was appointed for the Court of Admiralty in Ireland,
took his patent from the great seal of the English Admiralty,
which expressly limited his jurisdiction by the words "in and
throughout the kingdom of Ireland and parts thereof, and to
the same adjacent whatsoever." But since the English statute
6 Geo. 1, c. 5 (which had asserted the subordinate character of

Ireland), has been repealed by the 22 Geo. 3, c. 53, which was understood to be a recognition of her rightful independence; since likewise the 23 Geo. 3, c. 28, has taken away the appellate jurisdiction of the English Courts; and since, in fine, the Act of Union has practically admitted the independence of Ireland as a contracting party, it seems to follow that the Courts of Admiralty in England and in Ireland have now become mutually independent, and have therefore each the same jurisdiction in the waters of the other island which belongs to either in the waters of any foreign State.

4, 5, 6. Our answer is in the negative.

7. The proper title is "Admiralty of Ireland."

8. The commission under 12 & 13 James 1, c. 2, and 23 & 24 Geo. 3, c. 14 (both Irish), should be made out under the Great Seal of Ireland, in the manner and form pointed out by the latter statute.

9. We think that in England the warrant set forth in the case would have been held sufficient.

10. We think no proceeding for wearing illegal colours could be entertained by any Admiralty Court in Ireland, neither by the Instance Court, inasmuch as this is not a cause "civil or maritime" within the 8th Article of the Act of Union, nor yet by the commission under the Acts of James I. and George III., inasmuch as these Acts do not extend to any misdemeanors except confederacies.

11. This seems not to be a question of law.

J. S. COPLEY.

CHARLES WETHERELL.

W. C. PLUNKET.

J. LESLIE FOSTER.

Serjeants' Inn, August 18, 1824.   HORACE TWISS.

(10.) JOINT OPINION *of the King's Advocate,* SIR CHRISTOPHER ROBINSON, *and the Admiralty Advocate,* MR. ARNOLD, *on the Irish Admiralty Court.* 1825.

1. We are of opinion that the Irish Admiralty Court is not a Vice-Admiralty Court, nor in any way dependent on the High Court of Admiralty in England, and that in all matters over which it has jurisdiction there is no court superior to it, but there is an appeal from it to the King in Chancery in Ireland.

2. We think that the words "causes civil and maritime" comprehend all matters generally cognizable by Admiralty Courts, save only matters of prize and criminal jurisdiction.

3. Considering the description of the jurisdiction in the patent of the Judge before the statute 23 & 24 Geo. 3, c. 14 (Irish), and considering the words of that statute, which was made for the purpose of regulating this Court, we should be of opinion that the jurisdiction was limited and extended only, in the words of the patent, "in and throughout the kingdom of Ireland, and parts thereof, and to the same adjacent whatsoever." Of the full extent and effects of the recognition of Ireland as an independent kingdom by the statute of 1782 and the Union, we do not think ourselves qualified to give an opinion. We think that the High Court of Admiralty of Ireland is now to be considered as having general Admiralty jurisdiction, civil and maritime, as limited by the Articles of Union. But how far this will establish a concurrence with the High Court of Admiralty of England, considering the different circumstances that may be connected with their origin and practice, we cannot venture to say. In causes depending on particular statutes, and cases that might be put of appellate jurisdiction, it certainly would not.

4, 5, 6. Our answer is in the negative.

7. The proper title is "Admiralty of Ireland."

8. The commission under 12 & 13 James 1, c. 2, and 23 & 24 Geo. 3, c. 14 (both Irish), should be made out under the Great Seal of Ireland, in the manner and form pointed out by the latter statute.

9. We think that in England the warrant set forth in the case would have been held sufficient.

10. We think no proceeding for wearing illegal colours could be entertained in any Admiralty Court in Ireland—neither by the Instance Court, inasmuch as this is not a cause "civil or maritime" within the 8th Article of the Act of Union; nor yet by the commission under the Acts of James I. and George III., inasmuch as these Acts do not extend to any misdemeanor except confederacies.

11. This seems not to be a question of law.

CHRIST. ROBINSON.

Doctors' Commons, August 18, 1825.   J. H. ARNOLD.

(11.) JOINT OPINION *of the King's Advocate*, SIR CHRIS-
TOPHER ROBINSON, *and the Admiralty Advocate*, MR. ARNOLD,
*on the appointment of H.R.H. the Duke of Clarence to be Lord
High Admiral, and his Rights as such.* 1827.

The Lord High Admiral's patent grants to him the appointment of Vice-Admirals, and in law they are termed his Vice-
Admirals (5 Eliz. c. 6, s. 50). The practice has been invariable,
so far as we learn, that during the time of a Lord High Admiral
they shall be appointed in his name. That form was observed
in the time of Prince George of Denmark and the Earl of Pem-
broke.

These instances occurred subsequently to the statute of 2 Will.
& Mary 2, c. 2, and we refer to them more particularly because
that statute having declared the powers of the Commissioners to
be the same as those of the Lord High Admiral, has been supposed
to render the forms used under Commissioners applicable also to
acts done in the time of a Lord High Admiral. But it is to be
observed that during the vacancy of the office of Lord High Admiral, *the style and title of the office are merged in the Crown;* the
royal authority therefore alone is expressed.

In instruments issued in the reign of James II. in his name, the
reason is explained: "Cum nos officium Domini Magni Admiralli
Angliæ nomine nostro regio exerceamus."

In the form of the sentence of condemnation of droits in modern
times the condemnation also is expressed to be, "*and to our Sovereign Lord the King, he enjoying the rights of the Lord High
Admiral of Great Britain at present.*"

These instances, therefore, appear to confirm the right and
title of the Lord High Admiral, when there is such an officer, to act
in his own name in all things to be done under his patent, and
we cannot venture to advise that it would be safe to depart from
that form, otherwise than under the authority of the legislative
enactments, if it should be deemed expedient to make any alteration.

It may be proper to direct the other particulars referred to in
Mr. Swabey's letter, to be settled by the advice of counsel, or on
further application to the Secretary of the Admiralty, when his

Royal Highness' pleasure shall be signified on the form of the warrant.

CHRIST. ROBINSON.

Doctors' Commons, May 19, 1827.   J. H. ARNOLD.

(12.) OPINION *of* SIR RICHARD LLOYD, *Judge of the Court of Admiralty, on the proceedings in Jamaica against Deane the Pirate* (1).

MAY IT PLEASE YOUR LORDSHIPS,—In obedience to your Lordships' commands to report my opinion whether the trial and condemnation of John Deane for piracy by my Lord Vaughan, as Vice-Admiral to his Royal Highness in Jamaica, can be justified by law, as also what has been the practice of the High Court of Admiralty here before the statutes of the 27 & 28 Hen. 8, and since, as to the trial of pirates, I do most humbly certify your Lordships:—

1. That though it doth not appear by any instances out of the records in the Admiralty Court that pirates were *de facto* tried by the rules of the civil law (there being no record I can meet with to that purpose so ancient as the said statutes), yet I take it for granted they were so tried; for the said statutes were enacted, as in the preamble is expressed, to reform the trial that was by the civil law.

2. That ever since the said statutes, which were made when Henry, Duke of Richmond and Somerset, was High Admiral, neither the Lord High Admiral, nor his lieutenant or commissary, have (for aught appears) ever tried pirates but by commission of oyer and terminer under the Great Seal of England, directed to them and other justices.

3. There be upon the Bill multitudes of such commissions in the times of the several admirals to this very day.

4. The Lord High Admirals of England, ever since the said statutes, have a clause in their patents whereby there is granted to them all amerciaments, issues, fines, and perquisites, mulcts and pecuniary pains, or forfeitures of whatsoever recognizances before the said High Admiral, their deputy or deputies, or any justices of

(1) From a M.S. in the possession of Sir Travers Twiss, Queen's Advocate, which formerly belonged to Sir James Marriott. 1676.

the Admiralty, assigned or to be assigned by commission of the King's Majesty under the great seal, to hear and determine all treasons, felonies, robberies, murders, homicides, confederacies, &c., after the course of the laws of the land, and custom of the Admiralty.

5. That the very same clause is in his Royal Highness' patent, whereby he is constituted Lord Admiral of the Foreign Plantations.

6. That by the statutes and ordinances made by Edward Lord Clinton, afterwards Earl of Lincoln, Lord High Admiral in the reign of King Philip and Queen Mary, every vice-admiral or his deputy is required, within half a year after he is so constituted, to procure such a commission in due form to be made under the great seal to them and other justices therein named, to hear and determine matters of piracy, &c.

All which being considered, I do most humbly conceive, with submission, that my Lord Vaughan, as Vice-Admiral to his Royal Highness, has not regularly proceeded in the aforesaid trial and condemnation, for the Lord Admiral himself cannot, in his ordinary capacity, try piracy; but as he is chief in the commission of oyer and terminer, I must confess that Dr. Exton, in his book of the Sea Jurisdiction, cap. 17, doth affirm that the aforesaid statutes do not take away the Admiral's power of trial of the same offences by the course of the civil law, as had been formerly used, but leaveth him to proceed in causes of that nature either way, as the proof of the fact may be most fitly had or made, but I do not find that any have, since the said statutes, been otherwise tried than by commission. I am afraid his assertion will hardly be maintained. True it is that pirates and sea-rovers are, in the eye of the law, *hostes humani generis;* they are *diffidati* outlawed, as I may say, and out of the protection of the law of nations; every man is commissioned to seize and slay them, if they make opposition; but if they yield, or be taken, they are to be tried criminally according to the prescribed form, and the practice in such cases.

July 20, 1676.   RICHARD LLOYD.

(10.) JOINT OPINION *of the Attorney and Solicitor General,* SIR EDWARD NORTHEY *and* SIR WILLIAM THOMSON, *on the Pardon of Pirates in the Colonies.* 1717.

Quære 1. Whether the proclamation is a full and sufficient pardon to any persons who may have committed piracies and robberies upon the high seas in America within the time therein mentioned; or, if not, what steps must be taken to obtain it of the Governors in America?

Quære 2. Whether, by this proclamation, murders committed by such pirates are pardoned?

Quære 3. Whether the persons who have committed any robberies, or piracies, or any others, by that title can hold the monies and effects they may be so possessed of, and not liable to be prosecuted for them?

Quære 4. Whether, if any persons having notice of this proclamation, should, between such notice and the 5th of January next, commit any piracies or robberies, are entitled to the benefit of it?

To the Right Honourable the Lords Commissioners for Trade and Plantations.

MAY IT PLEASE YOUR LORDSHIPS,—In obedience to your Lordships' commands, signified to us by Mr. Popple, we have considered of the annexed *quæries,* proposed to us by your Lordships; and as to the first *quære,* "whether the proclamation is a full and sufficient pardon to any persons who may have committed piracies and robberies upon the high seas in America within the time therein mentioned, or, if not, what steps must be taken to obtain it of the Governors in America," we are of opinion, that the proclamation does not contain a pardon of piracy, but only his Majesty's gracious promise to grant pirates such pardon on the terms mentioned in the proclamation, on which every subject may safely rely; but, that it will be reasonable for his Majesty to give instructions to his Governors in America, to grant the persons surrendering themselves according to the terms of such proclamation, his Majesty's most gracious pardon for piracies and robberies on the high seas.

As to the second *quære,* " whether, by this proclamation, murders

I

committed by such pirates are pardoned," we are of opinion, that, where the murder is committed in the piracy, it was his Majesty's intention to pardon the murder so committed, and that, therefore, it may be reasonable, in the instructions to his Majesty's Governors, to direct them to insert in the pardons by them to be passed, of the piracies and robberies committed on the high seas, a pardon of all murders committed in the same.

As to the third *quære*, " whether the persons who have committed any robberies, or piracies, or any other, by that title can hold the monies and effects they may be so possessed of, and not be liable to be prosecuted for them," we are of opinion that, as to the proper goods of the pirates, they being pardoned, the same will not be forfeited; but, as to the goods of other persons which they have taken unlawfully from them, the property thereof by such taking is not altered; but the owners, notwithstanding any pardon, may retake them, or they may recover the same by an action to be brought against the robber for the same.

And as to the fourth *quære*, "whether, if any persons having notice of this proclamation, should, between such notice and the 5th of January next, commit any piracies or robberies, are entitled to the benefit of it," we are of opinion, that there is no exception of any notice in the proclamation, and his Majesty has been pleased to give his royal promise, which he will never break, to pardon pirates surrendering themselves, all piracies committed, or to be committed, before the said 5th day of January; and for preventing the mischiefs hinted at in this *quære*, his Majesty's officers are to be diligent in apprehending all pirates, for his Majesty has not been pleased to promise pardon to any pirates but such as surrender voluntarily, according to the terms of the proclamation.

EDW. NORTHEY.

November 14, 1717.   WM. THOMSON.

(11.) JOINT OPINION *of the King's Advocate*, DR. HAY, *and the Attorney and Solicitor General*, HON. C. YORKE *and* SIR F. NORTON, *on the Admiralty Jurisdiction in the case of Murder committed on the High Seas.* 1761.

GENTLEMEN,—I am directed by the Lords Commissioners for Trade and Plantations to send you the inclosed copies of a letter

which their Lordships have received from the Lieutenant-Governor
of New York, and of a report made to him by commissioners,
appointed by a special commission for the trial of the master,
mate, and several of the crew of a privateer, charged with the
murder of some men belonging to his Majesty's ship *Winchester*,
committed within a bay of that province.

I am further directed to acquaint you that the law of New
York upon which the commission for the trial of these persons
was founded, was repealed by Order in Council of the 5th of September, 1700, upon consideration of which, and of the statutes of
Great Britain which have reference to Admiralty jurisdiction, a
doubt has occurred to their Lordships whether there is in the
colony of New York, or in any other of his Majesty's colonies in
America (unless by laws which may have been passed in the said
colonies) any sufficient authority for the trial and punishment of
murder committed upon the seas within the Admiralty jurisdiction
in the said colonies; and, therefore, their Lordships desire the
favour of your opinion upon the following questions as soon as conveniently may be, to the end that if there should be a want of
such authority, some remedy may be provided as soon as possible :—

Question 1. Does the Act of 28 Hen. 8, c. 15, entitled "For
Pirates" (being passed before the establishment of any of the
British colonies), extend to the said colonies? and if it does, how
are the regulations therein set down to be executed?

We are of opinion that the statute 28 Hen. 8 does extend
to the case of murder committed anywhere on the high seas; and
consequently that a commission might issue in the present case
into any country within the realm of England, to try the offenders
who might be brought over for that purpose, and the witnesses
examined and a jury sworn before such commissioners, unless that
mode of inquiry and trial should be deemed inconvenient.

Question 2. Does the Act of 11 & 12 Will. 3, c. 7, entitled "An Act for the Effectual Suppression of Piracy," or the
7th section of the Act of 4 Geo. 1, c. 11, entitled "An Act for the
further preventing Robbery, Burglary, &c.," contain sufficient authority for the trial and punishment of persons guilty of murder
upon the seas or waters within the Admiralty jurisdiction in the
plantations?

We are of opinion that neither of the Acts of Parliament mentioned in this *quære* were intended to affect the case of murders; they relate merely to such felonies as are equal, or inferior, to the species particularly expressed.

Question 3. If the Act of 28 Hen. 8, c. 15, does not extend to America, and neither the Act of 11 and 12 Will. 3, c. 7, nor the 7th section of the Act of 4 Geo. 1, c. 11, do contain sufficient authority for the trial and punishment of persons guilty of murder upon the seas or waters within the Admiralty jurisdiction in the plantations; by what other authority and jurisdiction are such persons to be tried and punished in the said plantations?

We have already said, in answer to the first *quære*, that the statute of Henry VIII. does extend to the present case; but, if that method of trial and proceeding should be found inconvenient, it will be proper to apply to the legislature for some new provision adapted to such case.

G. HAY.

Whitehall, Nov. 5, 1761.   C. YORKE.

F. NORTON.

NOTES TO CHAPTER IV.

Jurisdiction of Vice-Admiralty Courts.   The jurisdiction of Vice-Admiralty Courts in Her Majesty's possessions abroad is regulated by statute 26 & 27 Vict. c. 24, extended and amended by statute 30 & 31 Vict. c. 45. Under sect. 16 of the latter Act, it is made lawful for Her Majesty to empower the Admiralty, by commission under the great seal, to establish Vice-Admiralty Courts in any British possession, notwithstanding that such possession may have previously acquired independent legislative powers. See as to Admiralty jurisdiction abroad, *Barton* v. *The Queen*, 2 Moore, P. C. 19 (Gibraltar); *Rolet* v. *The Queen*, L. R. 1 P. C. 198 (Sierra Leone); *Cassanova* v. *The Queen*, ib. 115 (as to the time limited for appeal).

Piracy.   Piracy is defined to be the offence of depredation on the seas without authority from any sovereign state, or with commissions from *different* sovereigns at war *with each other*: Wheaton, s. 122. It has been doubted how far it is lawful to cruise under commissions from different sovereigns *allied* against a common enemy; but the weight of authority seems to be in favour of the opinion that it is illegal, although not an act of piracy. The reason assigned is because the two co-belligerents may have adopted different rules of conduct respecting neutrals, or may be separately bound by engagements unknown to the party acting under the different commissions: *Ibid.* s. 123. It is not piracy if a privateer or other armed vessel commissioned against one nation, depredates upon another. Offences of this kind entitle the injured party to compensation, but the jurisdiction belongs to the vessel's sovereign who is responsible for the conduct of his officer: Wheaton, s. 122; Woolsey's Internat. Law, s. 137. As to the question whether rebels cruising in the high seas against the property of the parent state are to be considered as pirates, the reader may consult a long note (84) in Dana's 6th edit. of Wheaton, s. 124. It is not every act of plunder and violence on the high seas that constitutes piracy, but it must be said that the offenders at the time are, in fact, free from lawful authority, which they may be by their own deed—so as to be in the predicament of outlaws : see note 83 to Dana's 8th edit. of Wheaton. Thus an act of robbery or murder committed on board a ship on the high seas which remains under the lawful control of its officers is not piracy ; but if the control of the ship is unlawfully taken away, this is in itself an act of piracy, and so are crimes of plunder and violence committed by the crew of a vessel so unlawfully in their possession. " It is of no importance, for the purpose of giving jurisdiction, on whom or where the piratical offence has been committed; the pirate is one who by the law of nations may be tried and punished in any country in which he is found:" Kent's Com. i. 186. By statute 28 Hen. 8, c. 15, "treasons, felonies, robberies, murders to compel crews " committed on the sea were to be tried in such shires and places in the realm as should be limited by the King's commission; other statutes were passed with respect to the trial of such offences, but these have all been repealed, so far as they relate to the punishment of piracy, by 7 Will. 4 and 1 Vict. c. 88, which is now the governing Act on the subject. " Every man, by the usage of our European nations, is justiciable in the place where the crime is committed ; so are pirates, being reputed out of the protection of all laws and privileges, and to be tried at what ports soever they may be taken :" Sir L. Jenkyns's Works, ii. 714. It would seem to follow that a pirate, although a foreigner, is not entitled to a jury *de medietate.* So far we have been speaking of piracy by the law of nations ; but there may be piracy created by municipal law, and this can only be tried by the State within whose territorial jurisdiction and on board of whose vessels the offence so created was committed : Wheaton, s. 124. " When the crime consists in having overpowered the ship, it becomes a crime within the jurisdiction of every civilized nation ; but other cases of robbery on board a ship may be cases of piracy by the municipal law of a country, though not *de jure gentium :*" *per* Blackburn, J., *Re Ternan,* 33 L. J. (M. C.) 211. " Statutes in one country may declare an offence committed on board one of its own vessels to be a piracy, and such an offence may be punishable exclusively by the nation which passed the statute:" Kent's Com. i. 186; and see 7 Will. 4 and 1 Vict. c. 88, the Act there referred to. By stat. 4 Geo. 4, c. 113, slave-trading is created piracy : see *R.* v. *Zulueta,* 1 C. & K. 215. It has been decided that attainder of piracy does not work corruption of blood, " for it was no offence at common law :" *R.* v. *Morphes*, 1 Salk. 85 (1). It is not very easy to understand this, for by the old common law, piracy, if committed by a subject, was held to be a species of treason ; and if by an alien, it was felony—but after the statute 25 Edw. 3, c. 2, it was held to be only felony in a subject : 3 Inst. 113. See as to piracy, *R.* v. *Hastings*, 1 Mood. C. C. 82 ; *R.* v. *Macgregor*, 1 C. & K. 430, and several cases in the State Trials.

(1) Piracy, as is well known to the classical scholar, was not thought a disreputable calling in the heroic ages of Greece: see Homer, Od. iii. 73; Thucyd. i. 5. Cicero says : *Pirata non est in perduellium numero definitus, sed communis hostis omnium.*—De Off. iii. 29.

CHAPTER V.

ON CERTAIN PREROGATIVES OF THE CROWN.

(1) Lands in the Colonies; (2) Grants; (3) Escheats; (4) Mines; (5) Treasure Trove; (6) Royal Fish; (7) Felons' Goods; (8) Writ ne exeat Regno; (9) Proclamations (in note); (10) Cession of Territory; (11) Erection of Courts of Justice.

(1.) Joint Opinion *of the Attorney and Solicitor General,* Sir Edward Northey *and* Sir William Thomson, *on the King's Right to the Three Lower Counties on Delaware.* 1717.

Sir,—The Lords Commissioners for Trade and Plantations having, by your letter of the 13th of February last, required our opinion on the petition of the Earl of Sutherland, praying for a charter of certain lands lying upon Delaware Bay, in America, commonly called the three lower counties, whether it be in the power of the Crown to dispose of those lands petitioned for ; which petition had been referred to their Lordships by his Majesty ; and his Majesty having been also pleased to refer the said petition to us, we have made our report thereon to his Majesty, and enclosed, have sent you a copy of the said report, which may serve for an answer to the question proposed to us by their Lordships.

EDWARD NORTHEY.

October 28, 1717.   W. THOMSON.

To the King's Most Excellent Majesty.

May it please your Majesty,—In humble obedience to your Majesty's commands, signified to your Majesty's Attorney General by the Lord Viscount Stanhope, when Secretary of State, on the memorial of the Right Honourable John, Earl of Sutherland, and your Majesty having been pleased also to signify your commands by Mr. Methuen, when Secretary of State, to refer the said memorial to your Majesty's Solicitor General: we have jointly considered of the said memorial, whereby the said Earl of Sutherland represents to your Majesty, that there are considerable arrears due to him since the Revolution, amounting to above £20,000 ; that he has always testified his great zeal and activity for the Protestant succession, both before and since your Majesty's happy accession to the throne, and given singular proofs of his fidelity and affection to your Majesty, by his services in North Britain during the rebellion there ; in consideration whereof your Majesty was pleased to express your favourable intention of gratifying him upon any occasion: wherefore he most humbly prays your Majesty will be graciously pleased to grant him a charter of certain lands lying upon Delaware Bay, in America, commonly called the three lower counties, which he represents he is ready to prove do belong to the Crown. And we have given notice thereof to the persons concerned for William Penn, Esq., and several mortgagees and purchasers under him ; and also to the Lord Baltimore, who severally claim title to the said lower counties, being called Newcastle, Kent, and Sussex. And we have heard them and their agents thereupon, and we do most humbly certify your Majesty, that the said William Penn is entitled, under the grant of King Charles II., to the plantation of Pennsylvania; but that these counties are not included in such grant, and his title to Pennsylvania is not now contested.

And as to your Majesty's title, which the Earl of Sutherland has undertaken to make out, to the said three lower counties, he has insisted that the same were gained by conquest, by the subjects of your Majesty's predecessors, or granted to your Majesty's predecessors by the possessors thereof, and that thereby your Majesty's predecessors became entitled to the same ; for that a subject of the Crown could not make foreign acquisitions by conquest, but for the benefit of the Crown, and that the length of possession will be no bar to the Crown ; that for several years past Mr. Penn hath had the possession of the said lower counties, under a pretence of a grant thereof to him made, in the year 1682, by the late King James, when Duke of York, who then had the possession of New York and the said three lower counties; but had no right to the said lower counties, and therefore could not transfer any right in the same to the said Mr. Penn, which appears; for that the said late King, afterwards, when Duke of York, in the year 1683, obtained a warrant from the then King, Charles II., to pass a patent whereby the said three lower counties should have been granted to the said then Duke of York, and a copy of the bill to pass into a grant in April, 1683, to the said James Duke of York, of the said three lower counties, has been produced by the said Earl of Sutherland; and it is alleged the same was never passed into a grant; and that if the same had passed into a grant, it would not have made Mr. Penn's title to the said three lower counties to be good, the title of the said Mr. Penn under the Duke of York being precedent to the title of the said Duke of York; but that the same did remain in the said Duke of York, and is, consequently, now in your Majesty. And that your Majesty's title further appears; for that after, in May, 1683, when the then Lord Baltimore, by petition, opposed the passing the said bill under the great seal, Mr. Penn then appeared against the said Lord Baltimore, as agent for the Crown, and not on behalf of himself; and Mr. Penn, under his hand, has declared that your Majesty's royal approbation and allowance of the Deputy-Governor of Pennsylvania, and the three lower counties on Delaware River named by him, shall not be construed to diminish or set aside the right claimed by the Crown to the said three lower counties.

Besides, the said Earl of Sutherland insists, that in the grant of the said Duke of York, in 1682, to Mr. Penn, of the said three lower counties, there is a reservation of an account to be made of one moiety of the profits of the lands thereby granted, touching which, no account has yet been rendered by Mr. Penn; and that, therefore, if the said grant in 1682 were effectual, the said Mr. Penn is yet accountable to your Majesty for the moiety of all the profits of the lands so granted, from the year 1682, according to the said reservation; and that, if the said Earl of Sutherland cannot, by your Majesty's favour, be entitled to the said three lower counties, he humbly prays he may have the benefit of the said account.

In answer to which, on the behalf of Mr. Penn's mortgagees and other purchasers under him, it hath been alleged, that the late King James II., when Duke of York, was seised in fee of the said three lower counties ; and as one argument to prove such seisin, they have produced letters patent, dated the 29th day of June, 26 Car. II., whereby his said late Majesty, King Charles II., granted to the said James, late Duke of York, his heirs and assigns, all that part of the mainland of New England, beginning at a certain place called or known by the name of St. Croix, next adjoining to New Scotland, in America, and from thence extending along the seacoast unto a certain place called Pemaquinue or Pemaquid, and so up the river thereof, to the further head of the same, as it tendeth northward, and extending from the river of Kinebequim, and so upwards, by the shortest course, to the river Canada, northwards ; and all that island or islands, commonly called by the several name or names of Matewaicks or Long Island, situate and being towards the west of Cape Codd, and the Narro Higansetts, abutting upon the mainland, between the two rivers there called, or known, by the several names of Connecticut and Hudson River, together also with the said river called Hudson's River, and all the lands from the west side of Connecticut River to the east side of Delaware Bay, and also all those several islands called or known by the name of Martin Viniard and Nantacks, otherwise Nantukett, together with all the lands, islands, soils, rivers, harbours, mines, minerals, quarries, woods, marshes, waters, lakes, fishings, hawking, hunting and fowling, and all other royalties, profits, commodities, and hereditaments, to the said several islands, lands, and premises belonging and appertaining, with their and every of their appurtenances; and all his said late Majesty's estate, right, title, and interest, benefit, advantage, claim, and demand, of, in, or to the said lands and premises, or any part or parcel thereof, and the reversion and reversions, remainder and remainders, together with the yearly and other rents, revenues, and profits of the premises, and of every part and parcel thereof; at and under the yearly rent of forty beaver-skins, when they shall be lawfully demanded, or within ninety days after such demand, made with powers of government ; within the descriptions of which grant, it hath been agreed by both parties, that the said three lower counties are not contained.

But, on the behalf of Mr. Penn, it hath been insisted, that by the general words, " together with all the lands, islands, soils, rivers, harbours, &c., and all other royalties, profits, commodities, and hereditaments to the said several islands, lands, and premises belonging and appertaining, with their and every of their appurtenances," the said three lower counties did pass as belonging to the premises expressly granted by the said letters patent; for that the three lower counties were enjoyed by the said late Duke of York, together with New York, which was granted unto the said late Duke of York, until he granted the same to the said William Penn, in 1682, by the grants hereinafter mentioned, which seems difficult to us to be maintained, since the abuttal in the said letters patent exclude the three lower counties; but they presume the said late Duke of York might have some other grants thereof, which Mr. Penn might give an account of, but cannot, being under a lunacy. And we do further humbly certify your Majesty, that by indenture dated the 24th day of August, 1682, made between the said late Duke of York of the one part, and the said William Penn of the other part, the said late Duke of York, for the considerations therein mentioned, did bargain, sell, enfeoff, and confirm to the said William Penn and his heirs, all the town of Newcastle, otherwise called Delaware, and all that tract of land lying within the compass or circle of twelve miles about the same, situate, lying, and being upon the river Delaware, and all islands in the said river Delaware; and the said river and soil thereof, lying north of the southernmost part of the said circle of twelve miles, about the said town; together with all rents, services, royalties, franchises, duties, jurisdictions, liberties, and privileges thereunto belonging, and all the estate, right, title, interest, powers, property, claim, and demand whatsoever, of the said late Duke, of, in, or to the same, or to any part or parcel thereof, at and under the yearly rent of five shillings, with a covenant for further assurance; and the said late Duke did thereby constitute and appoint John Moll and Ephraim Harmon, or either of them, his attorney, with full power for him, and in his name and stead, to deliver seisin of the premises granted by the said last-recited indenture to the said William Penn and his heirs. And the said late Duke of York, by another indenture bearing date the said 24th of August, 1682, and made between the said late Duke of York of the one part, and the said William Penn of the other part, for the consideration therein men-

tioned, did bargain, sell, enfeoff, and confirm unto the said William
Penn and his heirs, all that tract of land upon Delaware River and
Bay, beginning twelve miles south from the town of Newcastle,
otherwise called Delaware, and extending south to the Whore Kills,
otherwise called Cape Henlopen; together with free and undisturbed use and passage into and out of all harbours, bays, waters,
rivers, isles, and inlets, belonging to or leading to the same;
together with the soil, fields, woods, underwoods, mountains, hills,
fens, isles, lakes, rivers, rivulets, bays, and inlets, situate in or belonging unto the limits and bounds aforesaid; together with all
sorts of minerals, and all the estate, interest, royalties, franchises,
powers, privileges, and immunities whatsoever, of the said Duke of
York therein, or in or unto any part or parcel thereof, at and
under the yearly rent of one rose; in which said last-mentioned
indenture is contained a covenant, on the part of the said William
Penn, his heirs or assigns, within the space of one year next ensu-
ing the date of the same indenture, to erect or cause to be erected
and set up, one or more public office or offices of registry, in or
upon the said last bargained premises, wherein truly and faithfully
to account, set down, and register, all and all manner of rents and
other profits, which he or they, or any of them, shall by any ways
or means make, raise, get, or procure, of, in, or out of the said last
bargained premises, or any part or parcel thereof; and also, at the
Feast of St. Michael the Archangel, yearly and every year, shall
well and truly yield, pay, and deliver unto the said late Duke of
York, his heirs and assigns, one full moiety of all and all manner of
rents, issues, and profits, as well extraordinary as ordinary, as shall
be made or raised upon or by reason of the premises, or any part
thereof; with power to the said late Duke of York, his heirs and
assigns, in case the same shall be in arrear twenty days, to enter
in and upon the same premises, or any part thereof, and there to
distrain, and the distresses to detain, until payment of the said
moiety and arrears thereof, together with all costs and damages for
the same.   And by the same indenture, the said John Moll and
Ephraim Harmon, or either of them, were appointed in like manner, attorney or attorneys, to deliver seisin of the last bargained
premises to the said William Penn and his heirs; both which said
indentures were entered in the Office of Records for the province of

ON CERTAIN PREROGATIVES OF THE CROWN.   125

New York, on the 21st of November, 1682, within which said grants the said three lower counties are contained, but the covenant to account extends only to what is included in the last-recited grant.

· That by an order by the Commander-in-Chief and Council of New York, dated at New York the 21st of November, 1682, reciting the said two recited indentures, and reciting that the said Commander and Council were fully satisfied of the said William Penn's right to the possession and enjoyment of the premises, had therefore thought fit and necessary to signify and declare the same to the several justices, magistrates, and other officers at Newcastle, St. Jones Deale, alias Whore Kill, at Delaware, or within any of the bounds and limits above mentioned, to prevent any doubt or trouble that might arise; and after having thanked the said magistrates for their good services, in their several offices and stations, during the time they remained under his said late Royal Highness' government, they declare they expected no further account, than that they should readily submit and yield all due obedience and conformity to the powers granted to the said William Penn, in and by the said indentures, which said order was, the 25th of October, 1701, entered in the Rolls' Office at Philadelphia.

It appears by the affidavit of Thomas Grey, who swears he lived in Pennsylvania from the year 1699 to the year 1707, and that he made out and saw many patents, or grants, and warrants, whereby considerable quantities of land lying in the said three lower counties, which, as he deposes, are esteemed to belong to Pennsylvania, were granted to divers persons and their heirs; some of which grants or warrants were signed by the said William Penn, and the rest by his agents or commissioners, and all sealed with the seal of the said province; and that he hath seen great improvements in building and planting, by persons claiming under such grants. That many of the said inhabitants, who were reputed to have settled upon lands in the said lower counties, by virtue of grants, or patents and warrants, either from the Swedes or Dutch, when the said counties were in their hands, respectively, or from the Governor of New York, under the said late Duke of York, when the same was in his hands, did, upon making their accounts up of quitrents due from them to the said William Penn, for their lands, accept new patents from the said William Penn, or his agents, and have since much increased their improvements thereof, both in building and planting.   That he hath seen patents or instruments for conveying lands, in the said lower counties, to divers of the ancient inhabitants thereof, as well from the Swedes or Dutch, as the Governors of New York, under the said late Duke, as also commissions under the hands of some one of the said Governors of New York, constituting magistrates and officers in the said lower counties.   That he believes that the patents of land in the said lower counties, granted by the said Governors of New York, were registered at New York, and that, if search were made in the Secretary's Office there, the same would appear so to be.   That he believes much the greatest part of the inhabitants of the said lower counties who have land there, hold the same by title under Mr. Penn, and that several who hold land there by other title, have delivered the same up, and have accepted new grants from Mr. Penn.   And it also appears, by the affirmation of Robert Hiscox, a quaker, that the Naval Store Company, in Bristol, have, by their agents, made several purchases of the said William Penn of 3120 acres of land in the county of Kent, and the said Company hath expended for purchasing lands, building thereon, and other improvements, and in carrying on their manufacture for raising hemp, upwards of £2000, and are, by their articles, obliged to lay out £5000, of which the said £2000 is part, and that he expects, in a short time, the greater part of the remaining £3000 will be laid out in the management and carrying on the said manufacture ; and that no benefit hath yet accrued to the said Company, for the money so expended ; and that he believes other purchases are already made for the use of the said Company.

And as to the said Earl of Sutherland's objection, that the Duke of York, in 1682, had no title to the lower counties, and therefore, those grants then made to Mr. Penn were void, which appears by a copy of a bill, dated 13th of April, 1683, in order to be passed into a grant of the said three lower counties to the said late Duke of York, which is after the grant by the Duke of York to the said William Penn, but never passed into a grant, and which bill recites a surrender of certain letters patent, bearing date 22nd of March then last past (which grant cannot be found), of the town of Newcastle, otherwise Delaware, and fort thereunto belonging, lying between Maryland and New Jersey, in America, and several other lands, tenements, and hereditaments therein mentioned, the said late King Charles II., for the considerations therein mentioned, did grant to the said late Duke of York, and his heirs, all that the town of Newcastle, otherwise called Delaware, and fort therein or thereunto belonging, lying between Maryland and New Jersey, in America; and all that river called Delaware, and soil thereof, and all islands in the said river; and all that tract of land upon the west side of the river and bay of Delaware which lieth from Schoolkill Creek upon the said river, unto Bombey's Hook, and backwards into the woods so far as the Minqua's country, and from Bombey's Hook, on the said river and bay, unto Cape Henlopen, now called Cape James, being the south point of a sea warmet (?) inlet, and backwards into the woods three Indian days' journeys, being formerly the claim or possession of the Dutch (or purchased by them of the natives), or which was by them first surrendered unto his said late Majesty's Lieutenant-Governor, Colonel Niccols, and which had been since surrendered unto Sir Edmond Andros, Lieutenant-Governor of the said James, Duke of York, and had for several years been in his possession, with the free use and continuance in, and passage into and out of all and singular ports, harbours, bays, rivers, isles, and inlets belonging unto or leading to or from the said tract of land, or any part or parcel thereof; and the seas, bays, and rivers, and soil thereof, bending eastward and southward on the said tract of land, and all islands therein; and also all the soil, lands, fields, woods, underwoods, mountains, hills, fens, swamps, isles, lakes, rivers, rivulets, bays, and inlets, situate and being within the said tract of land; and any of the limits and bounds aforesaid, together with all minerals, quarries, fishings, hawkings, huntings, and fowlings, and all other royalties, privileges, profits, commodities, and hereditaments to the said town, fort, tract of land and premises, or to any or either of them belonging or appertaining, with their and every of their appurtenances in America; and all his said late Majesty's estate, right, title, interest, benefit, advantage, claim, and demand whatsoever, of, in, or to the said town, fort, tract of land, and premises, or any part or parcel thereof, together with the yearly and other rents, revenues, and profits of the premises, and of every part and parcel thereof, to hold to the said Duke of York and his heirs, at and under the yearly rent of one beaver-skin, when demanded.

On the behalf of Mr. Penn, it is alleged that it is probable the said bill in 1683 might have been passed into a grant, for that they produced from the Hanaper Office, where entries are made of grants that pass the great seal, a certificate of an entry in that office, in the words following, viz. :—" April 6th, 1683 : a grant to James, Duke of York, of the town of Newcastle, alias Delaware, situate between Maryland and New Jersey, in America, to him and his heirs for ever," such entries not having been made at the Hanaper Office, but where letters patent do pass, which patent might happen not to be enrolled, as it is not, by the neglect of the six (?) clerk, called the riding clerk, whose business it was to see the same enrolled.

And as to the objection, that if the same were enrolled, that the same is a title subsequent to the grant to Mr. Penn, and that Mr. Penn appeared as agent for the Crown against the Lord Baltimore, they do humbly insist that Mr. Penn, having a grant then so lately from the said late Duke of York, might make use of the name of the said Duke, with his leave in trust, for the said Mr. Penn and his heirs, which they the rather apprehend, for that the possession was always suffered to remain with the said William Penn ; and that if the said grant was passed, and the said grant was in trust for the said William Penn, the same extinguished the said covenant of Mr. Penn for accounting in the grant to him thereof.

Besides, in the said last grant to the Duke of York, it is recited, that the lands were formerly the claim and possession of the Dutch, and had been surrendered unto the Lieutenant-Governor of the said Duke of York, and had for several years been in his possession, which might enable him to make the grants, in 1682, to the said Mr. Penn.

And, on the behalf of the purchasers, it has been insisted, that it would be very hard to put them to any trouble who have bought under the title and enjoyment of Mr. Penn, and have laid out great sums of money in improving their purchases.

And as to the title claimed by the Lord Baltimore, we are

humbly of opinion that the same has already received a full and
final determination; for that, 31st of May, 1683, Richard Burk,
gent., servant to Charles, then Lord Baltimore, praying that the
said bill of 1683 might not pass the great seal, until his then
Majesty should be satisfied of the extent of the letters patent
formerly granted to Cecil, Lord Baltimore, wherein the said town
and adjacent country is alleged to be comprised; which said petition being referred to the then Lords Commissioners for Trade and
Plantations, on the 13th of November, 1685, their Lordships made
their report, wherein they report that:—"Having examined the
matters in difference between the Lord Baltimore and William
Penn, Esq., on behalf of his then Majesty, concerning a tract of
land called Delaware, they found the land intended to be granted
to Lord Baltimore was only lands uncultivated, and inhabited by
savages; and that the tract of land then in dispute was inhabited
and planted by Christians at and before the date of the Lord
Baltimore's patent, as it had ever been since, to that time, and
continued as a distinct colony from Maryland, so that their Lordships humbly offered their opinion, that for avoiding further differences, the tract of land lying between the river and the eastern
sea, on the one side, and Chesapeake Bay on the other, be divided
into equal parts, by a line from the latitude of Cape Henlopen to
the 40th degree of northern latitude; and that one-half thereof,
lying towards the bay of Delaware and the eastern sea, be adjudged to belong to his Majesty, and the other half to Lord Baltimore;" which report his then Majesty was pleased to approve of,
and to order the said lands to be divided accordingly, and the
Lord Baltimore and William Penn required to yield due obedience
thereunto, which report was also confirmed, the 23rd of June,
1709, by her late Majesty, Queen Anne, in Council. However, this
petition, on behalf of the Lord Baltimore, is a very great argument that the Bill of 1683, to the late Duke of York, never passed
the great seal, as on Mr. Penn's behalf is supposed; for that it
being stopped, as must be presumed in that petition or grant, after
that matter settled, which was in 1685, in the reign of the said
Duke, when King of England, could not pass the great seal, in
the name of King Charles, to the Duke of York, then being King
of England; but the entry in the Hanaper Office might have been

K

made when the privy seal was brought to the great seal, to be passed into a grant.

On the whole matter, we humbly submit it to your Majesty's consideration, whether that it will not be reasonable that your Majesty's title should be established by the Court of Chancery, before any grant should be made of the premises; and if any grant should be made, we most humbly submit it to your Majesty, whether the claims of purchasers or grantees under Mr. Penn, who have improved part of the said three lower counties, should not be established; but if Mr. Penn should have a title to the three lower counties, by virtue of the two grants made to him by the late King James, in 1682, when Duke of York, we have not received any answer why he should not account, according to his covenant, in the last of the said deeds, for the moiety of the rents, issues, and profits, raised by virtue of that grant.

October 21, 1717.

EDW. NORTHEY.
WM. THOMPSON.

(2.) OPINION *of* MR. WEST *on the King's Right to the Woods in the Province of Maine.* 1718.

To the Right Honourable the Lords Commissioners for Trade and Plantations.

MY LORDS,—In obedience to your Lordships' commands, I have perused and considered of the several papers relating to the memorial of John Bridger, Esq., Surveyor-general of his Majesty's Woods in America, and I do find that the title which Mr. Elisha Cook doth, by his memorial, claim to be in the province of Massachusetts Bay, in opposition to the right of his Majesty, to all trees fit for masts, of the diameter of twenty-four inches and upwards at twelve inches from the ground, growing within the province of Maine, in America, is founded upon a supposed purchase of the said province of Maine, by the province of the Massachusetts Bay, of and from the assignees of Sir Ferdinando Gorges, the person to whom the said province was originally granted from the Crown.

I must beg leave to observe to your Lordships, that King Charles I. did incorporate the assignees of the patent, which King James I. did, in the eighteenth year of his reign, grant to the

Council established at Plymouth, in the county of Devon, by the name of the Governor and Company of the Massachusetts Bay, in New England, by which charter the said King did grant unto the said corporation power to have, take, possess, acquire, and purchase any lands, tenements, or hereditaments, or any goods or chattels, and the same to lease, grant, demise, alien, bargain, sell and dispose of, as other our liege people of this our realm of England, or other corporation or body-politic of the same, may lawfully do.

In the fifteenth year of King Charles I., the province of Maine was granted to Sir Ferdinando Gorges, his heirs and assigns, which province did descend unto Ferdinando Gorges, son and heir of John Gorges, who was son and heir of the said Sir Ferdinando Gorges, which Ferdinando Gorges did, in the year 1677, in consideration of the sum of £1,250, give and grant all his right and title in and to the said province, unto John Usher, of Boston, merchant, his heirs and assigns; but whether it was by way of absolute sale, or way of mortgage, doth not appear; and the said John Usher did afterwards, in the year 1678, convey the same unto the said corporation, as appears by the printed journal of the House of Representatives of that province which was sent to me by Mr. Dummer, their agent. It may, my Lords, be made a question in law, whether that corporation, which was created by King Charles I., could legally purchase the said province of Maine, inasmuch as the clause of license does go no further than that they might purchase lands, &c., as any other corporation or body-politic in England might lawfully do; and take it to be clear law, that no corporation whatsoever, in England, can purchase any lands which shall inure to themselves, unless an express license for that purpose be inserted in their charter of incorporation, or otherwise. Your Lordships will be pleased to observe, that this corporation is, by the charter, only subjected to the same laws as the corporations in England are; and that there is no license to purchase lands granted to them by express words. I need not observe to your Lordships, that nothing but express words is, in law, sufficient to take away the King's prerogative; but, indeed, I should not have made use of any argument of this nature, did I not think the maintaining the royal prerogative, in relation to the naval stores in America, of the utmost consequence to the kingdom; and that, therefore, any advantage, in point of law, ought to be taken, which does not injure any private persons.

But, admitting that corporation was fully enabled to purchase lands, yet that corporation is now extinguished, for the patent 4° Caroli primi, was, in the year 1684, reversed in Chancery, by a judgment upon a *scire facias*, and consequently the province, which was granted to that corporation, and all lands purchased by that corporation, were revested in the Crown; and, therefore, the inhabitants of New England can be no otherwise entitled unto the province of Maine, than by some new title which must have accrued unto them subsequent to their incorporation by King William, which it is impossible ever should have been, since there is no license granted unto them to purchase lands in or by their last charter. Their last charter was granted by the late King William, in the third year of his reign, in which charter, it is observable, that there is not a variation in the name of the incorporation, but in the thing itself. And so far is the old corporation from being revived, that, by this charter, they are not so much as erected into a corporation or body-politic, so as to be able to sue or be sued, &c.; but the very terms of the charter are, that the King does erect and incorporate the several countries mentioned in the patent, into one real province, by the name of our Province of the Massachusetts Bay, in New England. It is plain, to demonstration, that King William did, at the time of granting this patent, consider all the countries therein named, and particularly the province of Maine, as vested in himself, in the right of his crown, and, therefore, he does unite and incorporate all those countries, which were before several and distinct, into one real province, and does then grant all the lands included in that province, unto the inhabitants of the province of the Massachusetts Bay, in which denomination and grant the inhabitants of the province of Maine, &c., are as much included and concerned, as grantees, as the inhabitants of that part of the country, which was originally and singly known by the name of the Massachusetts Bay; all these provinces, therefore, are now to be considered as one, neither is it possible that one part of the province should be the private property of another.

It is true that the King does grant a power unto the General

Assembly of the said province, to make grants of lands, uncultivated, lying within the bounds described in and by the charter;
but that grant does noways extend to one part of the province
more than another, but is equal to them all; and, therefore, subject to the last clause in the charter, by which all trees of the
before-mentioned size are reserved to the Crown, and, consequently,
the General Assembly of that province cannot make any grant of
lands to private persons, without their being subject to that clause
of reservation.

The Act of Parliament, Nono Anne, page 387, extends no further
than the reservation in the charter does, only that prerogative,
which before subsisted singly on the charter, is now confirmed and
established by authority of Parliament; and therefore, upon the
whole matter, I am of opinion, that the King is legally entitled to
all trees of the prescribed size, growing in the province of the Massachusetts Bay, as it is described and bounded in the charter of
King William, and particularly in the province of Maine, excepting only those trees situated in lands which were legally granted
to private persons before the charter 4° Caroli primi was reversed;
and which I humbly certify to your Lordships.

November 12, 1718.   RICH. WEST.

(3.) JOINT OPINION *of the Attorney and Solicitor General,*
SIR DUDLEY RYDER *and* SIR WILLIAM MURRAY, *on the King's*
Right to certain Waste Lands in New Hampshire.   1752.

[State of the case with respect to the property of the waste and
   unimproved lands in the province of New Hampshire, within
   the limits of the grant made by the Council of Plymouth to
   John Mason, in the year 1629.]
   King James I., by letters patent, dated the 3rd of November,
1620, granted all that tract of country, since called New England,
lying between the latitude of 40 and 48 degrees north, to Sir Ferdinando Gorges, and thirty-nine others, under the name of the
Council established at Plymouth, in the county of Devon, for the
planting, ruling, and governing New England, in America.
   The Council of Plymouth, by indenture under their common seal,
dated 7th November, 1629, granted unto Captain John Mason, his

heirs and assigns, all that part of the mainland, in New England, lying upon the seacoast, beginning from the middle part of Merrimack River, and from thence to proceed northward along the seacoast to Piscataway River, and so forwards up within the said river, and to the farthest head thereof, and from thence northward until threescore miles be finished from the first entrance of Piscataway River, and also from Merrimack through the said river, and to the farthest head thereof; and so forward up into the land westward until threescore miles be finished, and from thence to cross overland to the threescore miles' end, accounted from Piscataway River.

This tract of country was, in consequence, and by express direction of the patent, called New Hampshire; and the grantee obliged himself to establish such government therein, as should be agreeable, as near as might be, to the laws and customs of the realm of England, with liberty for any person aggrieved to appeal to the said Council of Plymouth.

In consequence of this grant, Captain Mason was (as is alleged by him) at considerable expense in sending over persons to plant and settle in this country, and in erecting forts and other buildings and habitations; and it does appear, from several testimonies made use of, in some actions brought by his grandson against the very persons he had sent over, that considerable improvements were made.

In 1635, the Council of Plymouth, by letters patent dated the 22nd of April, confirmed their former grant of New Hampshire to Captain Mason, with an extension of the limits, which, in the said letters patent, are described in the following words: " All that part, purpart, and portion of the mainland of New England, beginning from the middle part of Naumkeck River, and from thence to proceed eastwards along the seacoast to Cape Ann, and round about the same to Piscataway Harbour, and so forward up within the river of Newwickwannock, and to the furthest head of the said river, and from thence northward till sixty miles be finished, from the first entrance of Piscataway Harbour, and also from Naumkeck through the river thereof, up into the land west, sixty miles, from which period to cross, overland, to the sixty miles' end, accounted from Piscataway, through Newwickwannock River, to the land north-westward, as aforesaid."

The eastern limits of the second grant appear to be the same as

those described in the first, but are extended to the south-west as
far as the river Naumkeck, which is about twenty miles to the
westward of Merrimack, the western limit of the former grant,
which tract of country lying between the said two rivers, and extending to three miles north-east of Merrimack, had been granted
by the Council of Plymouth, to the Massachusetts colony, in the
year 1728, prior to the first grant to Mr. Mason, and is now part of
that colony.

It is alleged that this last grant to Mr. Mason was ratified and
confirmed by the Crown, by a charter dated the 19th of August,
1635, with full power of civil jurisdiction and government; but no
such charter as this appears on record.

In the same year (1635), Captain Mason, having no immediate
issue then living (his only daughter, who had married Joseph
Tufton, Esq., being dead), by his will, dated the 26th of November,
devised, amongst other things, to his grandchild, John Tufton, and
his heirs, all his manor, messuages, lands, tenements, and hereditaments in New Hampshire, except some inconsiderable legacies,
upon condition of his changing his name to Mason; the remainder
to Robert Tufton, the brother of John Tufton, and other persons
mentioned in the will.

Upon the death of Captain Mason, in the same year, or soon
after, New Hampshire, by virtue of the afore-mentioned devise,
came to his grandson, John Tufton, but he dying without issue,
the limitation over to Robert Tufton took effect; but he being at
that time a minor, and not coming of age till 1650, the servants
and agents, which his grandfather, John Mason, had sent over to
New Hampshire, taking advantage thereof, and of the confusion of
affairs in England at that time, when no redress could be had,
embezzled and sold his stock and effects, and put themselves under
the government of the Massachusetts colony, who then exercised
jurisdiction in New Hampshire.

Soon after the Restoration, Mr. Robert Mason (for Robert Tufton,
the younger brother, had now taken upon him that name, in compliance with his grandfather's will), presented a petition to King
Charles II., setting forth the unjust and illegal encroachments of
the Massachusetts colony over his property, and praying that justice
might be done him; which petition was referred to Sir Geofry

Palmer, then Attorney General, to consider of his title to the country, who reported that his title was good; and nevertheless, in the year 1675, we find Mr. Mason presenting a second petition, to the same effect as the former, upon which his title was again referred to the consideration of Sir William Jones and Sir Francis Winnington, the then Attorney and Solicitor General, who, upon consideration of the several patents under which Mason claimed, reported that he had a good and legal title to the lands conveyed by them.

In 1679, the Crown took the government of the province of New Hampshire into its own hands; a commission passed the Great Seal, appointing a President and Council to govern the province, in which commission Mr. Mason's title is mentioned in the following words: " And whereas the inhabitants of the country have long been in possession, and are said to have made considerable improvements on the lands they hold, but without any other title than what hath been derived by the government of Boston, in virtue of their imaginary line, which title, as it has, by the opinion of the Judges here, been altogether set aside, so the agents of Boston have consequently disowned any right, either in the soil or government, from the three miles' line aforesaid; and as it appeared that the ancestors of Mr. Mason obtained grants from the great Council at Plymouth for this tract, and were at very great expense upon the same till molested and finally driven out, which hath occasioned a lasting complaint for justice by the said Mr. Mason ever since the Restoration; however, to prevent, in this case, any unreasonable demands which may be made by Mr. Mason, for the right he alleged to the soil, we have obliged Mr. Mason to declare under his hand and seal to demand nothing for the time past until the 24th of June, 1679, nor molest any in their possession for the time to come, but make out titles to them and their heirs for ever, provided they would pay unto him by fair agreement, in lieu of all rents, sixpence in the pound, according to the just and true yearly value of all houses built by them, and of all lands, whether gardens or orchards, arable or pasture, which have been improved by them, which he will agree should be bounded out unto every of the said parties concerned, and that the residue might remain to himself, to be disposed of for his best advantage;

but if, notwithstanding this overture from Mr. Mason, which seems
so fair to us, any of the inhabitants there should refuse to agree
with his agents upon these terms, you are empowered to interpose
and reconcile all differences, if you can; but if not, you are to send
home such cases fairly and impartially stated, together with your
opinions, that we may, at our council-board, with due regard to
Mr. Mason's ancient right, and the long possession, improvements,
or any other title of the inhabitants, determine therein according
to equity."

In 1680, Mr. Mason went over to the province to prosecute his
title, and although many of the inhabitants at first appeared willing to submit to it, yet, as the members of the Council were proprietors of the greatest part of the cultivated lands, they made use
of all their interest, and the influence which their situation and
character gave them, to prevent his getting possession; and they
so far prevailed, that he was at length obliged to commence suits
in the courts there, against some of the principal proprietors.
While these suits were depending, Mr. Mason, in order to strengthen
his interest at home, made a surrender to the Crown of all fines and
forfeitures in New Hampshire, and of one-fifth of the rents and
revenues for the support of government.

In 1781, a commission passed the great seal, appointing Edward
Cranfield, Esq., Lieutenant-Governor of New Hampshire, in which
Robert Mason, styled therein proprietor, and eight others are
appointed councillors; and there is a clause inserted in it, recognizing Mr. Mason's title in the same words as that inserted in the
former commission.

It does not appear that the authority or influence which it
might be supposed would be derived to Mr. Mason from this commission, had any effect to reinstate him in possession of his property, the inhabitants still continuing to contest his title, though
several judgments were given in his favour in the courts there—one
of which was, upon an appeal, confirmed by his Majesty in Council.

In or about the year 1685, Mr. Mason returned to England,
where he died, leaving the province of New Hampshire to his two
sons, John and Robert Mason, who, in 1690, sold it to Samuel
Allen, of London, for £2700, having first sued out a fine and
recovery, in Westminster Hall, in order to bar the entail.

The first mention made of Mr. Allen's title after this purchase, is the charter granted by King William to the Massachusetts Bay, in 1691, where his right is reserved in the following words, viz. :— " Provided also, that nothing herein contained shall extend, or be understood, or taken to impeach or prejudice any right, title, interest, or demand, which Samuel Allen, of London, merchant, claiming from and under John Mason, Esq., deceased, or any other person or persons, hath or have, or claimeth to hold and enjoy, of, in, to, or out of any part or parts of the premises situate within the limits above-mentioned; but that the said Samuel Allen, and all and every such person and persons, may and shall have, hold, and enjoy the same, in such manner, and no other, than as if these presents had not been had or made."

In 1691 Mr. Allen was appointed Lieutenant-Governor of this province, who brought many actions, in the courts of justice there, against the inhabitants in possession of the lands he claimed; but a verdict was given against him by the jury in every action.

In 1697, Lord Bellomont was appointed Governor of all New England, by which Mr. Allen's commission as Governor of New Hampshire was superseded.

In 1702, Colonel Allen brought an appeal to her Majesty in Council, from a verdict and judgment given against him in the superior court of judicature in New Hampshire, the 13th of August, 1700, in favour of Richard Waldron, who at that time possessed the largest quantity of land in New Hampshire, which said judgment was, upon a hearing of all parties, affirmed; but, in regard, the judgment was not final in its nature. The order directed that the defendants should be left at liberty to bring a new action in ejectment in the courts of New Hampshire, in order to try his title to the propriety of the lands in question, or certain quitrents payable out of the same; and that in case, upon such trial, any doubt in law should arise, the jury be directed to find the matter specially, that is, what title the appellant and defendant do severally make out to the said lands in question, and that the points in law should be reserved to the court before which the same should be tried, or if, upon such trial, any doubt should arise concerning the evidence given at such trial, such doubts should be specially stated and taken in writing, to the end that, in case either party should think to appeal to her Majesty in Council from the judgment of the Court therein, her Majesty might be more fully informed, in order to a final determination of the said case.

While this appeal was depending before her Majesty in Council, Mr. Allen presented a petition, praying to be put in possession of the waste and unimproved lands in the said province; and, on the 28th of January, 1702-3, his petition was referred to the Attorney General for his opinion: *first*, whether Mr. Mason had a right to the waste lands in the province of New Hampshire; *second*, what lands in that province were to be reputed waste lands; and *third*, by what methods her Majesty might put him in possession? Upon the 5th of April, 1703, the Attorney General reported his opinion, "that Samuel Allen had a good title to the waste lands of the province of New Hampshire; that all lands lying uninclosed and unoccupied were to be reputed waste, and that Mr. Allen might enter into and take possession of the same; and that, if he should be disturbed in the possession thereof, it would be proper for him (her Majesty having courts of justice within the said province), to assert his right, and punish the trespassers, by legal proceedings in those courts; and that it would not be proper for her Majesty to interpose in this matter, unless the question concerning the right should come before her Majesty by appeal from the judgments that should be given in the Courts in the said province, save it might be reasonable, as he conceived, to direct (if Mr. Allen insisted on it), on the trials that might be had for settling his right to the said province, that the matters of fact relating to his, and the title of others claiming the same lands, might be specially found by the juries that should be impannelled in the same trials, that the matters of fact might appear before her Majesty, if appeals should be made from the judgments that should be given in the said province."

In consequence of this opinion of the Attorney General, Colonel Dudley, then Governor of New England, was directed, by a letter from the Queen, that in case Mr. Allen should be opposed by the inhabitants, and hindered from entering quietly into possession of the waste lands, or should be disturbed in the possession thereof, whereupon any trial or trials should be brought before her Majesty's Courts there for settling the title to waste lands, and that on such

trial or trials the said Allen did insist that the matters of fact
should be specially found by the juries, that he should do all which
in him lay that the matters of fact should be specially found accordingly.

On the 20th of February, 1703-4, Colonel Dudley acquainted
the Assembly of New Hampshire with the orders he had received
relative to Mr. Allen's title; upon which the Assembly addressed
him to represent to her Majesty that they were sensible of her
regard to justice in the late trial between Mr. Allen and Mr. Waldron, which had for ever obliged them to a sense of, and resolution
in, their duty and obedience to her Majesty; that they only
claimed the property of such land as was contained within the
bounds of their towns, which was less than one-third part of the
province, and had been possessed by them and their ancestors for
more than sixty years; and that they had no objection to the other
two-thirds being adjudged to Mr. Allen.

On the 3rd of May, 1705, the inhabitants and terre tenants of the
province, at a general meeting held at Portsmouth, came to the
following resolutions with respect to Mr. Allen's title :—

"That they had not, on behalf of themselves, nor any the inhabitants of this province (whom they represented), any challenge
or claim to any part of this province extra the bounds of the four
towns of Portsmouth, Hampton, Dover, and Exeter, with the hamlets
of Newcastle and Kingstown, &c., appertaining, which were all
comprehended by a line on the western part of Dover, Exeter, and
Kingstown, already known and laid out, and should be forthwith
revised; but the said Samuel Allen, Esq., his heirs and assigns,
might peaceably hold and enjoy the said great waste, containing
forty miles in length, and twenty miles in breadth, or thereabouts,
at the heads of the towns aforesaid, if so should please her
Majesty; and that the inhabitants of this province, at all times,
should be so far from giving interruption to the settlement thereof,
that they declared on their behalf, and by the power given them,
that they desired, by all means, that the waste might be planted
and filled with inhabitants, the lands being very capable thereof, to
whom they would all give their assistance and encouragement as
far as they were able.

"That in case Samuel Allen should, for himself, his heirs, exe-

cutors, &c., for ever quit-claim unto the present inhabitants, their
heirs and assigns, for ever, of all that tract of land, and every part
and parcel thereof, with all privileges, &c., situate, lying, and being
within the several towns in this province, to the extents of the
bounds thereof; and also warrant and defend the same to the inhabitants against all manner of persons whatever, free from mortgage, entailment, and all other manner of incumbrances, and that
this agreement, and the lands therein contained, should be accepted
and confirmed by her Majesty; then, and in such case, they agreed
to allot and lay out unto Samuel Allen, his heirs and assigns, for
ever, 500 acres of land out of the townships of Portsmouth and
Newcastle, 1500 acres out of the township of Dover, 1500 acres
out of the townships of Hampton and Kingstown, and 1500 acres
out of the township of Exeter; all which lands should be laid out
to him, the said Samuel Allen, out of the commonages of the respective towns, in such place or places (not exceeding three places
in a town) as should be most convenient for Mr. Allen, and least
detrimental to the inhabitants of the town.

"And further, they agreed to pay to Samuel Allen, his heirs or
assigns, £2000 current money of New England—that is to say,
£1000 within twelve months after the receipt of her Majesty's
confirmation of this their agreement, and the other £1000 within
twelve months after the first payment.

"And further, that all contracts and bargains formerly made
between Mr. Mason and Mr. Allen, with any the inhabitants, or
other her Majesty's subjects, which were bonâ fide, for lands or
other privileges, in the possession of their tenants, in their own
just right, besides the claim of Mr. Mason or Mr. Allen, and no
other, should be accounted good and valid by these articles; but,
if any, the purchasers, lessees, or tenants should refuse to pay their
just part of what money should be agreed to be paid, referring to
this affair in equal proportion with the rest of the inhabitants,
according to the land they hold, then their share should be
abated by Mr. Allen out of the £2000 payable to him by this
agreement.

"And further, that upon Mr. Allen's acceptance and underwriting
of these articles, they promised to give good personal security for
the payments abovesaid.

" And further, that all actions and suits in the law depending, or thereafter to be brought, concerning the premises, should cease and determine, and be void, until her Majesty's pleasure should be further known therein."

These propositions having been finally settled and agreed to, were ordered to be presented to Mr. Allen for his acceptance; but his death, which happened on the next day, prevented it.

Upon the death of Colonel Allen, his son, Thomas Allen, petitioned the Crown that an appeal brought by his father to the Governor and Council against a judgment given in the inferior Courts in favour of Waldron, might be revived; which petition having been referred to the Attorney General for his opinion, whether it might be proper for her Majesty to grant the prayer thereof, the Attorney General, on the 23rd of March, 1705-6, reported his opinion, that, by the plaintiff's death, the writ of error was abated, and could not be revived.

Upon Mr. Allen's suing for writs of ejectment in his own name, he was cast with costs, whereupon he appealed to her Majesty in Council; but died before the appeal was determined, having first, by deed of sale dated the 28th of August, 1706, conveyed one half of his lands to Sir Charles Hobby, of Boston, in New England.

Upon the death of Mr. Allen, the half of New Hampshire which remained unsold devolved to two infant sons, but it does not appear that any application was ever made since that time by them, or any one in their behalf, or by any claiming under them, to be put in possession; and in the year 1716 Colonel Shute was appointed Governor of New England, with a power, in his commission, of granting lands in New Hampshire, in consequence whereof several townships were laid out; nor does it appear that any claim of property was set up until the year 1746, when John Tufton, who had taken upon him the name of John Mason, and who is one of the surviving grandsons of Robert Mason, pretending that the fine and recovery, sued out in Westminster Hall by John and Robert Mason, in 1691, previous to the conveyance by them to Samuel Allen, was illegal, as it ought to have been done in the Courts there, himself sued out a common recovery in the Courts of New Hampshire, in consequence whereof the sheriff put him in possession, and he sells his right by deeds to sundry persons in the province, who have taken upon them to grant lands, and lay out townships.

Question.—Whether the uniform silence and discontinuance of all sort of claim to the waste and unimproved lands, within the province of New Hampshire, for more than forty years successively, during the greater part of which time the Crown has occasionally made several grants of the unimproved lands of the said province, without exception or complaint from any person or family, does not prescriptively vest the waste lands of the province in the Crown? And how far can any private claim to these lands, so long deserted, be now revived against such an exercise of power over them in the Crown? If these waste lands are not in the Crown, to whom do they belong? And what will be the regular and best method of bringing this matter to a final legal determination?

It is impossible to give an answer to this *quære* without knowing many circumstances not appearing upon the state of this case.

First. It is asked to whom these lands belong? They were originally granted to Mason; they were afterwards conveyed to Allen. Whether that conveyance be good, depends upon the will of John Mason, not particularly stated; upon the fine and recovery said to have been levied and suffered, not particularly stated; upon the usage or laws in New Hampshire, in relation to barring estates tail, not stated at all; upon the infancy or other disability of the issue in tail; his acquiescence; the acts of limitation in New Hampshire, none of which matters are before us.

Second. It is asked, whether they belong to the Crown? We suppose, upon this ground, that neither the Masons nor Allens, for forty years past, have done anything till 1746. This depends upon a variety of circumstances: the nature and causes of the acquiescence; the acts done by the Crown in the meantime; the kind of possession taken in 1746; and what has been done since. We can only say that where persons, under grants from the Crown, have quietly possessed and improved, so great regard is always had to persons who have settled lands in America, that it is hardly possible for a stale title to be so circumstanced as to prevail against them; and here the length of time during which they have been permitted to improve is extremely material.

Upon the whole, we cannot advise anything so proper, as that the parties, if any suits are commenced in New Hampshire, should take care to have the evidence so laid before the Court, as to be transmitted over to England, in case of an appeal to the King in Council.

D. RYDER.

August 7, 1752.   W. MURRAY.

(4.) *Extract from the* JOINT OPINION *of the Attorney and Solicitor General,* SIR PHILIP YORKE *and* CHARLES TALBOT, *on the question whether the King's Right to the Lands of Pemaquid remain in the Crown.* 1731.

As to the question, stated in the Case, upon the effect of the conquest of this tract of country by the French, and the re-conquest thereof by General Nicholson, we conceive that the said tract, not having been yielded by the Crown of England to France by any treaty, the conquest thereof by the French created, according to the law of nations, only a suspension of the property of the former owners, and not an extinguishment of it; and that, upon the reconquest by General Nicholson, all the ancient right, both of the province and of private persons, subjects of the Crown of Great Britain, did revive, and were restored *jure postliminii* (1). This rule holds the more strongly in the present case, in regard, it appears by the affidavits, that the province joined their forces to those which came thither, under the command of General Nicholson, in this service.

(1) The *Jus Postliminii* in the Roman law was the right of recovering a thing lost to an enemy in war, and there were two heads of *postliminium;* for, as Pomponius says, "A man may either return himself or recover something:" Dig. 49, tit. 15, § 14. Cicero, in his Topica II., discusses the etymology of the word, and says that Servius considered the *liminium* merely as a prolongation of *post,* while Scævola derived it from *post* and *limen:* "*ut quæ a nobis alienata sunt, cum ad hostem pervenerint et ex suo tamquam limine exierint, dein cum redierint post ad idem limen, postliminio videantur rediisse.*" If a Roman citizen was captured in war, he became a slave, and suffered a *diminutio capitis maxima.* His rights over his children were said to be in abeyance, but revived on his return, *jure postliminii.* As to a wife the case was different; and the husband

For these reasons, we are of opinion that the said charter still remains in force, and that the Crown hath not power to appoint a particular Governor over this part of the province, or to assign lands to persons desirous to settle there; nor can the province grant those lands to private proprietors, without the approbation of the Crown, according to the charter. . . .

August 11, 1731.

P. YORKE.
C. TALBOT.

(5.) JOINT OPINION *of the Attorney and Solicitor General,* SIR DUDLEY RYDER *and* SIR WILLIAM MURRAY, *on the King's Right to make New Grants of Land in New Hampshire.* 1752.

[NEW HAMPSHIRE.—State of the case with respect to certain townships and tracts of land granted by the Governments of the Massachusetts Bay and Connecticut, in New England, which townships and tracts of land are now part of the province of New Hampshire, by the determination of the boundary-line between that province and the province of the Massachusetts Bay, in the year 1738.]

Disputes having for a long time subsisted between the provinces of the Massachusetts Bay and New Hampshire, with respect to

---

could not recover her, *jure postliminii,* but the marriage might be renewed by consent. Things taken by the enemy, when recaptured, reverted to their former owners. Arms, however, were not *res postliminii,* for it was a Roman maxim that they could not be honourably lost. A slave, who escaped from the enemy, became again the property of his master: see Dig. 28, tit. 15, § 5 ; Cic. de Orat. i. 100; pro Balbo ii. pro Cæcina, c. 34. According to modern law there is a difference between moveable and immoveable property as regards the *jus postliminii.* In maritime and land captures, when complete, it is excluded in the case of moveables, but applies in the case of real property. The purchaser of any portion of the national domain takes it at the peril of being evicted by the original sovereign, when he is restored to the possession of his dominion : see Wheaton's Internat. Law, 441 (n. 169 (9)) 495 (8th edit. by Dana); Woolsey, § 143 ; Kent's Comm. i. 108 ; Phillimore, i. 288 *et seq.*; Justinian's Institutes by Sandars, 124, 125, 175.

It has been held in the United States that a slave taken by his owner to a free-soil state, thereby became free, and could not be held to slavery on returning to the country of his owner, or to any other slave state: see Woolsey's Internat. Law, p. 70, note. In the case of the *Creole,* in 1841, some slaves who were being transported from one port of the United States, when the vessel was driven by

L

their boundaries, in 1733 a petition was presented on behalf of the
province of New Hampshire, praying that commissioners might
be appointed to ascertain the boundaries.

Upon hearings of both parties before the Attorney and Solicitor
General, the Board of Trade, and the Council, his Majesty was
pleased, by his Order in Council of the 9th of February, 1736, to
direct that a commission should be prepared and pass under the
great seal, authorizing commissioners to mark out the dividing
line between the provinces of the Massachusetts Bay and New
Hampshire, giving liberty to either party therein, who thought
themselves aggrieved, to appeal therefrom to his Majesty in
Council. In pursuance of his Majesty's said commission, commissioners met and reported their determination specially, upon
which both provinces appealed to his Majesty in Council; and
afterwards their Lordships reported to his Majesty, as their opinion,
that the northern boundaries of the Massachusetts Bay are and be,
a similar curve-line, pursuing the course of Merrimac River, at
three miles' distance from the north side thereof, beginning at the
Atlantic Ocean, and ending at a point due north of a place in the
plan returned by the said commissioners, called Pantuket Falls,
and a straight line drawn from thence due west, crossing the said
river till it meets with his Majesty's other Governments; and that
the rest of the commissioners' said report or determination be
affirmed by his Majesty. In 1738 his Majesty was pleased, with
the advice of his Privy Council, to approve of their Lordships'
report, and to confirm it accordingly; in consequence whereof, the
line has been marked out.

In the years 1735 and 1736, while the appeals from both the
Massachusetts Bay and New Hampshire were depending before
his Majesty, the General Assembly of the Massachusetts Bay

stress of weather into a port of the Bahama Islands, escaped on shore, and the
British Government refused to give them up as being free persons. It was intimated by the American Government that the law of nations exempts from foreign
interference property in vessels driven into foreign ports by disasters of the sea, or
carried there by unlawful force; but the argument was urged in vain.—*Ibid.*
This, however, was not a case of *jus postliminii.* In truth there was no legal
power in the Colonial or Imperial Government to order the slaves, who by landing
had become free, to go back to the vessel; and in the eye of the English law they
had been guilty of no crime.

granted above thirty townships between the rivers Merrimac and Connecticut, which townships, upon the running of the boundary-line in 1738, fell within the province of New Hampshire. The conditions of these grants were, that the grantees should settle the said townships within three years after the date of their respective grants; but this condition has been performed by very few, if by any, of the grantees; no obligation to pay quitrents, or a reservation of pine-trees fit for the service and supply of his Majesty's navy, are inserted in any of these grants, although no grant ought, in good policy, to be made of any lands in any part of North America, without both these provisions, which have been thought of so much importance and so absolutely necessary for the public service, that Mr. Wentworth, his Majesty's Governor of New Hampshire, was particularly instructed, in the year 1741, never to pass any grant of land, without enjoining express conditions of cultivation, the reservation of quitrents, and the preservation of such pines as are of size for the use of his Majesty's navy.

There are also about 60,000 acres of land situated on the west side of Connecticut River, which were purchased by private persons from the Government of Connecticut, to whom that land had been laid out by the Government of the Massachusetts Bay, as an equivalent for two or three townships which the Massachusetts Bay purchased from Connecticut Government. This tract of land, by the determination of the boundary-line in 1738, is become a part of New Hampshire, but the proprietors of it are subject to no conditions of improvement, and the land lies waste and uncultivated.

Question.—Whether the Crown can resume the lands granted by the province of the Massachusetts Bay, under condition of cultivation, those lands being now become a part of New Hampshire, by the running of the boundary-line in 1738, in cases where the proprietors have not performed the condition of their grants; and if the Crown can, what is the most advisable and regular method of making such resumption? Whether, in the case of the lands granted away by the province of the Massachusetts Bay to particular persons, without any condition of cultivation, the Crown can now enforce the proprietors of such lands to cultivate them, or oblige them to take these lands under new grants, upon the said

L 2

lands being made a part of the Province of New Hampshire, by the determination of the boundary-line in 1738?

We are clearly of opinion the Crown may resume the lands granted on condition of settling within three years, where there has in fact been no settlement. With regard to lands granted by the Massachusetts Bay, without any such express condition, where there has been no settlement, as they appear now to have been no part of that province, their grants are in themselves void as against the Crown, and there appears no ground to support them but on the foot of the direction, which we find to have been given in an Order of Council of the 22nd of January, 1735, when the commission for marking the dividing line between the two provinces was first directed—viz., "that due care should be taken that private property might not be affected by it." We do not find that this direction was continued, either in the Order of the 9th of February, 1736, on which the present commission issued, or in the commission itself; or that the commissioners have, in their report, taken notice of any such private rights; or that they are saved in the Order of Council that establishes the boundary-line. However, considering the manifest intent of these sort of grants, whether appearing from the general nature or the particular recitals or considerations of them—that the country may be settled and inhabited, and the tacit condition attendant upon them; that the lands should be settled in a reasonable time—we think due care will be taken of the private property arising from these grants, if his Majesty shall be pleased to give these sort of proprietors a reasonable time to come in, and accept new grants upon terms of settling the lands within a certain time, reserving the old quitrent, and pines fit for his Majesty's navy; and in case of their not accepting these terms, his Majesty may resume the lands.

The proper manner of making such resumption after such default, is, by making new grants to such as shall be willing to accept them, at such rents and on such terms as shall be thought most advisable.

August 14, 1752.

D. RYDER.
W. MURRAY.

(6.) JOINT OPINION *of the Attorney and Solicitor General,* SIR DUDLEY RYDER *and* SIR JOHN STRANGE, *concerning the Grants of Lands in Carolina, before and after the Purchase, by the King, of the Proprietors' Rights.* 1737.

Quære 1st,—Whether any of the patents granted after their Lordships had ordered the Land Office to be shut up, can be deemed valid, other than such as were granted by order in London?

We are of opinion that such patents may be good, notwithstanding that order to shut up the Land Office, if the Lords Proprietors were either made privy to those grants, or after they were made received the consideration for them; otherwise, we think they cannot be supported.

2nd,—Whether such patents as were granted after the King's purchase by the Lords Proprietors' Governor, before the new Governor arrived from the Crown, particularly such as appears to have been entered in the secretaries' books after advice received in the province of the King's purchase, are to be deemed good?

We are of opinion that none of the patents mentioned in the second *quære* can be deemed good.

3rd,—Whether, as the Act of Parliament made upon the Crown's purchase from the Lords Proprietors, that clause in it that was for quitting possession of grants takes notice of such only as bore date before 1727? If it does not give room for a strict examination into all such as were issued subsequent to that time, and if such grants appear to have been irregularly made, they ought not to be voided; but as to such as were granted for defraying the expense of running the boundary-line, if the Crown, in such case, ought not to bear the expense?

We think it proper to observe, that the clause referred to in this *quære* does not put it upon the patents bearing date, but being actually made before 1st January, 1727; and considering the extraordinary circumstances attending these grants, and that the Crown had no notice of them at the time of the purchase, there is great reason for a strict inquiry into the validity thereof, and to avoid them for such irregularities. But as those that were granted for defraying the expense of the boundary-line seem to stand in a much more favourable light, we think it reasonable some indulgence should be shown to such purchasers by regranting on the terms of the purchase what they or their assigns have actually cultivated, and by repaying a proportion of the consideration money for the rest.

4th,—Whether such patents as were drawn up and signed with blanks, and not registered in the secretaries' office for some years afterwards, shall be deemed good; if their not being registered is not an evidence of fraud?

We are of opinion, that in general such patents as were executed with such blanks as are mentioned in the case, though filled up afterwards, are void; but if they have been attended with a long possession, and not obtained fraudulently or irregularly in any other respect, we think they ought to be now supported; and as to the circumstance of not being registered in the secretaries' office for some years afterwards, it not being stated how far or within what time such registry is necessary to the validity of such grants, nor for how long it was neglected, we cannot form any judgment what influence that will have upon the patents.

5th,—Whether such patents as were given out without any description of the boundaries, and not preceded by regular surveys, returned into the secretaries' office, are to be deemed valid?

We are of opinion, that the want of a description of the boundaries, or of preceding regular surveys, is not of itself sufficient to destroy such patents, unless such circumstances were the known requisites necessary to such grants; and even in that case, if the proprietors have had the consideration, and the lands have been enjoyed accordingly, without fraud, we think such grants ought to be deemed valid.

6th,—Whether those grants issued by virtue of warrants that had lain by many years, are to be deemed good, notwithstanding the grants assigned them were taken out irregularly, and particularly those after 1727?

We are of opinion that the circumstance of there having been warrants many years before the grants issued is not, of itself, sufficient to support grants that would otherwise be irregular and void; though upon the general question of fraud, that circumstance may probably be of some service to the grantees, according to the particular circumstances of each case, whether such grants issued before or after the year 1727.

7th,—As it is alleged by the Governor that many of the people that hold lands by virtue of the patents formerly granted under the Lords Proprietors, possess much greater quantities than they ought to hold by the words of the said grants, has not the Crown power to re-survey such lands; and, in case any fraud should appear, what steps must the Crown take to recover its right?

We are of opinion, that whoever possesses a much greater quantity than they ought to hold by the words of a grant made since the 1st of January, 1727, is liable to have the same re-surveyed on behalf of the Crown. But, as to grants made before 1727, upon surveys actually made, we apprehend (if they were otherwise good in law,) they are excepted by the Act 2 Geo. 2, out of the sale to the Crown, and therefore not liable to be now re-surveyed; and as to such cases wherein a re-survey is proper, and yet the grants are valid in law, we are of opinion, that the proper remedy is by information in the name of the Attorney General of the province in a Court of Equity there, in order to have the real quantity set out, and the excess pared off for the benefit of the Crown.

8th,—In case any of these grants appear to be voidable in law, what is the proper method to have the same vacated?

We are of opinion that the proper method for the Crown to recover its right (except in the instances mentioned in the answer to the last *quære*), is by an information of intrusion in the proper Court of the province, and in case of error there by appeal to his Majesty in Council.

D. RYDER.

February 11, 1737.

J. STRANGE.

(7.) JOINT OPINION *of the Attorney and Solicitor General,* SIR PHILIP YORKE *and* CHARLES TALBOT, *on Grants that are void for Uncertainty.* 1730.

To the Right Honourable the Lords Commissioners for Trade and Plantations.

MAY IT PLEASE YOUR LORDSHIPS,—In obedience to your Lordships' commands, signified to us by letter from Mr. Popple, informing us that your Lordships having had under consideration several papers relating to the settlement of Carolina, and observing that some grants were made by the late Lords Proprietors of large tracts of land without any limitation therein as to the place where or time when the said land is to be taken up and seated; and transmitting to us the enclosed copy of a grant of that kind made to Sir Nathaniel Johnson in 1686, which hath never yet been put in execution, together with the enclosed copy of the original grant from the Crown to the Lords Proprietors of Carolina, for our further information; and desiring us to consider the same, and report our opinion, in point of law, whether such grants are legal and of force? We have considered the patent, whereby the said Lords Proprietors did grant to Sir Nathaniel Johnson the honour and dignity of a *Cassique, cum duabus baroniis quarum singula contineat duodecim mille acras terræ*; and are of opinion that, in regard, the place where the said lands lie is not described, nor any method provided by which the same may be ascertained, such grant of the two baronies is, by reason of the uncertainty thereof, absolutely void in law.

P. Yorke.

July 28, 1730.   C. Talbot.

(8.) Joint Opinions *of* Mr. Fane, *and of the Attorney and Solicitor General*, Sir John Willes *and* Sir Dudley Ryder, *on the Question of Taking Lands, under Old Grants, from the Proprietories of Carolina.* 1734.

To the Right Honourable the Lords Commissioners of Trade and Plantations.

May it please your Lordships,—In obedience to your Lordships' commands, signified to me by Mr. Popple, desiring my opinion, in point of law, whether the townships of Purrysborough, in Carolina, being, pursuant to his Majesty's instructions, set out for the use of certain people; and his Majesty having declared that all the land within six miles thereof shall not be taken up by any person claiming a right under old grants which have not been taken up, shall not be deemed such an effectual taking-up of the said land for his Majesty's use as to invalidate the claim of any person who shall, subsequent to the said instructions and proclamation, take up land there.   And, I humbly certify to your Lordships, that I think the grantees of the late Lords Proprietors, under the general power granted to them, of taking such quantities of land in such places as they shall think fit, since they neglected to do it previous to his Majesty's instructions and declaration, shall not now be permitted to pitch upon lands already settled, but must have the effect and operation of their grants upon lands now unsettled.

July 23, 1734.

FRAN. FANE.

The grant being general of 12,000 acres of land, and the same being not described therein, nor ascertained by any survey before the proclamation of Governor Johnson, we are of opinion that such grantee cannot now take up lands within six miles of Purrysborough. For the right of the Lords Proprietors is now vested in the Crown, and such general grant could certainly not have prevented the Lords Proprietors from making subsequent grants of any particular lands, provided there was still sufficient land left to satisfy such precedent grant; and yet this would be the necessary consequence if such general grantee might, at any time before his lands are let out, take them wherever he pleases, and disturb the possession of any subsequent grantee. This would not only be a great invasion of his Majesty's right, but would create very great confusion, and would tend very much to the disturbance of the peace of the country.

August 12, 1734.

J. WILLES.
D. RYDER.

(9.) JOINT OPINION *of the Attorney and Solicitor General,* SIR WILLIAM GARROW *and* SIR SAMUEL SHEPHERD, *on the Power of the Crown to alter the Tenure of Lands in Canada.*

2, Lincoln's Inn, January 22, 1817.

MY LORD,—We have had the honour to receive your Lordship's letter, dated the 18th instant, transmitting to us the copy of a despatch addressed by your Lordship to the Governor of Canada, and of the reply which has been received from Sir J. Sherbrooke, relative to the power of the Crown to accept the surrender of lands granted to individuals in Canada for the purpose of regranting them in free and common soccage; and your Lordship is pleased to desire that we will take the same into our consideration, and report to your Lordship our opinion whether there is, either under the statute of the 31 Geo. 3, c. 31, or under the law originally prevailing in the province, as referred to in the minutes of the Executive Council, any legal objection to changing the tenure of land in Canada in the manner recommended?

In obedience to your Lordship's commands we have considered the same, and we beg leave to observe that if it was intended to change the tenure of any lands without the consent or desire of the persons possessing such lands, or at once to effect a general alteration of tenure, there is no doubt that it could not be done without an Act of the legislative bodies, with the assent of his Majesty; but the question is, whether, if lands are surrendered to his Majesty, and thereby become revested in the Crown, his Majesty may not, by virtue of his prerogative, grant such lands to be holden by a tenure different from that by which they were formerly holden (provided the tenure on which they are so regranted be one which is lawful in the province). That a man holding of the Crown may surrender his land to the Crown of whom he holds, we conceive to be clear, and also that the Crown may regrant them upon such terms or tenure recognized by law as shall seem fit, unless restrained by some law or Act of Parliament. Looking at the British Acts which relate to the province of Canada, we do not find any such restriction of the royal prerogative as applicable to this case. By the 14 Geo. 3, c. 83, the title under which any lands were then holden was not to be affected by that Act, but was to remain as if the Act had never passed. But by the same Act a power to grant lands in free and common soccage by the Crown is recognized, because after the 8th section has directed that the laws of Canada shall be the rule of decision in all matters of controversy relative to property and civil rights, the 9th section provides that such provision shall not extend to any lands that have been or may be granted by his Majesty in free and common soccage. This statute imposes no restraint on the ordinary rights of the Crown, but merely leaves all subsisting tenure unaffected by that statute. There is, by the 43rd section of the 31 Geo. 3, c. 31, a restriction of the prerogative as to the tenure on which lands shall be granted in Upper Canada, because by that section his Majesty can only grant lands in free and common soccage; and all the consequences which follow such tenure by the law of England must follow such tenure in Upper Canada.

With respect to the province of Lower Canada, there is also a partial restriction upon the prerogative as to granting lands to be holden by any *other* tenure *than* free and common soccage—namely, where the grantee shall desire to have them granted in free and common soccage, there they must be so granted. These provisions, however, do not affect the right of his Majesty to accept a surrender of lands holden in seigneurie, and to grant such land in free and common soccage, though they compel his Majesty in certain cases to grant them to be holden by such last-mentioned tenure. The 44th section does not apply at all to this case, and neither enables nor restrains his Majesty as to any powers of granting lands in *Lower* Canada; but relates to the giving good and valid grants of lands in Upper Canada, holden under an incomplete or informal title by a mere certificate of occupation.   We do not consider that the message of Lord Dorchester, as far as we collect the contents from the papers, could be deemed restrictive upon the prerogative of the Crown to accept a surrender of lands holden in seigneurie, or to grant such lands after they have been revested in the Crown in free and common soccage.

The 36th section of the 31 Geo. 3, c. 31, does not, in terms or by inference, impose any restriction on the prerogative of the Crown to accept a surrender of lands holden in seigneurie, and to regrant them in free and common soccage; but we think it would be necessary that at the time of such new grant proportionable allotments should be made of other land for the support of the Protestant clergy equal in value to the seventh part to be specified in the new grant; for the regulations of that clause are general, and would apply to grants of lands which had become revested in the Crown by surrender, as well as to lands which had never before been granted.

It is stated by the Chief Justice, and not disputed by the Executive Council, that the King of France, before the conquest of Canada, might have accepted a surrender of lands and have regranted them; and indeed it would have been extraordinary if such had not been the law.   His Majesty, of course, must have the same power; and though the King of France might not have had power to grant in free and common soccage, if such tenure had not existed in Canada by the laws then in force (upon which we do not venture to form any opinion), yet his Majesty having power to grant in free and common soccage, and being bound so to grant at the request of the grantee, if he grants at all, we humbly report to your Lordship that there does not appear to us to be any *legal* objection to his Majesty's accepting a surrender of lands holden in seigneurie, and regranting them in free and common soccage either under the statute of the 31 Geo. 3, c. 31, or under any law which prevailed originally in the province before the conquest.

The Right Hon. Earl Bathurst,   W. GARROW.
&c.   &c.   &c.   S. SHEPHERD.

(10.) JOINT OPINION *of the Attorney and Solicitor General,* SIR J. CAMPBELL *and* SIR R. M. ROLFE, *as to the appropriation of Wild Lands in New Brunswick, by the Legislature of the Colony, in return for a Civil List.*

Temple, April 4, 1837.

MY LORD,—We have to acknowledge the receipt of your Lordship's letter of yesterday's date, requesting us to report our opinion, whether it is in point of law competent to his Majesty, with the advice and consent of the Legislative Council and Assembly of New Brunswick, to render the tracts of wild land in that colony which belong to his Majesty *jure coronæ,* subject to the appropriation of the Legislature of the province, for a fixed period or in perpetuity, in return for a Civil List, to be settled on the Crown for a similar term, or in perpetuity, as may be thought best?

We have the honour to report to your Lordship, that we are of opinion that it is competent to his Majesty to make such appropriation of his hereditary revenues in the colony of New Brunswick as is suggested in your Lordship's letter.

The Lord Glenelg,   J. CAMPBELL.
&c. &c. &c.   R. M. ROLFE.

(11.) OPINION *of the Attorney General,* SIR EDWARD NORTHEY, *on Escheats in New Jersey.* 1705.

To the Rt. Hon. the Lords Commissioners for Trade and Plantations.

MAY IT PLEASE YOUR LORDSHIPS,—In humble obedience to your Lordships' commands, signified to me by Mr. Popple, Jr., your secretary, I have considered of the annexed letter and papers therewith sent, and have perused the letters patent and surrender mentioned in the said letter; and am of opinion, that the fines, forfeitures, and escheats in New Jersey belong to her Majesty, and not to the proprietors of the soil of that colony; for, as to the fines and forfeitures for offences, they were not granted to his late Majesty King James II., when Duke of York, by the letters patent granted to him of the Jerseys and other lands, under which grants the present proprietors claim. And as to the escheats, the whole tract was granted in fee to the Duke of York, to be holden of the King in common soccage as of his manor of East Greenwich; and the inheritance of part being granted away by the assignees of the Duke, to other persons in fee, they hold of the Queen and not of the proprietors; and, therefore, the escheat must be to her Majesty.

As to the appointing of rangers of the woods, the inheritance of those woods being in the proprietors, assignees of the Duke of York, I am of opinion the right of appointing rangers in them belongs to the owners of those woods, and not to her Majesty.

October 19, 1705. EDW. NORTHEY.

(12.) JOINT OPINION *of the Attorney and Solicitor General,* SIR JOHN SOMERS *and* SIR THOMAS TREVOR, *on the Royal Right to Escheats in Virginia.* No date.

MAY IT PLEASE YOUR MOST EXCELLENT MAJESTY,—In obedience to an Order of Council, hereunto annexed, we have considered of the question: Whether escheats in Virginia may be granted before they actually accrue? And it does appear to us, that the tenure by which the lands in Virginia are holden of the Crown of England, is in free and common soccage as of the manor of East Greenwich. The consequence of this tenure is, that where any person dies without heirs his land will escheat to the Crown, as having the immediate seigniory; and we are of opinion, that escheats of this nature cannot be granted before they happen, otherwise than by a grant or alienation of the seigniory itself, which we suppose is not intended to be done.

There are other escheats upon attainder of treason, which are
not incident to the tenure, but belong to the Crown (as a prerogative royal), of whomsoever the land be holden. It seems to us to
be very doubtful, whether such royal escheats may, in any manner,
be granted before they happen ; but, if that might be done, we are
humbly of opinion that it is not advisable for the Crown to part
with such a right, and to put the forfeitures for treason in other
hands.
J. SOMERS.
THOS. TREVOR.

(13.) JOINT OPINION *of the Attorney and Solicitor General,*
SIR ROBERT RAYMOND *and* SIR PHILIP YORKE, *on the King's
Right to Mines in New Jersey.* 1723.

To the Right Honourable the Lords Commissioners of Trade and
Plantations.

MAY IT PLEASE YOUR LORDSHIPS,—In obedience to your Lordships' commands, signified to us by Mr. Popple, and requiring us
to consider the annexed extract of a letter from Mr. Burnet,
Governor of New Jersey, dated the 12th day of December, 1722,
in relation to gold and silver mines said to be found there, and to
report our opinion, in point of law, what right and title is remaining to his Majesty in the said gold and silver mines, and how far
the present proprietors have the right in the said mines, according
to their several grants? We have considered the case as stated in
the said extract of the letter transmitted to us, and have looked
into the charter granted to the proprietors of New Jersey, and do
certify your Lordships that we are of opinion that by the said
charter only the base mines within that province passed to the
grantees, and that the words of the grant are not sufficient to carry
royal mines, the property whereof still remains in the Crown, notwithstanding anything that has appeared to us ; but we beg leave
to inform your Lordships that we have not heard the proprietors,
or any person on their behalf, upon the subject-matter of this
reference, not being directed by your Lordships so to do.

November 30, 1723.
ROBT. RAYMOND.
P. YORKE.

(14.) JOINT OPINION *of the Attorney and Solicitor General,*
SIR J. S. COPLEY *and* SIR CHARLES WETHERELL, *as to the
Right of the Crown to Mines of Gold and Silver and other
Minerals in Nova Scotia.*

Serjeants' Inn, July 13, 1825.

MY LORD,—We have the honour to acknowledge the receipt of
your Lordship's letter of the 21st June last, stating that in the
province of Nova Scotia it is understood that very extensive mines
of iron, coal, and other minerals might be found, and would be
capable of being worked to advantage, and that it has therefore become an object of importance to ascertain how far the rights of the
Crown to these minerals are affected by the grants of land which have
already been made throughout the province in favour of individuals,
and that those grants have been numerous and extensive, but the
terms of them have not been always the same. In some cases an
express reservation has been made to the King, his heirs and successors, " of all coals, and all gold, silver, and other mines and minerals." That in other cases, the words of the reservation enumerate
merely particular metals, such as gold, silver, and copper, with the
addition of the general words, " and all other mines and minerals."
That in other cases, the enumeration of particular minerals is not
followed by any general words comprehending or referring to other
mines or minerals. That there are also cases in which the land
has been granted without any mention whatever of mines or minerals. That all these grants are made under the Great Seal of the
province, and are gratuitous on the part of the Crown, except that
the grantee is bound to the payment of an annual quitrent.

And your Lordship, in reference to the preceding statement, was
pleased to desire that we would report to your Lordship, for his
Majesty's information, our opinion how far in each of the several
cases above mentioned the King is deprived of his right to the
mines below the surface in the lands granted in the province of
Nova Scotia; and particularly whether the general exception " of
coals, and also gold, silver, and all mines and minerals " in some of
the grants, is to be understood in any sense more limited than the
words according to their ordinary signification would seem to
apply ; and whether when the general reservation " of all other
mines and minerals " immediately follows the enumeration of par-

ticular *metals* only, such as gold, silver, and copper, the words are
to be construed literally, or are to be understood as referring to
mines, and minerals, *ejusdem generis*, that is to metallic mines, and
not to mines of gold; and whether when the general words of the
reservation are omitted, and the reservation comprehends in terms
nothing more than certain enumerated minerals, all those minerals
which are not so enumerated must be considered as having passed
to, and become vested in, the grantee; and whether in those cases
where the grant is entirely silent on the subject of minerals, but
amounts to an absolute alienation of the fee-simple of the soil, the
minerals are to be considered as tacitly included in the terms of
such a grant, so as to divest the Crown of its right to them; and
whether there is any general principle of law which would enable
the Crown to resume, as improvident, a grant of lands in a waste
country, by virtue of which the minerals had passed to the grantee
tacitly, and by the mere operation of the general words of the
grant; if it should be subsequently discovered that there were,
beneath the surface, extensive and valuable mineral tracts of the
existence of which the Crown was ignorant at the time of making
the grant?

In compliance with your Lordship's directions, we beg leave to
report, for the information of his Majesty, that we are of opinion
that where the grant contains an exception of "coals, and also gold,
silver, and all mines and minerals," all mines and minerals of
every description under the surface of the land so granted remain
in the Crown. In those cases where the general reservation of *all
other mines and minerals* immediately follows the enumeration of
particular metals only, such as gold, silver, and copper, we think
the words *other mines and minerals* are not to be construed as signifying merely mines, &c., *ejusdem generis*, but that (in the case of
a grant by the Crown) they would embrace mines and minerals of
every description. Where the reservation is in terms confined to
certain specific minerals, without any *general* words, we think the
reservation cannot be extended beyond the minerals so mentioned,
with the exception of gold and silver, which, whether mentioned
or not, would be excepted as belonging to the King by virtue of
his prerogative. If the soil be granted *without any reservation* of
mines or minerals, either in general terms or by specific enumera-

tion, still mines of gold and silver would, upon the principle above mentioned, remain in the Crown. We are not aware of any general principle of law which would, under the circumstances above suggested in your Lordship's letter, enable the Crown to resume its grant.

To Earl Bathurst,   J. S. COPLEY.
&c. &c. &c.   C. WETHERELL.

(15.) OPINION of MR. FANE on the King's Right to Treasure-trove in the Bahamas. 1737.

To the Right Hon. the Lords Commissioners for Trade and Plantations.

MY LORDS,—In obedience to your Lordships' commands, signified to me by Mr. Popple, I have considered the two cases mentioned in the letter of Governor Fitzwilliams, dated the 12th day of November last—one relating to the right of administration to John Sims, a mulatto, who died intestate, leaving a wife, without any relations; the other relating to some treasure found at Providence by one of the inhabitants: and I beg leave to say, as to the first case, that John Sims, dying intestate without any relations, the moiety of such estate, which it is stated he died in the possession of, becomes the right of the Crown; the other moiety his wife will be entitled to, as he left no children.

As to the other case, if no person can legally prove a property in the treasure found, it will be deemed the property of the Crown.

February 27, 1736-7.   FRAN. FANE.

(16.) OPINION of the Attorney General, SIR EDWARD NORTHEY, on the Queen's Right to Royal Fish at New York. 1713.

The pleading is informal on both sides; for, first, the plea of the defendant, alleging a prescription in the inhabitants of the town of Southton to take whales on the high seas and coasts of the same, and convert them to their own use, is ill; for although royal fishes may be claimed by prescription, yet a prescription cannot be laid in the inhabitants; and New York being gained to the Crown of England within time of memory, no prescription can be there

M

against the Crown. Next, the traversing the day and year laid in
the information, and the whales coming to his hands by finding
and his conversion, is ill. The prosecutor's replication is also a
mistake—that royal fish cannot be claimed but by grant; and the
traverse of the prescription, which should have been demurred to,
because not well alleged.

The rejoinder, denying the Queen cannot be divested but by
grant, being taken by protestation, is well enough, that being
matter of law, and not fact; and joining issue on the traverse of
the prescription was well, and no occasion for the prosecutor's
demurrer; however, the plea of the defendant being ill, I am of
opinion judgment ought to be given for the Queen.

July 30, 1713.   EDW. NORTHEY.

(17.) JOINT OPINION *of the Attorney and Solicitor General,*
SIR PHILIP YORKE *and* CHARLES TALBOT, *on the grant by
Letters Patent of Felons' Goods, Fines, and Forfeitures.* 1727.

To the Right Hon. the Lords Commissioners for Trade and
Plantations.

MAY IT PLEASE YOUR LORDSHIPS,—In obedience to your Lordships' commands, signified to us by a letter from Mr. Popple,
referring us the state of the case between his Majesty and the proprietors of the Northern Neck in Virginia, together with the copies
of two charters granted by King Charles II. and King James II.,
and a letter from Major Drisdale, late Lieutenant-Governor of
Virginia, hereunto annexed, we have considered the same, and the
queries proposed in the said letter.

The first of which queries is: What shall pass by the grant of
felons' goods in the said letters patent of King James II.; and
whether the goods of a *felo de se* shall not pass thereby?

As to which we are of opinion that, by the grant of felons' goods,
all goods in possession belonging to any felon convicted, which are
within the district described in the grant, do pass; but it hath
been determined that those words do not extend to any debts or
rights of action, nor to any leases for years, or other chattels real,
belonging to such felon, nor to any goods or chattels whatsoever of
a *felo de se.*

The second question is: Whether fines imposed by the King's court upon persons residing within the said territory for contempt or otherwise shall not pass by the said letters patent; and what fines pass thereby?

As to this we are of opinion that no other fines pass thereby but such as are imposed by the King's courts held within the said territory; the fines imposed at the courts leet of the grantees are expressly granted to them by the letters patent of King Charles II.; and the fines imposed by the King's courts held without the said territory cannot, with propriety, be said to arise or accrue with the same.

The third question is: What shall pass by the word forfeitures in the said letters patent?

As to this, we are of opinion that all goods and chattels, real and personal, in possession, being within the said territory, and forfeited by reason of any judgment or convictions for misdemeanor or felony, and all interests in any lands lying within the said territory forfeited to the Crown by any attainder of felony, do pass by the word forfeitures; but this word is so general and extensive, and the cases which may arise upon it so various, that it is impossible to give an opinion thereupon, which may answer every event, without having the particular facts stated.

The only question contained in Major Drisdale's letter is: How far the Governor of Virginia may exercise the authority given him by his Majesty in pardoning offences and remitting forfeitures arising in the Northern Neck?

As to which we are of opinion, that nothing contained in the said letters patent restrain him from exercising the authority of pardoning such offences; and if the pardon be granted before any forfeiture incurred by judgment in cases of misdemeanor, or by flight, conviction, or judgment in cases of felony, the pardon will prevent any forfeiture; but if the pardon be granted after the forfeiture actually incurred by any of the means aforesaid, though the offence will be thereby discharged, the right of the grantees to the things forfeited will continue.

P. YORKE.

August 12, 1727.   C. TALBOT.

M 2

(18.) OPINION *of the Solicitor General*, SIR WILLIAM THOM-
SON, *on the King's prerogative of prohibiting his Subjects from
going abroad.* 1718.

SIR,—In obedience to the commands of the Lords Commissioners
of Trade and Plantations, signified by yours received this day, I
have perused the letters therein inclosed.   The King may prohibit
his subjects from going out of the realm without license, and the
5th of Richard 2, c. 2, forbids all persons to depart the realm
without license, except those sort of persons mentioned therein.
As to the particular persons intending to go abroad, a writ will be
granted from the chancery, upon a suggestion of such intention, to
prohibit them from going abroad, and security may be required by
virtue thereof that they will not depart the realm without license,
which, if they refuse, they may be committed till sufficient security
is found.   As to those already abroad, if they are required by
proclamation to return home, and do not obey, I do not know of
any method of getting at them by any process abroad; but it is
proper that the King's minister, residing in the country where
they inhabit, do require that they may be made to depart that
country in order to their return.

November 12, 1718.   WM. THOMSON.

(19.) OPINION *of the Attorney General*, SIR ARCHIBALD
MACDONALD, *as to how far the King may restrain his Subjects
from going abroad.* 1788.

A case of so much importance as the present, and not very
frequently occurring, would require more investigation than the
unavoidable shortness of the time permits me to make ; nevertheless, certain established principles furnish conclusions which, in
my judgment, forcibly apply to it.

The questions must be—first, whether the British seamen found
on board of the *Friendship* have committed any, and what offence,
and how it is punishable ?   Secondly, whether Brough, Taylor,
and Rising have committed any, and what offence, and how that
is punishable?   Thirdly, whether, in case an action should be
brought on account of the detention, there be a good defence to it ?

As to the first, disobedience to the King's lawful commands is, by the common law, an high misprision and contempt, punishable, upon indictment or information, by fine and imprisonment; and that the King may lawfully command the return of his subject when out of the realm, under the penalty of seizing his lands till he return, or may command any particular subject to remain within the realm, by his writ of *ne exeat regnum*, or all, or any part of his subjects by proclamation, has been long and often recognized as a part of the common law.   Fitzherbert, N. B. fol. 85, C. says, "that the King, by his proclamation, may inhibit his subjects that they go not beyond the seas, or out of the realm, without license, and that without sending any writ or commandment unto his subjects; for perhaps he cannot find his subject, or know where he is; and therefore the King's proclamation is sufficient in itself." And the Judges held (12th and 13th Ed.) that departing the realm without license was no contempt, though done with intent to live out of the Queen's allegiance; the departing having been before prohibition or restraint by proclamation, or writ of *ne exeat* awarded by the Queen; by which it is plainly implied that departing after proclamation would have been a contempt: and even so early as the reign of Edward I. several persons were impleaded for having acted contrary to a legal proclamation.   Lord Hale, in his treatise *De Portibus Maris*, part 2, c. 8, sums up the law upon this subject thus: first, at common law, any man might pass the seas without license, unless he was prohibited: secondly, at common law, the King might, by his writ, prohibit a person particularly from going beyond sea without license, and this may be done at this day; thirdly, at common law, in time of public danger, and *pro hac vice*, there might be a general inhibition by proclamation, restraining any from going beyond sea without license.   From another passage in a MS. of the same writer, he shows what kind of public danger he adverts to; for speaking of the general restraint, as distinguished from restraining an individual, he says, "This is clearly that restraint intended by the statute of Magna Charta, *nisi publici antea prohibit facient* (not as if it must be a prohibition by Act of Parliament), and this appears by the constant practice, especially in time of danger, when a free passage might either weaken the strength or disclose the secrets of the realm."   And after citing many instances, he adds, "and this prohibition the King may take off generally or particularly, as he pleaseth."

From these authorities, and the constant practice of prohibiting marines, by proclamation, from departing the realm for the purpose of entering into foreign service, at times when the state of Europe would render it dangerous to weaken the strength of the nation, I conceive that the British seamen on board the *Friendship*, who actually executed a contract for the 26th of March last, are guilty of a misdemeanor, for which, upon conviction, they may be fined and imprisoned : as the King, by his prerogative, may restrain all his subjects from departing the realm, he undoubtedly may such classes of them on which its strength depends.

Secondly, with respect to Brough, Taylor, and Rising, if the entering into foreign service, in breach of the proclamation, be a crime in the British seamen, I am of opinion that a conspiracy to entice and carry them into foreign service is also a misdemeanor, punishable by fine and imprisonment, if the evidence upon examination is sufficient.

Thirdly, with respect to the sufficiency of the defence to an action brought against the officers, I think they might justify the detention of the ship, so long as the British seamen were on board, and till they received directions upon the subject. The commander of a ship actually disobeying the law cannot, I apprehend, insist upon a clearance. By the 12th Ch. 2, c. 4, s. 12, power is given to the King to prohibit, by proclamation, the exportation of gunpowder, &c., but no specific mode of putting the Act in force, by preventing the exportation, is pointed out ; nor was any pointed out till the 29th George 2, c. 16, forfeited the gunpowder and inflicted a penalty. During the period which elapsed between the passing of those two Acts, I think the officers of the customs must have been justified in stopping a ship having gunpowder on board, after a proclamation, till such gunpowder was relanded ; and this proclamation is equally warranted by the common law.

July 31, 1788.   AR. MACDONALD.

(20.) JOINT OPINION *of the Attorney and Solicitor General,*
SIR PHILIP YORKE *and* SIR CLEMENT WEARG, *on Criminal
Jurisdiction in the Leeward Islands.* 1725.

William White, an inhabitant of the island of Spanish Town,
which is one of the Leeward Islands, *kills* one Cary there ; for which
being apprehended by the Governor of that island, he, the said
White, *petitioned the Chief Governor of all the Leeward Islands (by
whom all commissions of oyer and terminer within that Government
are issued) for a speedy trial in Spanish Town aforesaid,* or, if that
could not be, for want of proper officers in that island, that he
might be sent for to St. Christopher's, and tried there.

Spanish Town is an island where no courts or officers are established for the administration of justice.

The Chief Governor, therefore, caused the said White to be
brought up to St. Christopher's, where he was examined before
four of his Majesty's Council there, and they, thinking there was
great cause to suspect that White was guilty of the said murder,
the said Chief Governor awarded a special commission of oyer and
terminer for his trial in St. Christopher's, *and White has since been
convicted of the murder of Cary, before those commissioners, by a jury
of St. Christopher's,* and received sentence of death thereupon.

The statute 33 Henry 8, reciting that persons, upon vehe-
ment suspicion of treasons or murder, being many times sent for
to divers shires of the realm, and other the Kings' dominions, to be
examined before the King's Council upon their offences, and also
setting forth the charge of the Crown, and inconveniency of remanding such suspected persons, after their examination, back to
the places where their offences were committed, for trial, &c., enacts
that, if any person, being examined by the King's Council, or three
of them, upon any manner of treasons, misprisions of treasons, or
murders, do confess any such offences, or that the said Council, or
three of them, upon such examination, shall think any persons so
examined to be vehemently suspected of any treason, misprision of
treason, or murder, that then, in every such case, by the King's
commandment, his Majesty's commission of oyer and terminer,
under his great seal, shall be made by the Chancellor of England
to such persons, and into such shires, as shall be named and

appointed by the King, for the speedy trial, conviction, or deliver-
ance of such offenders; and that, in such case, no challenge for
the shire or hundred shall be allowed : which statute, though it be
repealed, by the 1st & 2nd P. and M., as to treason, yet, it is
apprehended, it is not as to murder.

Quære 1. Does not this statute make such an alteration in the
common law, and so enlarge the King's prerogative as to trials in
murder, as well in his colonies as in his kingdom of England, that
he may, if he thinks fit, appoint any man (charged with that offence
in any of his colonies, and examined as the Act directs) to be tried
in any place there, other than the place or island where the offence
was committed ?

Quære 2. If such power be in the King, can that power be
executed by his Governor in St. Christopher's, who is expressly
empowered by his Majesty's commission to erect courts of justice,
and issue commissions of oyer and terminer, within this government,
as he shall think fit; and can a commission, in the King's name,
under the seal of the Leeward Islands, and an examination before
the King's Council there (who are actually nominated by the King,
and, by his instructions, called his Council), be taken to be such a
commission and examination as is meant by, or comprehended
within, the words or designs of this Act ?

_ *Quære* 3. If this commission in this case be not warranted by
the statute, it is not, nevertheless, warranted by the King's prerogative in his colonies, and well supported by the powers *supra*,
which his Majesty, by his commission, has given to the Governor
of St. Christopher's; and, upon the whole matter, is the trial and
conviction of White legal or not ?

To Quære 1. We are of opinion that the statute of 33 Henry 8,
cap. 23, does not extend to the plantations, and that there is no
foundation, from that Act of Parliament, to grant special commissions of oyer and terminer, for trial of offences arising out of the
colony within which such commission is granted.

To Quære 2. This question depends upon the former, and is
answered under that.

To Quære 3. The legality of the commission upon which White
was tried will depend upon the constitution of the government of
the Leeward Islands, and the jurisdiction of the courts of judica-

ture in St. Christopher's, which is not sufficiently stated, so as to enable us to give any certain opinion thereupon. If the island of Spanish Town is dependent, as to its government, on St. Christopher's, and crimes committed in the former can be, and have usually been, tried by commissioners of oyer and terminer in the latter, then we conceive this commission was well warranted, and the trial and conviction were legal, in case there be no other objection against them; but if crimes committed in Spanish Town cannot, by the laws of that government, be so tried in St. Christopher's, then this commission, and the proceedings thereupon, were against law; and there being no settled courts of justice in Spanish Town, we apprehend the safest method of bringing White to justice is to send him over into England to be examined before the Privy Council, according to the statute of 33 Henry 8, whereupon a special commission of oyer and terminer may be issued under the Great Seal of Great Britain, for trying him pursuant to the directions of that Act; but as that may be attended with great trouble, if the Governor has authority, by his commission and instructions, to erect courts and constitute officers of justice in Spanish Town, and there are sufficient inhabitants within that island qualified to serve upon the grand and petty jury, then, we apprehend, the Governor may grant a commission of oyer and terminer, and appoint proper officers for summoning juries, and other purposes, in order to the trying of the prisoner within Spanish Town.

P. YORKE.

December 18, 1725.   C. WEARG.

(21.) JOINT OPINION *of the Attorney and Solicitor General,* SIR DUDLEY RYDER *and* SIR THOMAS STRANGE, *on the erection of a Court of Exchequer in the Colonies.* 1738.

Quære 1. Whether the Crown has by the prerogative a power to erect a Court of Exchequer in South Carolina; and in what manner such court should be erected?—We are of opinion that the Crown has, by the prerogative, power to erect a Court of Exchequer in South Carolina, which may be done by letters patent under the seal of the province, by virtue of his Majesty's commission to the Governor for that purpose.

2. What powers a court so established will have? whether they will extend as far as the Court of Exchequer in England; and whether the proceedings therein should be the same as in England? ·—We are of opinion that his Majesty may erect a Court of Exchequer in South Carolina, with the same powers as the Court of Exchequer here has: we think the proceedings in such new erected court should be agreeably, as near as may be, to the practice here.

3. Whether the Governor, by his commission or instructions, be sufficiently empowered to appoint a chief baron; and in what manner such chief baron should be appointed?—We think the general power of erecting courts of justice, as given by the commission to Mr. Horsey, would be sufficient to authorize him to appoint a chief baron; but as by the 39th instruction the Crown seems to reserve to itself the consideration, whether a standing Court of Exchequer should be erected or not, and as doubts have arose in the province touching the authority of the present Chief Baron, we conceive it is not advisable to rest the authority of erecting such court and appointing the chief baron on the present commission and instructions, but yet it would be more proper (if his Majesty shall be so pleased), by a special commission to his Governor, to authorize the establishment of such a court, and the constitution of the chief baron and other officers of it.

J. STRANGE.

June 12, 1738.   D. RYDER.

(22.) OPINION of the *Attorney General*, SIR DUDLEY RYDER, on the *King's power to erect Courts of Justice in Newfoundland.* 1749.

To His Grace the Duke of Bedford.

MAY IT PLEASE YOUR GRACE,—In obedience to your Grace's commands, signified to me by your Grace's letter of the 23rd instant, setting forth that your Grace had laid before the King a letter which you had received from Captain Rodney, late Governor of Newfoundland, wherein he desires, at the request of the principal inhabitants of that island, that your Grace would move his Majesty in their behalf, that power may be granted to take cognizance of capital crimes there; his Majesty had thereupon been pleased to command your Grace to transmit to me an extract of the said letter, that I should consider of the request of the said inhabitants, and report to your Grace my opinion, for his Majesty's information, in what manner I think his Majesty may comply with their request, consistent with the 13th article of the Act of Parliament of the 10th and 11th of the reign of the late King William, for the trial of persons guilty of capital crimes in the said island, in any shire or county in England, a copy of which your Grace was pleased to inclose: I have perused and considered the Act of the 10th and 11th of King William III. and the enclosed extract from Captain Rodney's letter, and am of opinion that his Majesty has a prerogative and right to erect courts of justice in Newfoundland for the trial and punishment of all sorts of crimes committed there, and that the Act of 10th and 11th of King William III. does not take away or affect that prerogative, so that his Majesty, notwithstanding that Act, may erect and constitute such court there for the trial of capital and other crimes as his Majesty shall, in his royal wisdom, think proper.·

I would only take the liberty of informing your grace, that about the year 1738, this matter was taken into consideration by the Board of Trade, in pursuance, I believe, of some reference to them from his Majesty, or a Committee of Council, and the Board did make a report concerning it, after having taken the opinion of myself, and his Honour the present Master of the Rolls, the then Attorney and Solicitor General; in which report they proposed inserting into the commission to the next Governor of Newfoundland, a clause to empower the Governor to erect a court of justice there, to the same effect as is inserted into the commission to other governors of his Majesty's American commission governments; but that clause, coming afterwards to be considered in Council, was rejected, as I have been informed.

January 30, 1749.   D. RYDER.

(23.) OPINION *of the Attorney General*, SIR DUDLEY RYDER, *that the King could not grant power to establish a Criminal Court at Newfoundland, but under the Great Seal.* 1750.

To the Right Hon. the Lords Commissioners for Trade and Plantations.

MY LORDS,—I have perused and considered the several papers your Lordships were pleased to transmit to me, with Mr. Hill's letter of the 26th instant, desiring my opinion, whether a power to take cognizance of capital crimes in Newfoundland can be granted to the Governor of that country by instructions only, signed by his Majesty in Council, or whether it ought to be inserted in his commission under the great seal; and whether, if such power must be inserted in the commission, the words proposed for that purpose in the year 1738, and which were sent me, are proper : I am of opinion, such power cannot be granted by instruction, or any otherwise than under the great seal, and, therefore, if thought advisable to be granted at all, ought to be inserted in the Governor's commission; but the manner of his exercising such power may be prescribed and limited by instructions, for any breach of which he will be answerable to his Majesty.

The form of words in the inclosed extract from the draft of a commission in 1738, is, I think, proper for the purpose, excepting that neither the power of trying, nor that of pardoning treasons, appear to me fit to be intrusted to the Governor, or a court to be erected by him.

March 27, 1750.   D. RYDER.

(24.) JOINT OPINION *of the Attorney and Solicitor General*, SIR JAMES SCARLETT *and* SIR N. C. TINDAL, *on the power of the Crown to create the office of Master of the Rolls in Canada.* 1827.

To the Right Hon. William Huskisson, &c.

SIR,—We have had the honour of receiving from Lord Goderich, a copy of the commission under the great seal, appointing the Earl of Dalhousie Governor of the provinces of Upper and Lower Canada, the draft of a proposed patent for the appointment of a

Master of the Rolls in the province of Upper Canada, and a copy
of the patent of Master of the Rolls in England, accompanied by a
letter from his Lordship, in which—after pointing out to our atten-
tention that the law of England has been generally adopted in
Upper Canada, that the custody of the seal intrusted to a colonial
governor has already been considered to invest him with the
office of chancellor, but that the governors of Upper Canada have
always declined assuming the judicial functions of chancellor, that
the want of a court authorized to enforce the execution of trusts, and
to protect the property of infants, has been productive of great inconvenience, of which representations have been made to his
Majesty's Government, although no attempt has been made to institute a court of equitable jurisdiction by any statute of the
Governor, Council, aud Assembly, for supplying which defect it had
been suggested, that the most appropriate remedy would be the
erection of the office of Master of the Rolls—his Lordship desires us
to take the proposed draft of a patent into our consideration, and
to report for his Majesty's information whether his Majesty can,
by letters patent under the great seal, or in any other manner, lawfully create the Master of the Rolls in Upper Canada, and whether
such letters patent could properly be passed in the form suggested,
and to make such alterations in the draft as may appear to us to
be necessary.

In compliance with his Lordship's desire, we have duly considered
the several matters referred to us, and have now the honour to
report, for his Majesty's information, that the result of our investigation leaves us in considerable doubt, whether his Majesty lawfully can, by letters patent under the great seal, or in any other
manner without the intervention of Parliament, or of the local legislature, create any new judge in equity, by whatsoever name he may
be called, in Upper Canada ; that the office of Master of the Rolls
in England is a very ancient office, deriving its authority and jurisdiction from usage, and the various relations by which that office
is connected with the general establishment of the courts both of
equity and common law; that the same office and the same relations, much less the same fees and emoluments, could not be transferred to Canada by the mere creation of an office of that name,
which would, nevertheless, be there a new office, the functions of

which ought to be specified in the law which authorized, or in the patent which created it; and we therefore humbly submit, that in order to prevent any misconception of the authority and jurisdiction of the office, by reason of analogies drawn from the name, it would be more expedient, if consistent with his Majesty's pleasure, that the intended equity judge should be called Vice-Chancellor to the Governor, and make his deputy for the desired purpose to which it is supposed the Governor's authority may be usefully employed in a court of equity. But in order to prevent doubts on the subject we would recommend this to be done by the aid of Parliament or of the local legislature.

We therefore beg permission to return the draft of the proposed patent, and to defer any alterations it may require, until his Majesty's pleasure be further known to us.

We take the liberty of submitting further to your consideration, as connected with this subject, whether, with a view to avoid the clashing of jurisdictions and the dissensions which may possibly arise upon the new establishment of distinct courts of equal power, but proceeding by different rules, it might not be expedient, instead of creating a distinct court of equity, to add to the judges who constitute the present common law court in that province, the proposed equity lawyer in the character of a puisne judge, and to give to the court so constituted, by the authority of Parliament, or of the local legislature, so much of an equitable jurisdiction as upon due consideration may be thought necessary or useful to the province, to be exercised as in the Court of Exchequer in England, in the same tribunal, and by the same judges who administer the common law.

J. SCARLETT.

September 25, 1827.   N. C. TINDAL.

NOTES TO CHAPTER V.

(1) Lands in the Colonies.   In 1852 an Act (15 & 16 Vict. c. 39) was passed to remove doubts as to the lands and casual revenues of the Crown in the colonies and foreign possessions of her Majesty. It recites that from the time of the passing of the Act 1 Will. 4, c. 25, the lands of the Crown in the colonies had been granted and disposed of, and the moneys arising therefrom had been appropriated by the authority of the Crown and of the legislature of the several colonies, as if the said Act and another

Act, 1 Vict. c. 2, had not been passed, and that doubts had arisen
whether such moneys might not be considered "hereditary casual
revenues" of the Crown, within the meaning of the said Act: and it
enacts that the provisions of the said Acts shall not extend to such
moneys, nor any sale or disposition of such lands, or any appropriation
of such moneys; and that nothing in the said Acts shall prevent the
appropriation of any casual revenues in the colonies or foreign possessions of the Crown towards public colonial purposes, provided that
the surplus not applied to such public purposes shall be carried to and
form part of the Consolidated Fund.

As to grants by the Crown of waste lands in the colonies, see *Latour* (2) Crown
v. *The Attorney General*, 11 Jur. (N.S.) 7. Grants.

In cases of grants by the Crown, the rule of law has been that they
are construed most strongly against the grantees, and that nothing
passes by them without clear and determinate words. *Stanhope's Case*,
Hob. 243, Bro. Abr. *Patent*, Pl. 62. But this must be taken with the
qualification that the words are really doubtful, and when the interpretation in favour of the Crown might be without violation of the
apparent object of the grant. In *Molyne's Case*, 6 Co. 5, it was held
that the King's grant should be taken beneficially for the honour of
the King and the relief of the subject; and Sir Edward Coke says there,
that the ancient sages of the law construed the King's grants beneficially,
so as not to make any strict or literal construction in subversion of such
parts: see also, 2 Inst. 497. As to grants by the Crown *ex certâ
scientiâ et mero motu*, see a valuable note to *The Case of Alton Woods*,
1 Co. 43 b., in the edition by Thomas and Fraser, vol. i. p. 110. The
rule of strict interpretation is said not to apply to royal grants made
upon a valuable consideration: Kent's Com. ii. 556.

At all events, whatever may have been the old rule, one consistent
with justice and common sense now prevails, and it has been expressed
in a recent case: "Upon a question of the meaning of words the
same rules of common sense and justice must apply, whether the subject-matter of construction be a grant from the Crown, or from a subject: it is always a question of intention, to be collected from the
language used with reference to the surrounding circumstances:" *Lord
v. Commissioners of Sydney*, 12 Moore, P. C. 497.

All grants from the Crown are matters of public record. "The King
cannot grant or take anything but by matter of record. . . . . . It hath
this sovereign privilege that it is proved by no other but by itself:"
3 Inst. 71. Royal franchises never pass by assignment without special
words in the Crown's grant (Year Book, 30 Edw. 1); and it is said that
a royal franchise does not pass to the assignee of him to whom it was
granted: *Ibid*. As to the necessity of express words to convey property of the Crown by reason of prerogative, see *Duke of Beaufort
v. Mayor of Swansea*, 3 Ex. R. 413, and *Attorney General v. Parsons*,
2 C. & J. 279. In the latter case the Court said: "The rules of construction upon grants from the Crown are much more favourable to-

the grantor than the rules of construction upon grants from ordinary persons." But this does not mean that a *forced* construction is to be put upon the words in favour of the Crown, but only that where there is a doubt they shall be interpreted in its favour contrary to the ordinary rule by which *verba fortius accipiuntur contra proferentem:* a rule, however, which the Court said in *Lindus* v. *Melrose*, 27 L. J. Ex. 329, ought to be applied only where other rules of construction fail. " If the King's grant can enure to two intents, it shall be taken to the intent that makes most for the King's benefit:" Com. Dig. *Grant* (G. 12): see *Jewison* v. *Dyson*, 9 M. & W. 540; *Doe* d. *Devine* v. *Wilson*, 10 Moore, P. C. 502.

In the absence of any reservation to the Crown of any right of killing or taking wild cattle on lands granted or demised in a colony by the Crown, such right is included in the grant or demise : *The Falkland Islands Company* v. *The Queen*, 2 Moore, P. C. (N. S.) 266.

In an opinion given by Sir A. Cockburn, A.G., and Sir R. Bethell, S.G., August 1854, on certain questions relating to the fishery revenues in Newfoundland, and including a question as to the extent of a Crown grant, they said : " The meaning of the term ' coast ' in the grant must, as it seems to us, be taken to mean the shore of what may be properly called the sea. Such is the ordinary acceptation of the term, and we see nothing to vary its sense in the present instance. We cannot therefore go to the length of the opinion given by Sir F. Pollock and Sir W. Follett, that the term ' coast ' will include the shores and bays, inlets and rivers, where the tide flows. It may or may not comprehend the shores of bays and inlets, according to circumstances. We think it does not include the shores of rivers. . . . . . The grant from the Crown vested in the owner all the soil, except a particular 500 feet. The sea having swallowed up the latter, there can be, so far as the grant is concerned, no pretence for calling on the owner to make good the loss, and there is no prerogative right in the Crown to land so circumstanced."

In *The Lord Advocate* v. *Hamilton*, 1 Macqueen, H. L. 55, where the Crown claimed the bed of a public navigable river, which by an Act of Parliament had been vested in trustees, on the ground that by a saving clause the rights of the Crown had been reserved, Lord Brougham said : " You cannot out of this saving clause construe any right to be given to the Crown. The right which the Crown had independently of it, and previously to it, is saved and nothing more. The Crown is not to have its right lessened or diminished ; but nothing whatever is *given* to the Crown by the saving clause, except the mode of ascertaining its rights by petition to the Court of Session. As, generally speaking, you cannot raise out of a proviso or an exception in a statute any affirmative enactment, so you cannot, generally speaking, raise out of a saving clause any affirmative or positive right whatever."

(3) Escheats.   There was formerly a doubt, while the East India Company possessed the territorial sovereignty of British India, whether they or the Crown were entitled to escheats of lands ; but the question was set at

rest by 16 & 17 Vict. c. 95, s. 27, which provided that all fines and penalties by the sentence or order of any court of justice within the territories under the government of the East India Company, and all forfeitures for crimes of any real or personal estate within the said territories, and all real and personal estate within the said territories *escheating* or lapsing for want of an heir or successor, should belong to the Company in trust for Her Majesty for the service of the Government of India. Since the passing of the Act for the " Better Government of India," 21 & 22 Vict. c. 106, these escheats belong to the Crown. And this applies to the estate of a Hindoo subject, though a Brahmin, notwithstanding the passage in the Mitacshara, chap. ii. sec. 7, which says, " Never shall a king take the wealth of a priest, for the text of Menu forbids it :" *Collector of Masulipatam* v. *Cavaly V. Narrainappah*, 8 Moore, Ind. App. 500. As to escheats in Jamaica, see *Mason* v. *Attorney General of Jamaica*, 4 Moore, P. C. 228.

According to the old French law, the Crown had the right to inherit the property of a foreigner who had no heirs in France. This was called the *jus albinagii*, or *droit d'aubaine*, which some have derived from *Albanus*, a Scotchman, and others, as Pothier, from *alibi natus;* but Dietz suggests that it comes from *alibi*, simply formed from that adverb after the analogy of *prochain*, *lointain*. The law was abolished by the Constituent Assembly in 1790, and re-established by the Code Napoleon, but afterwards again abolished in 1819, when the right of succession to foreigners in France was placed on the same footing as in the case of native-born Frenchmen (1).

By the common law, all mines of gold and silver within the realm belong to the Crown; so also mines of copper, tin, lead, iron, or other base metal, if they contain *aliquid auri aut argenti :* Com. Dig. *Waife*, H. 1. But by statute 1 Will. & M. c. 30, s. 4, no mine of copper, tin, iron, or lead shall be taken to be a royal mine, although gold or silver may be extracted out of the same : see also 5 Will. & M. c. 6, and 55 Geo. 3, c. 134. As to mines and minerals in Cornwall, see 21 & 22 Vict. c. 109. If the Crown grants lands in which mines are, and all mines in them, yet royal mines (*i.e.* mines of gold and silver) do not pass : Com. Dig. *Waife*, H. 1. But the Crown may, by apt words, grant mines of gold or silver to a subject : *Ibid. :* see *The Case of Mines*, Plowd. 313 a.

(4) Right of Crown to Mines.

In *Mayor of Lyons* v. *East India Company*, 1 Moore, Ind. App. 281, Lord Brougham, in delivering the judgment of the Court, said : " Mines of precious metals, treasure trove, royal fish, are all vested in the Crown, for the purpose of maintaining its power, and enabling it to defend the State. They are not enjoyed by the Sovereign in all or even in novel circumstances, and no one has said that they extend to the East Indian

(1) It appears from a fragment recently discovered of a work, *De Jure Fisci*, by an unknown jurist, that by the Roman law under the empire, if a person convicted of a crime alienated any part of his property, the Crown could recover it, together with fourfold its value—*ab eo, qui reus criminis postulatus adversam sententiam meruit tempore reatus quocunque modo alienata a fisco cum quadruplis fructibus revocantur:* Fragm. Vet. Jcti apud Gaii Inst. edit. Lachmann, p. 426.

N

possessions of the British Crown." This seems to throw a doubt upon the right of the Crown to the things here enumerated ; but whatever may be the law as to a prerogative right to treasure trove and royal fish in the colonies, I conceive that mines of gold and silver there do belong to the Queen, *jure coronæ*. At all events, I know of no rule or principle to the contrary ; and the opinion in the text given by Sir John Copley, A.G., and Sir Charles Wetherell, S.G., expressly states that such mines belong to the Crown by virtue of its prerogative. It is usual for the Crown to reserve a royalty on minerals raised from waste lands in the colonies. Thus, I find in the M.S. Council Register for 1847, p. 772, an Order in Council approving of instructions to the Governor of New Zealand for altering the royalty to be reserved on minerals in waste lands in that colony without specifying any particular kind, and therefore including all.

(5) Treasure Trove. Anciently the concealing of treasure trove was punishable by death : 3 Inst. 133. The term only applies to money, coin, gold, silver, plate, or bullion hid in the earth, "and in which no man has a property." These belong to the Crown ; but treasures found on the surface of the earth, or in the sea, belong to the finder : *Ibid.* ; Bac. Abr. *Prerog.* B. 8 ; *Constable's Case*, 5 Co. 108 b. Grotius calls the right of the Sovereign to treasure trove, *jus commune et quasi gentium :* De Jure, Bell. et. Pac. ii. c. 8, s. 7. There can be no *larceny* of such treasures until office found : see *R.* v. *Toole*, 11 Cox, Crim. Ca. 75, and *R.* v. *Thomas*, 9 Cox, Crim. Ca. 376. By the Hindoo law, according to the Institutes of Menu, c. viii., the King was entitled to half of the treasure anciently deposited underground by reason of his general protection, and because he was lord paramount of the soil ; but the other half he was to give to the Brahmins. By the Roman law treasure found by the owner of the soil belonged to him, but if found on another's property, one half belonged to the owner and the other half to the finder : Cod. *de Thesauris*, x. 15 ; Inst. *de Rerum Div.* s. ii., tit. i. s. 39. The French law is the same, and treasure is defined to be *toute chose cachée on enfouie, sur laquelle personne ne peut justifier sa propriété, et qui est découverte par le pur effet du hasard :* Cod. Civ. 716. When Pothier wrote, the old feudal system existed in France, and then treasure when found belonged, one-third to the *seigneur haut justicier*, one-third to the owner of the soil, and one-third to the finder : Pothier, Traité de Propr. art. 4, s. 2. A curious question once arose in France as to the right of ownership in a meteoric stone which had fallen from the sky—but I forget how it was decided. I remember, however, Lord Brougham asking whether no claim was put in by the man in the moon ! By the Roman law the finder was entitled only when he discovered the treasure by mere accident, and not after search, *non studio perscrutandi :* Cod. *de Thesauris*, x. 15.

(6) Royal Fish. The royal fish are whales and sturgeons, which, when either cast ashore or caught near the coast, belong to the Crown : Stat. de Prerog. Reg. 17 Edw. 2, c. 11 ; *Constable's Case*, 5 Co. 108 b. Blackstone

notices a curious distinction made by the old legal authorities, which is, that the whale is to be divided between the King and the Queen—the King taking the head and the Queen the tail; the reason assigned being, that the Queen might have the whalebone for her wardrobe, although in fact the whalebone is found in the head and not in the tail. In the *Case of Swans*, 7 Co. 16, it was held that the swan is a royal fowl, and that all *white* swans *not marked*, which have gained their natural liberty and are found swimming in an open and common river, may be seized to the King's use by his prerogative. Whether the same prerogative applies to *black* swans the authorities do not inform us.

It has been held that if the King grants certain *liberties*, and, amongst (7) Felons' other things, grants *omnia bona et catalla felonum de se* within such a ^Goods. place, the grant shall pass obligations, specialties, and debts due to the felon; for though in other cases, a grant of *omnia bona et catalla* by the King will not pass specialties and debts, yet in the grant of a liberty it will: 2 Roll. Abr. 195. So by a grant of goods and chattels of felons the grantee shall have the ready money of such felons: *Anon.*, 2 Show. 133. Stock and money in the funds will not pass by a grant of *bona et catalla felonum*, not being within a particular liberty: *R. v. Capper*, 5 Price, 217, 263; and see the notes to *The King v. Sutton*, 1 Wms. Saund. 275 (c.); *Jewison v. Dyson*, 9 M. & W. 540.

A *felo de se* forfeits all his chattels, real and personal, and all *choses in action* belonging solely to himself; but his lands of inheritance are not forfeited, nor is his blood corrupted, nor his wife barred of her dower: Hawkins, P.C., bk. i. c. 67; Steph. Com. iv. 549 (6th ed.). " I must repeat my conviction that, according to the understood law of this country, freeholds of inheritance which at the time of his death belong to a man who dies *felo de se*, do not escheat to the Crown, but pass to his heir-at-law:" *per* Lord Romilly, M.R., in *Norris v. Chambers*, 30 L. J. (Ch.) 290. The proposition in the Opinion in the text, that a grant of felon's goods and chattels does not pass the goods and chattels of a *felo de se*, was affirmed in *The King v. Sutton*, 1 Wms. Saund. 273. The reason assigned *arguendo* for this was, that the goods and chattels of felons are a different liberty from the goods and chattels of felons of themselves. In the case of a *felo de se*, nothing is vested in the Crown until the inquisition is found: *R. v. Ward*, 1 Sid. 150; *Toomes v. Etherington*, 1 Wms. Saund. 363. But in the case of other felonies, goods and chattels are forfeited on conviction. Lands are forfeited only upon attainder, which, however, relates back to the time of the offence committed, so as to avoid all mesne incumbrances. The offence of a *felo de se* is included in the commissions of justices of *oyer and terminer*, and of justices of the peace; and a presentment may be made before either of them, for the offence is included in their commission to try all felonies: *Toomes v. Etherington, ubi sup.* 363 (note). See, as to lands of felons attainted, Stat. de Prerog. Reg. 17 Edward 2, c. 16; and as to inquests by coroners, 6 Vict. c. 12.

The English law as to *felo de se*, and the forfeiture of goods and

N 2

chattels consequent upon suicide, does not apply to Hindoo and Mahommedan subjects in the East Indies: *Advocate-General of Bengal* v.
Ranee Surnomoye Dossee, 2 Moore, P. C. (N. S.) 22 (1).

(8) Ne Exeat   By the old common law of England, the Crown at its pleasure might,
Regno.   by a writ *de securitate inveniendâ quod se non divertat ad partes exteras*,
sine licentiâ regis, command a subject not to go beyond the seas or out
of the realm; and the reason alleged was, "because that every man is
bound to defend the King and the realm:" Fitz. *Nat. Brev.* 85. And
this might be done by proclamation (2): *Ibid.*

It was said *arguendo*, by Treby, in *East India Company* v. *Sandys*, 10
State Tr. 396, that this writ was originally for the clergy only, and
was properly granted for matter of State only—the reason for the prohibition assigned in it being *quod plurima nobis et coronæ nostræ præjudi-
cialia ibidem prosequi intendis*—and that it was only recently that it had
been extended to restrain a person in a private trust from going abroad.
Wilmot, C.J., in his "Opinions and Judgments," pp. 97–98, calls it "a
State writ to restrain people from going abroad—first used to hinder
the clergy from going to Rome; then extended to laymen machinating
and concerting measures against the State; now applied to prevent a
subterfuge from the justice of the nation, though in matters of private
concernment. . . . . . The legality of that application was settled in
Charles II.'s time, upon an usage first begun in the time of James I."

(1) For some curious information as to the practice of suicide amongst the ancients,
see Lecky's "History of European Morals." (London, 1869.)

(9) Proclama-   (2) The Queen's proclamations are binding on the subject "where they do not
tions.   either contradict the old laws, or tend to establish new ones, but only confine the
execution of such laws as are already in being, in such manner as the Sovereign shall
judge necessary:" Steph. Blackst. ii. 528 (1st edit.).   In a note to his published
Charge to the Grand Jury in *R.* v. *Eyre* (Ridgway, 1867), Lord Chief Justice Cockburn
says: "The law on the subject is fully discussed and settled by Lord Coke, with his
accustomed weight and learning, in a memorandum under the head of 'Proclama-
tinis,' in the 12th part of his Reports, p. 74.   The result of his reasoning, and of the
authorities he cites, may be briefly stated.   Besides such as are issued in furtherance
of the executive power of the Crown, proclamations which either call upon the subject to fulfil some duty which he is by law bound to perform, or to abstain from any
acts or conduct already prohibited by law, are perfectly lawful and right; and it is
said that if, after such a proclamation, the law is nevertheless broken, the disobedience of the royal command, if not of itself a misdemeanor, is at all events an aggra-
vation of the offence.   On the other hand, wherever a proclamation purports to be
made in the exercise of legislative power—as if the Sovereign grants a monopoly or
privilege against the rights of the rest of the community, or imposes a duty to which
the subject is not by law liable, or prohibits under penalties what is not an offence at
law, or adds fresh penalties to any offence beyond those to which it is already liable—
the proclamation is of no effect, for the Crown has no legislative power except such as
it exercises in common with the other two branches of the legislature.   'The King,'
says Comyn, 'cannot by proclamation alter any part of the common law, statutes,
or customs of the realm' (Dig. Title Prerogative, ii. 3)."

It has been laid down that every proclamation ought to be under the Great Seal,
sub magno sigillo Angliæ, and it is most safe and proper to be so pleaded (Cro. Car.
180).   The statute 31 Hen. 8, c. 8 (repealed by 1 Edw. 6, c. 12), which gave to the
King's proclamation, with the advice of his Council, the power of law, says nothing
about the Great Seal.

It has been laid down, that if a subject goes out of the kingdom, with or without the license of the Crown, and a messenger by command, under the great or privy seal, summons him to come back into the kingdom, and he does not return at the limited time, he forfeits all his goods and lands for his contempt : Dyer, 128 b; 3 Inst. 179 ; Com. Dig. *Prerog.* D. 35.   By stat. 5 Rich. 2. c. 2, " all persons, except only the lords and other great men of the realm, and true and notable merchants, and the King's soldiers," were forbidden to pass out of the realm without the King's special license, available only at certain specified ports.   But this statute was repealed by 4 Jac. 1, c. 1, s. 22 ; and see the expired stat. 13 Eliz. c. 3.   The writ *ne exeat regno* was originally a State writ granted by the Lord Chancellor on application from the Secretaries of State, but it is now granted in aid of the subject to help him to obtain his just debts : Com. Dig. *Chan.* 4 B. Fitz. *Nat. Brev.* 85 F.; 3 P. Wms. 313.   This writ is issued from the Court of Chancery.   It has been considered as in the nature of equitable bail ; and that where a party would not be entitled to bail at law, he could not have the writ in Chancery : *Haffey* v. *Haffey*, 14 Ves. 261.

In the United States the name of this writ is *ne exeat republica ;* but there it can be issued only for equitable demands, for when the demand is strictly legal the Court has no jurisdiction : 1 John's Ch. New York, 2. In this country it has been decided, that the writ could not be issued against a defendant who had been held to bail in an action at law : *Amsinck* v. *Barklay*, 8 Ves. 594.

As the Crown may restrain any of its subjects from going abroad, it may also command them, by writ under the great or privy seal, to return home ; and it is said that disobedience of the writ is the highest contempt, the punishment of which is the seizure of the offender's estate until he return.   But the Crown has only an interest in the lands until the party returns, and the restoration of them then is not a matter of grace but of right.   The contempt is incurred from the time when notice is given to the party by the messenger sent to serve it, who ought to make a certificate upon oath in Chancery of due service of the writ : Bac. Abr. *Prerog.* C. 4.

But the Crown has no power, by its prerogative alone, to send any one, whether he be a subject or an alien, compulsorily out of the realm. In a debate, however, in the House of Lords, in June, 1816, on the Alien Bill, which was introduced at the restoration of peace, Lord Ellenborough, C.J., contended that at common law the Crown has the right, by the royal prerogative, to send all aliens out of the kingdom ; and to prove this he cited a petition of the merchants of London in the reign of Edward I., praying that monarch to do so : 34 Parl. Debates, 1069.   But this is certainly not the law of England.

Alien Acts, of a temporary nature, have been from time to time Alien Acts. passed, to give the Executive this power with respect to foreigners.   The earliest is 33 Geo. 3, c. 4 (1793), which was in force until the end of the war.   Another was passed in 1806, 56 Geo. 3, c. 86 ; and a third in 1848, 11 & 12 Vict. c. 20, which was limited to one year and the end of the then next session of Parliament, nor has it been again renewed.

(10) Cession of Territory by the Crown.

Has the Crown the power by its prerogative to cede British territory to a foreign power except under a treaty of peace?—No doubt ministers who improperly advise such a cession may be impeached, but impeachment is punishment, and cannot invalidate the grant. If it is part of the prerogative of the Crown to cede territory by a simple grant, without any reference to treaty, then a foreign power has the right *jure gentium* to hold the ceded territory, however improperly it may have been granted. A treaty concluded with a foreign state by the President of the United States alone, without the consent of the Senate, would not, according to the Constitution, be binding on the nation, and the foreign state would derive no rights under it; and, in like manner, it may be contended that a foreign state derives no title to British territory ceded by the Crown as a free gift in time of peace, without reference to treaty.

There is no doubt that it is part of the prerogative of the Crown to make treaties with foreign powers, and Blackstone lays down the law correctly when he says that in doing so, " whatever contracts he (the Sovereign) engages in, no other power in the kingdom can legally delay, resist, or annul." Wheaton indeed says (Internat. Law, s. 542), that in Great Britain the treaty power is " practically limited by the general controlling authority of Parliament, whose approbation is necessary to carry into effect a treaty by which the existing territorial arrangements of the empire are altered." But in the case of treaties of peace following a state of war, there is no doubt that the consent of Parliament is *not* necessary to enable the Crown to alienate part of British territory to a foreign contracting power. Kent, in his Commentaries (vol. i. p. 175, 10th ed.), says that, " the power competent to bind the nation by treaty may alienate the public domain and property by treaty." The reason of this is, that if the nation has conferred upon its supreme executive without reserve the right of making treaties, the alienation is valid because made by the reputed will of the nation.

In *Conway* v. *Gray*, 10 East, 536, the Court said: " In all questions arising between the subjects of different states, each is a party to the public authoritative acts of his own Government; and, on that account, a foreign subject is as much incapacitated from making the consequences of an act of his own state the foundation of a claim to indemnity upon a British subject in a British court of justice, as he would be if such act had been done immediately and individually by such foreign subject himself." But the authority of this case was shaken by *Flindt* v. *Scott* (in Error), 5 Taunt. 674, as explained by Thomson, C.B., in *Bazett* v. *Meyer*, *Ibid.* 829; and it was overruled by *Aubert* v. *Gray* (in Error), 32 L. J. (Q. B.) 50, where the Court said: " The assertion that the act of the Government is the act of each subject of the Government, is never really true. In representative governments it may have a partial semblance of truth, but in despotic governments it is without that semblance."

Whether the Crown has the power to alienate British territory by treaty, not following the close of a war—as, for instance, by a commercial treaty—does, I confess, seem to me to be extremely questionable. I should doubt much whether the Crown, without the authority of Parliament, would have the *legal power* to cede by treaty the Channel Islands to France, there having been no war, and the cession not being made as part of the adjustment of a quarrel between the two countries. And to show how cautiously British statesmen have acted where there was a case of novelty with regard to the exercise of the prerogative of the Crown, even as regards peace and war, I may mention that when it* was resolved, in 1782, to recognise the independence of the North American Colonies, an Act of Parliament (22 Geo. 3, c. 46) was passed authorizing the Crown to make peace with the colonies, and to repeal and make void Acts of Parliament relating to them.   I may mention also, that although, by the constitutional Charter of 1830, the King of France had the power expressly given to him to make treaties of peace, the opinions of French jurists have been that he had not the power of alienating French territory.

But where there is no treaty, the opinion of jurists seems to be strongly against the supposition of such a power residing in the sovereign, except indeed in a purely despotic form of government: see Grotius de Jure Belli et Pacis, lib. ii. c. 6, ss. 3, 4, 7, 8 ; Puffendorf, lib. viii. c. 12; Vattel, lib. i. c. 20, s. 224 ; c. 21, s. 260; Liv. 4, c. 2, s. 11 ; Phillimore, part iii. c. 14, ss. 261, 262.

In the debate in the House of Lords on the preliminary articles of peace, January, 1783 (Parl. Hist. vol. xxii. pp. 430–1), Lord Loughborough said, with reference to the cession of East Florida to Spain, that no prerogative existed in the Crown to cede without the authority of Parliament any part of the dominions of the Crown in the possession of subjects under the allegiance and at the peace of the King. He was answered by Lord Thurlow, then Lord Chancellor, who said that if this doctrine were true, he should consider himself strangely ignorant of the constitution of his country, for till the present day of novelty and miracle, he had never heard that such a doctrine existed. " The learned lord (Lord Loughborough) resorted to the lucubrations and fancies of foreign writers, and gravely referred their lordships to Swiss authors for an explanation of the prerogative of the British Crown. He (Lord Thurlow), for his own part, rejected all foreign books on the point before them. However full of ingenuity or speculation Mr. Vattel and Mr. Puffendorf might be on the law of nations, and other points which neither were nor could be fixed by any solid and permanent rule, he denied their authority—he exploded their evidence—when they were brought to explain to him what was, and what was not, the prerogative of the British Crown." But we must remember that Great Britain had been at war with Spain, and the cession of Florida was under a treaty of peace ; so that the declamatory rhetoric of Lord Thurlow proves nothing for the point we are considering, which is whether by a mere grant—not under a treaty of peace—the

Crown can by its prerogative cede part of its dominions to a foreign power.

If such a power resides in the British Crown, we may ask for proofs of its existence by acts done. The only precedent I know of (with the exception of the Orange River Territory, to be noticed hereafter), is the sale of Dunkirk by Charles II., for which Lord Clarendon was impeached, and which can hardly be considered a constitutional precedent now. It would be easy to show that the Crown before the Revolution claimed to exercise, and did in fact exercise, prerogatives which were not constitutional, and which, independently of prohibitory statutes, would now be disallowed: for instance, the claim of the Crown to levy ship-money, the legality of which was, on the authority of precedents, maintained by Attorney General Noy, and upheld by the judges, but which by the statute 16 Chas. 1, c. 14, was "declared and enacted" to be contrary to law. So the claim of the Crown to suspend or dispense with penal statutes by a non obstante, as to which Mr. Broom says, in his "Constitutional Law," p. 507 : "The current of authority serves to show that the prerogative of dispensing by non obstante with Acts of Parliament was, subject to certain restrictions, recognized in former times as vested in the Crown." But by the Bill of Rights it was "declared" that "the pretended power of dispensing with laws by regal authority is illegal." So also the grants by the Crown of the right of exclusive trading, as in the case of the East India Company and the Hudson's Bay Company. In East India Company v. Sandys, 10 State Trials, 371, 554, the grant of sole trading was held to be good ; but it is difficult to believe that, even independently of the Statute of Monopolies, such a grant would be held to be good now.

In a debate in the House of Commons, February 1863, on the question of the relinquishment by the British Crown of the protectorate of the Ionian Islands, it was contended that they were a possession of the British Crown, and Lord Palmerston was asked whether it was competent, according to the Constitution, for the Crown to alienate them without the consent of Parliament. His Lordship answered that the Republic of the Seven Islands was, by the treaty of 1815, placed under the protectorate of the British Crown, and not given as a possession to the British Crown. He said that the distinction was "manifest and radical," and added : "But with regard to cases of territory acquired by conquest during war, and not ceded by treaty, and which are not therefore British freehold, and all possessions that have been ceded by treaty and held as possessions of the British Crown, there is no question that the Crown may make a treaty alienating such possessions without the consent of the House of Commons." He then instanced the cases of Senegal, Minorca, Florida, and the island of Banca, "all of them for a greater or less period of time possessions of the British Crown, and they were all ceded by treaty to some foreign power, therefore there cannot be a question as to the competency of the Crown to make such cessions:" Hansard, Parl. Deb. vol. clxix., pp. 230-1. But all these were cases of cession made by treaty of peace at the close of a war, as to which there never was really any doubt that the Crown could do so by virtue of its prerogative. They do not touch the question of whether the Crown has the power where there has been no war, and consequently no treaty of peace.

It has, I believe, been supposed that a distinction exists between territory acquired by the Crown by conquest or cession which has not been the subject of Parliamentary legislation, and territory to which Acts of Parliament have been applied, and it has been thought that the Crown may by its prerogative cede the former but not the latter to a foreign power

In 1853, a question arose as to the abandonment by the Crown of its sovereignty over the Orange River Territory, which had been assumed by proclamation of the Governor, and under the public seal of the colony of Cape of Good Hope, in 1848. By letters patent under the great seal, dated March 1851, Her Majesty ordained and appointed that the said territory should become and be constituted a distinct government to be administered by the Governor of the Cape, and that it should thenceforth be known by the name of the Orange River Territory. In 1854, the Duke of Newcastle, who was then Secretary for the Colonies, wrote to Sir George Clerk, the Governor of the Cape, and informed him that Her Majesty's Government had come to the conclusion, that the abandonment of the Orange River sovereignty could be legally and most conveniently effected by an Order in Council and proclamation. The letters patent of March 1851 were accordingly revoked by other letters patent, and the Queen, by Order in Council, dated January 30, 1854, approved of a proclamation, whereby Her Majesty did " declare and make known the abandonment and renunciation of our dominion and sovereignty over the said territory and the inhabitants thereof :" see Correspondence on the State of the Orange River Territory, presented to Parliament, April 10, 1854.

There are two instances of cession (independently of treaty at the conclusion of a war) by the East India Company to a foreign state previously to the Indian mutiny :—

1. In 1817, a cession by *treaty*, " in full sovereignty," to the Sikhimputtee Rajah of a part of territory formerly possessed by the Rajah of Nepaul, but taken by the East India Company, and ceded to them by a treaty of peace.

2. In 1833, a cession by *treaty* to Rajah Voorunder Singh of a portion of Assam, lying on the south of the Burrampooter River, by which the Rajah bound himself, " in the administration of justice in the country now made over to him, to abstain from the practices of the former rajahs of Assam, as to cutting off ears and noses, extracting eyes, or otherwise mutilating or torturing:" Treaties, Engagements, and Sunnuds, vol. i. p. 132.

This is not a very satisfactory precedent, and it shows the kind of risks to which British subjects might be liable in being transferred to a semi-barbarous power. But I may add that in that case the Rajah agreed to pay a large annual tribute, so that he became a sort of feudatory of the Company. Since the mutiny there have been several instances of cession of territory in India by grants, as rewards to native chiefs for fidelity to the British Government. And as to these it may be said that Indian necessities are peculiar, and cannot be judged of by European precedents. It is not, as generally with us, a foreign enemy, but it is the hostility and disaffection of the native population, a population enormously outnumbering the English, which may produce dangers quite as imminent and urgent, during apparent peace, as a foreign European war, and it may be urged that European precedents cannot be strictly applied to a state of things wholly different. It is right also to mention that boundary treaties have been made by the Crown without the authority of Parliament, and those treaties have in effect altered the nationality of territory to a certain extent, as in the case of the Washington Treaty in 1842, and the Oregon Treaty in 1846.

If cessions of territory by mere grant are valid, what becomes of the allegiance of the inhabitants? The rule of Roman law is thus stated by Cicero : " Jure enim nostro neque mutare civitatem quisquam *invitus* potest, neque si velit, mutare non potest, modo adsciscatur ab eâ civitate, cujus esse se civitatis velit:" *pro* Balbo, 11. It seems to be clear that the Crown cannot by its prerogative alone release subjects from their allegiance, nor *e converso* deprive them of the rights of British subjects. In the despatch of the Duke of Newcastle to which I have already referred, his Grace said : " With respect to the allegiance of the inhabitants who may have been born in British dominions either within or without the sovereignty, there is, I believe, little doubt that no measure resting on the Queen's prerogative only for its authority, could release them from the tie of such native allegiance. An Act of Parliament would be required for such a purpose. But, for the reasons already adverted to in my despatch of November 14 last, I do not consider it necessary to apply to Parliament on this ground. It is probable that the inhabitants of the future commonwealth would generally prefer to retain the rights of British subjects rather than become wholly aliens, and subject to the ordinary incapacity of aliens within Her Majesty's dominions." This part of the subject, however, will be more fully considered in the chapter on Allegiance, *post.*

(11) Erection of Courts of Justice.

" It is a settled constitutional principle or rule of law, that although the Crown may, by its prerogative, establish courts to proceed according to the common law, yet it cannot create any new court to administer any other law ; and it is laid down by Lord Coke, in the 4th Institute, that the erection of a new court with a new jurisdiction cannot be without an Act of Parliament :" *In re Lord Bishop of Natal,* 3 Moore, P. C. (N. S.) 152. The Crown, by its prerogative, may make what courts for the administration of the common law, and in what places, it pleases : Com. Dig. *Prerog.* D. 28. But the Crown cannot erect a Court of Chancery or Conscience, for the common law is the inheritance of the subject : *Ibid.* The erection of a new court with a *new jurisdiction* cannot be without an Act of Parliament : 4 Inst. 200. The Crown cannot grant to a court that it may proceed according to the civil law :

2 Rush. App. 77; nor can it by charter or commission alter the common law : *Ibid.* The Crown cannot give any addition of jurisdiction to an ancient court, and hence the Court of Queen's Bench could not, by virtue of the prerogative alone, have been authorized to determine a mere real action between subject and subject ; " so neither can the Court of Common Pleas, to inquire of treason or felony :" Bacon's Abr. *Courts.*

It is usual when courts of justice are established in the foreign possessions of the Crown to obtain the authority of an Act of Parliament empowering the Crown to establish them by letters patent or charter. George II., by letters patent dated January 18, 1753, granted to the East India Company his royal charter constituting and establishing courts of civil, criminal, and ecclesiastical jurisdiction at Bombay and Calcutta (1); but afterwards, in 1773, by statute 13 Geo. 3, c. 63, s. 13, it was enacted that it might be lawful for the Crown, by charter or letters patent under the great seal, to erect a Supreme Court of Judicature at Fort William (Calcutta), with power and authority to exercise civil, criminal, admiralty, and ecclesiastical jurisdiction. A charter was accordingly granted by the Crown, dated March 26, 1774, whereby a Supreme Court of Judicature was established at Fort William. In 1800, by statute 39 & 40 Geo. 3, c. 79, the Crown was similarly empowered to erect a Supreme Court of Judicature at Madras, under which a charter was granted for that purpose, dated December 26, 1800. And in 1823, by statute 4 Geo. 4, c. 71, the Crown was similarly empowered to erect a Supreme Court of Judicature at Bombay, under which a charter was granted, bearing date December 8, 1823. In 1861 an Act was passed, 24 & 25 Vict. c. 104, empowering the Crown, by letters patent under the great seal, to erect High Courts of Judicature at Fort William, Madras, and Bombay, and also in any portion of the territories within Her Majesty's dominions in India not included within the limits of the local jurisdiction of another High Court. Under this Act letters patent were granted, bearing date respectively, December 28, 1865, by which High Courts were established at Fort William, Madras, and Bombay ; and by other letters patent, dated March 17, 1866, a High Court was established for the North-western Provinces of the Presidency of Fort William.

The County Courts were established by statute 9 & 10 Vict. c. 95, and were thereby made courts of record, but their proceedings differ from those of the courts of common law : *Breese* v. *Owens,* 6 Ex. 419. Courts of quarter sessions are courts of oyer and terminer, and not inferior courts : *Campbell* v. *The Queen,* 11 Q. B. 841 ; *R.* v. *Smith,* 8 B. & C. 342–3.

Although it is not strictly relevant to the subject of this note, I may quote a useful dictum of Lord Abinger, C.B., in *Jewison* v. *Dyson,* 9 M. & W. 586, that "every person who administers a public duty has a right to preserve order in the place where it is administered, and to turn out any person who is found there for improper purposes."

(1) There was an older charter, in 1726, constituting Mayors' Courts at Calcutta, Madras, and Bombay; but this charter was surrendered, and a fresh charter granted in 1753, reconstituting the Mayors' Courts.

CHAPTER VI.

ON MARTIAL LAW AND COURTS MARTIAL.

(1.) JOINT OPINION *of the Attorney and Solicitor General,*
SIR ROBERT HENLEY *and* HON. CHARLES YORKE, *as to how
far the proclamation of Martial Law suspends the functions of
the Council.* 1757.

To the Right Honourable the Lords Commissioners for Trade and
Plantations.

MAY IT PLEASE YOUR LORDSHIPS,—In pursuance of your Lordships' commands, signified to us by Mr. Pownall, in his letter of the
22nd instant, acquainting us that your Lordships had received two
letters from Henry Moore, Esq., Lieutenant-Governor of Jamaica,
informing your Lordships that he had, in consequence of advices
which he had received of an intended invasion of that island, caused
martial law to be proclaimed; and that his Majesty's Council, upon
being summoned to meet in their legislative capacity, had refused
to do any business, alleging that neither they nor the Assembly
had any right to sit or transact business after the publication of
martial law; and also transmitting to us copies of the Lieutenant-
Governor's letters and two other papers, containing the reasons
assigned by the Council for their opinion, and their answers to
several questions propounded to them by the Lieutenant-Governor,
and desiring us to take the same into our consideration, and report
to your Lordships our opinion thereon: we have taken the same
into our consideration, and are of opinion that there is no foundation for the notion of the Council, that the proclaiming of martial
law suspends the execution of the legislative authority, which may
and ought to continue to act as long as the public exigencies
require.

Nor do we apprehend that by such proclamation of martial law, the ordinary course of law and justice is suspended or stopped, any further than is absolutely necessary to answer the then military service of the public and the exigencies of the province.

January 28, 1757.   ·   ROBT. HENLEY.
                                   C. YORKE.

(2.) OPINION *of* MR. HARGRAVE *on an Irish case involving the question of Martial Law* (1).

I have perused the several papers laid before me in the case of the high treason attainder of Mr. Cornelius Grogan after his death, by the Irish Act of October 6, 1798, which included Lord Edward Fitzgerald and Mr. Beauchamp Bagnel Harvey.

But previously to attempting the draft of a reversal bill, it is necessary that it should be fixed upon what principle the bill should be framed.

There are two ways of putting the case in the proposed bill of reversal.

One is, representing that Mr. Cornelius Grogan was under compulsion from the rebels, and so was free from all crime; and that the Irish Parliament was in great measure misled into a supposition of his guilt by his having been put to death on the judgment of a court of officers acting under what was conceived to be *martial law*. Looking to the case in this point of view, the minutes of the evidence before the Committee of the House of Commons in Ireland, appear to me to present a very strong case in favour of considering Mr. Cornelius Grogan as having acted under compulsion. I am impressed also that his having been tried and put to death, under a proceeding called *martial law*, so far from being ground for inducing an Act *for attainting him after his death*, should have operated in preventing such an *extraordinary* rigour. I so express myself because that extremity was resorted to against him previously to the Irish statute, made in the 39th of his present Majesty, for suppression of the rebellion in Ireland; and so, as I conceive, was applied when the doctrine, attributing to the Crown in time of rebellion a prerogative right of authorizing the trial of arrested rebels before a court-martial and by martial law, and the punish-

(1) Jurisconsult Exercitations, i. 401.

ment of them, by death or otherwise, as to the members of such court-martial should seem meet, had not, as I apprehend, received legislative sanction even in Ireland. Had I been consulted before the passing of that Act, I should have deemed it fully open to me, to express at least a doubt whether the prerogative of claiming and exercising martial law in time of actual invasion by a foreign enemy, or in time of actual rebellion, was not merely referable to the law for governing the royal army and all connected with it—that is, for governing those employed in defending the country against invasion, and in suppressing rebellion. I should have deemed it fully open to me to express at least a doubt—whether, under martial law, to try persons seized in rebellion, or seized upon suspicion of being rebels, before a court-martial constituted by the King's authority, and to punish them by death or otherwise, at the discretion of the members of such a court, was not an extension of martial law beyond its real object; and being so, was not an infringement of the law of England in a point of the most serious kind. But the Irish Act of the 39th of the present King, for suppression of the Irish rebellion, makes a vast difference; for in effect it contains recitals which not only recognized a royal prerogative of authorizing the trial and punishment of rebels by martial law, in the very harsh latitude I have already mentioned, but expressly authorized such application of martial law by new provisions for that purpose; and this Act, which was temporary, was afterwards continued for a further time by a subsequent Irish Act, and since the Union of Great Britain and Ireland, has been further continued with some amendments by Acts of the Parliament of the United Kingdom, the first of which is the 41st of the present King, chapter 15. With these statutes before me, I am forced to resist any contrary impressions I may have as to the real boundary of martial law. However, too, from previously settled notions, I may see these statutes as amounting to a melancholy change, first most unhappily generated in the code of Irish legislation by the heated atmosphere of civil convulsions in Ireland, and then insensibly, as it seems, insinuated into a code of English law through statutes of the United Kingdom of Great Britain and Ireland, not so much as stating the terrible prerogative I point at, but engrafting it by continuing Irish statutes, which, being mentioned by the

title only, are probably at this moment little known even to prac-
tising lawyers in England; yet to such high authority I must
succumb! [The rest of the opinion is not material.]

The foregoing Opinion, as published by Mr. Hargrave, in his "Jurisconsult Exercitations," is prefaced by the following remarks :—

The following small article includes, in some degree, matter of
very high importance, which, though of great notoriety in Ireland,
where the transaction occurred, is not so generally known amongst
us in England. It relates to the case of Mr. Cornelius Grogan, an
Irish gentleman of large fortune in the county of Wexford, who,
during the horrid rebellion in that part of Ireland in the year
1798, was taken up for high treason, under the circumstance of
there having been a previous proclamation authorizing martial
law, in aiding the rebels, and was tried by a court of officers, and
being found guilty, was put to death on the judgment of that
court; and was, shortly after his death, attainted of high treason
by Act of the Irish Parliament. Upon the case thus generally
stated, with a view to the trial of rebels by *martial* law, it is proper
to add that in 1799 an Irish Act of Parliament was passed, which
in *effect* appears to recognize that it is a part of the royal *prerogative* during the time of rebellion to authorize the King's general
and other commanding officers to *punish* REBELS *according to
martial law, by death or otherwise, as to them shall seem expedient.*
That an Act of Parliament may, for more effectually suppressing
rebellion, so extend trial by *martial law,* and so also give to generals
and other commanding officers a discretion of punishing rebels
found guilty upon such trial, either with *death,* or *indefinitely in
any other way,* is not to be doubted ; for when such an Act is passed,
though judges or others should ever so strongly feel either its
incongruity with the principles of our law, or its harsh latitude
otherwise, the Act must operate till it shall be revoked by the
same high authority as engrafts it upon the law of England. But
the question which forced itself, in a great degree, upon the
author's mind, when he was called upon professionally to write
opinions in answer to those who consulted him for the purpose of
seeking a repeal of the Grogan attainder, was whether, independently of the express warrant of an Act of Parliament, and on the
mere ground of *prerogative* power, authority could be given against

persons taken into custody for high treason during the heat of
rebellion, to try them by martial law for their offence, and to
punish them, either by death or in any other way, at the discretion
of the court-martial so trying them. Looking at that question,
he could not forbear avowing how his mind was affected. But he
so avowed himself under a conviction that *martial law* to such an
extent was not the law of England without an express Act of
Parliament. He saw the right of putting rebels to death in battle
while the battle lasted. He also saw the right to arrest those found
in actual rebellion or duly charged with being traitors, and to have
them imprisoned for trial and punishment, according to the law of
treason. But he could not see that trying and punishing rebels
according to martial law was, when Mr. Grogan was tried and put
to death, part of the English law as it was administrable in England, or even as it was administrable in Ireland. On the contrary,
he saw such a prerogative doctrine to be unconsonant with several
recitals and one enactment in that grand Act-of Parliament, the
Petition of Right in the 16th of Charles I. He saw it also to be
irreconcileable with the opinions declared by some of the greatest
lawyers of that time to a committee of the whole House of Commons sitting on martial law: namely, Sir Edward Coke, Mr. Noy
(afterwards Attorney General), Mr. Rolle (afterwards Serjeant-at-
Law, and author of the "Abridgement"), Mr. Banks (afterwards successively Attorney General and Lord Chief Justice of the Common
Pleas), and Mr. Mason, distinguished both as a lawyer and member
of Parliament; for which opinions the author begs leave to refer
to the preservation of them in the Appendix to Rushworth's third
volume. Further, the author found such a latitude of martial
law equally crossed by the doctrines of Lord Chief Justice Hale,
as expressed in his manuscripts and unprinted collections on the
prerogative. This the author trusts will, without for the present
looking further, sufficiently at least apologize for the strong terms
used in those parts of his following Opinion on the Grogan case
which relate to martial law, even though volumes of cruel and
irregular practice during the sad extremities of civil war should be
laboriously collected, to overcome the passing of the Petition of
Right, and of the high, grave legal authorities the author inclusively relies upon as speaking the same language.

(3.) *On Naval Courts Martial and Admiralty Jurisdiction* (1).

The first statute that gave power to admirals to exercise martial law at sea is an Act of 15 Ric. 2, where the admiral is empowered to arrest flotes for the public service, and shall have jurisdiction upon the said flotes during the said voyage only.

I should suppose that in virtue of this statute, the admirals made and executed ordinances for the good government of the fleet, which probably was the original foundation of the Articles of War.

Afterwards these powers were given occasionally by patent under the great seal, which was only a temporary power; though in these patents all crimes whatsoever, including high treason, were allowed to be tried by courts martial under the admiral.

By an ordinance of Edward III., anno 1348, the King gives power to the captain or general of his galleys to try all crimes, felonies, and transgressions by sea and land.

By a special commission from Charles I., in 1627, the Duke of Buckingham, then Lord High Admiral, is vested with full power in the fleet and army, to call a martial court and proceed according to the justice of martial law against soldiers and marines and other dissolute persons.

In the same reign, anno 1637, there is a special commission to the Earl of Warwick, who was going with a fleet to the West Indies, by which he is empowered, during the service, "to punish all offenders for treason, murder, or any notable mutiny, with loss of life, or otherwise, after the form or order of martial law, in such sort and manner as is commonly used and accustomed in our armies by land, and in our fleets and navies by sea."

In the same reign, in the year 1639, the Earl of Northumberland has also a commission under the great seal to hold courts martial or military courts, or direct them to be held by his deputies, to hear, examine, and determine and punish, all capital and criminal offences whatever; and all lesser crimes are to be punished by him or his deputies, at their discretion, according to the usage in the King's armies at sea and land.

It would seem, however, that when these special commissions

(1) From a M. S. in the possession of Sir Travers Twiss, Queen's Advocate, which formerly belonged to Sir James Marriott, King's Advocate. No date.

were not in force, capital crimes committed at sea were tried at the common law courts.

In the instructions from the Duke of York, then Lord High Admiral, to Sir John Mennes, Commander-in-Chief in the narrow seas, he is directed, if any seaman or other shall commit murder or manslaughter, that he shall send him in safe custody to the next gaol, to be there kept until he shall have his trial according to law.

In the time of the Commonwealth, if any capital crime was committed on board a man-of-war, the offender was sent to the next gaol, to receive his trial according to common law, as above-mentioned; but it is remarkable, that though, in the instructions given by the Committee of the Lords and Commons for the Admiralty in the year 1647, it is directed, as above, that criminals for murder or manslaughter should be sent to the next gaol till delivered by due course of law, in a subsequent order, in the year 1653, signed by Moncke and Penn, styling themselves Admirals and Generals of the fleet sent forth by the Parliament of the Commonwealth of England, that "the chief flag or commander of each squadron, with the assistance of his council of war, do fully determine, sentence, and punish all offences committed against any and every of the Articles of War and ordinances of the sea, provided that no execution or loss of life do proceed until we, the Generals, be made acquainted therewith."

In this state this matter seems to have remained till the 13th of Charles II., which brought the naval usages and ordinances into the form of a statute.

(4.) OPINION *of the Attorney General,* SIR JOHN S. COPLEY, *on the authority of the Military to take away life in suppression of a Riot in the Island of Barbadoes.*

Lincoln's Inn, January 18, 1824.

MY LORD,—I have had the honour to receive your Lordship's letter, dated the 6th instant, transmitting to me therewith a letter from Governor Sir Henry Warde, dated Barbadoes, the 4th of November last, together with a memorial from the Council of that island, requesting the opinion of the Law Officers of the Crown upon the question therein stated, viz.: " Whether there is any statute, passed before the settlement of that island in the year 1625, which authorizes the military, acting under the magistrate for the suppression of a riot, to take the life of rioters, if such a measure should be necessary, and, if not, is such a proceeding sanctioned by the common law of England?"

Your Lordship also enclosed despatches from the Governor, reporting the occurrences which had lately taken place in the island, and which had given rise to the present application. And your Lordship was pleased to state that you had received his Majesty's commands to desire that I would take the papers into consideration, and report to your Lordship as speedily as possible, for his Majesty's information, what instructions it might, in my opinion, be proper to transmit to the Governor upon the case stated.

In obedience to the commands of his Majesty, I have taken the papers as speedily as possible into my consideration, and beg leave to report to your Lordship that there is no statute passed before the settlement of the island of Barbadoes in the year 1625, and now in force, of the nature above alluded to; but by the common law the military may effectively act under the direction of the civil power in the suppression of riots. The late Chief Justice Mansfield, in the case of *Burdett* v. *Abbott*, in the Exchequer Chamber (4 Taunt. Rep. p. 449), in speaking upon this subject, observes that a "strange mistaken notion had got abroad, that because men were soldiers they ceased to be citizens. A soldier (he adds) is gifted with all the rights of other citizens, and is bound to all the duties of other citizens, and he is as much bound to prevent a breach of the peace or a felony as any other citizen. This notion is the more extraordinary, because formerly the *posse comitatus*, which was the strength to prevent felonies, must in a great proportion have consisted of military tenants who held lands by the tenure of military service. If it is necessary for the purpose of preventing mischief, or for the execution of the law, it is not only the right of soldiers, but it is their duty, to exert themselves in assisting the execution of a legal process, or to prevent any crime or mischief being committed. It is therefore highly important that the mistake should be corrected which supposes that an Englishman, by taking upon him the additional character

o 2

of a soldier, puts off any of the rights and duties of an Englishman." Soldiers, when called upon and required to aid the civil
magistrate in apprehending or opposing persons engaged in a riot,
will be justified in using the force necessary for that purpose; any
excess will be illegal, and for such excess the soldier, as well as
the mere citizen, will be responsible. In this respect the law as
applicable to both classes is the same. If, in executing the commands of the magistrate, opposition is made by the rioters, force
· may be opposed to force; but the same rule still applies, viz., that
the extent of the force used must be regulated by the necessity of
the occasion. The excess only is illegal. If the military, in obeying the lawful commands of the magistrate, be so assailed that
resistance cannot be effectually made without sacrificing the lives
of the rioters, they would in law be justified in so doing. It is
obvious, therefore, that each case must depend upon its own circumstances, and the only rule that can be given is that the force,
to be legal and justifiable, must in every instance, as far as the
infirmity of human passion will admit, be governed by what the
necessity of the particular occasion may require.

I beg leave to suggest that it will be proper to direct the
Governor to take especial care that a magistrate be present when
the military are called out for the purpose of suppressing a riot,
and that they act in his aid and by his command. Temper and
coolness upon such occasions, and forbearance as far as it can be
exercised consistently with the public safety, cannot be too strongly
recommended.

To Earl Bathurst,   J. S. COPLEY.
&c. &c. &c.

(5.) OPINION *of the Judge Advocate General,* SIR JOHN
BECKETT, *on a trial by Court Martial during the existence of
Martial Law in Demerara.*

Downing Street, February 10, 1824.

My LORD,—I have the honour to acknowledge the receipt of
your Lordship's letter of the 5th instant, transmitting to me the
report of certain proceedings against John Smith, of the London
Missionary Society, at a General Court Martial recently held in
Demerara, during the time that it was deemed necessary to place

that colony under martial law; and requesting that I would report to your Lordship, with all convenient despatch, for his Majesty's information, my opinion as to whether the proceedings referred to have been conducted with a due regard to every essential form of military law.

In compliance with your Lordship's request, I beg leave to report to your Lordship, for his Majesty's information, that the proceedings in question against John Smith appear to me to have been conducted, by the Court appointed to try him, with a due regard to every essential form of military law.

I think it right at the same time to make the following observation to your Lordship respecting two of the members of the Court.

On referring to the names of the several individuals who composed it, two of them are described as officers of the *militia there*— viz., the President, Lieutenant-Colonel Goodman, who is described as " half-pay 48th Regiment, and commandant of the Georgetown brigade of *militia*," and Lieutenant-Colonel Wray, who is described as " of the *militia staff*."

If *these* proceedings had taken place upon the *trial of an officer or soldier of the King's forces in the ordinary way*, under the provisions of the Mutiny Act and Articles of War, the forms required to be observed thereby would not appear to have been duly regarded, inasmuch as it is provided, by the 6th article of the 16th section of the Articles of War, that " no officer serving in the militia shall sit in any court martial upon the trial of any officer or soldier serving in any of our other forces; nor shall any officer in our other forces sit in any court martial upon the trial of any officer or soldier serving in the militia."

I am aware, of course, that martial law, as stated in your Lordship's letter of reference, was in force when the trial of John Smith took place in Demerara; nevertheless the terms of your Lordship's reference to me seem to require, that the circumstances above mentioned should be brought under your Lordship's notice.

The Earl Bathurst,   J. BECKETT.
    &c. &c. &c.

(6.) JOINT OPINION *of the Attorney and Solicitor General,*
SIR JOHN CAMPBELL *and* SIR R. M. ROLFE, *as to the power
of the Governor of Canada to proclaim Martial Law.*

Temple, January 16, 1838.

MY LORD,—We have to acknowledge the receipt of a letter from
your Lordship of yesterday's date, together with the copy of a letter
addressed by the Earl of Gosford to the Attorney and Solicitor
General of Lower Canada, and their reply, on the subject of the
power vested in the Governor of that province to proclaim martial
law : your Lordship desires that we should take these papers into our
consideration, and report to your Lordship our joint opinion whether
the views expressed by the Law Officers of the Crown in Lower
Canada are correct in point of law.   We have now the honour of
reporting to your Lordship that in our opinion the Governor of
Lower Canada has the power of proclaiming, in any district in
which large bodies of the inhabitants are in open rebellion, that
the Executive Government will proceed to enforce martial law.   We
must, however, add that in our opinion such proclamation confers
no power on the Governor which he would not have possessed
without it.   The object of it can only be to give notice to the inhabitants of the course which the Government is obliged to adopt
for the purpose of restoring tranquillity.   In any district in which,
by reason of armed bodies of the inhabitants being engaged in
insurrection, the ordinary course of law cannot be maintained, we
are of opinion that the Governor may, even without any proclamation, proceed to put down the rebellion by force of arms, as in case
of foreign invasion, and for that purpose may lawfully put to death
all persons engaged in the work of resistance ; and this, as we conceive, is all that is meant by the language of the statutes referred
to in the report of the Attorney and Solicitor General for Lower
Canada, when they allude to the "*undoubted prerogative of His
Majesty for the public safety to resort to the exercise of martial law
against open enemies or traitors.*"

The right of resorting to such an extremity is a right arising
from and limited by the necessity of the case—*quod necessitas cogit,
defendit.*   For this reason we are of opinion that the prerogative
does not extend beyond the case of persons taken in open resistance,
and with whom, by reason of the suspension of the ordinary tribu-

nals, it is impossible to deal according to the regular course of justice. When the regular courts are open, so that criminals might be delivered over to them to be dealt with according to law, there is not, as we conceive, any right in the Crown to adopt any other course of proceeding. Such power can only be conferred by the Legislature, as was done by the Acts passed in consequence of the Irish rebellions of 1798 and 1803, and also of the Irish Coercion Act of 1833.

From the foregoing observations, your Lordship will perceive that the question, how far martial law, when in force, supersedes the ordinary tribunals, can never, in our view of the case, arise. Martial law is stated by Lord Hale to be in truth no law, but something rather indulged than allowed as a law, and it can only be tolerated because, by reason of open rebellion, the enforcing of any other law has become impossible. It cannot be said in strictness to *supersede* the ordinary tribunals, inasmuch as it only exists by reason of those tribunals having been already practically superseded.

It is hardly necessary for us to add that, in our view of the case, martial law can never be enforced for the ordinary purposes of civil or even criminal justice, except, in the latter, so far as the necessity arising from actual resistance compels its adoption.

The Lord Glenelg,   J. CAMPBELL.
    &c. &c. &c.   R. M. ROLFE.

(7). JOINT OPINION *of the Queen's Advocate*, SIR JOHN DODSON, *and the Attorney and Solicitor General*, SIR JOHN CAMPBELL *and* SIR R. M. ROLFE, *on the liability of Foreigners invading Her Majesty's dominions to suffer the penalties of High Treason ; and on Martial Law.*

Doctors' Commons, August 21, 1838.

MY LORD,—We are honoured with your Lordship's commands, signified in your Lordship's letter of the 11th instant, with reference to your Lordship's letters mentioned in the margin, and to our answers of the 28th and 31st of May and 7th of June last, and transmitting therewith copies of two letters addressed to the Lieutenant-Governor of Upper Canada by the Chief Justice and the Law Officers of that province, controverting the opinions expressed by us as to the liability of foreigners invading Her Majesty's territories to suffer the penalties of high treason in the same manner as any of Her Majesty's natural-born subjects, or as aliens domiciled within the British dominions: your Lordship is pleased to request that we would take these documents into our consideration, and report to your Lordship whether we see any reason to retract or qualify the joint opinions which we formerly expressed on this subject. Should we continue to adhere to our former opinion, your Lordship is pleased to request that we would state the grounds of that opinion at length, for the information of the Judges and Law Officers of the Crown in Upper Canada.

In obedience to your Lordship's commands, we have the honour to report that, after a most attentive and respectful consideration of the objections of the legal functionaries in Canada, and an anxious reference to all the authorities to be found in the English law-books, we see no reason to retract or qualify the opinions we have before expressed on this subject.

We continue to think that an alien, a native of a State at peace with our Queen, and not in the service of a State at war with our Queen, who levies war against the Queen within her dominions, is liable to be tried for high treason, although he entered her dominions in a hostile manner. Treason certainly consists in the breach of allegiance, and where no allegiance is due there can be no treason. For this reason an alien enemy cannot be tried for treason, for while in arms within the British territory he owes allegiance only to his own Sovereign; and, while observing the laws of war, he is fully justified in any act of hostility which he may commit. But we conceive that an alien *amy* does owe allegiance to the Queen within her dominions, and both according to the technical form of an indictment for treason, and on principle, the question is, whether allegiance is *due* from him?—whether he owes obedience to the law of the territory which he has entered? The obligation of allegiance does not arise from the protection which, *de facto*, he has enjoyed, but from the protection to which he was entitled, and which he might have enjoyed if he had thought fit.

An alien enemy occupies a portion of the British territory, as the territory of his own Sovereign; the laws of his own country are supposed to prevail there as far as he is concerned, and he owes exclusive and undivided allegiance to his own Sovereign. If he is captured he is to be treated as a prisoner of war; he can in no shape be tried as an offender for any act of hostility in which he may have participated.

An alien *amy* is subject to the law of the country where he is, and he cannot be permitted, without authority from his own or any foreign Government, to absolve himself from this obligation by saying that he entered the country as an enemy.

He cannot claim to be treated as a prisoner of war, or to be ransomed or exchanged.

If he may not be tried for treason, he is guilty of no offence whatever; he is entitled to demand his immediate discharge, and, enjoying entire impunity, he may again repeat his hostile acts without any apprehension of punishment at any time before he has once submitted himself peaceably to the law of the country, and voluntarily sought its protection.

For hostilely invading a country to assist rebels and bring about a revolution he could not be tried for piracy; and if he were to kill an English soldier in action, we apprehend that he could not be tried for murder if he is not liable to be tried for treason.

In the old law-books there is much said about *martial law;* but in such a case as the present, this would afford no remedy. Martial law is merely a cessation from necessity of all municipal law, and what necessity requires it justifies. An alien *amy* hostilely invading the English territory while in arms, might lawfully be put to death, and when taken prisoner, if his immediate execution were necessary to the suppression of insurrection, he might be executed immediately, without any reference to municipal law. But the insurrection being quelled and tranquillity restored, and the ordinary tribunals proceeding regularly in the administration of justice, an alien *amy* who had been taken in arms could not be lawfully put to death, either with or without the form of being tried by a court-martial, and all who should take part in such an execution would be guilty of murder.

We think that the alien *amy* is liable to be tried for treason, in the same manner as if he were a native-born subject. Although he might have been put to death in a summary manner *flagrante bello,* he cannot complain that such a right is waived, and that he

is reserved to take his trial, as if he had been born within the
allegiance of the British Crown.

The case we have been considering is clearly distinguishable from
that of a foreigner assisting in a civil war.   Where an insurrection
against a Government has become so formidable as to assume the
aspect of an equally-balanced civil war, the laws of war are to be
observed between the Government and the insurgents ; and native-
born subjects taken prisoners could not properly be tried as traitors.
Even were the alien *amy* in the ranks of the insurgents, he would
be dealt with as a native-born subject.

But let us put the case of Her Majesty being at Brighton, and a
Frenchman landing from the opposite coast, instantly firing, or
preparing to fire, a pistol at her.   Were he tried for treason in
compassing the Queen's death, *contra ligeantiæ suæ debitum*, would
it be any defence to him that he had loaded the pistol at Calais,
that he had cocked it a league from the shore, and that he came
to England for the express purpose of putting the Queen to death ?

The conviction of an alien *amy* for treason, under such circumstances, would, we conceive, be in no respect contrary to the law
of nations, and could afford no ground of complaint to his own
Government.   Any State might pass a law enacting that if a
foreigner, the native of a friendly country, should within its territories attempt the life of the Sovereign, or levy war against him
within his dominions, the foreigner should be deemed guilty of a
capital offence, although he came for the express purpose of committing it.   Therefore if the Canadian Courts should hold the
associates of Sheller, who are American citizens, guilty of treason,
the Government of the United States could not complain or interfere.

The reasons for holding that an alien *amy* is liable to be tried
for treason, though entering the British territory with a hostile intent, appear to us so strong that they must prevail, unless there
be some decisive authorities in the books to the contrary.   But
the authorities when properly considered appear to us strongly to
support the view we have taken.

In Brooke's " Abridgment," a work of great authority, is the
following passage :—" Nota q̄ si alien nee de pays q̄ est in amitie
et peace ove cest realme veigne en le realme ove traitors Anglois

et leve guerre, c'est treason in touts, cont si le pays l' alien fuit in guerre vers Angliterre, quar dovques lalieu poet este occide: p. martial ley :" see title "Treason," 32.

In the case of Perkin Warbeck, referred to by Lord Coke in *Calvin's Case* (7 Rep. p. 6), it is said that he (Warbeck), being an alien, could not be tried by the common law, but before the constable and marshal who had special commission to hear and determine the same according to martial law. The judgment, however, was that he (Warbeck) should be hanged, drawn, and quartered, which is the judgment in treason; and Lord Bacon, in his " Life of Henry VII.," expressly says that Warbeck was executed for the *treasons* committed by him in this realm, so that the distinction seems to have been in the mode of trial, and not in the nature of the offence.

But the decisive authority in point is that of Shirley, a Frenchman, who was tried, convicted, and attainted of treason in 1557. The narrative of the facts is to be found in 3 Hollingshed, p. 1133, Stow, p. 630, and Godwin's Annals, p. 325. It appears from these writers that one of the sons of Lord Stafford collected in France a body of men, consisting partly of English fugitives, and partly of foreigners, and with this force invaded England, assuming the title of Protector, and succeeded in taking Scarborough Castle. This rebellion was soon put down, and several of the party (including Shirley) were taken; Shirley was thereupon indicted for high treason, and was tried and convicted, and had judgment of treason. A question arose as to the mode of trial in this case, which is to be found in the Reports of Chief Justice Dyer, p. 144, A., and towards the end of the report is this passage: " And note in the case above the indictment *was against the duty of his allegiance*, when he was not a subject of the realm, but that is of no signification. In this time of peace between England and France, to levy war with other English rebels was sufficient treason, and if it were in time of war he should not be arraigned, but ransomed."

This doctrine was recognized by the Parliament in the case of the Duke of Hamilton in 1649 (see State Trials, vol. iv. p. 1182), but, considering the state of things when that trial took place, we should not feel justified in placing much reliance on what was then done.

We are aware that Hawkins, in his "Pleas of the Crown," has a passage in his chapter on High Treason, which is opposed to the view we take of this subject. He says, in section 6 of that chapter: "But it seemeth that aliens who in a hostile manner invade the kingdom, whether their King were at war or peace with ours, and whether they come by themselves, or in company with English traitors, cannot be punished as traitors, but shall be dealt with by martial law;" and a similar doctrine is laid down in 5 Bacon's "Abridgment," p. 112. The authority of Hawkins is certainly very high, but it must be observed he speaks with evident distrust of what he is stating, and he refers to no authorities, except those we have already mentioned, and a passage in the 3rd Institute, which clearly does not warrant him in the doctrine he lays down.

We, for these reasons, cannot but adhere to the opinion we have already expressed. · We feel, however, that the scruples of the legal authorities of Upper Canada are entitled to great respect, and would therefore suggest that any cases of foreigners coming within the recent local statute of that province, should be tried by a court-martial as thereby directed, rather than as for treason by common law. That statute authorizes the court to award the punishment of death, or any milder punishment, and therefore secures all which could be done on a conviction for treason.

J. DODSON.

To the Right Hon. the Lord Glenelg,   J. CAMPBELL.

&c. &c. &c.   R. M. ROLFE.

(8.) JOINT OPINION *of the Attorney and Solicitor General,* SIR JOHN CAMPBELL *and* SIR R. M. ROLFE, *on the establishment of a Court in Canada for the trial of offences committed during an Insurrection in which Martial Law had been proclaimed.*

Temple, January 22, 1839.

MY LORD,—We have had the honour to receive your Lordship's letter of the 19th instant, transmitting to us the copy of a confidential despatch from Sir John Colborne respecting the measures which he had taken for the establishment of a court for the trial of offences committed during the late insurrection, the proceedings of that court, and his intention to allow the execution of two of the

persons who had been sentenced to death ; and, with reference to
the ordinance of the Governor and Special Council of Lower Canada,
2 Vict. c. 3, desiring us to take Sir John Colborne's despatch into
consideration, and to report to your Lordship our opinion, whether
the opinion entertained by the Solicitor General of Lower Canada,
of the incompetency of the Court established under the ordinance
in question to try prisoners under the charge of treason, rests on
any valid foundation.

Unfortunately we are not informed of the reasons which have
induced the Solicitor General of Lower Canada to come to this
opinion; but we have given the subject the most deliberate consideration, and we have to report to your Lordship that in our
opinion the Court established under the ordinance in question is
competent to try prisoners under the charge of treason.

We adhere to the opinion we have repeatedly expressed, that the
Special Council established in Lower Canada by 1 Vict. c. 9 is not
restrained from passing ordinances which may alter the criminal
law in Canada, and make it different from the criminal law of
England as it existed at the passing of the Canada Act, 14 Geo. 3.
We conceive that the power of the Special Council to legislate
respecting criminal law and the administration of it in Lower
Canada is supreme, as was the power of the former Legislature of
Lower Canada before it was suspended.   If this be so, it is impossible to make any distinction in point of law between an ordinance
altering the mode of trial of common assaults, and subjecting them
to the summary jurisdiction of a magistrate instead of being referred to a jury, and an ordinance altering the mode of trial in cases
of treason, and enacting that instead of a jury they shall be tried
by a court-martial.   In 1 Vict. c. 9 there is no exception with
regard to treason, and the mode of trying it may be altered as
much as of any other offence.

It has been said by Lord Denman that any ordinance of the
Special Council contrary to the first principles of equity and justice
is void; but this doctrine does not proceed upon any express restriction upon its powers, and must be equally applied to the acts
of any supreme legislature.   That the mode of trial prescribed by
the ordinance 2 Vict. c. 3 is such as cannot lawfully be prescribed
by a supreme legislature, it is impossible for anyone to contend in

a British court of justice after the late Irish Coercion Act, and various other Acts to be found in the Statute Book of the United Kingdom.

If necessity will justify what is called martial law by proclamation (which is a cessation of all law), while the necessity endures, no objection can reasonably be made, where the same necessity exists, to a modification and mitigation of martial law by legislative enactment.

The Lord Glenelg,   J. CAMPBELL.
&c. &c. &c.   R. M. ROLFE.

(9.) OPINION *of the Attorney General*, SIR RICHARD BETHELL, *on proclaiming Martial Law in Hong Kong.*

Lincoln's Inn, April 17, 1857.

SIR,—I have had the honour to receive the draft of your proposed despatch to Sir John Bowring, in answer to the despatch of Sir John Bowring, No. 9, of the 13th of January last.

I have read and considered the aforesaid draft of your proposed despatch, which appears to me to be in every respect right and proper, except that I would humbly submit to you that, under the circumstances, the last paragraph (No. 7) had better be omitted.

It appears to me, with submission, that this paragraph No. 7 may be construed as expressing an opinion that, instead of the ordinance, martial law ought to have been proclaimed; and also as containing something like a recommendation that, in any future emergency, resort had better be had to the proclamation of martial law.

I do not think it desirable to express any such opinion, or convey any such recommendation. Exception also may be taken to the accuracy of the language of part of the paragraph, in the parts underscored. If any recommendation be given to Sir John Bowring, I think it should be to augment the civil force by every means in his power (swearing in every resident, not being a Chinaman, as a special constable); during the day to have the military at hand to assist the civil power if necessary; and if these precautions be not sufficient for the protection of life and property, as a last resource, martial law might be proclaimed from sunset to sunrise in Hong Kong.

The Right Hon. H. Labouchere, M.P.,   RICHARD BETHELL.
&c. &c. &c.

NOTES TO CHAPTER VI.

Lord Chief Justice Hale says, in his "History of the Common Law," Martial law p. 54, that martial law "is sometimes indulged, rather than allowed, as a law ; the necessity of government, order, and discipline *in an army* being that which alone can give those laws a countenance—*quod enim necessitas cogit, defendit*. Secondly, this indulged law was only to extend *to members of the army*, or to those of the opposite army, and never was so much indulged as intended to be executed or exercised upon others." It is plain that Hale is here speaking of military law exercised by courts martial, which is a totally different thing from martial law in the sense in which it is used in the opinions in the text. He goes on to say, that " the exercise of martial law, whereby *any person* should lose his life, member, or liberty, may not be permitted in time of peace, when the King's courts are open for all persons to receive justice according to the laws of the land. This is, in substance, declared by the Petition of Right, 3 Car. 1, whereby such commissions and martial law were repealed and declared contrary to law." It thus appears that, according to Hale's opinion, even soldiers and sailors could not, so far as life or liberty was concerned, be tried by martial law in time of peace. And in this he agrees with Sir Edward Coke, who says (3 Inst. 32) : " If a lieutenant, or other that hath commission of martial authority, in time of peace hang or otherwise execute any man by colour of martial law, this is murder ; for this is against Magna Charta, c. 29, and is done with such power and strength that the party cannot defend himself, and here the law implieth malice ;" and see Hale's " Pleas of the Crown," p. 500.

But it must be remembered—and that is the explanation of the apparent discrepancy between the law as laid down by these eminent authorities, and the law as it is exercised at the present day—that there was then no Mutiny Act in existence ; and therefore military law, or martial law, as it was called, could only be enforced at common law, and the common law did not sanction its application in time of peace, even to those who were enlisted in the military or naval service of the Crown. And this is what Chief Baron Comyn means when he says, " Martial law cannot be used in England without authority of Parliament :" Dig. *Parliament*, H. 23. There was, moreover, then no standing army—at least none sanctioned by law ; for the Declaration of Rights, 1 Will. & M. s. 2, c. 2, declared that the raising or keeping a standing army in the kingdom in time of peace, unless it be with the consent of Parliament, is against law. Charles II. and James II. did, in fact, maintain standing armies in time of peace, but this is what the Declaration of Rights denounced as illegal. And so it was declared by the first Mutiny Act, 1 Will. & M. s. 2, c. 4, which Act first gave Parliamentary authority to punish *soldiers* by martial law. The Mutiny

Act, 2 & 3 Anne, c. 20, s. 37, first expressly reserved to the Queen the power of making Articles of War; but this Act also is confined to soldiers, being made for the government Hof er Majesty's land forces. The complaint in the Petition of Right (3 Car. 1, c. 1) was, that commissioners had been appointed with authority to proceed " according to the justice of martial law against such soldiers or mariners, or *other dissolute persons* joining with them, as should commit any *murder, robbery, felony, mutiny, or other outrage or misdemeanor whatsoever.*" Such commissions were thereby revoked and annulled; and it was further provided, that no commissions of like nature might issue, "lest by colour of them any of your Majesty's subjects be destroyed or put to death, contrary to the laws and practices of the land." It seems quite clear that this does not touch the question of martial law in the case of rebellion. It was directed against the illegal substitution of it for the ordinary course of law in time of peace to suppress crime. The nature of the commissions which exasperated the Commons, and against which they resolutely protested, may be seen in Rymer's Fœd. xviii. 254, 763, cited by Hallam, Const. Hist. i. 531, 3rd edit (1). The terms of these commissions were, " to proceed according to the justice of martial law against such soldiers, or other dissolute persons joining with them, as shall commit any robberies, felonies or mutinies, or other outrages or misdemeanors, which, by martial law, should or ought to be punished with death; and by such summary course and order as is agreeable to martial law, and is used in armies in time of war, to proceed to the trial and condemnation of such offenders, and them to cause to be executed and put to death according to the law martial." By the Petition of Right such commissions are declared to be wholly and directly contrary to the laws and statutes of the realm. In a charge delivered to the grand jury by Blackburn, J., in *R.* v. *Eyre* in 1868, the learned Judge said : " I think it would be an exceedingly wrong presumption to say, that the Petition of Right, by not condemning martial law in time of war, sanctioned it; still it did not in terms condemn it."

Proceeding by courts martial is something very different from martial law. "Martial law is quite a distinct thing (from ordinary military law), and is founded on paramount necessity, and proclaimed by a military chief:" Kent's Com. i. 377, 10th edit. Courts martial are part of the recognized judicatures of the realm, whose jurisdiction is confined to the military and naval forces of the Crown. In *Wolton* v. *Gavin*, 16 Q. B. 61, Lord Campbell, C.J., said : " None are bound by the Mutiny Acts or the Articles of War, except Her Majesty's forces ; and I am most anxious, as a constitutional judge, that this should be fully understood to be my opinion :" see *Wolfe Tone's Case*, 27 State Tr. 615. Under martial law the trial *may* be by court martial, but it is not necessarily so. A want of attention to this distinction has produced some confusion, even in the minds of judges. Thus, in *Grant* v. *Gould*, 2 H. Bl. 99, Lord Loughborough, C.J., said : " This leads me to an

(1) See these Commissions, given *in extenso* in the Appendix.

observation that martial law, such as it is described by Hale, and such, also, as it is marked by Mr. Justice Blackstone, does not exist in England at all. . . . Where martial law prevails, the authority under which it is exercised, claims a jurisdiction over all military persons in all circumstances. Even their debts are subject to inquiry by a military authority." Here it is obvious that the word "martial law" is used in two different senses. Hale and Blackstone were speaking of martial law during insurrection or rebellion; and Hale says (Analysis of the Law, p. 13): "The King may punish his subjects by martial law during such insurrection or rebellion, but not after it is suppressed." He further enumerates, strangely enough, "Commissions by Martial Law" amongst the "common heads of those liberties and rights that the people are to enjoy under the magistrate "! —*Ibid.* p. 37. But Lord Loughborough, in the latter part of the passage I have quoted from his judgment, is speaking of military law as administered by courts martial. And yet he was aware of the distinction, for he says also : " Where martial law is established and prevails in any country, it is of a totally different nature from that which is inaccurately called martial law merely because the decision is by a court martial, but which bears no affinity to that which was formerly attempted to be exercised in this kingdom, which was contrary to the Constitution, and which has been for a century totally exploded." That which was exploded, as contrary to the Constitution, was the issuing of commissions to try men in time of peace for ordinary felonies by martial law, which was declared illegal by the Petition of Right, and yet which Hale described as part of the liberties and rights which the people are to enjoy.

The distinction is pointed out in the following extract from an Opinion given by Mr. Cushing, Attorney General of the United States, February 7, 1857 (8 Attorney Generals' Opinions, 365) :—

" Sir Matthew Hale observes that martial law is not, in truth and reality, a law, but something indulged rather than allowed as a law; the necessity of government, order, and discipline in an army is that only which gives these laws a countenance. This proposition is a mere composite blunder, a total misapprehension of the matter. It confounds *martial law* and *law military ;* it ascribes to the former the uses of the latter, it erroneously assumes that the government of a body of troops is a *necessity* more than that of a body of civilians or citizens. It confounds and confuses all the relations of the subject, and is an apt illustration of the incompleteness of the notions of the common law jurists of England in regard to matters not comprehended in that limited branch of legal science.

" Even at a later day in England, when some glimmerings of light on the subject had begun to appear, the nature of martial law remained without accurate appreciation in Westminster Hall.

" Thus, in the great case of *Grant* v. *Sir Charles Gould*, Lord Loughborough said that ' the essence of martial law consists in its being a jurisdiction over all *military* persons in all circumstances.' And because military men are triable for many offences, and have their personal rights for the most part regulated by the common law, 'therefore,' he says, 'it is totally inaccurate to state martial law as having any place whatever within the realm of Great Britain.'

"All that is 'totally inaccurate.' *Military* law, it is now perfectly understood in England, is a branch of the law of the land applicable only to certain acts of a particular class of persons, and administered by special tribunals; but neither in that, nor in any other respect, essentially differing, as to foundation in constitutional reason, from admiralty, ecclesiastical, or indeed chancery and common law.

"It is not the absence of law supposed by Sir Matthew Hale, nor is it under any circumstances the martial law imagined by Lord Loughborough. It is the system of rules for the government of the army and navy established by successive Acts of Parliament. . . . . Martial law, as exercised in any country by the commander of a foreign army, is an element of the *jus belli*. It is incidental to the state of solemn war, and appertains to the law of nations. The commander of the invading, occupying, or conquering army rules the invaded, occupied, or conquered foreign country with supreme power, limited only by international law and the orders of the Sovereign or Government he serves or represents. For by the law of nations the *occupatio bellica* in a just war transfers the sovereign power of the enemy's country to the conqueror. Such occupation by right of war, so long as it is military only—that is, *flagrante bello*—will be the case put by the Duke of Wellington, of all the powers of government resumed in the hands of the Commander-in-Chief. . . . . I say we are without law on the subject. . . . . There may undoubtedly be, and have been, emergencies of necessity capable of themselves to produce, and therefore to justify, such suspension of all law, and involving for the time the omnipotence of military power. But such a necessity is not of the range of mere legal questions. When martial law is proclaimed under circumstances of assumed necessity, the proclamation must be regarded as the statement of an existing fact, rather than the legal creation of that fact. . . . As to the present case, therefore, it suffices to say that the power to suspend the laws, and to substitute the military authority in the place of the civil authority, is not a power within the legal attributes of a governor of one of the territories of the United States."

Hallam says (Const. Hist., i. 326, 3rd edit.): "It has been usual for all governments, during an actual rebellion, to proclaim martial law, *or the suspension of civil jurisdiction*." It supersedes all civil proceedings *which conflict with it*, but does not necessarily supersede all such proceedings: Bouvier's Law Dict., *Art.* "Martial Law" (an American work, of which it is difficult to speak too highly). It is founded on paramount necessity, and proclaimed by a military chief: Kent's Com. i. 377, 10th edit.

"Usurpari quoque interdum ista suprema auctoritas solita est, antequam belli facies se aperuerit, in subitis nimirum rebellium motibus, sed bonis et cordatis viris parum approbata. . . . . Absoluta hæc potestas *Castrensis* appellatur, quia semper fuit eritque apud militum turmas oppido necessaria :" Smith de Rep. Ang. ii., c. 4.

The Duke of Wellington said, in the House of Lords, on the 1st of April, 1851, on the question of the Ceylon rebellion in 1849 : "Martial law is neither more nor less than the will of the general who commands the army ; in fact, martial law is no law at all." And, on the same occasion, Earl Grey, after stating his agreement with the Duke, added : " I am sure I was not wrong in law, for I had the advice of Lord Cottenham, Lord Campbell, and the Attorney General (Sir John Jervis), and explained to my noble friend that what is called martial law is no law at all, but merely for the sake of public safety in circumstances of real emergency, setting aside all law, and acting under the military power." And see " The Evidence before the Ceylon Committee, 1849–50."

The following is an extract from an Opinion given by the late Mr. Serjeant Spankie, which will be found at length in " Hough on Courts Martial ":—

" The object of martial law, and the trial of offenders under it, is justly stated, in the Regulation X. of 1804 (1), to be immediate punishment 'for the safety of the British possessions, and for the security of the lives and property of the inhabitants thereof.' It is, in fact, the law of social self-defence, superseding, under the pressure, and therefore under the justification, of an extreme necessity, the ordinary forms of justice. Courts martial under martial law, or rather during the suspension of law, are invested with the power of administering that prompt and speedy justice in cases presumed to be clearly and indispensably of the highest species of guilt. The object is self-preservation by the terror and the example of speedy justice. But courts martial which condemn to imprisonment and hard labour belie the necessity under which alone the jurisdiction of courts martial can lawfully exist in civil society."

In his Charge to the Grand Jury in *R.* v. *Eyre*, in 1868, after quoting Hale's " Pleas of the Crown," i. 347, where that writer says, with reference to the case of the Earl of Lancaster, " From this record it will appear that in time of peace the Crown cannot enforce martial law ;" and, further, that "*regularly* when the King's courts are open it is a time of peace in judgment of laws " (2), Blackburn, J., said : " He is very cautious, you will observe, and puts it there in this way ; and certainly that is the opinion I have come to myself, that it has not yet been quite settled what is the Crown's prerogative in such cases, and what not. But I think this much is settled, that it is by no means that unbounded,

(1) By Regulation X. of 1804, the Governor-General of India in Council was empowered to establish martial law in time of war, or during open rebellion, in any part of British territory subject to the Government of the Presidency of Fort William.

(2) " And therefore, when the courts of justice be open, and the judges and ministers of the same may, by law, protect men from wrong and violence, and distribute justice to all, it is said to be time of peace " : Co. Litt. bk. iii., s. 412.

P 2

wild, and tyrannical prerogative which some persons have been lately
saying that it is. It must, if it exist at all, be strictly limited to
necessity."

In his celebrated Charge to the Grand Jury in *R.* v. *Eyre*, in 1867,
Lord Chief Justice Cockburn said : "So far as I have been able to discover, no such thing as martial law has ever been put in force *in this
country* against civilians, for the purpose of putting down rebellion."
But martial law has been several times proclaimed in Ireland. It was
proclaimed there in 1798 by the Lord-Lieutenant, and the proclamation
was signed by the Lord Chancellor, the Lord Chief Justice, and the
Law Officers of the Crown : Plowden's Historical Review of the State
of Ireland, ii. 690.

The Act of Indemnity, 37 Geo. 3, c. 11 (Irish Act), speaks of "the
use and salutary exercise of his Majesty's undoubted prerogative in
executing martial law." And the Irish Rebellion Act, 43 Geo. 3, c. 117,
(1803), declares that "nothing in this Act contained shall take away,
abridge, or diminish the acknowledged prerogative of his Majesty for
the public safety to resort to the exercise of martial law against open
enemies or traitors." That Act authorized the Lord-Lieutenant during
the continuance of the rebellion, "whether the ordinary courts of
justice shall or shall not at such time be open," to punish offenders
according to martial law, and to cause persons arrested to be tried by
courts martial. The same declaratory statement of the "undoubted
prerogative" of the Crown to resort to the exercise of martial law is
repeated in the statute 3 & 4 Will. 4, c. 4 (1833). After these distinct
assertions by Parliament of the existence of the prerogative, it would
seem to be difficult to deny it ; but it is right to notice the weighty
opinion of Lord Chief Justice Cockburn, who has expressed grave
doubts on the question in his Charge to the Grand Jury in *R.* v. *Eyre*,
p. 74, where he said : "So emphatic an expression of the opinion of
Parliament is certainly entitled to great and respectful consideration ;
but in my opinion it cannot and ought not to prevail against fact and
truth, if a thorough investigation of the subject should lead us to an
opposite conclusion, and satisfy us that Parliament has formed an un-
sound opinion upon it. Against it may be set the fact that Parliament
has passed Acts to indemnify persons who assisted in carrying martial
law into execution, and took care to shut the doors of courts of law to
those who could question its legality—enactments which would appear
to have been wholly uncalled for, if the power to put martial law in
force were as undoubted as it is thus described to be."

Coke said, in the debate on the Petition of Right, that a rebel may be
slain, in rebellion, but if he be taken he cannot be put to death by
martial law ; and Rolle (afterwards Lord Chief Justice) on the same
occasion, that if a subject be not taken in rebellion, and be not slain at
the time of his rebellion, he is to be tried by the common law : Rushworth's Collection, iii. App. 79, 81. "A rebel in arms stands in the
position of a public enemy, and therefore ·you may kill him in battle,

as you might kill a foreign enemy. . . . . If it be true that you can apply martial law for the purpose of suppressing rebellion, it is equally certain that you cannot bring men to trial for treason under martial law after a rebellion has been suppressed " (1) : Lord Chief Justice Cockburn's Charge to the Grand Jury in *R.* v. *Eyre*, pp. 25, 29. See *Wolfe Tone's Case*, 27 State Tr. 615, where a habeas corpus was granted after the prisoner had been tried and sentenced to death by a court martial. While the rebellion exists, and martial law is in force, the trial *may* be by court-martial, but need not be so. In fact, there is no legal necessity for any form of trial at all when the rebel is met with arms in his hands, *flagrante bello*, for he may be killed on the spot. But if, instead of being killed in open resistance, he were to be arrested, the gravest responsibility would be incurred if he were to be put to death without *some* form of trial, and analogy would obviously suggest a trial by court-martial.

Owing to the atrocities and excesses which were committed during the existence of martial law in Ireland, an Act of Indemnity was thought necessary, and this was accordingly passed, 37 Geo. 3, c. 11 (Irish Act). But notwithstanding the Act of Indemnity, where a sheriff had flogged a man against whom there was no charge or pretence that he was implicated in the rebellion, he was held liable in damages. The Court said: " The jury were not to imagine that the Legislature, by enabling magistrates to justify under the Indemnity Bill, had released them from the feelings of humanity, or permitted them wantonly to exercise power, even though it were to put down rebellion :" *Wright* v. *Fitzgerald*, 27 State Tr. 765 ; and see *Luther* v. *Borden*, 7 Howard (American Sup. Court Rep.) 46.

In *R.* v. *Pinney*, 3 B. & Ad. 958 (quoted by Blackburn, J., in his Charge to the Grand Jury in the case of *R.* v. *Eyre*, 1868), Littledale, J., said that " a party intrusted with the duty of putting down a riot, whether by virtue of an office of his own seeking (as in the ordinary case of a magistrate), or imposed upon him (as that of a constable), is bound to hit the exact line between excess and failure of duty, and that the difficulty of so doing, though it might be some ground for a lenient consideration of his conduct on the part of the jury, was no legal defence to a charge like the present. Nor could a party so charged excuse himself on the mere ground of honest intention." And *per* Blackburn, J., in the above-mentioned charge : " I think the officer is bound under such circumstances to bring to the exercise of his duty ordinary firmness, judgment, and discretion. I think he is bound to do that, and I think in such a case the jury have to determine upon the evidence—first, whether the circumstances were in fact such that what was done really was in excess of the duty of the officer ; and, secondly, whether a person placed in the position of that officer, having

(1) See *Geoffroy's Case* in France, 1832 ; and the argument of Mr. David Dudley Field, *In the Matter of M'Cardle*, Supreme Court of the United States, 1868 ; both in the Appendix.

the information that he had, believing what he did believe, and knowing what he did know, if exercising ordinary judgment, firmness, and moderation, would have perceived it was an excess." The law, in fact, requires and exacts from every man in such a responsible situation that he shall fulfil the character described by Horace:—

"Justum et tenacem propositi virum
Non civium ardor, prava jubentium,
Nec vultus instantis tyranni,
Mente quatit solidâ."

The right conclusion upon the whole matter seems to be this : Martial law may be justifiably imposed as a terrible necessity, and an act of self-defence; under it there is a suspension of civil rights, and the ordinary forms of trial are in abeyance. Under it a man in actual armed resistance may be put to death on the spot by anyone acting under the orders of competent authority; or, if arrested, may be tried in any manner which such authority shall direct. But if there be an abuse of the power so given, and acts are done under it, not *bonâ fide* to suppress rebellion and in self-defence, but to gratify malice or in the caprice of tyranny, then for such acts the party doing them is responsible (1).

By the Jamaica statute, 9 & 10 Vict. c. 35, it was enacted that martial law should not be declared except by the advice and opinion of a council of war, composed as therein directed.

In a circular despatch addressed by Lord Carnarvon, the Secretary of State for the Colonies, to the Colonial Governors, January 30, 1867, and containing the copy of a despatch which he had sent to the Governor of Antigua, requiring him to submit to the local legislature a bill for the repeal of an Act which authorized the proclamation of martial law, he said : " In giving you these instructions, Her Majesty's Government must not be supposed to convey an absolute prohibition of all recourse to martial law under the stress of great emergencies, and in anticipation of an Act of Indemnity. The justification, however, of such a step must rest on the pressure of the moment, and the Governor cannot by any instructions be relieved from the obligation of deciding for himself, under that pressure, whether the responsibility of proclaiming martial law is or is not greater than that of refraining from doing so."

Proceeding by courts martial. As to proceedings by courts martial, see *Grant* v. *Gould*, 2 H. Bl. 69 ; *R.* v. *Suddis*, 1 East, 306 ; *Wall's Case*, 28 State Tr. 51 ; *Harden* v. *Bailey*, 4 Taunt. 67 ; 4 M. & S. 400 (S.C. in Error). *In time of war* the Crown acts out of the limits of its dominions as regards the army by virtue of its prerogative : *Barwise* v. *Keppel*, 2 Wils. 314.

Duty of magistrates in case of riots and unlawful assemblies. As to the powers and duties of magistrates in case of riots and unlawful assemblies, see *R.* v. *Pinney*, 3 B. & Ad. 947 ; *R.* v. *Langford*, 1 Car. & Marsh. 602 ; *R.* v. *Furzey*, 9 C. & P. 431, which shows that contrary.

(1) See an able view of the subject in Finlason's Commentaries upon Martial Law (London, 1867).

stables and even private individuals are justified in using force to disperse an unlawful assembly; *R.* v. *Neale,* 9 C. & P. 431. Levying war against the Crown is where there is an armed force seeking to supersede the law, and gain some public object. There must be an insurrection, and a force accompanying it: *R.* v. *Frost,* 9 C. & P. 141.

In the Annual Register for 1768, vol. xi. p. 227, there is an account of a trial of a magistrate named Gilham, who was tried for his life for having given orders to the military to fire on the mob during the riots in St. George's Fields, after the Riot Act had been read. He was acquitted. Serjeant Glynn, who was counsel for the prosecution, said at the close of his evidence : " I am not now pressing this gentleman's conviction ; I opened the law that where it was absolutely necessary for suppressing a riotous mob, there the magistrate is justified."

What is the law with regard to a soldier firing upon a crowd and causing death? There can be no doubt that if the occasion justifies the command to fire, he is bound to obey it, and is not liable for the consequences. To disobey it would subject him to severe punishment, perhaps death, by court-martial. But suppose that the occasion does not justify the command—in other words, that the order to fire is improperly given, and unlawful—what then? A soldier is here placed in a most difficult dilemma. On the one hand, it is his military duty to obey the orders of his commanding officer ; on the other, he has by becoming a soldier not ceased to be a citizen, and is subject to the duties of a civilian. It is clear that he would not be justified in obeying *every* command of his superior ; as, for instance—to put an extreme case—supposing he were ordered to fire upon the Sovereign, or to desert to the enemy, or to commit a rape. There he must instantly recognize the form of a paramount obligation, and see that disobedience is a duty. But suppose that the command is such that, although in the eye of the law illegal, it is not obviously so. In such a case he surely ought to be held harmless for obeying it. Suppose now that he conscientiously believes the order to be illegal, although in fact it is not. If he disobeys it he would be tried and punished by a court-martial, and properly so ; for it would be very dangerous to allow a soldier to shelter himself against the charge of disobedience on the plea that he mistakingly believed the order of his commanding officer to be contrary to law. But there is yet a third case. Suppose he disobeys an order which is illegal, but not obviously so, as in the case of a command to fire where there is a riot, but not such violence as to justify the use of military weapons. Here he would only have done that which as a citizen he was bound to do, namely, to abstain from murder ; for, as was said by Bayley, J., in *R.* v. *Burdett,* 4 B. & Al. 323 : " The libel in question imports that the troops had killed men *unarmed, unresisting,* and had disfigured, maimed, cut down, and trampled on women. If that were done, if *unresisting men* were cut down, whether by troops or not, it is *murder,* for which the parties are liable to be tried by the law of the country." But would he have committed an offence against

The duty of soldiers.

the Articles of War? Those Articles provide that any officer or soldier who shall disobey the *lawful* command of his superior officer shall, if an officer, suffer death, or such other punishment as by a general court martial shall be awarded; and if a soldier, shall suffer death, transportation (now penal servitude), or such other punishment as by a general court martial shall be awarded.   It seems, therefore, that a court martial could not find him guilty of disobedience if the command was not lawful.   Perhaps, upon the whole, the right conclusion is this : a soldier *may* disobey an unlawful command, but he is justified in obeying all orders of his commanding officer, unless they are obviously, and in a manner patent to common sense, illegal.   The habit of discipline and obedience in a soldier is, I believe, more essential to the wellbeing of the State, than the possibility of his now and then executing an illegal order is injurious to it.   In *Keighley* v. *Bell*, 4 Fost. & Fin. 790, Willes, J., said : "I hope I may never have to determine that difficult question, how far the orders of a superior officer are a justification.   Were I compelled to determine that question, I should probably hold that the orders are an *absolute* justification in time of actual war—at all events as regards enemies or foreigners—and, I should think, even with regard to English·born subjects of the Crown, unless the orders were such as could not legally be given.   I believe that the better opinion is that an officer or soldier, acting under the orders of his superior, not being necessarily or manifestly illegal, would be justified by his orders."

Under what circumstances is a sentry justified in firing upon persons approaching him?   It seems to me that this is a question of discretion, in which much must be left to the judgment of the soldier.   If he fires wantonly and unnecessarily, and thereby takes away life,·he is guilty of manslaughter, if not of murder.   If, on the other hand, he allows himself to be assaulted and disarmed, or the property which he is stationed to defend to be plundered, he is guilty of a grave military offence, for which he might suffer death.   But between these two extremes there is a wide interval, in which his conduct must be regulated by circumstances.   If a sentry is attacked or threatened by an armed force, he certainly may use his firearms, if necessary to repel the attack and prevent the commission of crime.   On the approach of an unarmed body of men in a hostile attitude, more caution would be requisite; and it would be, I conceive, necessary to give the most distinct challenge and warning before firing, and then only provided the party continue to advance, and could not otherwise be prevented from carrying out his or their unlawful design.   That an attempt to deprive a sentry of his arms might be repelled by force, even to the extent of taking away life, provided the force cannot be otherwise successfully resisted, is, I think, clear from the circumstance that a sentry who improperly allows himself to be disarmed, is by the Articles of War punishable by death; so that in defending his arms he is in effect defending his own life.

CHAPTER VII.

ON EXTRA-TERRITORIAL JURISDICTION.

(1.) REPORT *by* SIR JAMES MARRIOTT, *King's Advocate, on the reference of the Letter of* SIR JAMES WRIGHT, *his Majesty's Minister at Venice, by the* EARL OF SHELBURNE (1).

MY LORD,—In humble obedience to his Majesty's pleasure, signified to me by your Lordship's letter of the 25th instant, referring to me an extract of a letter from Sir James Wright, and the case of felony, or murder, " which may eventually be committed by his Majesty's subjects on board English ships, or in the house or privileged circuit of his Majesty's accredited minister," for me to consider, in point of law, what directions are proper to be given thereupon, I have the honour to report to your Lordship, that in the case of murders or felonies committed upon the high seas, the parties charged therewith are proper objects of the jurisdiction of the High Court of Admiralty in England, and are to be sent home, to be delivered up to the proper magistrate here, and take their trials accordingly. But that when murders or felonies are committed in any port, river, creek, or haven of the territory of any foreign Power, those crimes do then fall under that particular local and territorial jurisdiction, which jurisdiction is always understood to reach as far as the power of protection reaches—that is to say, within the command of gunshot from the shore, for the power of punishment is always equal to and coincident with and inseparable from the power of protection.

With respect to such crimes or violences as may be committed within the house of a public minister, if he can give an asylum to foreigners (a privilege of which I doubt the justice and reciprocal utility, though some have asserted it), he might *à fortiori* protect persons of his own suite against a foreign jurisdiction, but certainly

(1) From a M.S. in the possession of Sir Travers Twiss, Queen's Advocate, which formerly belonged to Sir James Marriott, King's Advocate. No date.

he cannot execute himself any jurisdiction, touching life and limb, upon them, because he has no such commission, and he is under a necessity, from circumstances, to deliver them up of his own movement to be tried by the jurisdiction of the country in which he and they are resident, because otherwise the criminal would go unpunished, inasmuch as the criminal, being sent home, could not, by the common law of this land, be tried for crimes committed out of the realm, and which cannot be laid in the indictment to be done against the peace of our Sovereign Lord the King, his Crown and dignity.

There is, indeed, in our constitution a jurisdiction of the constable and marshal for things done out of the realm, but it appertains only to matters touching war and arms, and appeals from the provost-marshal or other military jurisdiction in the King's armies in a foreign territory.

With respect to murders, when persons die in a foreign country of a wound received within this realm, or die in this realm of a wound received in a foreign country, in either alternative the party giving the wound, and his accessory or accessories, by 2 Geo. 2, c. 21, must be tried in England, the statute considering the cause and effect as one continuity of action without interval, in order to found a domestic jurisdiction and to reach the crime.

To conclude, the law of nations does not delegate to any accredited minister, as Sir James Wright supposes, a full judicial power to determine, without appeal, upon all acts of violence and theft committed within the circle of his supposed district, by which only the walls of his own house can possibly be meant, which, by the law of nations, protects its inhabitants from insult, without having in it their definitive tribunal.

(2.) JOINT OPINION *of the Attorney and Solicitor General,* SIR PHILIP YORKE *and* SIR CLEMENT WEARG, *on a trial for Murder committed at Sea.* 1725.

Extract of a letter from Mr. Worsley, Governor of Barbadoes, to the Lords Commissioners for Trade and Plantations, dated the 24th of January, 1724–5 :—

" I have the honour to present to your Lordships an account of an accident that has lately happened here. On the 4th of December last, the St. Christopher's galley, James Newth, commander, sailed out of this port, and the forts fired some random shot at her to bring her to, in that she had not put up the proper signal that was given her, or any other, which is to show that she had cleared out of all the offices and had liberty to depart. The master, instead of bringing to, hoisted more sail, whence a matross of James's Fort, suspecting she had done something irregular (as they often do in this part of the world, one about twelve months ago attempting to carry away a custom-house officer), fired a shot into her when she was about two miles off, which happened, unfortunately, to kill the mate, and wounded another man. The vessel immediately returned into port, and as soon as the master informed me of it, I inquired into the fact, upon which I found she had not put up her signal, the master complaining it was not a proper signal, being a tarpauling hoisted upon the flagstaff; and though I found such signals had been sometimes given and had been put up, nevertheless, as I thought it a very improper one, that there might be no such precedents for the future, I suspended the captain of the fort for some time. However, if the master of the vessel had not liked the signal, he ought not to have gone under sail till he had got another, and ought to have brought to upon the fort's firing. The difficulty at present I lie under, is to know whether, and where, the matross that fired the shot from James's Fort is to be tried, or what court can take cognizance of it. The person that was killed by a gun from the shore was upon the high seas two miles off of the shore, where, I apprehend, my jurisdiction does not extend, and his Majesty's Attorney General here is of the same opinion."

Opinion.—We are of opinion that the matross who fired the shot cannot be tried for the death of the mate in any court of common law, but that he ought to be tried for the same either in the Court of Admiralty at Barbadoes, or by special commission under statute of 11 & 12 Will. 3, c. 7, which is now the most known and usual method of proceeding in cases of felonies done upon the sea in these parts.

P. YORKE.

April 17, 1725.   C. WEARG.

(3.) JOINT OPINION *of the Attorney and Solicitor General,* SIR SAMUEL SHEPHERD *and* SIR ROBERT GIFFORD, *as to the Jurisdiction of the Superior Court of New South Wales, in case of Persons not resident within the Territory; and as to the disability to sue of Prisoners convicted of Felony.*

Serjeants' Inn, May 13, 1818.

MY LORD,—We have had the honour to receive your Lordship's letter of the 4th of May, transmitting to us the copy of a letter which has been addressed to your Lordships' under-secretary by the Judge Advocate and Judge of the Supreme Court of the colony of New South Wales, inclosing a case for consideration, viz.: whether, by the present charter of justice under which the courts of civil jurisdiction are established in the colony, any person can sue or be sued therein, unless he be resident within the territory or its dependencies at least at the commencement of the action, as also whether convict prisoners, even though in the employ of Government, cannot sue and be sued in the courts there under the general terms of the legal charter; and your Lordship is pleased to request that we will take the same into consideration, and report on the cases in question.

We have the honour to report to your Lordship, that by the present charter of justice under which the courts of civil jurisdiction are established in the colony, it is necessary that the person sued should be resident within the territory or its dependencies at the commencement of the suit, but we do not think it is necessary that the party suing as plaintiff should be so resident, the restriction with respect to residence not applying to them; and the provisions of the statute 54 Geo. 3, c. 15, fortify us in this opinion. We think that prisoners convicted of felony, even though in the employ of Government, cannot sue in the courts of the colony; for, though the words of the charter are general, "any person or persons," yet we think they must be taken to mean any person or persons capable of suing, and felons convict are not so capable; but though they cannot be plaintiffs in a suit, they may be sued as defendants, since they cannot take advantage of their own disability.

S. SHEPHERD.
R. GIFFORD.

(4.) JOINT OPINION *of the Attorney and Solicitor General,*
SIR JOHN S. COPLEY *and* SIR CHARLES WETHERELL, *on the
Foreign Enlistment Act,* 59 *Geo.* 3, *c.* 69.

Serjeants' Inn, October 13, 1825.

MY LORD,—We have had the honour to receive your Lordship's
letter of the 30th ultimo, stating that his Majesty's Government
having received such information as induces them to believe, that
some of his Majesty's natural-born subjects, at present resident in this
kingdom, have either enlisted or intend to enlist themselves to serve
against the Government of Turkey, in the war at present carrying
on in various parts of Greece; and it being deemed expedient that
measures should be taken to prevent this violation of the law, your
Lordship was pleased to request our attention to the questions
which your Lordship proposed to us with reference to that subject,
and which questions are stated in the following terms:—

Supposing that any person, while resident in England, should
either enlist, or agree to enlist, in the service of the Greeks, or
should accept a commission as an officer or commander of a privateer in that service, or should contract to go to Greece with an
intent to serve in the military operations of that country either by
sea or land, or should hire persons to enter into such service; and
supposing, further, that in the prosecution of any such engagement
or design, such a person should arrive at Malta or Gibraltar, could
he be prosecuted and tried in the superior courts of criminal jurisdiction at those settlements, or must he be sent for trial to England?
If the trial might lawfully take place at Malta or Gibraltar, are the
civil authorities there to proceed precisely in the same manner as in
the ordinary administration of justice they would proceed on the
trial of any other offenders; or is any particular mode of proceeding
required by the statute? Or if, on the contrary, the trial is to take
place in England, in what method are the civil authorities in Malta
or Gibraltar (where the office of justice of the peace is unknown) to
proceed for the apprehension of the offender, and what measures
may they lawfully take for sending him to England?

In the case already supposed, would it be competent to the civil
authorities at Malta or Gibraltar, in pursuance of the statute 59
Geo. 3, cap. 69, to arrest or detain the vessel in which any such

offender might arrive at those settlements; and is any particular
course of proceeding to be observed for the purpose of effecting
such arrest or detention; or are the supreme courts of justice to
proceed for the arrest or detention of the vessel, in the same manner as in other ordinary causes, where vessels may be seized in those
settlements under judicial process? And in what manner is the
vessel to be disposed of after she had been thus seized and detained?

And your Lordship requested that we would report to your Lordship, for his Majesty's information, our opinion upon the questions
thus proposed to us at our earliest convenience.

In obedience to your Lordship's request, we beg leave to report,
for the information of his Majesty, that if any person, while himself in England, should enlist or agree to enlist in the service of
the Greeks, or should accept a commission as an officer or commander of a privateer in that service, or should contract to go to
Greece with an intent to serve in the military operations of that
country either by sea or land, or should hire persons to enter into
such service, such offences would be complete in England, and
could only be tried here; and that if such a person should arrive at
Malta or Gibraltar in the prosecution of any such engagement, he
could not, we think, be tried in those settlements for any of the
offences above enumerated. In the same section, however, of the
statute, it is enacted that if any natural-born subject of his Majesty
shall without leave, &c., go to any place beyond the seas with
intent to serve in any warlike or military operation, whether by
land or sea, in the service, &c., he shall be deemed guilty of misdemeanor. We conceive, therefore, that if any of the above-mentioned persons should, in the prosecution of their engagements, touch
at Gibraltar or Malta, places beyond the seas, they would, under
this part of the section, commit an offence for which they might be
tried at such places; for they would have gone to those places with
intent to serve in the military or naval operations of the Greeks.

No person offending against the Act could in any case be sent
for trial to England.

No particular mode of proceeding is required by the statute.
The civil authorities in the above-mentioned settlements must proceed in the same manner as in the ordinary administration of
justice against other offenders guilty of what in the law of England

are usually styled misdemeanors—that is, offences punishable by fine, or imprisonment, or both.

Though the office of justice of the peace may be unknown in Gibraltar and Malta, yet if, for offences of this class—that is, offences punishable in the manner above-mentioned—parties may be arrested and held to bail, the same course of proceeding may be adopted under this Act.

We have already stated that offenders against this Act cannot be apprehended and sent to England.

We are of opinion that any vessel which should arrive at Gibraltar or Malta, having any such offenders on board, might be lawfully detained and prevented from proceeding with such persons on her voyage. The vessel can only be detained for this purpose, and if the commander should put the offenders on shore he would be entitled immediately to proceed upon his voyage. But as long as the persons continued on board it would be lawful to detain the vessel. Authority is given for this purpose to the principal officers of his Majesty's customs, if there be any such ; and, if not, then to the Governor or person having the chief civil command. There must be an information upon oath to justify the detention, and such information must also state the facts upon which the knowledge or belief of the informer is founded. The officers who may be called upon to act upon this clause of the statute must be particularly directed strictly to conform to its provisions.

In a subsequent section (the 7th), authority is given to seize and *condemn* the vessels therein described, viz. :—vessels fitted out as transports or storeships, or cruisers for the service, or in aid of any foreign power, &c. The mode of proceeding in the seizure and condemnation of any such vessel, and the tribunal by which the adjudication is to be made will be the same as where a vessel is seized and condemned for any forfeiture incurred under the laws of customs or excise, or the laws of trade and navigation. The seizure may be by any officer of his Majesty's customs or excise, or any officer of his Majesty's navy who is empowered to make seizures for forfeitures incurred under the laws above-mentioned. The officers who may be required to act upon this section of the statute should also be directed to attend carefully to its provisions.

J. S. COPLEY.
CHARLES WETHERELL.

(5.) JOINT OPINION *of the King's Advocate*, SIR HERBERT JENNER, *and the Solicitor General*, SIR N. C. TINDAL, *as to whether Slaves escaping to a Foreign Territory could be brought back to a Colony to be there dealt with as Slaves.*

Doctors' Commons, May 30, 1829.

SIR,—We are honoured with your letter stating that during the last autumn three slaves belonging to the Bahama Islands obtained possession of a boat in which they effected their escape to Cuba. On their arrival at Cuba, they were seized by the authorities at that island and placed in confinement. The commandant of the port of Remedios, in Cuba, reported this transaction to the Governor of the Bahama Islands, offering to restore the slaves to their owners in that colony upon payment of the expenses which had been incurred. The Governor has applied for instructions for his guidance on this occasion, and has expressed a doubt whether, if the slaves were restored, they could lawfully be brought back to the Bahamas, there to be dealt with as slaves.

And you are therefore pleased to desire that we would report our opinion, whether these slaves could lawfully be brought back from Cuba to the Bahama Islands for the purpose, and with the intention, of dealing with them as slaves in those islands upon their return.

In obedience to your commands, we have the honour to report that we think, that these slaves, having made their escape from the Bahamas to a colony under foreign dominion, cannot, with reference to the provisions of the statute 5th Geo. 4, c. 113, be legally brought back into any of the territories or dominions belonging to his Majesty, there to be dealt with as slaves.

Right Hon. Sir George Murray,   HERBERT JENNER.
&c.   &c.   &c.   N. C. TINDAL.

(6.) JOINT OPINION *of the Attorney and Solicitor General,* SIR JOHN CAMPBELL *and* SIR R. M. ROLFE, *as to jurisdiction over offences committed in Territory outside of the Gates of Gibraltar.*

Temple, July 23, 1838.

MY LORD,—We have had the honour to receive your Lordship's letter of the 14th instant, transmitting to us various papers relating to the question, how far the courts established in Gibraltar are entitled to take cognizance of offences committed on any portion of the territory outside of the gates of the garrison, and requesting our opinion on this subject.

After attentively perusing all these papers, we entertain no doubt whatever that the courts established in Gibraltar are entitled to take cognizance of offences committed on any portion of the territory between the gates of the garrison and the extremity of the English lines. This territory is clearly held in full sovereignty by the English Crown, and is included in the charters establishing courts with jurisdiction over the garrison and territory of Gibraltar.

We entirely concur in the view taken of the subject by Mr. Attorney General Cochrane, and we do not see any foundation for the scruples of Chief Justice Field or his predecessors.

Even under the strictest interpretation of the Treaty of Utrecht, this ground, which is indispensably necessary for the occupation and defence of the fortress, is to be considered part of the fortress of Gibraltar; and by our exercising jurisdiction over it there is no pretence for saying that we assume any territorial jurisdiction, or open any communication with the surrounding country, against the stipulations of the treaty.

To gain the object desired by the Governor, as to the ground between the fortress and the British lines, there appears to us to be no occasion whatever for any new treaty with Spain, or any new charter from the Crown.

The Lord Glenelg,   J. CAMPBELL.
&c. &c. &c.   R. M. ROLFE.

(7.) JOINT OPINION *of the Attorney and Solicitor General,* SIR JOHN JERVIS *and* SIR JOHN ROMILLY, *that an assault on a Native in a Colony, by British Subjects, is not triable in the Court of Queen's Bench in England.*

Temple, April 16, 1850.

MY LORD,—We were honoured with your Lordship's command, contained in Mr. Hawes' letter of the 6th ultimo, in which he stated that he was directed by your Lordship to request that we would favour your Lordship with our joint opinion on the following questions:—

Certain officers of Her Majesty's 1st West India Regiment are charged with having given directions for the ill-usage of a native

Q

of Cape Coast Castle, named Robert Erskine, by torture, in order
to compel him to disclose an alleged robbery.

That the circumstances, as far as known to your Lordship, are
detailed in the statements of Robert Erskine, and certain other
parties, enclosed in a despatch from the Acting Governor of Cape
Coast Castle, dated October 22, 1849, a copy of which is annexed,
and also in the declarations of other parties taken before a Committee of the Aborigines' Protection Society, and likewise annexed.

That Captain Murray and Lieutenants Bingham and Stuart, the
officers whose names are mentioned in the account of this transaction, are now believed to be on service in the West Indies.

That the papers relating to this transaction have been submitted
by the Commander-in-Chief to the Judge Advocate General, whose
letter thereupon is likewise annexed.

That the questions which the Judge Advocate General recom-
mends to be submitted to us are—whether the persons who are
charged with having tortured Robert Erskine can be tried and
punished for it, either upon an information exhibited by the Attorney General, or upon an indictment found in the Court of
Queen's Bench in England; and would it be proper in a case of
this kind to resort to such mode of trial?

Mr. Hawes then stated that your Lordship requested that, in the
event of our being of opinion that such proceedings might be taken,
either on information or indictment, we would further favour your
Lordship with our opinion in what manner, and by what authority,
the examination of the witnesses and other preliminary proceedings should be taken, with a view to the committal of the accused
parties for trial?

In obedience to your Lordship's commands, we have perused the
several documents transmitted to us, and have the honour to report
that, in our opinion, the persons who are charged with having
tortured Robert Erskine cannot be tried and punished in this
country by information or indictment in the Queen's Bench; at
common law no such proceeding could be instituted in this
country, and we are of opinion that the case is not within the provisions of the statute 42 Geo. 3, c. 85.

The Right Hon. Earl Grey,   JOHN JERVIS.
    &c.   &c.   &c.   JOHN ROMILLY.

(8.) JOINT OPINION *of the Queen's Advocate,* SIR JOHN DODSON, *and the Attorney and Solicitor General,* SIR JOHN ROMILLY *and* SIR A. E. COCKBURN, *on the construction of the Statutes* 59 *Geo.* 3, *c.* 44 (*an Act relating to offences committed in Honduras*), *and* 12 *&* 13 *Vict. c.* 96 (*an Act to provide for the Prosecution and Trial in the Colonies of Offences committed within the Jurisdiction of the Admiralty*).

Doctors' Commons, March 14, 1851.

MY LORD,—We are honoured with your Lordship's commands, signified in Mr. Merivale's letter of the 5th instant, stating that he was directed to transmit to us an extract of a despatch from the Governor of Jamaica, with copies of so much of its enclosures as relates to the trial and conviction at a Commission Court held at Honduras of two persons for piracy on the high seas.

Mr. Merivale is pleased to request that we would take these papers into consideration, and report to your Lordship our joint opinion as to the validity of the objections which we should find to have been taken to the conviction in this case.

In obedience to your Lordship's commands, we have taken the papers into consideration, and have the honour to report that we think that the first objection, viz.: " That the Commission Court, according to the statute 59 Geo. 3, c. 44, and the letters patent of the Crown, by which it is constituted, has no jurisdiction to try, *eo nomine,* for 'piracy,' and that the subsequent imperial statute of the 12 & 13 Vict. c. 96, which the Chief Justice of Honduras seems to think has given that jurisdiction to the Court, only contemplated the trial by any colonial court of the same offences when committed on the high seas which the same court might previously have tried if committed upon any inland waters," is valid.

We are of opinion that the second objection, viz.: " That the crime of which the prisoners were convicted was committed before the Act of the 13 & 14 Vict. was passed," is invalid, inasmuch as the prisoners were charged after the passing of the statute of 12 & 13 Vict. c. 96.

We think that the third objection, viz.: " That British Honduras does not come within the meaning of the 5th clause of the 12 & 13 Vict., as being neither a colony, island, plantation, dominion, fort, or

Q 2

factory of Her Majesty," is not free from doubt; but upon the whole, notwithstanding whatever may have been the original state of things in that settlement, we are disposed to think that at present it has become a part of the dominions of Her Majesty, and that, consequently, the third objection is invalid.

J. DODSON.

The Right Hon. Earl Grey,   JOHN ROMILLY.

&c.   &c.   &c.   A. E. COCKBURN.

(9.) JOINT OPINION *of the Queen's Advocate,* SIR JOHN DODSON, *and the Attorney and Solicitor General,* SIR JOHN ROMILLY *and* SIR A. E. COCKBURN, *that British Courts have no Jurisdiction in respect of illegal acts committed against Emigrants on board Foreign Vessels.*

Lincoln's Inn, February 26, 1851.

MY LORD,—We were honoured with your Lordship's commands, contained in Mr. Merivale's letter of the 19th February instant, in which he stated that he had been directed by your Lordship to transmit to us an accompanying copy of a letter from the Colonial Land and Emigration Commissioners, suggesting a difficulty which might probably arise as regards the jurisdiction possessed by British or colonial courts over acts committed against emigrants on the high seas under a foreign flag; and he was to request that we would take this letter into our consideration, and report to your Lordship our joint opinion upon the point raised by the Commissioners.

In obedience to your Lordship's commands, we have considered the various documents submitted to us, and have the honour to report that we are of opinion, that if an emigrant be illegally treated on the high seas by the masters or officers of a foreign vessel, he would not be able to obtain redress from the colonial courts. In other words, that these courts would not, nor could any British courts, have jurisdiction over acts committed on the high seas under a foreign flag, and that the recent Act 12 & 13 Vict. c. 96, facilitating the trial in colonies of offences committed on the high seas would not meet the case.

J. DODSON.

The Right Hon. Earl Grey,   JOHN ROMILLY.

&c.   &c.   &c.   A. E. COCKBURN.

(10.) Joint Opinion *of the Queen's Advocate,* Sir J. D. Harding, *and the Attorney and Solicitor General,* Sir Fred. Thesiger *and* Sir FitzRoy Kelly, *on the same question.*

Doctors' Commons, September 21, 1852.

Sir,—We are honoured with your commands, signified in Mr. Merivale's letter of the 14th instant, stating that he was directed to request that we would furnish you with our joint opinion upon the following questions.

It appears that a number of Chinese, emigrating in a vessel under the American flag, have risen upon the captain and crew, murdered most of them, possessed themselves of the vessel, changed her course, plundered, and finally abandoned her.

It need hardly be said that they did not themselves hoist any flag, or assume any national character.

That an American officer, who has captured some of the supposed criminals, desires that they should be tried by the Supreme Court at Hong Kong; but, as the seizure of the ship and murder of the crew was effected by subjects of a foreign Power, and under a foreign flag, it appears very doubtful whether this can be done. That the acting Attorney General of the colony is of opinion, on the grounds stated in his letter (of which a copy is annexed), that it can; but, on a point of so much delicacy and importance, he is desirous of acting with the sanction of the Law Officers of the Crown in this country.

That the questions, therefore, on which our opinion is requested are :—

1. Whether any British authority could, consistently with the law of nations, take cognizance of such a case as that above described? and,

2. Whether the Supreme Court at Hong Kong possesses that authority?

That on the first of these questions it appears unnecessary to trouble us with any observations. That on the second, it is desirable to inform us that the Legislature of Hong Kong is, by the Governor's commission (from which an extract is annexed), authorized to make such laws and ordinances as may be required for the peace, order, and good government of the colony.

That by the colonial ordinance No. 6 of 1845 (of which a copy is annexed), a Supreme Court of judicature was established, to which, however, no Admiralty jurisdiction was, or indeed could legally be given. But by the Imperial Act 12 & 13 Vict. c. 91, s. 1, it is enacted that colonial courts of justice shall have the same authority to try offences committed within the jurisdiction of the Admiralty, as if these offences had been committed on any waters within the limits of the colony, and of the jurisdiction of the colonial courts.

In obedience to your commands, we have taken the papers into consideration, and have the honour to report, that we are of opinion—

1. That no British authority could, consistently with the law of England, or with the law of nations, take cognizance of such a case as that described.

2. It follows that the Supreme Court of Hong Kong has not the necessary authority to take cognizance of the case.

J. D. HARDING.

The Right Hon. Sir J. Pakington, Bart.,   FRED. THESIGER.
&c.   &c.   &c.   FITZROY KELLY.

(11.) JOINT OPINION *of the Queen's Advocate,* SIR J. D. HARDING, *and the Attorney and Solicitor General,* SIR R. BETHELL *and* SIR H. S. KEATING, *that a person charged in a Colony with any offence under 12 & 13 Vict. c. 96, cannot be sent to England for trial; nor can proceedings of such trial be revised in England.*

Doctors' Commons, December 21, 1857.

SIR,—We are honoured with your commands, signified in Mr Elliot's letter of the 6th November ultimo, requesting that we would furnish you with our opinion on the following questions:—

The Act of Parliament, 12 & 13 Vict. c. 96, provides that if a person shall be charged in any colony with any one of certain specified offences, committed within the jurisdiction of the Admiralty, the colonial judicature shall have the same powers for trying such offence as they would have possessed, and shall be authorized, empowered, and required to carry on such proceedings, for bringing the accused person to trial, as would and ought to have been carried on, if the offence had been committed within the jurisdiction of the colonial court.

Having regard to the provisions of the statute, we are requested. to inform you—

1. Whether a colonial court of judicature, before which a case is brought for trial under the provisions of the 12 & 13 Vict. c. 96, possesses, either at common law, or in virtue of any statute, the power of sending the accused person to England for trial? And,

2. Whether any means exist (other than those which may be provided by the law of the particular colony), by which the proceedings on such trial may be sent to England for revision? (1).

In obedience to your directions, we beg to report—

That having considered the questions submitted to us, we are of opinion that both must be answered in the negative.

J. D. HARDING.

The Right Hon. H. Labouchere, M.P.,   RICHARD BETHELL.

&c. &c. &c.   HENRY S. KEATING.

NOTES TO CHAPTER VII.

The general rule of law is thus expressed by Paulus, *Extra territorium* Extra-terri-*jus dicenti impune haud paretur*, Dig. ii. tit. 1, 20 : " It is true, beyond all torial jurisdi-doubt, that, as a matter of right, no State can claim jurisdiction of any tion. kind within the territorial limits of another independent State. It is also true that between two Christian States all claims for jurisdiction of any kind, or exemption from jurisdiction, must be founded upon treaty, or engagements of similar validity. Such, indeed, were factory establishments for the benefit of trade . . . . . The formality of a treaty is the best proof of the consent and acquiescence of parties, but it is not the only proof, nor does it exclude other proof; and more especially in transactions with Oriental States :" *Papayanni* v. *The Russian Steam Navigation Company*, 2 Moore, P. C. (N.S.) 181.

One mode of exercising extra-territorial jurisdiction is by permanent local tribunals, under treaty or by sufferance, in Mahommedan or barbarous countries. " One form of this jurisdiction, which has existed from the earliest times, is that of factories established for commercial purposes by a more civilized, in the territory of a less civilized, nation,

(1) Even if a colonial law were passed to enable the proceedings to be transmitted, I know of no authority which the courts here would have to deal with them.

with the consent of the latter. Factories have always been allowed to appoint magistrates of their own, and to exercise an independent jurisdiction, from the Greek factory of Naucrates in ancient Egypt, and the factories of the Genoese and Venetians in the Levant in the middle ages, to those of the English East India Company in Hindostan :" Sir G. Cornewall Lewis on Foreign Jurisdiction (London, 1859).

In an Opinion given in 1866 by the Attorney General, Sir Hugh Cairns, the Solicitor General, Sir William Bovill, and myself, on the question of erecting courts for the trial of British subjects in Indian territories not under the dominion of the Crown, we said : " Where no treaty exists between a foreign State and Her Majesty authorizing the creation of such tribunals as are here supposed, we are of opinion that the Governor-General in Council has no authority or power to establish it, and that no Act of Parliament could give him such power. We think that in order to create such tribunals treaties should be entered into with foreign States authorizing their establishment, and that, notwithstanding the Foreign Jurisdiction Act, it would be advisable to have an Act of Parliament passed which should enable the Governor-General of India in Council to establish them, after the assent of the foreign States in each particular case has been obtained."

And in a later Opinion on the same subject, given in 1867, by the Attorney General, Sir John Rolt, the Queen's Advocate, Sir Robert Phillimore, the Solicitor General, Sir John Karslake, and myself, we said : " We do not think that actual treaties are necessary for the establishment of courts of justice in dependent native States. It would be sufficient if the consent of the ruling powers were obtained, and this might be evidenced by acquiescence, usage, and sufferance."

The Royal Warrant first constituting a Judicial Assessor on the Gold Coast of Africa in 1847, recites that : " We have, by usage and sufferance, or by one or other of these, or by other lawful means, power and jurisdiction within divers countries and places not of, but adjacent to, our forts and settlements on the Gold Coast:" quoted by Sir G. Cornewall Lewis on Foreign Jurisdiction ; and see Earl Grey's Colonial Policy, ii. 270.   By the Foreign Jurisdiction Act, 6 & 7 Vict. c. 94, which recites that, " whereas by treaty, capitulation, grant, usage, sufferance, and other lawful means, Her Majesty hath power and jurisdiction within divers countries and places out of Her Majesty's dominions," but doubts had arisen how far the exercise of such power and jurisdiction is controlled by the laws and customs of this realm, it is enacted that Her Majesty may exercise any power or jurisdiction which she has within any country or place not her dominions in the same and as ample a manner as if such power or jurisdiction had been acquired by the cession or conquest of territory.   The same Act gives power to send persons charged with crimes in such countries or places for trial to any British colony.   The statute 3 & 4 Will. 4, c. 93, empowers the Crown to appoint Superintendents of Trade in China, and by Order in Council to give them power and authority to make regulations for the government of British subjects in China, and to impose penalties, forfeitures, or imprisonments for the breach of such regulations, and to create a court of justice with criminal and admiralty jurisdiction for the trial of offences committed by British subjects within the dominion of China and on the high seas within one hundred miles of the coast of China : see *Evans* v. *Hutton*, 4 M. & G. 954.

Many of the German States, some of the Swiss Cantons, Portugal, Russia, and Norway, punish all offences of their subjects committed in foreign parts, whether against themselves, their subjects, or foreigners : Woolsey's International Law, s. 78. The French law does not punish crimes of Frenchmen against foreigners, nor *delits* of one Frenchman against another, on foreign soil, nor "crimes" of Frenchmen against Frenchmen except on complaint of the injured party, but punishes offences against the Government and public safety of France, including the counterfeiting of its seal, coins, and paper money : *Ibid.* ; Wheaton's International Law, s. 120, n. 77 (8th ed. by Dana). The Italian monarchy punishes high crimes of its subjects committed abroad, but treats misdemeanors by the rule of reciprocity : *Ibid.* Belgium and Holland punish foreign crimes of their subjects against the State or their fellow-subjects, but only certain crimes of such subjects in foreign parts against foreigners : Woolsey, s. 78. Great Britain and the United States do not punish a foreigner found within their limits for a crime committed abroad against their Governments or their subjects, but France does, following the analogy of its treatment of its subjects under like circumstances.

It has been decided in France that French criminal law is for Frenchmen a personal statute, that it binds them in foreign countries, and that consequently when they have committed a crime or a misdemeanor in a foreign land, they can always be prosecuted for this crime or misdemeanor on their return to France : Speech of M. Portalis in the Chamber of Peers in 1842. (M. Portalis had been a member of the *Cour de Cassation* for many years.)

It is a general rule that a State will not try its own subjects for offences committed abroad against foreign States or their subjects ; Wheaton, *ubi sup.* Dana, in a note there, says that this seems to be a rule almost without exception. But an exception occurs in the case of Great Britain ; for by statute 24 & 25 Vict. c. 100, s. 9, where any murder or manslaughter shall be committed *on land* out of the United Kingdom, whether within the Queen's dominions or without, and *whether the person killed was a subject of Her Majesty or not*, every such offence committed by any subject of Her Majesty may be tried in any county or place, in England or Ireland, where the offender shall be apprehended or be in custody : see *R.* v. *Azzopardi*, 2 Moody, C. C. 288.

But by the common law of England no court of justice in this country has jurisdiction to try a crime committed abroad. With respect to crimes committed on the high seas by British subjects, the Court of Admiralty had jurisdiction by statute 28 Hen. 8, c. 15 ; 39 Geo. 3,

c. 37 ; 46 Geo. 3, c. 54 ; 4 & 5 Will. 4, c. 36 ; 7 & 8 Vict. c. 2. See
statute 12 & 13 Vict. c. 96, for the prosecution and trial in Her Majesty's
colonies of offences committed within the jurisdiction of the Admiralty.
This Act was extended to the East Indies by statute 23 & 24 Vict.
c. 88.

In a case submitted in 1849 to the Queen's Advocate, Sir John
Dodson, where a felonious assault had been committed on the high
seas by an inhabitant of the Virgin Islands, it was stated that the
Chief Justice of the colony was of opinion that there was no local court
of competent jurisdiction to try the offender, and that it would be
necessary that a commission under the great seal for the holding of
Admiralty sessions should be issued. The Queen's Advocate gave it
as his opinion that the case was one which might be tried under the
provisions of statute 12 & 13 Vict. c. 96, and that there was no necessity for the issue of a commission under the great seal for trial of the
offender. And in another case, in 1851, the Law Officers—Sir J. Dodson,
Queen's Advocate, Sir J. Romilly, A.G., and Sir A. Cockburn, S.G.—
were of opinion that the 12 & 13 Vict. c. 96 is an enabling statute, not
repealing any authority possessed by the Crown prior to it, and that
since the passing of that Act it remains in Her Majesty's power to
issue commissions, as was customarily done under the 46 Geo. 3, c. 54,
for the trial of offences specified in the later Act, and that commissions
issued before it passed were still in force. They added that, if there
could not be an impartial trial in the colony (Tortola), they thought it
was competent for the Governor to transfer the offenders for trial to
another colony, where there was a commission in force. Also in
another case, in 1851, where two persons had been tried and convicted
of piracy on the high seas, at a Commission Court held at Honduras, and
an objection was taken that the crime of which the prisoners were convicted was committed before the Act 12 & 13 Vict. c. 96 was passed,
the same Law Officers were of opinion that the objection was invalid,
inasmuch as the prisoners were charged after the passing of the Act.
They held, however, that an objection, that the Commission Court,
according to statute 59 Geo. 3, c. 44, and the letters patent of the
Crown by which it was constituted, had no jurisdiction to try eo nomine
for piracy, and that statute 12 & 13 Vict. c. 96 only contemplated the
trial by any colonial court of the same offences when committed on the
high seas which the same court might previously have tried if committed upon any inland waters, was valid: see the Opinion of the
Law Officers, p. 227, ante.

The Merchant Shipping Act, 1854 (17 & 18 Vict. c. 104, s. 207), enacts
that all offences against property or person committed at any place,
either ashore or afloat, out of Her Majesty's dominions by any British
seaman, who at the time of the offence committed, or within three
months previously, has been employed in any British ship, shall be
tried as if such offences had been committed within the jurisdiction of
the Admiralty ; and certain rules are given in the Act with respect to

offences committed on the high seas or abroad. The statute 18 & 19 Vict. c. 91, s. 21, enacts that if any person, being a British subject, charged with having committed any crime or offence on board any British ship on the high seas, or in any foreign port or harbour, or if any person, not being a British subject, charged with having committed any crime or offence on board any British ship on the high seas is *found*—that is to say, is found to be at the time of his trial : *R.* v. *Lopez,* 27 L. J. (M.C.) 48—within the jurisdiction of any court of justice in Her Majesty's dominions, which would have had cognizance of such crime or offence if committed within the limits of its ordinary jurisdiction, such court shall have jurisdiction to hear and try the case, as if such crime or offence had been committed within such limits : *R.* v. *Anderson,* 11 Cox C. C. 198 ; see *R.* v. *Sattler,* 27 L. J. (M.C.) 50. I have already referred to statute 24 & 25 Vict. c. 100, which applies to trials in England or Ireland for murder or manslaughter committed on land, whether within the Queen's dominions or without. And by statute 30 & 31 Vict. c. 124, s. 11, if a British subject commits any crime or offence on board a British ship, or on board a foreign ship to which he does not belong, any court of justice in Her Majesty's dominions, which would have had cognizance of such crime or offence if committed on board a British ship within the limits of the ordinary jurisdiction of such court, shall have jurisdiction over the case as if the said crime or offence had been committed as last aforesaid. But a foreigner who kills another foreigner abroad, on land out of the Queen's dominions, or on the high seas on board a *foreign* ship, is not amenable to the law of England, and cannot be tried here : *R.* v. *Lewis,* 1 Dear & B. C. C. 182. The criminal jurisdiction of the Court of Admiralty was transferred to the Central Criminal Court by statute 4 & 5 Will. 4, c. 36.

By statute 10 & 11 Will. 3, c. 25, s. 13, any capital crimes whatsoever, committed in Newfoundland or the islands adjoining, may be tried in any county in England. The statute 57 Geo. 3, c. 53, enacts that murders and manslaughters committed on land at Honduras, or in any place not within the dominions of the Crown, nor subject to any European State or Power, nor within the territories of the United States, by the master or crew of any British ship, or by any person sailing or belonging thereto, or that shall have sailed in, or belonged to, and have quitted any British ship to live in any of the said places, or that shall be there living, may be tried in any of the possessions of the Crown abroad.

By statute 36 Geo. 3, c. 57, if any person shall, within the realm or without, commit treason, he shall suffer death as a traitor.

By statute 9 Geo. 4, c. 83, s. 4, jurisdiction is given to the Supreme Courts of New South Wales and Van Diemen's Land over all offences committed on the sea or in any island or country in the Indian or Pacific Oceans, not subject to the British Crown, or to any European State or Power, by any British subject, having sailed in, or belonging to, or having quitted any British vessel to live in any such places, or that are there living. See also statute 6 & 7 Will. 4, c. 57, as to offences committed by British subjects in territories adjacent to the colony of the Cape of Good Hope.

See statute 6 & 7 Vict."c. 80, " An Act for the better government of Her Majesty's subjects resorting to China." In 1844 an Order in Council was made authorizing British consuls in China to exercise civil and criminal jurisdiction within their districts, over British subjects within such districts, and to send such subjects charged with the commission of crimes and offences to Hong Kong for trial: M. S. Council Register, 1844, p. 220.

It was held, in an old case, that a man who had committed in Ireland the crime of abduction, which was then capital there, although not so in England, could be sent to Ireland from this country to be tried: *Kimberley's Case*, 2 Stra. 848; see *Lundy's Case*, 2 Vent. 314.

As to an arrest made in a foreign country with a view to a subsequent trial here, see *Mure* v. *Kaye*, 4 Taunt. 34; *Ex parte Scott*, 9 B. & C. 446.

With respect to murder or manslaughter committed in foreign territory, see *R.* v. *Depardo*, Russ. & Ry. 134 (where the prisoner was an alien who had killed a British subject on shore at Canton); *R.* v. *Sawyer*, *ibid.* 224; *R.* v. *Helsham*, 4 C. & P. 394 (where the prisoner, a British subject, had killed another British subject in a duel in France); *R.* v. *De Mattos*, 7 C. & P. 458; *R.* v. *Azzopardi*, 2 Moo. C. C. 288; *R.* v. *Anderson*, 11 Cox C. C. 198 (where the prisoner, a foreigner, one of the crew of a British ship, committed manslaughter on board the ship in the Garonne, within the boundaries of the Empire of France) (1).

Crimes against foreign States.
There is no doubt that a crime committed in England against a foreign State in amity with the Crown of England—as, for instance, a plot to assassinate a friendly monarch—is punishable here. When Lord Palmerston introduced a Bill into Parliament in 1858, to amend the law with relation to the crime of conspiracy to commit murder, of which the immediate occasion was a plot against the life of the Emperor of the French organized in this country, it was rejected, because 'the House of Commons thought that the measure was brought forward at the dictation of a foreign Power. In reality the common law was sufficient for the purpose: see *R.* v. *Bernard*, 1 Fost. & Fin. 240. So it is a misdemeanor to subscribe in this country to aid a rebellion against a foreign Government in amity with the Crown. Lord Lyndhurst said in the House of Lords, on the 4th of March, 1853 : "If a number of British subjects were to combine and conspire together to excite revolt among the inhabitants of a friendly State—of a State united in alliance with us—and these persons, in pursuance of that conspiracy, were to issue manifestoes and proclamations for the pur-

(1) A curious question was submitted to the Law Officers of the Crown while Napoleon was a prisoner at St. Helena. He was fond of ball-practice, and fired very carelessly, one day killing a bullock. Supposing he had killed a person, under circumstances which would amount to manslaughter according to English law, what was to be done with him? An opinion was given, but I have not been able to find it. (See Forsyth's Napoleon at St. Helena and Sir Hudson Lowe, vol. iii. p. 311.)

pose of carrying that object into effect; above all, if they were to
subscribe money for the purpose of purchasing arms to give effect to
that intended enterprise, I conceive, and I state with confidence, that
such persons would be guilty of a misdemeanor, and liable to suffer
punishment by the laws of this country, inasmuch as their conduct
would tend to embroil the two countries together, to lead to remon-
strances by the one with the other, and ultimately it might be to war.
. . . . . . The offence of endeavouring to excite revolt among the subjects of a neighbouring State is an offence against the law of nations.
No writer on the law of nations states otherwise. But the law of
nations according to the decisions of our greatest judges is part of the
law of England." In *De Wütz* v. *Hendricks*, 2 Bing. 315, Best, C.J.,
said : " It occurred to me at the trial that it was contrary to the law of
nations (which in all cases of international law is adopted into the
municipal code of every civilized country) for persons in England to
enter into engagements to support the subjects of a Government in
amity with our own, in hostilities against their Government, and that
no right of action could arise but of such a transaction . . . . . . In
consequence of what I said, a note has since been handed to me of a
case that occurred lately in Chancery, in which the Lord Chancellor
is reported to have said that English courts of justice will afford
no assistance to persons who set about to raise loans for subjects of
the King of Spain, to enable them to prosecute a war against that
Sovereign."

The following are cases of criminal information filed against persons
in this country for libels against foreign sovereigns in amity with the
Crown : *R.* v. *Lord George Gordon*, 22 State Tr. 213 (a libel on the
Queen of France); *R.* v. *Vint*, 27 State Tr. 627 (a libel on the Em-
peror Paul of Russia); *R.* v. *Peltier*, 28 State Tr. 617 (a libel upon
Bonaparte when First Consul).

By the Foreign Enlistment Act (59 Geo. 3, c. 69), if any British sub- Foreign En-
ject, without license from the Crown, shall accept any military com- listment Act.
mission (see *Dobree* v. *Napier*, 2 Bing. N. C. 781), or enlist as a soldier
or a sailor in any foreign service, or shall go to any foreign country
with an intent so to enlist; and if any person within the dominions of
the Crown shall equip, furnish, fit out, or arm any ship or vessel for
the service of any foreign State, or with intent to cruise or commit
hostilities against any State with whom Her Majesty shall not then be
at war, or shall issue any commission for any such vessel, or shall alter
the number of guns of such vessel, or be concerned in augmenting the
force of any foreign armed vessel arriving in this country, such offender
shall be guilty of a misdemeanor, and may be punished with fine or
imprisonment, or both.

In an opinion given by Mr. Mellish, Q.C., in February, 1863, on the
question whether the building of a vessel for the Confederate Government, during the civil war in America, was an illegal act, he said : "I
am of opinion that Messrs. Laird had a right to build the ship which

has since been called the *Alabama* in the manner they did, and that
they have committed no offence against either the common law or the
Foreign Enlistment Act with reference to that ship. I am of opinion
that the simple building of a ship, even although the ship be of a kind
apparently adapted for warlike purposes, and delivering such ship to a
purchaser in an English port, even although the purchaser is suspected
or known to be the agent of a foreign belligerent Power, does not constitute an offence against the Foreign Enlistment Act (59 Geo. 3, c. 69;
s. 7), on the part of the builder, unless the builder makes himself a
party to the equipping of the vessel for warlike purposes. The
Alabama, indeed, appears to me to have been equipped at the Azores,
and not in England at all." And this opinion was confirmed by Sir
Hugh Cairns and Mr. Kemplay, who added that it would not be
altered if the fact were that the builders knew they were building the
Alabama for an agent of the Confederate Government. See the report
of the trial, *Attorney General* v. *Sillem*, "The *Alexandra*" (London, 1863).

Power of
Parliament to
legislate for
foreigners.

Parliament has no general power to legislate for foreigners out of the
dominions and beyond the jurisdiction of the British Crown, but it
may fix a time within which application must be made for redress to
the courts of justice. This is matter of procedure, and becomes part of
the *lex fori* : *Lopez* v. *Burslem*, 4 Moore, P. C. 300.

An Act was passed by Congress in 1850, to carry into effect certain
stipulations in the treaties between the United States and China,
Japan, Siam, Turkey, Persia, Tripoli, Tunis, Morocco, and Muscat, by
which the laws of the United States are extended over American
citizens in those countries, and ministers and consuls have full judicial
powers given to them. The President is authorized to appoint marshals to execute process : see Woolsey's Internat. Law, s. 65.

In an American case, *Rose* v. *Himeley*, 4 Cranch, 241, where a vessel,
after trading with rebels at St. Domingo, was seized more than ten
leagues from the coast by a French privateer, and taken to a Spanish
port and sold, and was afterwards condemned by a French tribunal at
St. Domingo under municipal law, the Court held that any seizure for
breach of a municipal regulation beyond the limits of the territorial
jurisdiction was not warranted by the law of nations, and invalid. "It
may be said," observes Dana, in a note to Wheaton's Internat. Law,
s. 180, "that the principle is settled that municipal seizures cannot be
made for any purpose beyond territorial waters. It is also settled that
the limit of these waters is, in the absence of treaty, the marine league,
or the cannon-shot." In the case of the *Cagliari* in 1857, the present
Queen's Advocate, Sir Travers Twiss, gave an opinion that, "in ordinary cases where a merchant ship has been seized on the high seas, the
Sovereign whose flag has been violated waives his privilege; considering the offending ship to have acted with *mala fides* towards the other
State with which he is in amity, and to have consequently forfeited
any just claim to his protection."

CHAPTER VIII.

ON THE LEX LOCI AND LEX FORI (1).

A CONTRACT valid by the law of the place where it was made is, Lex Loci. generally speaking, valid everywhere else. *Rectores imperiorum id comiter agunt, ut jura cujusque populi intra terminos ejus exercita teneant ubique suam vim, quatenus nihil potestati aut juri alterius imperantis ejusque civium præjudicetur.* —Huber, *de Conflict Leg.* ii. lib. i. tit. 3, s. 3.

The interpretation of contracts, and the legal rights arising out of them, are governed by the *lex loci* where they were made: *Wriggleworth* v. *Dallison*, 1 Doug. 201, 202 ; *Holman* v. *Johnson*, Cowp. 341 ; *Lacon* v. *Hooper*, 6 T. R. 224 ; *Webb* v. *Plumer*, 2 B. & Al. 746 ; *De la Vega* v. *Vianna*, 1 B. & Ad. 284 ; *Dalrymple* v. *Dalrymple*, 2 Hagg. Cons. R. 60, 61 ; *Donn* v. *Lipman*, 5 Cl. & Fin. 1 ; *Ferguson* v. *Fyffe*, 8 Cl. & Fin. 121 ; *Munroe* v. *Pilkington*, 31 L. J. (Q. B.) 81 ; *Peninsular and Oriental Steam Navigation Company* v. *Shand*, 3 Moore, P. C. (N. S.) 272 ; *Leroux* v. *Brown*, 12 C. B. 801. Where an action was brought in this country by the syndics of a French bankrupt, upon an *ordinance* in France whereby the defendant was adjudged to pay to the bankrupt a sum of money, the Court said: " This is a peculiar right of action created by the law of that country ; and we think it may by the comity of nations be enforced in this, as much as the right of foreign assignees, or curators, or foreign corporations, appointed or created in a different way from that which the law of this country requires :" *Alivon* v. *Furnival*, 1 C. M. & R. 296 ; see *Solomons* v. *Ross*, 1 H. Bl. 131, note.

(1) The subject of this chapter is naturally connected with that of the preceding one ; but I was not able to find any Law Officers' or other Opinions directly relating to it. I have, therefore, thought it better and more convenient to place these notes in the text.

In *Somersett's Case*, 20 State Tr. 1 (a case of *trover* for a slave), Lord Mansfield said: "I am quite clear that the act of detaining a man as a slave can only be justified by the law of the country where the act is done, although contracts are to be construed according to the law of the country where they are entered into, and the succession to personal property according to the law of the country where the deceased owner was domiciled at the time of his death."

Where contract illegal by Lex Loci. The principle of giving validity to contracts according to the *lex loci* where they are made, is said not to apply where that law is *contra bonos mores*, or contrary to the public law of the State where they are sought to be enforced, or to the general wellbeing of society. "It cannot apply," says Wheaton, s. 90, "where it would injuriously conflict with the laws of another State relating to its police, its public health, its commerce, its revenue, and generally its sovereign authority, and the rights and interests of its citizens." "There is no exception to the rule as to the universal validity of contracts; which is, that no nation is bound to recognize or enforce any contracts which are injurious to its own interests, or to those of its own subjects." Huber (*de Conflict Leg.*, lib. i. tit. 3, s. 2) has expressed it in the following terms:—"*Quatenus nihil potestati aut juri alterius imperantis ejusque civium præjudicetur :*" see Story, Conf. Laws, s. 244. In *Forbes* v. *Cochrane*, 2 B. & C. 471, Best, C.J., said, that the comity of nations "is a maxim that cannot prevail in any case where it violates the law of our own country, the law of nature, or the law of God. . . . . If the right sought to be enforced is inconsistent with either of these, the English municipal courts cannot recognize it." Woolsey (Internat. Law, s. 72), citing Savigny (Rom. Recht. s. 374), says: "Wherever a law of a strictly positive nature opposes the matter of the contract, the *lex fori contractûs* must be applied. Thus if a suit for interest due on money be brought in a place where the usury laws would render such a transaction void, the Judge must follow his own law." Story says (Conflict of Laws, s. 340): "In a very recent case the Supreme Court of the United States have adopted the doctrine, that when a contract is made in one place to be executed in another, it is to be governed as to usury by the law of the place of performance, and not by the law of the place where it is made. So that, if the transaction is *boná fide*, and not with intent to evade the law against usury, and the law of the place of performance allows a higher rate of interest than that permitted at the place of the contract, the parties may lawfully stipulate for the higher interest. But then the transction must be *boná fide*, and not intended as a mere error of usury." And again, s. 305 : "It has been said that if the principle be that a contract valid in the place where the contract is celebrated is void if it is contrary to the law of the place of payment, it must establish the universal proposition, that a contract void by the law of the place where it is made is valid, if good by the law of the place of payment. This would seem to be reasonable, and the doctrine is supported by the modern cases, notwithstanding the old cases have been supposed to lead to a contrary conclusion."

As to the rule of English law in such cases, see *Robinson* v. *Bland*, 2 Burr. 1077 ; *Holman* v. *Johnson*, Cowp. 341 ; *Pellecatt* v. *Angell*, 2 C. M. & R. 311 ; *Spence* v. *Chadwick*, 10 Q. B. 517, 2 Sim. 194 ; *Hyde* v. *Hyde*, L. R. 1 Prob. & Div. 131. An exception has been thought to exist in cases of contracts made in violation of the revenue laws: *Cas. temp. Hardwicke*, 85 ; 2 Rob. D. & M. 6 ; *Planché* v. *Fletcher*, 1 Douglas, 251 ; *Holman* v. *Johnson*, 1 Cowp. 341 ; *Pellecatt* v. *Angell*, 2 C. M. & R. 311. But the old idea that there is a distinction between statutes which have in view the protection of the revenue, and those which have in view other objects, if *the contract* is rendered illegal by them, is now exploded ; and a contract is rendered void where the statute only inflicts a penalty, for such a penalty implies a prohibition : *Cope* v. *Rowlands*, 2 M. & W. 157 ; see *Spence* v. *Chadwick*, 10 Q. B. 517. If the want of a stamp renders a contract made in a foreign country *void*, it cannot be enforced here: *Alves* v. *Hodgson*, 7 T. R. 241. *Aliter*, if the stamp is required only to enable the document embodying the contract to be given in evidence : *Bristow* v. *Sequeville*, 5 Ex. 275.

A contract by British subjects relating to the sale and purchase of slaves in a country where slavery is legal, may be enforced in the courts of this country, notwithstanding statute 5 Geo. 4, c. 113, and by the force of 6 & 7 Vict. c. 98, s. 5 : so held by a majority of the Court of Error in *Santos* v. *Illidge*, 29 L. J. (C. P.) 348, reversing the judgment of the Court below, 28 L. J. (C. P.) 317.

. R

Blackburn, J., said: "Assuming the taking to have been prohibited by a British Act, still the taking having been of property locally situate in a foreign country, in a manner lawful according to the laws of that country, I apprehend that the property actually passed by the sale, and vested in the purchasers, *though they committed a felony according to our law by taking it.*" See *Somersett* v. *Stewart*, Lofft., 17; *Smith* v. *Brown*, 2 Salk. 666; *Smith* v. *Gould, Ibid.*; *Mittelholzer* v. *Fullarton*, 6 Q. B. 989; *Madrazo* v. *Willes*, 3 B. & Al. 353—as to which it was said by Willes, J., in *Santos* v. *Illidge*, 28 L. J. (C. P.) 318, "That case has been wondered at;" *Buron* v. *Denman*, 2 Ex. 167.

"If the penal laws of a foreign country," said the Court in *Folliott* v. *Ogden*, 1 H. Bl. 135, "do not in themselves import a personal disability to sue in this, neither do they, by diverting the property of a person in that country, take away his right of action in England. . . . The penal laws of foreign countries are strictly local, and affect nothing more than that they can reach and can be seized by virtue of their authority; a fugitive who passes hither comes with all his transitory rights; he may recover money held for his use, stock, obligations, and the like, and cannot be affected in this country by proceedings against him in that which he has left, beyond the limits of which such proceedings do not extend."

A contract illegal in the place where it was made, is generally held to be invalid everywhere: *Robinson* v. *Bland*, 2 Burr. 1077; 2 Kent, Com. 458; Story, Conf. Laws, s. 243.

The question of disability to make a contract on account of infancy is decided by the *lex loci*: *Male* v. *Roberts*, 3 Esp. 163, where Lord Eldon said: "I hold myself not warranted in saying that such a contract is void by the law of Scotland (where it was made) because it is void by the law of England."

Foreign Court acting perversely.
Where a foreign Court acts perversely and in defiance of the comity of nations, by refusing to recognize a title to property acquired according to the laws of England, its judgment will not be regarded by the English Courts: *Simpson* v. *Fogo*, 32 L. J. (Ch.) 249; see *Cammell* v. *Sewell*, 29 L. J. (Ex.) 350; *Castrique* v. *Imrie*, 30 L. J. (C. P.) 177; *Woolf* v. *Oxholm*, 6 M. & S. 92.

Bills of Exchange.
The indorsee of a bill of exchange drawn, accepted, and pay-

able in England, can maintain an action here against the acceptor under an indorsement made in France, although the law of France gives no right to the indorsee to sue in his own name, and both he and the indorser were subjects of France, and domiciled and resident there when the bill was made and indorsed: *Lebel* v. *Tucker*, L. R. 3 Q. B. 77. See also, as to bills of exchange, *Snaith* v. *Mingay*, 1 M. & S. 87; *Crutchley* v. *Mann*, 5 Taunt. 529; *Rothschild* v. *Currie*, 1 Q. B. 43; *Hirschfield* v. *Smith*, L. R. 1 C. P. 340; *Allen* v. *Kemble*, 6 Moore, P. C. 314; *Gibbs* v. *Fremont*, 9 Ex. R. 25; *Sharples* v. *Rickard*, 26 L. J. (Ex.) 302.

Where the place for executing the contract is different from the place where it is made, everything which concerns its *execution* is determined by the law of the former place, but what concerns its *validity and interpretation* by the *lex loci contractûs:* Wheaton, s. 94. Story (Conf. Laws, s. 250) says that in such a case the contract, as to its validity, nature, obligation, and interpretation, is to be governed by the law of the place of performance. But Wheaton seems to point out the true distinction. Nor is what was said by Lord Mansfield in *Robinson* v. *Bland*, 2 Burr. 1077— namely, that "the law of the place can never be the rule where the transaction is entered into *with an express view to the law of another country, as the rule by which it is to be governed*"—inconsistent with this principle; for by the nature of the case it is assumed that it was part of the contract that it should be governed by the law of another country, and, of course, in such a case the maxim *volenti non fit injuria* would apply.

Where place of execution different from place where contract made.

"The *lex loci contractûs* is to govern in the construction of contracts, but that applies only when the contract is not express. If it be special, it must be construed according to the express terms in which it is made:" *per* Alderson, B., *Gibbs* v. *Fremont*, 9 Ex. R. 30; see *Munroe* v. *Pilkington*, 31 L. J. (Q. B.) 81; *Peninsular and Oriental Steam Navigation Company* v. *Shand*, 3 Moore, P. C. (N.S.) 272. But where the contract is to be performed generally without any stipulation, express or implied, as to the place, the law of the place of making it governs: Story, Conf. Laws, s. 282. And when a contract of affreightment does not provide otherwise, the law of the country to which the ship belongs must be taken to be the law governing liability in respect of sea-damage and

R 2

its incidents: *Lloyd* v. *Guibert*, L. R. 1 Q. B. 115 (in error). As to the liability here for collision on the high seas of a Frenchman, the member of a French marine company, by one of whose vessels the damage was occasioned, see *General Steam Navigation Company* v. *Guillou*, 11 M. & W. 877. Where a contract is made partly in one country and partly in another, it is said to be a contract of the place where the assent of the parties first concurs and becomes complete.

Discharge of liability.

A discharge from a debt or the performance of a contract under the *lex loci* is, in general, a discharge everywhere: Story, Conf. Laws, ss. 331–334; *Robinson* v. *Bland*, 1 W. Bl. 258; *Quin* v. *Keefe*, 2 H. Bl. 553; *Phillips* v. *Allan*, 8 B. & C. 477. But to this rule there is an exception, where there has been a confiscation of the debt, not justified by the law of nations: *Woolf* v. *Oxholm*, 6 M. & S. 92.

And where the statutes of limitation or prescription, as they are generally called, in a foreign country, not only extinguish the right of action, but the claim or title itself, *ipso facto*, and declare it to be a nullity after the lapse of the prescribed period, it seems that the statute may be pleaded here as a valid defence to show the extinguishment of the debt. "But this must be taken with the qualification stated by Story, Conf. Laws, that the parties are resident within the jurisdiction all that period, so that it has actually operated on the case:" *per cur. Huber* v. *Steiner*, 2 Bing. N. C. 211; see *Don* v. *Lippman*, 5 Cl. & Fin. 1. The question to be determined in each case seems to be this, whether the rule of foreign law applies *ad valorem contractús*, or *ad modum actionis instituendæ*. If the former, the action is not maintainable; if the latter, it is.

A discharge of a contract by the law of a place where it was neither made nor to be performed will not be a discharge of it in any other country. A foreign law cannot take away the right of a subject of this country to sue here upon a contract made here: *Smith* v. *Buchanan*, 1 East, 6; *Bartley* v. *Hodges*, 30 L. J. (Q. B.) 352; *Lewis* v. *Owen*, 4 B. & Al. 654; *Phillips* v. *Allan*, 8 B. & C. 477.

Marriage.

The general rule as to marriage is, that the contract is governed by the law of the place where it is celebrated, and the formalities to be observed are those of the *lex loci*, if any mode available to the parties is provided by that law: *Scrimshire* v. *Scrimshire*, 2 Hagg. Const. 395; *Harford* v. *Morris*, Ib. 423-436; *R.* v. *Inhabitants of Brampton*, 10 East, 282; *Kent* v. *Burgess*, 11 Sim. 361.

In *Ruding* v. *Smith*, 2 Hagg. Cons. R. 382, where the question was as to the validity of a marriage between British subjects at the Cape of Good Hope, not according to the *lex loci* of Holland, but celebrated according to the rites of the Church of England by the chaplain of the British forces, who then occupied the settlement under a capitulation, Lord Stowell said (p. 391): "It is true indeed that English decisions have established this rule, that a foreign marriage, valid according to the law of a place where celebrated, is good everywhere else; but they have not, *e converso*, established that marriage of British subjects, not good according to the general law of the place where celebrated, are universally, and under all possible circumstances, to be regarded as invalid in England. It is therefore certainly to be advised that the safest course is always to be married according to the law of the country, for then no question can be stirred; but if this cannot be done on account of legal or religious difficulties, the law of this country does not say that its subjects shall not marry abroad. . . . In my opinion, this marriage (for I desire to be understood as not extending this decision beyond cases including nearly the same circumstances) rests upon solid foundations: on the distinct British character of the parties—on their independence of the Dutch law in their own British transactions—on the insuperable difficulties of obtaining any marriage conformable to the Dutch law—on the countenance given by British authority and British ministration to this British transaction—upon the whole country being under British dominion, and upon the other grounds to which I have adverted; and I therefore dismiss this libel as insufficient, if proved, for the conclusion it prays."

In *Catherwood* v. *Caslon*, 13 M. & W. 264, it was said by Parke, B.: "It may be proper to advert to a dictum in Buller's Nisi Prius, p. 28, that a marriage according to any form of religion is a marriage *de facto*; and for this the case of *Woolston* v. *Scott* (*ibid.*). before Denison, J., in 1753, is quoted. Whether this marriage of Anabaptists before the Marriage Act was valid, is one of those doubtful disputations pressed on the House of Lords in *The Queen*

v. *Millis*, 10 Cl. & Fin. 534. The case before Denison, J., was probably upon a marriage prior to 1752, when all marriages were in the same condition. Both these marriages and Quakers', if valid at all, were valid as being formal marriages, and legal to all purposes."

The prevalent American doctrine is that a marriage valid in the State where it is contracted is good everywhere, even if prohibited by the *lex fori* or *domicilii*: see Bouvier's Dict. ii. 38.

But the rule that a "foreign marriage, valid according to the law of the country where it is celebrated, is good everywhere," applies in England only to the form and not to the essentials of the contract, which depend on the *lex domicilii*—that is, the law of the country where the parties are then domiciled, and in which they contemplate to reside. In *Brook* v. *Brook*, 9 H. L. 212, Lord Campbell, L.C., said: "It is quite obvious that no civilized State can allow its domiciled subjects or citizens, by making a temporary visit to a foreign country, to enter into a contract to be performed in the place of domicile, if the contract is forbidden by the law of the place of domicile as contrary to religion or morality, or to any of its fundamental institutions." And again, p. 218: "None of these cases can show the validity of a marriage which the law of the domicile of the parties condemns as incestuous, and which could not by any forms or consents have been rendered valid in the country in which the parties were domiciled."

In a case decided in the Ecclesiastical Court in 1838, where the parties went to Scotland fraudulently to evade the English law, the Court said that marriage was a natural right, and that what was done in aid of that natural right was not a fraud. It was an evasion of the law, but no fraud. And the learned judge cited a case where a man *in articulo mortis* actually married to prevent his property going to a particular person; and although it might be called a fraud as regarded the person thus deprived of the property, yet the marriage was held good upon the ground that it was a natural right (1): Ann. Reg. for 1838, vol. 80, Chron. p. 24; and

(1) I have read somewhere, but the reference has escaped me, of a lady of rank who, oeing pressed by her creditors, married a convict in prison under sentence of transportation; and having become a *femme covert*, she was released from her debts, and from liability to arrest. She took care, however, not to follow her husband to a penal settlement.

see remarks by Sir George Hay, in *Harford* v. *Morris*, 2 Hagg. Ecc. R. 433.

Where a statute is personal its force is recognized everywhere, and is as much respected in a foreign country as at home: Fœlix, Traité du Droit, s. 31.

Statutes creating personal disability.

Thus where a statute creates a *personal* incapacity of marriage between parties, this cannot be evaded by their going to a foreign country where there is no such restriction, and getting married there. This applies to the Royal Marriage Act, 12 Geo. 3, c. 11, by which the previous consent of the Sovereign is required: *Sussex Peerage Case*, 11 Cl. & Fin. 85; and to the Act, 5 & 6 Will. 4, c. 54, prohibiting marriage with a deceased wife's sister: *Brook* v. *Brook*, 9 H. L. 193. In France the age of consent required by the code is considered a personal quality of French subjects which follows them everywhere ; and it was upon this ground that in 1861, the Cour Impériale held the marriage of Jerome Bonaparte with Miss Paterson, contracted in the United States in 1803, to be invalid: see Wheaton, Internat. Law, s. 93, n. 55.

A curious question might arise as to the rights *inter se* in this country of a husband and wife, foreigners, and resident here, but married abroad in a country where the wife's property is not vested in the husband nor subject to his control, and where the property of neither is liable for the debts of the other. I suppose there is no doubt that, as regards creditors here, he would be liable for her debts contracted in England, and that her personal property (not settled to her separate use) would be considered as his, and so be liable to his debts. But if so, then they have not the benefit of the *lex loci* as regards their marriage rights, for one of those rights was that the property of neither should be seized for the debts of the other.

"What is to be done," asks Woolsey (Internat. Law, s. 74), "if the domicile is changed during marriage? Here some maintain that the law of the prior domicile, and others that of the new domicile, should be followed. Others still claim that the law of the new domicile should be applied to the property acquired since the change of residence, and the law of the earlier to all held before the change. Savigny holds that at the time of marriage

there was a tacit subjection of both parties to the law of their
habitation, which ought therefore to be enforced afterwards. A
new law might place the wife in a worse condition than she had
expected at the time of marriage:" see Story, Conf. Laws, ss.
145–199.

Divorce.   As to divorce, this is governed generally by the law of domicile:
Lolley's Case, 1 Russ & Ry. C. C. 236; *Warrender* v. *Warrender*,
9 Bligh, 122; *Tovey* v. *Lindsay*, 1 Dow. 117; *M'Carthy* v. *De Caix*,
2 Russ. & M. 614; *Conway* v. *Beazley*, 3 Hagg. Ecc. R. 639; *Argent*
v. *Argent*, 34 L. J. Prob. 133; Story, Conf. Laws, chap. 7.

Real property.   With respect to real property, the *lex loci rei sitæ* universally
Lex Loci rei
sitæ.   prevails: *Sill* v. *Worswick*, 1 H. Bl. 666; *Doe* d. *Birtwhistle* v. *Bar-
dill*, 5 B. & C. 438; *Tulloch* v. *Hartley*, 1 Y. & C. 114; *Brodie* v.
Barry, 2 Ves. & B. 127; *Coppin* v. *Coppin*, 2 P. Wms. 291; *Curtes*
v. *Hutton*, 14 Ves. 537; *Warrender* v. *Warrender*, 9 Bligh, H. L.
127; Story, Conf. Laws, ss. 365–428.

" The right to land in Chili must, no doubt, be determined by
their laws; but a contract entered into between three English
gentlemen, two of them domiciled and residing in England, and
the third residing in Chili, but not having acquired a foreign domicile, must, I think, be governed and construed by the rules of
English law": *per* Sir J. Romilly, M.R., *Coad* v. *Coad*, 33 L. J.
(Ch.) 278.

In *Frith* v. *Wollaston*, 7 Ex. R. 194, Parke, B., said: "At all
events it seems to be clear that the law of the Cape of Good Hope
cannot be taken to affect the debtor's real estate out of that country, which, being extra-territorial, is also out of the jurisdiction of
the Court where the judgment was obtained."

Wills.   Wills of personalty are governed by the law of the domicile of
the party at the time of the execution, but wills of realty, as to the
mode of transfer, by the *lex loci rei sitæ*: *Brodie* v. *Barry*, 2 Ves.
&. B. 127; *Price* v. *Dewhurst*, 8 Sim. 279; 4 Myl. & Cr. 76, S. C.;
Moore v. *Darell*, 4 Hagg. Ecc. R. 346; *Trotter* v. *Trotter*, 4 Bligh
(N.S.) 502; Story, Conf. Laws, s. 479 a.

Lex Loci as   As regards criminal law: "The *lex loci* must needs govern all
to crimes.
criminal jurisdiction, from the nature of the thing, and the purpose

of that jurisdiction :" *per* Lord Brougham, in *Warrender* v. *Warrender*, 9 Bligh (N. S.) 129. " It has been generally understood that whenever a crime has been committed, the criminal is punishable according to the *lex loci* of the country against the law of which the crime was committed :" *per* Heath, J., *Mure* v. *Kaye*, 4 Taunt. 43. This does not mean that in one country an offender can be punished for a crime committed in another, and that the trial must be had in the first country according to the law of the latter country, but only that by the comity of nations he should be surrendered. In *Keighley* v. *Bell*, 4 Fost. & Fin. 790, Willes, J., said : " It is the general rule and principle of law that crime is local in its trial, and that offences are to be tried where they are alleged to have been committed — a principle of universal application."

The *lex fori* applies to all modes of enforcing rights, and governs as to the nature, extent, and character of the remedy, including Statutes of Limitation and the right of set-off : *Imlay* v. *Ellefsen*, 2 East. 453; *General Steam Navigation Company* v. *Guillou*, 11 M. & W. 895; *British Linen Company* v. *Drummond*, 10 B. & C. 903; *Huber* v. *Steiner*, 2 Bing. N. C., 202; *De la Vega* v. *Vianna*, 1 B. & Ad. 284; *Bhaeechund* v. *Partabchund Manikchund*, 1 Moore, Ind. App. 172; *Lopez* v. *Burslem*, 4 Moore, P. C. 300; *Her Highness Ruckmaboye* v. *L. Mottichund*, 8 Moore, P. C. 4. Where a foreign statute of limitation not merely limits the remedy, but extinguishes the debt after the period of limitation has expired, it appears to be equivalent to a release, and to prevent an action in this country : *Donn* v. *Lippman*, 5 Cl. & F. 1; and see *per cur.* in *Huber* v. *Steiner*, 2 Bing. N. C. 211.

In *Williams* v. *Jones*, 13 East, 439, it was held that, assuming that the English Statute of Limitations, 21 Jac. 1. c. 16, applies to the East Indies (as it does : see *Her Highness Ruckmaboye* v. *L. Mottichund*, 8 Moore, P. C. 4), a plaintiff's right of action is not barred if he commences the action in this country within six years after the defendants return home, although more than six years have elapsed since the cause of action occurred in India, the defendant having remained there during that period. Lord Ellenborough asked in that case : " How is the plaintiff to be divested of this right by a charter which the King was empowered by statute to grant for the purpose of erecting courts of judicature in India?" With reference to the priority of creditors and distribution of assets the *lex fori* prevails: *Simpson* v. *Fogo*, 32 L. J. (Ch.) 249.

If the exemption from arrest and imprisonment enters into and forms an essential ingredient in the original contract by the law of the country where it is made, and is not merely contingent on the failure of the debtor to perform his obligations, it has been held that it cannot be enforced. Thus it was decided that an ordinary debt contracted in France, where the *contrainte par corps* is limited to commercial debts, could not be enforced by personal arrest in this country: *Melan* v. *The Duke of FitzJames*, 1 Bos. & Pul. 138. But this case is doubtful: see *Imlay* v. *Ellefsen*, 2 East, 453; *De la Vega* v. *Vianna*, 1 B. & Ad. 284; Voet, Comm. ad Pandect, lib. ii. tit. 4, s. 45.

And if a positive law intervenes in the country where the action is brought, affecting the subject-matter of the contract, the *lex fori* must be applied, although in effect it alters the terms of the contract. Thus, if a rate of interest were claimed upon a loan which, although legal in the place where the contract was made, was illegal by the usury laws in the place where the action to recover it is brought, the Court would decide against the claim: Story, Conf. Laws, s. 374. But compare ss. 303–5.

Where Lex Loci and Lex Fori conflict.   Jurists have laid it down that when the *lex loci contractûs* and the *lex fori* come into collision, as to conflicting rights acquired under each, the comity of nations must yield to the positive law of the land: Kent, Com. ii. 461 (3rd edit.); Story, Conf. Laws, s. 327. In *Potter* v. *Brown*, 5 East, 131, Lord Ellenborough, C.J., said: "We always import together with these persons the existing relations of foreigners as between themselves according to the law of their respective countries, except indeed where those laws clash with the rights of our own subjects here; and one or other of the laws must necessarily give way, in which case our own is entitled to the preference."

In an action brought in this country for an assault committed at Naples, the defendant pleaded, that according to the law of Naples he was liable to certain penal proceedings in consequence of the trespass, and that by that law no civil action could be maintained until after he had been found in such penal proceedings, and that no such proceedings had been instituted; but the Court said: "We think this furnishes no defence. It is a matter of procedure which was to be governed by the *lex fori:*" *Scott* v. *Lord Seymour*, 31 L. J. (Ex.) 457; affirmed in Error, 32 L. J. (Ex.) 61. But upon the question whether, if, by the Neapolitan law, no damages had been recoverable at law for such an assault, the action would be maintainable here, the Court of Error differed in opinion. Wightman, J., thought that a British subject would not be deprived of his right to sue here by such a foreign law; but Williams, J., said, that he was not prepared to assent to this; Compton, J., thought it a matter of very great difficulty and doubt; and Blackburn, J., said, that his mind was far from made up on the question, but he doubted very much whether such a plea would be a good bar. In a recent case the Judicial Committee said that it was alike contrary to principle and authority to hold that an English court of justice would enforce a foreign municipal law, and give a remedy in the shape of damages in respect of an act which according to its own principles imposes no liability on the person from whom the damages are claimed: *The Halley*, L. R. 2 P. C. 204.

In a case of collision on the high seas between a foreign and a British vessel, Dr. Lushington held that the Merchant Shipping Act, 1854, which limits the liability of owners in damages to the value of ship and freight, does not apply where the foreigner is defendant: *The Wild Ranger*, 32 L. J., P. M. & Adm. 49. And the Judicial Committee, reversing a decision of the Court of Admiralty, have determined that in an action founded on a tort committed in the territory of a foreign State (it was the case of a collision in Belgian waters), the party suing in a British court is not entitled to the benefit of the foreign law against the provisions of the statute law of England: *The Halley*, L. R. 2 P. C. 193.

CHAPTER IX.

ON ALLEGIANCE AND ALIENS.

(1.) OPINION *of the Attorney General,* SIR EDWARD
NORTHEY, *on the question of Alienage, and Trading with Her
Majesty's Enemies.* 1703.

To the Right Honourable the Lords Commissioners for Trade and
Plantations.

MAY IT PLEASE YOUR LORDSHIPS,—On consideration of the case
of Manasses Gillingham, who (being a natural-born subject of her
Majesty, but a settled inhabitant in the island of St. Thomas, belonging to the King of Denmark, and naturalized there) traded from
thence to and with the Spaniards, in war with her Majesty; I am
of opinion, his being naturalized without the license of her Majesty
will not discharge him from the natural allegiance he owes to her
Majesty; however, he being a settled inhabitant in the island of
St. Thomas, under the King of Denmark, and not having been
commanded to return into her Majesty's dominions, as he might
have been, though naturalized there, his trading with the Spaniards
from that island, in amity with the Danes, will not be a capital, if
any offence at all; and therefore I cannot advise the proceeding
against him criminally for such trading. If any inconvenience
happens from such trading, as is suggested by the Governor of
Barbadoes' letter, the Queen's subjects may be recalled to return
to her Majesty's dominions; and if they refuse, and after trade with
her Majesty's enemies, they may be proceeded against criminally
for such trading, as any of her Majesty's subjects residing in her
plantations may be proceeded against for trading with her Majesty's
enemies—that is, for a misdemeanor; for I do not take simple

trading with an enemy to be high treason, unless it be in such trade as furnishes the enemy with stores of war.

March 22, 1703-4. EDW. NORTHEY.

(2.) OPINION *of the Attorney General,* SIR FLETCHER NORTON, *as to whether the French and Spaniards who remained in the ceded Countries after the Peace of* 1763, *were Aliens or Subjects.* 1764.

To the Right Honourable the Lords Commissioners for Trade and Plantations.

MAY IT PLEASE YOUR LORDSHIPS,—In obedieuce to your Lordships' commands, signified to me by Mr. Pownall's letters of the 21st of December and the 1st of March last, stating that great difficulties had frequently occurred from the question whether the subjects of the Crowns of France and Spain, who remain in the ceded countries in America, are to be considered as aliens; and intimating more particularly, that a variety of doubts and difficulties had occurred as to the ability of aliens to acquire property in America, either by purchase, grant, or lease from the Crown; and also as to the situation in respect to the laws of this kingdom, of such subjects of the Crowns of France and Spain as, being inhabitants of Canada, Florida, and the ceded islands in the West Indies, remain there under the stipulations of the last definitive treaty; and therefore desiring my opinion, whether such of the French or Spanish inhabitants of Canada, Florida, and the islands of Grenada, Dominica, St. Vincent's, and Tobago, as being born out of the allegiance of his Majesty, and also remain in the said countries under the stipulations of the definitive treaty, are, or are not, under the legal incapacities and disabilities put upon aliens and strangers by the laws of this kingdom in general, and particularly by the Act of Navigation, and the other laws made for regulating the plantation trade; and if it should be my opinion that they are under such disabilities and incapacities, your Lordships, in that case, desire my sentiments in what manner such disabilities may be removed.

I have taken Mr. Pownall's letters into my consideration, and am humbly of opinion that those subjects of the Crowns of France and Spain, who were inhabitants of Canada, Florida, and the ceded islands in the West Indies, and continued there under the stipulations of the definitive treaty, having entitled themselves to the benefits thereof by taking the oaths of allegiance, &c., are not to be considered in the light of aliens, as incapable of enjoying or acquiring real property there, or transmitting it to others for their own benefit; for I conceive that the definitive treaty, which has had the sanction, and been approved and confirmed by both Houses of Parliament, meant to give, and that it has in fact and in law given, to the then inhabitants of those ceded countries, a permanent transmissible interest in their land there; and that to put a different construction upon the treaty would dishonour the Crown and the national faith, as it would be saying, that by the treaty they were promised the quiet enjoyment of their property, but by the laws were to be immediately stripped of their estates; but I think that no aliens, except such as can claim the benefit of the definitive treaty, or bring themselves within the 7th of his late Majesty, are by law entitled to purchase lands for their own benefit and transmit them to others, either from the Crown or from private persons, in any of his Majesty's dominions in North America or the West Indies.

But I submit to your Lordships, whether, as it is a matter of the highest importance that those countries should be settled, and perhaps not less so that such settlements should be made without draining this country of its inhabitants—whether it would not be proper to apply to Parliament for a Naturalization Bill for those places, under proper regulations, as well to encourage foreigners to go thither, as to quiet such aliens as may have already settled there, under the common received opinion that they were capable of holding lands there for their own benefit, and disposing of them in any manner they might think proper, in common with the rest of his Majesty's liege subjects.

Lincoln's Inn, July 27, 1764.   FLETCH. NORTON.

(3.) OBSERVATIONS *by* SIR JAMES MARRIOTT, *King's Advocate, on the Case of the Inhabitants of Dominica, sent to the Attorney and Solicitor General previous to a consultation with him thereupon* (1). *January* 5, 1765.

The case of the inhabitants of Dominica does not come under the description of the Treaty of Versailles; it being an island in partition, neither ceded nor restored, but now first occupied in full sovereignty by his Majesty and acknowledged by France.

The inhabitants of Dominica hold all they have now under the King; and their request to be at liberty to withdraw their persons, and dispose of their possessions, is not supported by the spirit of the treaty, nor the letter of it; nor consequently by the good faith of any express or tacit agreement of the King.

It has been disputed by writers on the law of nations whether any persons can withdraw themselves, and renounce the Government under which they were born, or fallen *en partage;* but be this as it may respecting their persons, it is certain that their possessions, under the protection of that Government and sovereignty, are the guarantees of their continuing their persons under it; for their possessions and effects may be confiscated to the State which they desert contrary to express injunctions.

It is stated that many of the inhabitants of Dominica have, since the treaty and Article of Partition, passed over to Guadaloupe, and now desire to withdraw their property as they have withdrawn their persons.

The King will be justified in refusing protection to their possessions, if they do not return to them on such conditions as his Majesty shall be pleased to grant them.

The terms of the treaty formally grant a privilege to the inhabitants of the islands ceded or restored, for withdrawing their persons and effects ; and it is a well-known rule of the civil law, which is the allowed interpreter of the law of nations—*Affirmatio unius est exclusio alterius;* therefore those islands, neither ceded nor restored, are excluded by necessary implication of the terms of the treaty.

(1) From a M. S. in the possession of Sir Travers Twiss, Queen's Advocate, which formerly belonged to Sir James Marriott.

2. They come within the intention of the treaty, because it is a known quality of all private and public compacts, of treaties more especially, *tantum disponunt quantum loquuntur*. In stipulations the intention of the contractor can only be judged by his words, as the sole indication of his sentiments. Silence then in one object, and affirmation in another, work a direct negative by implication equally to express words in every case not mentioned, and which is different in its nature and circumstances from the case affirmed to be privileged. Now all privileged cases are held universally to be *stricti juris*, and they cannot by the civil law be granted but by express words.

Those adventurers who have established themselves without lawful commissions from their respective Sovereigns are intruders upon public rights, and the law of nations adjudges them to have made such establishments at the peril of their own persons and properties.

This law is necessary for the repose of mankind, and the support of all civil associations and governments.

The settlers in Dominica, till this period without civil rights, their settlements disavowed by one Sovereign and prohibited by the other, are fallen to the King, who may make their possessions answerable for their conduct, if they withdraw their persons; for from him only, and from his royal grant and confirmation, can they derive any right to what they possess.

The fact represented of Admiral Knowles draws to no consequence in this question, unless it makes those inhabitants more subject by their own acquiescence to the King than they are now by partition. The fact urged by the memorialist is a made fact; it conferred no privilege on these inhabitants; but merely the protection of the Admiral *pro tempore*, on condition that they remained upon the island.

The protection of the King under the present circumstances of the island, and the inhabitants continuing upon it on such terms as it shall please his Majesty to dictate, is the question.

But if the utmost force is allowed to the declarations of an admiral, though made without orders from his Sovereign, yet the indecision of these islands by the treaty of 1660, called the treaty of League and Union, and by the agreements in the year 1733, and by the subsequent treaty of Aix-la-Chapelle, still kept in suspense the civil condition of those inhabitants; under that decided dependency into which they are now fallen by partition, they must necessarily abide, or lose the benefit of protection.

With respect to the inhabitants of Cape Breton, the treaty being silent, their condition falls under the terms of the particular capitulation for that island.

If the French King, notwithstanding the disavowals of his ministers, has made grants to French settlers in Dominica, it is unfortunate for them, but these grants cannot affect the right of his Majesty; and in a case between Sovereign and Sovereign, they must be considered relatively to them, and *comme non avenus*. The French settlers who have obtained such grants can only hope to obtain their indemnification from the same hand from which they obtained their grants.

The whole of this case depends upon his Majesty's good pleasure. All which is humbly submitted, &c.

(4.) OPINION *of* MR. CHALMERS *on the legal effects resulting from the acknowledgment of the Independence of the United States* (1).   1814.

The question is, whether the inhabitants of the United States, who had been born within the King's allegiance, and remained within the United States after they were acknowledged by the King to be independent and sovereign, continued subjects, having the rights of subjects; or became aliens, having the rights of aliens, from that acknowledgment?

During the year 1783, which forms the epoch of that event, I took the liberty of publishing my opinion of those effects. Whatsoever I may have seen or heard since that epoch, I have not in the least changed my opinion. And as abler men than I pretend to be have avowed and published very different sentiments from mine, it may, perhaps, be permitted me to restate and reinforce my original opinion, which first broke the ice that had been collecting and consolidating for so many years.

(1) The foot-notes to this Opinion are those of Chalmers, as given in his " Opinions of Eminent Lawyers."

S

The Act (1) which enabled his Majesty to conclude a peace or truce with certain colonies in North America, declared it " to be essential to the interests and the welfare and prosperity of Great Britain and the thirteen specified colonies, that peace, intercourse, and commerce should be restored between them."

The treaty, it must be allowed, is explicit enough as to the political associations that formed the States, which are expressly acknowledged " to be free, sovereign, and independent States ; and the King, for himself and his heirs and successors, relinquished all claims to the government, propriety, and territorial rights of the same, and every part thereof." The statute of the 22nd of the King does not take notice of what the world knew sufficiently, that thirteen of the British colonies had revolted ; neither does it notice, that the persons forming those colonies which had declared themselves in 1776 to be independent, were, and had always been, the King's subjects ; but it merely enables the King to make a peace or truce with any commissioners who might be sent by the said colonies, or any of them, or any bodies politic, or descriptions of men within those colonies ; and the treaty is altogether silent as to the individuals who formed those well-known confederations ; it admits the thirteen societies, in their associated capacity, to be free, sovereign, and independent, by relinquishing all claim of government over them ; yet it does not explicitly renounce the allegiance of those colonists, who, at the epoch of the war, were still British subjects, in contemplation of British law ; for it does not declare that the citizens of the United States shall be deemed aliens in future ; and it neither excepts nor disowns those faithful subjects who had retained their allegiance and adhered to their King and country.

The faithful colonists of Great Britain, as they had been born within the King's dominions, were, owing to this circumstance alone, constituted subjects of the King and freemen of the realm. By their birth within the allegiance of the Crown they acquired a variety of rights, which are called emphatically by lawyers their birthrights, and which can never be forfeited except by their own misconduct, and can never be taken away but by the law of the land. " No freeman," says the Great Charter, " shall be seized or

(1) 22 Geo. 3, c. 46.

imprisoned, or outlawed, or any way destroyed, except by the legal judgment of his peers, or by the law of the land."

It is, nevertheless, a very different consideration with respect to those colonists who, having achieved the late American revolution by their efforts, now form by their residence the United States. Rights may be undoubtedly forfeited, though privileges cannot be arbitrarily taken away ; a man's crimes, or even misconduct, may deprive him of those immunities which he might have claimed from birth, or derived from some Act of the legislature : he may be outlawed by the sentence of a court of justice, or he may be banished by the united suffrages of his countrymen in Parliament; the American citizens, who voluntarily abjured their Sovereign, avowed their design to relinquish their character of subjects, however contrary to law their relinquishment undoubtedly was. The American subjects who swore fidelity to the government of their own choice, thereby declared their election to be no longer connected with a State which had mortified their prejudices rather than bereaved them of rights; and by that conduct, and by those offences, the devoted colonists forfeited to the law all which the law had conferred on them. The American treaty virtually pardoned their misconduct in forming those associations which were admitted to be free : the Parliament, by its recognition, virtually legalized the election which the revolted citizens of those States had made.

But whether that treaty, or that Act of the British legislature, ought to be construed as a relinquishment of their allegiance, with the obedience that is inherent in it, or as a pardon of their faults, whatever were committed by forming those associations and taking oaths which were inconsistent with their allegiance, is a point which needs not be now very pertinaciously argued.

The term " nation " always supposes something collective, or a body-politic. A colony is also a body-politic, though inferior to a nation. Each of the revolted colonies, when it departed from its former character of a colony, became a State, or body-politic, and the association of those thirteen States which had departed thus from their character of colonies, formed a nation, or body-politic, under the name of the United States. The King, by the definitive treaty, acknowledged those States to be free, sovereign, and independent; he treated with them as such, and he relinquished for

s 2

ever all claims to the government, propriety, and territorial right of the same countries; the extent of those territorial rights or boundaries of the United States were distinctly ascertained and avowedly declared by a particular clause of the definitive treaty. On the same day that the King ratified by a formal Act that definitive treaty, the whole acts of trade, navigation, and revenue, attached upon those United States, as a nation free, independent, and sovereign. It did not now require to be a great lawyer to tell that the soil of such a nation was alien; that the products of such a soil were alien; that the ships of such a nation were alien; and that the navigators of such ships were, *ex primâ facie*, aliens.

As the King had now, by the treaty, relinquished for ever all claims to the government of the United States, so did he, incidentally, relinquish the obedience of the various people forming those United States. As the American citizens, who formed those bodies politic, now owed no subjection to the Crown of Great Britain, they were no longer British subjects, the terms subjection and subjects being correlatives—such as husband and wife, father and son, sovereign and subject, which must always have a reciprocal relation to each other. "It is one thing," says South, "for a father to cease to be a father by casting off his son, and another for him to cease to be so by the death of his son;" in this, the relation is at an end for the want of a correlative; and in the same manner, when the Sovereign relinquished by the treaty, in the due performance of a legal trust, all claim to the government of the United States, the relation of the American citizens ceased for the want of a correlative.

The first law opinion which has fallen into my hands on those topics was that of Mr. Kenyon, dated at Chester, on the 11th of October, 1783 (1); and without any hesitation he gave it as his opinion, that " the fair construction of the Act, as circumstances now stand, is, that goods, the produce of the United States, may be imported into this country from the place of their growth, upon payment of the duties payable by foreigners, and upon no other terms." The next opinion which has fallen in my way is that of Sir William

(1) The definitive treaty was signed on the 3rd of September, 1783. The case only stated to Mr. Kenyon the statute 12 Charles 2, c. 18, ss. 3, 8, 9, with this N.B. :—" These questions are put merely to know how the law stands upon those clauses, without any regard to any Orders of Council that may be made relative to the trade of America, under the Act of last session of Parliament."

Wynne, which was asked by the Board of Customs, whether ships of the United States were entitled to registers, as ships of the British colonies, which is such an opinion as was to be expected from such a jurist, against considering such ships as British, but as alien (1). The next opinion which has occurred to me is that of the Attorney General Ardon, in October, 1788, wherein he gives it as his judgment, that there can be no trade between the United States and the British West Indies, except such as was allowed by the King's proclamation. All those opinions go to prove, what is sufficiently obvious in itself, that the United States became free, sovereign, and independent, under the definitive treaty, and so must be deemed foreign and alien to the British nation; taking it for granted, that the people forming those United States must be necessarily aliens.

Yet are there books which propagate different doctrines, and persons of ingenuity who avow notions that lead them to consider those citizens who were born under the allegiance of the King to be still entitled to their birthrights, as subjects, under the well-known declaration of the Great Charter that has been already quoted.

But every nation and every State, under whatever name, must consist of individuals, men, women, and children, of whatever number; and it is those individuals who form the body-politic of every such nation and State. By the definitive treaty, the King, first, acknowledged the associations of individuals, forming the United States, to be free, sovereign, and independent; and, secondly, relinquished all claims to the government and territorial rights of the same. According to those notions, then, the country of the United States is relinquished, as sovereign, and the inhabitants thereof are admitted to be free and independent; yet are they said to be subjects, claiming from the laws of England their birthrights as British subjects, notwithstanding their own election to be free and independent, and the recognition of their election by their former Sovereign. Such a contradiction of character never existed in any code of law in any country; on

(1) It was dated on the 19th of October, 1785. The late Mr. Thomas Boone, the Chairman of the Board of Customs, assured me that the Attorney and Solicitor General concurred in Sir William Wynne's opinion.

the contrary, the Lord Chancellor Egerton laid it down as a principle, in delivering his judgment in the case of the *post-nati* : " In a true and lawful subject, there must be *subjectio, fides, et obedientia*, and those cannot be severed, no more than true faith and charity in a true Christian " (1). Now, the notions before mentioned would separate from the character of a true subject, the subjection, the fealty, and the obedience, which is so essential to the genuine character; and after those very citizens of the United States had relinquished their faith, allegiance, and obedience, and were acknowledged by the King to be free and independent, what subjection, what faith, what obedience could remain in such citizens ? We may now infer from the foregoing premises, that it is absurd in argument, and unfounded in law, for any person to claim the rights and privileges of a subject, without showing his subjection, professing his faith, and owning his obedience. Yes, the American citizens are free, and without subjection; yet how ? Not to do as they list; for they must so use their freedom and independence as not to prejudice the public (2): so says the law of reason and policy, *respublica præferenda est privatis ;* and so affirm many statutes (3).

The learned and elegant Craig traces back the doctrine of foreign birth alienage to the feudal law, of which this is the chiefest rule: *unus et idem duorum dominorum homo ligius esse non potest*—that is, one and the same person cannot be liegeman, or vassal, of two superior lords. He who is born under another prince, whose liege subject he is, because he cannot perform what he owes to his true lord, is put away from the fief in another country ; for he cannot keep his fealty untainted and inviolate to two lords—to him under whom he is born, and to his new Sovereign; neither is it possible for him, in case of war between them, to succour them both, to assist both as a soldier, to conceal the secrets of both princes, which is chiefly required by the feudal law.   This able writer considers this doctrine as universal in the several codes

(1) See Lord Egerton's speech, which he published in 1609, p. 64.
(2) Commentary upon Fortescue, p. 203.
(3) 27 Edw. 3, 12, 16 ; 28 Edw. 3, c. 5 ; 23 Hen. 8, c. 16 ; 25 Hen. 8 c. 13; 32 Hen. 8 c. 18, 19 ; 33 Hen. 8, c. 7 ; 35 Hen. 8, c. 4 ; 1 Edw. 6, c. 3, 5 ; 2 and 3 Edw. 6, c. 37 ; 1 & 2 P. & M. c. 5 ; 18 Eliz. c. 9, 15, 17 ; 8 Eliz. c. 3; 23 Eliz. c. 5 ; 27 Eliz. c. 19, &c.

of the European nations; it is even so by the law of nature: no man, said Our Saviour, can serve two masters, for he will hate the one and love the other (1). If the feudal law were a branch of the common law, then must the notion which attributes rights to the former subjects, after their subjection was relinquished by their Sovereign, be abhorrent to the common law.

The American citizens can, therefore, by no mode of speech, nor by any principle of law—of the law of nature, of the law of nations, of the feudal law, of the common law—be deemed British subjects, unless those associations of mankind are subjects who owe no allegiance to the British Crown, or any obedience to the British Government; that allegiance, which is said to include all the engagements owing from subject to Sovereign; that obedience which is styled, emphatically, the very essence of law. In the report of *Calvin's Case*, it is said to be a maxim that ligeance is a reciprocal tie, *quia sicut subditus tenetur ad obedientiam, ita rex tenetur ad protectionem* (2). But what reciprocity can there be, or what protection claimed, when subjects have renounced their allegiance, refused their obedience, and the King thereupon renounces their allegiance, and releases their subjection, by acknowledging their freedom and independence? The King gives protection to his subjects by his laws. An American citizen, claiming his birthrights, must apply to the King's laws; and, to entitle himself to legal protection, he must show that he is a subject, owning and yielding obedience. If he cannot do that, he must fail in his claims of rights, like the Frenchwoman in the time of Edward I., whose case is reported in Hengham: she brought a writ of *ayell* against Cobledicke, and declared of the seisin of Roger, her grandfather, and conveyed the descent to Gilbert, her father, and the same descent from her father to herself; and the tenant pleaded that the demandant was not of the ligeance of England, or of the fidelity of the King; and demanded judgment. This was held to be good and sufficient, for to the King fidelity and allegiance are due; and therefore, since she failed in that, she was not to be answered, and thereupon she prayed license to depart from her writ, and so she left her suit (3).

(1) Craig, "On the Succession of King James," p. 253.

(2) 7 Co. 5.   (3) The Lord Chancellor Egerton's speech, pp. 91–3.

It may be here worth inquiry, if something to this useful purpose may not appear on the face of the treaties with the United
States? By Article 4 of the definitive treaty, it was stipulated
that creditors on either side should meet with no lawful impediment to the recovery of their debts. After the re-establishment
of peace by that treaty, the subjects and citizens of the contracting parties were not at war, and being at peace, there could not be
any legal impediment to legal remedies for just debts; but in
contemplation of the treaty, the subjects of the one power and
the citizens of the other had become thereby aliens to each other.
The same observations may be made upon the 5th Article, which
provides that persons having any interest in confiscated lands,
either by debts, marriage settlements, or otherwise, should meet
with no lawful impediment in the prosecution of their just rights.
It may be moreover remarked that Adams and Jay, two of the
American negotiators, were lawyers—the first being Chief Justice of
Massachusetts, and the last Chief Justice of the United States—and
both Adams and Jay knew the meaning of their own terms, whatever the British negotiator may have done. This reasoning is
confirmed by an article in the commercial treaty between Great
Britain and the United States, which was negotiated in November,
1794, by Lord Grenville and the same John Jay; it was agreed
by Article 9 : "That British subjects who now hold lands in the
United States, and the American citizens who now hold lands in
his Majesty's dominions, shall continue to hold them, according to
the nature and tenure of their respective states and titles therein,
and may grant, sell, or devise the same, as if they were natives,
and that neither they, nor their heirs or assigns, shall, so far as
may respect the said lands, and the legal remedies incident thereto,
be regarded as *aliens* " (1). Is it not apparent, then, from the fore-

(1) The 37 Geo. 3, c. 97, was made for carrying into execution that treaty
of commerce. By section 24, the 9th Article above stated was ratified, any law,
custom, or usage to the contrary notwithstanding. The article before mentioned
was adopted by the negotiators of it, as they considered the people of Great Britain
and United States to be aliens to each other; and the Parliament confirmed this
article, *ex abundante cautela*, notwithstanding the well-known law, custom, and
usage to the contrary ; yet are there some who consider this statute as a proof
that the citizens of the United States are not aliens. There is another statute,
which also shows the sense of Parliament on this topic: the 30 Geo. 3, c. 27,

going intimations, that in the judgment of the negotiators of the several treaties between Great Britain and the United States, and in contemplation of Parliament, the subjects of the first country and the citizens of the last were considered as foreigners to each other?

Yet are we still told that those people of the United States, who were born British subjects, even now continue to be entitled to their original birthrights; and for this singular notion the Great Charter of English liberties is quoted, that no freeman shall be outlawed, or any way destroyed, except by the judgment of his peers, or by the law of the land. But is not this argument conceived upon too narrow principles to apply appositely to the present question, relative to thousands of men, rather than to one man? The fundamental principle is sound law, but it does not reach the case of the inhabitants of thirteen colonies, who revolted from the British Empire, who rose in arms against the King's government, renouncing their allegiance, and claiming their freedom from any further obedience to British laws, and acting thus against all law during seven years, were recognized by the King, in pursuance of the high trust invested in him by those laws, to be independent and sovereign, without subjection or obedience. Is it not a sufficient answer to such pretensions, as a claim of rights without submission *volenti non fit injuria :* you have elected to be aliens, and you have been recognized by the King, the fountain of all jurisdiction, to be what you have chosen for yourselves; and the laws, from which you claim your rights, cannot acknowledge you in any other character than you have chosen for yourselves and have been recognized to belong to you; you profess not to owe any allegiance to the King, or obedience to his laws, and under such circumstances you cannot receive protection from either, whatever rights you may have once possessed, *quod est inconveniens, aut contra rationem, non permissum est in lege* (1)?

In the argument of the instructive case of *Campbell* v. *Hall,* in Hilary Term, 1744, it was said by Mr. Alleyn, the learned

---

for encouraging the settling of the British colonies by inhabitants from the United States, required such emigrants to the British colonies to take the oath of allegiance upon their arrival and settlement; but in this case none but aliens would have been required to take the oath of allegiance to the King.

(1) Co. Litt. 178.

counsel for the plaintiff: "The technical learning of Westminster Hall can give but little assistance to the decision of this question. The great principles of the law of empire must determine it, and the political history of England affords particular illustrations of it." This course must again be pursued, in illustrating the question of the alienage of the American citizens, which may be inquired into under two heads:

1. How aliens may become subjects.
2. How subjects may become aliens.

As to the first head, it is in general true that an alien born, coming into England, and desiring to become a subject, cannot be naturalized but by Parliament, that is, without the consent of the nation: this seems to have been always the law of England, though it was otherwise of old in Normandy, where the prince might naturalize. An Act of Naturalization, thus obtained from Parliament, cures the alien's disabilities, as if he had been born in England, and by apt clauses an Act of naturalization may be so made as to cure other disabilities; yet is it inaccurate to say that a person may be naturalized by being born in any dominion of the King while he was King of England, or born upon the King's seas, or born under the statute of Edward III., *de natis ultra mare;* for such subjects never were aliens.

During the late reign the Parliament extended the benefits of naturalization to such foreign Protestants as should reside for a limited time in the King's plantations (1); and Protestant officers, being foreigners, were naturalized by Parliament upon performance of special services; and foreign seamen, upon performing nautical services on board British shipping. The colonial assemblies did pass Acts of Naturalization, which were limited in their operation by several statutes imposing disabilities on aliens and denizens; they were bound also by the limited nature of their jurisdictions, and at the beginning of the present reign, a general instruction was given by the King to his governors of colonies not to assent to any Act of assembly granting naturalization to any foreigners, as such Acts might trench upon the statute law of the land, and thus operate against the policy of the State.

(1) 7 Geo. 2, c. 21 ; 13 Geo. 2, c. 4 ; 20 Geo. 2, c. 45 ; 2 Geo. 3, c. 25 ; 13 Geo. 3, c. 25 ; 20 Geo. 3, c. 20.

Yet, Ventris hath reported Sir Matthew Hale, the Chief Baron, to have said in Lord Holderness' case, that "Naturalization, according to our law, can only be by Parliament, and not otherwise" (1). There must be surely some mistake here, as such a judge could not have so far allowed his vigilance of observation to have slumbered, as to say that naturalization cannot be otherwise than by Parliament. The Chief Baron, it seems, did not advert that thousands and tens of thousands, millions and tens of millions of people have been naturalized by the act and operation of law, and thus became subjects. Mr. Wallace, who argued for the defendant in the case of *Campbell* v. *Hall*, remarked, what may well be remembered: "It is not, as formerly, when the conqueror gained captives and slaves and absolute rights by the law of nations, but now the conqueror obtains dominion and subjects." This beneficial change probably took place as early as the age when the ravages of the Danes were softened by the introduction of Christianity, or prevented by the progress of civilization. There is, however, but little in our law-books, as hath been already intimated, of naturalization by conquest, for slow is the progress of jurisprudence as a science; yet was it said: "If the King of England make a new conquest, the persons there born are his subjects; but if it be taken from him again, the persons there born afterwards (after being conquered) are aliens" (2). This was saying but very little in advance of a more rational construction; as it is not said that the alien people who had been conquered by the arms of the Crown became subjects of the Crown by act and operation of the law. It is not easy to ascertain the epoch when the law became thus understood; I should guess that such a principle of law became prevalent soon after the arrival of the Normans, who argued very acutely about sovereignty and subjection. It was certainly understood as early as the reign of Henry II., when the people of Ireland were supposed to have become his subjects, from his conquest.

Let us now listen to the soft voice of Lord Mansfield, when delivering the judgment of the King's Bench, in the well-known case of *Campbell* v. *Hall*. "In the acquisition of conquests, it is limited by the Constitution," says he, "to the King's authority,

(1) 1 Vent. 419-20.   (2) Dyer, 224; Vaughan, 281-2.

to grant or refuse a capitulation ; if he refuse, and put the inhabitants to the sword, all their lands belong to him ; if he receive the
inhabitants under his protection and grant them their property, he
has the power to fix the conditions; he is entrusted with making
the treaty of peace, and he may yield up the conquest, or retain it,
upon such terms as he shall think fit to agree to." These powers
(in the King), no man ever disputed ; neither has it hitherto been
controverted but that the King might change part of the government of Grenada, or all the political form of the government of a
conquered dominion.   He afterwards added : " It is not to be wondered that an adjudged case in point has not been produced ; no
dispute ever was started before upon the King's legislative authority
over a conquest; it never was denied in Westminster Hall ; it
never was questioned in Parliament ; it was so decided in *Calvin's
Case.*" Lord Mansfield then ran over the history of the conquests
made by the Crown of England, in order to confirm and illustrate
his judicial doctrines ; beginning with that of Ireland and ending
with that of New York.   In all those cases of conquest, the previous aliens became subjects of the crown, by subsequent conquest ;
and of course were virtually naturalized by the act and operation
of law.   " The conquered inhabitants, once received under the
King's protection," said Lord Mansfield, in judgment, " became
subjects, and were to be universally considered in this light,.and
not as enemies *or aliens* " (1).

The first opinion which I have found on such topics is that of
John de Witt, in 1667, with the remarks thereon by Sir William
Temple, who was then ambassador in Holland. This opinion, which
was called a discourse, was given in consequence of the Treaty of
Breda (1667), whereby England ceded Surinam to Holland, and

(1) Cowper's Reports, 204.—But Lord Mansfield, while he paid the greatest deference to the opinions of the Law Officers of the Crown, when formally given, seems
not to have been aware of the opinion of the Attorney General Northey, in 1704,
with regard to the part of St. Christopher's then recently conquered. " Her Majesty
may," said Northey, " if she shall be so pleased, under her great seal of England,
direct that the like duty (of four-and-a-half per cent.) be levied, for goods to be exported, from the conquered part ; and that command will be a law there ; her Majesty,
by her prerogative, being enabled to make laws that will bind places obtained by
conquest, and all that shall inhabit therein." This proves also that those conquered people, being now obedient to her power, were subjects and not aliens ; as
she could only legislate for such a people, by Acts under the Great Seal of England.

Holland ceded New York to England, with plenary right of sovereignty, propriety, and possession. These expressions were deemed by De Witt, and tacitly acknowledged by Temple, of sufficient force to transfer the allegiance of the Dutch colonists at New York to the English Crown, who thereby became subjects, as Lord Mansfield remarked, and ceased to be considered as enemies and aliens. The next opinion which I have found is that of the Attorney General Pratt, in August, 1759, who, with the Solicitor General Yorke, was consulted by the Board of Customs on the effect of the recent capitulation of Guadaloupe. His opinion was, that this island must be considered as now one of the British plantations; the right of sovereignty being changed, the whole island is the King's, in right of conquest, and the whole colonists are become his Majesty's subjects. Mr. Solicitor General C. Yorke gave a separate opinion on that occasion to the same effect: " I am of opinion," said he, " that Guadaloupe is now to be considered as a plantation or territory belonging to the King by conquest; and the people thereof owed in consequence an allegiance to his Majesty, as his subjects resident in a plantation belonging to his crown. Yet some doubts being entertained, by persons abroad and at home, whether the French and Spaniards who remained in the ceded countries after the peace of 1763 were aliens or subjects, the Attorney General (Norton) gave it as his opinion to the Board of Trade, that " those French and Spaniards are not to be considered in the light of aliens, but as his Majesty's liege subjects." Yet the Bill in Parliament which he advised for quieting those doubts, was never passed, perhaps never proposed; as wiser men than Norton, probably, considered such advice as weak. The law being clear, who could doubt whether such French and Spaniards, being the King's subjects and not aliens, were not entitled to the rights of subjects? Lord Mansfield delivered it as the judgment of the Court of King's Bench, in the before-mentioned case of *Campbell* v. *Hall*, " that the law and legislative government of every dominion equally affects all persons and property within the limits thereof, and is the true rule for the decision of all questions arising there: whoever purchases, lives, or sues there, puts himself under the law of the place. An Englishman in the island of Minorca, the Isle of Man, or in the plantations, has no privilege distinct from the

270 CASES AND OPINIONS ON CONSTITUTIONAL LAW.

natives " (1). I have now delivered explicitly what has occurred to me on this first head of argumentation, how aliens may become subjects, which we now see must and may be done by Act of Parliament, or by the operation of the law. By such operations of law, it is not too much to assert, that there have been acquired to the British Empire, since the commencement of the present reign, forty millions of subjects.

Secondly, I will now proceed under this second head to inquire how subjects may become aliens? The persons and the property of the English people have been guarded with great anxiety by their laws, which have made surety, in those respects, double sure (2).

Yet did the common law, as we may learn from Bracton, allow of disfranchisement and of banishment: an individual might be interdicted his province, his city, or his town; or he might have been interdicted his kingdom for years, or for life; and abjuration was a legal exile, as well by the statute law as by the common law.

Yet neither the law of exile nor the law of security applies to the present operation, which relates to many subjects, not to one subject; and which turns upon circumstances of national policy, and not upon points of judicial practice; it involves this high consideration of public interest, whether, if the State be in danger, the rights of the few may not be sacrificed to the benefit of the many: and the foregoing considerations lead on to the inquiry, whether, as subjects may be obtained by the act and operation of law, subjects may not be relinquished also by the act and operation of law.

The King certainly cannot, by any special act, disfranchise a particular subject: though by his judges, sitting in his bench, a subject may be outlawed on proper process for that end, operating upon the demerits of the party; yet the King, by authority of that high trust wherewith he is invested by the Constitution of making war and peace, may relinquish, by treaty, the subjection of many subjects; as in the performance of this trust, the act of the King virtually includes the act of the nation, for if it were otherwise, by the understanding of the law of nations, treaties of peace could

---

(1) See the report of the case of *Campbell* v. *Hall:* Cowper.

(2) By the Great Charter, which has been so often confirmed, and by the greatest and best explanatory Act of the 28th Ed. 3, c. 3.

never be made between belligerent powers. *Rex et subditi sunt relativa*, said Lord Chancellor Egerton, in giving his judgment in *Calvin's Case* (1). There cannot, he adds, be a King of land, without subjects, for that were but *imperium in belluas*: so, neither can there be subjects without their King, for then the terms King and subject would not be correlatives. Hence we may infer, as the Lord Chancellor intimated, that the true correlatives are sovereignty and subjection (2): if the subjection be withdrawn, and so admitted, the sovereignty is gone; if the sovereignty be removed, then is the subjection gone; and the subjection being gone, the people, owing no subjection, are no longer subjects; for they are all correlatives, which cannot exist without each other.

On this second head, how subjects may become aliens, any more than on the first, it is not to be wondered, as Lord Mansfield remarked, that an adjudged case in point cannot be produced; no dispute was ever started before as to the King's power, in making a treaty of peace, to relinquish a province with the allegiance of the provincials.

But if we trace this point historically, the operation of law will become very apparent. The Lord Chancellor Egerton said, what all the Judges indeed affirmed, in arguing the case of the *post-nati*, that King Henry II. had England and Normandy by descent from his mother, the Empress Maud; and Anjou and Main by descent from his father, Geoffrey Plantagenet; and he that was born, the Chancellor went on to say, in any of the King's dominions, and under the King's obedience, is the King's liege subject, and born *ad fidem regis* (for that is the proper and ancient word, which the law of England hath used; *ad fidem regis Angliæ, ad fidem regis Franciæ*); and therefore he cannot be a stranger or alien to the King, or in any of his kingdoms; and by consequence is enabled to have lands in England, and to sue, and be sued, in any real action for the same (3).

King John, the youngest son of Henry II., lost all those French dominions to Philip, the French King, in 1204 (4). Upon this

(1) Lord Chancellor Egerton's speech, printed 1609, p. 104.
(2) *Ibid.* p. 73.
(3) *Ibid.* pp. 62, 64.
(4) Brady says, "by his negligence," Hist. i. 474. The President Hénault tells

transaction, whereby England lost so many provinces, what was
the operation of law? Is it not apparent, that the people of those
provinces no longer remained *ad fidem regis,* in obedience to John,
and that they must have sworn fealty to Philip? When the sovereignty of those provinces thus ceased to be in the King of England,
the subjection of the people within the same also ceased. We
may infer as much from the following records, M. 4, Henry III. in
dower, the defendant pleaded, *quod petens est de potestate regis
Franciæ, et residens in Francia; et provisum est a consilio regis,
quod nullus de potestate regis Franciæ respondeatur in Anglia antequam Angli respondeantur de jure suo in Francia:* (1) this the
plaintiff's attorney could not deny; and thereupon the judgment
was, *ideo sine die* (2). There is a record of the 7th Hen. 3 [1223],
Baronibus Normanniæ quod ad servitium regis redeant (3), which
evinces that the people of those French provinces, by the forfeiture
of John, became aliens to England.

The Lord Chancellor went on, in the progress of his argument,
to say that Henry III. had Aquitaine by descent from his grand-
mother Eleanor, the daughter of the Duke of Aquitaine; Edward I.
had the same by descent, and part of Scotland by conquest;
Edward II. and Edward III. had the same by descent; and
Edward III. claimed all France by descent from his mother, and
had the most part of it in possession; and so had Henry V. and

---

a somewhat different story : King John, who was a peer of France, was cited before
the Court of Peers in France, to be judged for the murder of Arthur : he did not
appear : he was declared a rebel for his contumacy, and, of consequence, his lands
were confiscated. He was condemned to death for the murder of his nephew, committed within the jurisdiction of France. Philip annexed Normandy and John's
other French dominions, all but Guienne, to the Crown of France.—Chron. Hist.
de France, i. 197–8; Consult du Tillet, Chron. Abr. les Roys de France, 48, under
the year 1204.

(1) Fitz. Dower, 179.

(2) The Lord Chancellor Egerton's speech on the *Post-nati,* pp. 13, 14.

(3) Rym. Fœd. i. 260 : the writ therein contained was tested, by the justiciary
of England, who knew the meaning of his own terms. Shard vouched the case of
a Norman, who, with some English, had robbed divers of the King's subjects in the
narrow seas ; and who being taken and arraigned, the Norman was found guilty
only of felony, and the rest of treason ; for that Normandy being lost by King
John, was out of the allegiance of Edward III., and the Norman was accounted
an alien. Shard quoted 40 Assize, pl. 24 ; and see *Calvin's Case,* 7th Report.

Henry VI. "Now," adds the Chancellor ," in those Kings' reigns the subjects born in those countries, being then under their obedience, were no aliens, but capable of holding lands in England " (1). History must tell how those Kings of England lost those dominions in France : did the obedience of the people of those dominions continue to England ? No ɟ when the sovereignty of the Kings of England was lost, the subjection of their French subjects also ceased, and they thenceforth became aliens to the Crown, and were therefore incapable of holding any lands in England ; as we may learn from the before-cited authorities and records, and even from Bracton.

But the aptest precedent for the American treaty, 1782–3, which can be found in the records of England, is the Treaty of Northampton (1328), that acknowledged the independence of Scotland (2). The three Edwards endeavoured, by the intrigues, the fraud, and force of more than forty years, to subdue Scotland. The country was again and again overrun; the people and their chiefs fell in the field, or bled on the scaffold ; and the limbs of the illustrious Wallace were exhibited on the public places. Yet such was the persevering spirit of the nation, such the skilful valour of their leaders, such the unconquerable magnanimity of their King, that after a struggle of more than forty years, they compelled Edward III., with the assent of his Parliament, to acknowledge the independence of Scotland (3). The sovereignty of England and the submission of Scotland were renounced; the people of Scotland were acknowledged to be free, and became of course aliens to England, as the subsequent events evince, as the Treaty of Perth (4) in 1335 plainly shows; and owing to those causes, the

(1) Lord Chancellor Egerton's Speech (1609), pp. 64, 65.

(2) There was a previous Act of Parliament, made at York on the 1st of March, 1327-8, entitled *Relaxatio superioritatis Scotiæ*, Rym. Fœd. iv. 337. This Act of Parliament went much beyond the mere release of the superiority ; it relinquished the country or kingdom according to its ancient limits, and it released all subjection, service, claim, or demand of the country or its people.

(3) See the cancelled Par. Rec. 85-7; 4 Rym. 337-8. Sir Edward Coke and Sir Matthew Hale, in discussing the connection of the English and Scots laws, wrote but idly, as they seem not to have known that the Treaty of Northampton was made under the authority of two Acts of Parliament ; but Sir Bulstrode Whitloke knew that it was, and says: "The peace between England and Scotland, 2 Ed. 3, was concluded by the Parliament at Northampton."—*Collectanea Juridica*, ii. 334.

(4) See the treaty in Avesbury, 24-27.

T

274 CASES AND OPINIONS ON CONSTITUTIONAL LAW.

people of England and of Scotland were aliens to each other at the
epoch of King James's accession, as the reasonings of the judges in
Calvin's Case demonstrate.

Come we now to the case of Calais, which is somewhat singular:
in 1347, it was taken by Edward III., who invited English merchants to settle in it; so that it now partook of a mixed nature—of
a conquest first, and of a colony afterwards, something like the
condition of St. Christopher's after its colonization and conquest.
In 1558, Calais was retaken by France, at the end of 211 years'
connexion. In 1559, under the Treaty of Château-Cambrensis,
Calais was to remain eight years in possession of France, and then
to be restored, provided Queen Elizabeth behaved well in the meantime (1). But Elizabeth and Cecil were meddlers by nature, and
they would interfere in the affairs of Scotland and of France: so
Calais remained in the hands of the conquerors. The sovereignty
of Calais seems thus to have remained during those eight years in
a sort of abeyance ; and during that period, persons who were born
there were clearly aliens, as they were born out of the ligeance of
the King, and in a country out of the possession of the Crown.
The whole people afterwards were considered as aliens, by operation of law; as the sovereignty of the town and the subjection of
the people were both lost to England for ever.

Let us now advert to the condition of Surinam and New York,
under the Treaty of Breda (1667), when England ceded the first to
Holland, in full sovereignty, propriety, and possession ; while
Holland, in the same manner, ceded New York to England.
During the effluxion of the preceding century, the law of nations
had been very much discussed by Grotius, Selden, and other eminent jurists; and statesmen now argued every case, arising from
events, with more accuracy, and decided with more precision. The
disputes arising out of the Treaty of Breda came to be settled by
John de Witt and Sir William Temple: De Witt gave his opinion
in a discourse, which is hereinafter printed: it was plainly insisted
on by the one, and tacitly agreed by the other, that the English
who remained in Surinam became Dutch subjects so completely
that they became aliens to England, and could not even apply
to their native country in any manner for aid or consideration

(1) 15 Rym. 505, &c. ; the President Hénault's Abr. Chron. i. 476-7.

consistent with the law of nations. In the same manner, the Dutch people at Manhattan, as New York was then called, became completely English subjects, and aliens to their native land (1).

The wars and the treaties of subsequent times do not supply much information, and throw scarcely any light on this head of our inquiry. The Peace of Ryswick (1697), by restoring generally what had been lost by either party to their former possessor, furnishes very little observation. The main point of that treaty was the direct acknowledgment of William III. as King of England and the dominions thereunto belonging. The Peace of Utrecht (1713), is much more instructive. The conquered part of St. Christopher's was now resigned in sovereignty and possession; Newfoundland, with its adjacencies, were resigned in full sovereignty to Great Britain. From this epoch the statute of William, regulating the government and fishery of this valuable island, attached upon both. Nova Scotia, according to its ancient boundaries, was resigned to Great Britain; but there was a proviso that the French subjects might remove if they should think fit; or if they should remain, to enjoy their religion as far as the laws of Britain allowed. This form of words shows in what manner an Act of Parliament limits the King's power of making treaties; and there was also a proviso that commissaries should be appointed to settle " who ought to be accounted the subjects and friends of Britain and of France," alluding chiefly to the American Indians, as the friends of both parties. From Spain, Britain obtained Gibraltar and Minorca, in full sovereignty, and the *assiento* trade, according to former stipulations; Gibraltar and Minorca have always been governed as conquests, but the *assiento* could not be received (*qu.* revived?), according to former stipulations, as it was opposed by the Acts of Navigation. Here are sufficient illustrations of two of our principles of law in respect to treaties.

The Peace of Aix-la-Chapelle (1748) does not supply, though it provides for mutual restorations, any instructive observation. Yet the war which was then ended ought to be deemed productive of

(1) It is to be regretted that Sir Lionel Jenkins, who was then the leading civilian, did not answer De Witt, as we should have had disclosed more law than Temple seems to have possessed. My researches lead me to suppose that there was no law opinion asked by the English Government on that occasion. The English people were afterwards removed from Surinam.

much information, if it produced nothing but the report of Sir
George Lee, the Judge of the Admiralty Court, and of the Advocate, Attorney, and Solicitor General, Paul, Ryder, and Murray, on
the Prussian ships carrying neutral property (1). There were published about that time various works on similar topics, which certainly made the Powers of Europe much better acquainted with the
instructive doctrines of the law of nations.

The Peace of Paris (1763), as it retained much, and gave but
little in return, left a wide field open for illustrative observation.
The French King again relinquished the whole of Nova Scotia,
with all its dependencies; Cape Breton, and the other islands in
the Gulf of St. Lawrence; Canada, with all its dependencies and
people. The King of Great Britain, on his part, granted to the
inhabitants of Canada the liberty of the Catholic religion. He
allowed the Canadians the freedom of selling their estates to his
subjects, and of retiring within eighteen months; but there is
nothing said on the ligeance of the Canadians if they should not
retire. The sovereignty, property, and possession of the country
of Canada was ceded by the Most Christian King, and, of course,
the subjection and faith of the inhabitants, who thereby became
subjects of the Crown, and who, of course, became entitled to the
several rights of British subjects. The King restored to France
the islands of Guadaloupe, Mariegalante, Desirade, Martinico, and
Belisle, with a proviso that the King's subjects, who might have
settled in any of those islands, might retire with their effects at
any time within eighteen months; but there is nothing said of the
King's subjects, whom he had conquered thereon, or who might
have been born after the conquest and before the restoration; they
were relinquished, by operation of law, as well as in fact. Those
clauses in this treaty, and those circumstances, come up fully to
the law which has been already intimated from Dyer and Vaughan:
"If the King of England make a conquest, the persons there born
are his subjects; but if it be taken from him (or he cede it), the

(1) *Collectanea Juridica*, i. No. 5.—There is herein a note stating that "this
report contains a thorough investigation and justification of the principles adhered
to by the Court of Admiralty in England, in cases of capture of the ships and property of neutral Powers in time of war. It was composed on a memorable occasion
by the united abilities of the great Law Officers of the Crown, and has ever since
been received as the standard authority in cases of that nature."

persons there born (after such cession or capture) are aliens " (1).
But how did they become aliens ?　The answer must be, by act and
operation of law.　This general principle may be illustrated by
other clauses of this memorable treaty.　The Christian King ceded
Grenada and the Grenadines to Great Britain, with the same stipulations in favour of the inhabitants, who might retire, but, if they
remained, became subjects.　The neutral islands were partitioned
in this manner: St. Vincent, Dominica, and Tobago remained to
Great Britain; St. Lucia was delivered to France; and from this
stipulation it followed that the French people became English subjects, and the English planters on St. Lucia became French subjects,
if they remained, by the act and operation of law.　Great Britain
and Spain arranged their conquests in this manner : Britain restored to Spain the Havana and part of Cuba ; Spain ceded to
Britain the Floridas ; and the island of Minorca was ceded to Britain
in the same condition as when conquered, so that the Spanish people
of this island, who had become English subjects when originally
conquered, became again English, by a sort of *jus postliminii* (2).

The treaties of Versailles (1783) are less glorious, but fully as
instructive.　Great Britain restored to France St. Lucia, and ceded
Tobago.　The British subjects in both were allowed to retain their
possessions, or to retire within eighteen months.　France restored
to Great Britain Grenada and the Grenadines, St. Vincent's, Dominica, St. Christopher's, Nevis, and Montserrat, with the same stipulations in favour of the French planters.　Great Britain ceded, in
full right, Minorca to Spain, with the same stipulations in favour
of British subjects.　Great Britain also ceded to Spain the two
Floridas, with a similar proviso that the British subjects might retire ; and Spain ceded to Great Britain the Bahamas, with a similar
stipulation in favour of the Spanish subjects who might there remain.　It is quite apparent from the foregoing facts and reasonings,
that those alterations of sovereignty changed the nature of the
ligeance of the people, so that they were aliens or subjects, according to the nature of their residence and subjection.

(1) Dy. 224; Vaugh. 281-2.

(2) The case of Fabrigas and General Mostyn, which was decided in 1773 by a
verdict of three thousand pounds against the General, evinces sufficiently that the
Spanish people of Minorca were English subjects.

After this full discussion of so many treaties, let us again advert to the definitive treaty with the United States. When this subject was considered in the House of Lords, Lord Loughborough said, that the King could not, in virtue of his prerogative, cede Canada or Florida without the sanction of Parliament. The Lord Chancellor, when he delivered his sentiments, treated Lord Loughborough's opinion with no great respect. What has been so often done before could not be done now. But what sort of logic is it to reason against facts? When the same subject was under consideration in the House of Commons, with respect to the powers of the prerogative, Mr. Wallace and Mr. Lee maintained that the King could not abdicate a part of his dominions, or declare any number of his subjects free from obedience to his laws. The contrary was asserted by the Attorney General; and both parties pledged themselves, if the matter should come regularly into discussion, to make good their several opinions (1). But the day of discussion never came, and all wise men saw that such extravagant doctrines, though they might have done very well at the sad epoch of civil war, could not be soberly maintained in time of domestic quiet. The King most undoubtedly enjoys from the Constitution the exclusive power of making war and peace. This is a fundamental principle of the law of nations; it is one of the pillars of society itself; and it has been argued by writers on the law of nature and nations, that though individuals, antecedent to all society (if such a state ever existed), had the right of war, this right was given up when they entered into society. It is said to be upon the same principle that the King enjoys the sovereign power of making treaties, leagues, and alliances with foreign States and princes (2). But was there not an Act of Parliament made to enable the King to make a peace with the United States? Yes; yet is it singular to remark, that the said Act was not used. It was neither recited nor alluded to

(1) Annual Register, 1783.

(2) If, however, it were necessary to lay on or take off taxes, the King cannot do this without the provision of Parliament; if regulations have been previously made under Parliamentary authority, as in the case of Newfoundland and fishery, a treaty cannot warrant the repeal of such regulations, as this must be done by Parliament or not at all; so, in making commercial treaties, regulations are to be made or repealed which can only be done by Parliament; and if Parliament disapprove of such a treaty, it must fall. All those cases are exceptions to the general principle of the royal power to make war and peace.

in either the preliminary or definitive treaty of peace with those thirteen States. The King's constitutional power was deemed sufficient, without the special statute, which had been suggested *ex abundante cautela* by the same spirit which suggested the repeal of the Stamp Act, and thereby created much of the mischief which was now pressed upon the nation for remedy.

The history of our diplomacy evinces the truth of the general principle which is recognised by every law. King William, by the Treaty of Ryswick, granted and received cessions of conquests in war. Queen Anne, by the Treaty of Utrecht, made some cessions, and received more. King George II., by the Treaty of Aix-la-Chapelle, agreed to cede and receive all conquests since the war commenced. King George III., by the Treaty of Paris, received much and ceded little. By the Peace of Versailles (1783), when the treaties in question were made and ratified, the King granted to France fisheries, factories, islands, and territories, and received much in return. The King ceded to Spain the island of Minorca, and the two provinces of the Floridas, and such other countries as might have been taken, and received in return from Spain the Bahamas. It was the opinion of Parliament that too much had been given to those several Powers, yet this opinion did not nullify or vitiate the treaties. It only operated upon the responsibility of Ministers, whom it virtually removed from the power of doing mischief. This is merely a collateral point, which, according to the wisdom of our Constitution, does not trench at all upon the King's authority to make war or peace.

Whether that vote of Parliament extended to the treaty with the United States is somewhat doubtful; but there can be no doubt whether that treaty were not the most exceptionable. Why relinquish, under the pretence of settling boundaries, countries larger than Great Britain, to which the United States had no pretensions? Why grant the Newfoundland fishery, which Britain guards as every man his nursery? They had no claim to anything beyond their independence. In the other treaties the rights of individuals were carefully guarded; in the treaty with the United States they were contemptuously disregarded. The statesmen who made this treaty pleaded in vain as a justification that the Congress would have the western countries—the Congress insisted on a right to the Newfoundland fishery; the Congress had only the power to recommend private persons and their claims to the particular States: yes, the Congress have done nothing since but make claims, and continue to make claims. If the Congress or the President had not complete authority to make war and peace, this defect had been a fatal objection to the full powers of the negotiators. This ought to be a beacon to such negotiators who may be appointed hereafter to treat with the commissioners of the United States, whose full powers ought to be carefully examined.

But whatever there may be in those objections and defences, the question still recurs—could the King, under the authority and trust which he possesses from the Constitution, acknowledge the independence and sovereignty of thirteen revolted colonies? Could he renounce the government of the people forming those United States in future? Could he renounce, of course, the subjection of the people? The answer must be in the affirmative; he renounced at the same time other provinces and islands, with British people thereon, and no doubt has been made whether those territories have not been legally ceded, and the subjection of the people constitutionally changed. After the restoration of peace an asylum was offered within the remaining colonies to those colonists who might think fit to retire from within the United States. Many did retire, but many more remained; and the question is, whether those who thus remained, and were acknowledged to be free from subjection and independent in their governments, could nevertheless claim the privileges of subjects? If they be aliens by the renunciation of their submission, they cannot claim the privileges of subjects; and that they are aliens is clear: since they do not possess any one of the characteristics of true and lawful subjects, they have neither *subjectio, fides, vel obedientia;* they lost all those characters of subjects by the act and operation of law, working upon their own actions; renouncing their allegiance, and electing to be aliens. What is done by treaty is *juridice factum;* so *non læsura populi:* but although the King never could, and cannot now, disfranchise any subject, yet his courts of justice could, at common law, disfranchise and outlaw his subjects on proper process issuing upon the delinquencies of the offending parties. In the same manner, when the King executes the great trust of making treaties of peace, whereby provinces are ceded, and the provincials, though unoffending subjects, are disfranchised, the law will justify and warrant what it empowers and enables the executive authority to perform and enforce; and a disfranchisement performed in this manner by the King's negotiators is as much done by the law of the land as an outlawry pronounced by the King's Judges in the Court of King's Bench: *Consuetudo regni Angliæ est Lex Angliæ.*

Mr. Professor Woodeson, indeed, informs us that when by a treaty, especially if ratified by Act of Parliament, our Sovereign cedes any island or region to another State, the inhabitants of such ceded territory, though born under the allegiance of the King, or being under his protection while it appertained to his Crown and authority, became effectually aliens, or liable to the disabilities of alienage, in respect to their future concerns with this country; and similar to this seems the condition of the revolted Americans since the recognition of their independent commonwealth (1).

Now let us listen to Mr. Professor Blackstone, who says that "Natural allegiance is a debt of gratitude, which cannot be forfeited, cancelled, or altered by any chance of time, place, or circumstance, nor by anything but the united concurrence of the Legislature" (2); yet Professor Blackstone had already well argued the King's constitutional authority to make war and peace, from the law of nature, from the law of nations, from the law of England: the Professor therefore wrote contradictorily without knowing this unlucky circumstance. His general position is sound law: that natural allegiance is such a debt from the subject that it cannot be altered or cancelled by the act of the party himself, even with the concurrent help of any prince or potentate or power: it must be relinquished by some act of law, which amounts to the assent of the King and nation, and a solemn treaty is that necessary act; but the conclusion of Blackstone's position is not law

(1) Woodeson's Vin. Lectures, i. 382.—This law has been collected into Bacon's Abr. 1798, i. 129. I have argued the several points upon common law principles. To introduce the ratification of Parliament is to weaken rather than strengthen the argument, from these principles: if Parliament decide, it is decided; no one argues with the omniscience of Parliament; no one contends with the omnipotence of Parliament.

(2) 1 Blacks. 369 (1st edit.).

as he words it, yet may it be made law by adopting the emphatical
language of the Great Charter: no freeman shall be destroyed or
disfranchised but by the lawful judgment of his peers, or by the
law of the land, which is the safest language, on occasions of this
sort, as the law will attach according to the necessity and nature
of the case before it.

Let us now hear what the Judges said in *Calvin's Case* (1): "So,
albeit the kingdoms of England and Scotland should by descent
be divided and governed by several Kings, yet was it resolved that
all those that were born under one natural obedience while the
realms were united under one Sovereign should remain natural-
born subjects, and no aliens; for that naturalization, due and
vested by birthright, cannot, by any separation of the crowns,
afterward be taken away; nor he that was by judgment of law a
natural subject at the time of his birth become an alien by such a
matter *ex post facto;* and in that case our *post-natus* may be *ad
fidem utriusque regis,* as Bracton saith."

This resolution is supposed and said to be decisive of the case
now in question, like other decided cases; but this resolve was not
the point before the Court, which was that of one Colvil, or Calvin,
as he is called, who had been born in Scotland, after the accession
of King James to the throne of England, and brought an action
for the recovery of a house and tenement in London. It was
pleaded in bar of his action that he was a Scotsman who was born
out of the allegiance of the King, and when the Court decided
that, being born after the accession of the King, Calvin was a subject, and not an alien, the case was decided in his favour, and, of
course, the resolution of the Judges on a supposed contingency, as
before-mentioned, was a mere extra-judicial opinion, which is no
authority at all, whatever there may be in the argument.

Let us now attend to the Lord Chancellor Egerton, when giving
his judgment in this very case of Calvin: "Wherefore of the many
and divers distinctions, divisions, and subdivisions, that have been
made in this case I will say no more, but *confusum est quicquid in*

(1) 7 Co. 27 b.—Coke's report of *Calvin's Case* was reprinted by James Watson,
at Edinburgh, in 1705, when parties ran high at the Union, "for the information
of such as would know the rights and privileges of Scotchmen residing in England,
and of Englishmen residing in Scotland." I have in my library a copy of this
reprinted report.

pulverem sectum est, and will conclude with Bishop Jewel, 'A man may wander and miss his way in the mists of distinctions' (1). As the King, nor his heart, cannot be divided, for he is one entire King over all his subjects, in whichsoever of his kingdoms or dominions he were born, so he must not be served nor obeyed by halves: he must have entire and perfect obedience of his subjects; for *ligentia* (as Baron Heron said well) must have four qualities: 1. *Pura* and *simplex*; 2. *Integra* and *solida*; 3. *Universalis non localis*; 4. *Permanens, continua*, and *illæsa*. Divide a man's heart, and you lose both parts of it, and make no heart at all; so he that is not an entire subject, but half-faced, is no subject at all." Apply this solid sense to the condition of the American citizens after their allegiance was renounced by the King's acknowledgment of the sovereignty of the United States, and the subjection of their citizens was also disowned by the King's solemn act, under a constitutional trust. Yes, say some, the United States are sovereign and independent, the American citizens owe no allegiance or subjection, yet do they claim their birthrights. The proper answer to such pretensions is: You have lost your birthrights by your own acts, and the operation of law upon your several acts; *ab assuetis non fit injuria*. When the King, acting in pursuance of a solemn trust derived from the Constitution, renounced all claim of government over you, and, of course, released your subjection, the King thereby signified the assent of the nation that you should be no longer subjects, but aliens; for in making every treaty the King, as trustee for the nation, binds the nation by his diplomatic acts, and *lex nil jubet frustra.*

Who sees not that the Lord Chancellor, in what he said above, glanced at the extra-judicial resolution and illogical reasoning of the Judges before mentioned? What sort of logic was it to reason in a circle? It never was a principle of the law of England that subjects could be *ad fidem utriusque regis*, as we have already seen in the learned Craig's discussions. It never was a principle of the law of nature, as we may learn from Our Saviour's declaration, though there might be exceptions to the general rule, under special privilege, as the Earl Marshal, who was mentioned by Bracton; so, in the Treaty of Utrecht, Art. 21, the French King engaged to

(1) His published speech, pp. 62, 102.

cause justice to be done to the family of Hamilton concerning the dukedom of Chatelherault, and to the Duke of Richmond concerning such requests as he had to make, and to Charles Douglass concerning some lands to be claimed by him, and so of others. Thus might the Duke of Hamilton, and the Duke of Richmond, and the Duke of Queensbury owe a double allegiance; but this exception only proves the general principle.

Well, but, says Sir Edward Coke, naturalization, due by birthright, cannot, by any separation of the crowns afterwards, be taken away; yet how was it before and after the Treaty of Northampton (1328), of which Sir Edward seems to have been but lamely informed? In the 21st of Edward I., Macduff, a Scotsman, appealed against a judgment of his Sovereign, John Baliol, to Edward, as his superior lord, and the King of England received the appeal and caused justice to be done (1); but when the sovereignty of England was renounced by that treaty, the homage of the Scottish King and people was determined, and they became aliens (2), and therefore no such appeal or suit can be shown in any record under the Treaty of Northampton, as Scotland was now alien to England, as hath been already shown; so after King John lost the Norman provinces, the two kingdoms, with their people, became aliens to each other, as hath been already shown, and as Bracton tells. Those two great precedents from well-vouched history and record clearly prove that a natural subject, by birthright, may become alien by such matter, *ex post facto*, and thus doth Sir Edward Coke fail in his argument. Then, as to the general resolution of the Judges, not upon the case referred to them, but upon a case which might by possibility happen in the progress of time and chance. What is it but a mere *petitio principii*, begging the very question which ought to be answered? How does it stand with the fundamental principle of the *feudal* law, which is quoted by Craig, the profound feudist, *unus et idem duorum dominorum homo ligius esse non potest?* How does it consist with the law of nature, as quoted by Our Saviour, " No man can serve two masters, for he will hate the one and love the other"? How does it quadrate with the general law as to alienage of European nations? Doth it not tear up by the roots the chief grounds of all

(1) Riley's Placita, 152, 157.   (2) Molloy, 375.

those laws in respect to alienage? Doth it not pretend to out-argue the historical facts which have been quoted as to the loss of the English dominion in Scotland, and in France? *Magis docet qui prudenter interrogat*, said the Lord Chancellor Egerton.

Lord Mansfield, indeed, in delivering the opinion of the King's Bench in the case of *Rex* v. *Cowle*, with regard to the legal state of Berwick, whether within the jurisdiction of that Court, and reprobating some *obiter opinions* in the case of Calvin, remarked of Sir Edward Coke, "that he was very fond of multiplying pre-cedents and authorities, and in order to illustrate his subject, was apt, besides such authorities as were strictly applicable, to cite other cases, which were not applicable to the particular question under his consideration."

After all those considerations, can it be doubted, within West-minster Hall or without, whether the Judges regard themselves as at all bound by manifest error? Lord Mansfield, in delivering the opinion of the King's Bench in the case of *Rex* v. *Cowle*, rectified two mistakes of very great lawyers: "It is manifest," said his Lord-ship, "that Coke is mistaken in saying, generally, 'that Berwick was not governed by the laws of England,' for in criminal matters the fact is undoubtedly otherwise;" and his Lordship added: "The Lord Chief Justice Hale is clearly mistaken in saying, 'that Ber-wick sends members to the Parliament of England by charter;' for it is by writ of summons that they send them thither, in con-sequence of their being a borough." We may thus perceive that the vigilance of even the greatest lawyers cannot always be awake; as the minds of men, according to Johnson's remark, cannot be con-stantly attentive to evanescent actions. We are told by Sir William Blackstone, that an appeal lies from the colonies to the King and Council (1). The commentator seems to have borrowed this form of words from Sir Matthew Hale's History of the Common Law; but great names and high authority cannot justify such in-accuracy of language and of law. The appeal is to the King in his Council. Sir Matthew Hale had said, that naturalization can only be by Parliament, and not otherwise (2). "Naturalization," saith

(1) Comment. 12th edit. i. 108.
(2) Vent. Rep. 419-20.—That position of Hale is true, in a particular sense, but is not true in a general sense.

Blackstone, "cannot be performed but by Act of Parliament," copying again Sir Matthew Hale, though without using his idle expression, and not otherwise ; but such general positions cannot stand against known facts as well as juridical policy, and it was overruled by the Court of King's Bench in the case of *Campbell* v. *Hall*, while the policy of considering aliens conquered in war, and ceded by treaty, as subjects, was confirmed as law. The whole observations of Sir Edward Coke, in support or explanation of the hypothetical resolution of the Judges before-mentioned, may be considered as mere mistakes, and extra-judicial inferences, leading to little information and to mischievous consequences. We all know the fatal effects of double allegiance during the latter periods of our domestic history (1). "Indeed," saith Blackstone (2), "the natural-born subject of one prince, to whom he owes allegiance, may be entangled by subjecting himself absolutely to another; but it is his own act that brings himself into those difficulties of owing service to two masters ; and it is unreasonable that, by such voluntary act of his own, he should be able at pleasure to unloose those bands by which he was connected to his natural prince."

But I have done. I have shown satisfactorily, I trust, in what manner millions of subjects may become aliens, by mere act and operation of law, as millions of aliens, by the same operation of law, may become subjects.

February 1, 1814.   G. C.

(5.) DISCUSSIONS *on the Question, "Whether Inhabitants of the United States, born there before the Independence, are, on coming to this Kingdom, to be considered as Natural-born Subjects?"* By MR. REEVES, *Author of the "History of the English Law"* (3). 1808.

I thought the affirmative of this question was acknowledged by all lawyers. One authority, it seems to me, is sufficient to sup-

(1) See Foster's Crown Law, 184, &c.
(2) Comment. i. 370.
(3) This opinion is given in Chalmers as by "a Barrister;" but he was the well-known John Reeves, who wrote the "History of the English Law." The foot-notes are his own.

port it. I mean what is laid down in *Calvin's Case*, on the supposition that the Crown of Scotland might possibly be separated from that of England, upon which point the Judges resolved: "That all those who were born under one natural obedience while the realms were united under one Sovereign should remain natural-born subjects, and no aliens; for that naturalization, due and vested by birthright, cannot, by any separation of the Crowns afterwards, be taken away; nor he that was by judgment of law a natural subject at the time of his birth become an alien by such matter, *ex post facto*, and in that case, upon such an accident, our *ante-natus* may be *ad fidem utriusque regis*" (7 Rep. 27 b.); or, to apply the words to the present case, our *ante-natus*, or American-born before the separation, may be *ad fidem regis*, and also a citizen of the United States (1).

Such a plain and explicit authority as this seems to make it unnecessary to search for any other; however, objections are raised to the claim of such persons to be considered as British-born subjects.

1. It is objected that, admitting the common law to be as laid down in the above resolution, there are circumstances in the American revolution that distinguish it from all other changes of sovereignty. The island of Jamaica, say they, may be ceded by the King, and this being done without the consent of the inhabitants, there is no reason why they should lose their birthright of British subjects; but the Americans, a whole people in arms, claimed to be released from the English Government, and the King at the peace consented to give up his authority: how can such a people be afterwards considered as British subjects?

2. It is objected that there are certain statutes and public Acts which stand in the way of the above-mentioned common law principle taking effect.

3. It is even objected by some that no principle of the common law can support so unwarrantable an anomaly as that the same persons should belong to two States, and that admitting them to levy war against the King in the character of American sub-

(1) The *post-natus* there, that is, one born after the union with Scotland, corresponds with the *ante-natus* here, that is, one born before the separation from America.

jects without being deemed traitors, and then allowing them to come into his kingdom in the character of British subjects, is an inconsistency which they think cannot be countenanced by the law of England.

To the first of these objections it may be answered, that the peace which put an end to the American war ought to be considered as putting an end to all the consequences that might be imputed to the Americans by reason of their rebellion; and, indeed, there is in the definitive treaty, Article 6, an express provision that no person should, on account of the war, suffer any future loss or damage, either in his person, liberty, or property.

Further, we should inquire what the Americans could be supposed to relinquish by making war, and what was the result of the King making peace? The Americans could not mean to renounce the privileges of British subjects; because they rebelled and made war in order to get something they had not, and not to surrender what they possessed; it was to release themselves from their allegiance; but no man can throw off his allegiance at his own option, as must be admitted by every one. Did the King, then, make peace with them in order to take away their rights as British subjects? But surely it is well known that the King alone cannot take away the rights of a British subject from any one. In the peace, therefore, made with the Americans there seems to have been no legal competency in the contracting parties to produce the effect supposed of making the Americans aliens. This must appear even upon general principles only. It will presently be shown that there was not, de facto, anything in the treaty upon the subject of British rights that warrants the supposition of their being taken away from the Americans.

There cannot, in a judicial point of view, be any difference between the supposed case of cession of territory without consent of the inhabitants, and the present case of cession to gratify the wishes of the inhabitants. The allegiance in both cases is of the same nature; the allegiance is not to the soil, but to the person of the King; and as no transfer or cession of the soil to a foreign prince makes any alteration in the allegiance of birthright of the subject, but the same still remains in the person of the subject, it imports nothing whether such cession is made with or without his consent. In both cases he becomes a British-born subject, living in a foreign land, and liable to the alteration of circumstances which everywhere attends a British subject when out of the King's dominions.

That going out of the King's dominions under the charge of criminality, at the choice of the party and by the King's consent, does not make a British subject an alien, is evinced from the old law of sanctuary in cases of felony, and abjuring the realm to save the felon's life. It is expressly laid down: " *Quod abjurat regnum, amittit regnum, sed non regem; amittit patriam, sed non patrem patriæ;* for notwithstanding the abjuration, he oweth the King his allegiance, and he remaineth within the King's protection; for the King may pardon and restore him to his country again. Allegiance is a quality of the mind, and not confined to any place." (*Calvin's Case,* fol. 9 b.)

As to what is now said of the Americans being a whole people in arms demanding to be released from their allegiance, it should be recollected that the language in this country during the whole of the American war was different. It was said, " the thinking part, those who had property and character," and some said, " the majority of the people," were against the violent measures which were driven on by an active minority of agitators. Is it, then, at all reasonable to infer upon those persons who were friendly to this country the consequences of such resistance and rebellion? Indeed, there is nothing so unjust in the law of England. The law does not consider the King's subjects in a mass, under the name of the people, in any number more or less. They cannot be considered in a legal view but as individuals. What is the law respecting one is the law respecting one million, and every man's case stands upon its own ground and circumstances. It is, therefore, utterly inconsistent with the law to impute to the Americans any disfranchisement as a people. If there is any such extinguishment of rights, it must be in some individual; and if it is not to be discovered in one, it is not to be found in a million.

Secondly, as to the statutes and public Acts which are supposed to stand in the way of the above-mentioned principle of common law: the principal statute which, I believe, is relied upon is statute 22 Geo. 3, c. 46. This is a Parliamentary authority enabling

290 CASES AND OPINIONS ON CONSTITUTIONAL LAW.

his Majesty to make peace with America—an authority which had become necessary, because the Parliament had passed some Acts of prohibition and penalty which might stand in the way of peace, as statute 16 Geo. 3, c. 5, and statute 17 Geo. 3, c. 7 (1), for prohibiting trade and intercourse with America, and for authorizing hostilities against the rebels. The American war having thus become a Parliamentary measure, it required the concurrence of Parliament to make peace, which in ordinary cases belongs to the King alone.

Accordingly, statute 22 Geo. 3, c. 46, authorizes the King to conclude " a peace or truce with the said colonies or plantations, or any of them;" and that the above-mentioned prohibitory Acts might not be an impediment to the progress of negotiation, the statute authorizes the King, " by letters patent under the great seal, to repeal, annul, and make void, or suspend the operation or effect of, any Act or Acts of Parliament which relate to the said colonies or plantations;" meaning under these general words, most probably, the above-mentioned prohibitory Acts, and none other.

There might be another reason for an Act of Parliament— namely, some hesitation as to the persons with whom the King's commissioners were to treat, whether they had competency : therefore the Act speaks of treating with commissioners named by the colonies, with any body or bodies politic, with any assembly or assemblies, or description of men, or with any person or persons whatsoever.

Such are the provisions of the Act for making peace with America, which is supposed to give authority to the King to take away the rights of British-born subjects from the inhabitants of the United States, and make them aliens. I can only ask those who allege this Act, to show us by what words, or by what construction of words, such power is given to, or is intimated to reside in, the King? And with such an appeal I dismiss this statute.

The next document that occurs, in course of time, is the definitive treaty made in September, 1783, in pursuance of such Parliamentary authority. In the first article of this treaty the King " acknowledges the United States (naming the several colonies) to be free, sovereign, and independent States; and for himself, his

(1) These Acts were afterwards repealed by stat. 23 Geo. 3, c. 26.

heirs and successors, relinquishes all claims to the government, propriety, and territorial rights of the same, and every part thereof." This leading and general provision being made, there follow in the treaty some few subsidiary stipulations, all tending to give effect to the above relinquishment of sovereignty, and to the confirmation of peace and amity. After reading these, I must again ask the like question as before—where is the provision in the treaty for doing that which I have not yet discovered the King was authorized by the Act to do? It appears from reading the treaty that the King has not, *de facto*, done that which he was not enabled by the Act, nor was otherwise authorized, *de jure*, to do. He has not taken away the rights of British-born subjects residing in the United States, nor has he renounced the allegiance of his natural-born subjects residing there; he has acknowledged the colonies to be free and independent, and relinquished all sovereignty over their territory: in doing so, he has departed with some of his own royal prerogative, and has circumscribed the claims he before had on the allegiance of his natural-born subjects residing there. This was his to give, and he has given it, but the rights of British subjects the King had no power to take away; nor was it a time for taking, but a time for giving and conceding: the Americans meant to add to what they already enjoyed. They would have felt it an injury if it had been proposed to them no longer to be deemed British-born subjects; and recollecting, as we must, the feeling and speculations in this country—looking forward, as many did, to the colonists quarrelling amongst themselves, and coming back, all or some of them, to their old connection with us— we may be sure no one in this kingdom would have ventured to propose that they should be stripped of the character of British subjects to which they were born, and be rendered aliens under circumstances which would indicate on our part a disposition to perpetual estrangement and enmity.

So far from this, I think, there is even in the treaty an express saving of the rights of a British-born subject, among other rights and claims. In Article 6, it is provided, "that no person shall on that account (meaning the preceding war) suffer any future loss or damage, either in person, liberty, or property." If an American comes to this kingdom, and is treated as an alien under the Alien

Act, he assuredly suffers in his person and liberty; and such suffering must be on account of the war, which those ought to allow who make the first of the above objections: he surely cannot be said to suffer by the peace, which was meant for conferring advantages, not for taking them away.

The next document, where we are to look for something which is to control the above principle of the common law, is the commercial treaty, 19th of November, 1794. But in this I can find nothing to the effect supposed, and I must put the like interrogation as before; yet with still less expectation of an answer, because in this treaty we have something more than negative evidence—we have here express testimony—that the rights of British-born subjects were intended to be continued to the Americans by the first treaty, and that it was intended by the commercial treaty to give them a longer continuance to their posterity. By the 9th Article it appears that the American citizens then held lands in the dominions of his Majesty; but they must be British-born subjects to hold lands, and not aliens. It appears, therefore, that his Majesty, in November, 1794, eleven years after the treaty of peace, recognized the citizens of the United States as British-born subjects. I lay this stress upon the declaration of the fact, because I cannot suppose a public and solemn instrument, as this treaty is, would speak of lands being holden in any other sense than that of being lawfully holden.

The framers of the treaty certainly understood it in that sense, because the provision they intended to make was to fortify the titles to these lands in future times, when certainly the title to them would become not lawful. They foresaw that although the present possessors were British-born subjects, their descendants, born in the United States, out of the King's allegiance, would be aliens (1). It was accordingly stipulated, "that neither they nor their heirs or assigns shall, so far as may respect the said lands and the legal remedies incident thereto, be regarded as aliens." If it should be objected, that the provision here speaks as well of the present possessor as the heirs, the answer is, that it would not have

(1) They might, for their sons and grandsons, have the benefit of stat. 7 Ann. c. 5, stat. 4 Geo. 2, c. 21, and stat. 13 Geo. 3, c. 21; but for after-descendants they needed a new provision.

been so well worded if the present possessor had not been named; and if he had not been named as well as the heirs, it might have been construed into an implication that he was to be excluded from the protection intended for the heirs only.

Another more probable reason for this stipulation was to bind the two nations not to make any disqualifying law, that, by rendering the others aliens, would disable them from holding lands. This future possibility, without any doubt about the then present state of the law, might be sufficient reason for such a cautionary provision.

Whatever observation may be indulged on this part of the article, the averment in the beginning of it remains unaffected; and this averment, of Americans being British-born subjects, is again published, ratified, and confirmed by Parliament, in statute 37 Geo. 3, c. 97, ss. 24, 25, which was made for carrying into execution the treaty. This article of the treaty is there recited at length, and the two clauses, ss. 24, 25, purport to carry it into execution.

If there is anything in this statute to control the effect of the common law position so often alluded to, I think it should be in these two clauses; yet I have not been able to discover such a meaning, and I must leave it to be demonstrated by those who have found it out. The clauses appear to me to have something particular in them; they omit the naming of heirs, which was the enactment most wanted, and they supply this omission by a winding wordiness in the proviso, that is not easily evolved. There is a grudging caution in the whole conception of these clauses: I believe the framers of them did not like the matter of them, being unwilling to bear this Parliamentary testimony to the legal conclusion, that *ante nati* Americans are British-born subjects, so as to hold lands.

As to the third objection—the anomaly and inconsistency of Americans being citizens of the United States while there, and being British-born subjects when here—this is not a novelty, nor is it peculiar to Americans. It may happen to any British subject, and it is allowable in our law, which recognizes this double character of a person being, as was before shown, *ad fidem utriusque regis*. British subjects may voluntarily put themselves in such a situation;

it is part of the privileges of a British subject to be at liberty so to do. Have we not British subjects who are naturalized in Holland, in Russia, in Hamburg, in various places on the continent of Europe? Do not British subjects become citizens of the United States? Some persons are born to such double character; children and grandchildren, born of British parents in foreign countries, are British-born subjects, yet these, no doubt, by the laws of the respective foreign countries, are also deemed natural-born subjects there.

Thus far of individuals; the like may happen to a whole community, a whole people. When the King relinquished his sovereignty over the United States, the land became foreign, while the inhabitants remained all British subjects. When the King's forces took Surinam and the other Dutch colonies, the land became British, but the inhabitants still continued foreigners. The personal character of alien, with which the Dutch colonists were born, still remains to them, and the indelible character of British subject, with which the Americans were born, remained to them after their country was made foreign.

I am aware of the difficulties which such persons may labour under, with those double claims of allegiance upon them. Such difficulties must be got through as circumstances will allow, and consideration should be had for the parties according to their respective situations; more especially with a distinction between those who brought themselves into such embarrassing situation voluntarily, and those who were born in it; and more particularly with regard to the difference between that which is the act of private individuals, and that which is a national proceeding involving a whole people. In weighing such circumstances, it will soon appear that these are all objections which relate more to facts than to the law of the case; they are inconveniences in the way of full exercise and enjoyment of the rights in question, but detract nothing from the rights themselves. On the one hand, the King cannot reckon upon the full and absolute obedience of such persons, because they owe another fealty besides that due to him ; on the other hand, the subject cannot have full enjoyment of his British rights. Indeed, it will be found, he will have as little of his own rights as the King has of his obedience; for if the rights of a

British subject are examined, it will appear that almost all of them
depend on a residence in the King's dominions, and that when he
removes into a foreign country, as they are without exercise or
application, they are suspended and have no apparent existence.

I have heard it asked, if the King was to send his writ to command the attendance of Mr. Jefferson in this kingdom?—I agree
he would not come; but that would be no test of the law upon the
subject; it is an inconvenience in point of fact. The law, in the
execution of it, is liable to many obstructions which prevail, and
yet the judgment of the law is not deemed thereby invalidated.
If the King had sent such a writ to General Washington, at the
head of his army, I suppose he would not have obeyed it, yet no
one would have deemed it a demonstration that he was not amenable to our law.   Why then should a pacific refusal from Mr.
Jefferson have in it more of the force of a legal argument? And
yet, I think, Mr. Jefferson might decline obedience to such a command, admit himself to be a British subject, and have the law on
his side too.

Mr. Jefferson might answer such a call upon him by saying:
" True it is, I was born a British subject, and I myself have done
nothing to put off that character.   But your Majesty has, by the
Treaty of 1783, relinquished all sovereignty over the United States;
and as your Majesty and all the world know, it was thereby intended that your subjects here should form a Government of their
own. We have so done, under the faith of your Majesty's grant and
covenant; and it has happened, in the progress of events, that I am
now exercising an office in that Government which necessarily requires my presence here. I am brought into this situation in
consequence af an act of your Majesty, by which it was designed
that myself, or some other of your subjects here, should come into
such a situation : being so circumstanced, I am no longer at liberty
to make a choice of my own.   There is a moral and political necessity, that makes it impossible, at present, to obey the commands of
your Majesty ; I pray your Majesty's forbearance; I plead your
Majesty's own covenant and good faith : and I rely upon them as
a justification, or excuse, for my disobedience."

Surely this would be a good plea in point of law, and Mr. Jefferson might have the benefit of his American citizenship, in perfect

compatibility with the claims upon him from British allegiance. Such *scintilla juris* in the King of England can, I should think, raise no flame in any American bosom.

There are much stronger cases of a similar kind that have never startled any one with their anomaly or incompatibility. Mr. Jefferson and other American citizens have entered into their offices, their engagements, and their situations, under the faith of the King and the Parliament. But how many British subjects have become citizens, burghers, burgomasters, and have taken other offices in foreign countries, voluntarily, upon speculations of private interest, and from various inducements, all of them of an individual and personal nature. If such persons had been called upon by the King's writ, they would not have had so good a plea as Mr. Jefferson, and yet, probably, none of them would have moved from their station. Was it ever heard that such persons, when returned to this kingdom, were deemed to be less of British subjects, because they had lived and risen to public stations in foreign States? No, certainly; they are considered as having exercised the liberty belonging to all British subjects, respecting whom there is no restraint but the considerations of prudence which are suggested by the occasion; and yet none of these volunteers in foreign service have so much to say for themselves as an American citizen who chooses to leave the United States, and to spend the remainder of his days in this kingdom. The local allegiance he has acknowledged to a foreign Government is recognized by the King and Parliament: he has never lived wholly out of the view of the sovereign power under which he was born; and the language, laws, and manners he has been conversant with during the whole of his residence in the ceded States of America, restore him to this kingdom, and to his original and natural allegiance, unchanged, and quite British. Why should a person of this description, an American citizen, be the only one rejected and excluded from the rights of a British subject, because he owes a local allegiance in another country?

There is a Parliamentary record testifying instances of such contumacy. In stat. 14 & 15 Henry 8, c. 4, it is recited tha Englishmen living beyond sea, and becoming subjects to foreign princes and lords, " will obey to none authority under the great seal of England, but they give themselves over to the protection and defence of those outward princes to whom they be sworn subjects." It is herein recorded by Parliament that Englishmen thus expatriated themselves and refused obedience to the King's writ; and yet no declaration or enactment was made by Parliament on that point of disobedience, so as to disfranchise them and make them aliens; but there is by that Act imposed on them merely a penalty in one particular article—that of importation of goods. Such persons, it seems, had abused their privilege as Englishmen, and had lent their name to cover the goods of persons of the foreign country where they resided. To put an end to such impositions, they were in future to pay alien duties, as the subjects of the country where they resided.

Compare these recusant absentees alluded to in the statute with the American now in question. The former voluntarily leave the kingdom, make themselves subjects of a foreign State, refuse obedience to the King's writ, abuse their privilege of natural-born subjects to defraud the revenue. The latter is born under the King's allegiance, in a country which the King has since ceded and made a foreign land. It does not appear this particular person had any concern in the public affairs of the country, till it was so settled by his Majesty's solemn covenant and grant. He chooses in the latter part of his life "to go home" (for such is the phrase in the United States to the present moment), and end his days here. No act of recusancy or contumacy is imputed to him.

Now compare the consequences in the two cases: the former, though solemnly noticed and censured by Parliament, is not marked by any penalty of disfranchisement, though thus alienated from his native country, but is merely mulct in the payment of alien duties; the latter is told he is an alien, and has lost his right of a natural-born subject.

The further we go, the more we find of precedent and principle against such a sentence of disfranchisement.

These are the answers which, I think, may be made to the above three objections (1). These answers seem to me sufficient, and nothing further need be done but to come round to the place from

(1) I recollect another objection: how is the question of American citizens to be tried? I see this was an objection in *Calvin's Case*: it is the second of the five inconveniences, and it is answered in the Report, fol. 26 b.

whence we set out—namely, the position of law resolved by all the Judges in *Caluin's Case*, according to which the *ante nati* in the United States continue still British-born subjects, and, coming here, are entitled to all the privileges of such. The plain and explicit principle laid down on that occasion has, I suppose, governed the minds of lawyers, whenever they have been consulted on the application of it to American citizens. It is owing, no doubt, to this uniformity of opinion, that the question has never been brought to argument in any court. During the space of twenty-five years, since the independence of America was declared, there has never been so much doubt on this claim as for any lawyer to advise a contest by suit. I deem this want of judicial determination, coupled with what follows, to be a great testimony for the affirmative of the question.

In the meantime lawyers have been consulted, no doubt very frequently, and written opinions are in the possession of many. I have been able to obtain a sight only of two. I have seen an Opinion of Mr. Kenyon, in 1784, where he declares, in few words and without hesitation or qualification, that American citizens may hold lands as British-born subjects. I have seen an opinion of the Attorney General Macdonald, in February, 1789, that engaging American seamen for foreign service should be prosecuted as the offence of enticing British seamen into a foreign service: the prosecution was commenced, the indictment found, but the Attorney General entered a *nolle prosequi* upon the party paying the costs.

Among the opinions of lawyers, I must mention what I received from Mr. ———, to whom I sent a statement of the case, with the view of learning whether any alteration had taken place in the opinions of lawyers of late days: I knew I should have from him the current opinion of Westminster Hall; he at once wrote with pencil on the back of the paper that such persons are British subjects; he seemed to answer it as if it was as known and as established as that the eldest son is the heir in feesimple.

I made inquiry at the Custom House, where, I was told, I might possibly find notes of some decisions at *nisi prius* in the Exchequer, which conveyed the Chief Baron's opinion, that a domiciliation in America took away the British character from a seaman employed in navigating a British ship. The solicitor said he knew of no such cases nor of such opinion ; on the contrary, he said, it was the usage of the Custom House to consider the *ante nati* in America as British-born subjects, and they were registered as owners of British ships : he informed me also of the above prosecution for enticing British seamen, and he gave me copies of the papers.

These authorities from the opinions of lawyers, and the practice of a public office, cannot be closed better than by an authority superior to all of them ; I mean (what has been already mentioned) the 9th Article of the treaty of commerce, and ss. 24 & 25 of statute 37 Geo. 3, c. 97, where there is a solemn declaration by the King and the Parliament, that American citizens did then hold lands, which they could not lawfully do unless they were deemed British natural-born subjects.

After such authorities, there does not seem to me any need to add a word more.

December 9, 1808.

Since writing the above I have been told that the subject of *ante nati* is no part of the present question, and what the objectors mean to urge is as follows: First, that the Americans, at the time of making statute 22 Geo. 3, c. 46, were in a state of legitimate war, bearing the character of foreign enemies, and not that of rebels. This is implied in the passing of such an Act, and in the wording of it. "Peace" and "truce" was not the language to hold to rebels, nor did the King need the authority of an Act of Parliament to proceed with traitors: the Act has no object if the Americans are not admitted to be foreigners in this transaction. Secondly, that after the peace made, it still remained for Americans, if they chose, to adhere to the British character; and it is not meant to deny that, *primâ facie*, the Americans are to be deemed British subjects. But those who domiciliated themselves in the United States, showed thereby a determination to become American citizens; and after such choice, they cease to be British subjects, and cannot resume that character.

If I have not stated the above points quite correctly, nor with all the advantage that belongs to them, I hope I shall be pardoned by those who made them, and who rely upon them: they were communicated to me in a rapid conversation only, for nothing on

that side of the question has been put into writing. I have done
my best to retain what I heard, and to state it fairly and fully.

I am totally at a loss to comprehend at what period of the war,
or by what modification of carrying it on, either on one side or the
other, or by what events or circumstances, that which was once
rebellion ceased to be so, and the traitors became changed into
aliens waging legitimate foreign war. As to the words "peace" and
"truce," I do not understand why they are not as applicable to war
coupled with rebellion, as to war not coupled with it. For war is
still war, whatever may give rise to it; and I do not see why the
war of rebels is not legitimate, *quatenus* war, and therefore needing
every consideration that attends all wars. Surely, in the time of
Charles I., there were treaties and truces and peace too ; there was
a peace for a short time, I think, in 1645, and yet the Lord Chancellor Clarendon entitled the narrative of these transactions a
" History of the Rebellion ;" and no man has ever doubted, be he
law-man or layman, that the war levied against Charles I. was
treason and rebellion; although it was attended with success, and
could command names, and although many amongst us have long
agreed in applying to it the qualified appellation of Civil War.

As to the necessity of making such Act of Parliament, and
giving thereby power to the King to make peace and truce, because the Americans were become alien enemies, and ceased to be
traitors and rebels, it is very curious that a different reason for
making it was given by the makers of the Act; that reason is
recorded in the Parliamentary debates of the time ; and the reason
so given seems to me to supersede the necessity of inventing any
new one like the present.

The Bill was called " The Truce Bill," and was brought into the
House of Commons on February 28, 1782, by the Attorney General
Wallace. It does not appear that it became a subject of debate in
any of its stages; the nation and Parliament were bent upon
peace, and any measure tending to bring it about was too welcome
to be questioned or criticised.—See Debrett's Debates, vol. vi.
pp. 341, 363.

However, this Act, which came into existence without a struggle,
afterwards was made a subject of discussion. When it had been
carried into execution, and the provisional articles with America,

together with the other preliminary treaties, came to be considered in Parliament in February, 1783, this Act was brought in question; and there was expressed great difference of opinion as to its original design, the construction to be put on it, and the effect it produced. In the first debate it was objected to the provisional articles that the King has no right by his prerogative, nor by the Act of last session—viz., statute 22 Geo. 3, c. 46—to alienate territories not acquired by conquest during the war. The gentlemen of the law being called upon by this objector (1), Mr. Mansfield answered, that certainly, by the Act of last session, the King was authorized to alienate for ever the independence of America.— Debrett's Debates, vol. ix. p. 280.

On a subsequent day, the same gentleman (Debrett's Debates, vol. ix. p. 312) again raised a question upon this Act. It appeared to him that no such power was given to the King by the Act; that any power to alienate part of his dominions, or abdicate the sovereignty of them, should be conveyed in express words, and not left to implication and construction. This brought up Mr. Wallace, who was the framer and mover of the Bill, and who declared that such power was given by the Act: he said he knew of no power in the King to abdicate part of his sovereignty, or declare any number of his subjects free from obedience to the laws in being. As soon, therefore, as the resolution for peace had passed the House, he had, with a view to enable his Majesty to make peace, drawn the Bill; and as the subject-matter of it was extremely delicate, he had been exceedingly cautious in wording it as generally as possible. But the whole aim of it was to enable his Majesty to recognize the independence of America; and that it gave the King such a power was, he said, indisputable, because by the wording of it that power was vested in the King, any law, statute, matter, or thing to the contrary notwithstanding.

This explanation, by the mover of the Act, did not satisfy the objector, who had been the seconder of it, but who now declared he had never supposed such an interpretation could be put on the Bill; and if he had thought it could, he would not have seconded it. But it was defended by the Attorney General Kenyon, who said the Act clearly gave authority to the King to recognize the

(1) Sir W. Dolben.

302 CASES AND OPINIONS ON CONSTITUTIONAL LAW.

independence of the Americans; adding that it was obvious, the Americans standing in the predicament of persons declared to be rebels at the time of passing the Act, it was necessary to word it in the general and cautious manner in which it stood upon the Statute Book.

Though the Attorney General Kenyon thus supported the late Attorney General Wallace in the construction and effect of his Act, he at the same time denied the position that the prerogative of the Crown needed any such special Act of Parliament to empower it to declare the American independence. Mr. Lee joined in opinion upon that point with Mr. Wallace.—Debrett's Debates, pp. 314, 315.

A like difference of opinion was discovered among the Law Lords in the discussions of the provisional articles and the preliminary treaties. It was maintained by Lord Loughborough that the King had no authority, without Parliament, to cede any part of the dominions of the Crown in the possession of subjects under the allegiance and at the peace of the King; and this, his Lordship said, could be proved by the records of Parliament. This doctrine was treated by Lord Thurlow as unfounded, and he strongly maintained the contrary.—Debates, vol. ii. pp. 88, 89.

The difference between the two lords had arisen, not upon the independence of the United States, but upon the cession of the Floridas to Spain; and it was on that account, no doubt, Lord Loughborough stated his proposition with the words "under allegiance and at the peace of the King," which was a proper description of the Floridas; but the same could not be said so fully of the United States, which, though under the allegiance, could not be so well said to be at the peace of the King. Lord Thurlow, it is plain, did not admit that this difference in circumstances made any difference in the power of the prerogative. It must surely be confessed that this cession of the Floridas to Spain, at the very moment that the American independence was acknowledged, makes a great breach in the hypothesis of Mr. Wallace, Mr. Lee, and Lord Loughborough, who thought statute 22 Geo. 3, c. 46, absolutely necessary for enabling the King to alienate part of his dominions. Indeed, the precedents are all against such a restriction on the prerogative; for when has there been a peace that some West India island has not been ceded, not only such as has been taken during the war, but those of ancient possession? In truth, this is another distinction that has no solid foundation in law, but is a mere conceit. It is well known that the laws of navigation attach upon a possession in America or Africa immediately on a surrender; and the territory is, to all intents and purposes, as much the King's as any ancient colony or plantation. It is therefore wholly assumption to raise the above distinction, and to consider such a conquest as less a part of the dominions of the Crown, and less under the protection of Parliament than the more ancient possessions.

But taking the judgment of Parliament (which finally approved all these treaties) for the supreme authority on this question of law, we are obliged to conclude that the King had power to relinquish to the King of Spain his sovereignty over the two Floridas without the special authority of any Act of Parliament enabling him so to do. This is a decision, after argument, when the objection had been taken and reasoned upon, and both sides heard openly and fully. It cannot after that, as I think, be doubted that the same Parliament would have recognized the King's power to relinquish his sovereignty over the United States, although there had been no such Act as statute 22 Geo. 3, c. 46. The relinquishing of sovereignty to the King of Spain, whereby he parts with all royal authority over his subjects in the Floridas; and the relinquishing of sovereignty over the colonies of New Hampshire, &c., &c., to the United States, whereby he parts with all royal authority over his subjects in New Hampshire, &c., &c.— where is the difference, in a juridical view, between these two cases? If you analyse them, and bring them down to their first principle, you will find it amounts to the same thing in both cases: to this, and nothing more, namely, that he makes the Floridas, and makes New Hampshire, &c., equally foreign dominions. Every consequence that follows upon the relinquishment of sovereignty is ascribable to that, and to that only. The inhabitants of the Floridas and of New Hampshire, &c., &c., become British subjects living in a foreign land, and lose all British advantages, now that British ground is taken from under them, in like manner, and in none other, as if they had removed themselves to the foreign soil of Spanish or Portuguese America.

Indeed, no one has ever pretended that the inhabitants of the
Floridas, who were British subjects born, were made aliens by the
cession, though some do mistakenly suppose this deprivation to
happen to Americans of the United States who were put under the
same circumstances at the same time, by the same or by a similar
operation, certainly for the same purpose—that of peace.

I say that the .cession has the single effect of making the
Floridas and the united States of New Hampshire, &c., &c., foreign
countries, and that no alteration is made in the birthrights of
British-born subjects, because what is covenanted, granted, and
agreed in the treaty, relates wholly to the former, and there is not
a word that relates to the latter. The Floridas are ceded to the
King of Spain ; that contains in it nothing so particular as to
raise a question : the material consideration is the case of America.
The definitive treaty begins by the King acknowledging the united
States of New Hampshire, &c., &c., to be free, sovereign, and independent States; and he relinquishes all claims to the government,
propriety, and territorial rights of the same : the King here parts
with the States—that is, the political machinery formed for the
government of those colonies, the Governor, the Assembly, &c., &c.—
and declares them independent ; to make this independence quite
clear and unclogged, he relinquishes all territorial sovereignty.
The thing given up by the King is his own superintendence and
authority over the local authority of those places; of the individuals his subjects there residing, he says nothing; there is not a
word in the treaty affecting their birthright as British subjects.

There is certainly not a word expressed upon that point; but I
think the great mistake in this discussion, and that which misleads
those on the other side, is an implication which they think necessarily arises upon this transaction of granting independence to
America; and they allow themselves to be carried away by the
force of expressions, which, without any defined meaning, seem to
signify something, and are repeated without examination into their
import. It has been said that, by acknowledging the independence
of the United States, the King dissolved the allegiance of the
Americans, and they of course were made aliens; this is an inference drawn from the independence, but it is wholly a fiction of
imagination among politicians. There is no such principle in the

law of England; it never was heard of; can any book, case, or dictum be shown, that gives the most remote intimation of any such operation? In the cession of territory, the King has always forborne to declare anything expressly on the article of allegiance, and never before has anyone raised the construction, that allegiance was ever surrendered by the King, any further than the nature of the cession did, in point of exercise and enjoyment, circumscribe the scope of it. As the King has in no case of cession made an actual relinquishment of allegiance due to him, so has he in no case of such cession ventured to take away what was not his, but belonged to the individuals his subjects; who were to suffer enough in being compelled thenceforward to live in a foreign land, and who might very well be indulged with the consolation of retaining their birthright of British subjects—a right which might be brought into enjoyment and exercise, whenever they should again come to live upon British ground.

With all the instances of cessions which are examples to the contrary, I cannot understand how anyone should entertain the imagination of their effect in dissolving personal allegiance, accompanied too with such an inconsequent result, as that the British subject so released becomes thereby an alien.

To return to the objection which I was to consider, in regard to the design and effect of stat. 22 Geo. 3, c. 46: it appears, from what I have before detailed out of the Parliamentary Debates, that the statute was deemed necessary, in order to satisfy the scruples of some persons, who thought that the King had not at common law power to alienate any part of his dominions; further, that it was necessary the King should have power to suspend the operation of certain Acts of Parliament, which it was foreseen might stand in the way of making peace. It was afterwards contended that the statute had also the special effect of authorizing the King to grant independence to the colonies; because, as it empowered him to make peace or truce, any law, statute, matter, or thing to the contrary notwithstanding, it of course, say these objectors, empowered him to grant independence, or indeed anything that should be deemed necessary towards making such peace or truce; meaning by such independence, disfranchisement, and converting the Americans into aliens.

x

After such explicit discovery as was before made of the nature and design of the Act, how are we to acquiesce in the construction thus put upon it in the objection? What reason is there for saying that the Act has no meaning or object, unless the Americans were admitted to be aliens and foreigners, in a state of legitimate war, and not rebels?

The second of these renewed objections to the grand common law position on which I build this argument, is, to my understanding, as extraordinary and as anomalous as the preceding; but it is not so novel. I admit I have before heard the notion of Americans domiciliating themselves in the United States, and being, in consequence of such election, pronounced to be no longer British subjects, but aliens and American citizens only; yet it always seemed to me to be an arbitrary and groundless assumption, totally irreconcileable to principle or precedent.

As to the precedent, I must again recur to the instances of the Floridas, Tobago, and other places that have been ceded to foreign Powers. Was it ever objected to the British-born subjects inhabiting those countries, that having domiciliated themselves there, they were considered as aliens in the British dominions? Where should men be domiciliated but where their home is? And did it ever enter into the mind of the King or his ministers, that, upon a cession of territory, the British-born subjects inhabiting there should migrate, at all hazard to their worldly affairs and the prosperity of their families? There are no such migrations, no such expectations of them; nor have they ever been deemed necessary for keeping alive the birthright of a British subject. Why then should it be necessary, for the first time, in the case of the inhabitants of the United States?

I think it erroneous in principle, because it makes that depend on the option and capriciousness of the person himself, which has ever been deemed an indelible character, one he is not at liberty to put off—that of a British subject. All the maxims that we have heard about birthright and natural allegiance are contrary to such a supposition, of a person choosing whether he will cease to be a British subject and begin to be an American citizen; but all those maxims are consistent with the construction which I contend for—namely, that such persons owe a local allegiance while in America;

and when they come here, their rights of British subjects revive, and their natural allegiance attaches: and it cannot be denied that in such a state of things there is a reciprocity of duty and protection between the Sovereign and the subject, which is quite commensurate with their respective situations.

This imagination of optional allegiance, and extinguishment of natural rights, is wholly inconsistent with the position resolved in *Calvin's Case*, which is laid down generally, without making the consequence of continuing the rights of birth to depend on any condition or observance whatsoever. Such absolute, entire, and indelible quality is what the common law ascribes to those rights of subjects that come to us by birth, and by birth only.

Such are the observations to which these two new objections seem to be open. These objections do not appear to me to have more force in them than the former; and I do not see anything in either of them to invalidate the resolution in *Calvin's Case*, ann the application of it, without any qualification or deduction, to citizens of the United States.

December 15, 1808.

In a conversation with a civilian upon this subject, I found he had made up his mind to the negative of the question; but it was upon principles wholly independent of the common law. He considered British-born subjects, residing in an island or country ceded by his Majesty, to become thereby aliens; he could not therefore, he said, doubt about the state of Americans, especially after the Act of Parliament which has been so often cited. He called for some case lately decided in the courts of Westminster, to contradict what he alleged of ceded countries; I had none to adduce, and could only refer to the common law principle, which had never been denied.

I perceive that the civilian went upon the law of his court, where they hold that persons take their character from the country where they reside; so, the ceded country becoming foreign, they deem the inhabitants foreign too. Such is the rule in prize causes, where hostility is to be regarded, which must ever be a national, not a personal consideration; accordingly, an enemy's country makes all the inhabitants enemies. So, indeed, at common law, the country

x 2

gives the character to the persons who inhabit it, in matters that
are governed by the character of the country. The British-born
subjects of a ceded colony lose their character of British colonists,
because their country has become foreign; they are restrained by
the Navigation Laws that before protected them; they cannot trade
as British colonists. They are foreigners, therefore, in everything
that relates to the country they live in, as the civilian contends;
but the common lawyer will add, they are in their own personal
rights still British subjects, as they were born; and they will be
entitled to claim the privileges of such whenever they remove from
the foreign country which obstructs the application and exercise of
them, and come to a place—that is, some place in the King's dominions—where alone the privileges of a British subject have their
exercise and application.

In truth, the character of a British-born subject is not merely
national and local, but personal and permanent. It is born with
him, and remains with him during life, never to be divested—un-
changeable, indelible. It is not so with what is called a British
subject; that does, indeed, depend upon locality and that is the
character which the civilian contemplates. I believe much of the
misapprehension upon this occasion has arisen from not preserving
the distinction between British subjects and natural-born British
subjects; they are not the same, though, I believe, they are reasoned
upon as if they were.

"British subject" and "alien" are not terms contradictory, because
the two characters may concur in the same person: the inhabitants
of the Dutch colonies, now in our possession, are British subjects;
they have taken the oath of allegiance, and they have the advantages of British colonists; but they are aliens, because they were
born out of the King's allegiance. The inhabitants of the Floridas,
born while those were British colonies, are, however, not now British
subjects, because they inhabit a foreign country; nor are they
aliens, because they were not born out of the King's allegiance;
but they are natural-born British subjects, because they were born
within the King's allegiance: so that it may be predicated of the
same person, that he is a "British subject," and an "alien;" that
he is "a natural-born British subject," and not a "British subject"
—accordingly as you speak of the local and national character, or

of the personal character. "British subject" is a term of common parlance, that has not properly a legal defined meaning: it serves sufficiently in ordinary discourse for "natural-born subject," but it can be properly applied only for intimating the local and national character. The true legal description is that of natural-born subject: this is the opposite to alien; and these are the terms that describe the personal character, which is the only one sought in the present inquiry, and the only one that is a subject of discussion in the books of the common law.

Through the whole of the argument, I have been insisting on this personal character of British-born Americans; but those who object to my conclusion in favour of them, from the common law principle (which principle, however, they do not pretend to dispute), keep their eye principally on the local and national character of the present Americans. Their two great topics are quite of that sort—namely, the stat. 22 Geo. 3, c. 46, for making peace or truce with the colonies and plantations; and the definitive treaty which acknowledges the independence of the United States, and relinquishes sovereignty, propriety, and territorial dominion. Surely all these are national and local ideas, riveted to the very soil, and limited by metes and bounds. Nothing is, by either instrument, said or done as to the personal character of the inhabitants; that was left, as the personal character of the inhabitants of the Floridas, to the sentence and disposition of the law, when any of the individuals residing there chose to remove himself into a situation where his personal character could be brought into question, and considered distinctly from local and national character, which the King of Great Britain had been pleased to superinduce upon him by ceding the country where he was born; that is, when any such individual should choose to come into the King's dominions, where alone his personal rights can have their application and exercise.

The only consideration for us, in this country, seems to be such personal character, whether it is the case of Florida, or a native of the United States, born within the King's allegiance.

December 16, 1808.

A passage has been cited by the objectors from Mr. Woodeson's

lectures; and as this is the only book authority they have been able
to adduce, it must not be let pass without observation, especially
as it has acquired a sort of reflected consequence, by being inserted
in Sir Henry Gwillim's edition of Bacon's Abridgment, title
"Alien." The passage is this: "But when by treaty, especially if
ratified by Act of Parliament, our Sovereign cedes any island or
region to another State, the inhabitants of such ceded territory,
though born under the allegiance of our King, or being under his
protection, while it appertained to his crown and authority, become,
I apprehend, effectually aliens, or liable to the disabilities of alienage,
in respect of their future concerns with this country. And similar to
this I take to be the condition of the revolted Americans, since the
recognition of their independent commonwealths." (Vol. i. p. 382.)

To those who insist on this as an authority for saying that such
persons become aliens and cease to be natural-born subjects, it might
be enough to reply, that a proposition laid down with an alternative,
as this is, has not in it sufficient precision to be authority for any
thing: "Effectually aliens, or liable to the disabilities of alienage,"
is a circumlocution that does not suit with the plainness required
in a juridical proposition. And yet, I think, the author has expressed
himself not unsuitably with another sense of the word alien, accompanied, as it here is, with an exposition. It seems to me that
"or" is not intended here to be a conjunction merely, but it bears
a sense that is not uncommon; it introduces a member of a sentence that is meant to be explanatory of the foregoing, and is the
same as "or in other words," "or to speak more plainly," "or to
speak more properly." In this sense of "or," he explains the
meaning of "effectually aliens," by showing they are liable to the
disabilities of alienage in respect to their "future concerns with this
country." Their "future concerns with this country" must be the
trade they carry on with this country—something which they
transact from a distant place, something that affects the whole
community, something that arises out of their locality and national
character. He is speaking of the local and national character
which we discussed before (in p. 694), and which was superinduced
on the inhabitants of these ceded countries, in respect of which
the inhabitants become a species of aliens, or (as the author ex-
presses it in an undefined epithet) "effectually aliens," or, I sup-

pose, " in effect aliens "—that is, in the case of trading with this country.

I take this to have been what the author's mind was then contemplating, the local and national character of such ceded colonists ; and by no means their personal character, that of natural-born subjects, which he knew, as well as all lawyers, can neither be surrendered nor taken away.

Mr. Woodeson has certainly not been sufficiently technical in expressing himself upon this occasion. It may be fit enough to oppose what he has said by an expression in the treaty of peace, which, though in like manner not technical, has evidently a meaning that cannot be mistaken, and that makes against his conclusion. In the 5th Article, it is agreed that Congress shall recommend to the legislatures of the respective States, to provide for restitution of confiscated estates which belong to real British subjects. Now, if there are " real British subjects," it is implied there are British subjects who are not real, that is, less so than the others. No one can doubt that the one expression means British subjects not comprehended within the new States, erected and recognized by the King's acknowledgment in the treaty ; the other must mean those inhabiting the United States. It is plainly indicated therefore, by this phrase, that both contracting parties in the treaty admitted that the inhabitants of the United States did remain, in some sort, British subjects ; and the mode in which they so continued can only be that which I have been contending for.

December 17, 1808.

According to the foregoing reasoning, I think the Law Officers, if consulted, would give an opinion somewhat to the following effect :—

Supposed Opinion of the Law Officers.

" In obedience to your Lordship's commands, we have considered the question, whether inhabitants of the United States, born there before the Independence, are, on coming to this kingdom, to be considered as natural-born subjects ; and we are of opinion, that such a person, coming to this kingdom, cannot be denied the character and privilege of a natural-born subject.

" In forming this opinion, we have given due consideration to all

the topics that have been suggested to us from different quarters
on both sides of the question, as well as to the principles of the
common law, which are to be found in books of known authority
amongst lawyers.

"Among the suggestions that have been made to us are statute
22 Geo. 3, c. 46, and the definitive treaty of peace with the United
States; and we find ourselves obliged to declare that nothing in
those two instruments appears to us to make any alteration in the
case of Americans when compared with others of his Majesty's subjects who reside in a ceded country.   In like manner as the inhabitants, natural-born subjects of his Majesty, in the two Floridas,
ceded to the King of Spain (at the same time that the independence
of the United States was acknowledged), are still deemed to retain
their privilege and character of natural-born subjects, so we think
these persons, being similarly circumstanced when they come into
this kingdom, cannot be denied to retain their original privileges
and character.

"Our reasons for thinking that the statute and treaty make no
difference or peculiarity in the case of the United States are these:
the statute, upon the face of it, appears to have been made for two
purposes: first, to enable the King to make peace or truce with
the colonies or plantations in question; secondly, to enable the
King to suspend the operation of certain Acts of Parliament that
might stand in the way of peace. The need of the second provision
is obvious—the need of the first is not so plain; but we are told,
in a debate in the House of Commons, by the Attorney General,
Wallace, who drew the bill and moved it, that it was intended to
give the King a power of alienating those colonies—a power
which he and some others considered the King as not possessing by
the common law. Without saying anything at present on the
justness of such opinion, we allege it as the best testimony to the
design of the Act. This design is perfectly consistent with the
conception and wording, and it does not appear to us necessary or
proper to suppose any other meaning in this Act. We conclude,
therefore, that there was no particular design, by this legislative
measure, to make any alteration in the character of the Americans
beyond that which necessarily must and always has followed upon
the cession of any of his Majesty's colonies.

"After these observations on the act for enabling the King to make peace, we come to the definitive treaty itself; and we find ourselves compelled to declare, that as we perceive no design in the Act to enable the King to alter the personal character of the Americans, so in the treaty we discover no declaration or provision that can be construed expressly, or impliedly, to alter their original character of natural-born subjects, and to make them aliens.

"In the first article of the treaty the King acknowledges the United States of New Hampshire, &c., &c., to be free, sovereign, and independent States; and he relinquishes all claim to government, propriety, and territorial rights of the same. It is upon this provision, and these words, that the separation and independence of those colonies are grounded. The effect of this provision appears to us to be confined wholly to the soil and territory, which is thereby made foreign, and ceases to be a part of the King's dominions. We cannot discover anything that at all affects the personal character of the natural-born subjects inhabiting such foreign territory.

"Indeed, we are much surprised that any such peculiar effect should be ascribed to this cession of territory to the United States (for so it is, in truth), when at the same peace the adjoining colonies, the Floridas, were ceded to the King of Spain; and no such consequences of the cession are supposed by anybody to affect the natural-born subjects residing there. We may here, too, remark that the cession of the Floridas was made, without any such enabling statute, by the King's common law prerogative, which demonstrates that in the opinion of the majority of Parliament, who approved the treaty, the Act of the Attorney General Wallace owed its origin, not to an absolute necessity in law, but to an abundant caution, or some scruple in politics, which deserves no regard in a judicial consideration of the subject. We are not able to discover any distinction in the two cases of the Floridas and of the United States. In both instances the soil was made foreign, and the inhabitants had superinduced upon them a new local and national character; that is, they became locally the inhabitants and subjects of a foreign nation, and they lost advantages of trade and benefits of various sorts which natural-born subjects must lose when they inhabit and make themselves subjects of a foreign land.

But, under the control of this new local and national character, their personal character of natural-born subjects still remains; and we see nothing in law to prevent it reviving and enjoying all its privileges when the person comes into the King's dominions, where alone the rights of a British-born subject have their full application and exercise.

"Having declared this our opinion that nothing is, *de facto*, done by the Act, or the treaty, to take away the personal character of natural-born subjects residing in the United States, it may seem unnecessary, though we think it not unsuitable, to add, that we know of no instance where the Crown has presumed to exercise the power of taking away the personal rights of a natural-born subject, neither have we met with any principle in the law of England that warrants such a supposition; nor can we conceive any proceeding by which such a divestment or extinguishment of natural rights can be enforced. As the common law recognizes no such principle as that of disfranchising a natural-born subject, the character has been deemed indelible; and the Parliament has never interposed, on the occasions of cession of territory, to take from the British inhabitants of such countries that which the common law has permitted them to retain.

"Such having been the construction of law in cases of cession, which have been made sometimes, no doubt, against the wishes of the inhabitants, and always without asking their consent, a principle of law has grown up and established itself, which it seems too late now to question in the case of the United States. We have given full consideration to the difference of circumstances which led to that cession, the rebellion and war that preceded it, and were the cause of it, and the claim of the colonists to be independent; but we think this difference of circumstances makes no alteration in the legal result arising from the new situation of the parties. Such matters are, as we think, wholly political; and as they are not of a nature to be subjected to any juridical examen, we do not see how they can be brought into the account when we are applying the legal principle before mentioned.

"Conformably, therefore, with the principle and practice that have long been acknowledged, and declaring that there appears no reason in law for not applying the same principle to the inhabitants of the United States, we repeat the opinion we before expressed, that the persons described in the question ought to be considered, in this kingdom, as natural-born subjects."

Such, I think, would be, or should be, the opinion of the Law Officers on the present question.

December 20, 1808.

Reply to observations on the subject of the foregoing argument:—

January 17, 1809.

First.—I cannot admit there is any straining to bring the Americans within *Calvin's Case*; and I maintain, the circumstances that distinguish them from the precise point in that case are fairly and fully considered by me.

It may not be necessary, in arguing with you, to adduce such authority as *Calvin's Case*, because you do not dispute it. But the persons I had to deal with were ignorant of the principles of that case, and I needed such an authority to set them right. I know no book case where the principles of allegiance and native rights are laid down and explained, except in that only instance; the principle and nature of allegiance and of native rights is the first step in the present argument, and the subsequent parts of it would have been without foundation if I had not taken that case for a basis.

The necessity for going so far back in the argument was shown to me by the civilian, who laid down the law, that the King's subjects of a ceded country become thereby aliens; when he called for some decided case to show the contrary, I had no decided case (you know there is none), but the resolutions and arguments of *Calvin's Case*. He felt this to be an important authority; and the piece of law, which you admit, I doubt whether you can ground upon any other authority in the books. The circumstances in *Calvin's Case* are different from those of the Americans; but the principle is the same (I mean the principle of the resolution that I quote); whether that difference in circumstances makes any difference in the application of the principle is the very question in hand.

Secondly.—You here admit that natural born subjects, continuing

316 CASES AND OPINIONS ON CONSTITUTIONAL LAW.

their residence in a ceded country, do not thereby become aliens; you go so far as to think that, if they joined in war with their new Sovereign against this kingdom, it would be treason in them. I will not say anything upon this point, except to remind you that my argument is wholly confined to an American coming to this country and residing here.

The other point in this part of your answer makes the main of your third article.

Thirdly.—Your third topic is, the difference between ceding a country to a foreign Power, and the constituting of a sovereignty from among British subjects, and ceding the country to such new-made sovereignty. You call it making a treaty with the subjects themselves, that they should hold the country as an independent State; " he ceded his sovereignty to them." You rely upon this difference in circumstances, which you make between ceding to a foreign Sovereign, and ceding to British subjects, as you term it; and you mention one certain result from this difference, that, in the former case, the levying of war by the natural subjects would be treason; in the latter case, it would not. I protest, I do not discern this distinction; in both cases, the subject is put into such peculiar situation by the act of the new Sovereign, and being so circumstanced, why should it be treason in an inhabitant of Florida, more than in an American, to obey the militia law of his new Sovereign, and bear arms against us, like the rest of his fellow-subjects ?

Some persons would argue differently from you on this point; those who distinguish the British subjects of the Floridas, because they were given up against their will, or without their consent, from the Americans, because these claimed to be independent, would not infer upon the former, who were wholly passive, the crime of treason, and acquit the latter, who sought and made choice of the peculiar situation of double allegiance in which they have placed themselves.

However, this point, as I before said, does not bear upon our present question, which relates to the American while he is in the King's dominions.

But you rely upon the difference of "the treating with the Americans, and giving up to British subjects the sovereignty of the country." I think there is in this an assumption and a reliance upon words which have no support from the real transaction. To come up to the representation you make about "them," and " they," there ought to be a covenant and grant from the King, to Mr. A., Mr. B., Mr. C.; and the said Mr. A., Mr. B., and Mr. C., ought to be plainly estopped and barred by what they took under such covenant and grant from the Crown. When we had thus ascertained who are legal parties to the transaction, and legally bound by it, we might then inspect the charter or instrument, and search whether the King, by the terms of it, relinquished his claims of allegiance wholly or in part; and whether the British subjects therein named had expressly relinquished, or were expressly deprived of their native rights, or whether such deprivation arose out of it by necessary construction.

I think such should have been the form of the transaction, in order to come up to your supposition; but when we examine it, we find it to be quite another sort of proceeding. As to Mr. A., Mr. B., and Mr. C., it is a matter *inter alios acta;* they are not parties not named, not alluded to; it does not appear to have been transacted by them. Let us consider the treaty of peace which must be the instrument, if any, that produces the supposed effect.

The treaty declares New Hampshire, &c., &c. to be free and independent States, and the King relinquishes the government of them. When this grant and covenant is brought to plain facts, it amounts to this, that the King will no longer send governors to those States, nor expect the legislative and executive authority to be subordinate to him. The King gives this to the States; but how can this be construed to take anything away from Mr. A., Mr. B., and Mr. C.? The King gives away the allegiance which the States owed him; it was his to give; but how should such free gift be construed to take away from Mr. A., and other individuals, the private rights to which they were born? Two questions arise upon this: first, are the native rights of individuals hereby, *de facto,* pretended to be taken away? Secondly, could the King *de jure* take away such rights?

To talk of " treating with them," and " they holding the country independently of the King," is speaking in a popular manner, and without sufficient regard to juridical circumstances. Any inference

818 CASES AND OPINIONS ON CONSTITUTIONAL LAW.

of that sort will not be allowed by law to deprive a man, living peaceably in his house in New Hampshire, of his British rights, that he was born to, and that are personal to him (namely, which he can carry about with him, and which do not depend on locality), merely because some daring men have forced the King to allow the States of New Hampshire to govern him, without enjoying any longer the right of appeal to the King. I say the law will not allow this, because personal rights of British subjects cannot be taken away from multitudes in a lump; they must be discussed in every individual case, and there must be a several judgment and execution against every person. Even the act of the King in this instance, though a national act, and relating to millions, is but a personal act; when he acknowledges them Free States, and re- linquishes the government of them, he acts only for himself, his heirs, and successors; and accordingly thereto, and agreeably with the true principles of the law, he alone is bound, and the sovereignty of those States ceases to be his. But where is the personal act of any American relinquishing his own rights? or if there was any such proceeding, in fact, show me the authority in law that recog- nizes any such principle, as that a natural-born British subject can divest himself of his native character; there is no such authority; and there is the known maxim of law against it, *nemo potest exuere patriam*.

I cannot, therefore, bring myself to distinguish the treaty with America from the ordinary case of cession to a foreign Sovereign: in both cases, it is a transaction between the two Sovereigns in which the inhabitants bear no part; and it seems to me a de- parture from principle to say that the American is thereby rendered an alien, while the inhabitant of Florida is allowed to be still a British-born subject.

Fourthly.—I have raised no question of the King's authority to make the American treaty. I agree with those who think he might have made it without the Act of Parliament; and I agree also with those who thought the treaty fell within the authority of the Act. I am satisfied with the treaty, whether with or without the Act; but I contend, that neither the Act nor the treaty had in contemplation to make the Americans aliens; and that neither one nor other of those instruments has, in point of law, the power of producing such an effect. I raise no question upon what passed in Parliament; if the Parliament approved the treaty, they left us to draw the inferences and make the construction that shall appear to belong to it.

Fifthly, and lastly.—You admit there are difficulties in deciding that "the treaty exempted the Americans from their allegiance, and excluded them from their rights as British subjects." In my opinion, these difficulties are made and increased by introducing phrases and raising constructions upon them, without looking to the real proceeding and adhering faithfully to the letter of it. You talk here of exempting the Americans from their allegiance. Why make a question of allegiance when the King does not claim it? And what consequences can be built on the affirmative or negative of this question? What is a subject's allegiance worth to the King, if he resides in America, although he is, *bonâ fide*, a native of London? It is worth nothing. And if he refuses to come home, what does the law say, and what did the Parliament do in a like case in statute 14 & 15 Henry 8, c. 4? Allegiance has nothing to do with the treaty. Allegiance is personal; the treaty is national and territorial. The treaty regulates land, its metes, and its bounds; and the government of it the treaty leaves and transfers to others, the States of the country; the persons and their allegiance remain unaffected. Allegiance is general or special, local or personal; these may, and do often, in fact, consist together in the same person; why not, then, in the instance of Americans?

It is for want of attending to this modification to which allegiance is subject, that some persons started the expedient which you here mention, and which seems to me to contain much more difficulty in it than the one it was meant to cure. You agree with those who think that such Americans, as " after a reasonable time allowed for election, subsequent to the ratification of the treaty, settled themselves in America, and chose their domicile there, became exempted from their allegiance, and excluded from their rights as British subjects."

This expedient of a "reasonable time," and "a domicile," for making a distinction between one American and another, seems to me to be a greater departure from principle than any of the other anomalies that I have observed in their argument. There are,

I admit, legal considerations that depend upon a man's local character, which may be changed by change of residence, and therefore must be ascribed to his own act and choice. But those are in cases of such a character as is capable of being acquired, and, as it is acquired, so it may be lost, by his own act; such is a man's local and national character. But the character of natural subject, which a man is born to, and to which is applied the maxim, *nemo potest exuere patriam;* to lay it down as a position of law, that it is in a man's own choice to decide whether he will put off this character or retain it, and that his continuing his native character depends upon altering his domicile—this is, surely, one of the most singular novelties that ever was attempted in the face of an acknowledged principle to the contrary. For which principle I must again refer to *Calvin's Case,* the whole doctrine and result of which is, that the personal rights of a subject, to which he was born, remain through life, and through all circumstances, unchanged and indelible; and that allegiance and native rights arise wholly from birth, and do not depend on actual local sovereignty for their continuance.

Such a device as this is not interpreting the law, but making it. A temporizing scheme, reduced to an Act of Parliament, for settling this national question, might very well be so modelled; it would be a half-measure that probably would be thought reasonable enough; but this very character of it is sufficient to discredit it as a piece of juridical reasoning: it is void of all steadiness of principle; it has not even in it the consistency of the former arguments and conclusions, that "relinquishing the sovereignty," that "acknowledging the States to be free," &c., &c., implied that there was an end of allegiance and of British rights. The device was, I believe, contrived by those who found they could not maintain the above bold conclusions in opposition to acknowledged principles of law; and, desirous of doing something, they were content to lower their notions to a medium between the two, which would sound, as they thought, reasonable in the effect of it, however unsupported it might be in principle.

So much for this half-measure of "reasonable time," and "domicile," which I have had occasion before to reprobate. I hope the difficulties, in point of law, with which this arbitrary notion is pregnant, will be avoided: if so, the other difficulties in point of fact, which you mention, will be escaped—namely, the necessity of inquiring in every particular claimant's case, when and how he was domiciliated in America, or in this kingdom.

Upon the whole I see nothing to distinguish, in a legal view, the condition of Americans from that of other British subjects residing in a ceded country; nothing done by the King, nothing by Parliament, nothing by themselves: and it seems to me, the person in question coming to this country is still entitled to the privileges of a natural-born subject.

January 17, 1809.

An authority is quoted for the notion of "optional domicile." It is said that Chief Baron Eyre has been heard, over and over, to lay it down, that Americans domiciled in the United States could not be deemed British subjects, so as to navigate a British ship. There may be good reason for such an opinion. The Chief Baron might have considered that, under the Order of Council for carrying on the American trade (it was before statute 37 Geo. 3, c. 97), American ships were to be navigated by subjects of the United States. He might consider domiciliation as the best evidence of being an American subject. It might appear to him reasonable, that such persons being allowed to navigate American ships, as American subjects, they should not be recognized occasionally as British subjects when navigating a British ship. Such a discrimination might appear to him to promote the principle of our navigation system, as no ships are allowed to be British-built, unless built in the King's dominions; it might seem to him an appropriate construction, to exclude from the character of British mariners all those who chose to domiciliate themselves in America, then become a foreign country.

Be it so; but can they report to us that the Chief Baron ever laid it down that persons who so made themselves Americans, by residing in the United States, might not afterwards be deemed British subjects and British mariners, by changing their domicile to some part of the King's dominions? Is there anything in the principle of domiciliation, which will enable them to say that the first choice is final, and the character thereby acquired cannot be

Y

put off? Is there not as much efficacy in a second, a third, or any other subsequent choice of domicile? And do not such persons become, *toties quoties*, successively British or American? And if not, why not?

If their notion is grounded on any principle, they should be able to explain to us why the first choice of domicile precludes the advantage to be derived from any subsequent choice.

Such are the queries that may be put on this piece of exchequer law, confined only to the very peculiar case of navigation and of mariners. There still remains the principal query, why should such a construction of the Navigation Act, supported as it is there by the special circumstances of the case, be adopted, and made to govern in the general question of natural-born subject, where there is nothing similar to make the application of it fit or colourable? Certainly domiciliation, or residence, temporary or permanent, never made a part of the consideration whether a person is a natural-born subject; but simply this was the question, whether he was born within the King's allegiance? However, if domiciliation weighs anything, the claimant in this case is resident here, and professes to make this kingdom his future residence. Perhaps the Chief Baron, upon a habeas corpus, would, in the case of this claimant, have deemed his present residence, and his determination declared to reside here in future, to be a sufficient choice of domicile within the principle of his exchequer decision; perhaps he might consider this case as standing on different grounds from the exchequer case, and to be decided on general principles, without regard to domiciliation.

We are so uninformed as to the extent of what the Chief Baron is supposed to have ruled at *nisi prius*, that it seems to afford no safe ground of reasoning.

January 21, 1809.

I have been desired, by a great lawyer, to look at the statute *De Prærogativa Regis*, c. 12, *de terris Normannorum*. I suppose he meant this should prove to me that on King John losing Normandy, the Normans became thereby aliens, and therefore the lands holden by them in England escheated to the King; but the statute does not import this, nor is it so understood by Staunforde.

On the contrary, Staunforde understands that the Normans still continued English subjects, and were *ad fidem utriusque regis*. The statute expressly speaks of those who were *non ad fidem regis Angliæ*, which must be such as were born after the severance of the two countries; and the design of the statute is to fix that the escheats, in the case of such *post-nati*, accrued to the King and not to the lord; and that the King was to grant them to be holden of the lord, by the same services as before.

This chapter, therefore, of the statute *De Prærogativa Regis* is an express authority that the severance of Normandy from the English Crown did not make the inhabitants there aliens, though their children, born after the severance, were aliens.

This authority becomes also an answer to another point maintained by the same great lawyer; he goes beyond the rest that I have had to contend with, except the civilian, and he holds, with the civilian, that the inhabitants of a ceded colony become thereby aliens. Yet in this I cannot but allow there is consistency, for the principle appears to me to be the same: those who call the Americans aliens ought to consider the inhabitants of Florida, ceded at the same time, in the same light; and those who consider the inhabitants of Florida as not deprived of their personal rights of Englishmen, ought to admit the American claim to continue natural-born subjects.

March 22, 1809.

Perhaps the objectors have never considered the persons to whom naturalization and denization are granted. In both cases, in the Act of Parliament and in the patent, the party is alleged to be born out of the King's allegiance, and in applying for either, he must allege the same in his petition; but an American cannot do this with truth. What then is to be the conclusion on the peculiar circumstances and situation of this supposed alien? Is he to be deemed an alien beyond all other aliens, that is, irredeemably such? Assuredly he is not susceptible of denization or naturalization in the ordinary course, because he cannot bring himself within the description which alone makes him the object of such favour; or may we conclude that, not having the defect which is to be supplied by such grant, he is already in possession of the character

Y 2

to be conferred by it; in other words, he is not an alien, but a
natural-born subject?

The latter appears to me the just conclusion, and I shall accordingly say with confidence, that there is the authority of the Lord
Chancellor in cases of denization, and of the two Houses of Parliament in cases of naturalization, for the proposition that birth
out of the King's allegiance is the only circumstance which constitutes an alien. We may be sure such forms would not have
been settled and constantly acted upon if they were not known
to be required by the general law of the land. Indeed, it is
nothing more than the definition of alien laid down in all the
books, whether elementary or practical; the following examples
are sufficient :—

" Natural-born subjects are such as are born within the dominion
of the Crown of England—that is, within the ligeance, or, as it is
generally called, the allegiance of the King; and aliens, such as
are born out of it."—Blackstone, book i. ch. 10.

" An alien is one who is born out of the ligeance of the King."—
Comyn's Digest, article " Alien."

" An alien is one born in a strange country."—Bacon's Abridgment, article " Alien."

And thus I conclude this discussion, as I began it; relying upon
established and known positions of law for maintaining juridical
truth against hypothesis and the speculations of political reasoning.

March 24, 1809.

(6.) JOINT OPINION *of the Attorney and Solicitor General,*
SIR JOHN S. COPLEY *and* SIR CHARLES WETHERELL, *on the
Status of a Citizen of the United States born before the Peace of*
1783, *and resident in Canada ; and also on the Status of his
Son, born in the United States after that date.*

Serjeants' Inn, November 13, 1824.

MY LORD,—We have had the honour to receive your Lordship's
letter, transmitting to us several documents relative to the case of

Mr. Barnabas Bidwell, a citizen of the United States, who had been returned as a member of the House of Assembly of the province of Upper Canada. And your Lordship was pleased to desire that we would take the same into our consideration, and report to your Lordship our opinion whether Mr. Bidwell has any right to sit as a representative in the Assembly of Upper Canada under the 31 Geo. 3, c. 31, or under any other Act of Parliament referred to in the accompanying case; and in the event of our considering that Mr. Bidwell has no claim to a seat in the Legislative Assembly, your Lordship was also pleased to desire that we would inform your Lordship whether we consider Mr. Bidwell's son, who was born in the United States of America since the Peace of 1783, as also ineligible.

In compliance with your Lordship's request, we beg leave to report that we are of opinion that Mr. Bidwell has no right to sit as a representative in the Assembly of Upper Canada under the 31 Geo. 3, c. 31, or under any other Act; and we are further of opinion that Mr. Bidwell's son is also ineligible.

We have considered the general question to be of very great importance, and as it has been for some time depending in the King's Bench, we were desirous of waiting the decision of that Court before we gave our opinion on it. The judgment has been lately pronounced, and after very elaborate argument it has been decided that a person in the situation of Mr. Bidwell is not a natural-born subject of his Majesty, but an alien; and that the son of such a person, born in the United States after the treaty of 1783, is also an alien (1).

This question, therefore, which has been so long and so frequently agitated, may at length be considered as finally determined.

The Right Hon. Earl Bathurst,   J. S. COPLEY.
  &c. &c. &c.   CHAS. WETHERELL.

(1) The case here referred to is *Doe* d. *Thomas* v. *Acklam*, 2 B. & C. 779. See also *Doe* d. *Auchmuty* v. *Mulcaster*, 5 B. & C. 771.

(7.) JOINT OPINION *of the King's Advocate,* SIR CHRISTOPHER
ROBINSON, *and the Attorney and Solicitor General,* SIR JOHN
S. COPLEY *and* SIR CHARLES WETHERELL, *as to the Status of
Slaves escaping to a British Settlement, and as to whether they
can be lawfully sent back to the Foreign Country from which they
have escaped.* 1826.

We are of opinion that a person held in slavery in a foreign
country, and effecting his escape to a British settlement, cannot,
under the statute 5 Geo. 4, c. 113, be lawfully sent back to the
foreign country whence he so escaped.   We see no reason to
change the opinion we have already given upon this point.   We
think the Act consolidating the laws respecting the Slave Trade has
not altered the state of the question.   The removal of slaves under
the circumstances above described comes within the general prohibitory words of the Act, and is not included in any of the exceptions.   We think the removal would be illegal whether the persons
were lawfully or unlawfully in slavery in the colony from which
they had escaped.   In answer to the remaining question, we are
of opinion that persons escaping to a British settlement from a
foreign country where they were lawfully held in slavery, and, of
course, not born under the King's allegiance, are aliens.   The rest
of this question, viz., whether they may be *dealt* with as aliens, is
so *general* that we cannot venture to answer it in its present form.
If your Lordship will be so kind as to state in what manner it is
proposed to deal with them, and under what law, we will return
upon this point an early answer to your Lordship for his Majesty's
information.
                                    CHRISTOPHER ROBINSON.
                                    J. S. COPLEY.
                                    CHARLES WETHERELL.

(8.) JOINT OPINION *of the Attorney and Solicitor General,*
SIR JOHN CAMPBELL *and* SIR R. M. ROLFE, *as to the Claims of
two Persons resident in the Mauritius before the Cession of the
Island to the Privileges of British Subjects after the Cession.*

                            Temple, December 28, 1838.
MY LORD,—We have been honoured with your Lordship's letter
of the 21st ult., transmitting to us the copy of a despatch received

by your Lordship from the Governor of Mauritius, forwarding a correspondence relative to the claims of two persons named Malvesgy and Bestel to the privileges of British subjects.

Your Lordship requests us to report our opinion whether, under the circumstances disclosed in these papers, these two gentlemen, or either of them, are or are not entitled to the character and privileges of British subjects.

We have now the honour of reporting to your Lordship, that the question whether these gentlemen, or either of them, are or is entitled to the privileges of a British subject, depends on the question whether they did or did not avail themselves of the right given by the Treaty of Paris to repudiate their allegiance to Great Britain, and to continue, as they were before the conquest of Mauritius, subjects of France: *primâ facie*, if they continued to reside at Mauritius for a period of six years (which was the term allowed by the treaty for parties to quit the ceded countries, and dispose of their property), they must be considered as having intended to become British subjects; and we are clearly of opinion that if they once became British subjects they could not afterwards divest themselves of that character by taking the oath of allegiance to France, or by any other act. In this respect we see no distinction between subjects who have become so by cession or conquest and natural-born subjects.

But if the circumstances of their residence at Mauritius were equivocal—if, for instance, they refused to take the oath of allegiance to Great Britain, or in any respect acted as being foreigners —then the circumstance of their subsequent residence at Bourbon would be strong to show that they never meant to become British subjects.

The circumstance, particularly (as to Mr. Malvesgy), that he accepted an office in Bourbon only tenable by a French subject would be strong, if other circumstances are equivocal, to show that he never became a British subject. But if he had previously become a British subject, he cannot have ceased to be so by subsequently taking the oath of allegiance to another power.

As to Mr. Bestel, the acts done by him out of the island of Mauritius seem to be by no means inconsistent with his character of a British subject; and if, therefore, he had, as we understand the

facts to be, resided in Mauritius as an inhabitant from 1814 to
1825, doing nothing to repudiate his character of a British subject,
we do not think that his subsequent residence for ten years in a
French colony for purposes of commerce can affect his right to be
considered as a subject of Her Majesty.

The Lord Glenelg,   J. CAMPBELL.
    &c.   &c.   &c.   R. M. ROLFE.

(9.) JOINT OPINION *of the Attorney and Solicitor General,*
SIR FREDERICK THESIGER *and* SIR FITZROY KELLY, *as to
whether an Inhabitant of the Mauritius was entitled to be considered a British Subject.*

Temple, August 15, 1845.

MY LORD,—We have the honour to acknowledge the receipt of
Mr. Hope's letter of the 14th of July, in which he was pleased to
state that he was directed by your Lordship to transmit to us the
copy of a despatch from the Governor of Mauritius relative to the
claim of one Louis Bonnier, an inhabitant of that colony, to be considered a British subject; and to request that we would report, for
your Lordship's information, our joint opinion whether, under the
circumstances stated in that despatch and its enclosures, Louis
Bonnier is entitled to the privilege of a British subject, or is to
be regarded as an alien.

In obedience to your Lordship's command, we have the honour
to report that in our opinion Louis Bonnier must be regarded as
an alien.   By the capitulation, cartels were to be provided to take
the French forces to France, and within two years the inhabitants
were to be at liberty to depart from the islands, and whoever did
so remained a French subject.   Louis Bonnier appears to have left
the island within the stipulated period in a cartel (which he could
only have done as a French subject), and to have proceeded to
France, and to have returned only in 1815, after the peace.   Unless
some satisfactory explanation is given of these circumstances we
cannot think that Louis Bonnier ever acquired the status of a
British subject.

To the Right Hon. the Lord Stanley,   FREDERICK THESIGER.
    &c.   &c.   &c.   FITZROY KELLY.

(10.) JOINT OPINION *of the Attorney and Solicitor General,* SIR WILLIAM FOLLETT *and* SIR FREDERICK THESIGER, *that the Crown may bestow the dignity of a Knight Bachelor on an Alien.*

Temple, December 9, 1844.

MY LORD,—We have the honour to acknowledge the receipt of Mr. G. W. Hope's letter of the 6th instant, requesting that we would consider and report to your Lordship, for Her Majesty's information, whether there was any objection in point of law to the dignity of a Knight Bachelor being conferred by Her Majesty on a person who is not a subject of her Crown.

It is also stated that, if no such objection exists, it is Her Majesty's purpose to confer that honour on an alien who has recently rendered important public services in the colony of British Guiana.

In humble obedience to your Lordship's commands, we have fully considered this case, and are of opinion that there is no objection in point of law to such dignity being conferred on an alien.

To the Right Hon. the Lord Stanley, . W. W. FOLLETT.
&c. &c. &c. FREDERICK THESIGER.

(11.) JOINT OPINION *of the Queen's Advocate,* SIR JOHN DODSON, *and the Attorney and Solicitor General,* SIR WILLIAM FOLLETT *and* SIR FREDERICK THESIGER, *on the Naturalization of an Alien Woman by marriage with a British Subject in Gibraltar.*

Doctors' Commons, April 15, 1845.

MY LORD,—We are honoured with your Lordship's commands, signified to us by Mr. Hope's letter of the 12th instant, stating that he had been directed by your Lordship to transmit for our consideration the copy of a despatch and of its enclosure, from the Governor of Gibraltar, submitting for the decision of your Lordship the question whether, under Act 7 & 8 Vict. c. 66, s. 16, aliens married to British subjects resident in Gibraltar become naturalized ?

Mr. Hope was pleased to desire that we would report to your Lordship our joint opinion whether the Act referred to extends to that garrison, and if so, whether the wife of Mr. Peter Francia is entitled, in virtue of it, to the privileges of a natural-born subject within the fortress and territory.

In obedience to your Lordship's commands, we have perused the despatch and its enclosures, and duly considered the same, and have the honour to report that we understand that Mr. Peter Francia is a natural-born subject of the British Crown; and this being so, we are of opinion that his wife has become naturalized, and is entitled to all the rights and privileges of a natural-born subject.

J. DODSON.

To the Right Hon. the Lord Stanley,   W. W. FOLLETT.

    &c. &c. &c.   FREDERICK THESIGER.

(12.) JOINT OPINION *of the Queen's Advocate*, SIR JOHN DODSON, *and the Attorney and Solicitor General*, SIR JOHN JERVIS *and* SIR JOHN ROMILLY, *that Aliens may be empowered by a Colonial Legislature to hold Offices of Trust.*

Doctors' Commons, July 3, 1850.

MY LORD,—We were honoured by your Lordship's commands contained in Mr. Merivale's letter of the 4th ultimo, in which he stated that he was directed by your Lordship to transmit to us the inclosed copy of an ordinance recently passed by the Legislature of the colony of Port Natal, "for imparting to aliens residing within the district of Natal some of the privileges of naturalization," in order to obtain our opinion on a question which this ordinance appears to raise.

By section 1 of this ordinance, it is provided that upon taking the oath, "and obtaining the certificate hereinafter prescribed, every alien now residing in, or who shall hereafter come to reside in, the district of Natal, with intent to settle therein, shall enjoy all the rights and capacities which a natural-born subject of Her Majesty can enjoy or transmit, except that such alien shall not be capable of becoming a member of the Executive or Legislative Councils of the said district."

By the Act 12 & 13 Will. 3, c. 2, s. 3 (enforced by 1 Geo. 1, statute 2, c. 4, s. 2), aliens are disabled, even after naturalization, from enjoying any office or place of trust, civil or military, and from having any grant of land from the Crown.

But by the Act 10 & 11 Vict. c. 83, for the naturalization of aliens, it is enacted (s. 2), "that all laws, statutes, and ordinances which shall hereafter be made and enacted by the legislatures of any of Her Majesty's colonies or possessions abroad, for imparting to any person or persons the privileges or any of the privileges of naturalization, to be by any such person or persons exercised and enjoyed within the limits of any such colonies and possessions respectively, shall within such limits have the force and authority of law, any law, statute, or usage to the contrary in anywise notwithstanding."

Mr. Merivale then stated that the question, therefore, on which he was instructed to request our opinion was, whether an alien naturalized in Natal according to the manner prescribed in this ordinance (which passed subsequently to 10 & 11 Vict. c. 83), would be able to enjoy an office or place of trust (except such as are specially excepted in the ordinance), and to take a grant of land from the Crown?

Mr. Merivale concluded by saying he was directed to subjoin a memorandum which was drawn up in the Colonial Office, on the legal status of colonial aliens prior to the passing of 10 & 11 Vict. c. 83; and a circular to the governors of the colonies, which was transmitted after the passing that Act; and also a copy of an opinion given by the Queen's Advocate General, and the Attorney and Solicitor General, on the 25th May, 1840, on the subject of a Mauritius Naturalization Ordinance.

In obedience to the commands of your Lordship, we have taken the papers into our consideration, and have the honour to report—

That in our opinion an alien naturalized in Natal, according to the manner prescribed in this ordinance, would be able to enjoy an office or place of trust, except such as are specially excepted in the ordinance, and to take a grant of land from the Crown.

The Right Hon. Earl Grey,
&c. &c. &c.

J. DODSON.
JOHN JERVIS.
JOHN ROMILLY.

(13.) JOINT OPINION *of the Queen's Advocate*, SIR JOHN DODSON, *and the Attorney and Solicitor General*, SIR A. E. COCKBURN *and* SIR W. PAGE WOOD, *that a " Liberated African " does not become*, ipso facto, *a British Subject.*

Doctors' Commons, October 21, 1851.

MY LORD,—We are honoured with your Lordship's commands, signified in Mr. Elliot's letter of the 13th instant, stating that he was directed to transmit to us the accompanying extract of a despatch from the Governor of Sierra Leone ; and to request that we would take the same into consideration, and report to your Lordship our joint opinion—

First.—Whether an African liberated from slavery by legal process in Her Majesty's Mixed Commission Courts becomes, *ipso facto*, a British subject in the full acceptation of that term ? and,

Secondly.—Whether a liberated African, in the event of his committing any offence out of the jurisdiction of a colony, would be amenable to the same jurisdiction by which a *bonâ fide* British subject could be tried within the territories of native chiefs with whom treaties may have been concluded ?

In obedience to your Lordship's commands, we have taken into consideration the extract of the despatch above referred to; and have the honour to report that, in our opinion, both questions should be answered in the negative.

	J. DODSON.
The Right Hon. Earl Grey,	A. E. COCKBURN.
&c. &c. &c.	W. P. WOOD.

(14.) JOINT OPINION *of the same* LAW OFFICERS, *that such an African may be comprehended in Treaties within the meaning of 6 & 7 Vict. c. 94.*

Doctors' Commons, February 21, 1852.

MY LORD,—We were honoured with your Lordship's commands, contained in Mr. Merivale's letter of the 4th instant, in which he stated that, with reference to our letter of the 21st of October last, on the subject of liberated Africans, he was directed by your Lordship to transmit to us copy of a despatch received by your Lordship from the Governor of Sierra Leone, to whom that letter had been communicated ; and he was directed to ask whether, in our opinion, although liberated Africans are not British subjects, yet, if treaties were entered into according to the recommendation of the annexed Order in Council of the 13th of July, 1850, with the constituted authorities of neighbouring territories to Sierra Leone, applying in terms to liberated Africans inhabiting the possessions of Her Majesty as well as to those who are strictly British subjects, it would not be competent for Her Majesty to authorize the punishment or trial at Sierra Leone of such liberated Africans under the provisions of 6 & 7 Vict. c. 94, and by virtue of such treaties?

Mr. Merivale annexed, for reference, the Order in Council of the 3rd of September, 1844, passed, in virtue of that Act, to regulate Her Majesty's jurisdiction within territories adjacent to Cape Coast Castle.

In obedience to your Lordship's commands, we have considered the several papers transmitted to us; and have the honour to report that, although liberated Africans are not British subjects, yet, if treaties were entered into, as suggested in the question put to us, it would be competent for Her Majesty to authorize the trial at Sierra Leone of such liberated Africans under the provisions of 6 & 7 Vict. c. 4, and by virtue of such treaties.

	J. Dodson.
The Right Hon. Earl Grey,	A. E. Cockburn.
&c. &c. &c.	W. P. Wood.

NOTES TO CHAPTER IX.

The English doctrine undoubtedly is that *nemo potest exuere patriam*— Allegi the obligation of allegiance is for life. Sir Travers Twiss says (Law of Nations, i. 231), that this "finds no countenance in the Law of Nations, as it is in direct conflict with the incontestable rule of that law." In the United States the current of judicial authorities has followed the rule of the English law, and it has been there held that neither a native nor a naturalized citizen can throw off his allegiance without consent of the State. See an able note on this subject in Dana's 6th edit. of Wheaton, 142, note 49, where he quotes a letter from Mr. Cass to the United States Minister at Berlin (July 8, 1859),

in which he says: " The doctrine of perpetual allegiance is a relic of
barbarism which has been disappearing from Christendom during the
last century."

The rule of the Roman law is thus stated by Cicero, *pro Balbo,* 11:
Jure enim nostro neque mutare civitatem quisquam invitus potest, NEQUE, SI
VELIT, MUTARE NON POTEST, *modo adsciscatur ab eâ civitate, cujus esse se
civitatis velit.*

In an Opinion given by the United States Attorney General Cushing,
in 1856 (Attorney Generals' Opinions, viii. 163), he said: " In truth,
opinion in the United States has been at all times a little coloured on
the subject by necessary opposition to the assumption of Great Britain
to uphold the doctrines of indefeasible allegiance, and in terms to forbid expatriation.   Hence we have been prone to regard it hastily as a
question between kings and their subjects.   It is not so.   The true
question is of the relation between the political society and its
members, upon whatever hypothesis of right, and in whatever form of
organization, that society may be constituted. . . . The admissibility
of change of allegiance in the United States without necessary *express*
co-operation of the foreign Government, is implied by the Naturalization Acts, which require conditions of residence, of personal character,
of publicity, and of actual abjuration of the foreign allegiance, as indispensable to the consummation of an act of expatriation. . . . Of course
the citizen cannot apply such implied consent to any act of pretended
emigration, which is itself a violation otherwise of the law, either
public or municipal, as in the case of illegal military enterprises;
nor by it can he escape the punishment of crime, nor appeal to it as
a mask to cover desertion or treasonable aid of the public enemy."

And in another opinion given by the United States Attorney General
Black, in 1859 (Attorney Generals' Opinions, ix. 360), he said that a
native and a naturalized American " are both of them American
citizens, and their exclusive allegiance is due to the Government of
the United States.   One of them never did owe any fealty elsewhere,
and the other at the time of his naturalization, solemnly and rightfully,
in pursuance of public law and municipal regulation, threw off, abjured,
and renounced for ever all allegiance to every foreign prince, potentate,
state, and sovereignty whatever, and especially to that sovereign
whose subject he had previously been.   If this did not work a dissolution of every political tie which bound him to his native country, then
our Naturalization Laws are a bitter mockery, and the oath we administer to foreigners is a delusion and a snare."

Allegiance by the English law is correlative with protection : *Calvin's
Case,* 7 Rep. 5 a; and where the Sovereign can no longer *de jure* protect
his subjects, their allegiance ceases.   Upon this principle allegiance is
changed by conquest, or by cession of territory under a treaty.

In *Fabrigas* v. *Mostyn,* Cowp. 161, Lord Mansfield said: " The objection made in this case, of its not being stated on the record that the
plaintiff was born since the Peace of Utrecht, by which Minorca was

ceded to this country, is untenable, for from the moment of the cession all the inhabitants of the island were under the allegiance and were entitled to the protection of the British Crown." But in the case of either conquest or cession, the former inhabitants have the option of continuing or transferring their allegiance. They may emigrate to the mother State, and in that case they remain its subjects, in accordance with the principle of the Roman law that *nemo mutare civitatem* INVITUS *potest*. But if they stay in the conquered or ceded territory, they will be considered to have elected to become the subjects of the new Government.

A case of some interest has recently occurred in Germany. Count Platen-Hallemund was prime minister of Hanover at the time of the capitulation of its army to Prussia in 1866. Hanover was afterwards forcibly annexed to Prussia, but before the annexation, Count Platen left Hanover in the suite of the ex-King, who, by the terms of the capitulation, was allowed to choose his own residence together with a suite of attendants. They took up their abode at Vienna ; and, while there, Count Platen was summoned to appear before the Supreme Court of Judicature (*Kammergericht*) in Berlin, on a charge of high treason, alleged to have been committed by him abroad "as a royal Prussian subject" after he had ceased to reside in Hanover. According to the law of Prussia, only a Prussian subject can be prosecuted before a Prussian court for an act of high treason committed abroad, and it was therefore necessary to assume that Count Platen had become a Prussian subject in consequence of the annexation of Hanover by Prussia. He by his counsel pleaded to the jurisdiction of the court on the ground that he had never become a Prussian subject ; and elaborate opinions were given by two German jurists (Professor Zachariæ of Göttingen, and Professor Neumann of Vienna), to the effect that he had not. The court, however, overruled the plea, and proceeded against the Count *in contumaciam*, sentencing him to penal servitude for fifteen years. The propositions which Professors Zachariæ and Neumann maintained in their opinions with much learning were, that the mere fact of conquest or forcible annexation did not create the relation of sovereign and subject between the conqueror and the conquered, but that there must be either an express or tacit submission for the purpose, and in "tacit submission" would be included the remaining within the sphere of the power of the new dominion and fulfilling the duties of subjects ; but that it must be entirely left to the choice of the subjects of the subdued State whether they would acknowledge the new sovereign power or not. Consequently they are at liberty to emigrate, but if they remain "they thereby tacitly declare that they enter the new State and population community; that is, the fact of their remaining is, according to the present law, considered as a silent declaration to that effect." See on this subject, Halleck, Internat. Law, 818 ; Heffter, Das Europäische Völkerrecht, ss. 178, 185 ; Schwarz, *De Jure Victoris in Res Incorporales* (1720) ; Vattel, Liv. iii. c. 13, s. 201.

The question discussed in some of the Opinions in the text was of a peculiar kind. The American colonies rose in rebellion, and at last Great Britain acknowledged their independence. But many of the inhabitants had remained loyal to the English Crown during the contest, and were they in consequence of the success of the rebellion to lose their rights and privileges as British subjects? The Treaty of Paris, in 1783, provided that there should be no confiscations or prosecutions against any persons for the part they had taken in the war, and that no persons should suffer on that account any future loss or damage; but it was silent on the subject of future allegiance, further than that his Britannic Majesty relinquished all claim to the government, propriety, and territorial rights of the United States.

Children born in the United States, after the recognition of their independence, of parents born there before that time, and continuing to reside there afterwards, were held to be aliens in *Doe* d. *Thomas* v. *Acklam*, 2 B. & C. 779. The Court held that the father of the lessor of the plaintiff, by his continued residence in the United States after the recognition of their independence, manifestly became a citizen of those States; and they said: "The inconvenience that must ensue from considering the great mass of the inhabitants of a country to be at once citizens and subjects of two distinct and independent States, and owing allegiance to the Government of each, was well commented upon in the argument at the bar. If the language of the treaty could admit a doubt of its effect, the consideration of this inconvenience would have great weight toward the removal of the doubt." The same point had been previously decided in the Supreme Court of the United States: *Blight's Lessee* v. *Rochester*, 7 Wheaton, 535.

But where the parents, at the time of the separation of the two countries, had adhered to the British Government, the children were held to be aliens: *Doe* d. *Auchmuty* v. *Mulcaster*, 5 B. & C. 771. There Bayley, J., distinguishing the case of *Doe* d. *Thomas* v. *Acklam*, said: "In that case it appeared that the parent through whom the claim was made, put off his allegiance at the time of the treaty which enabled him to do so." The Court therefore held that the lessor of the plaintiff was expressly within the statute 4 Geo. 2, c. 21, which provides that children born out of the ligeance of the Crown, whose fathers were natural-born subjects of the Crown, shall be adjudged and taken to be natural-born subjects of the Crown: see *Stewart* v. *Hoome*, 11 Morrison, Dict. of Dec. 4649. In *Re Bruce*, 2 C. & J. 450, the Court said that the plaintiff, "upon the treaty between this country and the United States, had the option of continuing a British subject, if he should elect Great Britain as his country, or of ceasing to be a British subject, and becoming to all intents and purposes an American; and it seems to us that he made his election for the latter." See *Jephson* v. *Riera*, 3 Knapp, P. C. 130 ; *Folliott* v. *Ogden*, 1 H. Bl. 124 ; *Doe* d. *Stansbury* v. *Arkwright*, 5 C. & P. 575. See also statute 37 Geo. 3, c. 97, s. 24 ; *Sutton* v. *Sutton*, 1 Russ. & M. 663.

A natural-born subject of this country who was also a citizen of the United States was held to be entitled to all the advantages of an American, under a treaty which permitted citizens of the United States to trade with the East Indies, although as a British subject he would not have been so entitled owing to the charter of the East India Company, which gave them the exclusive right of trading with those countries. In his capacity of British subject he was prohibited, but in his capacity of American subject he was permitted; and the Court decided that the circumstance of his being a natural-born subject here did not deprive him of the advantages of the treaty as a citizen of the United States: *Wilson* v. *Marryat*, 8 T. R. 31; *Marryat* v. *Wilson* (S. C. in Error) 1 B. & P. 430.

In *Drummond's Case*, 2 Knapp, 295, the Court held that the grandson of a natural-born British subject, although both himself and his father were born in a foreign country, might possess the characters of both a British subject under statute 3 Geo. 3, c. 26, and a French subject under the municipal law of France. That was a case of claim for compensation against the Commissioners for liquidating the claims of British subjects on France; and the claimants, who were the heirs of James Lewis Drummond, afterwards having obtained the opinion of six eminent French lawyers that he was not a French subject, petitioned the Lords of the Treasury for a re-hearing. The case was referred again to the Judicial Committee, who were of opinion that, admitting the correctness of the statement made by the French lawyers, James Lewis Drummond and his father "did sufficiently indicate by their conduct their intention to accept the character of French subjects, so that their estates could not be considered as ' *indûment confisqués.*' "

When Lord Brougham applied to M. Crémieux, the French Minister of Justice, under the Republic in 1848, to be made a French citizen, the Minister replied: " If France adopts you for one of her sons, you cease to be an Englishman ; you are no longer Lord Brougham, you become citizen Brougham." Lord Brougham replied: " I never doubted that by causing myself to be naturalized a French citizen I should lose all my rights as a British Peer and a British subject in France. I will retain my privileges as an Englishman only in England ; in France I should be all that the laws of France allowed to the citizens of the Republic." But M. Crémieux answered : " France admits no partition ; she admits not that a French citizen shall at the same time be a citizen of another country. In order to become a Frenchman you must cease to be an Englishman. You cannot be an Englishman in England, and a Frenchman in France ; our laws are absolutely opposed to it :" Lord Campbell's Lives of the Chancellors, viii. 552–3. It is hardly necessary to say that Lord Brougham renounced all idea of naturalization in France. The French law is in entire conformity with the Roman law in this respect — *Duarum civitatum civis esse, jure nostro civili, nemo potest : Cic. pro Balbo,* 11.

Woolsey says (International Law, s. 66) : " Most nations hold that this transfer of allegiance is possible, and embody the conditions of it in their naturalization laws. Even England, which retains the doctrine

z

of indelible allegiance, admits strangers to citizenship by special Act or grant. But, inasmuch as the conditions of naturalization vary, there may arise here a conflict of laws, and two nations may at once claim the same man as sustaining to them the obligations of a citizen. International law has not undertaken to decide in such conflicts, and the question is scarcely one of practical importance, except when the naturalized person returns to his native country, and when he is caught fighting against her. There is no doubt that a State having undertaken to adopt a stranger, is bound to protect him like any other citizen . . . Whether anything short of completed naturalization can sunder the tie to the place of origin may be a question. It is held that a domiciled stranger may not with impunity be found in arms against his native country :" see Kent's Com. i. 76.

There is a case known as *Koszta's Case*, cited by both Wheaton, p. 146 (Dana's 8th edit.), and Woolsey (International Law, p. 131), which it will be useful to notice. Koszta was a Hungarian, who had taken part in the rebellion against Austria, and fled to Turkey, where he was arrested, but released upon a promise to leave Turkey. He went to the United States, and took up his residence there, making the declaration preliminary to naturalization, but he did not become actually a citizen. He afterwards went to Smyrna for temporary commercial purposes, and placed himself under the protection of the United States consul there, and the Chargé d'Affaires at Constantinople, by both of whom he was furnished with a passport or certificate of American nationality. While at Smyrna he was seized by Austrian officials, and placed in confinement on board an Austrian vessel in the harbour. The Turkish authorities protested against this act as a violation of the sovereignty of the Sublime Porte. The commander of an American ship-of-war demanded the release of Koszta, and threatened to fire on the Austrian vessel unless he was given up. This led to an arrangement by which Koszta was put under the custody of the French Consul-General until the Governments which were at issue should agree what to do with him. He afterwards went back to the United States. In the course of correspondence on the subject the United States Government claimed the right to free a subject domiciled, although not naturalized, from arrest of his person made within the territories of a friendly State, where he was sojourning for business purposes, by the agents of another State, although that of his birth, and if necessary to resort to force for that purpose. Woolsey says (*Ibid.* p. 132) : " This was a case of collision between original and transferred allegiance—the latter in its incipiency, in which the obligation to protect the person clearly lay on the United States. How Austria could have dealt with him within her own limits is another question." The *Case of Tousig*, cited by Dana in his note to Wheaton, p. 146, shows that if Koszta had voluntarily returned to Austria, the conduct of the United States Government would have been different. Tousig, a subject of Austria, had acquired a domicile in the United States, but was not naturalized, and he voluntarily returned to Austria with a passport from the American Secretary of State. He was arrested in Austria on a charge of offences committed before he had originally left that country, and the American Government refused to interfere. The distinction between the two cases is obvious.

By statute 4 Geo. 2, c. 21, and 13 Geo. 3, c. 21, all children born out of .the King's ligeance whose fathers or grandfathers by the fathers' side were *natural-born* subjects are deemed to be natural-born subjects themselves to all intents and purposes, unless their said ancestors were attainted or banished beyond sea for high treason, or were at the birth of such children in the service of a prince at enmity with the Crown of this realm. This might seem to place the children and grandchildren of those persons who, born in Great Britain, have left their native country to settle permanently in a foreign State, in a very awkward predicament in case of their being found in arms on the side of their adopted country in a war between it and England. Many of those who fought under Napoleon I. against England must have been technically British subjects. Were they, therefore, guilty of treason, and if taken liable to be put to death as traitors? This would certainly have revolted every feeling of humanity, and perhaps the true solution of the difficulty is to be found in the explanation of the law given by Sir Roundell Palmer, in a speech he delivered in the House of Commons, March 20, 1868, when he said that Great Britain could not be supposed by any Acts to be imposing burdens upon the subjects of other countries; and he thought it impossible to read the two Acts of 4 Geo. 2, c. 21, and 13 Geo. 3, c. 21 together, without seeing that the Legislature as good as declared that all they intended by those Acts was to confer benefits, and not to impose burdens, upon the foreign-born children and grandchildren of natural-born British subjects. The second Act was merely passed to continue those privileges to the foreign-born grandchildren which were extended by the first Act to the foreign-born children of British-born subjects; there being no intention to fasten upon such persons, without their own concurrence, any burdens whatsoever. Sir R. Palmer stated this to be his distinct and deliberate opinion, and it seems to be sound law and good sense : see *Æneas Macdonald's Case*, 18 State Tr. 858.

The abjuration by a British subject of his allegiance to the Crown, and his promise of obedience to a foreign State, although they might have rendered him liable, under stat. 3 James 1, c. 4, ss. 22, 23, to the penalty of high treason, do not divest him of his character of a British subject, and therefore do not disqualify his children or grandchildren from inheriting as British subjects : see *Fitch* v. *Weber*, 6 Hare, 51.

It was decided in *Doe* d. *Duroure* v. *Jones*, 4 T. R. 300, that the son of an alien father and English mother born out of the realm could not inherit to his mother in this country. But now, by stat. 7 & 8 Vict.c. 66, s. 3, every person born out of Her Majesty's dominions of a mother a natural-born subject, shall be capable of taking any real or personal estate.

During the late civil war in the United States the military draft included citizens, native or naturalized, and " persons of foreign birth

340 CASES AND OPINIONS ON CONSTITUTIONAL LAW.

who shall have declared on oath their intention to become citizens:" United States Laws, xii. 731.

During the Canadian rebellion in 1838, Lord (then Sir John) Campbell, A.G., gave an opinion, which was acted upon, that an armed band of American citizens who invaded our territory without the authority of their Government were liable to be treated as traitors: see Lives of the Chief Justices, i. 197; and OPINION, p. 199, *ante*.

In *Craw* v. *Ramsay* (Vaugh. 281), Vaughan, C.J., said: "If the King of England enter with his army hostilely the territories of another prince, and any be born within the places possessed by the King's army, and consequently within his protection, such person is a subject born to the King of England, if from parents subjects and not hostile."

fects of rriage on alien- e.

Where a British subject married a Frenchwoman and became domiciled in France, where they resided until the outbreak of the Revolution, and the wife died in her husband's lifetime never having come into British territory, it was held that by the common law she was not a British subject: *De Wall's Case*, 12 Jur. (P.C.) 145. In the *Countess of Conway's Case*, 2 Knapp, 368, the Court said: "A Frenchwoman becomes in no way a British subject by marrying an Englishman; she continues an alien, and is not entitled to dower:" Co. Litt. 31 b. But by virtue of statute 7 & 8 Vict. c. 66, an alien woman who marries a British subject is now naturalized, and is not entitled to a jury *de medietate linguæ*: *R.* v *Manning*, 1 Den. C. C. 467. In *Derry* v. *Duchess of Mazarine*, 1 Raym. 147, it was held that if a husband is an alien *enemy*, he has no legal existence in this country; and his wife, resident here, so long as he remains such, is looked upon as a *femme sole*, and may be sued on contracts made by her as if she were a widow.

aturaliza- on.

Naturalization in this country is now regulated by statute 7 & 8 Vict. c. 66, and it may be effected by a certificate issued by the Secretary of State for the Home Department, which has the effect of granting to the alien all the rights and capacities of a natural-born British subject, except the capacity of being a Privy Councillor, or a member of either House of Parliament.

By the Constitution of the United States the power of naturalization is vested exclusively in Congress, and the State Governments have not the power: Kent's Com. i. 467, 8th edit. But no naturalized citizen of the United States is capable of being elected President.

aturaliza- on in the olonies.

The statute 10 & 11 Vict. c. 83, enacts that all Acts, statutes, and ordinances theretofore passed by the legislatures of any of Her Majesty's colonies and possessions abroad, for naturalizing persons within the respective limits of such colonies and possessions, shall within such limits be valid, and that all such Acts, statutes, and ordinances passed in future shall within such limits be valid, subject to confirmation or disallowance by Her Majesty. And the same Act enacts and declares that the Act 7 & 8 Vict. c. 66, "An Act to Amend the Laws relating to Aliens," does not extend to any British colonies or possessions abroad.

CHAPTER X.

ON EXTRADITION.

(1.) JOINT OPINION *of the Attorney and Solicitor General,* SIR JOHN CAMPBELL *and* SIR R. M. ROLFE, *as to the Detention and Extradition of Spanish Convicts wrecked on the Bahama Islands while proceeding under sentence of transportation from the Havannah to Cadiz.*

Temple, September 15, 1836.

MY LORD,—We have to acknowledge the receipt of your Lordship's letter of the 31st ultimo, enclosing copies of despatches from the Governor of the Bahamas, and of enclosures therein contained, relating to certain Spanish convicts wrecked on the Bahama Islands while proceeding under sentence of transportation from the Havannah to Cadiz, in which letter your Lordship requests that we would report our opinion how far the proceedings of the Lieutenant-Governor were consistent with the law of nations and with the municipal law of England.

We beg leave to state to your Lordship that the Lieutenant-Governor has no right by the law of England to detain in custody any persons merely on the ground of their having been guilty of offences against the laws of Spain. The convicts in question, having been wrecked on an island forming part of the territories of his Majesty, are entitled to be dealt with as free agents so long as they conduct themselves in conformity to the laws in force in the Bahama Islands. However reasonable the course recommended by the Attorney General of the island might be—namely, to deliver up to the Spanish authorities such of the convicts as had been convicted of the graver offences constituting *mala in se*, and to set at liberty those convicted of what were only *mala prohibita*—we are not aware of any law warranting such a course, or justifying a

British Governor in treating as criminals persons who have not violated the laws of the colony over which he presides.

The Lord Glenelg,   J. CAMPBELL.
&c. &c. &c.   R. M. ROLFE.

(2.) OPINION *of the United States Attorney General*, MR. LEGARE, *on the Extradition of Criminals* (1).

Attorney General's Office, October 11, 1841.

SIR,—I find among the papers left in this office by my predecessor a letter from his Excellency Governor Seward, consulting you upon the course which ought to be pursued in the matter of one Dewit, a fugitive from justice demanded of the Governor of New York by the Governor-General of Canada, together with a request from yourself that it be considered by the Attorney General. I have accordingly turned my attention to the subject as soon as other pressing avocations would permit me to do so, and now have the honour to give you an opinion upon it.

I think from the whole argument of the Bench in the case of *Holmes* v. *Jennison*, 14 Peters, 540, we may consider it as law : First, that no State can without the consent of Congress enter into any agreement or compact, expressed or implied, to deliver up fugitives from justice from a foreign State who may be found within its limits : secondly, that according to the practice of the executive department, as appears from the official correspondence both of Mr. Jefferson and Mr. Clay, your predecessors in office, the President is not considered as authorized, in the absence of any express provision by treaty, to order the delivering up of fugitives from justice. In the absence, therefore, of such treaty stipulations, I am of opinion that it is necessary to refer the whole matter to Congress, and submit to its wisdom the propriety of passing an Act to authorize such of the States as may choose to make arrangements with the Government of Canada or any other foreign State for the the mutual extradition of fugitives, to enact laws to that effect, or Acts approving such laws as may already have been passed in the several States to that effect.

(1) 3 Attorney Generals' Opinions, 661.

Whatever I might think of the power of the Federal Executive in the premises, were this a new question, I consider the rules laid down by Mr. Jefferson, and sanctioned after the lapse of thirty years by another administration, as too solemnly settled to be now departed from.

Hon. D. Webster, Sec. of State.   H. S. LEGARE.

(3.) CASE and JOINT OPINION *of the Attorney and Solicitor General,* SIR JOHN ROMILLY *and* SIR A. E. COCKBURN, *on the Act* 6 & 7 *Vict. c.* 79 (*an Act to carry into effect a Convention concerning the Fisheries in the Seas between the British Islands and France*); *and the Jurisdiction of the Royal Court of Jersey.* 1851.

Case.—Some British fishing-boats, including one from Jersey, were found fishing off the coast of France, within the French limits; and the French authorities being desirous that proceedings should be taken against the Jersey boat for an infraction of the Fishery Laws, the Lieutenant-Governor of Jersey referred the question to the Attorney General of the island, for his opinion as to whether the Royal Court there had jurisdiction in the case. The Attorney General said, in his Opinion: "I doubt if the Royal Court of this island has jurisdiction in the case, inasmuch as the occurrence took place within the limits within which the general right of fishing is stated to be exclusively reserved to the French. The jurisdiction in such cases appears to me to belong altogether to the French tribunal, under the 89th section of the Fishery Regulations, agreed upon by the two countries on the 23rd of June, 1843." A further question arose, as to whether the conduct of the crews of the other boats, in endeavouring to rescue her from the hands of the French, who had seized her, was punishable in Jersey, and on this point the Attorney General said: "As regards the second offence, neither the Act 6 & 7 Vict. c. 75 (to carry into effect the Extradition Treaty between Great Britain and France), nor the regulations above-mentioned, provide specifically for the case of a British fisherman resisting or obstructing a French officer or functionary; nor have we any other law under which such an offence could be tried in the Royal Court, nor is that Court empowered to send the supposed offenders to a French court for trial."

The case was then submitted to the Law Officers of the Crown, Sir John Romilly and Sir A. E. Cockburn, and they were asked whether, under the Act 6 & 7 Vict. c. 79, the Royal Court of Jersey had jurisdiction to try the parties for either, and which, of the alleged offences?

Opinion.—We think that the present case is one omitted in the provisions of the Act. The 11th section states that the magistrate to hear the charge is to be one having jurisdiction in the country or place in which, or in the waters adjacent to which, the offence shall be committed, or to which the offenders shall be brought. Here the offence was committed in French waters, and not in the waters adjacent to Jersey, and the offenders were not brought to Jersey, although they escaped thither. In these circumstances we are compelled to agree with the Attorney General of Jersey, and are of opinion that, under the Act 6 & 7 Vict. c. 79, the Royal Court of Jersey has no jurisdiction to try the parties for any one of the alleged offences mentioned in the above correspondence.

JOHN ROMILLY.

Lincoln's Inn, March 22, 1851.   A. E. COCKBURN.

(4.) OPINION *of the United States Attorney General,* Mr. CUSHING, *on the Extradition of Criminals* (1).

Attorney General's Office, August 19, 1853.

SIR,—I have examined the papers which you were pleased to submit to me in the case of *The People of New York* v. *Anson Wing,* from which it appears that the said Wing is under indictment for larceny alleged to have been committed by him in violation of the law of the State of New York, and is now a fugitive from justice in the British provinces; and application is made to you for process to obtain the extradition of said Wing.

Larceny is not among the cases provided for by any convention between the United States and Great Britain. The crimes enumerated in the treaty of 1842, which now governs the question, are murder, or assault with intent to commit murder, or piracy, or

_____
(1) 6 Attorney Generals' Opinions, 85.

arson, or robbery, or forgery, or the utterance of forged papers. It is, therefore, in these cases only that by treaty either Government can claim the extradition of fugitives from justice taking refuge in the dominions of the other.

It is the settled doctrine of the United States that, independently of special compact, no State is bound to deliver up fugitives from the justice of another State (see the authorities collected in Wheaton's Elements, p. 172).

It is true any State may, in its discretion, do this as a matter of international comity towards the foreign State; but all such discretion is of inconvenient exercise in a constitutional republic organized as is the Federal Union; and accordingly, it is the decided policy of this Government to refuse to grant extradition except in virtue of express stipulations to that effect (Mr. Legare's Opinion, October 11, 1841) (1).

I think it is unjust and unwise, in point of principle, for the United States to ask as an act of comity from any other Government what it refuses to do in the like case itself. We should, it seems to me, stand on the basis of complete reciprocity of right and equal justice in all our relations with foreign Governments, doing as we would be done by, and demanding of them only what we are prepared to concede in return. That was the public doctrine of this Government in the days of our relative weakness, and it should the more plainly be so now in the time of our relative strength.

Special reasons exist to dictate reserve in the matter of extradition. If the enumeration of cases for the claim of extradition in existing treaties be not sufficiently ample, it would seem better to enlarge the same by further mutual stipulations, rather than at the mere discretion of the President.

I am therefore of opinion, that to grant the present application would be contrary to the true doctrines of international law, and to the received practice of the United States.

The President.   CUSHING.

(1) See *ante*, p. 342

(5.) OPINION *of the same Attorney General on the same subject* (1).

Attorney General's Office, August 31, 1853.

SIR,—I have considered the question presented by your note of yesterday.

It appears that on application on behalf of the British Government, duly made to that of the United States, a mandate issued on the 12th inst., in the name of the President, calling on certain magistrates therein designated, or any one of them, to cause William Calder, charged with the crime of forgery committed in Great Britain, to be arrested as a fugitive from justice, and to examine the evidence of his criminality ; and, if the charge should be sustained, to certify the same to the President, to the end that said Calder may in such case be surrendered to the proper authorities of the British Government.

This mandate, the issue of which is a departure from the recently pre-existing practice of the Government, seemed to me to be called for by the action of the Supreme Court of the United States in *Kaine's Case* (*In re Kaine*, 14 Howard, p. 103) ; for although the necessity of such a mandate is not the thing specifically passed upon by the Court in that case, yet the views expressed by some of the members of the Court as to the true course of proceeding in such cases, and the analogy of the practice in Great Britain itself, led to the conclusion on the part of the President, that in case of claim for extradition falling within the scope of any treaty provision, it was proper for this Government, on being requested by the foreign Government desiring extradition of an alleged fugitive from its justice, and reasonable cause in the premises being shown, to move to action the proper judicial authorities of the country, in order to the arrest and lawful examination of the party charged with crimes and the investigation thereof for the information of the Government.

So that, whereas heretofore, the parties desiring the extradition of an alleged fugitive from the justice of a foreign Government went, *in the first instance*, to some one of the officers designated in the Act of Congress of the 12th of August, 1848, entitled " An Act for giving effect to certain treaty stipulations between this and

(1) 6 Attorney Generals' Opinions, 91.

foreign Governments for the apprehension and delivery up of certain Offenders," and sued out a warrant of arrest and pursued the other requisitions of that Act; now, in the opinions expressed' by Mr. Justice Nelson especially, in *Kaine's Case*, the party may, if he please, commence by applying to the President of the United States for a mandate, which being granted, the Act of Congress above cited then takes up the case, and pursues it to the conclusion corresponding to the particular facts and to our treaty obligations towards the given foreign Government.

I say here, in repetition, substantially, of the idea before intimated, that the foreign Government may, *if it please*, apply to the President for a mandate. The Federal Government does not require this, but only stands ready to do it if required by the foreign Government.

For, when carefully analysed, the decision in *Kaine's Case* appears to be this: Thomas Kaine, charged as a fugitive from the justice of Great Britain within the treaty, was arrested by one of the Commissioners in New York, appointed by the Circuit Court of the United States to take affidavits and examinations, and committed to abide the order of the President.

Thereupon a writ of habeas corpus in the matter was issued by the Circuit Court of the United States, and upon the hearing before the District Judge dismissed. After this another writ of habeas corpus was ordered by Mr. Justice Nelson at chambers, and a hearing thereon reserved by him to be had before the Supreme Court of the United States *in banco*. On the argument of the case, eight judges being present, four of these (Justices Catron, McLean, Wayne, and Grier) declared, through Mr. Justice Catron, that in their opinion the proceedings before the Commissioner were correct, and the party had been rightfully committed for extradition, but that the Supreme Court had no jurisdiction of the habeas corpus. Mr. Justice Curtis, for other reasons assigned by him, came to the same conclusion as to the precise question before the Court; and Mr. Justice Nelson, and the Chief Justice and Mr. Justice Daniel, for whom he spoke, were of opinion that the proceedings before the Commissioner were incorrect, and that the Supreme Court had jurisdiction of the writ of habeas corpus to revise the question of the lawfulness of Kaine's commitment.

Now, it was in the consideration of the question of *jurisdiction*, the only thing decided by the Court, that discussion came up *arguendo* as to the rightfulness of the proceedings before the Commissioner. Mr. Justice Nelson, with whom were the Chief Justice and Mr. Justice Daniel, expressed the conviction that a previous mandate from the President was necessary, and that no Commissioner could lawfully act unless appointed specially *ad hoc;* while the contrary was held by Mr. Justice Catron, with whom were Justices McLean, Wayne, and Grier; and Mr. Justice Curtis expressed no opinion upon these points. The only thing authoritatively adjudged, therefore, by five judges out of eight, was that the Supreme Court had no jurisdiction.

Now, the decision of *Kaine's Case* not definitively establishing the necessity of such a mandate, and that alleged necessity being a part of the argument only, and that of a minority of the Court, the minister of the foreign Government has the faculty still to go to some lawful magistrate in the first instance, and take his chance of what may be ultimately adjudged to be the law in the premises. But if the foreign Government desire to be relieved of this hazard, the President has the power, and in the exercise of a just comity, and especially in the discharge of his whole obligation to see to the faithful observance of treaties, he will, when occasion requires, proceed to give his mandate, by which the foreign Government will be relieved of the difficulty arising on the opinion of Mr. Justice Nelson and others of the judges of the Supreme Court of the United States.

In the present case, a warrant of arrest had been issued by the Honourable John W. Edmonds, of the Supreme Court of the State of New York, who certifies to the President, under date of the 23rd inst., that he has had the fugitive before him, and has heard the case upon evidence and argument, and is of opinion that there is not evidence enough of the criminality of the said Calder, according to the laws of the State of New York, to justify his apprehension and committal for trial for the offence charged, if the same had been committed in said State.

Mr. Justice Edmonds reports the evidence in the case, and supports his conclusion in a carefully-drawn opinion, independently of which the precise question before him was one exclusively within his province as a Judge to determine; and upon his report, whether his opinion of the effect of the evidence be erroneous or not, it is clear the President cannot order the surrender of the said Calder.

But another question arises upon a second report of Justice Edmonds; for it appears that a motion has been submitted to the Court to remand the party until new evidence can be obtained from Great Britain to maintain the charge—to grant which application the Court has decided not to be within its province, the same vesting, if anywhere, in the Government of the United States. Upon which the Minister of the British Government here applies to the Secretary of State, requesting "that directions may be given for the retention of the prisoner in custody for the time required" for the procurement of "further evidence"—and the inquiry which thus presents itself is of the duty and the power of the President in this behalf.

His general duty in this case, of course, is that which the 10th Article of the treaty with Great Britain imposes—namely, to "deliver up to justice all persons who, being charged with the crime of murder, or assault with intent to commit murder, or piracy, or arson, or robbery, or forgery, or the utterance of forged paper," committed within the jurisdiction of Great Britain, shall seek an asylum in the United States: Treaty of August 9, 1842, U. S. Stat. at Large, vol. viii. p. 576.

But this, by the terms of the treaty, is to be done upon such evidence of criminality as, according to the laws of the place where the alleged criminal shall be found, would justify his apprehension and commitment for trial, if the crime or offence had been there committed; and the judges, and other magistrates thereto lawfully authorized, are to cause the arrest of the party charged, hear and consider the evidence, and if on such hearing the evidence be deemed sufficient to sustain the charge, the examining judge or magistrate is to certify the same to the Executive.

In like manner the Act of Congress, which is in execution of and subordinate to the treaty stipulations of this class, commits to the judge or magistrate the duty and power of arrest of the party, his examination, the hearing of the evidence, and the determination of the questions upon which, if at all, the surrender of the alleged criminal is to be made.

That is to say, in the execution of this treaty, as of other treaties of the same class, the arrest, examination, and decision of fact, are judicial functions and acts. They are not, and they cannot be, performed by the President.

Now the arrest, examination, and decision being purely judicial acts, it follows, although the Act of Congress, like the treaty, is silent on this point, yet that the rules of precedure must conform to the law of the land in such matters. What is to be deemed "sufficient evidence" to sustain the charge is a question for the judge or magistrate to decide, according to the laws of the place where the criminal may happen to be examined. So also is the question, on what day he will sit, what adjournments he will grant, and whether he will remand the party charged for a further examination?

All these are things over which the President has no control, and as to which he can give no command. He cannot arrest the alleged criminal; he cannot judge the question of his guilt; he cannot regulate the discretion or conscience of the examining magistrate.

True the President may, as in this case, issue his mandate for the commencement of the proceedings in the United States, but that mandate is facultative only; it serves, on the hypothesis of the legal conclusions of Mr. Justice Nelson, to give jurisdiction; but that jurisdiction, when thus called into life by the President, rests exclusively with the magistrate making the arrest and examination. If he certifies the criminality of the accused, then the President is to order a surrender—otherwise there is an end, *pro hac vice*, of the duty and the power of the President.

Nor can appeal be taken from the decision of Mr. Justice Edmonds to any other Court so as to revise that decision. The judge or magistrate in this case acts by special authority under the Act of Congress; no appeal is given from his decision by the Act, and he does not exercise any part of what is technically considered the judicial power of the United States. (*Ex parte Metzger* v. *Howard*, 176; *United States* v. *Ferreira*, 13 Howard 40, 48, *per* Ch. J. Taney; *In re Kaine*, 14 Howard 103, 119, *per* Mr. Justice Curtis.)

Indeed, by the municipal law as well of England as of the United States, the judgment upon the evidence of the preliminary

examination of a party accused, as also the mode of conducting
the inquiry, including the question of remanding the party, are, in
general, matters within the discretion of the magistrate, that discretion being a wise one of course, and guided by the precedents
and doctrines of law; but still not subject to appeal, as such, to
another magistrate or Court. (1 Chitty's Crim. Law, by Perkins,
p. 89; 1 Archbold's Crim. Prac., by Waterman, p. 44; 2 New
York Revised Stat., p. 789.)

I feel constrained, therefore, to come to the conclusion that the
President has no power to revise the action of Mr. Justice Edmonds, or to order the detention of Calder.

However inconvenient this may be to the authorities of the
British Government in the present instance, the inconveniences
are obviously reciprocal and inevitable. The two Governments
have by treaty agreed to make the question a judicial one, and
they could not do otherwise; for the Government of the United
Kingdom is a constitutional one, as well as that of the United
States; and in both countries the writ of habeas corpus presents
itself as the safeguard, in the hands of the judges, of individual
freedom against all possible encroachments on the part of the
executive.

I do not perceive how a different conclusion could be reached
upon a similar case arising in the United Kingdom. The tenor of
the statute there is, that on the requisition of the United States,
any Principal Secretary of State, or certain executive authorities
designated, shall issue a warrant to signify that such requisition
has been so made, and to require all magistrates and officers of
justice to govern themselves accordingly, and to aid in apprehending the person accused, and committing him to gaol for the purpose of being delivered up to justice; and thereupon, proceeds the
statute, it shall be lawful for the proper magistrate to examine
upon oath any persons touching the truth of the charge, and upon
such evidence as, according to the law of the place, would justify
the apprehension and commitment for trial of the person accused
of the crime, had it been committed in that jurisdiction, the magistrate is to commit the accused to gaol, there to remain until
delivered up, in pursuance of the requisition of the United States
(6 & 7 Vict. c. 76, s. 1). There is no indication here of any power

on the part of a Principal Secretary to arrest the alleged fugitive, or to direct the examining magistrate, or to require the detention of the accused for further examination. All he is empowered by the Act to do, is to issue a warrant "to signify that such requisition has been made," upon which magistrates and other officers of justice are to govern themselves, according to the provisions of the treaty and the laws of the land.

One thing only, it seems to me, can be done in behalf of the British Government: Mr. Crampton may undoubtedly cause a new complaint to be entered against Calder, and apply for a new warrant of arrest, either with or without a new mandate from the President. Calder has not been tried. He has been examined by a magistrate, and the evidence is adjudged to be insufficient to justify his extradition. But upon a new complaint he may be examined anew by the same or by another magistrate, and the exhibition of additional evidence may lead to the conclusion of his criminality and the certificate thereof to the President.

Permit me, in conclusion, further to suggest, with all proper deference for the opinions of Mr. Justice Edmonds, whether he has not power to remand Calder; that is, if in his judgment the circumstances of the case and the present stage of the examination justify it. Of the general power of a magistrate to remand for examination, there can be no doubt, of course, it being the familiar practice of magistrates; and cases are not wanting of prisoners being detained more than twenty days between their first appearance and their commitment for trial, and being brought up for examination several different days during the interval. (Chitty's Crim. Law, by Perkins, vol. i. p. 73; Archbold's Crim. Prac., by Waterman, vol i. p. 36.) The authority to do this has been recognized in New York in the case of a State magistrate examining for a crime charged against the United States. (*Ex parte Smith* v. *Cowen*, 273.) In Massachusetts it is regulated and allowed by statute. (Rev. Stat., c. 135, p. 9.) It is true that some adjudications have been made in England which subject the magistrate who remands to an action for alleged unreasonableness of time, even when no improper motive is pretended. What is a reasonable time is a mixed question of law and of fact, depending upon the probability of obtaining further and competent evidence. "What is reasonable," Bayley, J., observes on one occasion, "does not rest in the discretion of the magistrate; there may be cases in which three days might not be a reasonable time, and yet there may be cases where three months might be reasonable" (*Davis* v. *Capper*, 4 Carrington & P. 443 n.). But the magistrate acts on the question of remanding under the peril that, on trespass being brought, a jury with proper instructions from the Court shall find the time of imprisonment to have been unreasonable (*Davis* v. *Capper*, *ubi sup.*; *Davis* v. *Capper*, 10 Barn. & Cr. 28), which the more conclusively shows that the whole question here is within the jurisdiction of Mr. Justice Edmonds. And if, having once decided the question of criminality, and made report thereon to the President, the Judge should be of opinion that it is too late for him to entertain a motion for delay, and to remand the party until further evidence be procured, it does not seem to me that his doing so can be subject to any just exception on the part either of his own Government or that of Great Britain.

Hon. Wm. L. Marcy, Sec. of State.   C. CUSHING.

(6.) OPINION *of the same Attorney General on the same subject* (1).

Attorney General's Office, April 21, 1854.

SIR,—Your letter of the 19th, referring a case of demand of extradition, would have received my attention immediately, but for my having been out of town for the last three or four days.

It communicates an application from James M. Ray, of the State of Indiana, for a requisition on the British Government to deliver up one Hamilton, charged as a fugitive from that State; and submits the question, "Whether the evidence here adduced is sufficient to justify the department in making the desired requisition?"

No evidence is adduced except an affidavit made by Mr. Ray himself, before a notary public, that at a certain time, Hamilton "feloniously stole, from the State Bank of Indiana, 1450 dollars in bank-notes of the State Bank," and so forth, and that Hamilton had probably fled into the British provinces.

(1) 6 Attorney Generals' Opinions, 431.

2 A

If this application depended on the question submitted, it would not be in my power to say that the evidence is sufficient, because it ought to have been passed upon by an examining and committing magistrate before being submitted to the President.

That defect in the papers filed might be cured; but there exists in the case another difficulty which seems to be insuperable.

The only crimes for which extradition is provided are "murder and forgery," by the treaty of 1794 (8 Stat. at Large, p. 129); and "murder, or assault with intent to commit murder, or piracy, or arson, or robbery, or forgery, or the utterance of forged papers," by the treaty of 1842 (8 Stat. at Large, p. 576).

The crime imputed to Hamilton by the affidavit of Mr. Ray is larceny, and that is not within the treaties.

It is the established rule of the United States neither to grant nor to ask for extradition of criminals as between us and any foreign Government, unless in cases for which stipulation is made by express condition. I cannot therefore advise that in the present case the desired requisition be made on the British Government.

Hon. Wm. L. Marcy, Sec. of State.   C. CUSHING.

(7.) OPINION *of the same Attorney General on the same subject* (1).

Attorney General's Office, November 2, 1854.

SIR,—I have received your communication of yesterday's date, transmitting to me the note of Mr. Hulsemann, of the Austrian Legation, in behalf of the Government of the Elector of Hesse Cassel, asking for the extradition, under the treaty of July 16, 1852, of one Maria Theresa Geêk, said to be convicted of murder within the territory of the said Elector, and a fugitive from the justice thereof, who it is supposed may have taken refuge in the United States.

The case, if duly proved, comes clearly within the purview of the treaty; and the gravity of the crime alleged to be perpetrated by the party, in addition to the obligations of the treaty and the sound reasons of public policy on which that is founded,

(1) 7 Attorney Generals' Opinions, 6.

make it desirable that, if it may be lawfully done, the application of Mr. Hulsemann should be granted.

But on a careful consideration of the only document filed in the case, it does not seem to me sufficient to justify the interposition of the President.

That document is, in fact, a mere notification of the fact, that such a party, guilty of such a crime, has escaped, and perhaps fled to the United States, and suggesting her extradition; said notification, a certificate, being under the seal of the criminal court of the city of Fulda. Such a document is not in conformity with what is required as between the different States of the American Union among ourselves, in the case of extradition of criminals under the Constitution of the United States, nor what is required as between us and those foreign States near us which have a known practice on the subject.

Thus, as between the States of this Union, the demand for extradition must come from the *executive* authority of the demanding State (Constitution Act, iv. s. 2), and the accompanying *justificatives pièces*—that is, the indictment, or record of convictions, or the testimony before the examining magistrate—must, in like manner, be certified by the executive authority of the demanding State (Act of Feb. 12, 1793, 1 Stat. at Large, p. 302). According to the municipal law, as well of England as of the United States, the mere seal of a local court on which to act—the seal and the authority of the court—must, in general, be proved, either by testimony of witnesses or by the great seal of the State (1 Starkie's Evidence, p. 285, and notes; 1 Greenleaf's Evid. s. 514).

In France all demands for the extradition of fugitive criminals must emanate from the executive authority of the demanding State, and be authenticated by the same (Ortolan, Le Ministère public en France, tom. ii. &c., p. 231; Foucart, Droit Pub. s. 211).

So it is in Spain, in the cases where that Government either claims or concedes the extradition of criminals, fugitives from justice. (Escriche, s. voc. Extrad.)

Without troubling you with further citations as to the practice of our own or of other Governments in this respect, it may be stated as the general rule, that the Government, of which extradition, whether comity only (Klüber, s. 66; Marten's Précis, s. 101), or by

2 A 2

treaty, is demanded, before it can be called upon to act, must have submitted to it reasonable *primâ facie* evidence of the guilt of the party accused, and the evidence thereof certified, as well as the demand made, by the executive authority of the demanding State. The document submitted here is deficient in all these respects. It is not what there ought to be in this case—an exemplification of the record of the accusation and conviction of the accused ; and the document is not properly authenticated by the Government of the Elector of Hesse-Cassel.

I suggest also for information, that if such cases were presented in this case as would properly justify the President in opening to him access to the courts of the country, and if the proper court, after hearing of the case, should thereafter return a certificate to the President in the terms of the Act of Congress making provision for the execution of extradition treaties (Act of August 12, 1818, 9 Stat. at Large, p. 303), then an agent of the Government of Hesse would be necessary to take possession of the criminal and convey her to Hesse ; and the testimony of such an agent might prove to be convenient, or even indispensable, at the preliminary examination of the case before the competent judicial tribunal of the United States.

Hon. Wm. L. Marcy, Sec. of State.   C. CUSHING.

(8.) OPINION *of the same Attorney General on the same subject* (1).

Attorney General's Office, June 18, 1855.

SIR,—I have the honour to acknowledge the receipt of your note of this date, communicating the application of M. Boilleau, Chargé d'Affaires of France, for authority to pursue the extradition of one Sucillon, a French subject, actually in New York, charged with the crime of forgery committed in France.

This application comes in due form through the Ministry of Foreign Affairs of the French Empire, and is founded on a *mandat d'arrêt*, issued upon suitable evidence, by the proper judicial autho-. rity in France, and setting forth the crime imputed to Sucillon.

The case comes within the treaty between the United States

(1) 7 Attorney Generals' Opinions, 285.

and France of November 9, 1843 (8 Stat. at Large, p. 581); and the only question is of the sufficiency of the papers.

It is clear that the *mandat d'arrêt* alone, without the proof on which it is founded, would not suffice to constitute that "evidence of criminality" which the statute requires as the basis of criminality —the certificate of the examining magistrate, upon which alone the final order of extradition is to be granted by the department.

I think, however, that the documents are sufficient to justify the preliminary action of the President, and therefore advise the delivery of the usual warrant to M. Boilleau. That will enable him to secure the person of the alleged fugitive from justice, leaving the ulterior question of his actual extradition to depend on the full evidence of criminality, which, as appears by the despatch of the Minister of Foreign Affairs, is now on its way from France to the United States.

Hon. Wm. L. Marcy, Sec. of State.   C. CUSHING.

(9.) OPINION *of the same Attorney General on the same subject* (1).

Attorney General's Office, October 4, 1855.

SIR,—I beg leave to refer to my communication to you of the 18th of June last, on the subject of the application of the Chargé d'Affaires of France in the case of Sucillon, an alleged fugitive from the justice of that country, and to say that M. Boilleau, having received a new set of papers in the case, suggests, in compliance with the advice of the Counsel for his Government—in which, by letter addressed to me by the District Attorney of the United States, it appears that the latter concurs—a desire to obtain from the State Department a new letter of authorisation to proceed in the case before the proper Commissioner.

I do not think a second document of this nature necessary, because, in my opinion, the first is valid and effective, until its virtue shall have been exhausted by the judicial examination of the party accused, and his release or condemnation; but I conceive it to be the duty of the Government of the United States to afford to other Governments every lawful facility, even though it be a superfluous

(1) 7 Attorney Generals' Opinions, 537.

one, in the execution of our treaty stipulations in this respect, and more especially to aid in removing those obstacles of pure technicality and form, the frequent recurrence of which, under the wretched system of criminal jurisprudence introduced into the United States from Great Britain, tends to render the administration of justice a game of sharps between the injured community on the one side and the criminal violation of the laws on the other side, in which contest chicanery too frequently gets the better of truth; and I therefore most respectfully recommend that new letters be issued in this case upon the papers now presented by M. Boilleau.

The object to be accomplished in all these cases is alike interesting to each Government—namely, the punishment of malefactors, the common enemies of every society. While the United States afford an asylum to all whom political differences at home have driven abroad, it repels malefactors, and is grateful to their Governments for undertaking their pursuit and relieving us from their intrusive presence.

Hon. Wm. L. Marcy, Sec. of State.   C. CUSHING.

(10.) OPINION *of the same Attorney General on the same subject* (1).

Attorney General's Office, February 28, 1856.

SIR,—The question of extradition presented by Mr. Joseph's papers is this:—

By a statute of the State of California, the act of fraudulent breach of trust by private persons is declared to be "grand larceny," and indictable as such. Mr. Joseph seeks the extradition of parties who have been indicted under this statute in the State of California, and who, it is supposed, have taken refuge in France.

It is clear that the act indicted is not embraced within the terms of the convention between the United States and France for the reciprocal surrender of criminals, and which of this class of offences applies only to embezzlement by public depositaries.

But Mr. Joseph supposes that the case may be provided for by the article additional to the above convention, which speaks of

(1) 7 Attorney Generals' Opinions, 643.

"crimes included under the French law, in the words *vol qualifié crime.*" Beyond all doubt he is mistaken in this supposition. The word *crime* in the French "*Code Pénal*" nearly corresponds to our technical term *felony*, while the French word *délit* is nearly equivalent to our law term *misdemeanor.* (Code Pénal, dis. prél., art. 1.) And in order to be qualified as *crime*, a *vol* must be committed with violence or menaces, or it must be committed in a dwelling-house, with circumstances either of night and of escalade, or of "effraction." Such, indeed, is the express tenor of the French duplicate of this additional article.

In truth, the case presented by Mr. Joseph is nothing but the "abus de confiance" of the laws of France. (Code Pénal, liv. iii. tit. 2, s. 2, § 2.)

I do not understand how it happened that, in the English duplicate of this article, this imperfect indication of a class of cases by description in French technical terms, was inserted. A literal translation of the corresponding clause in the French duplicate would have been a much better mode of expressing the undertaking of the United States in the premises.

Hon. Wm. L. Marcy, Sec. of State. C. Cushing.

(11.) Opinion *of the same Attorney General on the same subject* (1).

Attorney General's Office, September 30, 1856.

Sir,—Your communication of yesterday encloses the letter of the Count de Sartiges, envoy of the Emperor of the French, requesting "the extradition of six individuals, who, after having abstracted values for a considerable sum from the chest of the Northern Railroad Company, have taken refuge in the United States."

M. de Sartiges suggests that the administration of the Northern Railroad is an establishment authorized by the French Government, *subventioned* by it, and for these reasons entering into the class of public establishments mentioned in the convention between France and the United States.

(1) 8 Attorney Generals' Opinions, 106.

Permit me to observe, that neither the original convention of extradition (November 9, 1843), nor the supplemental convention, · speaks of "public establishments" (*établissements publics*).
The provision which M. de Sartiges had in his mind is undoubtedly that which speaks of "embezzlement by *public officers*, when the same is punishable with infamous punishment;" or, as it stands in the French copy, "*soustractions commises par les dépositaires publics*, mais seulement dans le cas ou elles seront punies de peines infamantes.*"

I begin with the expression "public officer" of the American copy. We can have no difficulty as to the meaning of the word "office." That, in its primitive sense, signifies *duty* merely; but derivatively, the right of some particular duty belonging to the party as a function.

The only question regards the word "public."

Functionaries of the Government, in all its departments, civil or military, supreme or subordinate, general or provincial, political or municipal, are undoubtedly "public officers."

Does the application extend beyond these persons, and reach the officers of corporate bodies created or authorized by the Government, and to which it contributes funds either as an associate or otherwise?

It cannot be successfully argued that the *nature* of the duties performed by the officers of such corporate bodies decides the question. A banking or railroad company, specially authorized and aided by the Government, subserves public uses; but so does a banking or other company existing spontaneously, or in virtue of general laws, as by the simple association of capitalists disconnected from the Government. Indeed, every merchant, manufacturer, book publisher, trader, and so forth, acts with relation to the whole community; and in that sense his *employés* are just as much public officers as are those of a railroad company.

In truth, the term "public," as applied to officers, must have meaning wholly independent of the question of greater or less *publicity* of the duties discharged, or acts performed; for there - may be a public officer with functions the most reserved, limited, and confidential—as, for example, an officer of the police or customs.

The case before us, it is true, is of corporations, which, in the popular sense of the term, may be called *public;* but they are public in the sense of their use only, not of their constitution. The distinction is indicated by the Court in the case of *Bonaparte* v. *The Camden Railroad Company.* " Generally speaking," says that Court, " public corporations are towns, cities, counties, parishes, existing for public purposes: private corporations are for banks, insurance, *railroads,* canals, bridges, and so forth, where the stock is owned by individuals, though their uses may be public " (1 Baldwin's C. C. Rep. 222).

Nor is the conclusion on this point different, though the State happens to hold a part of the stock, and thus to be a corporator, and, as such, to participate in the management of the company. (*Bank of the United States* v. *Planters' Bank of Georgia,* 9 Wheaton's Rep. 907 : *Turnpike Company* v. *Wallace,* 8 Watts, R., 316 : *Bank of United States* v. *McKenzie,* 2 Brockenbrough's, R., 395.)

I feel constrained to think, therefore, that we must look at " public officers" as meaning persons who discharge the functions of the Government as such, who are appointed by or officially responsible to it, and who thus enter into the organization of the Government.

At the same time it is in the highest degree important to the public interest that officers of these great corporations, who have in charge large sums of money, should not be able to take refuge in foreign countries, enriched by the fruits of the criminal embezzlement of the funds of a bank or railroad company, especially in view of the fact that crimes of less gravity, such as forgery, are generally provided for in treaties of extradition.

Meanwhile, though it would on the whole seem to me, that as the expression " public officers" is used in our law, it implies officers of the Government, it would not follow that the " embezzlement" intended by the treaty must be of the funds of the Government ; that is to say, the word " public," as here employed, refers to the political society as a whole, and in its political capacity (Cruise's Dig. by Greenleaf, vol. iii. 36 n.). Such is the precise force of the word as defined by jurists of the greatest authority (Com. Dig. " Officer E ").

362 CASES AND OPINIONS ON CONSTITUTIONAL LAW.

In the original convention between the United States and France, however, there is, we have seen, a notable difference of language in the two copies. The French has it, public "*dépositaires*," instead of public "officers," as it is in the English.

In France the term "*officier public*" is occasionally employed in the same sense with our term "public officer" (Ex. gr. Code Pénal, No. 172). But the more customary or technical phrase for the idea is "*fonctionnaire public*," or simply "*fonctionnaire*," denoting persons invested with some part of the authority of the State (Block, Dict. de l'Admin. Française, *sub voc.*: Dalloz, Dict. de Jurisp. *sub voc.*).

If the word employed in the French text were "*fonctionnaire public*," it would be necessary to conclude at once that the treaty does not apply to the case before me ; it being clear that an officer of the Northern Railroad Company is not, as such, an officer of the Government.

Can we ascribe any more available force to the term " *dépositaire public ?*" I hesitate to say so. I think the language of the "Code Pénal" leads to the opposite conclusion.

The section of the Code which has for its object to punish the case of the treaty, that is, " Soustractions commises par les dépositaires publics," is a sub-section (Liv. iii. tit. 1, c. 3, s. 2), the title of which is, " De la forfaiture et des crimes et délits des fonctionnaires publics dans l'exercise de leurs fonctions " (Tripier, 836); that is to say, the persons denominated by the law "dépositaires publics" are comprehended in and part of the class "fonctionnaires publics."

To the same effect is the tenor of the articles defining the crime. "Every collector," it says, "every clerk of collector, *public depositary*, or accountable person who shall have embezzled or converted to his own use moneys, public or private, or effects having the place of the same, or documents, title-papers, acts, personal effects, which were in his hands *in virtue of his functions*, shall be subject to the punishment of forced labour for a certain time" (Art. 169). Does not this language import public functionaries? So it appears to me. And although cases have come under my observation of persons comprehended within the penalties of this Act, who are not appointed directly by the Government—

a collector of certain *droits*, for instance—yet such persons are not the less public functionaries, in the understanding of the term in France, as they are also in the United States (Dalloz, tit. Fonc. Pub., art. ii. s. 5, No. 142).

This conclusion is confirmed by the consideration that other articles of the Code Pénal make provisions for the offence of embezzlement by persons not public functionaries, the designation of such an act by the law being "abus de confiance" (tit. ii. c. 2, s. 2, § 2). In conformity with which is the fact, that in the several *mandats d'arrêt* communicated in this case by M. de Sartiges, the offence charged is "abus de confiance," exclusively applicable to *private* depositaries by the very terms of the Code Pénal.

I should have been happy to come to a different result in the present inquiry, but it is not in my power.

Now to apply these conclusions to the case before me.

M. de Sartiges requests the extradition of six persons, two of whom are cashiers of the Northern Railroad Company. I apprehend, for the reasons given, that the articles of the original convention do not meet their case,—that the two cashiers were not either public officers or public depositaries; and certainly the terms of that convention do not reach the other four persons, their associates and confederates in the crime.

But the supplemental article of 1845 provides for the case. It authorizes the extradition, according to the American copy, of persons accused of burglary, "and the corresponding crimes included under the French law in the words *vol qualifié crime;*" which crimes, as more fully described in the French duplicate, constitute one of the forms of the very act committed by all these parties as charged in the *mandats d'arrêt*—namely, "vols commis à l'aide de fausses clefs dans une maison habitée." (See the Code Pénal, tit. ii. c. 2, s. 1.)

The *mandats d'arrêt* do not show whether the crime was committed in the night-time, so as to constitute the crime of burglary by our law; but that is probable; and if not, still it is the case of the "*vol qualifié crime,*" according to the laws of France of one text, and of the "vols commis dans une maison habitée," with the circumstance of technical "effraction" of the other text, and so clearly within both versions of the supplemental convention.

The *demand* of extradition is made in the present case upon sufficient authority—that is, a *mandat d'arrêt* duly certified and duly transmitted through the minister; but other proofs will be needed to procure from the judicial tribunals a decree on which to base an ultimate order of extradition by your department.

Hon. Wm. L. Marcy, Sec. of State.   C. CUSHING.

(12.) OPINION *of the same Attorney General on the same subject* (1).

Attorney General's Office, November 29, 1856.

SIR,—The communication of the French Minister, transmitted with your letter of the 24th, requesting the extradition of one David, presents a point of doubt requiring elucidation.

David is charged as an accomplice in an act of " vol commis la nuit, dans une maison habitée et à l'aide de fausses clefs." That is a crime comprehended in the terms of the supplement of Feb. 4, 1845, to the treaty with France of Nov. 9, 1843, and in that respect the case would justify action on the part of the President.

But, in the *mandat d'arrêt*, David is described as " *commerçant à* New York;" and in the letter of M. de Sartiges, it is only said of him, that " *il parait être actuellement à* New York;" and it is not expressly alleged in the papers that the acts of complicity were committed in France.

If David was guilty of the acts charged while in France, the fact that he was before, and afterwards, and at the time, a merchant or trader at New York would not prevent his extradition even if he were commercially domiciled in this country, nor would it though he had been naturalized here; and of course not if he remained a subject of France.

But it should, in my judgment, appear that the acts of complicity were committed by him while actually in France.

I have requested of M. de Sartiges explanation on this point, and meanwhile return the papers.

Hon. Wm. L. Marcy, Sec. of State.   C. CUSHING.

(1) 8 Attorney Generals' Opinions, 215.

(13.) OPINION *of the same Attorney General on the same subject* (1).

Attorney General's Office, January 10, 1857.

SIR,—I have received your note of this date, referring to me the question of the issue of a mandate for the institution of proceedings in extradition on the demand of the French Government in the case of sundry persons, and among others, Edouard David.

The present demand of extradition in his case, though for a different crime, is, in effect, a renewal of that made by the Count de Sartiges on the 23rd of November, acquiescence in which at that time was postponed, because the *mandat d'arrêt* described him as "*commerçant à* New York," and it did not otherwise appear that the acts of participation in crime with which he was charged had been committed in France.

These difficulties are removed by the communication of Count de Sartiges of the 9th instant.

David, it now appears, is a citizen of France, charged with having participated with Carpentier and the others in a series of acts of forgery which continued through a considerable period of time; and during the progress of these incidents, but after many acts of crime had been consummated, David left France and came to the United States.

The present proofs, therefore, dispose of the doubt previously existing, but suggest a new one, in the fact that David's departure from France had no ostensible or ascertained connection with the forgeries charged, it having been anterior to the detection of the forgeries, and of course to criminal proceedings on the part of the Government. He left France, it appears, *avowedly* for the cause of bankruptcy.

I am satisfied however, on reflection, that this fact is no impediment to the extradition demanded. The language of the convention is,—"persons who . . . shall seek an asylum, or *shall be found* in the territories of the other" (Art. 1). It was the manifest intention of the high contracting parties to provide for just such cases as this; that is, for the case of a crime committed, but not discovered, before the party leaves the country in which it is committed,

(1) 8 Attorney Generals' Opinions, 306

surrender American subjects rests, manslaughter is not one of the offences in respect of which extradition can take place.

A. E. COCKBURN.
RICHARD BETHELL.

(17.) CASE and JOINT OPINION *of the Queen's Advocate,* SIR J. D. HARDING, *and the Attorney and Solicitor General,* SIR FITZROY KELLY *and* SIR HUGH McC. CAIRNS, *on the surrender by the United States Government of a person charged with being accessory before the fact, in this country, to a Murder in France.*

Whitehall, March 12, 1858.

SIR,—I am directed by Mr. Secretary Walpole to request that you will submit the following statement to the Attorney and Solicitor General and the Queen's Advocate, viz. :—

A warrant has been issued by a police magistrate for the apprehension of Thomas Allsop, a British subject, upon the charge of being accessory before the fact, in this country, to the murder, by Orsini and others, Italians, of a Frenchman in Paris. Allsop has escaped to the United States of America ; and it is suggested that his extradition may be demanded of the American Government under the treaty between Her Majesty and the United States made in the year 1842.

And that you will move the Attorney and Solicitor General and the Queen's Advocate to refer to the treaty in question, and to advise whether Allsop is a person charged with the crime of murder committed within the jurisdiction of the British Crown within the meaning of the convention, whose extradition may be properly demanded.

H. WADDINGTON.

Opinion.—We are of opinion that Allsop is not a person charged with the crime of murder committed within the jurisdiction of the British Crown, within the meaning of the treaty of 1842, and that his extradition cannot properly be demanded of the United States under that treaty.

J. D. HARDING.
FITZ ROY KELLY.
H. McC. CAIRNS.

NOTES TO CHAPTER X.

There is a difference of opinion amongst jurists whether extradition, independent of treaty, is a matter of duty or discretion only. If the latter, then the refusal to surrender fugitive criminals is no ground of offence to the State demanding it. The former opinion is maintained by Grotius, Heineccius, Burlamaqui, Vattel, Rutherforth, Schmelzing, and Kent; the latter by Puffendorf (1), Voet, Martens, Klüber, Leyser, Kluit, Saalfeld, Schmaltz, Mittermeier, and Heffter : see Wheaton, s. 115, and Dana's note (73), *Ibid.* 8th edit.

Woolsey says (Internat. Law, s. 79) : "We conclude that there is a limited obligation of nations to assist each other's criminal justice, which only treaties, expressing the views of the parties at the time, can define." Heffter says (Droit Internat. p. 128) : " Early writers, such as Grotius and Vattel, declared extradition obligatory; but the negative is held by modern writers, and has prevailed in practice." Phillimore says (Internat. Law, i. 413) : " The result of the whole consideration of this subject is, that the extradition of criminals is a matter of *comity*, not of *right*, except in the cases of special convention."

The constitutional doctrine in this country is, that the Crown may make treaties with foreign States for the extradition of criminals; but those treaties can only be carried into effect by Act of Parliament, for the executive has no power, without statutory authority, to seize an alien here and deliver him to a foreign power. In a debate in the House of Lords, on February 14, 1842, on the case of the *Creole*, Lord Brougham said : " What right existed, under the municipal law of this country, to seize and deliver up criminals taking refuge there? What right had the Goverment to detain, still less to deliver them up? Whatever right one nation had against another nation—even by treaty, which would give the strongest right—there was, by the municipal law of the nation, no power to execute the obligation of the treaty." Lord Denman said he believed that all Westminster Hall, including the judicial bench, were unanimous in holding the opinion that in this country there was no right of delivering up, indeed no means of securing persons accused of crimes committed in foreign countries. The other Law Lords entirely concurred in this opinion : Hansard's Parl. Deb. vol. lx. pp. 317–327. And the law is the same in the United States : Kent's Com. ss. 39–42, 8th edit.

(1) In his Law of Extradition, p. 3, Mr. Clarke points out that Puffendorf (in the passage to which reference is usually made) does not explicitly deny the right. But in his De Officio Hominis et Civis juxta Legem Naturalem, lib ii. c. 16 (quoted by Mr. Clarke), he says, as to the question whether the harbouring of criminals is a *casus belli* : " Id magis ex peculiari pacto inter vicinos et socios, quam communi aliquâ obligatione provenit," which surely amounts to a denial that extradition is a matter of international *duty*.

It was said by Heath, J., in *Mure* v. *Kaye*, 4 Taunt. 43, that in Lord Loughborough's time the crew of a Dutch ship mastered the vessel, ran away with her, and brought her into Deal; and it was a question whether we could seize them and send them to Holland, and it was held we might. But I cannot understand how this could have been legally done without the authority of an Act of Parliament. In former times, however, there was a laxity of practice in many things which would not be allowed now. In 1749 the Court of Exchequer said: " The Government may send a person to answer for a crime wherever committed, that he may not involve his country, and to prevent reprisals": *East India Company* v. *Campbell*, 1 Ves. Sen. 247. And in an Opinion given by Attorney General Northey (*ante*, p. 36), he said : " As to the question whether her Majesty may not direct Jesuits or Roman priests to be turned out of Maryland, I am of opinion, if the Jesuits or priests be aliens, not made denizens or naturalized, her Majesty may, by law, compel them to depart Maryland." But this, certainly, is not sound law; and the direct contrary was decided by the Supreme Court of Madras, in the case of *R.* v. *Symons* (2 Strange's Madras Reports, 93), where the Court held that the Government of Fort St. George had no inherent power to send two alien Roman Catholic priests, against their will, out of the Presidency. In the able judgment delivered by the Court, they distinctly intimated their opinion that the King, by his prerogative, had no such power; but said : " Admit that he has it, it would not follow that this Government has it. It is not co-ordinate with his Majesty." In the debate on the Alien Bill, in May, 1818, Sir Samuel Romilly, speaking of the alleged prerogative of the Crown in such a case, said : " There was only the opinion of Judge Blackstone for such a doctrine."

In a letter I have received from Sir Frederick Pollock, he says: " When Follett was Solicitor General, and I was Attorney General, one or more slaves got into a boat and rowed to a British vessel of war, where they were received, of course, and where, to use Curran's words, 'their bodies swelled beyond the measure of their chains, which burst from around them,' and they became *free*. The American Government demanded them as *slaves*. The answer was, of course, that we knew nothing of slavery. They then said, ' We demand them as felons who have stolen a boat.' I remembered an old case in Foster's Crown Law, that to constitute *stealing* a thing must be taken *lucri causâ*, and the boat being taken *fugæ causâ*, there was no theft. We answered accordingly, and the matter ended." And in a debate in the House of Lords, on February 14, 1842, Lord Campbell said, that when he was Attorney General a slave had escaped from his master in the State of New York, and got to Canada. To facilitate his escape he rode a horse of his master's for a part of the way, but turned him back on reaching the frontier. The authorities of New York preferred a bill of indictment against him before a New York grand jury for stealing the horse, though it was clear the *animus furandi* was wanting.

The grand jury, however, found a true bill against him for the felony, and he was claimed under the treaty. Lord (then Sir John) Campbell, who was Attorney General, was consulted by our Government, and he gave an opinion that the man ought not to be given up, as no felony had been committed; and the fugitive was not surrendered : Hansard's Parl. Deb. vol. lx. p. 325. The extraordinary similarity between these two cases suggests the idea of some possible confusion between them.

It is an almost universal rule, that no country will surrender political Politi- fugitives (1). At the end of the war with Antiochus, King of Syria, refuge the Romans stipulated with him by treaty for the extradition of Hannibal, but he made his escape: Polyb. xxi. 14, cited by Sir Corne- wall Lewis, in his able work on Foreign Jurisdiction. Admetus, King of the Molossi, refused to surrender Themistocles. In his 3rd Inst., p. 180, Sir Edward Coke says : " It is holden, and so hath been resolved, that divided kingdoms under several kings in league with one another, are sanctuaries for servants or subjects flying for safety from one king- dom to another, and upon demand made by them are not by the laws and liberties of kingdoms to be delivered."

In 1798 Great Britain demanded, and ultimately obtained, from the Senate of the free city of Hamburg, the surrender of four political refugees—Irish rebels, one of whom was Napper Tandy: Marten's Causes Célèbres, iv. 106 (2). At the end of the Hungarian insurrection, in 1849, Russia and Austria demanded from the Sublime Porte the extradition of some Polish subjects of Russia and some Hungarian subjects of Austria, who had taken refuge in the territory of Turkey. The British Government was appealed to, and, in one of his despatches, Lord Palmerston, who was then Foreign Secretary, said : " The laws of hospitality, the dictates of humanity, the general feelings of man- kind, forbid such surrenders; and any independent Government which of its own free will were to make such surrender, would be deservedly and universally stigmatized as degraded and dishonoured :" State Papers, 1849–50, i. 1295. The Turkish Government nobly refused to surrender the fugitives.

Every extradition treaty with a foreign Power now provides that Extrad neither party shall surrender its own subjects. In the treaty of 1843, Treatie between England and France, there were no such restrictive words; but the French Government refused the extradition of the Baron de Vidil, on the ground of his being a Frenchman : see Correspondence respecting the Extradition Treaty, 1866, p. 14. " In the negotiation of treaties stipulating for the extradition of persons accused or con- victed of specified crimes, certain rules are generally followed, and

(1) Woolsey's "Internat. Law," s. 79, cites a passage from the oration of Demo- sthenes against Aristocrates, to show the feeling at Athens : κατὰ τὸν κοινὸν ἀπάντων ἀνθρώπων νόμον, ὃς κεῖται τὸν φεύγοντα δέχεσθαι.

(2) See a full account of the proceedings in that case in " Extradition Treaties," by F. W. Gibbs. London : Ridgway, 1868.

2 B 2

especially by constitutional governments. The principle of these rules
is, that a State should never authorize the extradition of its own
citizens or subjects, or of persons accused or convicted of political or
purely local crimes, or of slight offences, but should confine the practice
to such acts as are by common accord regarded as grave crimes:"
Wheaton's Internat. Law, s. 120.

There are only three extradition treaties, to which Great Britain is a
party, confirmed by Parliament—the first, made August 9, 1842, with
the United States; the second, February 13, 1843, with France (which
has now expired); and the third, April 15, 1863, with Denmark.
The treaty with the United States has effect given to it by statute 6 & 7
Vict. c. 76, and 8 & 9 Vict. c. 120. In *Re Ternan*, 5 Best & Smith,
643, S.C. 33 L. J. (M.C.) 201, where some men who had embarked on
board an American vessel and seized her, taken her to Honduras, and
there abandoned her after selling the cargo, were arrested at Liverpool
by direction of the Secretary of State, at the request of the United
States Minister, it was held by the majority of the Court, on a writ of
habeas corpus being issued, that the case did not come within the terms
of the treaty of extradition with the United States, and the Act 6 &
7 Vict. c. 76, providing for its execution. They thought that the treaty
was intended to apply only to crimes justifiable by one country and
not by the other; that the act of the accused was piracy *jure gentium*;
and that the word " piracy " in the treaty and Act was meant to apply
to acts made piracy by the statute law of America. Cockburn, C.J.,
was of opinion that the treaty and statute were not necessarily confined
to crimes of which the nation making the demand had exclusive jurisdiction. " Within the jurisdiction " did not necessarily mean " exclusive jurisdiction ;" and if it did, it referred to the area over which
the laws of a particular State prevail, and a ship is constructively such
a place, and within the jurisdiction of the State. Piracy, *jure gentium*,
would be committed " within the jurisdiction," not exclusive of the
demanding nation, if committed on board one of its vessels at sea.
The treaty and the Act 6 & 7 Vict. c. 76, include " forgery," and by a
statute of New York, the making of false entries in books of account
with intent to defraud is punishable as " forgery." A person charged
with that offence in New York was arrested here for the purpose of
extradition ; but as the offence was not forgery by the law of England,
or the law of the United States generally, the Court of Queen's Bench
held that it did not come within the Act, and that the prisoner must
be released. Blackburn, J., there said: " Two very high contracting
parties made a treaty on which the Extradition Act is founded; but
we must construe that treaty according to the words used by them
when fairly understood, especially when we find both peoples speaking
the same language. Forgery is one of the crimes specified, and that
must be understood to mean any crimes recognised throughout the
United States and in England as being in the nature of forgery. . . .
The meaning of the New York statute is, the party shall be punished

as if for forgery :" Re Windsor, 6 Best & Smith, 530. See *Anderson's Case,* cited in Dana's note (75) to Wheaton, p. 117, where a slave who had killed a white citizen of Missouri, who tried to arrest him while he was making his escape from that State, and who, having fled to Canada, was demanded by the American authorities, under the treaty, as a person "charged with murder." The Court of Queen's Bench in Canada upheld the requisition, but the Court of Common Pleas thought that the act did not come within the meaning of the treaty, and discharged the prisoner.

In that case the following Opinion was given by the Attorney and Solicitor General, Sir Richard Bethell and Sir William Atherton, on the 28th of March, 1861 : "Upon the assumption that the act proved to have been committed by the fugitive slave Anderson, in the State of Missouri, in killing Digges under the circumstances stated, amounted to murder by the law of Missouri, but would not have amounted to murder if it had been committed in Canada, we are of opinion that the Canadian Government is not bound by the 10th Article of the treaty of Washington (9th of August, 1842) to surrender Anderson, though demanded by the American Government with all due formalities, under the provisions of the treaty. The plain meaning of the article appears to us to be, that the facts proved in support of the particular charge, whatever its nature, must be such facts as, if they had occurred in the harbouring State, would, by the law of that State, have warranted the apprehension and commitment of the perpetrator to take his trial on such charge :" see *Re Anderson,* 30 L. J. (Q.B.) 129.

Under the statute 6 & 7 Vict. c. 75, for giving effect to the extradition treaty with France, it was held that a warrant to detain a party accused of the crime of fraudulent bankruptcy committed in France, "until he be discharged by due course of law," on the requisition of an agent of the King of the French, was insufficient, and the person imprisoned under it was entitled to his discharge on habeas corpus. Lord Denman, C.J., there said : "We are asked to remand the prisoner on our own authority as charged with a crime; but we have nothing of the crime, unless as it is brought before us by the warrant; or, I should rather say, we have no authority of the kind in such a case. If we could act in the manner suggested, the statute would have been unnecessary. The prisoner must be discharged :" *Ex parte Besset,* 6 Q. B. 481, 485. Wightman, J., said in that case : "Where a man is committed for any crime, at common law or by statute, for which he is punishable by indictment, he is to be committed till discharged by due course of law; but when it is in pursuance of a special authority, the terms of the commitment must be special, and exactly pursue that authority :" see *Mash's Case,* 2 W. Bl. 805.

In a case submitted to the Queen's Advocate (Dr. Twiss), and myself, in 1867, on the question whether a British subject who had committed an offence (alleged to come within the scope of the extradition treaty between Her Majesty and the United States in 1842, and the statute

6 & 7 Vict. c. 76) on board an American ship on the high seas, and
who had landed in Calcutta, ought to be given up on a demand of the
consul of the United States, we were of opinion that, as a British
court of justice would take cognizance of the offence by reason of the
nationality of the offender, the case was not within the scope of the
treaty or the Act. See Statute 30 & 31 Vict. c. 124, s. 11, which
provides that "if any British subject commits any crime or offence on
board any British ship, or on board any foreign ship to which he does
not belong, any court of justice in Her Majesty's dominions which
would have had cognizance of such a crime or offence, if committed on
board a British ship within the limits of the ordinary jurisdiction of
such court, shall have jurisdiction to hear and determine the case as if
the said crime or offence had been committed as last aforesaid."

By the treaty with China of the 8th of October, 1843, it is provided
that Chinese criminals flying to any of the five ports thrown open to
British trade shall be handed over to the Chinese authorities, and
that British subjects flying into Chinese territory shall be handed
over to the nearest British consular officer.

See on the subject of this note, Clarke's Law of Extradition (London,
1867).

CHAPTER XI.

ON APPEALS FROM THE COLONIES.

(1.) CASE *and* OPINION *of the Attorney General,* SIR EDWARD NORTHEY, *on the right of Appeal from the Colonial Courts.* 1713.

SIR,—By order of the Lords Commissioners for Trade t d Plantations, I send you the enclosed extract of a letter m Mr. Lowther, Governor of Barbadoes, upon consideration whereof their Lordships desire your opinion, as soon as may be, upon this following *quære,* viz. :

Quære.—Whether an appeal can, or ought to be brought, from the Court of Exchequer in Barbadoes to the Governor and Council there, as a Court of Chancery ?

WM. POPPLE.

Opinion.—I am of opinion the Governor, by virtue of his instructions, is to admit appeals as well from the Court of Exchequer as from other Courts in the island of Barbadoes to the Governor and Council there, and this plainly was the intent of the Governor's instructions, no appeal being directed to be allowed from any Court to her Majesty but from the Court of Chancery, which would have been provided for, to have been from the Court of Exchequer to her Majesty, if an appeal had not been intended to be first in the Chancery.

February 16, 1713.   EDW. NORTHEY.

(2.) OPINION *of the same Lawyer, on a question of Appeal.* 1717.

To the Right Honourable the Lords Commissioners for Trade and Plantations.

MY LORDS,—In obedience to your Lordships' commands, signified to me by Mr. Popple, I have considered of the petition of William

Cockburn, Esq., whereby he represents to your Lordships that he, being appointed by the Lord Archibald Hamilton, late Governor of Jamaica, to exercise the office of Secretary and Clerk of the Enrolment there (Mr. Page, who was the deputy of Mr. Congreve, who had those offices by patent, voluntarily absenting himself from that island), did execute the same from the 9th of March till the 6th of August, 1716, when he was removed by Mr. Haywood, the succeeding Governor of the said plantation; and thereupon a bill was brought against the petitioner by Mr. Beckford, who was appointed by the said Mr. Congreve to be his deputy, upon the death or absence of the said Mr. Page, and a decree was given against him in Jamaica for more money, as the profits of the said office, than he received during the time that he executed the same, without making any allowance to him for the execution of the said offices; against which decree the Governor cannot, by his instructions, allow an appeal, the demand being under the value of five hundred pounds sterling: humbly praying that his Majesty would be pleased, for the relief of the petitioner, to give directions for re-hearing of his cause, and the doing therein what to justice shall appertain.

And I do most humbly certify your Lordships, that the petition is unadvisedly framed, for that his Majesty cannot, by law, give a direction to any Court to re-hear any cause depending therein; but re-hearings are granted, or denied, by Courts of Equity, on petition of the parties grieved, to such Court as shall be judged proper.

And as to the instructions given to the Governor mentioned in the petition, whereby he is restrained from allowing an appeal in any case under the value of £500 sterling, that does restrain the Governor only from granting of appeals under that value, notwithstanding which, it is in his Majesty's power, upon a petition, to allow an appeal in cases of any value where he shall think fit, and such appeals have been often allowed by his Majesty; but I think the reference to your Lordships in that matter is improper, for petitions for appeal from decrees given in the Plantations have been always referred to a Committee of the Council for hearing the causes of the Plantations, and on their report that it is proper to allow the appeal prayed for, his Majesty in Council has usually allowed the same, and not in any other manner. I have perused the decree, and think the petitioner has great hardship therein, and that upon a proper application he may obtain an appeal in that cause.

December 19, 1717.   EDW. NORTHEY.

(3.) OPINION *of the Attorney General,* SIR EDWARD NORTHEY, *on appeals from the Admiralty Courts in the Colonies.* 1704.

To the Right Honourable the Lords Commissioners for Trade and Plantations.

MAY IT PLEASE YOUR LORDSHIPS,—In obedience to your Lordships' commands, signified to me by Mr. Popple, I have considered of the annexed petition of Peter Van Ball, praying the liberty of appeal to Her Majesty in Council from a sentence pronounced in the Admiralty Court of Nevis, and am of opinion, if that Court was held under the late King's commission for governing the Leeward Islands, as the petitioner takes it to be, alleging that the President and Council had power only to appoint, but not to sit themselves as a Court of Admiralty ; or if the sentence was given by the President and Council of Nevis, as the Council there in both cases, the appeal ought to be to her Majesty in Council; but if the President and Council held a Court of Admiralty, by authority derived from the Admiralty of England, the appeal is to be to the Court of Admiralty in England; and so it was lately determined by her Majesty in Council.

May 23, 1704.   EDW. NORTHEY.

(4.) OPINION *of the King's Advocate,* SIR NATHANIEL LLOYD, *on the same subject.* 1715.

MY LORDS,—In further obedience about the *Eagle* brigantine, condemned at New York, and appealed upon hither: I find that the appellants have thought fit to drop such appeal, and they proceed no further ; so the condemnation stands. Not but that the appellants might have re-heard the cause here, had they thought fit.

For by law appeals do lie from the Admiralty Courts in the Plantations to the Lord High Admiral of Great Britain, in the High Court of Admiralty in England, in common maritime causes, as in causes of prize property, as taken *jure belli*, to the Lords of the Council, as Commissioners for Appeals in causes of prize by the American Act.

March 13, 1715.   NATH. LLOYD.

NOTES TO CHAPTER XI.

peals from a Colonies civil cases. It is the settled prerogative of the Crown to receive appeals in all colonial cases : *per cur. Re Lord Bishop of Natal*, 3 Moore, P. C. (N. S.) 156; and see stat. 25 Hen. 8, c. 19, s. 4. The right of appeal is one of the rights of the subject with which the Crown, by its mere prerogative, cannot interfere; for, as was said in *Cuvillier* v. *Aylwin*, 2 Knapp, 78, the Crown has no power to deprive the subject of any of his rights; but the Crown, acting with the other branches of the Legislature, has the power of depriving any of its subjects in any of the countries under its dominion of any of his rights.

Appeals to Her Majesty in Council, and by her referred to the Judicial Committee of the Privy Council, are regulated by stat. 3 & 4, Will. 4, c. 41; and by s. 4 it is enacted that it shall be lawful for the Crown to refer to the Judicial Committee any matters whatsoever as Her Majesty shall think fit. See upon this section *Re the Nawab of Surat*, 5 Moore, Ind. App. 499 : see also stat. 6 & 7 Vict. c. 38 ; 7 & 8 Vict. c. 69, s. 9 ; 14 & 15 Vict. c. 83, ss. 15–16 ; and Rules and Regulations made by Order in Council, June 13, 1853. In *R.* v. *Suddis*, 1 East, 314, Lord Kenyon, C.J., said : " It has always been considered that the judges in our foreign possessions abroad are not bound by the rules of proceeding in our courts here. Their laws are often altogether distinct from our own. Such is the case in India and other places. On appeals to the Privy Council from our colonies, no formal objections are attended to, if the substance of the matter, or the *corpus delicti*, sufficiently appear to enable them to get at the truth and justice of the case." And *per* Lord Tenterden, C.J., in *Henley* v. *Soper*, 8 B. & C. 20 : " In considering the proceedings of a colonial court, we must look at the substance and not at the form, according to the rule adopted by the Privy Council. If we, sitting in England, were to require in the proceedings of foreign courts all the accuracy for which we look in our own, hardly any of their judgments would stand."

Appeals were granted where judgments had been obtained against the Crown in Victoria, in several actions in the nature of Petitions of Right, without imposing terms or requiring security for costs : *Re Attorney General of Victoria*, L. R. 1 P. C. 147.

peals in criminal cases. In *The Queen* v. *Eduljee Byramjee*, 3 Moore, Ind. App. 481, the Court said that not only in England, but throughout the dominions of the Crown, no right of appeal in felonies has ever existed. " Nor are we aware that in any one single instance the Crown has ever, by the exercise of its prerogative, granted leave to appeal in any such case." But it may now be considered as settled law, that an appeal to the Queen in Council from the colonies does lie in all criminal cases. "It seems undeniable that in all cases, criminal as well as civil, arising in places from which an appeal would lie, and where, either by the terms of a charter or statute, the authority has not been parted with, it is the inherent prerogative, right, and, on all proper occasions, the duty of the Queen in Council to exercise an appellate jurisdiction, with a view not only to insure, so far as may be, the due administration of justice in the individual case, but also to preserve the due course of procedure generally :" *R.* v. *Bertrand,* L. R. 1 P. C. 530. For instances of appeals in criminal cases, see *Ames and Others,* 3 Moore, P. C. 409 ; *The Queen* v. *Mookerjee,* 1 Moore, P. C. (N.S.) 272 ; *Falkland Islands* v. *The Queen, Ib.* 299 ; *Levien* v. *The Queen,* L. R. 1 P. C. 536 ; *The Queen* v. *Murphy,* L. R. 2 P. C. 35.

Under the several charters erecting supreme courts of judicature in the East Indies, it was provided that in all indictments, informations, and criminal suits and causes, the supreme courts respectively should "have the full and absolute power and authority to allow or deny" appeals; and it was decided by the Judicial Committee that where the Supreme Court of Bombay refused to grant leave to appeal in a case of conviction for felony, there was no power in the Crown to grant an appeal: *The Queen* v. *Alloo Paroo,* 3 Moore, Ind. App. 488. The charter in that case had been granted under the authority of the stat. 4 Geo. 4, c. 71, s. 7, and Lord Brougham, in delivering the judgment of the Court, said : " The Crown may abandon a prerogative, however high and essential to public justice and valuable to the subject, if it is authorized by statute to abandon it; and here it is in the execution of a power conferred by statute that this abandonment, if any abandonment has been made, has taken place." This had reference to what is said by the reporter in *Christian* v. *Cowen,* 1 P. Wms. 329—namely, that even if there be express words in a charter excluding the right of the subject to appeal, these words shall not be held to deprive him of his right. To this doctrine the Judicial Committee refused to assent, citing *Ash* v. *Bogle,* 1 Vern. 367 ; but, for the reason above given, they said that even if it were true it did not apply to the case before them.

CHAPTER XII.

ON THE REVOCATION OF CHARTERS.

(1.) OPINION *of Lord Chief Justice* HOLT, *that the King might appoint a Governor of Maryland, in a case of necessity, notwithstanding an existing Charter by which Lord Baltimore was appointed Governor.* 1690 (1).

To the Marquis of Carmarthen, President of the Council.

MY LORD,—I think it had been better if an inquisition had been taken, and the forfeiture committed by the Lord Baltimore had been therein found, before any grant be made to a new Governor; yet, since there is none, and it being in a case of necessity, I think the King may, by his commission, constitute a Governor, whose authority will be legal, though he must be responsible to Lord Baltimore for the profits (2). If an agreement can be made with Lord Baltimore, it will be convenient and easy for the Governor that the King shall appoint. An inquisition may at any time be taken, if the forfeiture be not pardoned, of which there is some doubt.

Serjeants' Inn, June 3, 1690.   J. HOLT.

(1) The Privy Council, on the 21st of August, 1690, issued an order, "That the Attorney General do forthwith proceed, by *scire facias*, against the charter of Lord Baltimore, the Proprietor of Maryland, in order to vacate the same." On the 5th of February, 1690-1, Lord Baltimore was heard, by counsel, against the King's appointment of a Governor for Maryland. On the 12th of February, 1690-1, there issued an Order of Council that the draft by a commission, which had been prepared by the Attorney General and approved by Lord Chief Justice Holt, constituting Lionel Copley Governor-in-Chief of Maryland, be transmitted to Lord Sydney, the Secretary of State, for the Queen's signature : note in "Chalmers's Opinions," i. 29.

(2) This cannot be considered sound law. The Crown had no power to revoke Lord Baltimore's charter, except upon or after an inquisition.

(2.) JOINT OPINION *of the Attorney and Solicitor General,*
SIR EDWARD NORTHEY *and* SIR SIMON HARCOURT, *that the*
Queen may resume a Government under a Royal Charter that
had been abused.

MAY IT PLEASE YOUR MAJESTY,—In humble obedience to your
Majesty's Order in Council, we have considered of the annexed extract of a representation from the Lords Commissioners of Trade
and Plantations, upon letters received from Colonel Dudley, your
Majesty's Governor of Massachusetts Bay and New Hampshire,
complaining of great inconveniences happening to him in that
government, from disorders in Rhode Island, for want of good
government there; and also upon letters received from the Lord
Cornbury, your Majesty's Governor of New York, complaining of
like inconveniences from disorders in the colony of Connecticut,
that and Rhode Island being charter Governments; and also of the
report of the Attorney and Solicitor General of the late King
William and Queen Mary, made in July, 1694: and we do concur
with them in their opinions therein mentioned, that upon an extraordinary exigency happening through the default or neglect of a
proprietor, or of those appointed by him, or their inability to protect or defend the province under their government, and the
inhabitants thereof, in times of war or imminent danger, your
Majesty may constitute a Governor of such province or colony, as
well for the civil as military part of government, and for the protection and preservation thereof, and of your Majesty's subjects
there, with this addition only, that as to the civil government, such
Governor is not to alter any of the rules of propriety, or methods
of proceedings in civil causes, established pursuant to the charters
granted, whereby the proprietors of those colonies are incorporated;
on perusal of which charters, we do not find any clauses that can
exclude your Majesty (who has a right to govern all your subjects)
from naming a Governor on your Majesty's behalf for those colonies
at all times.

EDW. NORTHEY.
SIM. HARCOURT.

(3.) OPINION *of the Attorney General*, SIR EDWARD NORTHEY, *on the Queen's prerogative to receive a surrender of the Pennsylvania Charter.* 1712.

To the Right Hon. Robert, Earl of Oxford and Earl Mortimer, Lord High Treasurer of Great Britain.

MAY IT PLEASE YOUR LORDSHIP,—In obedience to your Lordship's commands, signified to me by Mr. Harley, I have considered the report of the Lords Commissioners of Trade and Plantations upon the memorial of William Penn, Esq., Proprietor and Governor of Pennsylvania, proposing to surrender to her Majesty the powers of government wherewith he is invested; and I have also perused the grant of that government to him by King Charles II., with other deeds relating to Mr. Penn's title thereto, and to the government of the tract of land on Delaware River and Bay, now called the town or colony of Newcastle, alias Delaware, and he has made out to me his title thereto; and, according to your Lordship's commands, I have prepared a draft of a surrender of those powers from Mr. Penn and others, in whom the legal estate is, under him, to her Majesty, reserving to Mr. Penn his right to the soil of those colonies. In the letters patent of King Charles II. there are granted to Mr. Penn all mines of gold and silver in Pennsylvania, which, he says, he cannot surrender to the Crown, having made several grants thereof to several people which are not in his power, and therefore the surrender of them is not in the draft prepared, although, if it be insisted on, he may surrender and assign what is not granted.

There is, likewise, an instrument prepared for her Majesty's accepting the said surrender; and in it Mr. Penn is an humble suitor to her Majesty, that she would be pleased thereby to declare that she will take the people of his persuasion, as well as the other inhabitants of those colonies, in her Majesty's protection. I do not observe that there is any provision made for the support of the government there, by any act of Assembly or otherwise, without which the government will be a charge to her Majesty; but the Council of Trade and Plantations, in their report, have represented that Mr. Penn affirms he does not doubt but the Assembly will readily make provision for the same, and he acquaints me that the fines and forfeitures there, which have been and may be applied hereto, are considerable.

February 25, 1711-12.   EDW. NORTHEY.

(4.) CASE *and* OPINION *of the Attorney General,* SIR EDWARD NORTHEY, *on the surrender of the Bahama Charter.* 1717.

Whitehall, December 10, 1717.

SIR,—The Lords Commissioners for Trade and Plantations command me to remind you of my letter of the 21st of the last month, which was to acquaint you that there being six proprietors of the Bahama Islands, whereof two are minors, the other four have executed a deed of surrender of their right of government to his Majesty, and to desire your immediate opinion whether a surrender executed by four out of six, as aforesaid, be valid and effectual.

WM. POPPLE.

Opinion.—I am of opinion that a surrender by four where six are seised can only convey and extinguish thereby four parts in six of what the parties enjoyed.   However, his Majesty being entitled under four, to four parts of the government, which is entire, he may execute the whole.   And I do not know that the other two can be co-partners with his Majesty in governing, for which reason, and that there might not be an extinguishment by surrender, I apprehend, as this case is, a grant to the Crown of the four parts might be more proper.

December 10, 1717.   EDW. NORTHEY.

(5.) JOINT OPINION *of the Attorney and Solicitor General,* SIR FREDERICK POLLOCK *and* SIR WILLIAM FOLLETT, *on a proposed surrender of the Charter of the University of King's College, in New Brunswick, and the grant of an amended Charter.*

Temple, January 19, 1842.

MY LORD,—On the 11th of December last, we received a letter from Mr. Stephen, wherein he was pleased to state that the Council of the University of King's College, at Fredericton, in the province of New Brunswick, are desirous of obtaining a modification of the charter from the Crown, under which it is incorporated, with a view to render the institution more acceptable to the inhabitants, and thereby to increase its usefulness.

That Her Majesty's government are willing to consent to the modification, and, as a preliminary to granting an amended charter, require the surrender of that now held by the college.

Doubts, however, are entertained by Her Majesty's law officers in the province as to the competency of the corporation to make such surrender, and also as to the mode in which the change desired can be lawfully effected.

Mr. Stephen further stated he had been directed by your Lordship to transmit to us a copy of the college charter, together with a copy of the opinion delivered by the Attorney and Solicitor General of New Brunswick; and he requested that we would take the subject into our consideration, and report to your Lordship our opinion whether it is competent to the corporation of the college to surrender their present charter and accept a new one; if not, in what manner the desired alteration in the constitution of the college can be lawfully effected.

In obedience to your Lordship's commands, we have perused the papers mentioned in Mr. Stephen's letter, and have fully considered the whole matter referred to us; and we have now the honour to report to your Lordship, that we do not think it necessary, in order to effect the intended alterations in the constitution of the college, that its present charter should be surrendered as a preliminary to the granting of an amended charter; and we think there are objections to such a course. We would recommend that a new charter should be granted to the college, containing the proposed modifications of the existing charter, and this new charter, if accepted by the college, will become the governing one of the corporation. We think that this new charter should recite the grant of the former, and that the Crown, considering it for the advantage of the institution, has thought fit to grant another charter to the college, and the charter should then set out all the regulations which it may be deemed expedient to provide for the government of the institution.

To the Right Hon. Lord Stanley,   FRED. POLLOCK.
&c.   &c.   &c.   W. W. FOLLETT.

(6.) CASE and JOINT OPINION *of the Attorney and Solicitor General,* SIR FREDERICK THESIGER *and* SIR FITZROY KELLY, *as to the revocation of a Royal Warrant. granting the property of a deceased person which had devolved upon the Crown.* 1852.

Case.—By warrant, under the Royal sign-manual, dated the 31st of January, 1851, reciting (*inter alia*) that by virtue of a Royal Warrant, dated the 25th of July, 1848, letters of administration (with will annexed) of the goods, chattels, and credits of A. N., a spinster, and a bastard, deceased, had been granted to George Maule, Esq., as nominee, and for the use and benefit of Her Majesty, in the Prerogative Court of Canterbury, and that a memorial had been presented to the Commissioners of the Treasury, by C. N., praying, under the circumstances set forth in the said memorial, that a certain share of the said effects might be granted to the memorialist for the use and benefit of her minor grandchildren then residing with her, and under her care and charge, it was made known that Her Majesty did authorize and require the said George Maule to dispose of certain sums of stock, the property of the deceased, and pay over a portion of the proceeds to the said C. N., to be applied by her for the benefit of her grand-children. The payment, however, of the money to C. N. was suspended, owing to an application on behalf of the mother of the said minor children; and there being reason to believe that the facts set forth in the memorial of C. N. were not correctly stated, an application was made to the Lords of the Treasury to revoke the former grant to her, and make a new grant. A doubt was raised whether it was competent to the Crown to revoke the warrant, and also whether, as Mr. Maule had died in the interval, the duty and power of executing the warrant devolved, under the statute 15 Vict. c. 3, s. 3 (relating to the case of letters of administration granted to Mr. Maule, Solicitor of the Treasury, as nominee of Her Majesty), upon the Solicitor of the Treasury for the time being, or whether the death of the nominee named in the first warrant did not render a new warrant necessary.

Opinion.—1. We are of opinion that, upon the assumption suggested, it is competent to Her Majesty to revoke the former grant, and make a new one, without *scire facias* or any other proceeding.

2 o

2. We think that if the former warrant was still in force and unrevoked, it could not be executed by the successor of Mr. Maule, but that a new warrant would be necessary. It is certainly desirable that such warrants in future should be made in favour of the Solicitor of the Treasury and his successors.

FRED. THESIGER.

Temple, September 29, 1852.   FitzRoy KELLY.

(7.) CASE and JOINT OPINION *of the Attorney and Solicitor General, SIR A. E. COCKBURN and SIR RICHARD BETHELL, as to power of the Crown to revoke or accept the Surrender of a Grant of separate Quarter Sessions, made under the Municipal Corporations Act, 5 & 6 Will. 4, c. 76.*   1856.

Case.—The Town Council of Newcastle-under-Lyme, being desirous that a separate Court of Quarter Sessions should no longer be holden in and for that borough, the Law Officers were asked to give their opinion whether the Crown is empowered to revoke or accept a surrender of a grant of separate Quarter Sessions, which has been made under the Municipal Corporations Act (5 & 6 Will. 4, c. 76, s. 103).

Opinion.—It seems to us clear that the Crown has not the power in question. The Crown cannot, by virtue of the prerogative, abrogate courts of justice established by law. *À fortiori*, when a court is established by virtue of a power conferred by Act of Parliament, which conveys no power to abrogate, the Crown, having exercised, has exhausted its power, and cannot annul the Court it has once created.

Besides, the offices of Recorder and Clerk of the Peace, being during good behaviour, are freehold offices, and cannot be taken away by the revocation of the grant of the Court.

We are of opinion that the question put to us must be answered in the negative.

A. E. COCKBURN.

September 19, 1856.   R. BETHELL.

NOTES TO CHAPTER XII.

In *Legat's Case*, 10 Co. 113 a, it was resolved that the Crown may avoid its grant made upon a false insinuation or suggestion, and such letters patent by judgment of law shall be cancelled. "The King has an undoubted right to repeal a patent wherein he is deceived or his subjects prejudiced, and that by *scire facias :*" *R.* v. *Butler*, 3 Lev. 221. The power of the Crown to call back its grants when made under mistake is not like any right possessed by individuals; for when it has been deceived the grant may be recalled, notwithstanding any derivative title depending upon it; and those who have deceived it must bear the consequences. So laid down by Sir Thomas Plumer, M.R., in *Cumming* v. *Forrester*, 2 Jac. & W. 342 : see Com. Dig. *Grant*, G. 8; Vin. Abr. *Prerog.* O b.

All charters or grants of the Crown may be repealed or revoked when they are contrary to law, or uncertain, or injurious to the rights and interests of third persons; and the appropriate process for the purpose is by writ of *scire facias*. And if the grant or charter is to the prejudice of any person, he is entitled, as of right, to the protection of this remedy : *The Queen* v. *Hughes*, L. R. 1 P. C. 87. The writ of *scire facias*, to repeal or revoke grants or charters of the Crown, is a prerogative judicial writ which must be founded upon a record. These Crown grants and charters under the great seal are always sealed in the Petty Bag Office, and enrolled in the Court of Chancery, where they become records : *Ibid.* "To every Crown grant there is annexed by the common law an implied condition that it may be repealed by *scire facias* by the Crown, or by a subject grieved using the prerogative of the Crown upon the *fiat* of the Attorney General :" *per* Jervis, C.J., in *Eastern Archipelago Company* v. *The Queen*, 2 E. & B. 914.

It deserves notice that the Act for the dissolution of the greater monasteries in 1539, 31 Hen. 8, c. 13, recites that the abbots, priors, abbesses, and prioresses had, "of their own free and voluntary minds, good-wills, and assents, without constraint, co-action, or compulsion," granted their monasteries, abbeys, and priories to the King, and had renounced, left, and forsaken the same. The statement was false, but it served to veil the rapacity of the Crown.

In the reign of Charles II. an information in the nature of a *quo warranto* was exhibited in the King's Bench, for the purpose of having it declared that the charters of the city of London had been forfeited, and judgment was given for the Crown : *R.* v. *The City of London*, 8 State Tr. 1039. But this judgment was declared void by statute 2 Will. & M. c. 8. See the case of *R.* v. *Amery*, 2 T. R. 515, where it was decided that when the charter of a corporation has been forfeited by a judgment of seizure *quousque*, and a new charter granted creating a new

2 C 2

388 CASES AND OPINIONS ON CONSTITUTIONAL LAW.

body, a subsequent charter of restoration or restitution is void. "For though it be competent to the Crown to pardon a forfeiture and to grant restitution, that can only be done where things remain *in statu quo*, but not so as to affect legal rights properly vested in third persons." In the same case it was also held that the granting of a new charter inconsistent with the former amounts to a declaration on record that the Crown elects to take advantage of a forfeiture incurred under the old charter. The judgment, however, in this case was reversed in the House of Lords : 4 T. R. 122 ; but it is not stated on what grounds, nor how far the above propositions were dissented from or agreed to.

In 1820 the North-West Company of Canada presented a petition to the Privy Council, praying that a *scire facias* might be issued for repealing the letters patent granted to the Hudson's Bay Company, and it was referred to the Attorney and Solicitor General to consider it, and report their opinion thereon. The Hudson's Bay Company opposed it, and the application for the *scire facias* being withdrawn, no report was made on the subject by the Law Officers : M. S. Council Register, 1820–1821. By statute 31 & 32 Vict. c. 105, the Crown is empowered to accept a surrender of the charter of the Hudson's Bay Company.

The province of Nova Scotia was ceded by France to the Crown of England by the Treaty of Utrecht. The island of Cape Breton was, with Canada and other French colonies in America, ceded by France to England in 1763. In that year the Crown, by proclamation, annexed Cape Breton to the Government of Nova Scotia. In 1784 Nova Scotia was divided into two governments, New Brunswick and Nova Scotia, and Cape Breton was included in Nova Scotia; but a Lieutenant-Governor was appointed for that island, whose commission gave him the same powers as expressed in the commission of the Lieutenant-Governor "of the province of Nova Scotia, and the islands of St. John and Cape Breton, then and for the time being." The commission or letters patent of the Governor of Nova Scotia spoke of "our respective councils and assemblies of our province of Nova Scotia and our islands of St. John and Cape Breton under your Government ;" and, without expressly authorizing him, implied that he had the power to call an Assembly of Cape Breton. A Council was formed, but no General Assembly was ever convened for Cape Breton. In 1820 a new commission was given to the Governor of Nova Scotia, and that Government was described "as including the island of Cape Breton (which we do expressly direct and declare shall in future form part of our said province of Nova Scotia)," and no mention was made of a Council or Assembly, or any separate legislature for Cape Breton. The Governor of Nova Scotia, in accordance with his instructions, issued a proclamation declaring Cape Breton to be a county of the province of Nova Scotia, to be represented by two members in the General Assembly of Nova Scotia, and dissolving the Council of the island.

Against this annexation of Cape Breton and dissolution of the Council certain of the inhabitants of the island petitioned the Queen in Council; and the Judicial Committee, having had the petition referred to them, confined to the question whether the inhabitants of Cape Breton were by law entitled to the Constitution purporting to be granted to them by the letters patent of 1784, reported to Her Majesty their opinion that the inhabitants were not so entitled: *Re The Island of Cape Breton*, 5 Moore, P. C. 259.

CHAPTER XIII.

THE CHANNEL ISLANDS.

JOINT OPINION *of the Attorney and Solicitor General*, SIR
DUDLEY RYDER *and* SIR JOHN STRANGE, *on the King's
authority over Guernsey and Jersey.* 1737.

To the Right Honourable the Lords of the Committee of Council
for the Affairs of Guernsey and Jersey.

MAY IT PLEASE YOUR LORDSHIPS,—In obedience to your Lordships' order of the 21st of July, 1736, hereunto annexed, whereby
your Lordships were pleased to refer the memorial and papers
hereunto annexed, to his Majesty's late Attorney and Solicitor
General, to consider the same and report their opinion to your
Lordships upon the general case of extents from the Exchequer,
and of the process from the Courts of King's Bench, how the same
can be legally executed in the islands of Guernsey and Jersey,
and if not, what other remedy is left to the Crown for the recovery
of their debts in those islands—

We have considered of the matters so referred, and are humbly
of opinion, that no writ of extent out of his Majesty's Court of
Exchequer here, nor any process from the Court of King's Bench,
can, as the laws of those islands now stand, be executed there, they
being governed by laws of their own, subject to his Majesty's Order
in Council, and the subjects there are not amenable to the courts
here.

And we are of opinion, the only remedy the Crown has for the
recovery of their debts in those islands, upon the foot of the present
law, is by proceeding upon proper suits, to be instituted in the
courts there, according to the course of those courts, and sending
thither the proper evidence of the debt, unless his Majesty shall

think fit to interpose in his legislative capacity, and by an Order in Council make a new law concerning the method of recovering the Crown debts against the inhabitants there.

By this means his Majesty may, if he think fit, give such force to extents and other processes out of the courts here, as he shall judge convenient; but whether the single instance of inconvenience to the Crown, in the case of Carey's debt, mentioned in the memorial, is a sufficient ground to make any alteration in the laws of those islands, is humbly submitted.

D. RYDER.

August 12, 1737.   J. STRANGE.

NOTES TO CHAPTER XIII.

There are many cases reported in Knapp and Moore of appeals from the Channel Islands which can be easily found by referring to the indexes of those volumes; but I propose in this note merely to explain a few points relating to their history and constitution.

The islands of Jersey, Guernsey, Alderney, and Sark originally formed part of the Duchy of Neustria, or Normandy, which was ceded in the year 911 by Charles IV. to Rollo the Norman, as a fief of the Crown of France. From Rollo they descended, along with Normandy, to William the Conqueror. At his death, his second son, William II., succeeded to the throne of England; but the eldest son, Robert, obtained Normandy and the Channel Islands. Henry I. made war upon Duke Robert, and having conquered him, united Normandy and the islands to England. The Normans afterwards revolted under King John, A.D. 1204, and the islanders seem to have followed their example, although this is denied by some writers. John failed to reconquer Normandy, but the islands were recovered, and John formed them into one bailiwick and granted them a charter. Afterwards, under Edward I., and more fully under Henry VII., they were formed into two bailiwicks. The first Order in Council, enacting laws in the island of Jersey, is said to have been issued in 1571. Coke, speaking of Jersey and Guernsey, says: "Those isles are no parcel of the realm of England, but several dominions enjoyed by several titles, governed by several laws:" *Calvin's Case*, 7 Co. 21 a; and see Hale, Hist. Com. Law, 269 (6th edit.).

The Royal Court of Jersey is composed of a bailiff appointed by the Crown, and twelve jurats or justices, who are elected for life by the people, and occupy the double character of judges and political representatives of the people in the States.

The States are composed of the bailiff, the twelve rectors of the

392 CASES AND OPINIONS ON CONSTITUTIONAL LAW.

twelve parishes, the twelve jurats elected for life by the people, and the twelve constables of the parishes, who are elected by the people for three years.

The Lieutenant-Governor is appointed by the Crown on the recommendation of the Commander-in-Chief.

The power of the States to legislate is strictly subordinate to the Royal authority. "If the States should think it expedient to make the offence of burglary a capital offence, as it is by the law of England [or rather was, at that time], they may, if they be so advised, propose a new law for your Majesty's consideration, to be enacted and confirmed by your Royal sanction, after your Majesty shall have signified your allowance to have such a law enacted :" Order in Council, June 23, 1790.

A few years ago the States denied the right of the Queen in Council to legislate for the island without consulting the States, and they relied principally upon the ordinances of the Commissioners, Pyne and Napper, who were sent by Queen Elizabeth to Jersey in 1591, upon the Order in Council of the 28th of March, 1776, upon which the Jersey Code of Laws is founded, and the usage which has prevailed in modern times of Acts having been passed by the States, and afterwards sanctioned by the Crown. And they asserted that no Orders in Council of a legislative nature have become the law of the island which have not been issued at the suggestion or upon the request of the States, or have subsequently received the assent of the States. The question came before a Committee of the Privy Council for the affairs of Jersey and Guernsey upon a petition by the States of Jersey praying for the recall of three Orders in Council issued in February 1852—a case in which the author was counsel against the petitioners : *Re The States of Jersey*, 9 Moore, P. C. 185. The Committee did not express any decided opinion upon the general question, but they advised the recall of the Orders in Council, and the confirmation of certain Acts proposed to be substituted for them by the States. See *Re The Jersey Jurats*, L. R. 1 P. C. 94. Regulations for prosecuting appeals to the Queen in Council are contained in the Orders in Council dated July 15, 1835, and June 13, 1853 (1).

Whether Acts of Parliament extend to the Channel Islands depends upon the manner in which they are worded. Sometimes they are specially named, as in statute 14 Vict. c. 5 : " This Act shall extend to the islands of Jersey, Guernsey, Alderney, Sark, and Man ;" and in statute 18 & 19 Vict. c. 63 : " This Act shall extend to Great Britain and Ireland, and the Channel Isles, and the Isle of Man." When an Act is expressed to extend to all parts of the British dominions, it, of course, includes the Channel Islands. And yet the Copyright Act, 5 & 6 Vict. c. 45, *enacts* that the words " British dominions" in that Act shall be construed to mean and include the islands of Jersey and

(1) See "The Constitution of Jersey," by Le Cras, (Jersey, 1857); and "A Concise View of the Legislative Powers of the Crown over the Island of Jersey," by Dryden. (Peterham : London, 1854).

Guernsey, as if without such enactment they would not have been included in the words " British dominions." And by statute 31 & 32 Vict. c. 37 (the Documentary Evidence Act, 1868), " British colony and possession shall, for the purposes of this Act, include the Channel Islands." Another statute (5 & 6 Vict. c. 47) says, in its recital : " Whereas one of the said Acts (3 & 4 Will. 4, c. 51) was passed for the management of the Customs . . . And whereas the provisions extend to the island of Jersey so far as the same are applicable to that island according to the laws thereof, although the island is not specially named in the said Act." By the Limitation of Suits Act (3 & 4 Will. 4, c. 27, s. 19), they are not to be deemed beyond seas within the meaning of that Act. The Postage Act, 2 & 3 Vict. c. 52, s. 11, speaks of letters conveyed " between places within the United Kingdom, and between the United Kingdom and the islands of Man, Jersey, Guernsey, Sark, and Alderney."

The Act 12 & 13 Vict. c. 96, s. 5, provides that the word " colony" used in that Act " shall mean any island, plantation, colony, dominion, fort, or factory of Her Majesty, except any island within the United Kingdom and the islands of Man, Guernsey, Jersey, Alderney, and Sark." In *Craw* v. *Ramsay* (Vaugh. 281), Vaughan, C.J., said that Guernsey and Jersey " are dominions belonging to the realm of England, though not within the territorial dominion or realm of England, but follow it, and are a part of its royalty."

CHAPTER XIV.

ON THE NATIONALITY OF A SHIP, AND OTHER MATTERS RELATING TO SHIPS.

(1.) JOINT OPINION *of the King's Advocate*, SIR JAMES MARRIOTT, *and the Attorney General*, SIR WILLIAM DE GREY, *on the case of an Arrest in the Isle of Man on board a Ship of War* (1). 1770.

MY LORD,—In obedience to his Majesty's commands, signified to us by your Lordship's letter of the 29th June last, we have taken into our consideration the complaint of his Majesty's Governor of the Isle of Man against Lieutenant Whiston, of his Majesty's sloop *Ranger ;* and in answer to the question whether, as the case appears to us, the process was regularly executable on the said Lieutenant Whiston by the officer therein mentioned on board his Majesty's ship, and what directions it may be proper to give to the said Governor for his future conduct,—we have the honour to answer that it appears to us, from the return of Joseph Labat, deputy captain, or one of the peace officers of the Isle of Man under that denomination, that when he repaired, in consequence of the order of the Governor, alongside of his Majesty's said ship, she was then riding within the high-water mark, for which reason he did not think himself authorized to execute the arrest. It also appears to us, agreeably to report of the Attorney General and the magistrates of the island, that the jurisdictions of the said island are become vested in his Majesty ; and that the deputy-searchers who formerly executed arrests below the full sea-mark are now officers of the revenue only.

That in consequence thereof there are no peace officers now who

(1) From a M. S. in the possession of Sir Travers Twiss, Queen's Advocate, which formerly belonged to Sir James Marriott.

can execute arrests in any cause purely civil upon the sea in the flux and reflux thereof. But that the High Court of Admiralty upon the realm hath only jurisdiction upon the sea, and that the civil authority only extends to arrests on board of vessels above sea-water mark, that is, on board such as lie . . . . . . in the bed of the ooze or sand, being so left dry at land by the water being at low-water mark, so that the said ship may be intended or understood to be *infra corpus comitatus*. Upon the whole, as far as appears from the aforesaid case, it does not seem to us that any peace officer of municipal jurisdiction only could legally execute an arrest on board the ship in question, or of any ship (whether his Majesty's or not), under the same circumstances, riding upon the sea. With regard to the expediency or impropriety of permitting his Majesty's ships, or any other ships, to be asylums against actions of debt, or any other prosecutions, it is a matter which relates to the manning his Majesty's ships and the rules and regulations of the navy; and it is submitted to superior wisdom whether it may be fit by any new law to make alterations therein.

The Right Hon. the Earl of Rochford,   JAMES MARRIOTT.
&c. &c. &c.   WM. DE GREY.
December 1770.

(2.) OPINION *of the King's Advocate*, SIR JAMES MARRIOTT, *on the right of property in a Vessel derelict on the Ocean* (1). 1772.

To the Lords Commissioners of His Majesty's Treasury.

MY LORDS,—In obedience to your Lordships' commands, I have taken into my consideration a letter of Charles Lutwidge, Esq., together with the affidavits enclosed of Thomas Nunns, Robert Cornate, Castill Corus, and James Howard, belonging to the snow *Henry*, of Liverpool, Thomas Saratt, master, in regard to a ship found by them and others floating on the high seas about twenty-three leagues to the south-west of the rock called Tuscar, and by them brought to anchor in the Bay of Peel, in the Isle of Man,

(1) From the same M. S.

where she afterwards parted from her cables and was lost, but the
greatest part of the cargo was saved :—whether the ship and cargo
are to be considered as derelict, and as such the property of the
finders, under the reservation of the claim of the original owners,
if any shall appear ?—or, whether the same are flotsam taken upon
the high seas, and as such the property of his Majesty, under the
right of salvage, by the finders, according to the law and custom
of the Isle of Man ?

I have the honour to observe to your Lordships, that this case is
not to be considered as at all affected by the place where the cargo
was saved, but by the place where the vessel was first found ; for
to whomsoever the cargo and vessel belonged at the time of finding,
to that person the cargo saved must belong, subject to salvage as
usual, according to circumstances attending the degree of risk and
labour in saving; so that, if the ship and cargo belonged, at the
time and place when and where first found, to his Majesty or to
the finders, to the same will belong, being once vested, the cargo
which was saved after the ship was anchored in any harbour
wheresoever and afterwards cast away.

For the greater clearness and precision, the two questions may
be reduced into one,—In whom, whether in the King or the
finders, did the property vest when first found ?

The principal facts which seem to deserve attention are the distance of the vessel from the shore (twenty-three leagues), and that
the vessel was not in a wrecked condition at the instant of time
when found. These circumstances occasion a nicety in the question
in point of law.

On the authority of the cases in Lord Coke, *Sir Henry Constable's
Case*, pt. 5, fol. 107, 5 Co. 106 a—5 Co. 106 b. ; and of Bracton
on the Laws and Customs of England, lib. iii., c. 2, fol. 138, de
Corona ; and of Molloy, de Jure Maritimo, b. 2, c. 5, flotsam is
when the ship is sunk, or otherwise perished, and the goods float
upon the sea—viz., at the time of finding.

Now it is there said that the King shall have flotsam and jetsam,
what is flung out to lighten the ship, and lagan, what is sunk in
shoal-water when the ship perisheth, but *when the ship perishes
not, e contra*.

The authority of Bracton as to the common law of the realm i doubtless very great, who, according to Selden, was a Judge of the Common Bench or Pleas in the reign of Henry III., and wrote a book, *De Legibus et Consuetudinibus Angliæ.* He lived in the time Magna Charta was made, according to my Lord Coke (4 Instit. 72), and was a strong favourer of the liberty of the subject, as is said by Justice Crawley in Hampden's trial. In lib. iii., fol. 128, tit. de Corona, he makes it to be an essential quality of wreck in right of the King or his grantee, "Si navis *frangatur,*" that the ship should be broke to pieces unless any proprietor can be made out; so that if there is a dog alive, and a person can prove property in the dog, he shall be presumed to be the owner of the ship, and cargo too, so as to oust the Crown. However, the statute 3 Edw. 1, which was made after Bracton's time, gives no further effect to the circumstance of man, dog, or cat escaping alive out of a ship than that it shall suspend judgment of wreck for a year and a day, for persons having interest to prove their property for restitution, otherwise the goods to be seized for the King's use.

But that part of Bracton which is most applicable to the present question is, the distinction which he makes of distance from the shore. If, says he, the ship or goods are found at a great distance from the shore, so that it is perfectly uncertain upon what coast they might be cast, then whatever is found shall be the property of the finder—on this ground, because it cannot be said to be the property of any man, and which, therefore, by law is given to the taker, because no man hath privilege therein; and the King hath not any more than a private person: and the reason hereof is the uncertainty of the event where the goods may be stranded. I believe this is a tolerably exact translation of Bracton's Latin.

Now this, with submission to such great authority, I take not to be law, because it is founded upon a false reason, if true reason only makes law and false reason cannot alter it; for the property of the ship does not depend upon the uncertainty upon what shore and into what dominion the ship or cargo may be carried, but it depends upon the certainty of what dominion it is found in, and by whose subjects, for the dominion of the King is over all the narrow seas, as we assert even with respect to foreigners passing through them: and, *à fortiori,* it follows the person of the subject

there and everywhere else, so that over the whole globe the jurisdiction of the Admiralty, which is the jurisdiction of the Crown,
extends to every British subject both as to matters civil as well
as criminal—for what can be so high a degree of property as a
man's life, for which he is tried for offences committed on the high
seas?   Therefore, I conceive that the same analogy of the law of
the realm that holdeth for treasure-trove upon land, holdeth for
ships and goods found upon the high seas.   The law in both cases,
as I conceive it, goes upon the feudal principle of vassalage—all
property being an emanation of the supreme power paramount,
which is the complex of all association and government centred
in the person of the great public representative.   And, therefore,
the rule is just "*quicquid acquiritur servo acquiritur domino,*" unless
the former holds it by privilege of especial grant expressed by written deed, or tacit which is the common usage.   For all these reasons
I am induced to be of opinion that the ship and cargo in question,
being found within the narrow seas, and within the dominions of
the Crown of Great Britain, are a public acquisition by British subjects to the use of the Crown, and the same are to be deemed to be,
according to the course and style of the High Court of Admiralty,
a droit of Admiralty, but that the finders thereof are entitled to
the usual salvage, in the discretion of the Court, according to the
circumstances of the case.   I have further to observe to your Lordships, that although things so found are styled droits of Admiralty,
yet the same are not necessarily inherent in the Lord High Admiral,
nor in the Commissioners of the Admiralty, to whom, by the statute
and commission in consequence, the power to execute the office of
Lord High Admiral is granted; but that all droits and perquisites
of Admiralty, by the terms of his Majesty's present commission,
appear to be reserved " to the only use and behoof of his Majesty,
although," as it is therein set forth, "*they were heretofore granted
to the Lord High Admiral by express words.*"

In consequence of all which, I am of opinion that the cargo of
the ship in question must be proceeded against in the High Court
of Admiralty, according to due course of law, in his Majesty's name,
and that all persons having interest therein may appear to show
cause why the same should not be condemned as a droit and perquisite of the Crown ; otherwise, in pain and in default of appear-

ance, the sentence of condemnation to pass as usual with salvage to the finders.

Doctors' Commons, July 25, 1772.   JAMES MARRIOTT.

P.S.—*Vide* Britton, fol. 26. This distinction, grounded upon the authorities of Britton & Bracton, is taken by Lord Coke between treasure found at sea and land: 2 Instit. p. 168. But, says he, if treasure be found *in* the sea the finder shall have it at this day. Doubtless if foreigners find anything *upon* the main ocean, being independent of the King, they shall have it; but *quære*, as to a subject in the narrow seas within the jurisdiction of the Admiralty of England. As to treasure found *in* the sea, the finder may have it, although a subject, because that is not fortuitous, but gained by the peril and labour of the person in diving or fishing.

(3.) JOINT OPINION *of the Queen's Advocate*, SIR JOHN DODSON, *and the Attorney and Solicitor General*, SIR JOHN CAMPBELL *and* SIR THOMAS WILDE, *on the seizure of a Spanish Vessel which had put into a port of Jamaica in distress with Five Slaves on board.*

Doctors' Commons, March 2, 1841.

MY LORD,—We are honoured with your Lordship's commands, signified in Mr. Vernon Smith's letter of the 27th ultimo, stating that he was directed to transmit to us the copy of a despatch from the Governor of Jamaica, with its several inclosures, reporting the proceedings adopted in the case of a Spanish schooner, named the *Industria*, which had put into the port of Black River in that island in distress, with five slaves on board.

Mr. Vernon Smith further states that the vessel was seized by the local authorities, and subsequently released by order of the Governor; but doubts having arisen whether the vessel was not liable to seizure, the Governor referred the case to the Attorney General of Jamaica, who reported that he should not advise the re-seizure of the *Industria*, although his opinion seemed to be that she was liable to confiscation.

Mr. Vernon Smith is pleased to request that we would report to your Lordship, whether the vessel was liable to seizure and confiscation, and whether, after having been released, she could lawfully have been again seized and brought to adjudication ?

In obedience to your Lordship's commands, we have taken the papers into consideration, and have the honour to report that, assuming the *Industria* to have come into Black River, in the island of Jamaica, through distress, we apprehend that she could not be deemed to have thereby committed any offence against the laws of Great Britain, and therefore think that she was not liable to seizure and confiscation by the civil authorities of the island. We are, however, of opinion, that she might have been seized by a British cruiser, duly commissioned, under the treaty with Spain for the abolition of the slave-trade, and carried before a Court of Mixed Commission for adjudication.

The prior release of a vessel does not prevent a subsequent lawful seizure.

	J. DODSON.
The Right Hon. Lord J. Russell,	J. CAMPBELL.
&c. &c. &c.	THOS. WILDE.

(4.) *Extract from* OPINION *of the United States Attorney General,* MR. LEGARE, *in the case of the* Creole, *an American Vessel, which under stress of weather put into port at the Bahamas with Slaves on board* (1).

Office of the Attorney General, July 20, 1842.

. . . . . . The principle is, that if a vessel be driven by stress of weather, or forced by *vis major*, or, in short, be compelled by any overruling necessity, to take refuge in the ports of another, she is not considered as subject to the municipal law of that other, so far as concerns any penalty, prohibition, tax, or incapacity that would otherwise be incurred by entering the ports; provided she do nothing further to violate the municipal law during her stay. The comity of nations—which is the usage, the common law, of civilized nations, and a breach of which would now be justly regarded as a grave offence—has gone very far on this point. The law of Europe, barbarous as it was in many respects (*e.g.*, wrecks), furnishes examples of this exemption (see 2 Inst., 57 ; Coke's Com. on Magna

(1) 4 Attorney Generals' Opinions, 98.

Charta, and a citation of ancient Saxon laws). When a ship is driven into port by stress of weather, and there unloads her cargo, she is not bound to pay duties or customs in that place, because she came there by force; nor is she liable to forfeiture; neither are duties to be paid on goods forcibly driven into port. If there is a case in which the excuse of necessity would be regarded with suspicion, and received with disfavour, it is undoubtedly a breach of blockade, one of the extreme cases of the law of war, involving in its own nature a necessity that would seem to supersede all others. Yet Sir William Scott admits it to be a good plea when the facts fully support it (see 5 Rob. 27—the *Fortune*).

Under the English Navigation Act it has been settled, that coming in by stress of weather could not be an importation without reference to intention or *mala fides* (see the cases collected in 1 Chitty's Commercial Law, p. 245). What is this but an admission, by statute, that a ship in that category is, like a ship of war belonging to a friendly Power, considered by the law of England as not subject to the municipal law? This analogy of a ship of war, like that of a foreign Sovereign travelling in the dominions of a friendly Power, and of ambassadors of all classes, shows the principle of immunity, by reason of a *quasi* or fictitious extra-territoriality, to be familiar to the law. But put it on the ground of comity, it is plainly *juris gentium*. To show how sacred the duties of humanity have been considered in England, even as between enemies, Sir William Scott rejected with indignation a claim of capture by persons going on board in distress, allowing freight, expenses, and demurrage to the ship (1 Rob. 243—the *Yonge, Jacobi* v. *Bannerman*). Further, the distinction is plain between calling on the foreigner for help (though even that is not often refused in case of distress), and demanding of him only a temporary asylum. In the former case, we ask him to aid in executing our municipal law in his territory; in the latter, we ask to be exempted from his municipal law in our territory. Beyond all question, a ship on the high seas, beyond a marine league from shore, is part of the territory of the nation to which she belongs. Why should her being blown &c., within a marine league, by tempests, &c., make a difference? We affirm that to shut up our ports absolutely to vessels in distress, would be less hostile than to

2 D

admit them on such conditions. *Hospitio prohibemur arenæ* in
either case, and the relation is one of covert hostility. Suppose
the case of a British transport or cartel filled with impressed seamen
driven into our ports, or a convict ship into those of France (1).

(5.) CASE and JOINT OPINION *of the Queen's Advocate*, SIR
J. D. HARDING, *and the Attorney and Solicitor General*, SIR
FREDERICK THESIGER *and* SIR FITZROY KELLY, *on the seizure
of some French Vessels at the Gambia.* 1852.

Case.—In the year 1848 a French vessel and five canoes were
seized (at separate times), and in March, 1850, another French
vessel was seized, by order of the Governor of Gambia, in the
neighbourhood of, or above, the French factory of Albreda, which
is situate on the River Gambia, thirty miles above the town of
Bathurst, which is a British settlement.

In an account given by the Governor of the seizures (in a letter
addressed to Earl Grey), he said that he had seized the first of
those vessels, the *Nancy*, because she was French-owned, French-
manned, without papers, and trading above the highest limits to
which any French vessel was permitted to go in that river; and for
a breach of the Navigation Act, 8 & 9 Vict. c. 88, s. 14, being
neither British-owned nor British-navigated, s. 24 declaring, under
such circumstances, her cargo forfeited, and the 4th section of the
Registry Act declaring, under the same circumstances, the vessel
forfeited. He next caused to be seized several canoes, laden with
brown nuts, the produce of the Gambia river, and proceeding to
the French *Comptoir* at Albreda. They were either owned by or
hired by Frenchmen, and the seizure was made on the alleged
ground that it was illegal for any French boat, or boat hired by
the French, to trade or move, with or without cargo, on the waters
of the river beyond Gambia. The last vessel seized was the
Combo, a small cutter, which the Governor saw anchored in front
of the French *Comptoir*, and she was publicly seized as being
without papers or any avowed owner. No claim was made for any
of the vessels or canoes so seized by the Governor. In a despatch

(1) See the debate on the case of the *Creole* in the House of Lords, Feb. 14,
1842 : Hansard's Parl. Deb. vol. lx. p. 318.

from the Governor defending the seizure, he referred to the Treaty of Versailles (1783), which contains, amongst others, the following articles :—

Art. 9. The King of Great Britain cedes in full right, and guarantees to his Most Christian Majesty, the River Senegal and its dependencies, with the forts of St. Louis, Podor, Galam, Arguin, and Portendie ; and his Britannic Majesty restores to France the island of Gorée, which shall be delivered up in the condition it was in when the conquest of it was made.

Art. 10. The Most Christian King, on his part, guarantees to the King of Great Britain the possession of Fort James, and of the River Gambia.

Art. 11. For preventing all discussion in that part of the world, the two high contracting parties shall, within three months after the exchange of the ratification of the present treaty, name commissaries, who shall be charged with the settling and fixing of the boundaries of the respective possessions. As to the gum trade, the English shall have the liberty of carrying it on from the mouth of the River St. John to the bay and fort of Portendie inclusively : provided that they shall not form any permanent settlement of what nature soever in the said River St. John, upon the coast, or in the Bay of Portendie.

Art. 12. As to the residue of the coast of Africa, the English and French subjects shall continue to resort thereto, according to the usage which has hitherto prevailed.

In addition to the statutes above-mentioned, the Law Officers were referred to statute 12 & 13 Vict. c. 29, s. 20 ("An Act to amend the Laws in force for the encouragement of British Shipping and Navigation, 1849 "), and they were requested to advise upon the legality of the seizures in question.

Opinion.—We are of opinion that the seizures in question are not warranted by law.

These not being British vessels, there is nothing in the Acts in force relating to customs and navigation at the time of the seizure which renders any but British vessels liable to forfeiture ; although, by the 24th section of 8 & 9 Vict. c. 89, the goods on board the vessels in question became forfeited, and the master of each incurred a penalty of £100.

2 D 2

There appears to be nothing in the Treaty of Versailles (to which we are referred) which gives any right of seizure.

It may be worthy the consideration of Her Majesty's Government, whether such violation of the law of nations, and the spirit of our own statutes, ought not to be made punishable by statute with the forfeiture of the offending vessel.

J. D. HARDING.

Doctors' Commons, April 3, 1852.   FRED. THESIGER.'

FITZROY KELLY.

(6.) JOINT OPINION *of the Queen's Advocate,* SIR J. D. HARD-ING, *and the Attorney and Solicitor General,* SIR A. E. COCKBURN *and* SIR RICHARD BETHELL, *as to what constitutes loss of Nationality in a Ship.*

Doctors' Commons, August 6, 1853.

MY LORD DUKE,—We are honoured with your Grace's commands, signified in Mr. Merivale's letter of the 20th of April last, stating that he was directed to transmit to us copy of a despatch, with its enclosures, received from the Lieutenant-Governor of Nova Scotia, and to request that we would jointly report to your Grace, whether we agree in the view of the law taken by the Judge of the Admiralty Court at Halifax, in the case of the *Creole,* and if not, in what respect we differ from it?

Whether, also, it appears to us that such amendments of the law, as suggested by the Judge in his letter of the 31st of March, are called for or advisable?

We are also honoured with Mr. Merivale's letter of the 4th of June, stating that, with reference to the Queen's Advocate's letter of the 23rd of April, he was directed by your Grace to transmit to us the copy of a further despatch from the Lieutenant-Governor of Nova Scotia, supplying the documents and other information required to enable us to report our opinion upon the case of the *Creole,* seized for the infraction of the Fishery Regulations.

In obedience to your Grace's commands, we have taken the papers into consideration, and have the honour to report—

That we do not agree with the view of the law taken by the Judge of the Admiralty Court at Halifax, in the case of the *Creole;* and that we are of opinion that, inasmuch as the *Creole,* although originally a British ship, yet had fallen into the hands of foreigners, and been altered so as not to correspond with her original certificate, and not re-registered; and inasmuch as she was not navigated according to the British Navigation Laws, she had lost her nationality and become a foreign ship. We are further of opinion that the colonial statute on the subject is valid, for reasons hereafter given by us in our answer to the questions, and that the *Creole* was, on these grounds, liable to condemnation and forfeiture.

With respect to the several questions on the case of the *Creole*, framed by Mr. Attorney-General Uniacke, appended to his letter to Sir G. Le Marchant sent with the papers, we are of opinion—

1. That, with respect to forfeiture, under 59 Geo. 3, c. 38, although both cases are equally within the mischief which the Act was intended to guard against, yet, as the language of the Act is ambiguous, and as the Act is of a highly penal nature, we are of opinion that it will not be advisable to forfeit under it any but foreign vessels.

2. Even if the Imperial Act, 59 Geo. 3, c. 38, should be insufficient to give Her Majesty power to impose all or any of the rules and regulations in question (a question which we need not now consider), the authority of the local legislature appears to us to be sufficient to make them valid in effect, by its express legislative enactment of them. The authority of the local legislature extends (like that of the Imperial Parliament) over the space of the three miles upon the high seas next the coast, which is, by the comity of nations, part of the country to which it is adjacent; and we are of opinion that, upon this general principle, and irrespective of the convention, the imperial statute, or the regulations of the Sovereign in Council, the colonial legislature was legally entitled to legislate as it has done relative to the fisheries, and that its enactments are valid and binding.

3. We are of opinion that such a vessel is, under the circumstances stated, liable to forfeiture under the express provisions of the colonial statute already referred to.

4. We are of opinion that the effect of 8 & 9 Vict. c. 89 is controlled by 12 & 13 Vict. c. 29, s. 17, and that it is no longer necessary that the owner of a vessel shall be resident within the

Queen's dominions in order to satisfy the requirements of the British Navigation Laws.

5. The master in all cases, and, besides the master, either three-fourths of the crew, or one seaman to every twenty tons, by the 12 & 13 Vict. c. 29, s. 27, must be British subjects.

6. A foreign fishing-vessel, duly registered and manned as a British vessel, may legally prosecute the fishery, as suggested, by virtue of 12 & 13 Vict. c. 29.

7. Such a ship will be liable to forfeiture and condemnation, if deficient in any requirement absolutely necessary to her nationality —as, for instance, if she be not registered or navigated as a British ship; but she will not be liable to forfeiture for deficiencies in other points of mere regulation, which involve only specific penal-ties—as, for instance, if she has not her tonnage carved on her beam, or her name painted on her stern.

J. D. HARDING.

His Grace the Duke of Newcastle,   A. E. COCKBURN.

&c. &c. &c.   RICHARD BETHELL.

(7.) JOINT OPINION *of the same Law Officers in the same Case, that indemnity for unauthorized seizure of a Foreign Vessel in Colonial Waters, for contravention of a Convention between Great Britain and a Foreign Country, ought to be paid by Great Britain.*

Doctors' Commons, November 12, 1855.

SIR,—We are honoured with your letter of the 22nd September last, stating that, with reference to our report of the 6th August, 1853, on the subject of the judgment given in the Vice-Admiralty Court at Halifax, in the case of the *Creole*, you were directed by the late Sir William Molesworth to send us a copy of a despatch from Lieutenant-Governor Sir Gaspard Le Marchant, enclosing a petition from Mr. Elliot, one of the claimants of the vessel in that case, for indemnity for damages; and to request that we would take the same into consideration, and report our opinion whether we consider such pecuniary indemnity ought to be given, and, if so, whether by the Home Government or by the Govern-ment of Nova Scotia.

In obedience to the above commands we have the honour to report—

That, in our opinion, the pecuniary indemnity sought by the owner of the *Creole* ought to be given. The question, in order to decide which the *Creole* was captured, arose out of a Convention between Great Britain and the United States, and she was captured by one of Her Majesty's ships, under instructions from the Imperial Government. The matter was therefore one of imperial concern, and we are of opinion that the indemnity must be paid by the Imperial Government, and not by that of Nova Scotia.

To Fred. Elliot, Esq.
&c. &c. &c.

J. D. HARDING.
A. E. COCKBURN.
RICHARD BETHELL.

(8.) OPINION *of the United States Attorney General,* MR. CUSHING, *on the seizure by the French Authorities in the Port of Marseilles of Seamen on board an American Ship charged with Crime* (1).

Attorney General's Office, September 6, 1856.

SIR,—I have examined the correspondence between Mr. Mason, the envoy of the United States in France, and the President of the Council of State of the French Empire, charged, *par interim,* with the Ministry of Foreign Affairs, M. Baroche, as communicated to me by your note of the 5th instant, and have reflected on the pertinent questions of public law which you suggest for my consideration.

Without entering into recapitulation of all the facts involved in the discussion, it will suffice for the present purpose to state such only as are essential to the right understanding of the points now remaining to be determined.

It appears that while the American merchant ship *Atalanta* was on a voyage from Marseilles to New York, and on the high seas, out of the municipal jurisdiction of any Government, acts of insubordination and violence occurred on the part of her crew, by whom the ship was forced to put back to Marseilles.

On her arrival in port, the criminal parties were, on the appli-

(1) 8 Attorney Generals' Opinions, 73.

cation of the American consul, received and imprisoned on shore
by the local authorities.

Afterwards a certain number of them were released absolutely,
with assent of the consul. Thirteen of the crew thus remained.
Of these a portion, six in number, were, on the application of the
consul, taken from the prison and placed on board the *Atalanta* for
conveyance to the United States, under charge of crime. Then—
with notice to the consul, it is true, but in spite of his remon-
strances—the local authorities went on board the *Atalanta*, and
forcibly resumed the possession of the six prisoners, and replaced
them in confinement on shore, where they now remain, together
with the seven others not taken on board, the subject of the
pending correspondence.

It does not distinctly appear of what nationality these men are,
but it is implied, by the tenor of the discussion on both sides, that
they are neither citizens of the United States nor citizens of France.

The acts of criminality with which they stand charged constitute
the crime of revolt, and also that of felonious assault, under circumstances which bring the case within the jurisdiction of the
judicial authorities of the United States (Act of March 3, 1835).

To the same effect undoubtedly is the French law, which assumes,
as ours does, that the ship is a part of the territory of her country,
and provides specially for the punishment of crimes committed on
board (Ord. de 1681, liv. ii. tit. 1, art. 22; Valin, Comment. tom. i.
p. 449; Decret. du 24 Mars, 1852; De Clercqq, Formul. tom. ii.
p. 348).

To this it is wholly immaterial, by our law, whether they were
citizens of the United States or not (*United States* v. *Sharp*,
1 Peters C. C. R. 118, 121).

Nor is it material whether, in their shipment on board the
Atalanta, the master did or not infringe the Navigation Laws of the
United States.

The practical inquiries are—

1. Whether, in view of the stipulations of the consular convention between the United States and France of February 23, 1853,
or of the rules of international law, the French authorities acted
rightfully in going on board the *Atalanta*, to retake the six seamen
placed there for transmission to the United States.

2. Whether the American Government may now, in virtue of treaty or of the law of nations, rightfully demand the extradition of these thirteen men for transmission to the United States, there to be tried in due course of law for their imputed crimes ?

It is due to the Emperor's Government to say, that the questions made in the case are manifestly presented by it in goodwill and in all comity, as regards the United States, and may, therefore, be dealt with by all, unreservedly, in their legal relations.

1. Of the rightfulness of the retaking of the men from on board the *Atalanta*.

I perfectly agree with M. Baroche, that it was not the object of the consular convention to confer on the consuls of either nation the *jurisdiction* of crimes in the ports of the other.

It is also undeniably true, that by the general rules of public laws, at least as they are understood and received in the United States, we do not claim for ourselves, nor concede to other nations, the right of ex-territoriality for merchant ships in the territorial waters.

If, in concluding this convention, the two Governments had designed to establish as between themselves a new rule in this respect, they would have said so expressly; and if they had so declared expressly, the convention would not have been confirmed on our side, for no State of the Union probably would have consented thus to surrender its own municipal jurisdiction in its own waters to the consuls of France.

But in treating the question as one either of the criminal jurisdiction of consuls, or of the ex-territoriality of merchant vessels on the territorial waters, do we not assume for it too broad a scope ?

I conceive the true question to be a much narrower one. It is whether, when a crime has been committed on the high seas on board an American ship, that crime being of the sole competency of the United States, and the ship is compelled, by her contract of destination, by stress of weather, or by the crime itself, to touch at a French port—whether, in such case, the criminal may be forcibly withdrawn from the ship by the local authorities, or by the order of the Government?

This question presents itself here in three different forms:—

First.—The French authorities take the temporary custody of the parties at the request of the American consul.

Secondly.—The French authorities re-deliver a portion of the prisoners to the consul to be held on board the *Atalanta*; and

Thirdly.—They retake the latter prisoners from on board the *Atalanta*.

In my opinion, when the *Atalanta* arrived at Marseilles, the master of that ship had lawful power, with aid of the consul, if required, to retain these men on board. Though not citizens of the United States, they were American seamen under voluntary contract for a voyage to New York, whom the local authorities had no just power to discharge from their contract.

The consideration that they had committed crimes on board the ship, but not within the local jurisdiction, for which crimes they were liable to be punished on her reaching New York, did not give to the local authorities any just right to interfere. If crime had been committed while the ship lay in the territorial waters, then the local authorities, and they alone, would have had jurisdiction, and might have gone on board to seize the prisoners by force, but not when no act had been done by them to give jurisdiction of the case to France.

I transfer the question to the United States, and proceed to suppose that a French merchant ship, on her way to Marseilles, puts into New York, in distress, having at the time mutinous members of her crew confined on board. Could such persons in such a case be lawfully taken away from the custody of the master by the local authorities, with instrumentality of the writ of habeas corpus or otherwise? I think not.

Now, by the consular convention, and by the law of nations without it, the consul represented the master, and his country alone, in matters calling for the intervention of the authorities of Marseilles. This representative duty, and this only, the consul undertook to discharge in the present case. He did not claim or assume to exercise any power, judicial or other, in derogation of the territorial sovereignty.

I think the consul acted lawfully, when, at the first stage of the transaction, he requested the local authorities to take temporary charge of these prisoners.

I do not say the local authorities were bound to assume the responsibility of such custody; but they might well in comity do it; nay, it was their duty, in my opinion, at the call of the consul, at least to lend him their aid in this respect, by the express terms of the convention.

I concede in the fullest terms the integrity of the local sovereignty, and that, instead of contradicting, seems to corroborate my view of the subject; for how shall the consuls maintain the internal order of the merchant vessels of their nation—how in the foreign port shall they imprison persons, save through the assistance of the local authority? Are they to do it by their own unaided force in the presence of the local jurisdiction?

Surely to allow this would be to produce the greatest disorders, which can be avoided only by having recurrence to the local authority for its own lawful action in behalf of the consul.

However this may be, my conviction is clear that the local authority, even if it may refuse to aid, cannot lawfully interpose to defeat, the lawful confinement of any members of the crew by the master, on board the ship, with advice and approbation of the consul.

If the parties confined have the lawful right to be discharged from such custody, they may obtain it on application to the consul. That is one of his legitimate, exclusive, and ordinary functions.

That the right and the power of the local jurisdiction are such only as here suggested, is the opinion of the jurists of France.

Ortolan states the doctrine as follows: " As to ships of commerce, we know that when they are in the territorial waters of a foreign State, they are not exempt from the local police and jurisdiction, *except as to facts happening on board which do not concern the tranquillity of the port, or persons foreign to the crew.* For all other facts, they remain subject to this police and this jurisdiction. Hence it follows that the local authority has the right to pass on board these vessels, there to pursue, search for, and arrest persons who have been guilty, either on shore or even on board, *of acts amenable* to the territorial justice " (Diplomatie de la Mer, tom. i. p. 335).

In the present case the crimes committed on board the *Atalanta* were not " amenable to the territorial justice ;" they did not concern the " tranquillity of the port," nor did they affect any persons " foreign to the crew."

The rule of law, as thus laid down by Ortolan, seems to have been drawn from a decision of the Council of State in the time of the Emperor Napoleon I., to the point that the local authority will not intermeddle with acts, even crimes, committed on board a foreign ship in such circumstances (Ortolan, tom. i. p. 450, annexe ii.).

Nay, the French laws do not hesitate to prescribe that when crimes are committed on board a French vessel in a foreign port, *by one of the crew against another of the same crew*, the French consul is to resist the application of the local authority to the case (Ord. du 29 Oct. 1833, tit. iii. art. 22 ; De Clercqq, Form. tom. ii. p. 65).

This doctrine has become so firmly fixed in France, that the best writers assume it as a rule of international law (see MM. de Clercqq et de Vallet, Guide Pratique, tom. i. p. 366).

Indeed, the recent legislation of France confers on her consuls unmistakable *jurisdiction* in these matters (Decret du 24 Mars, 1852 ; see De Clercqq, Formulaire, tom. ii. p. 348).

Previously, their duties were in the nature of *surveillance* rather than jurisdiction (Moreuil, Guide des Agens Cons. p. 389).

We do not go so far in this as France. I admit, as already stated, the local authority in regard to crimes committed on board a merchantman in the territorial waters ; but I deny that the local authority has any right to interfere with persons lawfully detained on board the ship by the laws of the country to which she belongs, as for a crime committed on the high seas among members of the crew, and not justiciable by the foreign jurisdiction. France, at least, cannot deny to us, it would seem, this exemption, when she herself claims to extend it so much further, and make it comprehend occurrences internal to the crew, even though happening in port.

The doctrine of the public law of Europe on this point is well stated by Riquelme, as follows : " Crimes committed on the high seas, whether on board ships of war or merchantmen, are considered as committed in the territory of the State to which the ship belongs, because only the laws of the latter are infringed, and consequently only the jurisdiction of the same is called upon to adjudicate, whether the accused be of the nationality of the ship or a foreigner, and whether the crime were committed against a fellow-countryman or between foreign passengers.

"If the ship on board of which the crime has been committed arrives then at a port, the jurisdictional right of the territory to which the ship belongs over the accused does not on that account cease. So that if one of these were a foreign subject to which the port at which the ship stops belongs, even in that case it is the right of the captain to detain him on board, that he may be judged by the tribunals of the ship's country. And if this passenger should get on shore, and should institute before the tribunals of his country proceedings against the captain, the local authority will be incompetent to judge the foreign captain, because the fact in question occurred in a foreign country—that is, on board a foreign merchantman on the high seas—and because, by embarking in that ship, the party is presumed to have submitted himself to the laws of the foreign territory of which the ship constitutes a part.

" When the crime is not committed on the high seas, but while the ship is in territorial waters, then it is necessary to distinguish between ships of war and merchantmen. In the first case the principle of ex-territoriality covers the ship from all foreign intervention or investigation . . . .

" In the second case, when the crime has been committed on board a merchantman in a foreign port, the resolution is different, because the condition of a merchantman in a foreign port is different from that of a man-of-war. The rule in these cases, in default of treaties or inducements of reciprocity determining it, is, that if the offence affect only the interior discipline of the ship, without disturbing or compromitting the tranquillity of the port, the local authority ought to declare itself incompetent unless its assistance is requested, because the true regulator of these questions, in which the local authority has no interest, is the consul.

" But if the offence has been committed by one of the crew against a subject of the country or another foreigner; or if, occurring among those of the crew, it be of a nature to compromise the tranquillity of the port, then the territorial jurisdiction is entitled to punish the crime, even although the accused undertake to claim the protection of the ship" (Riquelme, Derecho Internacional, tom. i. pp. 243, 245).

These are just and reasonable views applicable to the present case.

I confess myself wholly at a loss, therefore, to see on what assignable ground of strict international right it was that the local authority at Marseilles proceeded in withdrawing these parties from their lawful confinement on board the *Atalanta*.

If indeed it were the intention of France to try these men for their crime, and it had been committed in the territorial waters so as to be capable of being tried there, then indeed we might see cause for withdrawing them from the custody of the ship or consul. But no such thing is proposed in the despatch of M. Baroche.

If the legality of what has been done be admitted, then municipal crimes perpetrated on the high seas will much of the time escape unpunished. One term of every voyage is a foreign port. If a crime other than piracy be committed while on the way thither, and the criminal cannot be detained on board the ship or on shore, subject to the discretion of the consul, he cannot be tried; for the local authority cannot try him, and if he is to be withdrawn from the custody of the ship, he cannot be tried in the country to which she belongs, and which alone has jurisdiction.

Thus the effect of the course entered upon by the local authority at Marseilles, if it should be sanctioned by the Emperor's Government, and admitted by the United States, would be to discharge these criminals without punishment, to set the example of immunity of crime in all such cases for the future, and tend to the most calamitous consequences as respects the safety of the commercial marine of both France and the United States.

The public evil in this respect would be sufficiently serious when considered in relation to the case of ordinary voyages; but in other cases, such as that of vessels forced into port by stress of weather, or other common perils of the sea, it would grow to be intolerable, and more especially in the case of acts of insubordination on the part of the crew. Meanwhile seamen would have nothing to do but to seize the ship and make for a foreign port, there to be released by the local authority. It would be to hold out inducements and temptations to mutiny and murder on the high seas.

The superior intelligence of M. Baroche cannot fail to see this, and to impel him to suggest to the diplomatic agents of any other Government who have made representations on the subject, that, in seeking for whatever plausible reason to abstract these men from the only jurisdiction which can try the offence, they do irreparable prejudice to the interests of all the maritime States of Europe and America.

It cannot be for the interest of Sardinia, for instance, of Austria, of Spain, to have it established as a rule of public law, that seamen who have committed crimes appertaining to their penal jurisdiction, and to no other, shall be set free the moment the ship in which they may be touches at a foreign port. It is for the common benefit of the civilized world to see to the condign punishment of all crimes committed on the high seas.

Permit me to add, that the United States, while recognising the local authority generally in the case of merchant ships, have never claimed nor conceded it as to things not appertaining to the territorial jurisdiction. We have constantly affirmed our right to detain on board our ships, even in a foreign port, persons held to such detention by the laws of the United States (see Mr. Legare's opinion of July 20, 1842; also Wheaton's Elements by Lawrence, p. 156, note).

Permit me also to remind you of the recent case of the ship *Corsica* at Calcutta (Opinion, June 25, 1856), which greatly resembles this in many respects, involving the question of extradition as well as detention, and which was disposed of by the British Government on both points as claimed by us here—that is, as a matter appertaining to the jurisdiction of the United States.

I have discussed this part of the subject, as you will have perceived, in points of view which are independent of any seriously debateable matter in the construction of the consular convention. Before leaving it allow me to say a few words on that question.

The relevant stipulations of the convention are contained in the 8th Article, as follows:—

"The respective consuls-general, vice-consuls, or consular agents, shall have exclusive charge of the internal order of the merchant vessels of their nation, and shall alone take cognisance of differences which may arise, either at sea or in port, between the captain, officers, and crew without exception, particularly in reference to the adjustment of wages and the execution of contracts. The local authorities shall not, on any pretext, interfere in these differences, but shall lend forcible aid to the consuls when they may ask it, to arrest and imprison all persons composing the crew whom they may deem it necessary to confine. Those persons shall be arrested at the sole request of the consuls, addressed in writing to the local authority, and supported by an official extract from the register of the ship, or the list of the crew, and shall be held during the whole time of their stay in port at the disposal of the consuls . . . . Their release shall be granted at the mere request of the consuls made in writing. The expenses of the arrest and detention of these persons shall be paid by the consuls."

I conceive that, regarding this article as we should—that is, as a part of our public law, adapted to and cohering with other parts of our public law—all the difficulties in its construction vanish.

The national sovereignty of the United States, like that of France, is complete within its own territory. Neither nation confers ex-territoriality on foreign merchant ships within its waters. Neither nation asserts for its consuls judicial authority for the trial of crimes, except in countries without the pale of Christendom. But each nation does by the general rule of public law, and more especially by this convention, as between France and the United States, concede to the consuls of the other a certain authority of discipline, and to the ships of the other a certain privilege in its ports.

As to questions of mere *civil* right, internal to the ship and to her crew, even if the latter be on shore, we agree that the consuls are to have cognisance, and are to be aided by the local authorities in this respect.

But now as to *criminal* matters?

These, it is clear, cannot be *tried and judged* by the American consul in Marseilles, nor by the French consul in New York.

Is the consul, for this reason, stripped of all power, and the ship herself of all immunity, in respect of persons subject to detention for any cause, either civil or criminal? I think not. I think when the convention says that the respective consuls "shall have exclusive charge of *the internal order* of the merchant vessels of their nation," the word "internal" imparts perfect precision to the proposition.

What is internal in this context? Plainly it seems to me everything which does not appertain, either by the law of nations or the municipal law, to the local jurisdiction. If the acts of *disorder*, if the "differences," be matters of local jurisdiction, then, as *questions*, they are jurisdiction external to the ship.

Apply the test to this or any other case of the same principle and it reconciles all controversy. Where there is in what occurs on board the ship no infringement of the laws of France, or of the United States, there the local authority has no concern in the matter, save, in the terms of the article, to support the consul, in maintaining the authority and executing the laws of his own Government.

I do not mean to say that the local authority may not, in either case, inquire into the legality of any alleged act of detention on board the foreign ship; but on ascertaining such legality, there the local authority is bound to stop. And surely no detention could be more thoroughly lawful than that of a mutineer on his way to the place of examination and judgment.

2. As to the extradition of the thirteen men still held in prison at Marseilles—I doubt whether it is, properly, a question of extradition.

It is manifest that these men are not fugitives from the justice of the United States seeking refuge in France.

In truth, these men have either been wrongfully taken from our national custody by inadvertence of the local authority, which ought in the mere correction of error to return them to our custody; or else they are to be regarded as prisoners held by the local authority, *pro tanto*, acting for us under the consular convention, and bound to retransfer them on demand to the direction of the consul in order to be replaced on board the *Atalanta*.

But if it be a case of extradition, then they are subject to it by the terms of the convention of November 9, 1843. That convention, it is true, does not provide for the crime of revolt or mutiny on board ship; but it provides for that of "attempt to commit murder"

2 E

(*tentative de meurtre*). That crime was committed in this case; it was committed within the putative territory of the Union; it is justiciable by the Federal courts, and by them alone; and you may, in my judgment, rightfully demand their extradition for this cause.

At the same time the convention speaks of "persons who shall be found within the territories of the other," and therefore the case comes within the letter of the convention.

It has been held in some parts of the United States that a misdemeanor is merged in a felony, and that a party guilty of the higher cannot be charged with the lower offence.

But that doctrine is losing ground; and it has never been held that, where an act involves two distinct felonies, the party may not be charged on either, at the election of the prosecuting officers of the Government.

I concur with Mr. Mason in opinion that the local authority of Marseilles exceeded its lawful power in the present case, in substance as well as in form.

The latter fact is implied by the new order of the Minister of Marine of June 24, 1856, regarding the visitation of foreign merchant ships in the ports of France.

This order, supplemental to those of July 26, 1832, and January 24, 1855, admits that theretofore the visitation should be made with concurrence of the consul.

It is material to observe, however, that the subject-matter of such visitation, in the face of all these orders, is perquisition into acts in violation of the laws of France. No such acts are pretended in this present case.

At the same time I do entire justice to the motives of the Emperor's Government in this transaction. They are frankly stated by M. Baroche.

The guilty parties are subjects of other nations, which, like us, are in amity with France, who seeks only to discharge her public duty to each with perfect impartiality. It is objections of theirs, rather than his own, which M. Baroche brings to the notice of Mr. Mason. Allow me to submit two or three legal suggestions applicable to this point.

I do not conceive that another nation, Sardinia for instance, can, simply because these men are her subjects, interpose in the question for any purpose except to see that they be lawfully tried. If a subject of Sardinia, having committed a crime in the United States, flee to France, can Sardinia justly object to his extradition? Surely not.

If indeed the Sardinian be a fugitive from the justice of Sardinia, having committed a previous crime there, and his extradition be demanded simultaneously by Sardinia and by the United States, then indeed France might be embarrassed by the conflicting appeals to her treaty engagements and her loyalty.

But this embarrassment only applies to the case regarded as a question of extradition. Taking the other and, as it seems to me, the truer view of the subject, there is no conflict of duties on the side of France; for the guilty parties have been from the beginning, and are still, in the constructive if not in the actual custody of the United States. That consideration furnishes a complete answer to the reclamations of any other Government.

Hon. Wm. L. Marcy, Sec. of State.　　　　C. CUSHING.

NOTES TO CHAPTER XIV.

The nationality of a merchant vessel depends upon—1, the construc- Nationality of tion or origin of the vessel ; 2, the owners to whom it belongs; 3, the ships. captain, and officers, and crew: Ortolan, tom. i. 180 ; see " Wildman on Search, Capture, and Prize," chap. iii.

In some countries a territorial character is allowed to foreign mer- Territorial chant vessels in their ports—limited, however, to offences committed by character of members of the same crew against one another on board the vessel : Or- ships. tolan, tom. i. 295. In France a distinction is taken between such offences where the peace of the port is not thereby disturbed, and where they are committed against persons not forming part of the officers and crew, or by any other than a person belonging to the same, or where the peace of the port is disturbed. In acts of the first class, the French courts decline jurisdiction ; in the others they assert it : Wheaton, Internat. Law, s. 102. But no such distinction exists in the English law, which exercises jurisdiction over *all* criminal offences committed on board foreign merchant ships in British ports.

On the question whether the vessels of a nation on the high seas are part of the territory of that nation, see some sensible remarks by Woolsey, Internat. Law, s. 54. He says that it is unsafe to argue on the assumption that they are altogether territory, but, on the other hand, they have certain qualities resembling those of territory : (1) as against

their crews on the high seas; (2) as against foreigners who are excluded on the high seas from any act of sovereignty over them, just as
if they were part of the soil of their country.   Vattel considers ships
on the high seas as part of a nation's territory: Liv. i. c. 19, s. 216 ; ii.
c. 7, s. 80.   As to ships of war, they are, even in foreign ports, exempt
from this local jurisdiction.   " It seems now established both in England and America, that no vessel or other property used by the Government for public purposes, whether those purposes be military, fiscal,
or of police, are subject to judicial proceedings without the consent of
the Government :" Wheaton, Internat. Law, s. 63, note 63 (8th edit.) :
see *The Lord Hobart*, 2 Dods. Adm. 103; 7 Attorney Generals' Opinions, 122.   Woolsey observes (Internat. Law, s. 54): " In both cases,
however, it is on account of the crew rather than of the ship itself that
they have any territorial quality.   Take the crew away—let the
abandoned hulk be met at sea; it now becomes property, and nothing
more."

In *R.* v. *Lopez*, 27 L. J. (M. C.) 49, it was said, *arguendo*, by the
counsel for the Crown, that it is a general principle of international
law that a ship, public or private, on the high seas is, for the purpose
of jurisdiction over crimes, a part of the territory of the country to
which it belongs, and that a foreigner going voluntarily on board an
English ship, and serving as one of her crew, is as amenable as a
British subject on board the ships, and, like a British subject, would be
liable in this country for a crime by statute 28 Hen. 8, c. 15, and 7 & 8
Vict. c. 2 : see Notes to Chapter VII. on Extra-territorial Jurisdiction,
p. 233.   And it was contended that the same principle governs the
law of America and France, in support of which the following authorities were cited : *The United States* v. *Palmer*, 3 Wheat. Rep. 609 ; *The
United States* v. *Holmes*, 5 *Ibid.* 112; Vattel, book i. c. 19, s. 216 ;
Fœlix, Traité du Droit Internat. Privé, ss. 544, 573 ; 2 Ortolan,
Régles Internat. de la Mer ; *R.* v. *Depardo*, 1 Taunt 26 ; *R.* v. *Serva*,
1 Den. C. C. 104.   In *R.* v. *Desley*, 29 L. J. (M. C.) 101, it was said,
per cur. : " It is clear that an English ship on the high seas, out of any
foreign territory, is subject to the laws of England; and persons,
whether foreign or English, on board such ship are as much amenable
to English laws as they would be on English soil.   The same principle has been laid down by foreign writers on international law."

" They went on board an English ship (of war), which for the purpose may be considered a floating island, and in that ship they became
subject to the English laws alone :" *per* Holroyd, J., *Forbes* v. *Cochrane*,
2 B. & C. 464 ; and see *per* Byles, J., in *R.* v. *Anderson*, 11 Cox C. C. 205.

But although merchant ships on the high seas have some of the
attributes of territory, when they arrive in a foreign port they have no
privilege, and are considered merely as the property of aliens.

The Court of Admiralty has jurisdiction in an action brought by a
British subject against a foreign ship for a collision in foreign waters :
The Griefswald, Swabey, Adm. 430.

CHAPTER XV.

ON THE POWER OF THE CROWN TO GRANT EXCLUSIVE RIGHTS OF TRADE (1).

(1.) OPINIONS *of* SIR WILLIAM JONES, SIR F. WINNINGTON, *and* MR. J. KING, *on the Statute of Monopolies*, 21 *James* 1, *c.* 3, *as to how far an action would lie, in the Barbadoes Courts, for seizing goods of the African Company.* 1676.

An action is brought against B in the Barbadoes, upon the Statute (21 Jac. 1, cap. 3) of Monopolies, for seizing certain goods imported thither from Guinea, contrary to the immunities and privileges granted by his Majesty to the Royal African Company.

Quære 1. Whether, in this case, the action lies upon that statute for treble damages, considering the proviso that exempts all charters granted to any companies or societies, erected for the maintenance or ordering of any trade or merchandize out of that statute?

I am of opinion, that this proviso doth exempt any charter, granted to any society of merchants, for the maintenance or ordering of trade, from being within the penalty of the statute; for that proviso, as it doth not confirm such charters, but leaves them to stand and fall by the common law, so it doth not inflict any new penalty upon them: wherefore, I think, an action will not lie upon this statute for treble damages, for doing anything in execution of such charter.

Quære 2. If any action lies upon the statute, can it be brought in any other courts but the King's Bench, Common Pleas, or Ex-

(1) Some of the views expressed in the Opinions in this chapter would certainly not be considered sound law at the present day, but I have thought it right to insert the Opinions in my work, as it is interesting and useful to see the change that has taken place in the mode of regarding some of the alleged prerogatives of the Crown.

chequer at Westminster, the statute seeming to restrain the subject to those courts?

It cannot be brought within any of the inferior courts within England; but if the law of the Barbadoes doth enact all statutes made in England to be of force there (for a statute made in England doth not of itself extend to any of the foreign plantations, unless the statute doth particularly name them), then an action will lie within their courts there upon a statute made here, though confined to the principal courts here; but, upon the answer given to the first *quære*, I think no action will lie upon this statute, for putting in execution this charter, but it will stand or fall by the common law.

November 13, 1676.   WM. JONES.

The second *quære* is out of the case, by the resolution of the first; for if this statute, as to the recovery of treble damages, extends not to the Royal African Company (as I conceive it doth not), then no action can be brought in Barbadoes or anywhere else.

November 16, 1676.   F. WINNINGTON.

I conceive no action lies upon this statute against the Company, or any agent of theirs, for any matter done in pursuance of their charter.

November 16, 1676.   J. KING.

(2.) OPINION *of the Attorney General*, SIR ROBERT SAWYER, *concerning Interlopers in the East Indies.* 1681.

REPORT OF THE ATTORNEY GENERAL CONCERNING INTERLOPERS.

In obedience to your Majesty's Order in Council of the 10th of November, whereby I am commanded to consider of the petition of the East India Company, and to report how the law stands, and whether such a proclamation may be granted as is desired: I humbly conceive that, by law, your Majesty's subjects ought not to trade or traffic with any infidel country not in amity with your Majesty, without your license; and that your Majesty may signify your pleasure therein, and require your subjects' obedience thereunto, by your royal proclamation. I am likewise of opinion, that the license given to the Company to trade into India, with a prohibition to others, is good in law, and the penalties of forfeitures of goods may therein run upon any goods which shall be seized within the limits of the Company's charter, as for breach of a local law made by your Majesty, which I conceive *your Majesty may make in the foreign plantations and colonies* inhabited by your Majesty's subjects by your permission. I am of opinion that your Majesty may issue such proclamation as is desired.

November 16, 1681. R. SAWYER.

(3.) OPINION *of* MR. WEST, *Counsel to the Board of Trade, on the question of establishing British Manufactures in France, and on the Prerogative of the Crown to restrain Trade.* 1718.

To the Right Honourable the Lords Commissioners of Trade and Plantations.

MY LORDS,—In obedience to your Lordships' commands, signified to me by Mr. Popple, I have perused and considered the several letters relating to the establishing several manufactures in foreign parts by British artificers; but, as the case is not particularly stated unto me, it will not be possible for me to give a direct answer to the question proposed. I shall therefore beg leave of your Lordships to consider it something at large, and to lay down some general positions which I take to be agreeable to the law of England; a right application of which, I believe, will in a great measure amount to an answer to such inquiries as may be made.

1. That particular subjects should have an uncontrollable liberty of all manner of trading, is not only against the policy of our nation, but of all other Governments whatsoever. I do, therefore, take it to be law, that the Crown may, upon special occasion, and for reasons of state, restrain the same; and that not only in cases of war, plague, or scarcity of any commodity, of more necessary use at home, for the provision of the subject, or the defence of the kingdom, &c. (in which cases the King's prerogative is allowed to be beyond dispute), but even for the preservation of the balance of trade; as, suppose a foreign prince, though in other respects preserving a fair correspondence and in amity with us, yet will not punctually observe such treaties of commerce as may have been

made between the two nations; or, in case there are no such treaties existing, refuses to enter into such a regulation of trade as may be for the mutual advantage and benefit of both dominions. On such occasion, I am of opinion that the King, by his prerogative, may prohibit and restrain all his subjects, in general, from exporting particular commodities, &c.; or else, generally, from trading to such a particular country or place; since trade does not only depend upon the will or laws of the prince whose subjects adventure abroad to carry it on, but also of that prince into whose country the commodities are exported, and with whose subjects commerce is negotiated and contracted. Without such a power, it is obvious that the Government of England could not be upon equal terms with the rest of its neighbours, and since trade depends principally upon such treaties and alliances as are entered into by the Crown with foreign princes; and, since the power of entering into such treaties is vested absolutely in the Crown, it necessarily follows that the management and direction of trade must, in a great measure, belong to the King.

2. Things of this nature are not to be considered strictly according to those municipal laws, and those ordinary rules, by which the private property of subjects resident within the kingdom is determined; but a regard must also be had to the laws of nations, to the policy and safety of the kingdom; the particular interest and advantages of private men must, in such cases, give way to the general good; and acting against that, though in a way of commerce, is an offence punishable at the common law.

3. Foreign trades carried on by particular subjects for their private advantage, which are really destructive unto, or else tending to the general disadvantage of the kingdom, are under the power of the Crown to be restrained or totally prohibited. There may be a prohibition of commerce without open enmity, as an actual declaration of war; and particular subjects, who, for private gain, carry on a trade abroad, which causes a general prejudice or loss to the kingdom, considered as an entire body, in doing so, manifestly act against the public good, and ought not only to be prohibited but punished. Carrying on such trades is, in truth (what some Acts of Parliament have declared some trades to be), being guilty of common nuisances: and if the Crown, which in its

administration of government is to regard the advantage of the whole realm, should not be invested with sufficient power to repress and restrain such common mischiefs, it has not a power to do right to all its subjects. If the public mischiefs, from such a way of trading, be plain and evident, there is the same reason for restraining particular persons from carrying on a trade that draws such consequences after it (though it be a trade that of itself is not prohibited by any particular law), as there is that a private subject shall not make such a use of his own house or land (in which he has an absolute propriety and a legal title to it) as will turn to the common annoyance and public detriment of the rest of the kingdom.

4. The general trade of the nation, and the maintaining of the customs and duties granted to the Crown for the support of it, are things of so public a concern, that whatsoever has a direct and evident tendency to the discouragement and disadvantage of the one, or to the diminution of the other, is a crime against the public. As an instance of which, I shall mention it as a kind of precedent, that raising and spreading a story that wool would not be suffered to be exported upon such a year (probably by some stock-jobbers in those times), whereby the value of wool was beaten down, though it did not appear the defendants reaped any particular advantage by the deceit, was, upon the account of its being an injury to trade, punished by indictment; and a confederacy, without any further act done, to impoverish the farmers of the excise and lessen the duty itself, has been held an offence punishable by information. If, therefore, the consequence of this present undertaking should prove what is apprehended from it, there can be no doubt but that the Crown has so much interest and concern for the trade of the nation and its own revenue, as to be able to put a stop to the carrying on a thing so mischievous to the one and the other by the advice and assistance of his Majesty's own subjects.

5. As to the particular subjects so employed abroad, there is no doubt but that the King, by his prerogative, may restrain them; it is agreed on all hands that the Statute of Fugitives is but an affirmance of the common law; that the Crown may, at its discretion, require the personal presence and attendance of the subject, lest the kingdom should be disfurnished of people for its defence,

as it is said in some books; and not only so, but upon a suspicion or jealousy that he is going abroad: *Ad quam plurima nobis et quam pluribus de populo nostro prejudicialia et damnosa ib⁻ prosequenda* (as the writ framed upon that occasion expressed it). The Crown is, by law, entrusted to judge what things those are which shall be looked upon to be mischievous and prejudicial to the Crown and people, and what caution is to be taken against them; and by that writ it appears it is equally criminal to do anything of that kind by any other hand as to do it personally himself; and therefore, after the writ has commanded his not going abroad, it adds: *Nec qui quicquam ib⁻ prosequi attemptes, seu attemptari facias, quod in nostrum seu dictæ coronæ nostræ præjudicium cedere valeat quovis modo: nec aliquem ib⁻ mittas ex hac causa.*

6. Upon the very foot of trade itself, it is necessary that the Crown should have a power over the persons and dealings of their subjects in foreign parts. By the law of nations, a Government, if they have no other redress, take goods from any of the same nation by way of reprisal for injustice done by one of the nations; so that Englishmen suffered to reside abroad, by their misbehaviour may endanger more than their own persons and estates. But, as the stating to your Lordships the power which the Crown has to prohibit the subject from going abroad, when there is reason to suspect that designs prejudicial to the kingdom are carrying on, alone is not sufficient to answer your Lordships' purpose, I shall beg leave to remind your Lordships of a case parallel to this, which has already had a determination at the board: anno 1705, several English merchants were concerned in a design to set up the manufacturing of tobacco in Russia, to which purpose they had carried over the necessary workmen and instruments; but, upon application to the Board of Trade, the then Lords Commissioners did represent it to the Queen in Council as their opinion, that the persons who had been already sent to Moscow might be recalled by letters of Privy Seal directed to her Majesty's envoy for that purpose, and that the engines and materials of working should be broken and destroyed in the presence of the said envoy, and that the persons at home who were concerned in sending the said workmen over should be enjoined not to send over any more workmen or materials, &c.

Upon inquiry, my Lords, I am informed that the said works and materials were actually destroyed in Russia, and the workmen sent back again by the direction of the envoy, who took the advantage of the Czar's absence from the place where they were established. What was then done may certainly be repeated. It is not the business of a lawyer to consider how such a method of proceeding may be relished by a foreign Court, but only to give it as his opinion that it may be *justified* as against particular subjects who are guilty of so high a crime against their country.

December 5, 1718.   RICH. WEST.

(4.) OPINION *of the Attorney General,* SIR PHILIP YORKE, *relating to English Subjects being engaged in the East India Company of Sweden.* 1731.

To the Right Honourable the Lords Commissioners for Trade and Plantations.

MY LORDS,—I received your Lordships' commands, by letter from Mr. Popple, signifying to me that your Lordships having some papers under your consideration relating to an East India Company lately erected in Sweden, wherein several Englishmen are thought to be engaged, not only as having shares in the said Company, but as captains, supercargoes, and sailors, had desired I would let your Lordships know what laws are now in force to restrain his Majesty's subjects, either in or out of this realm, from being anyways engaged as aforementioned, and what penalties they are subject to, as also my opinion whether his Majesty has any power to recall his subjects (other than artificers and manufacturers) from foreign parts, and if they are liable to any penalty upon their refusing to return.

As to the first question—what laws are now in force to restrain his Majesty's subjects, either in or out of the realm, from being engaged either as sharers in the said Company, or as captains, supercargoes, or sailors under them ?—I humbly certify your Lordships, that the Act made in the fifth year of the reign of his late Majesty King George I., entitled, " An Act for the better securing the lawful trade of his Majesty's subjects to and from the East Indies, and for the more effectual preventing all his Majesty's subjects trading thither under foreign commissions," expired at the end of the session of Parliament.

But the Act of the ninth year of his said late Majesty's reign, entitled, "An Act to prevent his Majesty's subjects from subscribing, or being concerned in encouraging or promoting, any subscription for an East India Company in the Austrian Netherlands, and for the better securing the lawful trade of his Majesty's subjects to and from the East Indies," is still in force, whereby it was (*inter alia*) enacted, that if any subject of his Majesty, his heirs or successors, should subscribe, contribute to encourage, or promote the raising, establishing, or carrying on, any foreign company or companies afterwards to be raised, formed, or erected for trading or dealing to the East Indies, or other parts within the limits of trade granted to the English East India Company, or should become interested in, or entitled unto, any share in the stock or capital of such company or companies—every person so offending shall forfeit all his and her interest, share, and concern in the capital stock or actions of such company, together with treble the value thereof, to be recovered and distributed as that Act directs.

Penalties are also inflicted by the said Act upon any of his Majesty's subjects who should know of any share or interest which any other subject had in any such company without discovering the same, or who should accept of any trust in any share or interest in any such foreign company.

It is also enacted, that if any subject of his Majesty, his heirs or successors (other than such as are lawfully authorized thereunto), should go, sail, or repair to, or be found in or at the East Indies, or any of the places aforesaid, every person so offending should be guilty of a high crime and misdemeanor, and should be liable to such corporal punishment or imprisonment, or to such fine as the Court where such prosecution should be commenced should think fit; and should and might be seized and brought to England, and upon their arrival here be committed until they should find security to answer for such offence as this Act requires.

By an Act made in the seventh year of the reign of his late Majesty King George I., c. 21, all contracts entered into by any of his Majesty's subjects for loans, by way of bottomry, on any ships of foreigners bound for the East Indies, and for loading or supplying such ships with a cargo or provisions, and all copartnerships or agreements relating to any such voyage or the profits thereof, and all agreements for wages for serving on board any such ships, are declared void.

Besides the particular penalties and provisions of these Acts, every subject of his Majesty offending by trafficking or adventuring to the East Indies, or visiting or haunting the parts aforesaid, under colour of being concerned in, or employed by, any such new company, will incur the penalties inflicted by the Act 9 & 10 Will. 3, c. 44—viz., the forfeiture of all ships and vessels employed in such trade, with the guns, tackle, apparel, and furniture thereunto belonging, and all the goods and merchandizes laden thereupon, and all the proceeds and effects of the same, and also double the value thereof, to be seized, sued for, and distributed, as by that and several subsequent laws is directed.

As to the second question, whether his Majesty hath any power to recall his subjects (other than artificers and manufacturers) from foreign parts, and whether they are liable to any penalty upon their refusing to return, I am of opinion that his Majesty may, by letters under his Privy Seal, require any of his subjects going into foreign parts without his royal licence (except merchants) to return home within a limited time upon their allegiance; and also merchants, in case they are guilty of any practices contrary to the duty of their allegiance or the laws of the land; and if any person, after such letters of Privy Seal served upon him, shall not return into Great Britain within the time thereby prescribed, he will forfeit the rents and profits of all his lands and tenements during his life, and all his personal estate.

As to seamen, his Majesty may, by a general proclamation under his Great Seal, command all seamen, being his natural-born subjects, who shall be in the service of any foreign prince or State, or employed on board the ships of foreigners, to return home upon the duty of their allegiance, and under the peril of being guilty of a contempt of his royal authority; and also prohibit all seamen to go into any foreign service, or to serve on board the ships of foreigners—and such proclamations have been frequently published in former reigns.

November 27, 1731.   P. YORKE.

(5.) OPINION *of* MR. FANE, *Counsel to the Board of Trade, on the Privileges of the Russia Company carrying on a Trade to Armenia.* 1734.

To the Right Honourable the Lords Commissioners for Trade and Plantations.

MY LORDS,—In obedience to your Lordships' commands, signified to me by Mr. Popple, inclosing extract from the charter of the Russia Company, and desiring my opinion whether the privileges therein granted to the said Company, particularly those of importing through Russia the produce and manufactures of Armenia Major or Minor, Media, Hyrcania, Persia, or the countries bordering on the Caspian Sea, do still subsist, notwithstanding the Acts of Navigation and the charter of the East India Company, confirmed by Acts of Parliament subsequent to the Russia charter: I have considered the several charters and the Act of Navigation, and I am humbly of opinion that the privileges granted to the Russia Company of importing through Russia the produce and manufactures of Armenia Major or Minor, Media, Hyrcania, Persia, or the countries bordering on the Caspian Sea, ceased by the Act of Navigation, by which all goods of foreign growth and manufacture are prohibited, under severe penalties and forfeitures, from being brought into England, Ireland, &c., from any place or places, country or countries, but only from those of their said growth or manufacture, or from those ports where the said goods can only, or are, or usually have been, first shipped for transportation, and from none other places or countries. This subsequent Act of Parliament, I think, therefore, very fully determines these privileges; but if there could be any doubt upon it, I apprehend the subsequent exclusive charter of the East India Company, confirmed by Act of Parliament, whereby the sole trade to those countries is granted to that Company, entirely takes away all pretences to those prior privileges.

June 17, 1734.   FRAN. FANE.

(6.) JOINT OPINION *of the Attorney and Solicitor General,* SIR DUDLEY RYDER *and* SIR JOHN STRANGE, *on an Act of Georgia about Trade with the Indians.* 1737.

To the Right Honourable the Lords Commissioners for Trade and Plantations.

MY LORDS,—We have considered the *quæries* sent to us by your Lordships, in Mr. Popple's letter of the 21st of June last, the first of which is: "Whether the Act of the Trustees of Georgia, or of any assembly, passed in the colonies abroad, and confirmed by the Crown, can grant to any of the said provinces an exclusive trade with the Indians dwelling within the respective provinces ?"

And, as to that, we are of opinion that, as an absolute exclusive trade with the Indians would be destructive of that general right of trading which all his Majesty's subjects are entitled to, and therefore repugnant to the laws of Great Britain, no Act of the Trustees of Georgia, or of any assembly, passed in the colonies abroad, and confirmed by the Crown, can grant to any of the said provinces an exclusive trade with the Indians dwelling within the respective provinces, though the method of trading within each respective province may be regulated by the laws thereof.

And as to the second *quære*—which is, whether the Act above mentioned excludes all persons whatsoever, whether inhabitants of Georgia or not, from trading with the Indians settled within the bounds of the province of Georgia, as described by the charter, except such as shall take out licences according to the direction of the said Act ?—we are of opinion that the Act there inreferred to does exclude all persons whatsoever, whether inhabitants of Georgia or not, from trading with the Indians settled within the bounds of the province of Georgia, as described by the charter, except such as shall take out licences according to the direction of the said Act; that Act and the reason of it extending *to all persons whatsoever,* and such taking out of licences being no more than a proper regulation of the trade within the said province.

D. RYDER.

July 28, 1737.　　　　　　　　　　　　　J. STRANGE.

432 CASES AND OPINIONS ON CONSTITUTIONAL LAW.

(7.) JOINT OPINION *of the Attorney and Solicitor General,*
SIR DUDLEY RYDER *and* SIR WILLIAM MURRAY, *on a Petition
which had been referred to the Privy Council, praying that the
Petitioners might be incorporated, and that the Crown would
grant to them the Property of all the Lands they should discover,
settle, and plant in North America, adjoining to Hudson's Bay,
not already occupied and settled by the Hudson's Bay Company,
with the like Privileges and Royalties as were granted to that
Company, with the Right of exclusive Trade.* 1748.

. . . . We have taken the same (petition) into consideration, and
have been attended by counsel both on behalf of the petitioners and
the Hudson's Bay Company, who opposed the petition, as it interferes
with their charter. The petitioners insisted on two general things:
that the Company's charter was either void in its original creation,
or became forfeited by the Company's conduct under it; that the
petitioners have, by their late attempts to discover the north-west
passage and navigation in those parts, merited the favour petitioned
for. As to the first, the petitioners endeavoured to show that the
grant of the country and territories included in the Company's
charter was void for the uncertainty of its extent, being bounded
by no limits of mountains, rivers, seas, latitude or longitude; and
that the grant of the exclusive trade within such limits as these
were was a monopoly, and void on that account. With respect to
both these, considering how long the Company have enjoyed and
acted under this charter without interruption or encroachment, we
cannot think it advisable for his Majesty to make any express or
implied declaration against the validity of it until there has been
some judgment of a court of justice to warrant it; and the rather
because, if the charter is void in either respect, there is nothing to
hinder the petitioners from exercising the same trade which the
Company now carries on. And the petitioners' own grant, if obtained, will itself be liable in a great degree to the same objection.
As to the supposed forfeiture of the Company's charter by nonuser
or abuser, the charge upon that head is of several sorts—viz., that
they have not discovered, nor sufficiently attempted to discover,
the north-west passage into the South Seas or Western Ocean;
that they have not extended their settlements through the limits

of their charter; that they have designedly confined their trade to a very narrow compass, and have for that purpose abused the Indians, neglected their own forts, ill-treated their own servants, and encouraged the French.

But in consideration of all the evidence laid before us by many affidavits on both sides (herewith inclosed), we think these charges are either not sufficiently supported in point of fact, or in a great measure accounted for from the nature and circumstances of the case. As to the petitioners' merit, it consists in the late attempts made to discover the same passage, which, however as yet unsuccessful in the main point, may probably be of use hereafter in that discovery, if it should ever be made, or in opening some trade or other, if any should hereafter be found practicable, and have certainly cost the petitioners considerable sums of money. But, as the grant proposed is not necessary in order to prosecute any further attempt of the like kind, and the charter of the Hudson's Bay Company does not prohibit the petitioners from the use of any of the ports, rivers, or seas included in their charter, or deprive them of the protection of the present settlements there, we humbly submit to your Lordships' consideration whether it will be proper at present to grant a charter to the petitioners, which must necessarily break in upon that of the Hudson's Bay Company, and may occasion great confusion by the interfering interests of two companies setting up the same trade against each other in the same parts under the like exclusive charters.

All which is humbly submitted to your Lordships' consideration.

D. RYDER.
August 10, 1748.   W. MURRAY.

NOTES TO CHAPTER XV.

The right of the Crown to grant to a subject an exclusive right of trading with foreigners was upheld in *East India Company* v. *Sandys* (10 State Tr. 371). In that case the defendant pleaded the statute 18 Edw. 3, sess. 2, c. 3; but the Judges held that this was limited to the trade in wool, which was the subject-matter of the Act. They agreed, however, that the clauses in the charter of the Company imposing penalties and forfeitures on persons invading their privileges

2 F

were invalid. The Judges in the same case also decided that the Statute of Monopolies (21 Jac. 1, c. 3) did not extend to the case of trade with foreigners. But it seems certain that such a grant would at the present day be held to be invalid at common law, if not by statute; and Lord Campbell, in his Life of Lord Jeffreys (Lives of the Chancellors, vol. iii. p. 581), says that to maintain its validity " is contrary to our notions on the subject." Formerly, however, a different opinion certainly prevailed, and charters granting an exclusive right of trade have at various periods been granted by the Crown. Amongst these, the most notable were the charters granted to the Russia Company by Philip and Mary; to the East India Company, by Elizabeth, in 1600; and to the Hudson's Bay Company, by Charles II., in 1670. But in 1693 the House of Commons resolved, that "it is the right of all Englishmen to trade to the East Indies, or any part of the world, unless prohibited by Act of Parliament;" and since that period there does not appear to have been any exercise of the assumed power of the Crown to grant a monopoly of foreign trade. When such a grant has been made it has been by the authority of an Act of Parliament. The statute 1 & 2 Geo. 4, c. 66, enacts that it shall be lawful for the Crown to make grants or give license to any body corporate, or company, or person, for the exclusive privilege of trading with Indians in certain parts of North America; and all such grants and licenses shall be good, "any law to the contrary notwithstanding." But no such grant or license is to be made or given for a longer period than twenty-one years.

In the case of the East India Company the right of exclusive trading to the east of the Cape of Good Hope, which was granted to them by the charter of William III. (1698), under the authority of statute 9 & 10 Will. 3, c. 44, s. 62, was from time to time continued by various Acts of Parliament, and was finally taken from them, in 1833, by statute 3 & 4 Will. 4, c. 85.

In 1857 a case was submitted to the Law Officers of the Crown (Sir R. Bethell, A.G., and Sir H. S. Keating, S.G.), on the question of the validity of the Hudson's Bay Company's charter,* and they said, in their Opinion: "The questions of the validity and construction of the Hudson's Bay Company's charter cannot be considered apart from the enjoyment that has been had under it during nearly two centuries, and the recognition made of the rights of the Company in various acts, both of the Government and the Legislature. Nothing could be more unjust, or more opposed to the spirit of our law, than to try this charter, as a thing of yesterday, upon principles which might be deemed applicable to it if it had been granted within the last ten or twenty years. These observations, however, must be considered as limited in their application to the territorial rights of the Company under the charter, and the necessary incidents or consequences of that territorial ownership. They do not extend to the monopoly of trade (save as territorial ownership justifies the exclusion of intruders), or to the right of an exclusive administration of justice . . . . But with respect to any rights of Government taxation, exclusive administration of justice, or exclusive trade, otherwise than as a consequence of the right of ownership of the land, such rights could not be legally insisted on by the Hudson's Bay Company as having been legally granted to them by the Crown. This remark, however, requires some explanation. The Company has, under the charter, power to make ordinances (which would be in the nature of bye-laws) for the government of the persons employed by them, and also power to exercise jurisdiction in all matters, civil and criminal; but no ordinance would be valid that was contrary to the common law, nor could the Company insist on its right to administer justice, as against the Crown's prerogative right to establish courts of civil and criminal justice within the territory. We do not think, therefore, that the charter should be treated as invalid, because it professes to confer these powers upon the Company; for to a certain extent they may be lawfully used, and for an abuse of them the Company would be amenable to law." This opinion will be found *in extenso* in the Appendix to the Blue Book, Report on the Hudson's Bay Company, 1857.

CHAPTER XVI.

ON THE WRIT OF HABEAS CORPUS.

JOINT OPINION *of the Attorney and Solicitor General,* SIR JOHN CAMPBELL *and* SIR R. M. ROLFE, *on certain proceedings relating to the issue of a Writ of Habeas Corpus in Canada.*

Temple, January, 1839.

MY LORD,—We have had the honour to receive your Lordship's letter of the 19th instant, transmitting to us the copy of a despatch from Sir John Colborne, with respect to the suspension of Messrs. Panet and Bedard, two of the Puisne Judges of the district of Quebec, from their offices, and requesting our opinion whether the proceedings of these Judges, on the occasion referred to, were consistent with law.

Having perused all the documents connected with this case, and maturely considered the subject, we have to report to your Lordship, that, in our opinion, the proceedings of Messrs. Panet and Bedard, on the occasion referred to, were not consistent with law.

We think that the writ of habeas corpus to bring up the body of John Teed, was improperly issued by M. Panet, on the 21st of November, 1838, and that his judgment and that of M. Bedard, on the return of this writ, holding that it had properly issued, are entirely erroneous.

The warrant of T. A. Young, on which Teed was in custody, showed that he was committed on suspicion of high treason ; therefore the Judge before whom a copy of the warrant was laid, had notice that the ordinance passed by the Special Council on the 8th of November, took away the power of bailing the prisoner, and if that ordinance was valid, the writ ought to have been refused. The doctrine is well settled that, whether a writ of habeas corpus be applied for before the full Court, or a single Judge, and whether under the statute or at common law, some probable ground for granting it must be disclosed by affidavit; and if it appears that when the prisoner is brought up he must, on his own showing, necessarily be remanded, the writ ought not to be granted.

We consider it unnecessary to discuss the question whether the Habeas Corpus Act, 31 Car. 2, was introduced into Canada by 14 Geo. 3. The writ of *habeas corpus ad subjiciendum* was unquestionably introduced into Canada as part of the criminal law of England; but there is great difficulty in saying that the specific regulations respecting that writ, and for bringing to trial persons charged with offences introduced into England by 31 Car. 2, were applicable to Canada before the provincial ordinance of 1784.

Assuming, however, that 31 Car. 2 was introduced into Canada by the authority of an Act of the Parliament of the United Kingdom, we are of opinion that it was suspended by the ordinance of the 8th of November, made under the imperial statute of 1 Vict, c. 9. The two Judges have picked out and relied upon a particular expression to be found in this statute, instead of looking to the general frame and scope of the statute, and the other enactments which it contains, wholly at variance with the construction they put upon the particular expression.

The proviso respecting Acts of the Parliament of Great Britain is evidently to be confined to Acts of the same nature as those expressly mentioned, and cannot be supposed intended to prevent the Special Council from passing any ordinance at all to vary the criminal law of Canada from what was the criminal law of England in the 14th year of King George III. If the extended sense were given to the proviso, the Special Council would be wholly inadequate for the purposes for which it is declared to have been created, and several of the most important enactments in 1 Vict. c. 9 would be entirely nugatory.

We think the two Judges would have been right in deciding that the return to the habeas corpus by the gaoler was insufficient, if the writ had properly issued; but their judgment upon the invalidity of the ordinance of the 8th of November is contrary to law.

As to the habeas corpus directed to Colonel Bowles, if the proceedings upon it are disconnected from the proceedings upon the habeas corpus directed to the gaoler, they appear to us to be regular. Affidavits were laid before M. Bedard, showing an unlawful detention of Teed, without disclosing that he had been committed on suspicion of treason, or showing anything to bring his case within the ordinance of the 9th of November. Supposing the writ to have lawfully issued to Colonel Bowles, he was in contempt for disobeying it, and subject to an attachment.

Considering, however, that there was upon the files of the Court an affidavit clearly showing that Teed had been committed on suspicion of high treason, that this affidavit had previously been brought to the notice of M. Bedard as well as of M. Panet, and that both Judges knew that Teed had been transferred to the custody of Colonel Bowles upon the original charge against him, we are bound to say that, in our opinion, the habeas corpus to Colonel Bowles ought not to have issued, and that the subsequent proceedings against him were unjustifiable.

The Lord Glenelg,   J. CAMPBELL.
&c.   &c.   &c.   R. M. ROLFE.

NOTES TO CHAPTER XVI.

It has been often said that *Jenkes's Case*, in 1676, 6 State Tr. 1189 —where so many difficulties were thrown in the way of his obtaining a writ of habeas corpus that he lay for several weeks in prison—was the cause of the passing of the statute 31 Car. 2, c. 2, known as the Habeas Corpus Act. But Hallam has satisfactorily shown that this is a mistake: Const. Hist. of England, iii. 15 (3rd edit.). The arbitrary proceedings of Lord Clarendon, in causing persons "to be imprisoned against law in remote islands, garrisons, and other places, thereby to prevent them from the benefit of the law," to quote the fourth article of his impeachment, really gave rise to it. So much importance was attached to the writ at common law long before the statute of Charles II., that we read of a Bishop of Durham who, in the 31st year of the reign of Elizabeth (1588), was fined £4000 for returning that he was a Count Palatine and therefore not bound to answer the writ: Bac. Abr. *Hab. Corp.* 6; and see *R. v. Pell*, 3 Keb. 279.

The old common-law remedy, where a person was improperly restrained of his liberty under no legal process, was the writ *de homine replegiando*, which did not issue of course, but was applied for by petition to the Great Seal, and upon affidavit disclosing the foundation on which it was prayed: Wilmot's Opinions and Judgments, p. 92. And when the writ was granted, an action was brought to determine the right of detention. Thus the defendant might plead that the plaintiff was his villein, and the plaintiff had to find sureties to deliver his body to the defendant in case the jury found the fact against him. The writ issued to the sheriff, commanding him to replevy the plaintiff, and the question between him and the person who had restrained his liberty was tried in the same way as in the case of a distress of chattels: Fitzherb. Nat. Brev. Writ *de Hom. Repleg.* It has been said that it does not appear when the writ of habeas corpus, which seems to have been adopted from the writ *de homine replegiando*, was first applied to relieve against private restraints: *Ibid.*

Chief Justice Wilmot declared the writ of habeas corpus to be " a remedial mandatory writ, by which the King's Supreme Court of Justice and the Judges of that Court, at the instance of a subject aggrieved, commands the production of that subject, and inquires after the cause of his imprisonment; and it is a writ of such a sovereign and transcendent authority, that no privilege or person can stand against it:" Opinions and Judgments, p. 88. For *Court*, however, in the passage just quoted, we may read *Courts.*

The writ of habeas corpus may issue either at common law, or under one of the statutes applicable to it. Where it issues under the statute 31 Car. 2, c. 2, it is marked *per statutum tricesimo primo Caroli secundi regis*, as sect. 3 of that Act provides. It must, however, be borne in mind that the Habeas Corpus Act, 31 Car. 2, c. 2, applies *exclusively* to cases of persons committed " for criminal or supposed criminal matters," and not to cases of restraint of liberty otherwise than for such matters. These latter cases are specially provided for by statute 56 Geo. 3, c. 100, which, however, excepts persons imprisoned for debt or by process in any civil suit: see *per* De Grey, C.J., in *Brass Crosby's Case*, 3 Wils. 188; S.C. 19 State Tr. 1138. Thus, a person confined as an alleged lunatic, or under any kind of private duress, cannot be relieved under stat. 31 Car. 2, c. 2, but must apply for a writ of habeas corpus at common law, or under stat. 56 Geo. 3, c. 100, with respect to the operation of which it was said by Patteson, J.: "That statute excludes criminal matter and process in civil suits—meaning, as I understand it, to except all cases of proceedings at law, and to include merely cases where parties are detained without any authority:" *Carus Wilson's Case*, 7 Q. B. 1010.

In the opinion given by Chief Justice (then Mr. Justice) Wilmot, in 1758, to the questions proposed to the Judges by the House of Lords, on the second reading of a Bill "for giving a more speedy remedy to the subject upon the writ of habeas corpus," he said: "I am of opinion that in cases not within the Act of the 31 Car. 2, writs of *habeas corpus ad subjiciendum*, by the law as it now stands, ought not to issue of course, but on probable cause, verified by affidavit. A writ which issues upon a probable cause verified by affidavit is as much a writ of right as a writ which issues of course. . . . . There is no such thing as writs of grace and favour issuing from the Judges; they are all writs of right, but they are not all writs of course. . . . . Writs of habeas corpus upon imprisonment for criminal matters were never writs of course; they always issued upon a motion grafted on a copy of the commitment; and cases may be put in which they ought not to be granted. . . . . If malefactors under sentence of death in all the gaols of the kingdom could have these writs of course, the sentence of the law might be suspended, and perhaps totally eluded by them. The 31 Car. 2 makes no alteration in the practice of the courts in granting them. . . . And in cases out of the Act, which take in all kinds of confinement and restraint, not for criminal or supposed criminal matter, and to which this question relates, it has been the uniform uninterrupted practice, both of the Court of King's Bench and of the Judges of that Court, that the foundation upon which the writ is prayed should be laid before the Court or Judge who awards it :" Wilmot's Opinions and Judgments, 81–129 (1). A case is afterwards mentioned by the learned Judge, to show that the whole facts ought to be fully disclosed on the motion for the writ. A man obtained the writ, directed to his wife's mother, to bring up his wife, upon an affidavit of detention by her; the fact

(1) The Bill was rejected by the House of Lords.

being, that he had entered into articles of separation, which had determined his right to the custody of his wife.

At common law the writ of habeas corpus is not grantable as of course. This was decided in *Hobhouse's Case*, 3 B. & Al. 420, where Abbott, C.J., said: "It would be a very strange inconsistency in the law of England if we were bound to do an act nugatory in itself; and that would be the case if, upon a view of the copy of the warrant, a writ was of course to issue, the only effect of which would be, that upon the return to it the prisoner must be remanded." And he referred to the opinion delivered by Wilmot, C.J., in 1758, in the House of Lords, where he said that writs of habeas corpus upon imprisonment for criminal matters were never writs of course; and cases might be put in which they ought not to be granted. In the same case Holroyd, J., said: "Even upon 31 Car. 2, c. 2, I should think it very questionable whether the writ was grantable of course, for that Act directs a Judge to grant in vacation upon view of the copy of the warrant." And, *per* Best, J.: "The cases in which prisoners have a right to the writ are where they are detained in prison, and when they are entitled to be admitted to bail. . . . In cases which come under this statute, a single Judge may perhaps be obliged to grant the writ as of course, but in no other; and the provisions of this law do not apply to writs grantable by the Court in term time."

Thus the writ has been refused in the case of a prisoner of war: *Case of the Spanish Sailors*, 2 W. Bl. 1324; and even a writ of *habeas corpus ad testificandum* in such a case: *Furby* v. *Newnham*, 2 Doug. 419, where Lord Mansfield said that the presence of witnesses under like circumstances was generally obtained by an order of the Secretary of State. In that case, however, it seems that the order had been applied for without success. When Napoleon Bonaparte was on board the *Bellerophon*, and it was known that his destination was St. Helena, a plan was proposed for getting him on shore by the issue of a writ of *habeas corpus ad testificandum*, on the pretence of some action in which he would be required as a witness; but the idea was not carried into execution.

The Habeas Corpus Act specially excepts from the benefit of its provisions persons committed or detained for treason or felony plainly expressed in the warrant of commitment, and persons convict or in execution by legal process. The Court of Exchequer refused to grant the writ for the purpose of charging in execution a person under military arrest. They said: "We have only civil jurisdiction, and have no authority to change the custody in such a case as this:" *Jones* v. *Danvers*, 5 M. & W. 234. But the writ was granted in the case of a military officer who was tried and convicted of manslaughter by a general court-martial in the East Indies, and sentenced to four years' imprisonment; but who was afterwards removed and sent in military custody to England, to undergo the remainder of his sentence: *Re Allen*, 30 L. J. (M. C.) 38. A writ of habeas corpus is not grantable in general where the party is in execution on a criminal charge after judgment on an indictment according to the course of the common law: *per cur. The Queen* v. *Lees*, 27 L. J. (Q.B.) 407.

In the reign of Charles II. the Court of King's Bench refused to bail a man committed on a charge of murder in Portugal: *Rex* v. *Hutchinson*, 3 Keb. 785. Also where a man was charged with a felony in Ireland contrary to the Irish statute: *Rex* v. *Kindersley*, 2 Stra. 848; see *Case of Canadian Prisoners*, 5 M. & W. 32; *Leonard Watson's Case*, 9 Ad. & Ell. 731; *Ex parte Newton*, 24 L. J. (C. P.) 148; *The Queen* v. *Lees*, 27 L. J. (Q. B.) 403, where the Court refused to grant the writ in the case of a prisoner convicted of a crime in St. Helena, and in execution of a sentence passed for that offence. The prisoner was in St. Helena when the writ was applied for. Where several persons were detained without any warrant on board a ship of war, having been captured in a smuggling vessel on suspicion of murder, the Court refused to discharge them or inquire into the facts of the case, but ordered them to be committed to the custody of the marshal, in order that they might be taken before a magistrate to be examined and further dealt with according to law: *Ex parte Kraus*, 1 B. & C. 258. The Court refused the writ to bring up a wife, it appearing that she was living apart from her husband by her own free will, and was under no restraint whatever: *Ex parte Sandilands*, 21 L. J. (Q. B.) 342. The Courts of Exchequer and Common Pleas both refused to grant the writ in the case of a person who had been committed by a Court of Assize for a contempt in refusing to answer a question put to him as a witness during a trial: *Ex parte Fernandez*,

30 L. J. (C. P.) 321. For instances where the writ has been granted, and the prisoner discharged in the case of extradition treaties, see *Re Fernan*, 33 L. J. (M. C.) 200; *Re Windsor*, 34 L. J. (M. C.) 163. In *Ex parte Wideman*, 14 L. T. (N. S.) 719, the writ was refused. When the return is substantially bad the Court will discharge the prisoner, and will not allow him to be arrested on another charge before due effect has been given to their judgment by his being allowed to leave the Court: *In the Matter of Douglas*, 3 Q. B. 825.

Where a prisoner had been committed for high treason under a warrant of the Secretary of State, and being brought up into the Court of King's Bench was charged with an indictment and re-committed by rule of Court, he afterwards applied for a writ of habeas corpus, and two out of the three Judges who were present decided that he was not entitled to it, as the Habeas Corpus Act speaks only of commitment by warrant, the prisoner was committed by rule of Court: *Rex v. Leonard*, 1 Stra. 142. But Parker, C.J., was of a different opinion. The Court refused also the writ where a person had been arrested in England for treason committed in Scotland, on the ground that the prayer for the writ "is only to be tried, and we cannot try a treason committed in Scotland:" *Rex v. Mackintosh*, 2 Stra. 308.

In *Carus Wilson's Case*, 7 Q. B. 984, a writ of habeas corpus was issued by a Baron of the Court of Exchequer in vacation under the seal of and returnable in the Court of Queen's Bench, and directed to the keeper of a gaol in Jersey, to bring up the body of the prisoner. An application was made to the Court of Queen's Bench to quash the writ, and it was contended that a Baron of the Exchequer had no such power as had been exercised; but the Court of Queen's Bench held that he had, and reliance was placed upon the statute 1 & 2 Vict. c. 45, s. 1, which provides that every Judge of the three superior Common Law Courts shall have juris-diction relating to any suit or proceeding in any of those Courts, or relating to the granting writs of certiorari or habeas corpus, "in like manner as if the Judge transacting such business had been a Judge of the Court to which the jurisdiction of law belongs." The Court said that the learned Baron (Rolfe) "had a discretion as to the Court where the writ would be made returnable, and might lawfully on these affidavits send the matter before the Queen's Bench."

It seems to have been once doubted whether the Court of Common Pleas could issue the writ at common law, owing to certain *dicta* that that Court could only grant it if the person were privileged there, or in order to charge him with an action. But it has been decided that it has co-ordinate jurisdiction in this matter with the other Courts: *Wood's Case*, 2 W. Black. 745; and see *Bushell's Case*, Vaugh. 154.

Whatever doubts may formerly have been entertained as to the power of a Judge of one of the three Courts of Common Law to issue the writ in vacation, returnable before himself at chambers, in the case of a prisoner committed in execution for a criminal offence, and therefore not within the statute 56 Geo. 3, c. 100, it is now settled that he has the power: *Leonard Watson's Case*, 9 Ad. & Ell. 731; and see Bac. Abr. *Habeas Corpus*, B. 1. That the Court of Chancery has the power in vacation as well as in term had been previously decided by Lord Eldon in *Crowley's Case*, 2 Swanst. 1.

Another question is, ought the rule for issuing the writ to be a rule *nisi*, or absolute in the first instance? In *Carus Wilson's Case*, 7 Q. B. 1001, the Court of Queen's Bench said: "We do not intimate that a previous inquiry would be wrong where there is reason for supposing the prisoner to be under sentence of a court. On the contrary, we think such a course the most desirable, and may conjecture that the learned Judge would probably, on more reflection, have granted a rule nisi for that purpose."

How writ obtained.   In order to obtain a writ of habeas corpus an affidavit is necessary, and it ought to be made either by the party himself who claims the writ, or by some other person, so as to satisfy the Court that the prisoner is so coerced as to be unable to make it: *Canadian Prisoners' Case*, 5 M. & W. 32. In the case of the *Hottentot Venus*, 13 East, 195, the affidavits were made by the secretary and members of a society called "The African Institution;" and although it does not so appear in the report, it was said by the Court of Exchequer in the *Canadian Prisoners' Case*, that a reason was there assigned for not producing an affidavit from the party herself. The Court ordered that she should be examined by the coroner and attorney of the Court, who reported that she was a free agent, and the rule nisi was discharged. See *In re Thompson*, 30 L. J. (M. C.) 19; *Cobbett* v. *Hudson*, 15 Q. B. 988.

An important question arises, whether, on a return to the writ, The return to affidavits are admissible to controvert the statements either in the the writ. return or the order of commitment, and show that they are not true ? A distinction must be here taken between cases under statute 31 Car. 2, c. 2, or at common law previous to statute 56 Geo. 3, c. 100, and cases to which the last-mentioned statute applies. The rule previous to that statute is thus laid down by Hawkins (Pleas of Crown, bk. ii. c. 15, s. 78) : "It seems to be agreed that no one can in any case controvert the truth of the return to a habeas corpus, or plead or suggest any matter repugnant to it. Yet it hath been holden that a man may confess and avoid such a return by admitting the truth of the matters contained in it, and suggesting others not repugnant, which take off the effect of them." Upon this point, see the cases cited in *Leonard Watson's Case*, 9 Q.B. 788–90. Wilmot, J., says: "In case the facts averred in the return to a writ of habeas corpus are sufficient in point of law to justify the restraint, I am of opinion that the Court or Judge before whom such writ is returnable cannot try the facts by affidavits in any proceeding grafted upon the return to such writ of habeas corpus :" Opinions and Judgments, p. 106. But it would seem that this doctrine ought now to be limited to cases of commitments for matter of a criminal nature (as in returns to writs under 31 Car. 2, c. 2), or commitments under civil process; for by sect. 3 of statute 56 Geo. 3, c. 100 (commonly called *Onslow's* Act)—which provides for the issuing of the writs of habeas corpus in vacation time, in the case of persons confined or restrained of their liberty, "otherwise than for some criminal or supposed criminal matter, and except persons imprisoned for debt or by process in any civil suit " —it is enacted that the Judge before whom *such* writ is returnable may examine into the truth of the facts set forth in the returns by affidavit, and " do therein as to justice shall appertain ;" and by sect. 4, " the like proceeding may be had *in the Court* for controverting the truth of the return . . . . . although such writ shall be awarded *by the said Court itself*, or. be returnable therein." Under the authority of this statute affidavits controverting the

truth of the return were admitted in the case of persons imprisoned
on a charge of smuggling: *Ex parte Beeching*, 3 B. & C. 136.
There, Abbott, C.J., said: " The habeas corpus in this case was a writ
issuing by virtue of the common law; and I think that under such
circumstances the 56 Geo. 3, c. 100, s. 4, gives to the prisoners
the right to controvert the truth of the return." But more recently, when a defendant had been committed to prison by order
of the Master of the Rolls, for not putting in an answer to a bill in
Chancery, the Court of Queen's Bench refused to allow affidavits
to be used, on a return to a writ of habeas corpus, to show that the
statements contained in the order were not true: *In the Matter of
Clarke*, 2 Q. B. 619. Patteson, J., there said: " There is no case
in which a party has been allowed in this way directly to contradict facts set forth in an order ; all that the Courts have permitted has been to allege a collateral extrinsic fact, confessing
and avoiding, as it were, the disputed order."

Here the distinction does not appear to be adverted to, between
a commitment for a criminal matter to which statute 56 Geo. 3,
c. 100, does not apply, and such a commitment as was then before
the Court; unless, indeed, it could be deemed an imprisonment " by
process in a civil suit," and so taken out of the operation of that Act.
An additional reason was, however, given by Lord Denman, C.J.,
for rejecting the affidavits, which puts the matter on a different
and more tenable ground. He said: " The adjudication of any
competent authority deciding on facts which are necessary to give
it jurisdiction is sufficient. *It would be different if the affidavits
tended to show that the magistrate's order was obtained by fraud, or
that he was not really exercising the functions which he professed to
exercise.*" And *per* Wightman, J.: " No case is cited in which
parties have been allowed to controvert a fact directly decided by
a Court of competent jurisdiction."

Where a prisoner is in custody under the sentence of a Court of
competent jurisdiction, no inquiry will be made by the Court on
the return to a writ of habeas corpus as to the validity of the sentence and lawfulness of the custody. As was said by Lord Denman,
C.J.: " When it appears that the party has been before a Court
of competent jurisdiction, which Court has committed him for a contempt, or any other cause, I think it is no longer open to this Court

to enter at all into the subject-matter. . . . . . The security which the public has against the impunity of offenders is, that the Court which tries must be considered competent to convict:" *Carus Wilson's Case,* 7 Q. B. 1008.   See also *In the Matter of Clarke, ubi sup.*; *R.* v. *Suddis,* 1 East, 306 (sentence of a court-martial); *Brass Crosby's Case,* 3 Wils. 199 (commitment by the House of Commons); *R.* v. *Flower,* 8 T. R. 325 (commitment by the House of Lords).   This, however, must not be taken to mean, that where it appears on the face of the return that the commitment was wrong, the Court will not discharge the prisoner.   In *Bushell's Case,* Vaugh. 135, the return was that the prisoner was a juryman who had been fined and imprisoned by the Court of Session at the Old Bailey (a Court of oyer and terminer), for giving a verdict contrary to evidence ; and he was discharged on the ground that the sentence was illegal.   And in the case of *Burdett* v. *Abbot,* 14 East, 150, Lord Ellenborough, C.J., said : "If a commitment appeared to be for a *contempt* of the House of Commons *generally,* I would neither in the case of that Court, or of any other of the superior Courts, inquire further : but if it did not *profess* to commit *for a contempt,* but for some matter appearing upon the return, which could by no reasonable intendment be considered as a contempt of the Court committing, but a ground of commitment palpably and evidently arbitrary, unjust, and contrary to every principle of positive law or national (*qu.* natural?) justice; I say that in the case of such a commitment (if it ever should occur, but which I cannot possibly anticipate as ever likely to occur) we must look at it and act upon it as parties may require from whatever Court it may profess to have proceeded."

What then, it may be asked, is the safeguard of the subject ? For the committing Court may suppress in its warrant the particulars of the cause of commitment, and then the Court which issues the writ of habeas corpus cannot inquire into it, or discharge the prisoner.   The only answer seems to be that conveyed in the judgment of Lord Denman, C.J., in the case of *The Sheriff of Middlesex,* 11 Ad. & Ell. 292, which had reference to a commitment by order of the House of Commons, but is in principle applicable to all commitments : "Indeed (as the Courts have said in some of the cases), it would be unseemly to suspect that a body, acting under such sanctions as a House of Parliament, would, in making its warrant, suppress facts which, if discussed, might entitle the person committed to his liberty." The truth is, that in many cases much must *necessarily* be left to the discretion and good sense of tribunals acting under the authority of the law, and responsible to public opinion. As was observed by De Grey, C.J., in *Brass Crosby's Case* (3 Wilson, 202 ; S. C. 19 State Tr. 1150-51): " It is better to leave some Courts to the obligation of their oaths. In the case of a commitment by this Court (Common Pleas), or the King's Bench, there is no appeal. Suppose the Court of King's Bench sets an excessive fine upon a man for a misdemeanor, there is no remedy, no appeal to any other Court. We must depend upon the discretion of some Courts. . . . Some persons, some Courts, must be trusted with discretionary powers."

A distinction must be taken between a commitment under a final sentence, or judgment, and a commitment for the purpose of trial. In the latter case the Court will examine on affidavits the circumstances under which a prisoner has been committed for trial, in order to see whether it is proper that he should be held to bail: see Bac. Abr. *Hab. Corp.* (B) 11: see *In the Matter of Douglas*, 3 Q. B. 825.

In a false return, it is said there is no remedy against the officer, but an action on the case at the suit of the party grieved, and an information or indictment: Bac. Abr. *Hab. Corp.* (B) 8. A writ of attachment will, however, issue against him as for a contempt: *Leonard Watson's Case*, 9 Ad. & Ell. 797.

The return to the writ ought to set out the warrant of commitment. In *Bushell's Case* (Vaugh. 137), Vaughan, C.J., said : " The cause of the imprisonment ought, by the return, to appear as specifically and certainly to the Judges of the return as it did appear to the Court or person authorized to commit ; else the return is insufficient." This, however, is stated too broadly. It certainly is not necessary to specify the particulars of the offence which led to the commitment, which may be quite unknown to the person to whom the writ is directed, and whose means of information are confined to the contents of the warrant itself. See the observations of the Attorney General (Sir V. Gibbs), *arguendo*, in *Burdett* v. *Abbot*, 14 East, 91, and the doubts thrown by Lord

ON THE WRIT OF HABEAS CORPUS.   449

Ellenborough, C.J., on the correctness of the proposition laid down
by Vaughan, C.J. Thus a commitment by a competent Court for
a contempt need not specify the nature of the contempt, and on a
return to the writ stating contempt generally, the Court will not
inquire into its nature and see whether it is sufficient to justify
the imprisonment. This was solemnly decided in the important
case of *The Sheriff of Middlesex*, 11 Ad. & Ell. 273, which was the
case of a commitment by order of the House of Commons, and
where all the authorities were elaborately reviewed (1). There
Littledale, J., said: "If the warrant declares the grounds of adjudication, this Court, in many cases, will examine into their validity;
but if it does not, we cannot go into such an inquiry." And in the
previous case of *Burdett* v. *Abbot*, 14 East, 1, 150,—as to which Lord
Denman, C.J., in the case of *The Sheriff of Middlesex, ubi sup.* 289,
declared that there is perhaps no case in the books entitled to so
great weight,—Lord Ellenborough, C.J., said: "If a commitment
appeared to be for a contempt of the House of Commons generally, I would neither in the case of that Court or of any other
of the superior Courts inquire further."

In the case of a commitment under a writ *de excommunicato
capiendo*, it was held that the cause of excommunication must be
set forth in the writ; and the reason assigned was that by statute
5 Eliz. c. 23, the writ is made returnable in the Court of Queen's
Bench, "which could be to no purpose if the cause were not to be
set forth in the writ, and this Court judge of that cause:" *R.* v.
Fowler, 1 Salk. 293, 350; and see *R.* v. *Snellor*, Vern. 24.

The return need not be, and in practice never is, supported by
affidavits: *Leonard Watson's Case*, 9 Ad. & Ell. 731–794.

We have seen that under a writ of habeas corpus the warrant of

(1) By an order of the House of Commons, 23rd of June, 1647 (the Long
Parliament), the sergeants and keepers of persons were directed to make returns
to writs of habeas corpus, with the causes of detention; but the judges were
ordered not to proceed to bail or discharge the prisoners without notice to the
House: 5 Com. Jour. 221; see May's Parliam. Pract. 71, n. 5 (3rd edit.). It is
needless to say that, so far as it applies to the Judges, such an order would, at the
present day, be entirely disregarded, and they would act in the spirit of Willes,
C.J., who said, in *Wynn* v. *Middleton*, 1 Wils. 128: "I declare for myself that
I will never be bound by any determination of the House of Commons against
bringing any action at common law for a false or a double return; and a party injured may proceed in Westminster Hall, notwithstanding any order of the House."

2 G

commitment (or a copy of it) must be returned. But in several cases, such as commitments by Courts for contempts, and in passing sentence on persons convicted of crimes, there is no warrant, but merely the oral authority of the Court to keep the prisoner in custody. In *Carus Wilson's Case*, 7 Q. B. 1011 (the case of a sentence of imprisonment for contempt, pronounced by a Court in Jersey), Patteson, J., said : " No warrant was necessary. Courts in such cases seldom act by warrant. We never do. If a party is brought up we sentence him in open Court. The same course is pursued at the assizes and at the sessions. When a man is sentenced to be hanged no warrant issues." (But if sentence is not awarded in open Court, the service of a written warrant is necessary : see *per* Parke, B., in *Ely* v. *Moule*, 5 Ex. R. 925. And when a justice of the peace commits for contempt, a warrant is necessary : *Mayhew* v. *Locke*, 7 Taunt. 63.) What then in such cases is the gaoler to do when called upon to make a return to the writ ? This question is answered by what was said by the Court in *King* v. *Clerk*, 1 Salk. 349 : " Where a commitment is in Court to a proper officer there present, there is no warrant of commitment, and therefore he cannot return a warrant *in hæc verba*, but must return the truth of the whole matter under peril of an action."

A defect in form in a commitment by a Court of oyer and terminer will not entitle a prisoner to his discharge where there appears a good cause for his commitment: see *Bethell's Case*, 1 Salk, 348, where the Court said : " Before *Bushel's Case* (6 State Tr. 999), no man was ever by habeas corpus, without writ of error, delivered from a commitment of a Court of oyer and terminer ;" and see *Hammond's Case*, 9 Q. B. 92. As was said by the Court of Queen's Bench in *Leonard Watson's Case*, 9 Ad. & Ell. 787 (where reliance was placed on the authorities—*Barnes's Case*, 2 Ro. Rep. 157 ; *R.* v. *Suddis*, 1 East, 306 ; and see *Beenan's Case*, 10 Q. B. 492) : " Returns to the writ of habeas corpus do not require minute correctness if the substance of the facts is stated." But in an earlier case, Bayley, J., said : " In these cases the greatest certainty is requisite, for the Court must see distinctly that the party who is brought up is justly deprived of his liberty :" *Deybel's Case*, 4 B. & Al. 246. Perhaps, however, these apparently conflicting statements may be reconciled by making a distinction between commitments by regular Courts of competent jurisdiction and commitments under a special authority given by Act of Parliament. In the case to which the observations of Mr. Justice Bayley applied, the prisoner had been impressed as a seaman as a penalty for having been engaged in smuggling by virtue of the provisions of statute 59 Geo. 3, c. 121.

An error in the return may be amended: *Re Clarke*, 2 Q. B. 619; *Leonard Watson's Case*, 9 Q. B. 731. As was pertinently observed by Lord Eldon, L.C., in 2 Russ. 584, "It would be a strong thing to say, that the merits of a committal are to be tried merely by the return to the writ, however erroneous that return may be. The return ought to show by whose order the commitment was made, and a return alleging that the prisoner is a deserter, and detained under statute 5 & 6 Vict. c. 12, ought expressly to show that he is a soldier and ought to be with his corps:" *Re Douglas*, 3 Q. B. 825.

In *Carus Wilson's Case*, 7 Q. B. 1001, the Court of Queen's Bench said: "We find from the Master of the Crown Office that the Court held more than once, in 26 Geo. 3, that no writ of habeas corpus should be quashed for matter that can be properly returned to it. As a general order, that is certainly the most convenient course—most just to the party applying for the writ, and most in furtherance of the great object for which our Constitution has appointed it."

As to the right of action for refusal of copy of the commitment or warrant, see *Hudson* v. *Ash*, 1 Stra. 167.

If no return is made to the writ, the Court will grant an attachment *nisi*, without a rule to return the writ: *R.* v. *Wright*, Stra. 915. It will not, however, grant an attachment to accompany the writ in the first instance: *R.* v. *Earl Ferrers*, 1 Burr. 631.

The penalty of £500, imposed by stat. 31 Car. 2, c. 2, s. 10, Penalty. applies only to a refusal of the writ by a Judge *in vacation time*. The statute, says Hawkins, "leaves it to their discretion in all other cases to pursue its directions in the same manner as they ought to execute all other laws, without making them subject to the action of the party:" Pleas of Crown, bk. ii.

The writ should be directed to the person who has the actual custody of the prisoner, and ought not to be in the disjunctive—as,

2 G 2

for instance, to " the sheriff or gaoler :" *R.* v. *Fowler*, 1 Salk. 350. In execution in civil cases, the custody is that of the sheriff, but in criminal that of the gaoler : *Ibid.*

Where the writ runs. It is laid down that the King may send his writ of *habeas corpus ad subjiciendum* to whom he pleases, and he must have an answer of his prisoner wherever he be : Bacon Abr. *Hab. Corp.* (B) 6. And it runs at common law to all the dominions of the Crown : *Calvin's Case,* 7 Co. 20 a ; *R.* v. *Cowle,* 2 Burr. 856 ; Bac. Abr. *Hab. Corp.* (B) 2 ; *Re Anderson,* 30 L.J. (Q.B.) 129, where the writ was granted to bring up the body of a British subject in Canada alleged to be illegally in custody there. The Court said : " The more remarkable cases are the instances in which the writ of habeas corpus has issued into the islands of Jersey, Man, and St. Helena, all these in very modern times." Lord Denman, C.J., in delivering the judgment of the Court in *Carus Wilson's Case,* 7 Q. B. 998, said : " That the writ of *habeas corpus ad subjiciendum* has legal force in the island of Jersey, and must be obeyed there, is now admitted on all hands. It was held that the writ lay to Calais, when that town was subject to the Crown of England—Bacon Abr. *Hab. Corp.* (B) 2— and to the Isle of Man : *Crawford's Case,* 13 Q.B. 613 ; *Re Brown,* 33 L.J. (Q.B.) 193, where it was held that the Isle of Man is not a *foreign* dominion of the Crown."

Now, however, by stat. 25 & 26 Vict. c. 20, no writ of habeas corpus shall issue out of England, by authority of any Judge or Court of Justice therein, into any colony or foreign dominion of the Crown, where Her Majesty has a lawfully established court or courts of justice, having authority to grant and issue the writ, and to ensure the due execution thereof throughout such colony or dominion.

Suspension of the writ. The following are instances of suspension of the writ of habeas corpus by Act of Parliament : 1 Will. & M. stat. 1, cc. 7, 19 ; 7 & 8 Will. 3, c. 11 ; 6 Anne, c. 15 ; 1 Geo. 1, cc. 8, 30 ; 17 Geo. 2, c. 6 ; 19 Geo. 2, c. 1 ; 17 Geo. 3, cc. 3, 9 ; 34 Geo. 3, c. 54 ; 35 Geo. 3, c. 3 ; 38 Geo. 3, c. 36 ; 39 Geo. 3, c. 44 ; 39 & 40 Geo. 3, c. 32 ; 41 Geo. 3, c. 26 ; 57 Geo. 3, cc. 3, 55 ; 11 & 12 Vict. c. 35.

CHAPTER XVII.

ON CERTAIN POINTS RELATING TO CRIMINAL LAW.

(1.) JOINT OPINION *of the King's Advocate*, SIR CHRISTOPHER ROBINSON, *and the Attorney and Solicitor General*, SIR ROBERT GIFFORD *and* SIR JOHN COPLEY, *on an application by the United States Government, that certain Proceedings of Outlawry in Canada might be revoked.*

Doctors' Commons, May 15, 1823.

MY LORD,—We are honoured with your Lordship's commands of the 3rd instant, transmitting a letter from Lord Francis Conyngham, inclosing the copy of a note which has been addressed to Mr. Secretary Canning by the American Minister in this country, requesting that certain proceedings of outlawry which have been passed in Upper Canada, against John M'Donnell, may be revoked; and your Lordship is pleased to request that we would take the same into consideration, and report to your Lordship our opinion, as to the steps necessary to be pursued in the event of his Majesty deeming it expedient to comply with the application of the American Government.

In obedience to your Lordship's commands, we have the honour to report that, in the event of his Majesty deeming it expedient to comply with the application of the American Government, the effect of the outlawry against John M'Donnell, the legality of which does not appear to be questionable, may be removed, either by a *nolle prosequi* being entered upon the indictment, by the Attorney General of the province, on the part of his Majesty, or by a general pardon to be granted to Mr. M'Donnell.

CHRIST. ROBINSON.
R. GIFFORD.
J. S. COPLEY.

To the Earl Bathurst,
&c. &c. &c.

(2.) JOINT OPINION *of the Attorney and Solicitor General,* SIR JOHN COPLEY *and* SIR CHARLES WETHERELL, *on a Petition presented to the Governor of the Colony of the Cape of Good Hope containing libellous matter, and as to how far it was privileged* (1).

Serjeants' Inn, April 28, 1825.

MY LORD,—We have had the honour to receive your Lordship's letter, dated the 13th instant, requesting our opinion upon the following questions, viz.:

1st. Whether under the statute 1 Will. & M. c. 2, or under any general principle or maxim of the law of England, it is competent to a natural-born British subject of his Majesty resident in the colony of the Cape of Good Hope, to present with impunity to the Governor of that settlement a petition for redress of grievances, containing statements which, if published to the world at large, would, according to the principles both of Dutch and English law, have been libels in the Courts of the colony; and which, according to the principles of Dutch law, would be punishable as libels, even though communicated exclusively to the Governor?

2nd. Whether the impunity of the petitioner in such a case depends upon the statements in question being relevant to the objects of his petition; or whether libellous statements, if clearly irrelevant and unnecessary, would subject him to a criminal prosecution for libel?

3rd. Whether any distinction is to be made between petitions presented to the Governor in his judicial character, and those addressed to him as the chief executive officer of Government in the colony?

4th. Whether his Majesty's subjects born in Great Britain enjoy any privileges in this respect, while actually in the Cape of Good Hope, distinct from those of the Dutch inhabitants who have become his Majesty's subjects by the cession of the colony?

In compliance with your Lordship's request, we have taken into our consideration the statement and questions contained in your Lordship's letter, and beg leave to report, as our opinion upon the first question, that a British subject born within the United Kingdom, but resident at the Cape of Good Hope, could not so act with

(1) See page 86, *ante.*

impunity, but would be subject to punishment according to the laws of the colony in which he was resident; and as to the second question, we think the circumstance of the libellous statements being irrelevant and unnecessary would not in England subject the party to punishment in the case of such a petition as would be deemed a privileged communication.

As to the third question, it would with reference to this subject be difficult to separate the characters of Governor and Judge, and to say that any petition of this description was presented to the Governor merely in his judicial capacity. But even if such separation could be made, and it were clear that the petition was presented to him solely in his judicial character, still if he had authority to interfere in the matters to which the petition related, such petition would, we think, according to the law of England, be a privileged communication.

As to the fourth question, we are of opinion that his Majesty's subjects born in Great Britain do not enjoy any privileges in the above respects, while actually resident at the Cape, distinct from those of the Dutch inhabitants who have become his Majesty's subjects by the cession of the colony.

To Earl Bathurst,   J. S Copley.
&c. &c. &c.   Chas. Wetherell.

(3.) Joint Opinion of the King's Advocate, Sir Herbert Jenner, and the Attorney and Solicitor General, Sir Charles Wetherell and Sir Nicolas Tindal, on a trial of Pirates at Malta; on a Jury de medietate, and Right of Challenge in that case.

Doctors' Commons, April 24, 1828.

Sir,—We are honoured with your commands, signified in your letter of the 8th instant, transmitting a case which has been prepared under your direction, respecting certain persons who have been capitally convicted of piracy before the Court for the trial of pirates at Malta; and you are pleased to request that we would, with the least possible delay, report for his Majesty's information our opinion upon the question proposed for our consideration at the conclusion of that case.'

In obedience to your commands, we have the honour to report

that we think the sentence against the three convicts mentioned in the preceding statement may be legally carried into effect. For we conceive the object of the Legislature in passing the 46 Geo. 3 was to substitute a trial by the common course of the law in England where persons are charged with piracy in colonies and other places beyond sea, instead of a trial by the course of the civil law, which had been directed by the statute 11 Will. 3; and we think the Act must have a reasonable construction put upon it, and that it must intend a trial by jury, so far as the forms of that trial are practicable in the country where it takes place.

Indeed, to construe the Act as requiring the trial by jury in all the exact forms for naming and summoning the jury prescribed by the law of England would be to make the statute a dead letter. It appears that the charge was first submitted to persons summoned in the nature of a grand jury, and found by them to be a true bill. The number, indeed, of such jurors is not expressly stated, but we assume that twelve of the jurymen concurred in such finding of the bill, and that such twelve constituted a majority. The trial then took place by twelve persons, half being subjects of his Majesty and half being aliens, and chosen out of a number summoned to serve on the jury amply sufficient to allow of all the challenges to which the prisoners were entitled (1). We are of opinion, therefore, that the Act has been complied with as closely as circumstances would allow, for a mode of naming and summoning the jury more conformable to the English law is stated to be impracticable in the island.

As to the objection that two of the alien jurymen were disqualified upon the ground of their having been attainted of treason and felony, and outlawed in consequence thereof by the law of a foreign country, we see no reason to believe that parties so circumstanced come within the scope of the exception in 6 Geo. 4, c. 50, s. 3, which we think must be interpreted as descriptive of persons attainted and outlawed by the English law. And, at all events, in the present case the objection came too late, for it was properly the ground of challenge only, which must be made before the jury-

(1) In the Notes to Chapter IV. (p. 117, *ante*), I have expressed an opinion that pirates, although foreigners, are not entitled to be tried by a jury *de medietate*; but I do not feel at all sure on the point.

men are sworn, and cannot be insisted upon afterwards. And here it appears by the statement that the prisoners must have been aware of the objection before the trial, inasmuch as we collect that it was taken and proved before the jury was discharged. Upon the whole, therefore, assuming the grand jury to have been constituted as above supposed, we think the inquiry and trial has been according to the common course of the law of England within the meaning and construction of the Act. Upon the other part of the statement in the petition, which appeals to a merciful consideration of the case, we do not of course presume to give any opinion.

HERBERT JENNER.

The Right Hon. Mr. Sec. Huskisson,   CHAS. WETHERELL.
   &c. &c. &c.   N. C. TINDAL.

In case it should upon further investigation be ascertained that the prisoners and their counsel were unacquainted with the ground of challenge at the time when such challenge ought to have been taken, we think it right to state that that circumstance will not, in strictness of law, make any difference whatever, as the challenge must be taken before the trial begins. But at the same time, as a reasonable doubt may be raised that the prisoners, from inadvertency or ignorance, have lost an advantage, it may be matter of discretion for the Crown whether the severest measure of punishment should be inflicted in that case.

HERBERT JENNER.
CHAS. WETHERELL.

April 30, 1828.   N. C. TINDAL.

(4.) JOINT OPINION *of the Attorney and Solicitor General* SIR THOMAS DENMAN *and* SIR WILLIAM HORNE, *on the Right of Slaves to claim Benefit of Clergy, and degree of certainty required in an Indictment.*

Lincoln's Inn, January 24, 1832.

MY LORD,—We feel ourselves bound to take the earliest opportunity of answering your Lordship's letter of the 18th instant, which submits to our consideration a case respecting the trial of certain slaves in the island of Tortola, because the doctrines on which the claim to benefit of clergy on the part of slaves in Tortola has been resisted in that island, go the whole length of depriving that class of all protection from the law, except where special enactments have been made in their favour.

According to those doctrines, the inquiry whether a slave has been lawfully convicted before he is put to death must always be superfluous, for he is boldly declared to derive no protection from the common law, and to be out of the King's peace. Not only the public executioner, therefore, but any private individual is at liberty to treat him in any way he may think proper, subject only to such penalties (if any) as may have been specifically provided for the fact committed, and to such damages as the owner may recover for the injury done to his property in the slave.

These doctrines do not appear to have been universally adopted. The Commissioners for legal inquiry have in their reports distinctly pronounced their opinion that slaves, as subjects of his Majesty, are entitled to the protection of the common law, and many lawyers in the colonies have plainly viewed the subject in the same light. We do not hesitate to inform your Lordship that such is also our opinion, and it follows that to deprive a slave of life without lawful authority must be murder or manslaughter, according to the circumstances of the particular case.

Having cleared away this preliminary difficulty, which would have precluded all further inquiry, we beg leave to state that we have read the case attentively, and think the questions correctly propounded at its close,—whether the indictment against Sam Fahie, Andrew Fahie, Johnns Purcell, Jacob Kierney, and Mac-Daniel (otherwise called McDonald), is sufficiently precise and definite to be sustained in point of law ; and, secondly, whether the slaves ought to be admitted to their benefit of clergy.

We entertain no doubt on the first point. The indictment is, in our opinion, completely worthless, as giving the accused no notice of the offence with which he stands charged. The first principles of law require that the charge shall be so preferred as to enable the Court to see that the facts amount to a violation of the law, and the prisoner to understand what facts he is to answer or disprove.

No argument is necessary to show that this indictment is insufficient, and unavailing for either purpose.

If sufficient overt acts had been set forth, and the jury had found the prisoners guilty, we are inclined to think, on the very technical point relating to benefit of clergy, that the prisoners would not have been entitled to that privilege. But we deem this discussion unnecessary, after giving a deliberate opinion on the nature of the indictment.

But, with a view to the future administration of criminal law in Tortola, and in other colonies where similar laws may have been made, we crave permission to express our serious doubts whether the law of 1783 is not in its own nature too vague, indefinite, and unintelligible to be capable of enforcement in any case: in other words, whether it is not, like some other legal instruments canvassed in courts of justice, void for uncertainty.

We also conceive that this law may well be challenged as being contrary to natural justice. The crime to be punished is thought not even requiring to be evinced by any overt act. The only overt act mentioned (and that as a separate crime) is speaking words tending to mutiny, &c. But unless they should be wilfully spoken it is against reason to punish the utterer.

Sir Edward Coke, in the eighth part of his Reports (page 118), records the opinion of the Court of King's Bench, that " in many cases the common law will control Acts of Parliament, and sometimes adjudges them to be utterly void ;" and though Blackstone (1 Com. 85) questions the right of the judicial authority to overrule the legislative, he exemplifies the manner in which the former may easily elude the latter.

For avoiding such collisions, and for establishing a criminal law which may admit of no difficulties in the execution, we respectfully suggest the propriety of a speedy change in that upon which the questionable indictment against the five slaves has been founded.

To the Right Hon. Visct. Goderich,	T. DENMAN.
&c. &c. &c.	WM. HORNE.

(5.) JOINT OPINION *of the Attorney and Solicitor General,* SIR WILLIAM HORNE *and* SIR JOHN CAMPBELL, *on the Power of the Crown to grant a Conditional Pardon.*

Lincoln's Inn, December 26, 1832.

MY LORD,—We have the honour to acknowledge the receipt of your Lordship's letter of the 28th November last, transmitting to us a copy of a despatch dated 31st May last, which your Lordship received in the month of June from the Governor of Antigua ; and the copy of a despatch from yourself to the Governor, dated 19th of the same month ; the copy of a despatch from the Governor to your Lordship, dated 30th August, and of two enclosures contained in it—these papers comprising the answer of the law officers of the Crown of Antigua to three questions proposed by your Lordship for their consideration, and requesting us to report to your Lordship our opinion with reference to these questions. We beg to state to your Lordship that we entirely concur in opinion with the law officers of Antigua upon the several questions submitted to us.

1st. We think that the introduction of the slave Mary into Antigua from Saint Bartholomew, under the circumstances stated, was not a violation of the Act for the abolition of the slave trade ; as this Act could not be meant to prevent a fugitive slave, who had absconded from his master to a foreign island, from voluntarily returning or being brought back by the person who induced his clandestine departure.

2nd. The Colonial Act on which this indictment proceeded appears to us to define with sufficient clearness the offence for which the prisoner was tried.

3rd. We are of opinion that if the party, after accepting the conditional pardon, should in breach of the conditions return to the island, he might in strictness be referred back to his original sentence, and, his identity being proved, execution might be awarded against him.

There is hardly anything to be found respecting conditional pardons in the old English law-books (1) ; but the authority of the Crown to grant a conditional pardon in capital cases is distinctly recognized in statute 5 Geo. 4, c. 84, s. 2 ; and it has been several times decided by the English Judges, that where the condition on which a pardon was granted has been broken, the offender may be referred to his original sentence. But we feel it our duty to add that this power, in our opinion, could only be properly used for compelling a performance of the condition.

To the Right Hon. Visct. Goderich,   W. HORNE.
&c.   &c.   &c.   J. CAMPBELL.

(1) The Crown may extend its mercy on what terms it pleases, and consequently may annex to its pardon any condition that it thinks fit, whether proce-

(6.) Joint Opinion *of the Attorney and Solicitor General,* Sir Frederick Pollock *and* Sir William Follett, *on the commutation of Sentence of Death to Transportation, with consent of the Convict.*

Temple, August 31, 1842.

Sir,—We beg to acknowledge the receipt of your letter of the 10th instant, wherein you state that George Hiscock, a soldier of the 76th Regiment, having been sentenced by the civil courts in Nova Scotia to death for the crime of firing at a sergeant of that corps with intent to kill, the Lieutenant-Governor of the province, at the instance of the jury, recommended a mitigation of the sentence.

The Lieutenant-Governor was in consequence authorized to commute it for transportation for life: on consulting, however, the Attorney General of the province, that officer has suggested doubts as to the mode in which the proposed mitigation of punishment can be lawfully carried into execution.

You were pleased to enclose for our information a copy of the despatch from the Lieutenant-Governor, communicating a copy of the report made by the Attorney General; and you further stated that you had been directed by Lord Stanley to request that we would take the subject into our early consideration, and state to his Lordship our opinion respecting the steps to be taken for giving effect to Her Majesty's directions in favour of the prisoner.

In obedience to his Lordship's commands we have taken this matter into our consideration, and have the honour to report that we think a pardon ought to be granted under the Great Seal of the province, in which the condition of transportation and the place to which the convict is to be transported should be clearly expressed. The consent of the convict in writing should be previously obtained;

---

dent or subsequent, on the performance whereof the validity of the pardon will depend: Hawkins P. C. Bk. ii. c. 37, s. 45; see *R.* v. *Miller,* 2 W. Bl. 797; *R.* v. *Madan,* 1 Leach, C. C. 223; *R.* v. *Dickie, ib.* 390; and the Opinion of the Law Officers, p. 76, *ante.* See also Stat. 16 & 17 Vict. c. 99, s. 5. As to cases where the Crown extends mercy to a prisoner convicted of a capital offence upon condition of his being kept to penal servitude for any term of years, or for life, see *The Queen* v. *Baker,* 7 Ad. & Ell. 502; *Leonard Watson's Case,* 9 Ad. & Ell. 783.

after this we think the convict may lawfully (under 5 Geo. 4,
c. 84, s. 17) be brought to England in order to be conveyed to the
place to which the transportation applies (1).

G. W. Hope, Esq.   F. POLLOCK.
&c. &c. &c.   W. W. FOLLETT.

(7.) JOINT OPINION *of the Attorney and Solicitor General,*
SIR A. E. COCKBURN *and* SIR RICHARD BETHELL, *that commutation of sentence from Transportation to Imprisonment without consent of the Convict is illegal.*

Temple, May 3, 1854.

MY LORD DUKE,—We were honoured with your Grace's commands, contained in Mr. Merivale's letter of the 20th ultimo, in
which he stated that he was directed by your Grace to transmit to
us copy of a despatch and its enclosure from the Governor of Barbadoes, reporting the commutation of a sentence for manslaughter;
also copy of the section of the Barbadoes Act referred to (5 Will. 4,
c. 9, s. 9); also of a further despatch, enclosing a letter addressed
to your Grace by the counsel for the prisoner, in his behalf.

Mr. Merivale further stated that he was directed to request that
we would take these papers into our consideration, and report
whether we considered that the commuted sentence of nine years'
imprisonment was legally awarded in this case; and if not, what
steps it would be proper for the Governor of Barbadoes to take?

In obedience to your Grace's command, we have taken the
several papers transmitted to us into our consideration, and have
the honour to report that we are of opinion that the commutation

(1) It has been laid down that no man can contract for his own imprisonment:
Clark's Case, 5 Rep. 64 a; *Foster v. Jackson,* Hob. 61; *Case of James Sommer-
sett,* 20 State Tr. 50. But, as was determined by the Court of Queen's Bench in
Leonard Watson's Case, 9 Ad. & Ell. 783, this has no application to the case of a
man charged with a crime, but permitted by the law to confess it before arraignment, and so enabled to obtain a pardon, by which his life is spared, but he binds
himself to undergo a less severe punishment. In that case the Legislature of
Canada had passed an Act authorizing the Governor to grant a pardon to such persons charged with high treason as should before arraignment confess their guilt
and petition for a pardon, on such conditions as should seem fit; and the prisoner
was so charged and so pardoned on condition of being transported to Van Diemen's
Land for life.

of the sentence of transportation to imprisonment for nine years is illegal.

The Crown has no power, except when such a power is expressly given by Act of Parliament, to commute a sentence passed by a court of justice. Practically, indeed, commutation of punishment has long taken place under the form of conditional pardons. For the Crown, having by the prerogative the power of pardon, may annex to a pardon such conditions as it pleases. Thus, for offences for which the punishment was death, where it was not deemed advisable to carry the sentence of death into execution, the course, from an early period, was to grant a pardon on condition of the convict being transported to some settlement or plantation.

But this could only be done with the consent of the felon. The Crown cannot compel a man, against his will, to submit to a different punishment from that which has been awarded against him in due course of law.

The sentence of transportation passed in the present case cannot, therefore, be changed into one of imprisonment, unless the substituted punishment be assented to by the prisoner as a condition of the remission of the sentence of transportation.

Even then, as the law has fixed the maximum of imprisonment, as corresponding to the maximum of transportation, at four years, it seems to us, that if the sentence of transportation be commuted into imprisonment, it would be desirable to act in consistency with the principle adopted by the legislature as to the relative proportions of the two punishments, and not to insist on a longer term of imprisonment than four years.

His Grace the Duke of Newcastle,   A. E. COCKBURN.
    &c. &c. &c.   RICHARD BETHELL.

(8.) JOINT OPINION *of the same Law Officers, that in such a case the Original Sentence may be carried into execution.*

Temple, July 5, 1854.

SIR,—We were honoured with his Grace the Duke of Newcastle's commands, contained in Mr. Merivale's letter of the 12th ultimo, in which he stated that, with reference to our letter of the 3rd of May last—wherein we reported that the commutation, by the Governor of Barbadoes, in a case of manslaughter, of a sentence of transportation for life into one of imprisonment for nine years, was illegal under the law of the island—he was directed by his Grace to request that we would favour him with our further opinion, whether the original sentence of transportation may now be legally carried into execution.

In obedience to the above request we have again considered the subject, and have the honour to report—

That, inasmuch as the commutation by the Governor of Barbadoes of the original sentence into one of imprisonment for nine years was null and void, not being warranted by law, we are of opinion that the original sentence remains, and may be legally carried into execution. Under the circumstances, we think an offer should be made to the convict to commute the original sentence into a sentence of four years' imprisonment with hard labour; and if the convict refuses to assent thereto, that the original sentence should be carried into effect.

The Right Hon. Sir G. Grey, Bart.,   A. E. COCKBURN.
&c.   &c.   &c.   RICHARD BETHELL.

(9.) JOINT OPINION *of the Attorney and Solicitor General,* SIR JOHN CAMPBELL *and* SIR R. M. ROLFE, *that a Witness ad-mitted to give Evidence for the Crown cannot refuse to answer questions on the ground that his answers may criminate himself, and that a Conviction obtained after such refusal is bad.*

Inner Temple, October 12, 1835.

MY LORD,—We have to acknowledge the receipt of a letter from your Lordship, dated the 29th ultimo, together with a despatch from the Governor of the Windward Caribbean Islands, dated the 22nd of July last, with various enclosures relating to the case of George Lindsay, a prisoner in the common gaol of St. Vincents, who was tried by the supreme criminal court of that island for stealing a musquet—in which letter your Lordship is pleased to desire that we should report whether there was any valid objection, in point of law, to the conduct of Lindsay's trial, or to his conviction? We beg leave, therefore, to state to your Lordship that, in compliance with your Lordship's desire, we have taken this case into our consideration, and we are clearly of opinion that the trial of Lindsay was not conducted according to law.

The chief witness against Lindsay was a man of the name of Welbank, an accomplice, who was admitted as evidence for the Crown. Being so admitted, he was bound to disclose the whole truth relative to the charge in question, without regard to the consequences to himself, and he could not refuse to answer any question on the ground that it would show him to have been engaged in the same theft for which Lindsay was tried.   The Court, however, permitted Welbank to decline answering many of the questions put to him, on the plea that he would be thereby criminating himself, and thus let his evidence go to the jury in an imperfect state.

We think this was clearly wrong, and consequently that the conviction was improperly obtained.

J. CAMPBELL.

R. M. ROLFE.

(10.) JOINT OPINION *of the Attorney and Solicitor General,* SIR JOHN CAMPBELL *and* SIR R. M. ROLFE, *on the illegality of an Ordinance passed by the Governor and Council of Lower Canada, directing certain persons to be transported to Bermuda and detained there.*

Temple, August 6, 1838.

MY LORD,—In answer to your Lordship's letter of the 4th instant, requesting our opinion whether there is any objection, in point of law, to the confirmation by Her Majesty in Council of an ordinance passed by the Earl of Durham and the Special Council of Lower Canada, on the 28th June last, entitled, "An Ordinance to provide for the security of the Province of Lower Canada," we have to state that, in our opinion, so much of this ordinance as directs the class of persons therein first enumerated to be transported to Bermuda, and to be kept under restraint there, is beyond the power of the Governor and Special Council, and void ; but that all the rest of the ordinance is within their power and valid.

The imperial stat. 1 Vict. c. 9, s. 2, authorizes the Governor and the Special Council to make such laws or ordinances for the peace, welfare, and good government of the province of Lower Canada, as the Legislature of Lower Canada as there constituted was empowered to make, with certain exceptions which do not affect the validity of the ordinance in question.   The Legislature of Lower

2 H

Canada, as constituted by 31 Geo. 3, c. 31, had conferred upon it a general sovereign legislative power within the province, and it is expressly enacted that all Acts passed by this legislature shall be valid and binding, to all intents and purposes, within the province in which the same shall have been passed.

We conceive, therefore, that the old legislature might have lawfully passed an Act for banishing from the province the first class of persons described in this ordinance, and enacting that if any of this class or of the second class should return to the province without the leave of the Governor, they should be deemed guilty of treason, and being convicted thereof should suffer death. This could not be done by the proclamation of the Governor, but it is an act of legislation for which there are precedents in the Parliaments of Great Britain and of Ireland. There is no pretence for saying that if this part of the ordinance really were put in force the parties who suffer would be put to death without trial. Before they could suffer they must be indicted for having returned to the province without leave of the Governor, which by law is made treason, and they could only suffer on being duly convicted of the offence laid to their charge. Of course we are only considering the regularity of such a proceeding in strict law, without giving any opinion as to its being expedient or proper.

With respect to that part of the ordinance which is to be executed beyond the limits of the province of Lower Canada, we are of opinion that it would acquire no force by being confirmed by Her Majesty, and we humbly conceive that in confirming the ordinance by Her Majesty that part of it which exceeds the power of the Governor and Special Council ought to be expressly excepted.

The Lord Glenelg,   J. CAMPBELL.
&c. &c. &c.   R. M. ROLFE.

(11.) JOINT OPINION *of the Attorney and Solicitor General,* SIR JOHN JERVIS *and* SIR JOHN ROMILLY, *on the power of Police Constables to arrest in certain cases without Warrant.* 1849.

Case.—Whether police constables are authorized to arrest and detain, without warrant, persons charged with the offences mentioned in the 64th and 65th sections of the Police Act (2 & 3 Vict. c. 47), upon the mere statement of the party making the charge, unsupported by any corroborative circumstances or evidence; or under what circumstances such arrests without warrant are justifiable?

Opinion.—This question presents difficulties which can only be solved by prudence on the part of the officer. On the one hand, it would be highly improper to act in cases where the consequence is so serious upon mere suspicion; while on the other, if the police were only to apprehend parties charged with such offences upon the view, or in cases where corroborating evidence was forthcoming, offenders would escape and the public would be dissatisfied. Upon the strict construction of the statute no corroborative evidence is essential. If the constable has "good cause" to suspect, he may arrest upon the statement of one witness only. But whether the cause of suspicion is good or not must in such case depend upon circumstances. For instance, if an interval unexplained by the accuser have elapsed between the assault and the complaint, the constable should not act without a warrant. So of course, if in the inquiry the constable have reason to doubt the truth of the complainant's story, or believe that he has entrapped the accused for the purpose of the charge, the cause of suspicion would not be good, and the constable ought not to act without a warrant. On the other hand, if the constable be attracted to the spot by the cries of the complainant, or if the accused give a contradictory or unsatisfactory account of himself, the constable should act without a warrant. We have mentioned these different circumstances only in illustration of what we have above said—viz., that much must be left to the prudence and discretion of the officer; and repeat that, in strictness, no corroborative evidence is necessary, but that the circumstances and charge must be such as would justify a reasonable man in suspecting that the offence had been committed (1).

JOHN JERVIS.

Temple, December 31, 1849.   JOHN ROMILLY.

(1) A private individual may justify an arrest for *felony* without warrant, if he can show either that a felony was in fact committed by the person arrested, or that a felony was committed by some one, and that he had probable cause to

(12.) JOINT OPINION *of the Attorney and Solicitor General,* SIR A. E. COCKBURN *and* SIR RICHARD BETHELL, *as to the illegality of the delivery up of Russian Sailors (Deserters), and the conveyance of them back to their ships.*

Case.—Some Russian sailors were found wandering in the streets of Guildford without any visible means of subsistence, and were locked up for the night by the superintendent of police. They were afterwards identified by a Russian naval officer as deserters from a Russian man-of-war which had arrived in England, and they were conveyed by him to Portsmouth with the assistance of the superintendent. The Law Officers were requested to advise as to the legality of the proceeding.

Temple, January 3, 1854.

Opinion.—We are of opinion that the delivering-up of the Russian sailors to the lieutenant, and the assistance offered by the police for the purpose of their being conveyed back to the Russian ship, was contrary to law.

A. E. COCKBURN.
RICHARD BETHELL.

(13.) JOINT OPINION *of the same Law Officers, as to how far Statute* 16 & 17 *Vict. c.* 99, *abolishing Transportation in certain cases, is in force in the Colonies.*

Temple, December 5, 1858.

SIR,—We were honoured with your commands, contained in Mr. Merivale's letter of the 15th ultimo, in which he stated that he was directed by you to transmit to us the accompanying despatch from the Governor of New South Wales, with its enclosures, and to request that we would favour you with our advice on the following point:—

That, referring to the letter of the 20th of February last, from

suspect the person arrested to be the felon. "It is lawful," said Abbott, C.J., in *Ex parte Kraus*, 1 B. & C. 261, "for any person to take into custody a man charged with felony, and keep him until he can be taken before a magistrate:" *Mure* v. *Kaye*, 4 Taunt. 34 ; *West* v. *Baxendale*, 6 C. B. 141. A constable is justified in arresting any person whom he has probable cause to suspect of having committed a felony, even although the prisoner is found not guilty, or it turns out that no felony was committed by anybody : *Beckwith* v. *Philby*, 6 B. & C. 635.

the Horse Guards to the General Officer commanding at New South Wales, and to our own opinion, as stated in that letter, as to sentences of transportation passed on military offenders, were we of opinion that the same principle applies to sentences of transportation passed by the ordinary Courts in the colonies on the other offenders, insomuch that all such sentences, passed since the 16 & 17 Vict. c. 99 came into operation, and which, if passed in England, would have been invalid by reason of that Act, were invalid and could not be enforced?

In obedience to your request, we have taken the subject into our consideration, and have the honour to report—

That, in our opinion, the question whether the principle embodied in our opinion as to sentences of transportation passed on military offenders applies to sentences of transportation passed by the ordinary Courts in the colonies, and whether, consequently, such sentences, passed since 16 & 17 Vict. c. 99, which, if passed in England, would have been invalid under that Act, are invalid and cannot be enforced, must depend materially on the constitution of the particular colony, and whether the law is administered in such colony under the authority of the British Crown, or under the laws passed by the local legislature. Generally speaking, Acts of Parliament do not apply to the colonies, unless the latter are expressly specified therein; but some classes of statutes, which appear to be of imperial concern, and to affect the whole of the dominions of the Crown, have been held to be excepted from this rule.

In the case of military offences, the trial takes place under the martial law, as established by the Mutiny Acts. In such a case there is no doubt that the 16 & 17 Vict. c. 99 applies, though the trial takes place in a colony. We are disposed to think, looking to the general scope and purport of the Act in question, that it would apply generally to sentences passed in the ordinary Colonial Courts also; but, as we have just pointed out, there may be circumstances of local legislation or law, which may make the local application of this statute, in which no reference is made to the colonies, very questionable.

We concur with the Law Officers of New South Wales in thinking that legislative provision should be made that statutes passed in this country, unless expressly declared to take effect from a particular period, should not take effect in a colony till promulgated there.

The Right Hon. Sir G. Grey, Bart.,   A. E. COCKBURN.
&c.   &c.   &c.   RICHARD BETHELL.

CHAPTER XVIII.

ON MISCELLANEOUS SUBJECTS (1).

(1.) LETTER *from the Lord Chancellor*, LORD THURLOW, *to* SIR JAMES MARRIOTT, *King's Advocate, on the necessity of Declaration of War before Hostilities* (2).

December 12, 1778.

I need not explain to you the Attorney General's doubts: he has stated them to you, and it would be too long to discuss them in a billet.

Without enquiring in books whether a nation may commence hostilities before declaration of war, or may seize the property of another, or may sell or otherwise use it when seized; without resorting to the present practice of France, as being next at hand, for the justification of such proceeding, I believe, if it were well searched, these facts would be found—that orders had been given to the King's ships to make prize, letters of marque and reprisals issued, proclamations to offer such letters to the King's subjects, commissions to the Admiralty to issue them, commissions to the Admiralty to appoint judges for trying them, distribution among the captors, and perhaps more acts of the same kind than I can enumerate.

The proclamations of war since the Revolution are—

May 7, 1689 . . .	France.
May 4, 1702 . . .	France and Spain.
Dec. 16, 1718 . . .	Spain.

(1) The Opinions in this chapter relate to various matters which could not properly be classed in any of the preceding chapters. I have therefore collected them together here.

(2) From a M. S. in the possession of Sir Travers Twiss, Queen's Advocate, which formerly belonged to Sir James Marriott.

Oct. 19, 1739 . . . Spain.
Mar. 29, 1744 . . . France.
May 17, 1756 . . . France.
Jan. 2, 1762 . . . Spain.

On July 10, 1739, letters of reprisal were granted, and I believe that period would furnish instances of all the kinds I have mentioned before.

These suggestions are hinted to you, rather to explain my own ideas than to assist you, who are much better acquainted than I am with them; but, as I know your diligence, perhaps you will be so good as to order enquiries in the Council Office, Admiralty, and Secretary of State's Office (1).

THURLOW.

(2.) JOINT OPINION *of the Queen's Advocate,* SIR JOHN D. HARDING, *and the Attorney and Solicitor General,* SIR A. E. COCKBURN *and* SIR RICHARD BETHELL, *that Her Majesty's mere Declaration of War with a foreign Power does not place the Ionian Republic in a state of war with that Power; and that it does not appear to be illegal for an Ionian to trade with a country with which Great Britain is at war.*

Doctors' Commons, July 11, 1855.

MY LORD,—We are honoured with Mr. Merivale's letter of the 9th June last, stating that he was directed by your Lordship to transmit to us a copy of the shorthand writer's notes of the judgment recently pronounced in the Court of Admiralty in the case of the *Leucade*; that the *Leucade* was an Ionian vessel, sailing

(1) By the modern law of nations, no declaration or other formal notice to the enemy of the existence of war is necessary to legalize hostilities. The ancients were more punctilious, and, as is well known, heralds were employed to announce an impending war. As to Greece, see Paus. iv. 5, 8; Polyæn. Strateg. iv. 7, 11; Ostermann, *De Præcon. Græc.* Cicero lays down the principle: *Nullum bellum esse justum nisi quod aut rebus repetitis geratur, aut denuntiatum ante sit et indictum:* De Off. i. 11. The last example of a declaration of war by heralds at arms, according to the forms observed in the Middle Ages, was by France against Spain, in 1635: Wheaton, Internat. Law, s. 297. Woolsey sensibly remarks (Internat. Law, s. 115), that the disuse of these declarations does not grow out of an intention to take the enemy at unawares, but out of the publicity and circulation of intelligence peculiar to modern times.

under the Ionian flag, destined to Taganrog, a Russian port, which
was not blockaded, laden with an innocent cargo; that the question
raised was, whether this vessel, so sailing, laden and bound, was
liable to capture, Great Britain and Russia being at war; that the
points bearing upon this question, determined by the Court of
Admiralty, were these, shortly stated:—

1st. That the declaration of the Ionian Senate, warning all
protected subjects of the Queen of Great Britain belonging to the
Ionian States to be guided by Her Majesty's declaration, dated
London, 28th March, 1854, was not an act placing the Ionian
States in the state of warfare with Russia.

2ndly. That with reference to the Treaty of Paris, 1815, which
settled the national status of the Ionian Islands, those islands were
declared to form a single, free, and independent State, and the
Ionian flag acknowledged as the flag of a free and independent
State; that consequently it was not the intention of the contracting
Powers, or the construction of the treaty, that the Ionian islanders
were to be taken either as British subjects, or as necessarily the
allies of the Crown of Great Britain in any war, and particularly
in a war with one of the Powers which guaranteed that very treaty.

3rdly. That, as in the Convention with the Netherlands in 1852,
and in the treaty with Tuscany in December 1854, it was deemed
necessary to mention expressly and distinctly the Ionian Islands;
so, in order to affect Ionian islanders with any obligations or duties
consequent upon a state of warfare between Great Britain and
Russia, they should be specially named.

4thly. That no such special reference has been made in respect
to the present war with Russia. That, incidentally, reference was
made to the Order in Council of the 15th of April, 1854; and that
the Court held that Ionian vessels were not "British vessels,"
within the terms of that order:—1st, under the municipal law;
2nd, under the British flag; 3rd, or as British-owned, though under
neutral flag;—and that reference was also made to the provision
requiring that every Ionian vessel should be navigated under the
pass of the Lord High Commissioner; that the final decision was
that Ionian subjects had a right, in the existing state of things, to
trade with Russia, and the ship and cargo were restored.

Mr. Merivale was pleased to refer us to the opinions given by us on the 19th of May, 1854, and on the 10th of May last, on the subject of the position of the Ionian States and Ionian subjects in the present war, and to annex a copy of a despatch from the Lord High Commissioner on the case of the *Leucade*, with the enclosure; that in the judgment in question, Dr. Lushington says : " I am strongly inclined to think that the necessary and inevitable consequence of such a condition (that created by the second article of the Treaty of Paris, November 5, 1815), is that the King of Great Britain has the right of making war and peace." And Mr. Merivale was further pleased to request that we would report to your Lordship our opinion whether we agree in the view here indicated by Dr. Lushington; and if we do so agree, in what manner should the exercise of this right be declared, so as legally to constitute a state of war (assuming, for the present, on the authority of the judgment, that such a state does not now exist) between the Ionian States and Russia, and by what authority publicly notified in the Ionian Islands?   If, on the contrary, we are of opinion that any declaration, or other formal notification of war, should be made by the authorities of the Ionian States, then we are requested to advise in what manner, and by what authorities, regard being had to the language of the Ionian charter?

In obedience, to your Lordship's commands, we have the honour to report that, although the questions put to us refer more immediately to the right of the Sovereign of Great Britain of making peace and war with reference to Ionia, and, if such right exists, to the mode in which it should be exercised ; yet we infer, from the reference to the case of the *Leucade*, and the judgment of Dr. Lushington thereon, that it is desired that we should state our view as to the liability of vessels belonging to Ionians, trading with an enemy of this country, to seizure and condemnation.

As regards the right of the Sovereign of Great Britain to prescribe to the Ionian State its course of political action, we fully adhere to the opinion contained in our report of May 19, 1854, as to the relation of the Ionian Islands to this country.   We are, however, of opinion that a mere declaration of war by the Sovereign of Great Britain, will not have the effect of placing the Ionian Republic in a state of warfare with the foreign Power against which such declaration of war is made.   It is necessary to observe that the relation between the Crown of Great Britain and the Ionian Republic is certainly anomalous in its character, and questions regarding it scarcely admit of being tried by the application of ordinary rules and principles. The right of appointing the supreme Governor of the States, the military occupation and possession of the islands, the command of the Ionian forces and the power of augmenting them in time of war, the right of conducting all the foreign relations of the Republic, and the power of convoking and dissolving the Senate, are the chief prerogative rights secured to and vested in the Crown of England by the Treaty of Paris and the charter of the Ionian States; and we think they necessarily involve the power of declaring war and making peace. On the other hand, the internal government of the country is in the hands of the Ionian Legislature and of the Senate, in the latter of which bodies (independently of the British Commissioner), the civil executive is vested. Thus the Ionian State is, as regards its foreign relations, dependent on this country, while with reference to its internal government it remains an independent State. Hence a double executive—the British Commissioner representing the State in its foreign relations and military government, the Senate conducting the civil affairs of the country.

It becomes necessary to bear in mind this distinction and division of powers, in considering the effect of what has hitherto been done with respect to the relation of Ionia towards Russia, or what it may be further necessary to do. It appears that all that has hitherto been done is that Her Majesty's proclamation of war against Russia, as Sovereign of Great Britain, has been transmitted to Ionia, and has there been published by the Senate for the guidance of Ionian subjects.

It appears to us that this is insufficient to place the Ionian State in a state of war with Russia. The Ionian Senate possessing no authority whatever with reference to the foreign relations of the country, no act of theirs can have any efficacy towards placing the subjects of Ionia in a state of warfare with Russia. A proclamation of war, or an act of which the purpose is to place Ionia in such a relation, should proceed either immediately from the Sovereign of Great Britain as the protecting Power, or from the Lord High Commissioner as the representative of the Sovereign in

Ionia with reference to the external relations of the country. It remains to be considered whether a mere declaration of war by the Sovereign of Great Britain, as such, produces any and what effect with reference to the inhabitants of the Ionian Islands. By the criminal code of the Ionian State, it is declared to be high treason in an Ionian subject to adhere to the enemies of the Ionian State or of the protecting Power. We have no doubt that, after Her Majesty's declaration of war, an Ionian subject entering into the service of Russia, or otherwise assisting the enemy, would be guilty of high treason, and liable to be punished accordingly. This, however, does not lead to the conclusion that Ionian subjects are prohibited from trading with an enemy of this country. The criminal code to which we have referred, is minute in its enumeration of the particular acts which amount to an adhering to the foreign enemy. It does not include amongst them the trading with the enemy: and although by the general laws of this and other countries, the act of trading with an enemy, though not amounting to treason, is nevertheless prohibited, as incompatible with the duties of the subject during war; yet as the relation of the Ionians to Her Majesty is not that of subjects, we think it more than doubtful whether such a principle would apply to them as flowing by implication from the provisions of the criminal code to which we have above referred. No doubt, if by the exercise of the power vested in the Sovereign of determining the foreign relations of the Ionian State, the latter should be placed in a state of warfare with Russia, the right of trading with the enemy would thenceforth be determined; but it must be borne in mind that by the Order in Council of the 15th of April, 1854, liberty has been given even to British subjects to trade with the enemy, provided such trade be not carried on in British vessels: under such circumstances, it would probably be thought right (if Ionia should be placed in a state of war with Russia) to extend a similar permission to Ionian subjects.

With regard to the case of the *Leucade*, upon which the question as to the relation of Ionian subjects to this country has more immediately arisen, we are of opinion that that vessel was not properly subject to seizure and condemnation—firstly, because, for the reasons we have above detailed, we do not consider Ionians as British subjects, or as prohibited, under existing circumstances, from trading with the enemy; secondly, because, if Ionians were to be considered as British subjects, and prohibited from so trading, they would be entitled to the benefit of the concession to the British subjects of the right to trade with the enemy otherwise than in British ships; and we are clearly of opinion that in no sense can an Ionian vessel be held to be a British vessel. Therefore, although we cannot bring ourselves to concur in much of the reasoning in the judgment of the learned Judge of the Admiralty Court in the recent case of the *Leucade*, we find ourselves compelled to concur in the conclusion at which he has arrived, that the ship of an Ionian subject trading with Russia, but without breaking blockade, is not, under existing circumstances, liable to seizure and condemnation.

<table>
<tr><td></td><td>J. D. HARDING.</td></tr>
<tr><td>The Right Hon. Lord J. Russell, M.P.,</td><td>A. E. COCKBURN.</td></tr>
<tr><td>&c. &c. &c.</td><td>RICHARD BETHELL.</td></tr>
</table>

(3.) JOINT OPINION *of the same Law Officers, that the Queen can, by her Declaration of War, place the Ionian Republic in a state of hostility towards another country.*

Temple, August 21, 1855.

SIR,—We were favoured with your letter of the 23rd ultimo,. stating you were directed by Lord John Russell to refer us to the following passage in our report of the 11th July on the case of the *Leucade*:—

"A proclamation of war, or an act of which the purpose is to place Ionia in such a relation (*i.e.*, of warfare with Russia), should proceed either immediately from the Sovereign of Great Britain as the protecting Power, or from the Lord High Commissioner as the representative of the Sovereign in Ionia with reference to the external relations of the country."

You also stated you were to request that we would inform Lord John Russell, whether it is our intention by this passage to affirm that the Queen, as protecting Power, has the right to constitute by her own act this state of hostility?

And whether, if such is our opinion, the annexed draft of a declaration (with any amendment we might suggest) appears to us sufficient to constitute such a state? Or, in the event of our being of opinion that the Lord High Commissioner should be instructed to issue a declaration, what is the form we should suggest for this purpose?

In obedience to his Lordship's commands, we have the honour to report that it was our intention, by the recited passage of our former report, to affirm that the Queen, as protecting Power of the Ionian States, has the right to constitute by her own act a state of hostility between that country and any other State.

The proposed draft of a declaration, with the amendments we have suggested (and we have thought it right to omit all the recitals, as uncalled for and inexpedient), will, in our opinion, be sufficient to constitute such a state of hostility.

But we think it advisable that the Lord High Commissioner should issue a proclamation in the islands, setting forth Her Majesty's declaration, and calling upon all Ionian subjects to take notice thereof, and to demean themselves accordingly.

J. D. HARDING.

Herman Merivale, Esq., &c. &c. &c.

A. E. COCKBURN.

RICHARD BETHELL.

(4.) *On the Right of War, and Booty, and Prize* (1).

It is certain that the right of war is lodged in the Sovereign. Wars are undertaken either to recover the rights of private subjects, which the enemy wilfully refuseth to pay, or upon some public cause. In the first case, the principal thing to be taken care of is, that the persons upon whose wrongs the war began may be restored to their rights of the overplus in this instance; and in wars that begin from a public cause, all that is taken is acquired to the Sovereign, whatever hands it first fell into—whether the mercenary soldiers, or subjects obliged to military service without receiving pay. But because war lies heavy upon the subjects, whether they are only taxed to support it, or are obliged to serve in it themselves, it is no more than a good prince that had a love for his subjects would yield to, that the subject should be allowed, in

(1) From a M. S. in the possession of Sir Travers Twiss, Queen's Advocate, which formerly belonged to Sir James Marriott. No date. Most probably the opinion of Sir James Marriott.

return, to make some advantage by the war—either by assigning them pay from the public when they go upon any expedition, or by sharing the booty among them, or giving everyone leave to keep the plunder he gets himself, or else, by giving the booty to the public, to ease the subjects of taxes for the future. Mercenary soldiers have no right to anything above their pay. What is given them above that is matter of bounty or reward to the good service, or encouragement to their valour. As to Grotius's distinction of acts of hostility in public and private acts, it may be very justly questioned whether everything taken in war by private hostilities, or by the bravery of private subjects, that have no commission, belongeth to them that take it. For this is also part of the right of war, to appoint what persons are to act in a hostile manner against the enemy, and no other. Consequently, no private person hath power to make devastations in an enemy's country, or to carry off spoil, or plunder, without permission from his Sovereign. And the Sovereign is to determine how far private men, when they are permitted, are to use that liberty of plunder, and whether they are to be sole proprietors in the booty, or only to have a part of it. For to be a soldier, and to act offensively in a hostile manner, a man must be commissioned by public authority; and therefore Cato used to say, " that no man has any right to fight an enemy that was not a soldier."

(5.) CASE and OPINION *of the Attorney General,* SIR CHARLES PRATT, *as to the Grant of a Marriage Licence* (1). 1760.

Case.—If application is made to an ecclesiastical Judge, duly authorized to grant marriage licences, for a licence to solemnize a marriage between parties of full age and free condition, who reside within his jurisdiction, and have complied with every requisite prescribed by the Act for the better preventing clandestine marriages, and with all the forms prescribed by the canons—is the Judge compellable to grant such licence as a matter of right, or is it a matter of favour, which of his own mere will he arbitrarily can refuse; or has the subject a right to a *mandamus,* or any other and what remedy ?

Opinion.—I am of opinion that this licence is not a matter of

(1) From the same M. S.

right, but favour only, and may be refused by the ecclesiastical
Judge; for it is a power lodged with the Ordinary and Metropolitan,
for their advantage only, to dispense with the forms required by
the rubric, whereby the marriage, as well as by the canonical law,
ought to be publicly celebrated after a due publication of banns.
Therefore, neither the party nor the public can be interested in the
refusal, because the proper and truly legal method is still left free,
viz., to marry by banns.

February 5, 1760.   C. PRATT.

    (6.) LETTER *from the Lord Chancellor*, LORD THURLOW, *to*
SIR JAMES MARRIOTT, *King's Advocate* (1).

DEAR DOCTOR,—I have read over your observations many times
with great attention, and I agree to many particulars; yet, upon
the whole, I cannot help remaining persuaded that the King in
Parliament gives as full a commission as under the Great Seal.
The necessity of applying to Parliament at all upon the subject I
do not maintain, unless it was to vest the prizes in the captor clear
of the Admiralty rights. As to the expediency, I am no judge of
it. Your thinking it necessary will be enough to make it expedient.

                                       THURLOW.

    (1) From the same M. S. No date.

APPENDIX.

RYMER'S FŒDERA, XVIII. 254.

"CHARLES, by the Grace of God, &c., to our right trusty and right wellbeloved cousin Edward, Viscount Wimbleton, Lord Marshall of our Army, and to our trustie wellbeloved Sir William St. Leger, Knight, Serjeant Major of our Army [and 23 others]:

"Whereas upon the Retourne of our Fleete, Wee have alreadie directed that non of the Soldiers imployed in that Service, and which shall retourne in any of those Shipps, shall be disbanded or departe from their Colours, but shall continue under the Commaund of those under whom they then served, Wee having present occasion to use their Services again, and yet Wee shall be inforced for a time to lodge and billett the said Soldiers in severall Places in and about Our Towne of *Plymouth* and in Our Counties of *Devon* and *Cornwall*, where with most Conveniencie for the Soldiers and least Trouble to the Countrey itt may best be performed, untill Wee shall have Opportunitie to ymploye them, which We intend to doe with all Expedition; And to the end that all Disorders and Outrages, to the Disturbance of our Peace and the Prejudice of our loveing Subjects, may be tymely prevented, Wee, being more desireous to keepe our People from doeing Mischiefe than to have Cause to punish them for doeing the same:

"Have, of the speciall Trust and Confidence We have reposed in your approved Wisdomes and Fidelities, appointed you to be our Commissioners, and by theis Presents doe give unto you, or any three or more of you, full Power and Authoritie in all Places within our said Counties of *Devon* and *Cornwall* and either of them, as well within the said Town of *Plymouth* or anie other Towne Libertie or Place as without, within our said Counties of Devon and Cornwall or either of them, to proceede according to the

2 I

Justice of Marshall Lawe against such Soldiers or other dissolute
Persons joyneing with them or anie of them, as dureing such Time
that anie of our said Troopes or Companies of Soldiers shall re-
mayne or abide thereabouts, and not be transported thence, shall
within any the Places or Precincts aforesaid att anie time after
the Publication of this Our Commission, committ any Robberies,
Felonyes, or Mutynies, or other Outrages or Misdemeanors, which
by Marshall Lawe should or ought to be punished with Death, and
by such summarie Course and Order as is agreeable to Marshall
Lawe, and is used in Armies in tyme of Warres, to proceed to the
Triall and Condempnation of such Delinquents and Offendors, and
them to cause to be executed and putt to Death according to the
Lawe Marshall for an Example of Terror to others, and to keepe
the rest in due Awe and Obedience.

" To which Purpose Our Will and Pleasure is that you cause to
be erected such Gallowes and Gibbetts, and in such Places within
the said Counties or either of them, as you shall think fitt, and
thereupon to cause the same Offenders to be executed in open
View, that others may take warning thereby to demeane themselves in such due Order and Obedience as good Subjects ought to
do, straightlie chargeing and commanding all Mayors, Sherriffs,
Justices of Peace, Constables, Bayliffs and other Officers, and all
other Our loveing Subjects whatsoever, upon their Allegiance
to Us and Our Crowne, to be ayding and assisting to you, or
such three or more of you as aforesaid, in the due Execution of
this Our Royal Commaundment; and theis Presents shal be unto
you and everie of you a sufficient Warrant and Discharge for the
doeing and executing, and causing to be done and executed, all and
everie such Act and Acts, Thing and Things, as anie three or more
of you as aforesaid shall find requisite to be done concerning the
Premisses.

" In Witnes whereof, &c.
Witnes, &c.
Teste Rege Apud *Hampton Court vicesimo octavo Die
Decembris.*
Per Breve de Privato Sigillo, &c.
A. D. 1625."

RYMER'S FŒDERA, XVIII. 763.

Similar Commission " to proceed according to the Justice of Martiall Lawe against such Soldiers or Marriners, or other dissolute Persons joyneing with them or any of them, as within the said County [of Kent] or any Parte thereof, shall at any tyme after the Publication of this Our Commission committ any Robbery, Felony, Mutiny, or other Outrage or Misdemeanor, or which shall withdrawe themselves from their Places of Service or Charge as aforesaid, or shall be found within the said Countie or any Parte thereof, which by the Martiall Lawe should or oughte to be punished with Death and by such summary Course," &c., *ut supra*.

" Witnes Our Selfe at Canbury the fourth day of October [1626]. Per ipsum Regem."

GEOFFROY'S CASE, IN FRANCE (1832).

Cour de Cassation, June 29, 1832 (24 *Journal du Palais, p.* 1218, *seqq*).

The laws and decrees in regard to creating a state of siege, must be carried into execution in all points not contrary to the Constitutional Charter.

But Art. 103, *Decree of* 24*th December,* 1811, *being irreconcileable with Arts.* 53 *and* 54 *of the Charter of* 1830, *placing a city in a state of siege, cannot have the effect of conferring jurisdiction on military commissions (conseils de guerre) over persons who are not in the army, nor impressed with a military character. Law* 22 *Messidor, year IV., Art.* 1.

GEOFFROY *vs.* LE MINISTÈRE PUBLIC.

A royal order, dated June 6, 1832, had put Paris in a state of siege ; it was based on the necessity of repressing seditious assemblages which had appeared in arms in the capital, during the days of June 5th and 6th; on attacks upon public and private property ; on assassinations of national guards, troops of the line, municipal guards, and officers in the public service ; and on the necessity of prompt and energetic measures to protect public safety against the renewal of similar attacks.

2 I 2

The Cour Royale, called to meet in extra session by order of the First President, to pass by way of review (*evocation*) or otherwise, upon the political occurrences of the 5th and 6th of June, rendered the following judgment on the 7th of June, all the chambers being united: On hearing the Procureur General on his motion, deciding on the proposition of one of its members, to cause to be transmitted for review, the record relative to criminal acts committed on the 5th and 6th of the present month: Whereas, by the order dated yesterday, the city of Paris has been placed in a state of siege, and whereas, by the terms of Art. 101 of the Decree of December 24, 1811, passed to carry out the laws of July 8, 1791, and 10th Fructidor, year V., the effect thereof is to transfer to the military commandant the power vested in the civil judges for the maintenance of order and police:

"And whereas the occurrences which occasioned the placing of the city of Paris in a state of siege must be subjected to this rule of law, although anterior thereto:

"It is declared that no ground for a review exists."

The publicity encountered by this decision raised the question of the constitutionality of the order, and the no less weighty question of the jurisdiction of military commissions over acts done and ended before the order declaring the state of siege was inserted in the " Moniteur " and the " Bulletin des Lois."

As early as June 10, the *Gazette des Tribunaux* published a carefully-considered opinion on these points by M. Ledru Rollin, of the Paris bar. The ball thus being opened, the opposition press soon after collected the opinions of several notabilities of the Order of Advocates of the Court of Cassation, and the concurring opinions of a number of the bars of the kingdom. All these opinions increased the arguments against the constitutionality of the order, its retroactive force, and the jurisdiction of military commissions.

The military commissions having taken cognizance of the cases, the successive defendants at their bar excepted in vain to their jurisdiction. The exceptions were entered of record, saving the right to pass upon them in deciding upon the merits. But it must be noted that this answer to the exception, on the ground of want of jurisdiction, did not afford a decision on the exceptions. According to the law of the 13th Brumaire, year V., which prescribes the procedure to be pursued before military commissions, the latter must give judgment without adjournment; military judges are both judges and juries; they have but one question to answer (Art. 30 of the law cited): " Is N., the accused, guilty ?" Being thus bound under the law which created them, by the double duty of giving judgment without adjournment, and of answering a complex question, the question of their jurisdiction could not be explicitly decided by the military commissions themselves; judgments of "not guilty" left the point vaguely undecided; on the other hand, the counsel for the defence being unable, after discussing it, to avoid a discussion of the merits without putting the fate of the accused in jeopardy, relied upon the exercise of the discretionary power which might be adopted by military judges from the new law, permitting juries to put questions upon trials for the purpose of discovering extenuating circumstances.

However, more than one capital sentence was pronounced. Among the accused, Michael Augustus Geoffroy, designer, of Paris, was by a decision of the second military commission of Paris, on the 18th of June, by a majority of 6 to 1, declared guilty of an attack with intent to subvert the government and to excite civil war. He was consequently condemned to death, in accordance with Arts. 87, 89, and 91, of the Penal Code and the law of 18th Germinal, year VI.

Geoffroy immediately appealed to the Council of Revision and the Court of Cassation.

[The latter court made an interlocutory order that the record should be brought into their clerk's office to await their further judgment. This having been done, and the reporting counsellor having stated the question raised, M. Odilon Barrot, of counsel for the appellant, stated and argued three propositions as the grounds of his appeal, as follows:]

" 1st. Placing the city of Paris in a state of siege by a mere order, when the city has not been invested, and the communications have not been interrupted, is an illegal act, and deemed not to exist.—2nd. In case the state of siege be considered legal and constitutional, it is impossible that it should result in withdrawing citizens from their natural judges, and in obliterating, as regards them, the 53rd and 54th Articles of the Charter."

[The third point related to the retroactive effect of the order.]

1st. How is the question in this case to be stated? Can any
one ask whether the government is authorized to despoil its
citizens of the guaranties of a jury, not only for ordinary misdemeanors, but even for violations of the laws of the press? This
would be doing violence to the Charter which establishes trial by
jury. Will anyone put the question thus: Is the city of Paris
besieged? This would be doing violence to common sense.
Where, I ask, are the rebels investing the city and putting it in a
state of siege? Are not the communications unobstructed? No,
the city is not besieged; there is no state of siege; the siege is a
fiction; this fiction is not lawful.

2nd. The laws of Prairial, year III., and Ventose, year IV., are
those on which the pretended jurisdiction of military commissions
is founded. A military commission, it is said, is not an extraordinary special tribunal. It is a permanent court. This assertion
is refuted by the statutes and decisions. The laws of the years III.
and IV. were re-cast and re-enacted by the law of Pluviose,
year IX., which created special tribunals, and subsequently by that
of 1815, which created provost's courts as a part of the ordinary
administration of justice. This has been distinctly decided by the
Court of Cassation in the cases of military emissaries and spies; of
enticements to desert; of highway robbers; and of all persons
brought within the scope of the laws conferring special jurisdiction.
I add, that according to these laws, the decisions of this court did
not bring within the jurisdiction of military courts such individuals
as were prosecuted for having formed a part of an armed assem-
blage, except in those cases where they were taken in the assem-
blage itself.

Therefore, as regards the persons placed by the events of June
in the hands of the Executive, some exceptional, extraordinary
jurisdiction was required, and it is this very jurisdiction which the
53rd and 54th Articles of the Charter have banished never to return. Listen to M. Dupin commenting on these articles from the
rostrum: "In order to prevent every possible abuse, we have added
to the former text of the Charter, 'under what name or denomination soever;' for specious names have never been wanting for bad
things, and without this precaution the title of 'ordinary tribunal'

might be conferred on the most irregular and extraordinary of courts." This is the principle which was applied in the Ordinance of 1830, relating to juries in Corsica. This ordinance declares that the acts of the government which had created in Corsica, not a military tribunal, but a supreme court, an ordinary jurisdiction, created by a senatus-consultum, confirmed by divers decrees, and sanctioned by a crowd of decisions, be and remain abrogated. Then, if the jurisdiction of judges for life, surrounded by guaranties, deciding with the solemnity of ordinary justice, has been considered extraordinary, what shall military commissions be called, which decide without adjournment, as soon as the case is before them, without any body similar to a grand jury having first declared the existence of the indictment—which decides without confronting witnesses, without a challenge, and whose judgments are executed within twenty-four hours? The most enormous of exceptions, the most monstrous of special jurisdictions, is a court which judges a non-military person by accidental authority. This tribunal, to use the epithet of the decree of the Convention of the 28th Thermidor, year III., can render nothing but revolutionary judgments—judgments which, by returning to true principles, were declared null and void by the Convention itself.

It is objected that the special laws concerning states of siege have survived the Charter, and that they compel the establishment of military justice. No; even putting aside the Charter of 1830, there is no law which, within the land, and excepting the case of an investment, permits a military chief to place a people beyond the pale of their constitutional guaranties. There are three laws which relate to a state of siege—that of 1791, that of the year V., and the Decree of December 24, 1811. The Law of 1791 provides what shall be done as regards places of strength, in the three situations in which they may be placed—peace, war, siege; it derogates in no respect from the Constitution of 1791, according to which no person can be accused or condemned except in virtue of a declaration of a jury on the facts, and of judges on the law. The law of the 17th Fructidor, year V., fills a void in the Law of 1791; it provides for the case where a place of strength in the interior should be in an analogous position to that of a place of strength, that is, invested by forces of the enemy, or by rebels. How is it

possible to make out of a war measure, a measure of public safety;
a measure of suspending the constitution, and of creating a dic-
tatorship towering above the institutions of the country? Can any
one at this day give the name of law to an act which sanctioned
the 18th of Fructidor, and the establishment of renewed proscrip-
tions? As to the Decree of 1811, that, in its letter and in its
spirit, was no measure of public safety, but an act of military
police prescribing a rule in regard to places of strength; this decree has perished like all exceptional measures, by which the Head
of the Government had arrogated to himself the power of modifying
the Constitution; it was one of the causes of his downfall.

[The public prosecutor replied to the first ground taken by the
defence, as follows:]

*   *   *   *   The right to declare a state of siege is con-
fided exclusively to the chief magistrate, or the executive power:
to the King, under the responsibility of his ministers, by the Law of
1791; to the Executive Directory by the laws of the year V., under
the duty of informing the legislative body, which, at that time,
was to be in permanent session; to the Emperor by the Decree of
1811; in a word, always to the executive power, as governed by
the necessities of the case and the law of public safety, and solely
capable of appreciating the demand for the measure.

[To the second ground:]

*   *   *   *   What is the character and nature of the
Charter? It is the usual and ordinary constitution of the country,
the basis of our public law. What is a state of siege? A violent,
extraordinary state of things, based upon the necessity of defence,
and of providing for the common safety, attacked or threatened to
be attacked by a war, or aggression of some kind. At such a time
ordinary misdemeanors and crimes may become military misdemeanors and crimes, subject to the laws of war, and triable by its
courts. The authority of military commissions is therefore necessarily connected with a state of siege. Without it a state of siege
would be nothing but an abstraction; the laws which govern it
belong to a state of things entirely outside of ordinary law. The
53rd and 54th Articles of the Charter are cited against us. Art.
53 merely reproduces Art. 62 of the Charter of 1814, and it has
always been held that the "natural judges" of a person accused,

are those fixed by the law for the case or person to be judged. Art. 54 strengthens the prohibition contained in Art. 53. But, in the first place, permanent military commissions are not extraordinary commissions, newly and specially created for specific cases; they are recognised by a course of legislation; they are not abolished by the Charter. This has been held several times by this court under the Charter of 1830, as well as that of 1814. These tribunals are not an exception to the usual order of things—they are the usual rule of a different order of things. The Charter did not, and could not, provide for a state of siege; and never intended that the Government should stand disarmed, where circumstances have once showed the necessity of this exceptional state, outside of ordinary law. It follows that military commissions do not take cognizance by force of the Order of the 6th of June, but as a consequence of the state of siege, and because military tribunals belong to a state of siege, and are the usual judges, recognized as such by law, in cases by which this state is created and constituted, which is not the normal state provided for by the Charter.

[On the 29th of June the Court gave judgment as follows:]

Per cur. (After advisement in the council-chamber.) Whereas neither the Charter nor any subsequent law treats of the laws and decrees which govern a state of siege, and whereas these laws and decrees must therefore be carried into execution in all points not contrary to the Charter; having considered the Art. 77, L. 27 Ventose, year VIII, in these words: "No appeal can be taken against final judgments of *juges de paix*, except for want of jurisdiction or for exceeding the same, nor against the judgments of military tribunals of land and sea, except for the said causes, taken by a citizen not in the army and not impressed by law with a military character by reason of his duties;" Art. 1, L. 22 Messidor, year IV., as follows: "No crime is military, unless committed by a person forming a part of the army; no other person can be brought, as a defendant before judges appointed by military law;" Arts. 53, 54, and 56 of the Charter: "No person can be withdrawn from his natural judges." "Consequently, extraordinary commissions and tribunals cannot be created under what title or name soever." "The institution of juries is continued;" Art. 69, which extends the cognizance of juries to crimes of the press, and political crimes,

and the law of October 8, 1831, which defines political crimes;
Art. 103, Decree of December 24, 1811, as follows: "As regards all
crimes the cognizance of which the commandant has not decreed
fit to be left to the ordinary courts, the duties of officers of judiciary police are performed by a military provost, chosen as far as
possible from the officers of *gendarmerie*, and the ordinary courts
are replaced by the military courts;" and whereas this provision is
irreconcileable with the letter and the spirit of the above-cited
articles of the Charter; and whereas military commissions are
ordinary tribunals solely for the judging of crimes committed by
the military, or persons impressed by law with a military character,
and become extraordinary tribunals when they extend their jurisdiction to crimes or misdemeanors committed by non-military
citizens; and whereas Geoffroy, brought before the second military
commission of the first military division, is neither in the army
nor impressed with a military character, yet nevertheless said tribunal has implicitly declared itself to have jurisdiction and passed
upon the merits, wherein it has committed an excess of power,
violated the limits of its jurisdiction and the provisions of Art. 53
and 54 of the Charter, and those of the laws above cited: On these
grounds, the Court reverses and annuls the proceedings instituted
against the appellant before the said commission, whatsoever
has followed therefrom, and especially the judgment of condemnation of the 18th June instant; and in order that further proceedings be had according to law, *remands* him before one of the judges
of instruction of the court of first instance of Paris, &c.

Supplement à la Répertoire du Journal du Palais (1857), *vol. I.,
p.* 707, *Arts.* 50, 54, 55.

"The questions of jurisdiction, etc., discussed in 1832, arose
again in consequence of the events of June, 1848, and new appeals
were taken to the Court of Cassation; the Court was no longer
confronted by the Charter of 1840, and this time declared that
military commissions had jurisdiction to try persons, though not of
the army, accused of having taken part in the insurrection of
June 1848. (*Journ. du Palais, vol. I.,* 1850, *p.* 223.)

"Art. 106 of the Constitution of 1848, for the purpose of putting
an end to all judicial controversies as to the legality of a state of siege

and its consequences, declared that a law should be passed to fix the cases in which a state of siege might be declared, and determined, at the same time, the forms and effects of this measure. This law was passed by the Legislative Assembly, and promulgated August 9, 1849 [which enacts as follows: 'Art. 2. The National Assembly solely can declare a state of siege, except as hereinafter excepted. Art. 3. In case of prorogation of the National Assembly, the President of the Republic may declare a state of siege, with the advice of the Council of Ministers. The President, when he has declared a state of siege, must immediately form the Commission created by virtue of Art. 32 of the Constitution, thereof, and, according to the importance of the circumstance, convoke the National Assembly. The National Assembly, from the time when it meets, maintains or abolishes the state of siege '], and still governs this important matter, except however one modification, resulting from Art. 12 of the Constitution of June 14, 1852, as regards the authority invested with the right of declaring a state of siege. By the terms of the Constitution of 1852, 'the Emperor has the right of declaring a state of siege in one or more departments, provided that he inform the Senate thereof, with the least delay.'"

MR. DUDLEY FIELD'S ARGUMENT IN McCARDLE'S CASE.

ARGUMENT of Mr. DAVID DUDLEY FIELD, before the Supreme Court of the United States (March 6th and 9th, 1868), In the Matter of WILLIAM H. McCARDLE, ex parte, Appellant.

Mr. FIELD—May it please the Court:

If I were ambitious to connect my name with a great event in the constitutional history of my country, I should desire no better opportunity than that which this case affords. What is here transacted will remain in the memory of men long after the feet which are treading the halls of this Capitol have made their last journey, and the voices now so loud are for ever silent. Although the part borne by the Bar in this transaction is inferior to yours, yet even they assume a portion of the responsibility, while the words that are to fall from you will stand for ever in the jurisprudence of the land.

In approaching the argument of so great a cause, it is of the first importance to exclude from it every extraneous or disturbing element. We should be lifted, if we may, above the strifes and passions of the hour into a serener air, overlooking a wider horizon. With the struggle for office, with the rise or fall of parties, with the policy of President or Congress, we have nothing to do. Within the walls of this chamber of justice we look only to the law and to the Constitution. That, however, does not prevent our taking care that the independence of the Bench and of the Bar be not menaced; or, if that happen, that the menace be repelled. I say this the rather, because one of the gentlemen who argued against us, saw fit to declare that it was the duty of counsel to admonish the Court. Admonition of what? Of impeachment, because you differ from Congress upon a constitutional question; of packing the Court at some future time; of enactment that two-thirds or three-fourths of the whole shall be necessary to decide, or the exclusion of the Court from its chamber? Admonition from whom? We know that the President has none to give; he disclaims it. Admonition from Congress? I have the highest respect for the members who perform the function of legislation for this country; but they are representatives, all of them, of States or districts. And when I reflect that from the great States of New York, New Jersey, Pennsylvania, Ohio, and California, they represent but a minority of the people, and that from ten States there are no representatives in either House: and when I reflect, further, that this legislative department for nearly two years submitted to the suspension of the Habeas Corpus by the Executive alone; that afterwards, when it passed an Act on the subject, it suffered the Secretaries of State and War to disregard and disobey its injunctions; that it enacted, besides, " That any order of the President, or under his authority, made at any time during the existence of the present rebellion, shall be a defence in all courts to any action or prosecution, civil or criminal, pending or to be commenced, for any search, seizure, arrest or imprisonment, made, done, or committed, or acts omitted to be done under and by virtue of such order "—a law which has scarce a parallel in history, save that of Denmark two centuries ago, which made a formal surrender to the Crown of all right and function of government: when I reflect on these things, the admonition, even were it otherwise proper, which it is not, appears to me shorn of all its force.

As a pendant to the admonition, we are told that this Court is not a co-ordinate department of the Government. Not a co-ordinate department? Is it meant that there is no department co-ordinate with Congress? This is the first time when it has been suggested here that the judicial department is not co-ordinate with either of the others. And certain I am, that in the great convention, where sat the conscript fathers who made this Constitution, such an idea never entered. For I find that at the beginning, for the original plan, it was resolved, as the first resolution of the convention, that "it is the opinion of this Committee that a national government ought to be established, consisting of a supreme legislative, executive, and judiciary." Turning to the comments of the founders of the Government, I find in the "Federalist," the forty-eighth and fifty-first numbers, written by Mr. Madison, this remarkable exposition, written as if in the spirit of prophecy:

"I shall undertake in the next place to show, that unless these departments be so far connected and blended as to give to each a constitutional control over the others, the degree of separation which the maxim requires as essential to a free government can never in practice be duly maintained."

*　　*　　*　　*　　*　　*　　*　　*

"It will not be denied that power is of an encroaching nature, and that it ought to be effectually restrained from passing the limits assigned to it."

*　　*　　*　　*　　*　　*　　*　　*

"The legislative department is everywhere extending the sphere of its activity, and drawing all power into its impetuous vortex."

*　　*　　*　　*　　*　　*　　*　　*

"In a representative republic, where the executive magistracy is carefully limited, both in the extent and the duration of its power; and where the legislative power is exercised by an assembly which is inspired by a supposed influence over the people, with an intrepid confidence in its own strength; which is sufficiently numerous to feel all the passions which actuate a multitude, yet not so numerous as to be incapable of pursuing the objects of its passions by means which reason prescribes; it is against the enterprising ambition of this department that the people ought to indulge all their jealousy, and exhaust all their precautions."

*　　*　　*　　*　　*　　*　　*　　*

"To what expedient, then, shall we finally resort for maintaining in practice the necessary partition of power among the several departments, as laid down in the Constitution? The only answer that can be given is, that as all these exterior provisions are found to be inadequate, the defect must be supplied by so contriving the interior structure of the government, as that its several constituent parts may by their mutual relations be the means of keeping each other in their proper places."

* * * * * * * *

Let me now turn to the case before the Court. The appellant, McCardle, a citizen of Mississippi, was there arrested in October, 1867, and brought before a military commission, which assumed to act under the authority of the United States, to be tried, for publishing in a newspaper, of which he is editor, criticisms upon military officers, and advice to the electors not to vote, or how to vote, upon public questions. This citizen was not in the army or navy, nor connected with the military service, nor impressed with a military character. *And the question is, whether he was rightfully brought before that commission to answer for that act:* in other words, according to the Constitution and laws of this country, could a military commission, sitting in Mississippi, under Federal authority, bring to trial and judgment a civilian of that State, for words published concerning Federal military officers, and the duty of the electors? The words may have been coarse and intemperate. That does not enter into the question. But it may be observed, in passing, that they were not coarser or more intemperate than other words daily uttered concerning the highest civil officers of the country—the President, the Judges of this Court, and Members of Congress—not only by the public press, but in public bodies which call themselves respectable.

The act of this military commission is defended in this Court by counsel deputed by the Secretary of War. The defence rests upon certain Acts of Congress, commonly known as the Military Reconstruction Acts. And the point to be decided is, therefore, whether these acts are or are not reconcileable with the supreme law of this land? If they are, our great forefathers made a charter of government, intended to last for all generations, of such a character, that within eighty years from its adoption that Federal body to which the States—originally sovereign and independent—surrendered a portion of their power, is able to take upon itself the whole government of a State, and govern it by the army alone. Such is the question which, in the last resort, is brought before you, the supreme judges of the land.

There are three of these Military Reconstruction Acts—one passed March 2, 1867 ; the second, a supplementary Act, passed March 23, 1867 ; and the third, a further supplementary Act, passed July 19, 1867. The first begins in this manner :

" Whereas no legal State Governments or adequate protection for life or property now exist in the rebel States of Virginia, North Carolina, South Carolina, Georgia, Mississippi, Alabama, Louisiana, Florida, Texas, and Arkansas ; and whereas it is necessary that peace and good order should be enforced in said States until loyal and republican State Governments can be legally established : Therefore,

" Be it enacted by the Senate and House of Representatives of the United States of America, in Congress assembled, That said rebel States shall be divided into military districts, and made subject to the military authority of the United States as hereinafter provided."

And after providing for the assignment of an officer of the army to the command of each district, the Act proceeds in the third section thus :

" And be it further enacted, That it shall be the duty of each officer assigned as aforesaid, to protect all persons in their rights of person and property ; to suppress insurrection, disorder, and violence ; to punish, or cause to be punished, all disturbers of the public peace and criminals : and to this end he may allow civil tribunals to take jurisdiction of, and to try offenders ; he shall have power to organize military commissions or tribunals for that purpose ; and all interference, under colour of State authority, with the exercise of military authority under this Act, shall be null and void."

The supplementary Act of March 23, 1867, is not material to the present inquiry.

The first, second, and tenth sections of the supplementary Act of July 19, 1867, are as follows :

" Section 1. Be it enacted by the Senate and House of Representatives of the United States of America in Congress assembled, That it is hereby declared to have been the true intent and meaning of the Act of the second day of March, One thousand eight hundred and sixty-seven, entitled ' An Act to provide for the more efficient government of the rebel States,' and of an Act supplementary thereto, passed on the twenty-third day of March, in the year One thousand eight hundred and sixty-seven, that the governments then existing in the rebel States of Virginia, North Carolina, South Carolina, Georgia, Mississippi,

Alabama, Louisiana, Florida, Texas, and Arkansas were not legal State governments, and that thereafter said governments, if continued, were to be continued subject in all respects to the military commanders of the respective districts, and to the paramount authority of Congress.

"Section 2. And be it further enacted, That the commander of any district named in said Act shall have power, subject to the disapproval of the General of the Army of the United States, and to have effect till disapproved, whenever in the opinion of such commander the proper administration of said Act shall require it, to suspend or remove from office, or from the performance of official duties and the exercise of official powers, any officer or person holding, or exercising, or professing to hold or exercise, any civil or military office or duty in such district, under any power, election, appointment, or authority derived from, or granted by, or claimed under, any so-called State or the government thereof, or any municipal or other division thereof; and upon such suspension or removal, such commander, subject to the disapproval of the General as aforesaid, shall have power to provide, from time to time, for the performance of the said duties of such officer or person so suspended or removed, by the detail of some competent officer or soldier of the army, or by the appointment of some other person to perform the same, and to fill vacancies occasioned by death, resignation, or otherwise.

"Section 10. And be it further enacted, That no district commander or member of the Board of Registration, or any of the officers or appointees acting under them, shall be bound in his action by any opinion of any civil officer of the United States."

The first and principal question hinges on the preamble to the original Act, and the enactments which I have just quoted.

There is the preamble, and here is the conclusion. I deny both. I deny that the preamble is true in a constitutional sense, or as a justification for assuming the government of a State; and I deny that, if the preamble were true in every one of its parts, it would justify this military government.

The propositions advanced against us are, in short: The preamble is true, and the enactments are justified by the preamble. We dispute both propositions. We say that the preamble is not true; but, if it were, that the conclusion would not follow.

It seems most convenient to reverse the order of the propositions, and to discuss the latter first; for if the conclusion does not follow from the premises, the Court need hardly trouble itself about them. I shall, however, not only resist the conclusion, but when I have done that, I shall examine and disprove the premises.

Let me first ask attention to the proposition, that because "no legal State government, or adequate protection for life or property, now exists" in the State of Mississippi, therefore that State can be placed by Congress under absolute and universal martial rule. Where is the authority of the Government of the nation for taking upon itself the government of a State, however disordered and anarchical, and carrying on that government by the soldiery? We know that whatever power is possessed by Congress, or any other department of the Federal Government, is contained in a written Constitution. Within its few pages are comprised, either in express language or by necessary intendment, every power which it is *possible* for the Federal authorities of any kind to exercise under any circumstances. Show me then, I say, the power to erect this military government. You cannot find it *expressed* in any one of the eighteen subdivisions of the eighth section of the first Article—that section which contains the enumeration of the powers of Congress. If it is *implied* in any of them, tell me in which one. I cannot find it.

Turn then to the fourth section of the fourth Article—that which declares that "the United States shall guarantee to every State in the Union a republican form of government, and shall protect each of them against invasion, and, on application of the Legislature, or the Executive (when the Legislature cannot be convened), against domestic violence."

Is a military government here sanctioned? Certainly it is not *expressed*. Is it *implied?* Supposing, for the sake of the argument, that the United States, uninvited by its Legislature or Executive, can go into a State for the purpose of repressing disorder or violence, or of overthrowing an existing State government, on the ground that it is not republican, I deny that they can introduce a military government as the means to such an end. To avoid misapprehension, I carefully distinguish between the use of military power in aid of the civil, subordinate to it, and military government. The two systems are opposed to each other. In one case the civil power governs, in the other the military. In one the military power is the servant of the civil, in the other it is the master. My proposition is, that a military government cannot be set up in the United States for any of the purposes mentioned; and

2 K

the reason is this—*military government is prohibited by the Constitution.* Not disputing the proposition that Congress may pass all
laws necessary or proper for carrying into effect any of the express
powers conferred upon any department of the Government, and
that Congress is in general the judge both of the necessity and the
means, the proposition is to be taken with this qualification or
limitation—that is, that the means must not be such as are prohibited by other parts of the Constitution. A lawful end, an end
expressly authorized by the Constitution, cannot be obtained by
prohibited means.

This proposition should seem to be beyond dispute. Let us de-
vote a few moments to its examination. The framers of the Government could not foresee all the exigencies which might arise in
the future, and therefore, after expressing the great ends for which
the Government was formed, and the powers conferred upon it,
they meant to leave the choice of the means generally to the discretion of Congress; but fearing that in seasons of excitement and
peril measures might be adopted not compatible with civil liberty,
or consistent with the rights of the States or of the people, various
express prohibitions were inserted in the original instrument, and
their number was greatly increased by the subsequent amendments. Thus, in the ninth section of the first Article, the one immediately following the list of granted powers, is a series of prohibitions, seven in number; and among them that relating to the
suspension of the privilege of habeas corpus, prohibiting it, "unless
when in cases of rebellion or invasion the public safety may require
it," and another relating to bills of attainder and *ex post facto* laws,
prohibiting them altogether. Stopping for a moment to consider
these clauses of the original instrument, before going into the
amendments, we see clearly that, in the choice of means for carrying into execution any of its powers, Congress could not pass an
act of attainder, or an *ex post facto* law, or (except in cases of rebellion or invasion) suspend the privilege of habeas corpus, however
great might be the exigency or the peril, and though not only
Congress, but the great majority of the country, should think these
means the most appropriate, the most sure, and the most speedy
for meeting the exigency or avoiding the peril.

Passing then to the amendments, we find eleven articles, every one of which contains a prohibition of the use of particular means to obtain a permitted end. If the end be not permitted, the prohibition is unnecessary; it is only when the end is lawful, and there is a choice of means, that the prohibition becomes effective. The manifest design was to prohibit the particular means enumerated in the amendments, however desirable might be the end. Among these prohibitions are the following: that Congress cannot abridge the freedom of speech or of the press; cannot infringe the right of the people to keep and bear arms; cannot subject any person not in the military service to answer for infamous crime, but upon the previous action of a grand jury; cannot bring an accused person to trial but by a jury; and cannot deprive any person of life, liberty, or property, without due process of law. Therefore, in the choice of means for obtaining an end, however good, Congress cannot authorize the trial of any person, not impressed with a military character, for any infamous crime whatever, except by means of a grand jury first accusing, and a trial jury afterwards deciding the accusation.

This prohibition is fatal to the military government of civilians wherever, whenever, and under whatever circumstances attempted. Such a government cannot exist without military courts, military arrests, and military trials. The military government set up in Mississippi could not exist a day without them.

Thence it follows, that even if Congress had authority to take upon itself the government of a State, this government could not be a military one; and for this reason, if there were no other, the whole scheme of these military reconstruction statutes fails, and the statutes themselves are unconstitutional and void. If the statutes are void, all acts done under them are illegal.

To illustrate: suppose there were no legal State government in Mississippi, and no adequate protection for life or property—that the State were utterly disorganized—could Congress, for those reasons, pass an Act of attainder? Is there any lawyer in this country who will stake his reputation in asserting it? Let us put the strongest possible case. Suppose that Jefferson Davis, the great leader of the rebellion, were in Mississippi to-day, creating anarchy and opposing the reconstruction of the South, so that unless he were got out of the way there could be no reconstruction of

2 K 2

the State : I ask whether any lawyer will say that Congress could
pass an Act of this tenor, reciting that, whereas there is no State
government in Mississippi, and total disorganization prevails; and
whereas the continuance of this Union depends upon the reconstruction of the State; therefore, be it enacted that Jefferson
Davis be attainted, and that the marshal be directed to take him
forthwith and execute him? I suppose a case as strong as you
may choose to put, and I defy any man to show that Congress has
the power to pass such an Act. Why not? Because our fathers,
jealous of authority—knowing from their own experience and from
the history of the world that power is liable to be abused, and that
in the excitement of party, in the storm of war, the active departments of the Government, Congress or the President, might be
tempted to use means dangerous to freedom—have provided these
safeguards, declaring that under no circumstances, and for no end,
however desirable, shall any such means be adopted.

It will be observed, that I have argued thus far without referring
to the *Case of Milligan*, decided by this Court more than a year
ago. I might have saved myself labour by citing that case in the
beginning. But, if I have stated the argument in part anew, I
nevertheless rely upon the authority of that great judgment—a
judgment which has given the Court a new title to the respect of
the world, and which will stand for ever as one of the bulwarks of
constitutional freedom. We may not even yet know how much
we owe to the Court for that decision. There was danger that the
public conscience would become debauched, by the spectacle of
irregular and usurped power going on without punishment or re-
buke. Some persons had come to believe that war, even as to
non-combatants, overturned the institutions of peace. Many were
disposed to palliate the wrong, if they could not justify it. A
larger number had ceased to consider these usurpations, as they
were, in fact, great crimes. All this is happily changed. Your
judgment recalled the people to a sense of the crimes which had
been committed against them in the name of loyalty, and to the
necessity of preserving at all times intact the defences of constitutional liberty. Men no longer think that what is called martial
law can be established by executive power, or applied to civil life.
We agree with Goldwin Smith, that " of that phrase ' martial law,'

absurd and self-contradictory as it is, each part has a meaning. The term 'martial' suspends the right of citizens to legal trial; the term 'law' suspends the claim of an enemy to quarter and the other rights of civilized war. The whole compound is the fiend's charter; and the public man who connives at its introduction, who fails in his day and in his place to resist it at whatever cost or hazard to himself, is a traitor to civilization and humanity, and though official morality may applaud him at the time, his name will stand in history accursed and infamous for ever!"

It is true that the judgment in *Milligan's Case* did not *in terms* embrace the rebel States, for the discussions at the Bar, as well as the opinions from the Bench, appear to have been carefully guarded from their disturbing influence; but it is nevertheless to be observed, that the principles declared are universal in their application. Four propositions were decided applicable to the present case. One was that the Judges will of themselves take notice that where the Courts are open there is peace in judgment of law. Another, that the guarantees in the Constitution of trial by jury, habeas corpus, &c., were made "for a state of war as well as a state of peace, and are equally binding upon rulers and people at all times, and under all circumstances"—a sentence which deserves to be written in letters of gold and placed in the chambers of justice, as sentences of Magna Charta are written in the judicial halls of England. A third was, that a civilian could not be subjected to military trial; and a fourth, that "neither the President, nor Congress, nor the Judiciary can disturb any one of the safeguards of civil liberty incorporated into the Constitution, except so far as the right is given to suspend in certain cases the privilege of the writ of habeas corpus."

I repeat, therefore, that if it were conceded that Congress could, in some possible circumstances, take upon itself the government of a State, it is certain that it could not govern by the army.

Before I proceed from this part of my argument to the next, which is to attack the premises upon which this military legislation is founded, I will make a short digression to consider the objections which have been urged, by the learned counsel who last addressed you, against the jurisdiction of the Circuit Court. These objections are very brief, and can be very briefly answered. In fact, they have been answered, as I think, in the opinion pronounced by the Chief Justice a few days ago, upon the motion to dismiss; in which he said, with reference to the Circuit Courts, in his own emphatic language, that it was impossible to widen their jurisdiction.

The objections are—first, that the Act of March 2, 1867, under which the application for discharge was made to the Circuit Court, does not apply to any case to which the 14th section of the Judiciary Act of 1789 applies; and secondly, that it does not apply to this case, because the offence charged against McCardle is a military one. The first objection arises out of a misconstruction of the Act of 1867. The Judiciary Act of 1789 authorized the writ of habeas corpus in favour of any person restrained of his liberty under the authority of the United States; the Act of 1867 authorizes it in favour of any person restrained of his liberty, in violation of the Constitution or laws of the United States. Here, it is quite true, both conditions exist: McCardle is restrained of his liberty under the authority of the United States, and he is restrained in violation of the Constitution. But, says my learned friend, because the Act of 1867 declares that the power which it gives is " in addition to the authority already conferred by law ;" therefore, if the Circuit Court could have issued the writ under the Act of 1789, it could not issue it under the Act of 1867. Is not this, however, mistaking the form for the substance, and confounding the means with the end? The design of both Acts is to release from unlawful custody, not to ordain the useless ceremony of issuing writs. The process might undoubtedly be issued in *McCardle's Case* under the old law, but it would be ineffectual; it may also be issued under the new law, and will then be effectual. He is restrained of his liberty under the authority of the United States, but the restraint is also in violation of the Constitution of the United States. Hence his right to discharge, and to the writ as a means to an end.

But, says the counsel, his was a military offence, and a military offence was not within the Act. A military offence! The statute says : " It shall be the duty of each officer, assigned as aforesaid, to protect all persons in their rights of person or property; to suppress insurrection, disorder, and violence ; to punish, or cause to be punished, all disturbers of the public peace and criminals: and to this end he may allow civil tribunals to take jurisdiction of and try offenders; he shall have power to organize military commissions or tribunals for that purpose:" and therefore, argues my learned friend, every case which can be brought before a military commission is a military offence. Then all crimes are military offences, because all criminals can be brought indiscriminately before "civil tribunals" or "military commissions." Even though an act be an offence against the penal code of Mississippi or of the United States, the offender can be brought before a military commission and tried by military rules. I have a great respect for the learned counsel, but really I cannot argue this point. A military offence is one committed by a military man, or which in some way affects the government of military men.

For these reasons, I submit to you as beyond dispute, that the Circuit Court had jurisdiction to hear McCardle's petition for a discharge, and that his case is rightfully here on appeal from its decision.

It is said, I know, that he is not accused of an infamous crime, and therefore that he is not within the purview of the prohibitions which I have mentioned. To this I answer—first, that if the offence with which he is charged be not infamous, he is still within all the prohibitions, except that contained in the 5th amendment; but, secondly, that he is accused of an infamous offence, because he can be subjected to infamous punishment. Under these Reconstruction Acts he can even be hanged by sentence of the military commission. There is no limit to its authority. He is therefore on trial for a capital crime. Besides, under the Act of Congress of July 17, 1862, inciting insurrection is made punishable by imprisonment for a period not exceeding ten years, or by a fine not exceeding 10,000 dollars.

It is said, again, that Mississippi is not a State of the Union, and for that reason the prohibitions do not apply. Mississippi not a State? I shall discuss that question by-and-by. But granting now, for the sake of the argument, that it is not a State, it is yet within the United States, and this protecting power of the Constitution covers every foot of soil over which the flag of the country floats from the eastern to the western ocean. It is felt in Massachusetts Bay and on the borders of the Lakes; it is borne on the

winds that sweep the western prairies; you stand on the pinnacle of
the Rocky Mountains and still it hangs above you; it travels with
you through the passes of the Sierra Nevada; it watches beside
you in California; and, if you go thence northward toward the
pole to far Aliaska—there, even there, it flashes over you like the
Northern Light.

In the case of *Dred Scott* v. *Sanford*, 19 Howard, 449, will be
found the following language of the Chief Justice, delivering the
opinion of the Court:—

" But the power of Congress over the person or property of a citizen
can never be a mere discretionary power under our Constitution and
form of government. The powers of the Government and the rights
and privileges of the citizen are regulated and plainly defined by the
Constitution itself. And when the territory becomes a part of the
United States, the Federal Government enters into possession in the
character impressed upon it by those who created it. It enters upon
it with its powers over the citizen strictly defined and limited by the
Constitution, from which it derives its own existence, and by virtue of
which alone it continues to exist and act as a Government and sovereignty. It has no power of any kind beyond it; and it cannot, when
it enters a territory of the United States, put off its character and
assume discretionary or despotic powers which the Constitution has
denied to it. It cannot create for itself a new character separated from
the citizens of the United States, and the duties it owes them under
the provisions of the Constitution. The territory being a part of the
United States, the Government and the citizen both enter it under the
authority of the Constitution, with their respective rights defined and
marked out; and the Federal Government can exercise no power over
his person or property beyond what that instrument confers, nor lawfully deny any right which it has reserved.

" A reference to a few of the provisions of the Constitution will illustrate this proposition.

" For example: no one, we presume, will contend that Congress can
make any law in a territory respecting the establishment of religion
or the free exercise thereof, or abridging the freedom of speech or of the
press, or the right of the people of the territory peaceably to assemble
and to petition the Government for the redress of grievances. Nor
can Congress deny to the people the right to keep and bear arms, nor
the right to trial by jury, nor compel anyone to be a witness against
himself in a criminal proceeding.

" These powers, and others, in relation to rights of person, which it
is not necessary here to enumerate, are, in express and positive terms,
denied to the general Government; and the rights of private property
have been guarded with equal care. Thus the rights of property are

united with the rights of person, and placed on the same ground by the fifth amendment to the Constitution, which provides that no person shall be deprived of life, liberty, and propeity without due process of law. And an Act of Congress which deprives a citizen of the United States of his liberty or property, merely because he came himself, or brought his property, into a particular territory of the United States, and who had committed no offence against the laws, could hardly be dignified with the name of due process of law.

" So, too, it will hardly be contended that Congress could by law quarter a soldier in a house in a territory, without the consent of the owner in time of peace, nor in time of war but in a manner prescribed by law. Nor could they by law forfeit the property of a citizen in a territory who was convicted of treason, for a longer period than the life of the person convicted, nor take private property for public use without just compensation.

" The powers over person and property of which we speak are not only not granted to Congress, but are in express terms denied, and they are forbidden to exercise them. And this prohibition is not confined to the States, but the words are general, and extend to the whole terri- tory over which the Constitution gives it power to legislate, including those portions of it remaining under territorial government, as well as that owned by States. It is a total absence of power everywhere within the dominion of the United States, and places the citizen of a territory, so far as these rights are concerned, on the same footing with citizens of the States, and guards them as firmly and plainly against any inroads which the general Government may attempt, under the plea of implied or incidental powers. And if Congress itself cannot do this—if it is beyond the powers conferred on the Federal Government—it will be admitted, we presume, that it could not autho- rize a territorial Government to exercise them. It could confer no power on any local Government, established by its authority, to violate the provisions of the Constitution."

Let it not be said of this language that the case of *Dred Scott* has been so much criticised as to weaken the authority of every part of it. This is the judgment of the Court, delivered by the Chief Justice, and concurred in by six of his brethren. The two dissenting opinions, Mr. Justice McLean and Mr. Justice Curtis, use on this point similar language. The opinion of Mr. Justice McLean is on page 542, as follows: " No powers can be exercised which are prohibited in the Constitution, or which are contrary to its spirit; so that whether the object may be the protection of the persons and property of purchasers of the public lands, or of communities who have been annexed to the Union by con- quest or purchase, they are initiatory to the establishment of State governments, and no more power can be claimed or exercised than is necessary to the attainment of the end. This is the limitation of all Federal powers. Congress has no right to regulate the internal concerns of a State as of a territory; consequently, in providing for the government of a territory, to some extent the combined powers of the Federal and State governments are necessarily exercised."

The opinion of Mr. Justice Curtis, on page 614, referring to the clause about the territory of the country, says: "If, then, this clause does contain a power to legislate respecting the territory, what are the limits of that power? To this I answer, that in common with all the other legislative powers of Congress, it finds limits in the express prohibitions of Congress not to do certain things; that, in the exercise of legislative powers, it cannot pass an *ex post facto* law or bill of attainder, and so on in respect to the other prohibitions contained in the constitution."

In the opinion of Mr. Justice Nelson there is no dissent, although he confined himself to a view of the case which did not make it necessary to enter into this discussion.

I have, therefore, the opinion of every member of the Court against the existence of the power upon which the whole argument of the defendants rests. Congress, though it had the right to do in Mississippi everything it could do if the country had been gained from Spain yesterday, or from the most unlimited government on earth, yet could not govern it by the army. And, as I have already said, even in the new territory, just purchased from that vast empire which has no constitution, but an autocrat legislating according to his will alone, and we have succeeded that government; even in that territory, if there be any vitality in our constitution, Congress cannot pass a law making the people subject to a military government. If that be so, is there not an end to this argument?

A parallel argument is contained in the case of *Houston* v. *Moore*, a case to which the gentlemen referred. There the question was whether a citizen of Pennsylvania, being ordered to rendezvous in pursuance of the direction of the President and by order of the Governor, refusing to attend, could be brought before a court-martial. The court-martial was held under the authority of the

State of Pennsylvania. And though the judgment is not relevant to this case, I refer to it for the purpose of showing that in the dissenting opinion of Mr. Chief Justice Story, he declared that if a person summoned to the rendezvous could not be considered as in the service of the United States, he could not be tried except by a jury. That is on page 62, 5th Wheaton:—

"The fourth section of the Act of 1795 makes the militia employed in the service of the United States subject to the rules and regulations of war; and those include capital punishment by court-martial. Yet one of the amendments (Article 5) to the Constitution prohibits such punishment, unless on a presentment or indictment of a grand jury, except in cases arising in the land or naval forces, or in the militia when in actual service."

In short, there does not appear to be a dissenting opinion anywhere from the doctrine, that a trial for crime of a person in civil life can only be by jury; and when it is for an infamous crime, it can only be on the accusation of a grand jury. That binds the United States and all its departments conjoined. For let it be understood that the Government of the United States means all the departments, and not one. Congress is not the government any more than this Court. But neither the whole Government of the United States, nor any department of it, can, by any law or act possible under the Constitution, subject a single citizen not in the military service, however high or however low, of whatever race or previous condition, to a trial for crime except by a jury of his peers. That being so, the whole scheme of the Reconstruction Acts falls to the ground. Here is a military government, resting upon military courts, and enforced by military executions. Congress has not chosen to intervene except by the army; its judges are men with epaulettes; its sheriffs are soldiers with bayonets; and its scaffold is the greensward, with a platoon paraded.

This is the first part of my argument, and here, as I think, the whole argument might end; for if military government be a thing prohibited by the Constitution, we need go no further, nor trouble ourselves to inquire whether Congress has judged rightly in its reasons for intervention. The question is whether McCardle, being a citizen of Mississippi, under the dominion of the United States, regarding Mississippi either as a State or as a territory, can be subjected, under the authority of the Government of the United States, to a military trial, which involves his imprisonment or his life, no matter under what pretence or for what end. It is the particular kind of intervention, that is to say, intervention by military power, that I have been objecting to; and if I have shown that to be inadmissible and unconstitutional, it matters little whether the reasons for intervention put forth in the preamble be sufficient or insufficient, or whether any other reasons have been, or could be, advanced for the interference of Congress in the government of Mississippi.

But I will now proceed a step further: and supposing, for the sake of the argument, that a military government is not a prohibited, but a rightful, constitutional means of intervention, I submit that the preamble furnishes no reason for any kind of intervention whatever, and this for two reasons—first, because it is not true, in a constitutional sense; and secondly, because, if true, it is not a constitutional reason for intervention.

It is not true in a constitutional sense. Of course I am not going into any question of personal veracity, nor into questions of fact, except such as the Court may take notice of judicially. The preamble asserts as facts, first, that there is no legal State government in Mississippi; and, secondly, that there is no adequate protection for life or property. These two asserted facts are separable and separately stated. There may be a legal State government, though that government may not fulfil, and may not be able to fulfil, all its duties for the protection of life and property. It is most convenient to consider these assertions separately.

Was there, or was there not, on the 2nd of March, 1867, a *legal State government* in Mississippi? This inquiry involves another, antecedent to everything else, which is, whether the declaration of Congress is conclusive upon this Court: or, in other words, whether you are at liberty, after this declaration, to make for yourselves inquiry on the subject; or whether you must accept the declaration as conclusive, whatever may be your own knowledge or information. This question may perhaps best be answered by supposing a case. Suppose an Act of Congress passed to-morrow, with a similar preamble, concerning the State of Massachusetts, would you accept it as absolute verity? If it declared that, whereas no legal State government exists in Massachusetts, therefore it be made a military district, and subject to the military power of the United States, just as Mississippi is made subject by the Act in question, and the commanding general of the district were to seize the ancient State House and Faneuil Hall, and the editors of the Boston newspapers were to be arrested and tried by military commissions for protesting against these violations, would you be obliged to hold that Massachusetts has no legal State government? Would you tell her that, though you do not see why she has not a legal State government, Congress has decided otherwise, and that is sufficient for you? I am supposing an extreme case; but an extreme case is a good test of a universal principle. If, as a principle universal in its application, the declaration of Congress is conclusive upon the other departments of the Government, then, in the case supposed of Massachusetts, it would prevail. If the principle is not universal, then there are cases in which this Court could inquire for itself, notwithstanding the declaration of Congress.

Is it true that under this government of ours it is competent for Congress to declare that a State in this Union, the State of Massachusetts, has not a legal government, and therefore can be governed as a territory? I deny it altogether. Where is the authority of Congress to declare whether a State has a legal or illegal government? I am not now discussing the question whether it is or is not republican. I repeat, where does Congress get the power to declare whether or not a State has a legal government? Take my State. Has Congress the power to say she has not a legal government? What do you mean by ".legal"? Legal, according to what law?—Federal law or State law?—military law or civil law? For legal means, according to some law. Mr. Justice Nelson knows that the Constitution of New York has been changed several times, he himself having been a member of two of the constitutional conventions that made those changes; and he will remember that the opinion of the Supreme Court of the State was taken on the question whether the convention to frame the present Constitution was constitutionally called, and they decided it was not, because the convention was not called in the mode provided by the former Constitution of 1821.

Now, I ask my friends, any of them, has Congress the power to declare that my State has not a legal State government? Everybody will say no. Congress has no more power to come into New York and tell us that we have framed a Constitution contrary to our previous Constitution than to declare that the first government of New York was a void government. And if they should presume to come to us in that way, I think they will get an answer which will be quite sufficient. Let me tell them that New York chooses to frame her government in her own way, and will alter it as she pleases, subject only to the provision that it shall not be anti-republican in form; and until that question arises, the Congress of the United States can have nothing to do with us any more than we can have to do with them.

The true rule I apprehend to be this: the Court will take judicial notice of the fact of an existing government in every State of the Union: such a government will be presumed to be legal till it is shown to be illegal: the declaration of Congress may be one of the sources of evidence which enter into the case, but not the conclusive or the only one. If there be two rival governments in a State, Congress may have the right to decide between them, and certainly must decide which is to send representatives to Congress, and that decision so far will be binding; but that is a very different thing from asserting that no government whatever exists, or that an existing government is *de facto*, and not *de jure*. The authority to *declare* a fact is only coextensive with the right to *decide* it; or, in other words, the declaration has no force, except as a decision. This, therefore, is the question: Has Congress authority to decide that *the existing government* of Massachusetts, or of any other State, is not a *legal* government? To this there should seem to be but one answer. No power is given Congress to interfere with the government of the States, any more than power is given the States to interfere with the government of the United States, except in this one respect, that the United States shall guarantee to each State a republican form of government. But this preamble does not deny that Mississippi has a government republican in form. That she has a government is stated more than once in these Acts of Congress: it is there called an existing government; and while it is pronounced not to be *legal*, it is nowhere pronounced not to be *republican*.

Having shown, as I trust, that the declaration of Congress is not conclusive upon this Court in respect to the existence of a *legal* State government, little need be said respecting the conclusiveness of the declaration, that there is no adequate protection for life or property. It is not for Congress to decide whether New York fulfils her duty to her citizens of protection for their lives and property; and therefore the declaration of Congress on that subject, in respect to New York or Mississippi, has no force whatever.

Now, laying aside the declaration of Congress contained in this preamble as of no constitutional force, though entitled to great respect because coming from one of the departments of the government; laying that aside, as not authoritative, I ask you to consider for yourselves whether or not the government of Mississippi was a legal government on the 2nd of March, 1867 ? First, let us see what evidence these Reconstruction Acts themselves furnish. Though the original Act declares that there is no legal State government in Mississippi, yet it provides, in the third section, that the military commander may allow the local civil tribunals to take effect. There is a government, then, as matter of fact. "And all interference, under colour of State authority, with the exercise of military authority under this Act shall be null and void." There is some State authority then. And in another section it is provided, that the citizens may have provisional governments only until they shall be entitled to representation. There is, then, a provisional government.

The supplementary Act of July 19, 1867, is still more explicit. The first section of that Act speaks of "the governments then existing in the rebel States of Virginia, North Carolina, &c., as not legal State governments." They were existing governments, be it understood. There is no doubt about that. They were *de facto* governments of the rebel States. The State of Mississippi had at the time a *de facto* government, which was exercising all the functions of government. Here—and this is additional and conclusive evidence—here are its statutes, and here are its reports. This (holding up the volume) is but one of the two volumes of the reports of the highest Court of Mississippi during the time of the rebellion, excepting the time when the State was occupied by the Federal army, which forbade the Courts to assemble. And it may

not be out of place to say, that in this, the last volume, is a decision upon the question whether they have a legal government;
that is to say, whether the government adopted under the provisional governor is a legal State government. Now, if, according
to the doctrine of the case of *Luther* v. *Borden*, you are to follow
the decisions of the highest court in the State as to the legality of
their own government, then the decision of the highest court in
Mississippi is conclusive upon the action of this Court. Indeed, it
is impossible to shut our eyes to the fact, that however censurable
and criminal may have been the conduct of the legislatures of the
rebel States during the rebellion, there were, nevertheless, established governments during all the time, carrying on their operations with regularity.

Let me turn aside for a moment to consider this case of *Luther*
v. *Borden*, about which so much has been said, to show that, so
far from being an authority against us, it is an authority in our
favour.

The contest in that case was between two rival parties, each
claiming to have the lawful government of the State. The contesting party claimed that its government had been adopted by the
vote of the whole people, exercising for the first time the elective
franchise; the party in possession, having admitted to the exercise
of the franchise only a part of the people, rested upon that part
for its authority; and the Judges were asked to decide that the
government of the contestants was the true one, on the ground
that it had received the sanction of the whole people.

By whom was the martial law mentioned in that case established?
By the State of Rhode Island. Under the charter of Charles II.
the legislature of that State had no limitation whatever; it could
exercise its powers in a legislative, executive, and judicial capacity
untrammelled, and the case has no application to the question
whether Congress can establish martial law. The Court, by Chief
Justice Taney, decided that "the question, which of the governments was the legitimate one—viz., the charter government or the
government established by the voluntary convention?—had not
heretofore been regarded as a judicial one in any of the courts;" that
"the courts of Rhode Island had decided in favour of the validity
of the charter government, and the courts of the United States

adopted and followed the decisions of the State courts in questions which concern merely the constitution and laws of the State." Here is language so very pertinent to the present inquiry, that I will ask your attention to it particularly: "The fourth section of the fourth article of the Constitution," says the Chief Justice, "provides, that the United States shall guarantee to every State in the Union a republican form of government, and shall protect each of them against invasion, and on the application of the Legislature, or of the Executive (when the Legislature cannot be convened), against domestic violence. Under this article of the Constitution it rests with Congress to decide what government is the established one in a State. For, as the United States guarantee to each State a republican government, Congress must necessarily decide what government is established in the State before it can determine whether it is republican or not." So that all that the Government of the United States, according to this case, can decide, is, as between two contesting governments, which is the established one.

And again: "No one, we believe, has ever doubted the proposition that, according to the institutions of this country, the sovereignty in every State resides in the people of the State, and that they may alter and change their form of government at their own pleasure. But whether they have changed it or not, by abolishing an old government, and establishing a new one in its place, is a question to be settled by the political power. And when that power has decided, the courts are bound to take notice of its decision, and to follow it."

The Congress is to decide what? Not that the State has not a legal State government, but to decide which is the established government of the State. It must decide what government is established, before it can decide whether it is republican or not. Now, see the argument that is pressed here: if Congress goes on with its reconstruction scheme, and there is set up another government in Mississippi, it can decide between the new government and the present one; therefore, Congress can set up the new government. Was there ever a claim of power more unfounded? Because you have the right to decide between contesting governments, therefore, when there is only one existing, you can set up

2 L

another to contest with the first and decide between the two. That is the whole of the argument.

Whether there is "*adequate* protection for life and property" in the State of Mississippi I do not know, as I do not know what is meant by *adequate* protection. According to European ideas, there is not "adequate protection for life or property" in some of the most loyal States of this Union. Should we, ourselves, say that there was adequate protection for life or property in the anti-rent districts of New York for the ten years between 1840 and 1850? Is there now adequate protection for life or property in the mining districts of Pennsylvania? How is it in the new settlements? Is it meant by adequate protection that crime is punished with celerity, certainty, firmness, and impartiality? If that be the measure of adequate protection, and Congress may interfere for the want of it, I fear they will have their hands full.

Having thus shown that neither part of the preamble is true in a constitutional sense, I add, that if both parts of it were true, they would not furnish a constitutional reason for assuming, even by civil officers of the United States, the civil administration of Mississippi. What I have to say in support of this negative proposition will be given more at length hereafter, as I proceed with my argument; and I will content myself here with observing, that the States are, both by the letter and the spirit of the Federal compact, exempt from all Federal control or interference, except in pursuance of the Constitution, and that nowhere, expressly or by implication, is power given to assume the government of a State, for either or both of the causes set forth in this preamble.

Thus far, if the Court please, I have gone on the path which I had marked out for myself at the commencement, in considering whether the preamble of the original military Reconstruction Act is true in a constitutional sense, and whether, if it be true, it justifies the Act; and I flatter myself that I have shown, that whether the preamble be true or not, it does not justify this intervention for the government of Mississippi by military power; and, in the second place, going back to the preamble, that it is not true in a constitutional sense, and, if true, would not justify assumption of the civil administration.

But my learned friends go further, and suggest other reasons, as they suppose, for these military governments. Now, I ask, in the first place, is the citizen permitted to go beyond an Act of Congress to find reasons for the Act? Congress has said in the Act itself, that whereas no legal State governments exist, and there is no adequate protection for life or property, therefore be it enacted, &c. Confining myself to this, I say that, standing alone, the preamble does not justify this Act. My learned friends have departed from this preamble, and say, virtually, that it does not state half the case—that there are other reasons which justify the Act.

To these other reasons I must ask your attention. First, I will consider some of those which are given in debate, though not specially urged by the other side. I propose, therefore, to consider the reasons generally given‾ for these military acts, and then the reasons given by the counsel who have argued the case.

Four reasons have been most insisted upon in political debate: one, that Congress is the sole judge of what is a republican form of government, and when it adjudges the government of a State not to be republican, it may force a military government upon it; the second, that the rebel States were conquered, and, being so, may be governed by the same military force which conquered them, so long as Congress sees fit to continue such government; the third, that by the rebellion the government and people of the Southern States forfeited all their rights; and the fourth, that Congress may now govern the rebel States, in the exercise of belligerent rights. Each of these reasons will be considered by itself, in the order in which I have stated them.

First.—The United States are to guarantee to each State a republican form of government.

What does this mean? To guarantee, in its ordinary sense, means to warrant something already existing, the performance of an existing contract, the continuance of an existing state of things. The first treaty made between this Government and France, negotiated by Franklin, provided that the United States should guarantee to France the possession of her West India Islands, and that France should guarantee to us the possession of our independence. The guaranty of the Constitution here is the guaranty of an existing form of republican government—that is to say, of a form of

2 L 2

republican government, the same being now in existence—and no
more justifies the claim to intervene in the government of a State
for the purpose of reconstruction, than for the purpose of creating
an Emperor.

Under colour of this power, can the Federal authorities destroy
existing State authorities? Our construction is the only one compatible with the public safety. To give the Federal Government
the unlimited power of destroying any State government upon the
allegation that it is not republican, is to give to the central authority a control over the local authorities greater than was ever
dreamed of before, and is to make way for a consolidation fatal to
the rights of the States and the liberties of the people.

The history and cotemporaneous exposition of this clause of the
Constitution, will show that it has no such meaning as the other
side claim for it.

The subject was first brought before the Convention which
framed the Constitution by Mr. Randolph, who proposed this form:
" Resolved, that a republican government, and the territory of
each State, except in the instance of a voluntary junction of
government and territory, ought to be guaranteed by the United
States to each State " (2 Mad. Papers, 734). Afterwards, "alterations having been made in the resolution, making it read: 'That
a republican constitution, and its existing laws, ought to be
guaranteed to each State by the United States,' the whole was
agreed to, *nem. con.*" (2 Mad. Papers, 843).

On a subsequent day, after considerable debate, Mr. Wilson
moved as a better expression of the idea, " 'That a republican form
of government shall be guaranteed to each State; and that each
State shall be protected against foreign and domestic violence.'
This seeming to be well received, Mr. Madison and Mr. Randolph
withdrew their propositions, and on the question for agreeing to
Mr. Wilson's motion, it passed, *nem. con.*" (2 Mad. Papers, 1139).
The language was afterwards changed to the form which it now
bears in the Constitution.

In the 43rd number of the "Federalist," written by Mr. Hamilton,
is the following exposition: " In a confederacy founded on republican principles and composed of republican members, the
superintending government ought clearly to possess authority to

defend the system against aristocratic or monarchical INNOVATIONS.
The more intimate the nature of such an union may be, the
greater interest have the members in the political institutions of
each other, and the greater right to insist that the forms of government, under which the compact was entered into, should be *substantially* maintained.

"But a right implies a remedy; and where else could the
remedy be deposited than where it is deposited by the Constitution? Governments of dissimilar principles and forms have been
found less adapted to a federal coalition of any sort than those of a
kindred nature. 'As the confederate Republic of Germany,' says
Montesquieu, 'consists of free cities and petty States, subject to
different princes, experience shows us that it is more imperfect
than that of Holland and Switzerland.' 'Greece was undone,' he
adds, 'as soon as the King of Macedon obtained a seat among the
Amphictyones.' In the latter case, no doubt the disproportionate
force as well as the monarchical form of the new confederate had
its share of influence on the events. It may possibly be asked,
what need there could be of such a precaution, and whether it
may not become a pretext for alterations in the State governments
without the concurrence of the States themselves? These questions admit of ready answers. If the interposition of the general
Government should not be needed, the provision for such an event
will be a harmless superfluity only in the Constitution. But who
can say what experiments may be produced by the caprice of
particular States, by the ambition of enterprising leaders, or by
the intrigues and influence of foreign Powers? To the second
question it may be answered, that if the general Government should
interpose by virtue of this constitutional authority, it will be of
course bound to pursue the authority. But the authority extends
no further than to a *guaranty* of a republican form of government,
which supposes a pre-existing government of the form which is to
be guaranteed. As long, therefore, as the existing republican
forms are continued by the States, they are guaranteed by the
Federal Constitution. Whenever the States may choose to substitute other republican forms they have a right to do so, and to
claim the Federal guaranty for the latter. The only restriction
imposed on them is, that they shall not exchange republican for

APPENDIX.

anti-republican constitutions—a restriction which, it is presumed, will hardly be considered as a grievance."

The purpose of this guaranty of republican government was, therefore, to protect the States against "*aristocratic or monarchical innovations.*" Who would have thought that in less than eighty years this clause would be invoked as authority for forcing upon the States the most radical *innovations* in the opposite direction? It is not for me in this place to say whether I think these innovations good or bad, nor is my opinion of any importance. If it depended upon me, and so far as I could constitutionally act, I would make every human being equal before the law. But I would not break the Constitution of my country for any innovations whatsoever.

Other forms of government, where there are different orders in the State, may be kept up by a balance of power, each struggling to prevent the preponderance of the other. But a republican government in a vast country is an impossibility without a written constitution. An instrument which is not kept inviolate is so far not a constitution. The choice for us, if we are to maintain a united government in this country, is between a written constitution, sacredly kept, preserved inviolate against all attacks, and a monarchical government. History has taught us nothing if it does not teach us that we cannot maintain a consolidated government on this continent but by an emperor or a king, and that no other government can exist than a consolidated one, except under a written constitution. Therefore, whoever maintains the integrity of this constitution sacred and inviolable against all opposers, maintains for himself and his posterity the freedom and unity of his country.

Secondly, we are told that we may govern the Southern States by the right of conquest. This right of conquest is the ground upon which the first counsel placed himself; the right of war is the ground upon which the last placed himself. "We have conquered the people," says the first. "It is well for them to know what is the temper of the North," he says, in conclusion. "They are conquered and we are the conquerors, and we will give them such a government as we choose." Is this argument a sound one? How have we conquered the Southern States? In the sense in which

the word conquest is used in this argument, we have conquered the
rebel armies, thanks be to God, and there is not a hostile force
marshalled, there is not a hostile hand raised against us, between
the two oceans. But does that operate to transfer the sovereignty
from the conquered to the conqueror? Is the conquered sovereign
displaced, and the conquering sovereign seated in his stead?
Mississippi was a sovereign before, in a qualified sense. The
United States were sovereign before, in a qualified sense also. But
when the United States overcame the rebel armies, did they suc-
ceed to the sovereignty of Mississippi?

The suppression, by the former, of the rebel forces of the latter,
was entirely consistent with the relations which previously existed
between the two sovereigns: neither the war nor the victory
changed the double allegiance of the citizen—one to his State, and
the other to his Nation.

The laws of conquest have no application to a civil war. When
a rebellion is subdued, the sovereign is restored to the exercise of
his ancient rights. If a county of New York is declared to be in a
state of insurrection, force is applied to put the insurrection down;
and when that is done, the law resumes its sway. The legal relations of the county to the State are not permanently changed,
though their operations may have been suspended for the time
being. By the laws of war between sovereign and independent
States, when one has taken possession of the other, the will of the
conqueror becomes the law, because his only relations to the conquered States are those of conqueror and master. If, however,
there were antecedent relations, which the war has not broken,
they are resumed the moment the war is over. The only inquiry in the present case, is whether the rebellion or the war has
abolished or changed the *legal relations* of the State to the Union.
Now, as we maintain that no act of the Federal Government can
exclude a State from the Union, so no act of the State can withdraw it from the Union. The war found it in the Union, subject
to its laws; the war left it in the Union, subject to the same laws.

In barbarous times, the laws of war authorized the reduction to
slavery of a conquered people. These laws have been softened
under the influences of Christianity and civilization, till now it is
the settled public law of the Christian and civilized world, that

the conquest of one nation by another makes no change in the property or the personal rights and relations of the conquered people. "The people change their allegiance," says Chief Justice Marshall (7 Pet. 87, *U. S.* v. *Churchman*); "their relation to their ancient sovereign is dissolved, but their relation to each other and their rights of property remain undisturbed." One change only is effected, and that is that one sovereign takes the place of the other. *In a civil war sovereigns are not changed* unless the rebellion is successful.

It is very true that the rebel States themselves renounced their allegiance to the nation, or rather they denied that they owed any such allegiance, and maintained that their relation to the Union was that merely of parties to a compact. We, however, denied their theory, and insisted that they owed allegiance which they could not renounce; and for the support of these opposite theories, each side took up arms. Now that we have won, it is not for us to deny the cause for which we fought. We are striving to maintain the supremacy of the Constitution in the Southern States, not so much for their sakes as for our own.

A little reflection will satisfy us that the opposite doctrine may lead to the most alarming consequences. Suppose that, in Shay's rebellion, the insurgents had got the better of the State government, and the troops of the United States, having been brought in, had suppressed the rebellion—would Congress, in that event, have been justified by the Constitution in imposing its own government upon Massachusetts? If the Federal Legislature may impose a government with one view, it may with another. It may impose one with a design to restrict the suffrage, as well as to extend it. Suppose, hereafter, a negro insurrection to occur in a southern State, or even a peaceable change to be made in its constitution for the purpose of excluding a majority of the whites from the government, and domestic violence and revolt thence to ensue, resulting in Federal intervention and suppression—would Congress, in that event, be justified by the Constitution in assuming the government of the State and restricting the suffrage to the whites? Let me put this question. Suppose Mississippi, in a war between the United States and Great Britain, had been conquered by the latter, and then retaken by the United States—would this Government hold the State as conqueror, or as Federal sovereign under the Constitution? Most clearly the latter. The doctrine of *postliminy* rests on that foundation.

Let us look abroad and see what crimes have been committed under the plea of conquest. Ireland is a memorable example. " To the charge of arbitrary government in Ireland," says Goldwin Smith, " Strafford pleaded that the Irish were a conquered nation. They were a conquered nation, cries Pym. There cannot be a word more pregnant and fruitful in treason than that word is. There are few nations in the world that have not been conquered, and no doubt but the conqueror may give what law he pleases to those that are conquered; but if the succeeding acts and agreements do not limit and restrain that right, what people can be secure? England hath been conquered, and Wales hath been conquered, and, by this reason, will be in little better case than Ireland. *If the King, by the right of a conqueror, gives laws to his people, shall not the people, by the same reason, be restored to the right of the conquered, to recover their liberty if they can ?"*

Hungary is another example. The House of Hapsburg was deposed by the Estates of the kingdom. A bloody war followed, and the Estates were conquered. Then ensued a strife between the Emperor and his subjects, whether he was King of Hungary by the conquest, or King by the Constitution—till, after long years, ending with the disastrous day of Sadowa, he was compelled to yield, and the Hungarians are now resting in the shelter of their ancient Constitution.

Therefore, I insist that the right of conquest gives no countenance whatever to the idea that Congress can take into its hands the government of Mississippi. I need not add to what I have already argued, that if Congress had any such right it could not exercise it by the military power.

The *third* reason given for the military government of Mississippi, is that the rebel States and their people forfeited their rights by the rebellion. This is the language—the State of Mississippi and the people of Mississippi have forfeited all their rights; that is to say, they are outlaws. How have they forfeited all their rights? Have they forfeited them by the attempt to withdraw from the United States—the peaceable act of secession, if there could be such a thing—that is to say, by the mere act of renouncing their allegiance? Most certainly not. They have denied the right of the Federal Government to keep them in the Union. But does that result in the change of our rights? It is not so in the case of private contracts. One cannot be absolved from a contract without the consent of the other party. Does war produce these results? When war exists, then there is a levying of war against the United States. But levying war is treason? Did they forfeit their rights by treason? Undoubtedly, there is a forfeiture when there is a conviction, but not before. Though every man in Mississippi were guilty of treason, not one could be touched by an Act of Congress, except upon conviction; because, as we all know, Congress is expressly forbidden to pass an Act of attainder. There may be in Mississippi a million of people; Congress has not the power to pass an Act against one of them, declaring that whereas he has been guilty of treason he may be taken and punished without conviction. Still less can they pass an act against the whole people.

There is a fallacy in the assertion, so often made, that the rebel States and people have forfeited their rights by the rebellion. The proposition is stated in its strongest form when it is said that the *war* of the rebels was treason, and that traitors have no rights. But it is not true that traitors have no rights; they have all their rights until they are judicially condemned—or perhaps the better form of stating the proposition is, that they are not to be accounted traitors until they are convicted of treason. The Constitution has carefully defined treason to consist in levying war against the United States, or adhering to their enemies, giving them aid and comfort; and has declared that no person shall be convicted of this crime unless on testimony of two witnesses to the same overt act, or upon confession in open court. So there can be neither treason, nor penalty of treason, until after conviction; and Congress has not competency to convict, however great and manifest may be the crime.

There is another answer to the argument of forfeiture, and that is that treason is a *personal* crime. There can be no treason of a State, though there may be of all the persons who compose it. Whatever may have been the misconduct of the citizens of Mississippi, even though every one of them were guilty, the State, the corporate body, did not, because it could not, commit the crime of treason.

The *fourth* reason given for governing Mississippi by military power is belligerent right. It is said that Congress may assume the government of Mississippi by virtue of this right. The first answer to that argument is this :—There can be no belligerent right where there is no belligerent, and there is no belligerent because the war is ended. There are no belligerents because there is no *bellum*. That is the first answer. The next is, that during the war, *flagrante bello*, it was not competent for the United States to assume the entire government of a State which they occupied with their forces. Let me ask your attention to this position for a few moments. What could the United States do by virtue of their belligerent rights? They could wage war as other wars are waged; they could ravage and kill—could fight the armies of their enemies, and capture cities—could make assaults upon forts and subdue them. But could they govern?—that is to say, could they take into their own hands the whole government of a State which they had succeeded in occupying with their forces? I am not asking what they could do in the act of waging war; but I am supposing that they have occupied the whole State of Mississippi, so that there is not a hostile arm lifted in the State, and that they are carrying on their hostile operations beyond the State. I deny that they have then the power to assume the government of Mississippi to themselves. What authority has an army of a sovereign, occupying his own territory, when every hostile force is subdued, to take into its own hands the government of the country by a right paramount to his antecedent right?

Suppose, however, they say—and this is the way in which the argument is put—suppose that there is utter anarchy; suppose that in the State of Mississippi, during the occupation of it by our armies, there is such anarchy that no law is enforced, and not a magistrate is sitting in the State. I am supposing a case which does not exist. It seems to me a very idle discussion; but my learned friends have made an argument upon it, and therefore I must notice it. I therefore ask, what may an occupying army do? The occupying army may keep the peace, and that is all. Is it to

APPENDIX.

force institutions upon the country? What right has New York, I should like to know, to force its institutions upon Mississippi under any circumstance whatever? War does not give the right. What does? Is it anarchy? Then the question comes to this: Does a condition of total anarchy in one State give the other States a right to go in there and construct their government? I deny it. I am not discussing the right of revolution. I admit that the people of nine-tenths or three-fourths of the States have the right, by an act of revolution, to invade and subdue a State, because the law of self-preservation is above all others. But that is not the question. The question here is one of constitution. I deny that, even in a condition of absolute anarchy, the State of Iowa can be forced to take the institutions of New York; the people of New York cannot go there to demand that the people of Iowa shall receive their form of municipal or State government. It is for Iowa to determine for herself. The fundamental doctrine of our government is, that the people have a right to change their own form of government as they please. That is set forth in almost every one of our State constitutions, and from that it results that no other State has a right to intervene.

But, as I said, this is, after all, but a speculative discussion; it is one that should not enter into this case at all, and one which I should not have entered upon if I had had the opinion just read by Mr. Chief Justice Nelson, where the revolutionary government of the Confederacy is said to have been a government *de facto*, with all its departments, legislative, judicial, and executive, having every function of government in full operation. If that is so, then the States that compose it had the same, and Mississippi was among the rest. They had *de facto* governments, with all their departments, and the argument from the necessity of assuming the government by reason of anarchy is one that has no foundation whatever. But one of the learned counsel says, these *de facto* governments were not governments *de jure*, because their members had not taken the oath of allegiance to the United States. Let us look at that. I admit that they were not governments *de jure* in a Federal sense, for they had renounced their allegiance. They could not send members to Congress. They had legislatures not acknowledging fealty to the United States, and for that reason they could not send senators, and for a similar reason their people could not send members to the House of Representatives. But is it true that because they had thrown off their allegiance all their acts of legislation were null? Look at Mobile; is every act of the city council of Mobile since the war began a nullity? When did the Virginia Legislature resolve not to take the oath of allegiance to the United States? How long ago? Before the war, I believe. Has not Virginia been a legal State government since that time, I ask? The obligation to take the oath is directory; that is all. If their members do not take the oath they are none the less governments. The Constitution of the United States provides that all legislative and judicial officers shall take oath to support the Constitution. Now, if nullity is the consequence of not taking the oath, there has been no lawful judge upon the Bench in the South since the war began, and there has been no judgment which is not a nullity from 1861 to 1864. Is that so? Is any man in his senses prepared to assert that?

This should seem to be a sufficient reason, but as the argument is much insisted on, I will follow it further. The question of belligerency and belligerent rights received great attention in the prize cases, where the Court laid down certain fundamental propositions. One of them, relating to the fact of civil war existing, was this: "The true test of its existence, as found in the writings of the sages of the common law, may be thus summarily stated: 'When the regular course of justice is interrupted by revolt, rebellion, or insurrection, so that the courts of justice cannot be kept open, *civil war exists*, and hostilities may be prosecuted on the same footing as if those opposing the Government were foreign enemies invading the land'" (2 Black. 667).

Applying this rule to the present case, it follows that civil war can no longer be recognized as existing in Mississippi, because the courts are open. Therefore, whether, during the war, the just exercise of belligerent rights would have authorized the Federal Government to take into its hands the entire government of that State or not, there is no warrant for any such exercise now.

Another proposition in that case was, that the Courts will take judicial notice of the beginning and progress of the civil war. Of course, for the same reason, they will take judicial notice of its end.

The Court says: "By the Constitution, Congress alone has the power to declare a national or foreign war. *It cannot declare war against a State*, or any number of States, by virtue of any clause in the Constitution. *The Constitution confers on the President the whole executive power.* He is bound to take care that the laws be faithfully executed. He is Commander-in-Chief of the army and navy of the United States, and of the militia of the several States, when called into the actual service of the United States. *He has no power to initiate or declare a war either against a foreign nation or a domestic State.*"

A further proposition of that case was, that by exercising belligerent rights the United States did not lose those which were sovereign. If their sovereign rights remained, their duties as sovereign remained also. The exercise of belligerent rights was, in fact, for the purpose of regaining the complete enjoyment of their sovereign rights, and for no other purpose.

Here is the language of the Court: "The parties belligerent in a public war are independent nations. But it is not necessary to constitute war that both parties should be acknowledged as independent nations or sovereign States. A war may exist where one of the belligerents claims sovereign rights as against the other."

It should not be forgotten, that belligerent rights are to be exercised by the Executive, and not by Congress. In the present instance the Executive exercises, and attempts to exercise, none against the State of Mississippi, or any of her people. Indeed, he disclaims any such authority; these military acts were passed over his veto; and if the argument from belligerency should prevail, we should have the extraordinary spectacle of the Legislature exercising an executive function without the consent and against the protest of the Executive.

It has been already observed, that while the war lasted, their belligerent rights did not authorize the United States to carry on the entire government of Mississippi. They might govern their own armies and subdue the armies of the rebels. As soon as that was done, or as fast as they advanced, they could proceed to organize their own displaced government in its former estate, open the Federal courts, run the Federal mails, collect the Federal revenue— in short, do all that they could do before. But might they not do something more? That depends upon their rights and their duties under the Constitution. This Government is a limited one, and its rights and duties are defined and limited by the Constitution; and if you cannot find there the warrant for its action, it cannot act at all. If a State of this Union should fall in great disorder, so that her finances should become ruinous, her treasury bankrupt, her roads be infested by robbers, property and person be insecure, with an impotent executive, a babbling legislature, and a venal judiciary, could Congress step in and take the government of that State into its own hands? I can perceive no authority for their doing so; and if authority be necessary, it must be sought by an amendment of the Constitution. It is as clear as noonday that the theory of our present Constitution is, that the States shall organize themselves, and that Congress has nothing to do with it; except that, if in such organization the States should introduce aristocratic or monarchical innovations, it might then interfere to insist upon their going back to their republican forms.

But it may be asked, cannot the Federal army, which goes into a State to suppress a rebellion, govern the parts into which it advances? I answer, as a similar question was answered in *Milligan's Case*, "*necessitas, quod cogit, defendit.*" The advancing and occupying army must govern itself by the laws of war; it must keep the peace within its own lines, and for that purpose it must govern the people within them, so far, and so far only, as ordinary civil government is impossible. For example, when the city of New Orleans was taken by the Federal forces, all the Federal laws applicable to the port and district went again into operation; but if there were no State officers competent to administer or execute the State laws, the commanding officer of the occupying forces must, of necessity, for the safety of his own army, as well as of the society within his lines, preserve order, and might make regulations for that purpose. This, I suppose, is the rule, and the whole of it.

Even this power ceases with the necessity of its exercise. The moment the military occupation (*occupatio bellica*) ceases, that moment the right to govern, even within the narrow limits which I have explained, ceases also. Is there no period, then, after the cessation of hostilities, during which the military occupation may

continue?—no intermediate state between the state of war and
the state of peace?—no interval after hostilities, and before the
re-establishment of civil government? To this question, as applicable to this case, I answer:

I. The occupying forces must have reasonable time to retire
with their war material; and so long as they necessarily remain
for that purpose, so long the reason of the rule applies, and therefore the rule itself; but they have no right to remain longer.

II. The *Federal* civil government is of course capable of being
put into full vigour as soon as the rebellion is suppressed. To
guard the Federal property, to protect the Federal officers, to assist
in the execution of Federal process, the troops may always remain,
in peace as in war.

III. If no State authorities whatever are left, and the people are
absolutely without magistrates or officers of any kind, so that the
withdrawal of the Federal troops would be the signal of a general
massacre or pillage, then the troops may remain, just as any other
body of men may remain, in the interest of humanity, and upon
principles of common or universal law, to prevent the commission
of crime or violent injury to person or property. If the captain
of an American frigate in a Chinese port finds a condition of
anarchy and general pillage on shore, I suppose he may land the
ship's company to stop the violence and rapine; but that does not
imply any right in the captain to govern the town.

IV. If there be an existing State government, *de facto* or *de
jure*, the question cannot arise. There was such a government in
Mississippi when the war closed. The retirement of the Federal
troops would have left the State impoverished and exhausted, no
doubt, but not without a government.

If this Court is not bound by the declaration of Congress, that
there are no legal State governments in the South, no more is it
bound by the declaration of the President, that there were none
when the war closed. Indeed, if I might venture the suggestion,
which I do with great diffidence, the true course at the close of the
war was to consider the governments then in existence as governments *de facto*, which could become governments *de jure* on taking
the oath of fidelity to the Federal Constitution. Congress would
not have felt itself obliged to admit any but loyal representatives

to seats. This suggestion is not important to my argument, but candour obliges me to say, that I think the source of all the difficulty that has since been encountered, was in the departure from the true theory of our Government when the rebel army surrendered. Indeed, I cannot help thinking, that the general form of capitulation arranged by General Sherman was, without reference to its details, constitutional and statesmanlike.

Having thus shown that the occupation of a State by a conquering army did not effect any such change in the rights and duties of the people as is supposed in the defendants' argument, even if the two contending parties were regarded as independent States, and the war what is called by jurists a public war, I might add, as an additional and conclusive argument of itself, that in a civil war there can be, strictly speaking, no such occupation—*occupatio bellica.* "In a civil war," says Phillimore, "there could be no *occupatio*" (3 Phill. Int. Law, 704). "A civil war," says Grotius, "is not of the same kind, concerning which this law of nations was instituted." (Grotius, lib. iii. c. 8, § iv.)

Halleck, in his work on International Law (p. 806, § 29), says: —"In the civil war between Cæsar and Pompey, the former remitted to the city of Dyrrachium the payment of a debt which it owed to Caius Flavius, the friend of Decius Brutus. The jurists who have commented on this transaction agree that the debt was not legally discharged—first, because in a civil war there could be, properly speaking, no *occupation ;* and secondly, because it was a private and not a public debt."

In a late case in North Carolina, where it was attempted to apply the principles of the "*occupatio bellica*" to the sequestration, by acts of the insurgent State, of a debt due to a citizen of a loyal State, the Court rejected the defence, and said: "These acts did not affect, *even for a moment,* the separation of North Carolina from the Union, any more than the action of an individual who commits grave offences against the State by resisting its officers and defying its authority can separate him from the State. Such acts may subject the offender even to outlawry, but can discharge him from no duty, nor relieve him from any responsibility."

After this opinion of the Chief Justice, let me read from the opinion of Mr. Justice Sprague, in the case of the *Amy Warwick*

2 M

APPENDIX.

(24 Law Rep. 498): "An objection to the prize decisions of the
district courts has arisen from an apprehension of radical consequences. It has been supposed that if the Government have the
rights of a belligerent, then, after the rebellion is suppressed, it
will have the rights of conquest; that a State and its inhabitants
may be permanently divested of all political privileges, and treated
as foreign territory acquired by arms. This is an error—a grave
and dangerous error. The rights of war exist only while the war
continues. Thus, if peace be concluded, a capture made immediately afterwards on the ocean, even where peace could not have
been known, is unauthorized, and property so taken is not prize of
war, and must be restored (Wheaton, Elements of International
Law, 619). Belligerent rights cannot be exercised when there are
no belligerents. Titles to property or to political jurisdiction,
acquired during the war by the exercise of belligerent rights, may
indeed survive the war. The holder of such title may permanently
exercise during peace all rights which appertain to his title; but
they must be rights only of proprietorship or sovereignty—they
cannot be belligerent. Conquest of a foreign country gives absolute and unlimited sovereign rights. But no nation ever makes
such a conquest of its own territory. If a hostile power, either
from without or within a nation, takes possession and holds absolute
dominion over any portion of its territory, and the nation by force
of arms expels or overthrows the enemy and suppresses hostilities,
it acquires no new title, but merely regains the possession of what
it had been temporarily deprived. The nation acquires no new
sovereignty, but merely maintains its previous rights (Wheaton,
616). During the war of 1812 the British took possession of
Castine, and held exclusive and unlimited control over it as conquered territory. So complete was the alienation that the Supreme
Court held that goods imported into it were not brought into the
United States, so as to be subject to import duties (*U. S.* v. *Rice,*
4 Wheat. 246). Castine was restored to us under the treaty of
peace; but it was never supposed that the United States acquired
a new title by the treaty, and could thenceforth govern it as merely
ceded territory. And if before the end of the war the United
States had, by force of arms, driven the British from Castine and
regained our rightful possession, no one would have imagined that

•

we could thenceforth hold and govern it as conquered territory, depriving the inhabitants of all pre-existing political rights. And when, in this civil war, the United States shall have succeeded in putting down this rebellion and restoring peace in any State, it will only have vindicated its original authority, and restored itself to a condition to exercise its previous sovereign rights under the Constitution. In a civil war, the military power is called in only to maintain the Government in the exercise of its legitimate civil authority. No success can extend the power of any department beyond the limits prescribed by the organic law. That would be not to maintain the Constitution, but to subvert it. Any Act of Congress which would annul the rights of any State under the Constitution, and permanently subject the inhabitants to arbitrary power, would be as utterly unconstitutional and void as the secession ordinances with which this atrocious rebellion commenced. The fact that the inhabitants of a State have passed such ordinances can make no difference. They are legal nullities; and it is because they are so that war is waged to maintain the Government. The war is justified only on the ground of their total invalidity. It is hardly necessary to remark, that I do not mean that the restoration of peace will preclude the Government from enforcing any municipal law, or from punishing any offence against previous standing laws."

Thus, if the Court please, have I gone over these four reasons, and I close what I have to say upon them with a single example from the Federal Government itself. What was done by that Government itself as it advanced? I take its own acts. Although the rebel capital was at Richmond, although the rebel flag was floating within sight of this Capitol, senators were received from Virginia into the Senate, and representatives from Virginia into the House of Representatives, upon the ground that as we advanced into the country the part occupied immediately reverted to its old condition, and was entitled to its civil government and to have representation in Congress. This is the way in which we dealt with the part which we occupied. We could not hold Alexandria for a moment but by bayonet and cannon; we did so hold it, and we received representatives elected by the people within our lines.

Now, let me pass, with your leave, from the consideration of these

2 M 2

four reasons, as they have been stated in debate, for the assumption
by Congress of the government of the State of Mississippi, and
ask your attention to the particular reasons given by my learned
friends who have argued on the other side.   But before I do that
let me turn aside for a moment, to answer what I suppose was intended to be an *argumentum ad hominem*, but which I think entirely
fails in this place.   This is the argument: The President, at the
close of the war, declared that there was no civil government in
the rebel States, and proceeded to organize governments.   The
brief of one of the counsel is much occupied with the correspondence between the President, the Secretary of State, and the provisional governors, and the steps taken to govern the States pro-
visionally.   The answer to that argument is, that we have nothing
to do with the action of the President on the subject; and whether
he was right or not, whether he took a constitutional view of the
case or not, it makes no difference to us.   But there is a further
answer, which is this: whether the provisional governments established under the authority of the Executive were or were not
legally established, *de facto* governments were established under them
which were recognized by the people, and were in possession of all
the attributes of sovereignty; had legislative, judicial, and executive
departments, and were going on as regularly as any States in the
Union at the time these Reconstruction Acts were passed; and,
consequently, it would not advance the argument at all to show
that the antecedent provisional governments were not warranted
by the Constitution.   I therefore pass over that argument because
it has no place here.   It is enough for us that the governments of
the States were in operation.   And we know by the reports of the
General of our army that order prevailed throughout the South
before these Acts of Reconstruction were passed.

I am now ready to examine the terms of the particular propositions which have been stated by the counsel on the other side in
support of their case.   There are six of them, thus expressed:—

1. "That Mississippi has no State Government which is entitled
to be recognized by the United States as a State of this Union,
and that this has been determined by the political departments of
this Government.

2. "That the decision so made is binding and conclusive upon

this Court, notwithstanding the Judges may think the decision
erroneous.

3. "That it is the undoubted right and duty of the United
States to aid the loyal people of Mississippi in establishing a
republican State government for that State, and that the United
States is now engaged in the performance of that constitutional
duty.

4. "That the grant of power to the United States to 'guarantee
a republican form of government' to the States of the Union, not
being restricted by the Constitution as to the means which may
be employed to execute the power, Congress is the exclusive judge
of what means are necessary in a given case.

5. "That the Act in question, with the Act supplemental
thereto, regarded as embodying the means adopted by Congress
for this purpose, violates no provision of the Constitution of the
United States.

6. "That inasmuch as Congress entered upon the prosecution of
the war against the rebel States in 1861, this Court is and will be
bound judicially to recognize war as still existing until Congress
shall declare peace to be restored, or shall cease to exercise any
belligerent right towards those States."

The fifth of these propositions is merely a supposed conclusion
from other propositions, and need not be separately considered.
The fourth is met by what I have already said about the use of
prohibited means to secure an end, however constitutional and
desirable that end may be. I have shown that military government is prohibited. So that, even if the first three and the sixth
propositions were all conceded, these military Reconstruction Acts
could not be defended.

The third proposition has already been sufficiently answered.
The first two and the sixth alone remain to deserve particular
attention; and even in respect to the sixth, I have already shown
that belligerent rights cannot continue to be exercised unless the
war can be prolonged by a fiction.

The discussion of these three propositions—that is, the first
second, and sixth—may be separated into four divisions:—

1. Is Mississippi, in fact and in law, a State of the Union, having regard only to the conditions of rebellion and war, without

reference to the declaration of the legislative and executive departments of the Government upon the question? In other words, did the rebellion, or the war, or both, put Mississippi, *as a State*, out of the Union?

2. Is war, in fact and in law, still subsisting between the United States on one side, and the State, or State government, or people of Mississippi, on the other side, without reference to the declaration of the legislative and executive departments of the Government upon the question?

3. What has been the declaration of the legislative and executive departments upon these two questions?

4. What is the legal effect of such declaration?

In the first place, did the rebellion, or the war, or both, put Mississippi, *as a State*, out of the Union?

This raises what I may call the *metaphysical* question. Horne Tooke protested that he had been the victim of a preposition. If the Southern States are to be held by this military government, after every hostile army has been surrendered, and every unfriendly hand has been lowered, they will be the victims of metaphysics imported into politics.

Mississippi was a State of the Union once. When did she cease to be such? Was it when she adopted the Ordinance of Secession, on the 9th of January, 1861, before a shot had been fired?—that is to say, did the act of renouncing her allegiance alone take her out of the Union? Was a *resolution* so potent as to dissolve her relations to the United States?

The day after that ordinance was passed was she not still a State in this Union? Suppose the Chief Justice had been holding court at Jackson the day after secession was declared, and a citizen of Ohio had sued in the Circuit Court of the United States a person in Mississippi as a citizen of that State—would the Judge have been obliged to hold that there was no such person as a citizen of the State of Mississippi? The jurisdiction of the Circuit Court could not have been maintained unless one of the parties was a citizen of a sister State, and the other party a citizen of Mississippi. Were the judgments of the courts in Mississippi no longer judgments to be recognized in the other States of this Union? Were the judgments of the other States in the Union no longer to be recognized in the Circuit Court of Mississippi? I do not ask what the people of Mississippi may have thought, but what this Court would have been bound to hold. Of course the statement of the proposition in this form answers it. It is so absurd that nobody will pretend that the Act of Secession carried the State out of the Union. In fact and in law, Mississippi was as truly a State in the Union after secession as before.

The denial of one's obligations can never *legally* effect his release from them, or change his legal relations to the one to whom the obligations are due. In this complex government of ours the effect of a change of the legal relations of the State to the Union would be a change of the legal relations of the different States to each other. Let us look at some of the consequences. The mere Act of Secession of Mississippi, not followed by any collision of forces, would have the effect of depriving a citizen of Wisconsin or Illinois, going there, of his equal rights in Mississippi; would render the judgments in the courts of Mississippi no longer conclusive in the courts of Wisconsin or Illinois, and so of the judgments of those States in Mississippi; would make a judgment in the highest court of Mississippi no longer examinable in this Court, however repugnant to the Federal Constitution and laws; would deprive a citizen of Wisconsin or Illinois of the right of suing in the Circuit Court of the United States for the Mississippi district; in fact, would drive that court out of Mississippi, for certainly it cannot sit there if that State is not as such in the Union. These are but examples; the list may be increased indefinitely.

And how could this state of things be remedied? You could not send the army there; for, in the case supposed, there would be no resistance to overcome. The consequences would be then, in effect, the withdrawal of a State from the Union without a blow.

Would a collision of forces change the *legal* relations, so as to effect by war what was not effected by secession? That depends upon the change which war produces; that is, it depends upon the nature and effect of belligerent rights. But these I have already considered, and I have shown, as I think, that the rights of the United States, as belligerents, give Congress no constitutional authority to pass these military statutes.

Let me now recur to the supposed principle upon which the counsel on the other side deduce the result, that Mississippi is no longer a State of the Union. It is this, as I take it from their own language: Mississippi is not a *State* of this Union, because she "has no *State government* which is entitled to be recognized by the United States as a 'State' of this Union." Here is a fallacy at the outset, arising from a confusion of ideas. A *State* and the *Government* of a State are two different things—as much so as a corporation and its governing body, or board of directors, are two different things. The original idea of a State is a community independent of all other communities. The States of the American Union, being originally independent, became united by the surrender of a portion of their sovereignty to a nation composed of all the States. Whether their relations to this nation can be dissolved or impaired depends upon the nature of the Union—whether it be, or be not, indissoluble. We agree that it is indissoluble. No argument is necessary, or would be permitted, on this point.

But it is asked, might the State of Mississippi send senators to Congress during the war? I answer, as I have already answered in effect, "No," for the simple reason, that there was nobody competent to send them. They must be sent by legislatures, acting under the Constitution of the United States. The Senate is the judge of the election and qualification of its own members, and is not bound to receive those who come in upon contempt of their authority, or with a feigned submission. There may be a State in this Union with a disloyal State government, although State magistrates who reject the *Federal authority* are thereby rendered incapable of executing any *Federal function*. This proposition answers the argument made against us.

A State does not change with a change of its Government. One of the fundamental doctrines of public law is, that the State is immortal. Governments, sovereigns, dynasties appear and disappear, but the State remains. The debts contracted by France under Napoleon I. were the debts of France under Louis XVIII., under the Citizen King, and under the Republic.

The proposition of the other side, which we are considering, contradicts, in fact, their fourth proposition; for, if Mississippi be not a State of the Union, Congress has no power under the clause authorizing it to "guarantee to *every State in the Union* a republican form of government."

If you can blot out a State, then of course she ceases to be; but she is not blotted out by any change whatever in her State government. New York might make this peaceful revolution a hundred times, so that she be still republican in form, and she would be still the same sovereign State in this Union.

Next—Is war, in law and in fact, still subsisting between the United States on the one side, and the State and people of Mississippi on the other, laying aside the declarations of the Executive and of Congress? You yourselves, in the decisions of the prize cases, have given the answer, by holding that war does not exist when the Courts are open—that is to say, when the Federal courts are open. You know that the Federal courts are open throughout Mississippi, and you know, therefore, that there is no war, whatever declarations may be made to the contrary. You know that the district courts are sitting throughout the South; you know that some of your own body sit there; you know that this is an appeal from a Circuit Court in Mississippi. And yet we are told that the United States are at war with Mississippi—that there is a state of war existing which authorizes martial rule.

But, further, what has been the declaration of the legislative and executive departments of the Government in respect to Mississippi and the other rebel States, for I consider them together? At the risk of wearying you, I must call your attention to various documents, by which I shall show that Congress has recognized these States, Mississippi among the rest, as being in the Union, by many Acts since the war commenced, and down to the very day when the first Reconstruction Act was passed. As to the executive department, you need no documents to be referred to. That this department has recognized Mississippi as being a State in the Union you know. We have had proclamation after proclamation, under the hand of the Executive, to that effect.

What has Congress done? The Constitution provides, as you remember, that "representatives and direct taxes shall be apportioned among the several States which may be included within this Union." You cannot apportion representatives and direct taxes except among the States of the Union. What do we find

among the first Acts of Congress on this subject after the rebellion
began? On the 5th of August, 1861, Congress passed an Act:—
"That a direct tax of $20,000,000 be and is hereby annually laid
upon the United States, and the same shall be and is hereby apportioned to the States respectively, in manner following: To the
State of Mississippi, $413,804 2-3." This was in August; Missis-
sippi seceded in January preceding. Was not that a declaration
of Congress that Mississippi was one of the States of this Union at
that time, six months after the Act of Secession, and during flagrant
war? These Acts have been regularly continued from year to year
down to 1866, as you will see by reference to the Statute-book.
So that Congress has regularly provided for the apportionment of
direct taxes among the States which are included in this Union,
Mississippi among the rest. Is not that a recognition? Next, in
the Act of July 16, 1862, the rebel States are all divided into districts for the different Circuit Courts; that could not be unless
they were States in the Union. On the 2nd of March, 1867 (chapter 185), an Act was passed in respect to appeals from rebel States;
that could not be unless they were States in the Union. Then
the laws as to the public lands show the same recognition; there
are several of them. The Non-intercourse Acts show the same.
Look at the joint resolution of the 8th of February, 1865, relating
to the electoral colleges. Let me read it, to show how completely
Congress kept in view the constitutional relations of the States
down almost to the day when it passed the first Reconstruction
Act:—

"Whereas the inhabitants and local authorities of the States of Virginia, North Carolina, South Carolina, Georgia, Florida, Alabama,
Mississippi, Louisiana, Texas, Arkansas, and Tennessee rebelled against
the Government of the United States, and were in such condition
on the 8th day of November, 1864, that no valid election for electors
of President and Vice-President of the United States, according to
the Constitution and laws thereof, was held therein on said day: therefore,

"Be it resolved, &c., That the States mentioned in the preamble to
this joint resolution are not entitled to representation in the Electoral
College for the choice of President and Vice-President of the United
States for the term of office, commencing on the 4th day of March,
1865; and no electoral votes shall be received or counted from said
States concerning the choice of President and Vice-President for said
term of office."

Look at the constitutional amendment—that great amendment abolishing slavery. Congress proposed it by the requisite majority, and ordered it to be sent to the Legislatures of the several States, not excluding any State from the consideration of the proposition. It was sent to every State in the Union, and here is the proclamation of the Secretary of State in regard to its adoption, made as early as December, 1865, in respect to which no dissent has ever been expressed by either House of Congress:—

"Know ye that whereas the Congress of the United States, on the 1st of February last, passed a resolution which is in the following words, namely—(reciting the constitutional amendment abolishing slavery):

"And whereas it appears, from official documents on file in this department, that the amendment to the Constitution of the United States, proposed as aforesaid, has been ratified by the Legislatures of the States of Illinois, Rhode Island, Michigan, Maryland, New York, West Virginia, Maine, Kansas, Massachusetts, Pennsylvania, Virginia, Ohio, Missouri, Nevada, Indiana, Louisiana, Minnesota, Wisconsin, Vermont, Tennessee, Arkansas, Connecticut, New Hampshire, South Carolina, Alabama, North Carolina, and Georgia, in all twenty-seven States:

"And whereas the whole number of States in the United States is thirty-six; and whereas the before specially named States whose Legislatures have ratified the said proposed amendment constitute three-fourths of the whole number of States in the United States:

"Now therefore, be it known that I, William H. Seward, Secretary of State of the United States, by virtue and in pursuance of the second section of the Act of Congress approved the 20th of April, 1818, entitled 'An Act to provide for the publication of the Laws of the United States, and for other purposes,' do hereby certify, that the amendment aforesaid has become valid, to all intents and purposes, as a part of the Constitution of the United States."

Among the ratifying States are Louisiana and South Carolina, without whose votes the amendment would not have been adopted. Consider for a moment the decision of the Chief Justice in North Carolina. I am not able to say, from the report of the case, whether one of the parties was designated as a citizen of one State, and the other of North Carolina.

The Chief Justice:—They were.

Mr. Field, resuming:—Tell me, then, if that be a legal judgment or not? The Chief Justice here made a memorable decision which satisfied the legal mind of the country, when, if the argument of our learned opponents be sound, he had no more jurisdiction than I. There was in the case supposed no citizen of North Carolina, because there was no State of North Carolina, and the judgment was void. But I have not yet done. Has there been a legal government of this Union during the war? Are the Acts upon the Statute-book of Congress binding? Is it not a familiar principle that the verdict of a jury in order to be valid must be a verdict of twelve men, and it becomes good for nothing if one member be added to the jury, making the verdict of thirteen? During all this war, up to the time when the Reconstruction Act was under consideration, there were two senators in the Senate Chamber from the ancient State of Virginia. But Virginia is said now not to be a State in this Union, and of course never has been since the war began, or since she seceded. If so, you have had two members in the Senate of the United States all the time who had no right to be there. What is the effect of that upon legislation? Has that been considered? By what sort of legerdemain, I ask, is it that Virginia, which had seats in Congress up to 1866, is now declared not to be entitled to any representation? It had four members in the Lower House during nearly the whole war—this State of Virginia, which is now alleged not to be a State in the Union at all. Where under the Constitution is there power to give any man a vote in the House of Representatives unless he be from a State? Congress is receding and going back upon its own footsteps. We are arguing for constitutional, regular governments; our opponents are the revolutionists. Tennessee is another State. There was one senator at least who stood his ground, "faithful among the faithless," and he remained in the Senate after the secession of his State, I think, two years, till 1863—yes, two years and over—and that senator was Andrew Johnson. What right had he to be in the Senate if Tennessee was not a State in this Union? Will you tell me? Were any laws passed with his concurrence and by the help of his vote? If we go into the House of Representatives, we find that Tennessee had two members there, Clemens and Maynard—Maynard continuing during the whole war. And yet, if you look at the most remarkable joint resolution of the 24th of July, 1866, you may infer that Tennessee has been out of the Union all the time. Here it is :—

" Whereas, in the year 1861, the government of the State of Tennes-

see was seized upon and taken possession of by persons in hostility to
the United States, and the inhabitants of said State, in pursuance of an
Act of Congress, were declared to be in a state of insurrection against
the United States ; and whereas said State government can only be restored to its former political relations in the Union by the consent of
the law-making power of the United States ; and whereas the people
of said State did, on the 21st day of February, 1865, by a large popular vote, adopt and ratify a constitution of government whereby slavery
was abolished, and all ordinances and laws of secession, and debts contracted under the same, were declared void ; and whereas a State
government has been organized under said constitution which has
ratified the amendment to the Constitution of the United States abolishing slavery, also the amendment proposed by the Thirty-ninth Congress, and has done other acts proclaiming and denoting loyalty :
. therefore,

"Be it resolved by the Senate and House of Representatives of the
United States of America in Congress assembled, That the State of
Tennessee is hereby restored to her former proper political relations to
the Union, and is again entitled to be represented by senators and
representatives in Congress."

Was there ever such a document as that since the world began ?
"Whereas the State of Tennessee has ratified the constitutional
amendment, therefore she may be restored," forgetting that if she
was not a State, with a legal State government, the ratification was
just so much waste paper. Let us go to Louisiana. She is in the
same predicament. We have had in the House from Louisiana,
Flanders and Hahn, from March 1863 to March 1865. What
will our friends say to that?

I will now ask your attention to the action of the legislative and
executive departments of the Government in respect to the question of existing war or peace. You remember that the argument
of my learned friend was, that we are now in a state of war ; that
we have a right to exercise the rights of war ; and that, exercising
the rights of war, we can govern the State of Mississippi as we will.
Here is a list of Acts and Resolutions of Congress to show that they
have recognised war as ended and peace as restored throughout the
United States. The Statute-book is full of references to "the late
war," and "the war that has closed," and "the war that is happily
ended." Among these Acts is one of March 2, 1867, passed the
same day the first Reconstruction Act was passed, increasing the
pay of non-commissioned officers and soldiers, as follows :—

"Sec. 2. And be it further enacted, That section 1 of the Act entitled 'An Act to increase the pay of soldiers in the United States army, and for other purposes,' approved June 20, 1864, be and the same is hereby continued in full force and effect for three years from and after the close of the rebellion, as announced by the President of the United States by proclamation bearing date the 20th of August, 1866."

Here is the proclamation of the President, to which this Act refers, reciting the previous proclamations, and ending as follows: " I do further proclaim that the said insurrection is at an end, and that peace, order, tranquillity, and civil authority now exist in and throughout the whole United States of America." Can anything be imagined more extraordinary than that the same persons who passed these Acts should come here to maintain that we have a right to deal with the South as if there were no peace, but flagrant war to this very hour? There is another comprehensive Act which, I should think, might alone determine the question as to the state of the South. It is an Act passed the same 2nd of March. In the desire of Congress to indemnify everybody, they ratified everything that the President had ever done. The Act is as follows:—

" An Act to declare valid and conclusive certain proclamations of the President, and acts done in pursuance thereof, or of his orders, in the suppression of the late rebellion against the United States.
" Be it enacted, &c., That all acts, proclamations, and orders of the President of the United States, or acts done by his authority or approval after the 4th of March, Anno Domini 1861, and before the 1st day of July 1866, respecting martial law, military trials by courts martial or military commissions, &c., during the late rebellion, are hereby approved in all respects."

Finally, I will read a very appropriate resolution of thanks, as follows, passed in May, 1866:—   •

" Resolved by the Senate and House of Representatives of the United States of America in Congress assembled, That it is the duty and privilege of Congress to express the gratitude of the nation to the officers, soldiers, and seamen of the United States, by whose valour and endurance, on the land and on the sea, the rebellion has been crushed and its pride and power have been humbled, by whose fidelity to the cause of freedom the government of the people has been preserved and maintained, and by whose orderly return from the fire and blood of

civil war to the peaceful pursuits of private life, the exalting and en-
nobling influence of free institutions upon a nation has been so signally
manifested to the world."

Have I not said enough to show that the legislative department
of the Government, as well as the executive, has recognized, first,
the State of Mississippi as being in the Union; secondly, has
recognized a government as there existing; and, thirdly, has recognized the war as ended, and peace, order, tranquillity, and civil
authority as existing throughout the land ?

Finally, it has thus become unimportant to consider further
what would have been the effect of the declarations of Congress
and the President, if they had, in the face of incontestable fact,
declared that Mississippi was no longer a State in this Union, and
that war still raged between her and the United States ; and I will
waste no time upon that subject.

These are my answers, if the Court please, to the propositions
brought forward by the learned counsel, and elaborately argued ;
and I hope that I have given—imperfectly, I grant—a sufficient
answer to them all.

There yet remains another point, not in the brief, nor do I find
it in any written paper, but very much urged in the argument, and
constantly referred to in public speeches, and that is—NECESSITY.
These military governments of the South, they say, are legal, because they are necessary. The usual phrase is, " This government
has a right to live, and no other government has a right to contest
it : and whatever Congress determines as necessary to this national
life is right, and therefore the Executive and this Court are to
recognize it as so." What necessity do they speak of? There is
no Federal necessity. The Federal courts are open ; the Federal
laws are executed ; the mails are run ; the customs are collected.
There is no interference with any commissioner or officer of the
United States anywhere in the country. There is no necessity,
therefore, of a Federal kind for an assumption of the government
of Mississippi. What, then, is the necessity ? " Why," they say,
"these are unrepentant rebels." Is that the reason why the military government is there ? If you are to wait until you get repentant rebels—or, I should perhaps rather say, if you wait until
you make rebels repentant by fire and sword—you will have to

wait many generations. Of all the arguments, that of necessity
is the most remarkable, and has the least force. " We will not
allow the Southern States to govern themselves, because, if we do,
the government will fall into the hands of unrepentant rebels."
Well, what is that to you, if they obey the laws—if they submit to
your government? Do you wish to force them to love you? Is
that what you are aiming at? Of course, it should be the desire
and the aim of all governments to make the people love, as well
as obey; but to give that as an argument for a military government,
is an extraordinary one. " Well, then," they say, " we must protect the loyal men at the South, and therefore the military government, which is the only one adequate to the end, must be kept up."
To that I answer, first, that the General of your armies, the person
upon whom this extraordinary power has been thrown, himself certified that there was order throughout the South, so far as he could
observe. But are there no other means than military coercion?
The Union men of the South, we have been told, are in the majority,
and have ever been in the majority, and it is the minority by which
the people were driven into secession. Is government by the United
States necessary to sustain the majority against the minority? A
majority, we are told, of the white people! They say that secession
was carried by a minority of the white people against the majority,
and that the majority have always been loyal. That is a perfect
answer, then, to the objection. Necessity is the staple reason given
by tyranny for misgovernment all the world over. It was the reason given by Philip II. for oppressing the Netherlands by the
Duke of Alva; it was the reason given for the misgovernment
of Italy by Austria; it was the reason given for the misgovernment
of Ireland by England.

" This nation has a right to live." Certainly it has, and so have
the States, and so have the people. Every one of us has the right,
and the life of each is bound up with the life of all. For who
compose my nation, and what constitutes my country? It is not
so much land and water. They would remain ever the same, though
an alien race occupied the soil; there would be the same green
hills and the same sweet valleys, the same ranges of mountains,
and the same lakes and rivers; but these, all combined, do not make
up my country. They are the body without the soul. That word,

country, comprehends within itself, place and people, and all that history, tradition, language, manners, social culture, and civil polity have associated with them.   This wonderful combination of State and nation, which binds me to both by indissoluble ties, enters into the idea of my country.   Its name is the United States of America.   The States are an essential part of the name, and of the thing.   They are represented by the starry flag, which their children have borne on so many fields of glory, the ever-shining symbol of one nation and many States.   They are not provinces or counties, they are not principalities or dukedoms, but they are free republican States, sovereign in their sphere, as the United States are sovereign in theirs ; and all essential elements of that one undivided and indissoluble country, which is dearer than life, and for which so many have died.   As the State of New York would not be to me what it is, if, instead of the free active commonwealth, it were to subside into a principality or a province ; so neither would the United States be to me what they are, if, instead of a union of free States, they were to subside into a consolidated empire.   For such an empire we have not borne the defeats and won the victories of this civil war.

I will here venture to call attention to an argument put forth with great force and ability by a learned gentleman now deceased, Mr. Loring, who, I think, was the first to propose this mode of dealing with the South, and who has attempted to justify it in a pamphlet, which I have now before me, and from which I will read one paragraph.   He says :

" The power to wage war upon a State in rebellion, for the preservation of the Union, is a constitutional power necessarily invested in the Government, solely for that purpose, and limited for that necessity.   It cannot, therefore, be exercised for any other end, nor beyond the means justly and reasonably required for its accomplishment. ; It cannot justify the holding of the territory of a State, as conquered or as provinces, under military rule, or deprive them of the rights of civil government, any further than may be necessary to enforce present obedience to the Constitution and laws, and for security against danger of future like disobedience and revolt."

That is the argument in the best form in which it can be stated. Now, I take leave to say that this is full of fallacies.   In the first place, there is no power to wage war against a State for the pre-

2 N

servation of the Union. This is a misstatement of the proposition. The power to wage war is to overcome resistance to the execution of the Federal laws and the Federal Constitution, and that is all. You cannot wage war against a State upon the abstract proposition that you are to preserve the Union. The Union takes care of itself when you execute its laws; and you execute its laws when you overcome resistance, and that is the only end for which you can begin or continue war. And, furthermore, what right have you to wage war for the purpose of obtaining security against the "danger of future like disobedience and revolt?" Is that a constitutional right? Let us put it to the test.

In 1860, when we saw, as clearly as men could foresee a future event, by the little cloud rising to darken finally the whole horizon, that war was coming, would it have been a constitutional exercise of power in the general Government to wage war upon the South? Have we ever had a President ready to do that, or a Congress ready to undertake it? Can you send armies into a State of this Union for the purpose of guarding against the danger of future rebellion, and war against it? You may have your armies ready, may garrison your forts, and strengthen your outposts. That you can do and ought to do; but you cannot wage war. If you can, then we have no guarantees, for it will rest for ever in the discretion of Congress to order an army to make war upon a State whenever it may determine that there is danger of something being one which ought not to be done.

A short time since, a proposition was made to take into the hands of the Federal Government the whole State of Maryland and the whole State of Kentucky, upon the ground that their people were disloyal in heart, that they did not mean sincerely to obey, and there was danger that hereafter they would give aid and countenance to a new rebellion. I deny most explicitly that this limited government of ours has power to wage war against a State upon any suspicion or theory of an intended insurrection against the Government. We are limited to our constitutional duties and our constitutional rights, which are to enact laws as authorized by the Federal Constitution, and to execute those laws by the courts of justice and the executive arm.

Let it not be imagined for a moment that I have the least sympathy with the rebels. As I detested the rebellion, so do I censure those who rebelled. But while I censure, I remember that they are still my countrymen, and, remembering also that rights and duties are correlative, as I would exact from them performance of the duties, so I would concede to them the rights of citizens. To close up the gaping wounds of civil war is the consummate art of statesmanship, and, if history teaches us aright, that end can never be accomplished by proscription. Conciliation is more potent than severity, and forgetfulness than the remembrance of wrongs.

These military governments of the South are said to be only temporary. How do we know that? Is it constitutional to do a thing as a temporary expedient which Congress may continue as long as it pleases? The conditions annexed to this first Reconstruction Act contemplated that the military power should remain in the South until the amendment proposed should be ratified by three-fourths of the States. The argument of danger is an argument of very little force on either side.

It is not speaking too strongly to say, that this Court stands now in the very gateway against the usurpation of military power dangerous to our liberty. What have we seen, and what do we now see? We have seen the Chief Justice of this Court, before whose robes all bayonets should be lowered, taking his place in a Circuit Court in North Carolina, after explaining to a Committee of Congress that he would not hold his Court where it was not supreme over all military as well as civil officers, and receiving assurances of the subordination of the military, and, upon appearing, announcing to the Bar as a reason why his Court had not been held at an earlier day, that it was beneath the dignity of a Court of the United States to sit where its process might be resisted by military power, and yet we have seen the execution of the process of this very Court forbidden by military officers. Of course, if the Chief Justice had taken his seat again upon that bench, he would have punished the offenders as they deserved. We have seen, in a printed document submitted to Congress, the testimony of the Secretary of War, asserting his belief that the decision of this Court in the *Milligan Case* was erroneous; that it was not founded in law, though it was the unanimous decision of the Court; and maintaining still the right to establish military commissions in

2 N 2

loyal States. We have seen an Act pass through one House of
Congress, which proposes to vest in the General of the army unlimited control over all these eleven States; and we have also seen
introduced into the Lower House an amendment to an appropriation bill, proposing to make your hall a place guarded by soldiers!
Here is the proposition, which I will read: "Provided that from
and after the close of the current fiscal year the police and protection of the Capitol building and grounds shall be under the direction of the engineer department of the army, and the Secretary of
War shall detail for that service from the garrison at Washington
such number of non-commissioned officers and privates, not exceeding forty, as may be deemed necessary for the purpose by the
Chief Engineer; and soldiers, when so employed, shall have an
extra allowance of twenty-five cents per day for privates, and thirty
cents per day for non-commissioned officers." If we go on as we
thus begin, instead of these guardians at your door you will find
soldiers with bayonets, and there will be soldiers with bayonets
before the Houses of Congress. We must resist now! We will
not have military government; it is against the Constitution, and
we stand upon the Constitution of our country. We will not have
it for an instant, for an instant's voluntary submission to unlawful
power is dishonour. An instant may expand into a day, a day into
a month, a month may lapse into years, and years into a genera-
tion. If we submit for a moment, we forget· the lessons of our
fathers, and despoil our inheritance.

We were threatened by the counsel that if in New York we did
not conform ourselves a little more diligently to what was required
of us we should have the General of the army there. One of them
called it "that infernal city of New York!" Pardon me if I repel
the calumny. My city is misgoverned, I admit; but that misgovernment, be it remembered, comes chiefly from the premature
admission to the suffrage of those not here accustomed to exercise
it. Among her people are as much virtue, as much patriotism, as
much honour as exist anywhere. You, sir, when you came to a
discredited treasury, know how your hand leaned upon her, and
how her merchants came forward with the most lavish offers to
sustain this Government; how, at the first summons of the President,
the flag of the country floated out from window and tower, and her

people called with one voice, bidding loyal men to rise everywhere throughout the land.   For social culture, for intellectual activity, for the magnificence of her commerce, for the grandeur of her enterprises, and, not least, for her abounding charities, she stands unapproached on this Continent, and unapproachable even by that younger sister of the Pacific through whose golden gate lies the highway to India.   New York sits upon her island rock, and there is no American who, returning to his country, sees her spires above the waters, but rejoices in her prosperity and is proud of her.

But we are told that this is a *political* question, which is beyond the competency of the Courts to determine.   A fortnight ago this objection would have come with more force than it comes now. The experience of a few days has taught many, what was understood by thoughtful observers before, that this Court is the great peacemaker, and that nothing but its peaceful interposition can prevent collisions of force.

What is a political question?   Is it one which affects the policy of parties, or is decided by partisan views?   Such a question is the very one that is most likely to lead the legislative department into excesses, which it needs the judicial to correct.   If Congress were to pass an act of attainder, with a purely political motive, or for a purely political end, does any one suppose that this Court is not competent to pronounce it unconstitutional and void? A political question, I apprehend, is one which the political department of the Government has exclusive authority to decide.

Is it a political question whether McCardle can be imprisoned by military order and tried by a military commission?   There are political questions undoubtedly—that is, questions which the political department of the Government has a right to decide, and, being decided there, the Courts will follow.   But whether or not a man can be imprisoned and tried by a particular tribunal is always a judicial question which the Judges will determine for themselves. The question, however, has received its final answer in the opinion of this Court, delivered by Mr. Justice Nelson, upon the Bill exhibited by Georgia against the Secretary of War and others; and it would be presumptuous in me to debate now what is there decided so satisfactorily to all friends of constitutional government, and so authoritatively for us all.

Finally, sir, may I say that I have shown : —

1. That there is no reason whatever for the proposition that Mississippi is not now a State of the American Union :

2. That not only is she a State of the Union, but her people have the rights of citizens of a State :

3. That whether she be or be not a State, or her people have or have not the rights of citizens of a State, that people cannot be subjected to military government by the Congress of the United States : and

4. That therefore the petitioner, McCardle, is entitled to his release from the military commission which presumed to sit in judgment upon him.

And when your judgment is pronounced, as I hope and pray it may be, in the petitioner's favour, it will, I trust, be the en- deavour of all good men to promote by their counsel and example the acquiescence of the other departments of the Government. As it is your right in the last resort, upon all cases that come before you, to give final interpretation to the Constitution, so it is the duty of all citizens to respect and accept your interpretation. There is no need to strain the authority of the Government. The constitu- tional amendment not only abolishes slavery, and makes freedom the rule throughout the country, but it gives Congress the power to enforce that article by appropriate legislation, and to see that the freedom of every man of every race and condition is maintained.

It was the boast of an English orator and statesman, on a memorable occasion, when he delivered a message from the King to his faithful Commons respecting the expedition to Portugal, that " wherever the standard of England is planted, there foreign domi- nation shall not come." If we will firmly maintain the Constitution of our fathers, as modified by the great amendment, we shall be able to make it our higher boast, that where the standard of America is planted there shall be neither foreign domination nor domestic oppression.

MARTIAL LAW.

CASE *and* JOINT OPINION *of* MR. EDWARD JAMES, Q.C., *and* MR. FITZJAMES STEPHEN, Q.C., *on Martial Law, with reference to the Jamaica Insurrection.* 1866.

Case submitted by the Jamaica Committee.—The Committee desires to be advised what steps are open to them to assist their fellow-subjects in Jamaica to obtain the protection of the law; and, if the law has been broken, to bring the guilty parties to justice; and also what steps are open to them, as Englishmen, to vindicate constitutional law and order, if constitutional law and order have been illegally set aside by the local Government in Jamaica.

With this are sent copies of the despatch from Governor Eyre to Mr. Secretary Cardwell, on the 20th of October, 1865, and also of the Address of the Governor to the Jamaica House of Legislature, at the annual meeting which took place on the 7th of November. Copies are also sent of such reports of the military officers as have appeared in the papers.

Considering for the present nothing but these official documents, and taking for granted that the statements they contain are all true, counsel is requested to advise:

1. What is the meaning of the term "martial law," and what is the legal effect of a proclamation of martial law?

2. Are there grounds for concluding that Governor Eyre has acted illegally and criminally in the mode in which he states that he has proclaimed and enforced martial law, and especially in removing the Hon. G. W. Gordon from Kingston to Morant Bay, and there handing him over to Brigadier-General Nelson, to be tried by court-martial?

3. Could Mr. Gordon be legally convicted and punished by court-martial for any act done prior to the proclamation of martial law, or for any act done beyond the boundaries of the proclaimed district?

4. Are officers acting in enforcing martial law exempt from all control beyond the instructions they receive from their superior officers? If not, are there any principles acknowledged by martial law, or by the British Constitution, which would render it illegal—

(*a*) to continue for several days shooting down men, and flogging men, women, and children, and burning their habitations, in the absence of any appearance of organized resistance; (*b*) to inflict punishment without or before trial; (*c*) to inflict punishment for the purpose of obtaining evidence; (*d*) to inflict death for or on the evidence of looks or gestures?

5. In case Governor Eyre or his subordinate officers have been guilty of illegal acts in the course of the late proceedings in Jamaica, what are the proper modes of bringing them to trial for such illegal acts?

6. Are any, and (if any) what, proceedings for the above purpose open to private persons in this country?

7. The last question has reference to a bill of indemnity, if one should be passed by the Jamaica Legislature.

Opinion.—The questions asked in this Case all depend more or less upon the general question, " What is the nature of martial law, and what power does it confer?" We will, therefore, state our view of this subject before answering the specific questions asked, and we must do so at some length, on account both of the importance and the obscurity of the subject. The expression " martial law " has been used at different times in four different senses, each of which must be carefully distinguished from the others :—

1. In very early times various systems of law co-existed in this country—as the common law, the ecclesiastical law, the law of the Court of Admiralty, &c. One of these was the law martial, exercised by the constable and marshal over troops in actual service, and especially on foreign service. As to this, *see* an essay on the " Laws of War," by Professor Montague Bernard, in the " Oxford Essays " for 1856.

2. The existence of this system in cases of foreign service or actual warfare, appears to have led to attempts on the parts of various sovereigns to introduce the same system in times of peace on emergencies, and especially for the punishment of breaches of the peace. This was declared to be illegal by the Petition of Right, as we shall show more fully immediately. (*See* Hallam's " Constitutional History," vol. i. p. 240, 7th edition, ch. v., near the beginning.)

3. When standing armies were introduced, the powers of the constable and marshal fell into disuse, and the discipline of the

army was provided for by annual Mutiny Acts, which provide express regulations for the purpose. These regulations form a code, which is sometimes called martial, but more properly military law. (Grant and Gould, 2 H. Blackstone, 69.)

4. Although martial law in sense (1) is obsolete, being superseded by military law, and in sense (2) is declared by the Petition of Right to be illegal, the expression has survived, and has been applied (as we think, inaccurately and improperly) to a very different thing—namely, to the common-law right of the Crown and its representatives to repel force by force in the case of invasion or insurrection. We shall proceed to develope and illustrate this view of the subject.

The provisions of the Petition of Right on Martial Law (3 Car. 1, c. 1), are contained in ss. 7, 8, 9, 10. These sections recite that commissions under the Great Seal had lately been issued to certain persons to proceed in particular cases " according to the justice of martial law;" and that thereby persons had been put to death who, if deserving of death, ought to have been tried in the ordinary way, whilst others, pleading privilege, had escaped. Such commissions are then declared to be illegal; and it is provided that henceforth no commissions of like nature may issue forth to any person or persons whatsoever.

The commissions themselves explain the nature of the system which the Petition of Right prohibited. Three, which were issued shortly before it passed, are given in 17 " Rymer's Fœdera " (pp. 43, 246, 647). They are dated respectively 24th November, 1617; 20th July, 1620; 30th December, 1624. The first is a commission to certain persons for the government of Wales, and the counties of Worcester, Hereford, and Shropshire. It directs them to call out the array of the county, and then proceeds to direct them to lead the array—

" As well against all and singular our enemies, as also against all and singular rebells, traytors, and other offenders and their adherents, against us our Crowne and dignitie, within the said principalitie and dominions of North Wales and South Wales, the marches of the same, and counties and places aforesaid, and with the said traytors and rebells from tyme to tyme to fight, and them to invade, resist, suppresse, subdue, slay, kill, and put to execution of death, by all ways and means, from tyme to tyme by your discretion.

" And further to doe, execute, and use against the said enemies, traytors, rebells, and such other like offenders and their adherents afore-mentioned, from tyme to tyme as necessitie shall require, by your discretion, the law called the martiall lawe according to the law martiall, and of such offenders apprehended or being brought in subjection, to save whom you shall think good to be saved, and to slay, destroie, and put to execution of death, such and as many of them as you shall think meete, by your good discretion, to be put to death."

The second empowers Sir Robert Maunsel to govern the crews of certain ships intended for the suppression of piracy, and gives him " full powers to execute and take away their life, or any member, in form and order of martial law."

The third is a commission to the Mayor of Dover, and others, reciting that certain troops, then at Dover, were licentious, and empowering them—

" To proceed according to the justice of martial law against such soldiers with any of our lists aforesaid, and other dissolute persons joining with them, or any of them, as during such time as any of our said troops or companies of soldiers shall remain or abide there, and not be transported thence, shall, within any of the places or precincts aforesaid, at any time after the publication of this our commission, commit any robberies, felonies, mutinies, or other outrages or misdemeanors, which by the martial law should or ought to be punished with death, and by such summary course and order as is agreeable to martial law, and as is used in armies in time of war, to proceed to the trial and condemnation of such delinquents and offenders, and them cause to be executed and put to death according to the law martial, for an example of terror to others, and to keep the rest in due awe and obedience."

The distinctive feature of all these commissions is, that they authorise not merely the suppression of revolts by military force, which is undoubtedly legal, but the subsequent punishment of offenders by illegal tribunals, which is the practice forbidden by the Petition of Right. In illustration of this we may compare the proceedings described in Governor Eyre's despatch with the course taken by a Lieutenant-general and his Provost-marshal in the reign of Queen Elizabeth, under one of the commissions declared to be illegal by the Petition of Right. In 1569 the Earls of Northumberland and Westmoreland had risen and besieged and taken Barnard Castle, and committed other acts of open treasonable warfare. The rising took place, and was suppressed, in the course of the month of December. The Earl of Sussex received from the Queen a commission, evidently similar to the one already cited, and appointed Sir George Bower his Provost-marshal. Sir George Bower made a circuit through Durham and Yorkshire, between the 2nd and the 20th of January, 1569, and executed at various places 600 persons. (Sharpe's "Memorials of the Rebellion," No. 1569, pp. 99, 113, 121, 133, 140, 143, 153, 163.)

It appears from Governor Eyre's despatch, passing by earlier portions, which contain instances of acts done by the so-called courts-martial, susceptible perhaps of a construction different from those which follow, that at daybreak on Monday, the 16th of October (paragraph 41), the last definite act of violence mentioned having taken place on the 15th (see paragraph 33), a court-martial sat to try prisoners, and twenty-seven were found guilty and hung. By the 18th (paragraph 55), many rebels had been captured, and several courts-martial had been held and capital punishment inflicted. On the 19th (paragraph 57), all was going on well in camp, more rebels had been captured or shot. Afterwards, on the 23rd of October, Mr. Gordon was hung. As Governor Eyre mentioned no acts of violence subsequent to that above referred to, it would appear that these executions were punishments for past offences, and not acts required for the suppression of open insurrection. The measures adopted thus resemble those taken by Sir George Bower, in 1569, under the authority of the commission declared illegal by the Petition of Right. As to the legal character of such punishments, Lord Coke observes (3rd Inst., c. 7, p. 52) : " If a lieutenant, or other that hath commission of martial authority in time of peace, hang, or otherwise execute any man by colour of martial law, this is murder; for this is against Magna Charta, c. 29. (See too Hale, Hist. C. L. 34.)

These authorities appear to show that it is illegal for the Crown to resort to martial law as a special mode of punishing rebellion.

We now proceed to consider the authorities which look in the
other direction. In 1799, an Act of the Irish Parliament (39
Geo. 3, c. 11) was passed, the effect of which was to put the parts
of the country which were still in rebellion under military command, according to a system therein described. The preamble
states that the rebellion had been already suppressed, and it sets
forth that on the 24th of May, 1798, Lord Camden did, by and
under the advice of the Privy Council, issue his orders to all
general officers commanding his Majesty's forces, to punish all
persons acting, ordering, or in any way assisting in the said rebellion, according to martial law, either by death or otherwise, as to
them should seem expedient, and did by his proclamation of the
same date ratify the same. It further goes on to recite, that " by
the wise and salutary exercise of his Majesty's undoubted prerogative in executing martial law, for defeating and dispersing such
armed and rebellious force, and in bringing divers rebels and
traitors to punishment in the most speedy and summary manner,
the peace of the kingdom has been so far restored as to permit the
course of the common law partially to take place," &c. And in
the body of the Act (section 6) there is contained a proviso that
" nothing in this Act shall be construed to abridge or diminish the
undoubted prerogative of his Majesty, for the public safety, to
resort to the exercise of martial law against open enemies or
traitors."

It is impossible to suppose that such a declaration as this should
operate as a repeal of the Petition of Right as regarded Ireland,
though the language of the two Acts appears to be conflicting. As,
however, it merely declares an " undoubted prerogative of the
Crown," it cannot refer to what the Petition of Right expressly denied to exist, and therefore it must probably be construed to mean
only that the Crown has an undoubted prerogative to attack an
army of rebels by regular forces under military law, conducting
themselves as armies in the field usually do. This construction is
strengthened by the fact that traitors are coupled with open enemies. Now, the force used against an invading army is used for
the purpose, not of punishment, but of conquest, and thus the
words in the Irish Act would mean only that the Crown has an
undoubted prerogative to carry on war against an army of rebels,

as it would against an invading army, and to inflict upon them such punishment as might be necessary to suppress the rebellion, and to restore the peace, and to permit the common law to take effect.

As soon, however, as the actual conflict was at an end, it would be the duty of the military authorities to hand over their prisoners to the civil powers. This was affirmed by the case of Wolfe Tone, who, having been captured when the French surrendered, was sent up to Dublin Barracks, tried by a court-martial, and sentenced to death. The Court of King's Bench immediately granted a habeas corpus, and directed the sheriff to take into custody the Provost-marshal and officers in charge, and to see that Mr. Tone was not executed (27 St. Tr. 624-5). No doubt many military executions took place during the Irish rebellion, but an Act of Indemnity was passed in respect to them, and it must also be remembered that by the laws of war (which are a branch of morals rather than of law proper, and prevail not over soldiers, but as between contending armies), many severities may be justified, such as the refusal of quarter, and the putting to death of soldiers who surrender at discretion; and thus, in a war like that in 1798, much might be done which might pass under the name of martial law, but which in reality would be no more than incidents of ordinary warfare conducted with unusual rigour.

Another argument is drawn from the annual Mutiny Acts. They contain a declaration that "no man can be forejudged of life or limb, or subjected to any punishment within this realm by martial law, in time of peace." This has been construed to imply that in times of war or disturbance martial law is legal. As to this, however, it must be remembered that in its original meaning, the phrase "martial law" included what we now understand by military law, and that one principal object of the commissions declared to be illegal by the Petition of Right, was the creation of military tribunals without Parliamentary authority. Hence the words "in peace," which were not in the first Mutiny Act, probably mean that standing armies and military courts were, in time of peace, illegal, except in so far as they were expressly authorised by Parliament.

The whole doctrine of martial law was discussed at great length

before a committee of the House of Commons, which sat in the
year 1849, to inquire into certain transactions which had taken
place at Ceylon. Sir David Dundas, then Judge Advocate General,
explained his view upon the subject at length, and was closely examined upon it by Sir Robert Peel, Mr. Gladstone, and others.
The following answers, amongst others, throw much light on the
subject:—

" 5437. The proclamation of martial law is a notice, to all those
to whom the proclamation is addressed, that there is now another
measure of law and another mode of proceeding than there was
before that proclamation."

" 5459. If a Governor fairly and truly believes that the civil and
military power which is with him, and such assistance as he might
derive from the sound-hearted part of the Queen's subjects, is not
enough to save the life of the community, and to suppress the
disorder, it is his duty to suppress by this (i.e., by martial law) or
any other means.

"5476. (Sir Robert Peel.) A wise and courageous man, responsible for the safety of a colony, would take the law into his own
hands, and make a law for the occasion rather than submit to
anarchy?—A. I think that a wise and courageous man would, if
necessary, make a law to his own hands, but he would much rather
take a law which is already made ; and I believe the law of England is, that a Governor, like the Crown, has vested in him the
right, where the necessity arises, of judging of it, and being responsible for his work afterwards, so to deal with the laws as to supersede them all, and to proclaim martial law for the safety of the
colony.

" 5477. (In answer to Mr. Gladstone.) I say he is responsible,
just as I am responsible for shooting a man on the King's highway
who comes to rob me. If I mistake my man, and have not, in the
opinion of the judge and jury who try me, an answer to give, I am
responsible.

" 5506. My notion is, that martial law is a rule of necessity, and
that when it is executed by men empowered to do so, and they act
honestly, rigorously, and vigorously, and with as much humanity
as the case will permit, in discharge of their duty, they have
done that which every good citizen is bound to do."

Martial law has, accordingly, been proclaimed in several colonies —viz., at the Cape of Good Hope, in Ceylon, in Jamaica, and in Demerara.

The views thus expressed by Sir David Dundas appear to us to be substantially correct. According to them the words "martial law," as used in the expression "proclaiming martial law," might be defined as the assumption for a certain time, by the officers of the Crown, of absolute power, exercised by military force, for the purpose of suppressing an insurrection or resisting an invasion. The "proclamation" of martial law, in this sense, would be only a notice to all whom it might concern that such a course was about to be taken. We do not think it is possible to distinguish martial law, thus described and explained, from the common-law duty which is incumbent on every man, and especially on every magistrate, to use any degree of physical force that may be required for the suppression of a violent insurrection, and which is incumbent as well on soldiers as on civilians, the soldiers retaining during such service their special military obligations. (On this subject *see* Lord Chief Justice Tindal's Charge to the Grand Jury of Bristol, in 1832, quoted in 1 Russ. on Cr. 286 n.) Thus, for instance, we apprehend that if martial law had been proclaimed in London in 1780, such a proclamation would have made no difference whatever in the duties of the troops or the liabilities of the rioters. Without any such proclamation the troops were entitled, and bound, to destroy life and property to any extent which might be necessary to restore order. It is difficult to see what further authority they could have had, except that of punishing the offenders afterwards, and this is expressly forbidden by the Petition of Right.

We may sum up our view of martial law in general in the following propositions:—

1. Martial law is the assumption by the officers of the Crown of absolute power, exercised by military force, for the suppression of an insurrection, and the restoration of order and lawful authority.

2. The officers of the Crown are justified in any exertion of physical force, extending to the destruction of life and property to any extent, and in any manner that may be required for this purpose. They are not justified in the use of excessive or cruel means, but are liable civilly or criminally for such excess. They are not

justified in inflicting punishment after resistance is suppressed, and after the ordinary courts of justice can be reopened. The principle by which their responsibility is measured is well expressed in the case of *Wright* v. *Fitzgerald*, 27 St. Tr. p. 65. Mons. Wright was a French master of Clonmel, who, after the suppression of the Irish rebellion, in 1798, brought an action against Mr. Fitzgerald, the sheriff of Tipperary, for having cruelly flogged him without due inquiry. Martial law was in full force at that time, and an Act of Indemnity had been passed, to excuse all breaches of the law committed in the suppression of the rebellion. In summing up, Justice Chamberlain, with whom Lord Yelverton agreed, said :—

" The jury were not to imagine that the Legislature, by enabling magistrates to justify under the Indemnity Bill, had released them from the feelings of humanity, or permitted them wantonly to exercise power, even though it were to put down rebellion. They expected that in all cases there should be a grave and serious examination into the conduct of the supposed criminal, and every act should show a mind intent to discover guilt, not to inflict torture. By examination or trial he did not mean that sort of examination and trial which they were now engaged in, but such examination and trial—the best the nature of the case and existing circumstances should allow of. That this must have been the intention of the Legislature was manifest from the expression ' magistrates and all other persons,' which provide that as every man, whether magistrate or not, was authorized to suppress rebellion, and was to be justified by that law for his acts, it is required that he should not exceed the necessity which gave him that power, and that he should show in his justification that he had used every possible means to ascertain the guilt which he had punished ; and, above all, no deviation from the common principles of humanity should appear in his conduct."

Mons. Wright recovered £500 damages ; and when Mr. Fitzgerald applied to the Irish Parliament for an indemnity, he could not get one.

3. The courts-martial, as they are called, by which martial law in this sense of the word is administered, are not, properly speaking, courts-martial or courts at all. They are mere committees formed for the purpose of carrying into execution the discretionary

power assumed by the Government. On the one hand, they are not obliged to proceed in the manner pointed out by the Mutiny Act and Articles of War. On the other hand, if they do so proceed, they are not protected by them as the members of a real court-martial might be, except in so far as such proceedings are evidence of good faith. They are justified in doing, with any forms and in any manner, whatever is necessary to suppress insurrection, and to restore peace and the authority of the law. They are personally liable for any acts which they may commit in excess of that power, even if they act in strict accordance with the Mutiny Act and Articles of War.

Such, in general, we take to be the nature of martial law.

We now proceed to examine the Act of the Jamaica Legislature under which Governor Eyre appears to have acted, as we presume, regularly.

The Act is 9 Vict. cap. 30, and is a consolidation of the laws relating to militia. The sections bearing on the subject of martial law are as follows: Sect. 95 constitutes a body called a council of war; sect. 96 is in these words: "And whereas the appearance of public danger, by invasion or otherwise, may sometimes make the imposition of martial law necessary, yet, as from experience of the mischief and calamities attending it, it must ever be considered as one of the greatest of evils: Be it therefore enacted, that it shall not in the future be declared or imposed but by the opinion and advice of a council of war, consisting as aforesaid, and that at the end of thirty days from the time of such martial law being declared, it shall *ipso facto* determine, unless continued by the advice of a council of war as aforesaid." Sect. 97 empowers the governor, with such advice as aforesaid, to declare particular districts to be under martial law, and to except others. Sect. 117 says that "This Act shall continue to be in force notwithstanding and during martial law."

It is a grave question whether, if this Act be considered to confer upon Governor Eyre any other power than he already possessed at common law, the Act itself would be valid. The powers of the Jamaica Legislature are derived, not from Parliament, but from Royal Commission. As the Crown cannot authorize legislation inconsistent with the law of England, it could not authorize the

2 o

Jamaica Legislature to confer upon the Governor, or anyone else, powers inconsistent with the provisions of the Petition of Right. It is indeed provided by 28 & 29 Vict. c. 63, ss. 1, 2, and 3, that no colonial law shall be deemed to be void on the ground of repugnancy to the law of England, unless it is repugnant to the provisions of any Act of Parliament applicable to any such colony by express words or necessary intendment. We apprehend, however, that if the Act of the Jamaica Legislature be construed as authorizing or recognizing anything declared illegal by the Petition of Right, it is repugnant to a provision of an Act of Parliament extending by necessary intendment to the colony of Jamaica.

It appears, however, that the Act does not create any new power, but only limits the existing power, and provides regulations under which it is to be exercised. It provides that the Governor shall not proclaim martial law without the advice and consent of a council of war, constituted in a certain way, and that when proclaimed it shall expire, *ipso facto*, in thirty days. It also provides that its operation may be limited (as in the present case it was) to certain districts.

We now proceed to the consideration of the specific questions contained in the case :—

2. and 3. The legality of the conduct pursued towards Mr. Gordon depends, according to the principles stated above, on the question whether it was necessary for the suppression of open force, and the restoration of legal authority, to put him to death. We see nothing whatever in Governor Eyre's despatch which affords any ground for thinking that such could have been the case. The fact that Kingston was exempted from martial law shows conclusively, as against Governor Eyre, that in his opinion no necessity for the assumption of arbitrary power existed then and there. The fact that Mr. Gordon was in lawful custody shows that he was at all events disabled from doing further mischief, however guilty he might previously have been. It would perhaps be too much to say that no conceivable state of things could justify the treatment which he received, but no such facts are mentioned in Governor Eyre's despatch. As to the legal power of the officers sitting as a court-martial at Morant Bay, we are of opinion that they had no powers at all as a court-martial, and that they could justify the

execution of Mr. Gordon only if, and in so far as they could show
that, that step was immediately and unavoidably necessary for the
preservation of peace and the restoration of order. They had no
right whatever to punish him for treason, even if he had committed
it. Their province was to suppress force by force, not to punish
crime.

4. This question is answered in our introductory observations.
Cases might be imagined in which some of the acts specified might
be justified. In a case, for instance, where the loyal part of the
population were (as in the case of the Indian Mutiny) greatly out-
numbered by a rebellious population, measures of excessive severity
might be absolutely essential to the restoration of the power of the
law; but this would be a case, not of punishment, but of self-preservation. No facts stated in Governor Eyre's despatch appear to
us to show any sort of reason for such conduct in Jamaica.

5. They may be indicted in Middlesex under the provisions of
42 Geo. 3, c. 85. See, too, 24 & 25 Vict. c. 100, s. 9. They may
also be impeached in Parliament.

6. Any person in this country may prefer a bill of indictment.

7. This is a question of great difficulty. As Governor Eyre's
consent would be necessary to such an Act, and as he could not
pardon himself, we are inclined to think that such an Act would be
no answer to an indictment in England. Besides this, if Governor
Eyre has committed any crime at all, it is a crime against the law
of England. Whilst Governor, he could not be made criminally
responsible in Jamaica (*Mostyn* v. *Fabrigas*, 1 Smith's "Leading
Cases," p. 543, 4th ed.). It is not competent to the Legislature of
Jamaica to pardon crimes committed against the laws of England.

To obviate all difficulty, we should advise that if such an Act
were passed, a petition should be presented to Her Majesty, praying
her to refer to the Judicial Committee of the Privy Council the
question whether the Act ought to be disallowed, and that the
petitioners might be permitted to show cause by counsel why it
should be disallowed. Unless and until they are disallowed by the
Queen, the Acts of the Jamaica Legislature are valid.

EDWARD JAMES.

Temple, January 13, 1866.   J. FITZJAMES STEPHEN.

INDEX.

PIRACY: statute 28 Hen. 8, c. 15, " For Pirates," extends to murder on the high
    seas, 115.
    slave-trading created piracy by statute 4 Geo. 4, c. 113, 117.
    attainder of, does not work corruption of blood, 117, 118.
    not an offence at common law, *ib.*
    not thought disreputable by the ancients, 118.
    whether pirates entitled to be tried by a jury *de medietate*, 117, 455-7.
PLANTATIONS, meaning of the term. " British plantations in America," in statute
    5 Geo. 2, c. 7, include the West Indies, 63.
PLATEN-HALLEMUND, COUNT, case of, whether he became a Prussian subject by
    seizure of Hanover by Prussia, 335.
POLITICAL FUGITIVES not to be surrendered, 371.
PREROGATIVE. See CROWN.
PRIVILEGED COMMUNICATION in case of public officers, 86, 454.
PROCLAMATIONS, legal effect of, 180 (note).
PUBLIC OFFICERS, actions against, 85.

QUO WARRANTO for declaring charters of City of London forfeited, 387.

REAL PROPERTY governed by *lex loci rei sitæ*, 248.
REBEL in arms may be killed as a foreign enemy, 212.
REVENUE, statutes relating to, as affecting contracts, 241.
REVOCATION OF CHARTERS, 380–389.
ROMAN CATHOLIC priests in the colonies, 35.
    bishops in Canada, appointment of, 49, 51.
    college in Prince Edward's Island, incorporation of, 51.

ST. HELENA, power of colonial legislature to enable foreigner to hold land there, 11.
SCIRE FACIAS to repeal grants or charters from the Crown, 387.
SENTRY, when justified in firing, 216.
SHIPS, nationality of, 394–420.
    privilege of ships of war, 394.
    derelict in ocean, right of property in, 395.
    jurisdiction over, when driven into foreign port by stress of weather, 400.
    what constitutes loss of nationality in, 404.
    jurisdiction over crimes committed on board of, 235, 407–419, 420.
    territorial character of, 419, 420.
SLAVES, compensation for, legal assets, 63.
    escaping to a free soil, 145 (note), 223, 326.
    contract for sale and purchase of, by British subjects, when legal, 241.
    whether " liberated African " becomes a British subject, 332.
    escaping by means of horse or boat, where no *animus furandi*, 370.
    on their right to claim benefit of clergy, 457.
SOLDIERS, authority of, to take away life in suppression of riot, 194.
    duty of, 214.
    do not cease to be citizens, 195.
STATUTES applicable to the colonies, 18–20.
SUPERINTENDENT of trade in China, 232.
    of Honduras, power of pardon not vested in, 77.
SYNODS of dissenting ministers, 36, 62.

LONDON : PRINTED BY WILLIAM CLOWES AND SONS, STAMFORD STREET AND CHARING CROSS.

CPSIA information can be obtained
at www.ICGtesting.com
Printed in the USA
LVHW100719210622
721748LV00003B/99